A passionate breed of men and women, they lived

THIS SIDE OF INNOCENCE

Amalie—Lovely, wilful, ready to marry for money—but demanding far, far more.

Alfred—His passion for one woman's beauty brought him to the edge of destruction.

Philip—A sufferer, he made pain his most powerful tool—to be inflicted on those he hated, and loved.

"A GIFT OF STORY-TELLING WHICH IS ALL TOO RARE"
—*Virginia Kirkus Review*

Also by Taylor Caldwell and available from
Popular Library

NEVER VICTORIOUS, NEVER DEFEATED
08435-9 $1.95

TENDER VICTORY   08298-4 $2.25

YOUR SINS AND MINE   00331-6 $1.75

Taylor Caldwell

This Side Of Innocence

POPULAR LIBRARY • NEW YORK

To Freda and Felix Muehlner

A garden was the primitive prison, till man, with
Promethean felicity and boldness, luckily sinned
himself out of it. Thence followed Babylon,
Nineveh, Venice, London, haberdashers, goldsmiths,
taverns, playhouses, satires, epigrams, puns—
these all came in on the town part, and the thither
side of innocence.

—Charles Lamb

THIS SIDE OF INNOCENCE

Published by Popular Library, a unit of CBS Publications, the
Consumer Publishing Division of CBS Inc., by arrangement with
Charles Scribner's Sons.

ISBN: 0-445-08434-0

PRINTED IN THE UNITED STATES OF AMERICA

25   24   23   22   21   20   19   18   17   16

PART ONE

CHAPTER ONE

It seemed to Jerome Lindsey that disagreeable news invariably arrived when he and New York weather were in execrable moods.

Yesterday, the air had been beguilingly mild and balmy, for all it was the middle of December, and the sun had had a misty golden effusion about it. This had all fitted nicely into the background of his own buoyancy: a particularly desirable and delectable young lady had given every promise of succumbing to a long siege in the evening. Yesterday, then, Jerome had appeared much younger than he did today. He had actually felt sparkle and exuberance. But that was yesterday.

Today, he felt more than senile. It was a senility mixed with various sensations of anguish. He was almost prepared to admit that champagne did not agree with him. But that plebeian confession still hovered uneasily about in a head that gave ominous indication that somewhere, somehow, during the night, it had been stepped upon, hard, by a brace of draft horses. The lady, unfortunately, had not stepped upon him. She had been much more amenable even than he had hoped. He wished, now, that she had shown a little restraint.

The weather matched his mood and his sensations. Sleet obliterated the brown buildings opposite in skeins of gray and swirling wool. Wind shrieked at his windows. The pavements were aslush, and a few wayfarers scurried along under pallidly gleaming umbrellas.

Nor, as he lingered over pots of coffee, and coffee only, did his mail touch his life with a glimmer of brightness. There were a few dull invitations. But the mass was almost entirely composed of bills. He regarded them, unopened, with pain, screwed up his lined face, and threw them into his wastebasket. Jim, his man, would later salvage them and lay them in a neat, but unobtrusive pile, upon his desk. In the meantime, he did not care to look at them. Just as he did not care to look at his face, which would inevitably suggest that he was much older than his thirty-four years, and much more repellent than he actually was in less head-cracking moments.

He was still unshaved. He could never bear to shave after a particularly hectic night. It only increased his suspicions that his skull was ready to fall into brittle fragments. His eyes watered, felt hot and rough and sore. He blinked them, bending forward to examine the last letter or two by the light of a very pretty alabaster lamp which he had bought in Italy the summer before.

There was a letter from his sister, Dorothea. He scowled. He was about to toss the letter aside, to be read in a less painful hour, when he noticed that the envelop was thick and bulging. Dorothea was not in the habit of writing long letters. One thin tissue sheet was usually enough for her, and even that one sheet required considerable mental bracing on the part of Jerome. But his curiosity overcame his involuntary wincing at the idea of reading one of Dorothea's letters, and he opened it. As he did so, he shouted to Jim to bring him more coffee. He began to read Dorothea's letter:

"Hilltop,
Riversend, New York,
15th December, 1868

"My dear Jerome:

"In the same post with my letter you will doubtless receive Papa's epistle with news that may seem to you merely amiable and pleasant, and of which you may possibly approve, in your careless way. I am afraid, however, that it will do little more than to stir your most casual interest, for you have never displayed that family solicitude and loyalty which are so important in dear Papa's life. You will forgive me, I trust, for recalling to your memory your unremitting amusement at Papa's sense of family and tradition, for it has always deeply wounded me. Even when you were only a schoolboy you appeared to find Papa's sentiments little less than ridiculous, and my heart is still scarred at the remembrance of your remarks to him on the subject on your seventeenth birthday. As if tradition and family pride and honor were somehow reprehensible and jejune, and not to be countenanced by young gentlemen with worldly and sophisticated pretensions!

"I am afraid that my sensibilities are so disturbed by this memory, and the memory of others hardly less insensible, that I am diverging from my subject. But I wish to assure you that only my agitation and distress impel me to write this letter to you, for we have been somewhat less than friends, though brother and sister. Then, my conscience sometimes disturbs me with a sense of guilt. I am four years your senior, and it was to my care that our dear mama consigned you before she was called Home. Have I failed in my duty? Are there hidden reproaches you could address to me but do not do so out of fraternal delicacy? But no, I hardly believe this. Delicacy was never one of your more prominent traits of character. Surely, I pray Heaven, I am not guilty of your curious sense of humor, your reckless way of living, your extravagance and irresponsibility, your debts and your foolish aspirations for an artistic career. If I am guilty at all, it is because I have never understood you, and that my precepts of integrity, honor, and an edifying and genteel manner of living failed to make any impression upon you.

"I hope and pray in my heart that darling Mama will not greet me with sad reproaches when I join her in those quiet fields of peace after my earthly journey is completed. I have done my best, and I may say this in all humble sincerity."

"Dear, dear Dorothea!" said Jerome, taking up another thin sheet of paper with its closely written lines in thin purple ink.

"It is to be understood" (Dorothea continued in writing that rapidly became more agitated) "that as you have taken so little interest in family affairs in the past years, because of your peregrinations through Europe, your long and indifferent sojourns in New York, Boston and Philadelphia, and your residence among worldly ladies and gentlemen without probity and a serious regard for the problems of the world, that the news that our cousin, Alfred, is about to marry again will do little more than to cause you to raise an eyebrow. I beg of you to give thought for just a moment to the implications of the matter."

"Good God!" exclaimed Jerome, aloud, and laughing immoderately, "is that stick about to propose for old Dotty after all?" He bent closer to the lamp that was shining brighter now in the December dusk. He had been reading with that amused indifference to everyone but himself which his sister found so insufferable, but now his interest was awakened.

"It is my constant prayer" (Dorothea went on) "that I shall always remember that I am a Christian gentlewoman, that I must harbor in my breast only the most Christian sentiments of charity and forbearance, and as our dear, late lamented President has urged, 'malice towards none.' I am certain that not even my worst enemy can accuse me, with truth, of forgetting those axioms of pious conduct implanted in my youthful heart by darling Mama. So, I implore you not to dismiss what I must say in the belief that any anxieties on my part rise from uncharitable motives or prejudice.

"I possess none of those snobberies and pretensions which so afflict those who have no securities of genteel birth and traditions and antecedents. From the elevation of our mutual ancestry, I can afford to be tolerant and kind, but just, I pray.

"Doubtless it will inflict ennui upon you if I remark, as I have remarked to you so often before, that Papa's sense of family and traditional pride are the supreme motivations of his life, and I revere him for them. I should be less than his daughter if I did not do so. It was his hope that he might be blessed by many sons and daughters who would live about him, and present to him flourishing families to share with him his reverence for property and the continuity of his blood and the immortality of his elevated traditions. But God, in His inexplicable wisdom (which I must confess I do not comprehend) saw fit to deprive Papa of these blessings, and allowed dear Mama to present to Papa only two children, you and myself. I do not reproach Heaven, but I find it a little difficult to understand——

"When I began this letter, so onerous and so bitter, under the circumstances, I warned myself sternly that I must not reprove you, nor remind you of things best forgotten. But in order to clarify what I must say, I am compelled to recall to you that though you are now nearly thirty-four years of age you have not seen fit to marry some genteel young lady of our mutual acquaintance, and that you have repeatedly declared, in Papa's hearing, that you will never wed and give to Papa those grandsons for which he yearns so silently and so patiently. If I have any reproach at all to address to Papa, it is that he was always so tolerant with you, and displayed for you an affection which is very bewildering to me. Never did he urge upon you that conduct for which any gentleman with sensibility and filial devotion would have needed no urging. He allowed you to dissipate the seventy-five thousand dollars which Grandma Holden left to you, indiscreetly, without a single suggestion or reproach, and in his tenderness was really convinced that you were gifted. Nevertheless, as the years passed, I saw his sadness and regret, though not a single word of this, I am certain, ever reached you from his pen. Rather, he sent you large cheques at intervals, doubtless at your imperative request. You will recall that I am Papa's secretary and housekeeper, and these cheques, in due time, all passed through my hands.

"You once told me that as Papa had adopted his brother's son, Alfred, that relieved you of any responsibilities towards Papa, and that he now had a son who would do his duty for the family. Your indifference to the implications of this appalled me, but I kept silent. Not that I do not cherish Alfred as dearly as a brother——"

"And slightly more so," remarked Jerome, with an unpleasant grin.

"—and do not rejoice that he has filled Papa's remaining years with pleasantness and comfort and peace. I am sure you will not deny this. But Alfred's first marriage, to Martha Winchester, resulted in nothing but poor young Philip who has neither the strength nor the possibility in him to give Papa great-grandsons, in due course of time. When Martha died, upon Philip's birth, it seemed that our hopes vanished forever with her."

"Not your hopes," said Jerome, with disagreeable derision. "Poor old Dotty."

"We have cherished Philip, and I have been a mother to him," Dorothea continued. "He has repaid both Papa and me with gentle affection, as if he understood that his deformity has been such a bitter disappointment to us.

"As time passed, and Philip grew older, we were resigned to our fate. Alfred displayed no anxiety to marry again, and we all settled down to tranquil existence."

"Not you!" said Jerome, laughing nastily. "You were after him day and night, in the most refined way possible, of course!"

"And then," wrote Dorothea, and now her writing was so agitated as to be scarcely legible, and blotted suspiciously here and there, "like a bolt from the blue, Alfred announced his intention to wed again."

"Ah, ha!" exclaimed Jerome, turning up the lamp. "Now this is going to be very interesting indeed! So it is not old Dotty, after all, thank God!" His expression brightened with malice and something very like gloating cruelty.

"Naturally, Papa and I were astounded. But I pray you to understand that I was not disturbed. On the contrary. Riversend has its adequate supply of marriageable and acceptable females of the proper age, for, after all, Alfred is nearly thirty-nine. But though I named them all to Alfred, he only shook his head and smiled. At length, we became conscious that he was uneasy, and that he kept glancing at Papa with a look that implored forgiveness in advance and affectionate tolerance.

"As you know, Alfred is now Papa's vice-president at the Bank. Then Alfred told us an incredible tale that froze my blood. It seems that a certain young female without antecedents, and an entire stranger, appealed to him a few months ago for financial assistance. This young female, who, it is hinted, possesses the most mediocre if not sinister past (it must be so, for she speaks rarely of her former life) comes from Thorntonville, that very miserable little farm village thirty miles away. She had been engaged to teach our local rural school, for which she was paid forty dollars a month. She claims to be but twenty-two years of age, but I am positive she is much older, for not only are her features hard and calculating, and the expression of her eyes exceedingly unpleasant, but she has a certain boldness of manner and speech which argues for more years than she admits. Also, her dress is not that acceptable in a teacher, and is of finer stuff and fashion than her salary could conceivably allow, though she declares that she makes all her garments herself, with patterns from Godey. I will concede this, in charitableness, but my heart speaks differently."

"Oh, no doubt," said Jerome.

"After the first stunning effects of the news had left me, I journeyed alone to Thorntonville to investigate this young female, whose name is Amalie Maxwell. To my horror, my first premonitions about her were justified. Her father had been a drunken tenant farmer, and his wife had cleaned and washed for local respectable families until she died some ten years ago. Mr. Maxwell was later arrested for drunkenness, and suspected of numerous thefts. Two of the latter charges were proved, and he was sent to State's prison, where he died seven years ago, leaving Miss Maxwell (if her claimed age is correct) to support herself at the age of fifteen. It would be suspected that a young female of that age, conscious of her background, would have entered service and there, with meekness and industry, would have tried to live down her past and elevate herself in the esteem of her mistress. But this she did not do. She decided, she says, to be a teacher. She declares that from her earliest youth she was disturbed by the 'illiteracy' of the poor, and that she intended to alleviate this with her own labors. When I remarked to her that God, in His wisdom, designates to each man his proper station in life, and that it is impious impudence to attempt to overturn this all-wise Design, she laughed coarsely in my face.

"Coarseness, I may say now, is her dominant characteristic. She has no modesty, no gentility, no presence, no graces. She utters language that no female of delicacy and breeding would utter. She has the boldness of an uneducated man, and I have often heard her swear like a groom. Alfred, in his fatuousness, finds her amusing and refreshing, and he dotes on her like the elderly man he is, as though she were his daughter! But I have discerned at times that she embarrasses him. In his lack of a sense of proportion he actually pleaded with me to be a 'mother to the girl,' though I am but thirty-eight, myself, and certainly possess too much breeding to associate with one so bereft of all genteel traits!"

"Good old imbecile Alfred!" cried Jerome, with enjoyment.

"Alfred must feel some lack, Jerome, or he would not have made this insulting and preposterous request of me, and the further request to teach Miss Amalie the most rudimentary arts of proper social intercourse and behavior. I promised to accede to his request, and, crushing down my sense of grief and outrage, I invited the young woman to sojourn with us until her marriage to Alfred, which has been marked for Christmas week. She willingly enough abandoned her mission to elevate the children of the poor, which proves her innate hypocrisy and wiliness, and has now taken up residence in the rose suite.

"To prove to you her complete lack of understanding of all delicacy and propriety, she accepted nearly a thousand dollars from Alfred, and went to New York, in my company, to purchase for herself a most flamboyant and indiscreet wardrobe! This is her trousseau. Such bonnets, such daring gowns, such colors, not at all befitting the future wife of Alfred Lindsey! Such lack of taste and discretion! There is a certain red gown of which the less said the better——

11

"Jerome, I implore you to understand! You know Alfred, his sobriety, his integrity, his single-heartedness, his sense of duty and responsibility, his soundness of principle, his probity, his devotion to family tradition and to dear Papa, and his position at the Bank! And think, then, of this reprehensible female, without background, delicate education and decorum, the daughter of a drunkard and a washwoman, as our Alfred's wife! I beg of you to believe that had this creature possessed the slightest humble knowledge of her overwhelming good fortune, had she appeared aware that her guardian angel had conferred upon her the most astounding fate, had she admitted that she was deeply fond of Alfred, and was preparing to make him a devoted and docile and grateful wife, I might have forgiven her, and attached myself to her as an older sister. But, incredible though this seems (and I hardly expect you to believe me under the circumstances), her attitude indicates that it is *Alfred* who has been singularly blessed, that it is *Alfred* who has been selected by Heaven for great good luck, and that while she is moderately attracted to him, it required months of the most sedulous courtship and pleading on his part to induce her to consent to be his wife! I know that you will laugh incredulously and with anger at this, and despise this creature for her lies and shamelessness. When I, concealing my pain and disbelief, indulgently asked her why she had finally consented, she laughed and said: 'My room is so cold in the winter, and I'm getting tired of meat once a week!'

"She is coarse, full of impertinence and effrontery and arrogance. I cannot impress this too deeply upon you. Think, Jerome, of the significance of all this. She will be Alfred's wife, the mother of his children, who will then inherit the Bank. You have long assured Papa that you wanted no active part in the Bank, that nothing would induce you to live in Riversend. But I beg of you to think of this woman, and her heirs, as inheritors of the Bank founded so long ago by Great-grandpapa, who was second cousin to Lord Brandon, in England. Can you contemplate such an interloper in our life, such an abandoned creature? Does it not stir your careless blood to conceive of her children as the recipients of the wealth and prestige of our family? What shall we, the true descendants of Great-grandpapa, inherit? We shall be defrauded and thrown out by the children of a woman whom charity forbids me to describe too fully."

Jerome lifted his eyes from the letter and stared before him. For the first time his face was grim. "Damn," he muttered,

12

scowling. His hand fumbled absently at the silver box of cheroots at his elbow. He found a cheroot, put it to his lips, but did not light it. An excellent diamond twinkled on his hand in the lamplight. Good God! Now, this was something not to be regarded with laughter or ridicule! It was damnably serious. He cared nothing for the Bank, so long as the cheques came regularly. But—would the cheques come so regularly after Papa's death? What a fool he was not to have thought of this before. It seemed incredible to him that he had been possessed of such folly. He was not even young; he was thirty-four. There was no excuse for such confounded lack of intelligence. An adventuress, by God! A trollop and a strumpet, entering that old house on the hill and wielding sway over the household —and over the money! What possessed that incredible ass of an Alfred? What possessed his father?

Now his disturbed and irascible eye fell on another letter. It was from his father, he knew. He flung Dorothea's many tissue pages upon the floor and seized eagerly on the other missive. His hands trembled somewhat, with a chronic tremor. This annoyed him, for the first time. He saw that the first two fingers of his right hand were darkly stained with tobacco, and he grimaced. His tongue was thick, his stomach nauseated. Five hundred dollars spent last night, and all he had, in return, was buckets of ice-cooled champagne, grinning strumpets, and a sojurn in a bed not his own! And now, this. He tore open his father's sealed letter, and began to read, bent towards the light. The letter was comparatively short, and full of quiet dignity. Jerome's livid face softened, involuntarily, as he read, and he did not notice the green slip of paper that fell from the pages. "My dear Jerome:

"I am sending you the thousand dollars you requested, and I hope this will be enough for a time. But, dear boy, do not hesitate to ask for more if it is necessary, even though your customary allowance is not due until February.

"I write this now to ask you to a wedding. Does this surprise you? You know I have long urged Alfred to remarry, and it had been my secret hope that he would ask for our Dorothea, who has long been the mainstay of my existence, and is eminently suited to be Alfred's wife. I believe I do nōt violate her inmost heart when I suggest that she has always been very attached to Alfred, and that his marriage to Martha was a blow to her. After Martha's death I began to hope again. She has been so devoted to young Philip, and Alfred was sincerely grateful. The marriage would have been ideal.

13

"But it was not to be, evidently. He has chosen a young woman, a schoolteacher in the village. To my regret, she is not a real resident of Riversend, and has no family of position. Moreover, she is very much younger that Alfred; seventeen years, in fact. I would have chosen otherwise, had it been in my hands, but one does not quarrel with circumstance.

"However, I am not too unhappy. Miss Amalie is a young lady of spirit and originality, she is very talented with brush and canvas, and can play the pianoforte with amazing sympathy. Her gifts are all natural, and entirely uncultivated. She has a surprising wit and intelligence, and amuses me for hours together, which is very kind of her. (I find my invalidism too confining for my taste, at times.) I might suggest that a little more restraint in her manner would be agreeable, and a little more refinement in deportment and language. But I am old, and possibly my taste is old-fashioned, also, and not modern in all particulars. Since the war, young people have developed a freedom not acceptable in my day, and the females, especially, display a certain intrepid boldness which makes one wonder. However, one cannot restrain the times. Doubtless I appeared very alarming to my own parents, and I do recall that my father regularly prophesied my doom.

"As for Miss Amalie's family, or lack of it, that ought not to militate against her. Is this not a country of vitality, where the strangest men rise to positions of esteem and honor? Miss Amalie's background is not disturbing to me. She is full of health and vitality, and is very shrewd. I predict she will present me with the grandchildren I long have wanted. They will be comely, I know, and even handsome, for she is a young lady of much presence, and with the loveliest face. Though Dorothea disagrees with me vehemently, I believe I find a resemblance in Miss Amalie to that portrait of my grandmother which hangs in the library. The eyes are identical in coloring, though Grandmother had a certain gentleness of expression not possessed by Miss Amalie. The hair is amazingly the same, black and curling and luxurious, and there is a startling similarity of carriage and figure. Had you known your great-grandmother, you would agree with me, I know.

"I do hope you will be able to come to Riversend for the wedding. I know that you and Alfred never possessed mutual understanding and sympathy in your youth. But I hope time has alleviated that, and that you will meet again with agreeable sensations of brotherhood. You have not seen each other for nearly five years. Am I correct in this?

14

"As for myself, I have not been overly well since Mr. Lincoln's assassination. I confess that it was a most frightful blow to me, for we were friends, if you remember. But I am able to ride in my carriage for an hour a day without too much exhaustion, and I contemplate the future of our country with more optimism than in years. We must discuss all this. I confess that I look forward eagerly to your arrival, for we have not come face to face for nearly two years, and that was when I visited you in New York.

"You do not speak in your last letter of the old wound in your leg, and I am anxious. I have not forgotten my pride in you, when you were a captain in the New York First Infantry, nor my terrible anxiety for you in the war years. How is the leg now?

"Dorothea is ordering your old apartments to be made ready, and I am taking it for granted that you will rejoice me by being present at the wedding. Will it be possible for you to arrive a few days before Christmas?

                    "Your loving father,
                                        "William Lindsey."

Jerome put his father's letter on the table beside him, but the palm of his tremulous hand lay gently upon it. Why, the poor old boy was all broken up! It was like him to make the best of a bad bargain, but his distress was evident in every line of this quiet letter. My God, what a calamity was this!

Jerome stood up. He swayed a little, for a racking pain went through his head. The door opened and, as if summoned, a wizened small man appeared, with a face like a nut and a completely bald head. That face was lewd and knowing, full of slyness and humor. The man wore a quiet black livery; there was a monkeylike agility about him, a monkeylike quickness and sprightliness.

"Jim," said Jerome, "pack our bags. We're off and away for a wedding, unless I can prevent it. And, damn it, I'll prevent it or die in the attempt."

CHAPTER TWO

The mild weather of the first two weeks of December had been whirled away in the smoking spirals of a fierce snowstorm. Now over a landscape that had been unreasonably green and soft gray the storm rode in on wild and tempestuous white horses. Boiling and twisting clouds rolled over the high foothills; the long low valley filled rapidly with mounds and dunes of snow, fuming as if with white sand. Ramparts of black pines groaned, bent, reared, were flung back like waves under the battering onslaughts of terrible winds, and their tortured and roaring voices were heard like bassoons over and below the screams and howlings of the gales. Everything was lost in a gray and coiling mist beneath the gigantic and tumultuous dark heavens, which reverberated like an enormous struck harp.

Riversend (formerly River's End, but corrupted on the lazy tongues of the local citizenry) cowered at the mouth of the valley, a huddle of small houses, miniature churches, bleak little shops and a stately mansion or two. It seemed to draw together, shivering, so that the streets appeared narrowed, closing in hour by hour, contracting like the chilled muscles of a living body. Houses dwindled, pulling in their walls upon themselves, the windows diminishing like frightened eyes. Here and there, a yellow light flickered timidly behind curtains, and the gaslamps on the corners of the streets flared and sank like candles in the wind, showing briefly, in their crescendoes, the sharp-edged and rising dunes of snow. Not a creature was abroad, not even a sparrow or a homeless dog. Moment by moment, the village gave the impression of sinking deeper and deeper into the drifts, like a lost thing burrowing for safety.

The station roof was already weighted with eighteen inches of fine white snow, sparkling sugarlike in the light of the station lantern which swung high and wide near the tracks. The New York train smoldered, and belched in a muffled voice, at the platform. Its smoke lay straight back over its long black length, battered by the winds, and the sallow glow of the lights in the coaches showed faintly through streaming windows. A bell rang warningly, though only two passengers descended. Then the train seemed to gather its strength together; it shuddered; the bell raised a thin clamor, sparks flew from the smokestack, lights flared up, and with a long groan the train pushed on into the formless black-and-white dark of the night. Now the gleaming tracks were empty, and the gales took over in triumph.

The two passengers bent their heads and bodies against the wind and scrambled into the odoriferous warm shelter of the station, stamping their boots, wiping their eyes, rubbing their stung cheeks. One of them was a tall young man in furred greatcoat and high hat and furred gloves. He carried a whimpering little dog under his arm. The other man, much older and smaller, and less elegantly dressed, set down numerous bags on the tobacco-stained floor. He went at once to the pot-bellied coal stove, took off his cap and shook it, hissing, near the fuming heat. The younger man put down the little dog, who whimpered and trembled near his polished boots.

"Well," said the young man, looking about him with disfavor, "no one's here to meet us, I see. They must have received my telegram. I sent it two days ago." He scowled at the empty counter. "Not even the damned stationmaster."

He turned to the older man, who was shaking the collar of his coat, bending sideways. "Jim, you remember the telegram?"

"Yes, sir, I do that. You went out especially, I remember. You said: 'Expect me and man on Tuesday, on the evening train——' " He paused, gaping monkeylike at his master. "It *was* Tuesday you said, warn't it, sir?"

"Tuesday it was, Jim."

Jim chuckled hoarsely. "Well, 'tis Monday now, sir. Tuesday's tomorrow."

The young man stared at his servant, emptily. Then he said softly: "Well, I'll be damned. Why didn't you remember what day it was, Jim?"

The nutlike face of the other wrinkled into its usual monkeyish expression. "Sir, it warn't until we was almost here that you mentioned—begging your pardon, sir—that the telegram said Tuesday. I allus thought it was Monday, until on the train you mentioned it."

The young man somberly regarded the little dog writhing miserably at his feet. "Shut up, Charlie," he remarked absently. Then he began to laugh. "We've gotten ourselves into a fix, it seems." He raised his voice and shouted. "Where's that damned stationmaster?"

The door opened on a blast of wind and snow, and a short and sturdy man entered, swearing. He was a stranger, unknown to the passengers. The younger man said abruptly, as the stationmaster paused and stared at them with surprise: "Where's old Thompson?"

The other replied: "Why, sir, he died a year ago. I'm his nephew, takin' over. You got off the train, sir?"

"No, we blew in on the wind, from the North Pole. Look here, my man, there's been some mistake. I was to be met by a carriage from Hilltop. I'm Jerome Lindsey. But there's no one here."

The man hastily pulled off his cap with a servile gesture.

"Well, now, sir, it's glad to see you I am, though we've never met before. But I know all the folks on Hilltop. They was to meet you, you say? Ain't seen any sign of a rig about." He trotted to a window, rubbed the steaming pane, and peered into the night. "No, sir, no rig—nothing. And it's five miles to Hilltop, and there's no one to send to notify 'em." He turned helplessly and apologetically from the window. "You can't walk it, neither, sir. Not in this storm, through the snow."

Jerome lifted his coattails slowly and elaborately, examined the single bench with suspicion, and sat down. The little dog promptly sprang upon his knees, huddling against him. The creature was snuff-colored, with long silky hair and bloodshot bad-tempered eyes. He snarled at the stationmaster from his safety. "Nice little beast," offered the man, lamely. He sighed. "No, sir, not in this storm and dark."

Jerome glanced pointedly at his servant, who blandly ignored his look and made much ado over rubbing his hands at the stove. "Never was here, myself, unfortunatelike. Wouldn't know the way. I'd be fair swamped before quarter of a mile. They'd be digging out my cor'se at dawn."

The stationmaster suddenly brightened, and snapped his fingers. "I have it, sir! Hobson's wagon'll be here in half an hour or so, with the milk, for the Syracuse train. He never misses, come hell nor high water. Course, the wagon's open, and it'll be a nasty ride, in the wind and snow, but it's better than nothin', ain't it? He has a farm one mile from Hilltop, and for a little consideration he'll take you to the Hill. Couldn't climb it, though, the weather bein' what it is."

"Pleasant prospect," remarked Jerome, frowning. He stroked the dog's wet head. "But we can't sit here until tomorrow night, either. I know! Your friend Hobson could notify Mr. Lindsey, and then they could send a carriage for us at once."

The stationmaster shook his head dolorously. "The storm like it is, sir, and getting worse by the minute, the rig'd never make it. At the best it'd be hours, and then how'd they get back? No, sir, best to go with Hobson, before the storm gets worse."

He threw a scuttle of coal into the stove. This frightened Charlie, the dog, to such an extent that he went off into a hysteria of barking. "Give him some meat," said Jerome, wearily. Jim opened a wicker basket, brought out a paper parcel of liver and assorted dainties, and offered a few morsels to the dog in his brown and shriveled hand. But the dog was so

18

disturbed that he snapped viciously at the man's fingers and refused the delicacies. "Filthy little devil," said Jerome, stroking him fondly. "Shut up, Charlie."

The coal-oil lamp swayed fitfully from the dirty ceiling. The stove crackled. The wind beat heavily against the windows. They could see the high rim of the snow on the sills. The glass was rapidly frosting, and the traceries of white ferns spread higher and higher by the moment. Now icy fingers of cold blew through the small and fetid room, and Jerome shivered. Seeing this, the stationmaster remarked dolefully: "Temperature's dropping, too. It's only three above zero. In an hour it'll be worse. Freeze the heart out of you soon."

He lifted the granite pot which was steaming on top of the stove, and remarked with more brightness: "Coffee's ready, sir! You'll have a cup, against the weather?"

Jerome frowned at the pot, but sniffed. "Thanks, I will." He rubbed his lip with his gloved hand. "Looks as if we have no other choice but going with Hobson. If this isn't hell——"

He threw back his richly furred coat, scowling, and plucked a few dog hairs from his fine black broadcloth pantaloons. The stationmaster, while washing a cracked cup in the bucket of water near his counter, peeped at him curiously. This would be the New York son, then, the one that was rumored to be so gay and spending, the artist. The one that never came home to see the old gentleman, but let that stiff-necked cousin of his take over with all the money. A bad-tempered devil, from the looks of him, and his manners so hoity-toity and elegant. Citified. Look at that greatcoat, now, brown like a leaf, with all that fur, like a woman's. And lined with fur, too, by God. And the gloves, and the polished pointed boots, and the gray gaiters. And that cane, there, with the gold head, leaning beside him as if it knew it was too good for the likes of us. And, if it isn't diamonds all over his fingers, now he's taking his gloves off. These city men, with their ways! And a servant he's got, too. A valley, they call 'em.

The stationmaster wiped the cup furtively with a dingy piece of cloth. His study of Jerome concentrated as he saw that the young man had sunken into his scowling thoughts. Yep, a bad-tempered cuss. And dark as if he'd worked in the fields, but half-starved for good wholesome farm food, looks like. Thin as a fence rail. No meat on his legs or on his face, which looks like it's been whittled out of brown oak. And those black thick eyebrows pulled together in a frown that's fastened there permanent. I don't like his eyes, though I guess the

19

women-folk'd think them very fine and black and sparkling, and they'd love them small flat ears of his, and all that black curlin' hair. No, sir, I don't like them eyes. He'd be bad with a horse, or a man, if he got in his way. And where'd he get that thin beak of a nose, like a hawk's? The old gentleman, bless him, don't have such a nose, and neither does Miss Dorothea. He's got a mouth like a hawk's, too, for all it smiles easy. I suppose he thinks he's the fine elegant figure of a man, with his white hands with the rings, and his high-toned way of talkin', and his languid ways that's all put on. He's the kind like a whip, lashin' out unexpected, and no mercy, either. That color on his cheekbones, too: water never put it there. I've seen drinkers in my time.

Jerome was gazing somberly at the fire. He did not turn his head. But he said quietly: "I hope you like what you see, my man."

The stationmaster, dumbfounded, flushed, and stared. Jim, at the stove, chuckled with hoarse malice, glancing over his neat small shoulder at the discomfited man. Jerome continued to regard the stove, not moving except for the rhythmic stroking of his dog.

"I'm sorry, sir," stammered the stationmaster. "I was just curious——"

"Well, look, damn you, and satisfy your curiosity. Where is that coffee?"

His hands shaking, his heart beating with indignation, the stationmaster poured the steaming brown fluid into the cup, shook a little sugar into it from a striped paper bag which stood on the counter, stirred it with an iron spoon. He brought it to Jerome. Charlie, the dog, growled. Jerome took it languidly, sniffed at it suspiciously. He put it to his lips, drank a little, grimaced, then drank some more. The two other men watched him earnestly. "Not bad," he remarked. "Full of chicory, though. And coffee's not so dear. Thank you."

He held the cup in his hands, warming them against the sides. He glanced at his servant. "And you, Jim?"

Jim bowed to the stationmaster, who disliked him thoroughly. "If there's no tea——"

"There's no tea," answered the stationmaster, on surer ground with this servant. "We don't like tea, much, in these parts. But there's more coffee." His blood flowed warmer with his hate and indignation. He glared at Jim. "You can have coffee, if you've a mind to." An Englishman, eh? Well, no Eng-

20

lishman could put it over on a good sound American, damned if he could.

"Coffee, and thank'ee, my good man," smirked Jim, grinning. Like a weasel, thought the stationmaster, gathering confidence.

Jerome rose and walked over to a window. The stationmaster observed that he had the slightest limp in his right leg. Wasn't there some story that he'd been an officer in the war, and got wounded? Yep, he walked like a soldier, and had shoulders like one, and that commanding air, too. One couldn't believe it, with all that fine elegance, but the story must be true. Must've been a devil with his men, by the looks of him. A bad un. Yet, he was lettin' all that money, and the Bank, get away from him, though if he, Jack Thompson, knew anything about men that was a greedy point on this fine gentleman's nose, and a hard hungry line or two around that hawk's mouth. Was he gettin' his dander up now, about the money, or was he just a'comin' for the weddin'? Didn't look the sort to be traipsin' into the country at this time of the year just for a weddin', and not for his cousin's sake, either. Stories had it there was bad blood between 'em. Trust the devil, himself, to come smellin' around when there was money! And this was the devil in flesh, and no mistake.

Jerome had bent his head, and was peering through the window, rubbing a dainty hole in the frost. He began to whistle, tonelessly, as he peered. Jim drank his coffee. The dog pattered, whining, after his master. Jerome looked down at him and smiled. The stationmaster was surprised. It was a humorous and charming smile, and showed a flash of strong white teeth. Jerome picked up the dog and returned to the bench. He was easier now, and indolent. He crossed his knees and favored the stationmaster with another friendly smile.

"You live in Riversend?" He had a beguiling voice now, gentle and ingratiating, with a deceptive note of sympathy in it. It was an actor feller's voice, thought the stationmaster, but without resentment.

He replied eagerly: "Yes, sir, Mr. Lindsey. Down near the blacksmith's. It was my uncle's house. You remember it?"

Jerome shook his head, regretfully. "I've been away a long time. Funny I don't remember you."

"Oh, I lived in Thorntonville until the old man died, my uncle."

The name struck at Jerome's memory. "Thorntonville." He paused. "Then you must know Miss Maxwell, the young lady

21

who is to marry my cousin?"

The stationmaster drew nearer. "Indeed I do, sir. A handsome young lady, much admired." His voice had a note of familiarity in it which caused Jerome to scowl, briefly. He averted his head, pursed his lips, and whistled tonelessly again. Jim pricked up his pointed, faunlike ears, and grinned. His bald round head twinkled in the lamplight.

There was a bustle at the door, which burst open violently. A burly farmer in cap and coat entered, swearing, brushing off his snow-covered arms. Charlie set up a wild and furious barking from Jerome's knee.

The stationmaster turned to the newcomer in relief. "Oh, there you are, Bill! Look'ee, are you goin' back up to the farm, tonight?"

Bill Hobson was staring frankly at the strangers and did not answer for a moment. Then he muttered: "Yeh. Got to. Old woman's down with the rheumatism and can't milk in the mornin'." He looked at the stationmaster inquiringly.

"Well, these gentlemen've got to go up to Hilltop. They was to be met, but no one came. You've got a place for them in the wagon, Bill?"

Bill gaped, amazed. Then he said: "For the weddin'?" He shook his head. "They couldn't stand it, open like it is. Best wait for morning and a rig or sleigh. Yep, best wait for a sleigh."

Jerome stood up, and gathered his dog under his arm. "We'll go with you, Bill, if you don't mind."

CHAPTER THREE

It was a world of hellish and bellowing darkness through which the open wagon heaved and groaned and stalled. The lantern that swung near the plank seat glared fitfully on millions of swirling white fireflies, but revealed nothing of the frozen and drifted road. The three wretched passengers, huddled close together on the plank, could see no shadow of the climbing pines, but could hear their roaring voices challenging the bitter gales. The two horses whined and panted as they struggled through the valley, and their smoking breath blew backwards along their haunches. The wagon might have been a small and laboring boat adrift on black and falling seas, and two of the passengers, at least, clung desperately to the plank and huddled their faces deep into their collars. Soon, their hands and feet were numb, and the spreading coldness crept up their limbs. They could feel their warm thick hearts beating deep within them. Sheltered by a lap of Jerome's coat, curled up between Jerome's lean warm thighs, Charlie, the dog, whimpered and burrowed against his master. The luggage jolted and smashed and rolled impotently in the rear of the wagon.

Conversation was impossible. One could only endure, grimly, blinking the freezing snow from eyelids, feeling the weight of the furious snow gathering on shoulders and arms, averting the head sideways to escape as much as possible from the tearing wind. Breath was sucked away, so that the passengers gasped frequently. There were no blankets to shelter them. The icy straw on which their feet rested only heightened their misery.

The wagon made the five miles to Hilltop in two hours, two hours of incredible endurance and grim suffering. Jerome cursed softly to himself, his voice lost in the tumult. The melting snow on his shoulders seemed to seep through the fur down to his very bones. What a fool he had been, to undergo this! He would have lung fever before morning, if he was lucky enough to arrive at Hilltop, and was not lost for days in the drifts. He could hear the hissing of the snow against the wheels, the groaning of the axles. Sometimes, for minutes at a time, the wagon was stalled, and the horses heaved and neighed in their struggles. Bill Hobson cracked his whip, shouting, suffering with his horses. But he dared not stop even for a moment.

He had informed Jerome that he would not attempt to climb up to Hilltop. Ice was thick under the snow. The wagon would never negotiate that long steep slope. The two passengers must walk up the hill as best they could.

Jerome had not been in Riversend since he had been invalided home from the war over five years ago. He had returned then only because of his father's unusual insistence and pleading. It had not been the happiest of times. In fact, he could not recall that many occasions at Hilltop had been happy. In conversations with his friends and acquaintances he was fond of saying, ruefully and with humor, that Riversend was the dullest spot imaginable, that his family was insuperably complacent and middle-class, and that, contrary to the fixed belief of mankind, there were some places in the world where time stood still. Notably Riversend. During more than thirty years it had less than doubled its population, and now boasted only ten thousand souls, including the farms of its township. Yet, villages within a day's radius of Riversend had increased to the dignity of towns, and a few had actually become small cities. What was wrong with Riversend, which barely replaced its dead with the newborn? Jerome did not know. Perhaps the reason lay in the fact that its middle class was stupid and stuffy, hating change, cautious of allowing new industry to enter the village, suspicious of strangers, and sunken in apathy and drowsing inertia. Certainly, it discouraged enterprise. For instance, during the war a "foreign" concern wished to build a mill for the manufacture of army blankets, for the river was a highroad to other towns and cities and labor was plentiful. After long and minute discussion among the local gentry, a site for the building of the factory was refused, and the "foreigners" were given to understand, with pointed politeness, that their departure would be appreciated. Jerome's family's own Bank took an active part in this refusal. The whole, if secret, reason, Jerome believed, was that the locally powerful were afraid that the farm labor and village labor might get "ideas" brought on by good wages, and thus inconvenience the local employers.

"We wish to keep the idyllic atmosphere of old Riversend unimpaired," the Mayor had said smugly, to the applause of his friends. "There are more things in life than factories, and high wages, and bustle and hustle. Let us maintain the Old World quality of our peaceful life in Riversend; let us maintain this quiet air of contentment and calm and contemplation. Let us cherish our retreat, our contentment."

The fact that the poor of Riversend found no contentment, and did not appreciate this quiet opportunity to remain chronically hungry and ill-clad, was a matter of no importance, naturally. Farm and village girls served in the stolid mansions for less than eight dollars a month, and excellent gardeners and grooms and coachmen could be obtained for ten and board. The feudal air of the village and the farms delighted the residents of fat estates. Lying snugly in its long and level valley, protected by the high foothills, Riversend seemed destined to pass its life in a dream. It had only one anxiety: the younger folk, who had palpably been created by a wise Deity for service to their masters, showed a disquieting new tendency to leave the farms and the village for distant towns and cities, for employment on "public works." This was the fault of the new railroad, of course. The owners of Riversend had fought despairingly to prevent the coming of the branch line, and success was apparently to be theirs until the incredible day when the "old gentleman," Mr. William Lindsey, suddenly displayed an ancient energy and demanded that the line be allowed to enter the village. This stunned his friends. For years, he had delegated all authority to his adopted son and nephew, Alfred Lindsey, and had not interfered with any of his mandates or decisions. Yet, on this occasion, his frail voice was heard like a stern command from the grave, and the branch line made its appearance in due time. He would not explain nor discuss the matter. After that one severe intrusion into the affairs of his own Bank and community, he retired into arthritic silence again.

The direst prophecies were fulfilled, and the young and able men and women began to leave Riversend for more lucrative employment. Now the farms, almost exclusively, supplied the local labor, and this was not always to be had. It was easy to board a train, and to ride in comfort to distant towns and cities, whereas even the hardy would consider long and thoughtfully a two or three days' journey by wagon or on foot. Without a railroad to bring in newspapers and periodicals regularly from the larger cities, the young folk would have had no stimulation for their "rebellious ideas."

Jerome had been at Hilltop during this controversy, and he had enjoyed it immensely. He loved to see his adopted brother and cousin thwarted, though Alfred was not of the character to express his disappointment and regret with any vehemence, and was the soul of filial respect and obedience. Alfred, however, was no fool. He suspected, and with considerable shrewdness, that Jerome had had some influence in bringing the railroad to Riversend. The "old gentleman" loved his real son, and though Alfred would have been the last to deplore this, and never by word or gesture or expression endeavored to turn his uncle's regard from Jerome, he regretted that his cousin possessed such power over his father. It was not a power for good, Alfred was convinced. What good could such as Jerome Lindsey possess? He was profligate and dissipated, egotistic and selfish, conceited beyond endurance, and as ruthless and devious as a serpent for all his languid and amiable ways. Whenever he interfered with the affairs of the community, however infrequently, convulsions ensued. Worst of all, Alfred firmly believed that Jerome did not interfere altruistically, and did not care a snap of his fingers for local welfare. It was all done in a spirit of mischief. Unfortunately, Alfred was quite correct in his gloomy surmises.

It was a matter of real concern to Alfred that such congenital antagonism existed between him and his cousin. It had disturbed him from his earliest years. At all times, he had been scrupulously polite to Jerome, deliberately and anxiously friendly, tolerant and just. Yet it had been evident, even in Jerome's childhood, that he was maliciously hostile to Alfred, that it amused him meanly and cruelly to disturb, shock, and frustrate him, even in the most inconsequential matters. However, when Uncle William had adopted Alfred, Jerome said nothing. He had not even written, protesting. He had displayed no interest whatsoever. That had amazed and bewildered Alfred, for a word of dissent from Jerome would have turned old Mr. Lindsey from his plan at once. Alfred simply could not understand. Dorothea had suggested that Jerome did not care to have any part in the affairs of the Bank or the community, and though no other solution of the enigma was more valid, Alfred could hardly credit it. Did not Jerome constantly demand, and receive, large sums of money from his father? Was he not extravagant, irresponsible, and avaricious? How, then, could he be so indifferent? Alfred, as adopted son, would share equally in any estate, would encroach on Jerome's property. It was not to be explained.

Had Jerome and Alfred been affectionately attached to each other, had they been old friends, Alfred might have understood in a measure. But Jerome had always amusedly hated his cousin, had consistently ridiculed and plagued him, laughing at his uprightness, his integrity, his stony "conscience," his stern piety. Alfred, to his credit, had always struggled despairingly to reach some rapport with his cousin, had tried to soften him, had undertaken long walks with him, had talked endlessly to him, with diffidence and in an earnest endeavor to establish a friendship, had written him long and frequently during his army service, and even afterwards, and had scrupulously attempted to create an atmosphere of goodwill and family regard. But Jerome had received all his overtures with derision and malevolence, had laughed openly at Alfred's "sentimentality," had derided and made much fun of him in private and public. There was nothing one could do with such a character. It was demoniacal. It was past all comprehension. It was only after long struggle against conviction that Alfred surrendered to the conclusion that Jerome was naturally evil and hardhearted, obdurate against the simplest human emotions, arrogantly disdainful of family feeling, and contemptible. How else explain his repudiation of all cousinly advances, and his shameful life? How else explain his neglect of his ailing father, his scorn of his old home, his indifference to family affairs?

It had been Alfred who had paid off an insistent lady, in the sum of ten thousand dollars out of his own pocket, rather than agitate Uncle William. Jerome had not asked him to do this service. The lady, from Syracuse, had written to Uncle William, and Alfred had intercepted the letter. Mr. Lindsey had been dangerously ill at that time, and Alfred had done this to spare him. When he later informed Jerome, in New York, of what he had done, Jerome had laughed long and excessively, with pure enjoyment. He had informed Alfred frankly that he was a fool, and that he hoped that his cousin had received some personal gratification from the lady in exchange for the money. There was no remorse in him, no conscience, no kindness, no decency. When Alfred, shocked and shaken, had suggested that it was most probable that the lady's child was Jerome's, Jerome had only shrugged, and had made some obscene remark.

Alfred, however, had his consolations. Uncle William was dearly fond of him and trusted him. And he had a strong and fanatical ally in his cousin, Dorothea. He often thought that if only Jerome would remain away from home forever, life would be very pleasant. When this thought occurred to him, he would sternly repress it, as unworthy of his innate loyalty to all the family and his strong sense of justice. Only one thing endlessly and sadly disturbed him: why did Jerome hate him? No one else had anything for him but affection, regard and respect. He had even asked Jerome this agitating question, and had received the usual immoderate laughter in answer. Yet Alfred continued to write his cousin with quiet affection, relating everything that might be of interest to the exile. However, Jerome never replied. Alfred suspected that he did not read his letters, and this distressed him. This did not prevent him from continuing the one-way correspondence. His conscience would not permit it.

As he precariously clung to his seat in the wagon, Jerome began to think of all these things and laughed aloud. No one heard his mirth in the gale, but Jim and the dog felt the prolonged shaking of his body. Jim tried to see his face in the darkness, but nothing could be seen.

The English servant had his own thoughts. He had been Jerome's familiar for three years, and though his wages had a curious way of not being paid regularly, Jim's devotion to Jerome was not shaken. He had the English servant's reverence for true gentry, for "fine" and careless gentlemen. Further, whenever Jerome was in funds, he was lavish with gifts for his

27

valet, and Jim never forgot that during a prolonged illness it was Jerome who cared for him with tenderness, anxiety, and unremitting affection. Jim was not horrified at his master's escapades. Such things were expected of young gentlemen, and he exercised his own natural wit and resourcefulness in extricating his master. In fact, he thoroughly enjoyed his precarious and unpredictable life with Jerome, and would not have exchanged it for twice the wages and twice the security. "A chap's got to 'ave some fun in his life, he has," he would think, of himself. "And life's as gay as a pantomime with Mr. Lindsey." No two days were alike, with Jerome. None of this quiet life, with regular duties, that was so tiring to one with an adventurous heart.

Jim was anxious, now, not for himself, but for Jerome. He pondered whether the greatcoat were sufficiently warm and thick to repel the snow and wind. Bluebloods caught "humours" such as never afflicted those of coarser fiber, like himself. He cursed the farmer for not providing blankets. He considered, with distress, that Jerome's fine kid boots were probably well wet by now, and that lung fever was easily contracted. Jerome must have felt his thoughts. (He was always so subtle and sensitive.) Jim felt the gloved hand touch his arm, squeeze it comfortingly. Jim's wizened heart swelled, and he blinked. Let them that would say that Mr. Lindsey was "bad" and "rash." They were fools, they were. Dull clods as would never be able to understand true gentry. He, Jim, knew better. In all his service in America he had never before worked for a gentleman.

Jerome moved closer to his servant, put his mouth to his ear, and shouted: "Hell of a place in winter!"

Yes, this was hell, Jim reflected, completely numb and wretched with cold. But he did not regret his coming. No one else would be able to care for Jerome so well as himself, in the very probable event of lung fever. Jim scowled fiercely in the darkness. Let one of 'em just try to hover round his sickbed! He'd show 'em, drive 'em off, he would!

All at once, the wagon lurched and rocked and stopped. There was a sudden lull in the wind. The farmer shouted: "Here we are! At the foot of the hill. Can't go no further."

Jim looked about him, incredulously. But the darkness was still thick, and the snow was heavier than ever. He could feel its bitter constant kisses on his forehead and cheeks. When he tried to move, he was as stiff as iron. He glanced upwards, despairingly. Far up, in the direction of the sky, a few yellow lights twinkled, winked out, reappeared, like candles seen at a distance. But the night hid everything else. Jerome was bestirring himself, swearing voluptuously. Jim forced himself to climb down slowly, on feet without sensation. He reached blindly in the darkness for the bags. He heard Charlie's faint whimpering. He put the bags down in the snow. And then, though he still saw nothing, he heard the rattle and lurching of the wagon as it went on in the night. He and Jerome were alone, unseen by each other. "Follow me!" shouted Jerome. "Put your arm against mine. Curse those bags, anyway!" He took one from the hand of his servant.

Jim never forgot that long and torturous climb through snow, gale and dark. Only the bumping of Jerome's arm against his own kept him in touch with moving life. He floundered in drifts over his knees; sometimes he slipped, and fell into the deep and burning snow. Slowly, however, the snow became visible as faint white dunes, and the lights above brightened, came closer. At length, they were so near at hand that one could see yellow shafts wavering over the swelling whiteness, and a dark bulk loomed near and above them.

Now they were staggering through smoother drifts over what was evidently the walk. The towering black shapes of pines appeared, twisting and bending in the storm. Step by step, panting, slipping, cursing, the two men pushed their way towards a great arched door. Then Jerome was beating upon it with his fists and shouting. Charlie, from the shelter of one of Jerome's large pockets, set up a thin and furious barking.

A light twinkled behind the little window in the door. There was a sound of bolts being drawn. Then the door opened cautiously, and a young woman's face appeared, frightened and wary. Jerome wiped away the snow from his face and addressed her,

"Open up, for God's sake. I'm Mr. Lindsey. Open up, I say."

He pushed the door rudely, and the servant girl fell back, squealing. Jim saw a great panelled hall with a tiled red floor, an immense grandfather clock glimmering in warm lamplight, and a mighty oaken staircase. "Just like the old country," he thought, pleased and surprised. A fire burned against a far wall, its big logs red and glowing, and above it was a dark portrait. Jerome set down his dog, who viciously barked at the girl, causing her to retreat with fresh squeals. Jim put down the bags, and glared longingly at the fire. Jerome was shaking his coat, and removing it, and stamping the snow from his feet. "Where is Mr. Lindsey, my father?" he demanded.

The girl fled silently through a door to the left. The two men were alone. Smiling, Jerome turned to his servant. "Well, here we are, home at last. That fire looks excellent." He moved to the fire, and Jim followed eagerly. His withered hands were drawn and blue. He extended them to the warmth. The abandoned luggage dripped unheeded on the shining dark-red tiles. Charlie yipped and leaped about his master, shivering, his reddened eyes adoring. Then he rushed about the hall, sniffing loudly and suspiciously.

Jerome was glancing about him with open satisfaction. "Always the same. It never changes. God, I'm glad to be here, after all that!" He looked up at the portrait of a young and pretty woman, who was smiling down at them from over the fireplace. His face changed a little. "That's my mother, Jim."

Jim looked at the portrait courteously. A lovely frail little thing, it was. And not in the least like Master Jerome.

A door to the right opened, and Jerome, wearing his charming smile, turned to it, thinking to greet his father. But a young woman stepped into the hall, then seeing these unexpected two, stopped short with a slight exclamation, her hand still on the doorknob. Jerome's smile faded, and he stood in silence, staring at her.

"Yes?" she murmured. Then her face changed. "Oh," she said flatly, "you must be Jerome. We didn't expect you until tomorrow. Was there some mistake? Does Mr. Lindsey know you are here?"

Jerome did not like her manner, which was repressed and haughty, and not in the least friendly. He did not answer her. Charlie rushed at her, barking savagely. She lifted a heavy fold of her gown and swept him aside, disdainfully. Jim regarded her furtively, and there was a quickening in his monkey eyes. This must be the baggage, then, of which Mr. Jerome had told him. A proud piece, and an imperious one. Charlie, indignant and alarmed, returned to the safety of Jerome's feet, and from there snarled at the young woman.

She moved into the hall, towards the fire. She repeated, with some impatience: "Does Mr. Lindsey know you are here? If not, I shall find him at once. He came down to dinner tonight." Her voice, Jim noticed with approval, was deep and low, with great potentialities. She stood in the light of the fire and of the newel lamp and regarded Jerome questioningly, as though she were already mistress of this great warm house, and he, an unwelcome intruder.

Jerome remained obdurately and nastily silent. Then she

30

smiled, and her white teeth flashed in the quiet light. "I'm sorry. I'm Amalie Maxwell."

Jerome bowed ironically. He lifted his head and stared at her full and derisively. His brows drew together, in his contemptuous scrutiny and boldness. She was no longer smiling. She answered his look, lifting her head, not at all abashed, but challenging.

The firelight flared up; there was a strong drumming of the wind in the broad chimney. The light revealed Amalie Maxwell fully. Jerome was very still. His contempt faded, was replaced by fascinated wonder. My God, what a face, what a figure! And all this for that stick of an Alfred, that stocky, desiccated stone of a man!

Amalie was tall, so tall, indeed, that her eyes were almost on a level with Jerome's. She had the most superb figure, slender yet swelling, and cunningly set off by a bustled and draped gown of thick gray velvet, touched here and there, at the throat and wrist, with bright coral. The tiny buttons that ran from her throat to her waist were coral, also. Her basque bodice, tight and sleek, rose and fell over a wonderful and delicately formed bosom, drew in lovingly at a perfect waist, then disappeared in the folds and draperies of her gown. Her shoulders were smooth, faultless; her carriage, beyond reproach, regal yet supple.

A connoisseur of female figures, Jerome was all amazement and reverence. Very slowly then he lifted his eyes, and encountered hers. She was smiling, and the smile was dark and knowing. What eyes, he thought, astonished. They were very large and of a deep purplish tinge, vivid and flashing, passionate with intelligence, and not in the least soft and tender, as women's eyes ought to be. They were set amid thick short lashes, very black and heavy. Above them was a low white forehead, a pair of smooth and satiny black eyebrows. The nose was short and straight, with flaring nostrils, and the mouth below it was rather too full and wide, and moistly red. Despite this, however, it was a somewhat hard mouth, too firm, too resolute, for a woman. Jerome, studying her as openly as though she were a work of art rather than a human being, surveyed the lines of her face critically. It was all strong angles and planes, heroic in concept, rather pale, though translucent. Too much hard strength there, he reflected, objectively, too much understanding of life. It was, for all its amazing beauty, the face of a fighter, and it was more than a little repellent in expression.

31

He decided that, though she was admirable and astonishing and almost unbelievable, he did not like her. In fact, he hated her on sight. Oh, he knew all about such trollops! Women cast adrift, unprotected, forced to fight for themselves, and expecting and giving no quarter. He had seen them in London, New York and Paris, hard strumpets who knew what they wanted, and took it ruthlessly. He had never admired them, though he had enjoyed them frequently, and appreciated their natural wit and knowingness and lack of illusion. A man would never be bored with them, and a clever man could always conquer them. They were exciting. They were endlessly amusing and titillating. But a man of the world never married them.

She spoke tartly, in the silence which had been unbroken except for the sound of the wind in the chimney, and the dismayed snarling of Charlie: "I hope you like what you see—Jerome."

Jerome stared. But Jim broke out in a hoarse giggle. She did not condescend to notice his existence. She put out her hand straightly, like a man, and Jerome took it, after a moment's deliberate, and meaningful, hesitation. Her hand was large and white, and unexpectedly soft, and the fingers were of a beautiful contour. On the ring finger of her left hand an exceptionally beautiful emerald sparkled. His mother's ring, thought Jerome, and something burned in him like a furious still anger.

Then she smiled again, and the strong hard planes of her face melted into lines of entrancing softness and amusement. She shook her head slightly, as if in denial. Her hair, thick and black and shining like glass, sloped back in long waves to a chignon at the nape of her long white neck, and the firelight danced on it.

Where had he seen that face, that hair, that bosom before? Jerome asked himself. Then he was surprised again, and angered, and he, too, shook his head as if in denial. He was bewitched by his father's letter. Surely, there was no resemblance between this young woman and the portrait of his great-grandmother in the library! It was all delusion.

He said, in his insolent and languid voice: "Were you ever in New York? I seem to remember——"

She withdrew her hand. He had not been conscious of holding it all this time. She said: "No, I have never been in New York."

The carved door at the left opened suddenly and quickly, and Alfred appeared, exclaiming, advancing with outstretched hand. "Jerome! For goodness' sake! Your telegram said Tuesday. Was it an error? Oh, these telegraph offices! Good heavens! How did you get here in this storm? You are soaked to the skin. How are you, Jerome, my boy?"

Jerome turned to him, smiling easily. The same old Alfred, carefully effusive on the proper occasion, forthright and simple! It had been three years since Jerome had seen him last, and that had been on the occasion of the regrettable affair of the exigent lady from Syracuse. But Alfred had changed little. He was somewhat taller than Jerome, but appeared a little shorter, because his body, though straight and firm, was of a larger frame. The stiff white linen collar and wide black cravat seemed slightly too tight for his powerful neck. He wore discreet black broadcloth, expertly tailored and of fastidious cut. He had a broad but angular face, completely colorless, but firm and resolved and open. It took a perceptive observer to discover that it was also narrowly relentless of expression. There were many who called it a "good, Christian face, exhibiting his fine virtues." Jerome found it excessively dull and lightless. The pale gray eyes between light lashes were certainly not full of sparkle, for all their resolute and candid regard. Jerome thought they resembled the agate marbles of his youth, for they were streaked with slashes of yellowish brown. They revealed nothing of a very good, if uncompromising, mind, and one of little imagination. The nose was well-shaped, short and wide, with thick and insensitive nostrils. The wide thin mouth betrayed, besides integrity, a tendency towards bigotry and obduracy. Jerome often called him an "ascetic and infernal Puritan," and the description was maliciously apt. There was a cold dignity about the man, an unshakable strength.

For the rest, Alfred had a smooth fine quantity of light-brown hair, cropped short above wide temples and over a round big head. He disdained personal adornment of any kind, and his only jewelry was the excellent pearl pin in his cravat, the pearl studs at his wrists, and the elaborate gold chain of his watch, extended over his black satin waistcoat.

He was all real, if reserved, pleasure at the sight of his adopted brother and cousin. He took Jerome's deliberately flaccid hand with enthusiasm, overcoming a slight and wary hesitation. He was always awkward with Jerome, and tried to compensate for this by an unusual and dignified affability.

"Let me look at you," he said. "How well you look, after that horrible journey in the storm. How did you get here?"

"On an open farm wagon," replied Jerome, easily. "No matter," he added, as Alfred uttered a word of consternation. "We're here, and that is the main thing."

Alfred immediately subsided into polite and sedate competence. "This is your man, I presume, about whom you telegraphed us. Your rooms are ready." He started. He had not at first noticed the dog, which again snarled and barked. "A dog?" he said uncertainly. "I trust—I hope——"

"Oh, he's housebroken. No indiscretions," said Jerome. Miss Maxwell laughed softly.

Alfred, recalling her in his confusion, turned to her. "Amalie, my love, this is my—my cousin, Jerome Lindsey."

She inclined her head sardonically. "We've introduced ourselves, Alfred."

"Miss Maxwell, my fiancée," added Alfred, lamely, and his pale cheek flushed. Jerome invariably made him feel boorish. Jerome bowed in the girl's direction.

Alfred resumed, with formality: "Amalie, will you summon a servant and order Jerome's man, and the bags, conducted to the prepared rooms?"

Amalie moved towards the door to the right, and Jerome watched her go with furtive admiration. What a carriage was this, regal and composed, yet also young and quick! Then he was annoyed. These two were already assuming the rôles of master and mistress of the old Lindsey mansion, and all that was in it. Well, he would soon alter this, he thought grimly.

"Would you care to go up to your rooms, also, and change your clothes?" asked Alfred.

Jerome looked down at his wet boots and the damp bottom regions of his pantaloons. He said: "No. I want to see my father."

He threw his hat, coat and cane towards Jim, who caught them deftly. But he tucked Charlie under his arm and turned towards the library door. "Are you taking the dog?" asked Alfred, with disapproval, for he disliked all animals.

"Why not? Certainly." Jerome walked to the library door. The flush deepened on Alfred's cheek. But he allowed Jerome to open the door and to precede him into the library.

CHAPTER FOUR

The immense room was warm and dim, with here and there a quiet lamp glowing on ancient dark oak. Books completely covered the high walls. Jerome's feet pressed deep into dark red carpeting. Before the enormous black marble fireplace was spread a huge white-bear rug, and on this rug were grouped several red and black leather chairs, with footstools. The great wide windows were completely covered, now, with crimson damask curtains. Over the fireplace was the famed portrait of Jerome's great-grandmother. It was an austere but inviting room, full of peace and dignity, and this atmosphere was enhanced by the glow and blaze of a mighty log fire.

Two people were seated before the fire, in a companionable silence, their faces turned towards the door. One was a tall, very thin, and quite elderly gentleman, a cane at his emaciated knee. The other was so small as to appear to be a very young child, but, as he stood up, pushing himself painfully from his chair, it was to be seen that he was a humpback, and about fourteen years of age.

The elderly man was visibly vibrating with his eager excitement. In a voice calm, but suprisingly strong, he exclaimed: "Jerome! Jerome, my boy!" And he extended to the young man a long white hand of delicate shape.

Jerome went to him quickly, and grasped the extended hand. Quite naturally, and without affectation, he bent over his father and kissed the thin and sunken cheek. "Papa," he said, and then could say nothing more. The two looked at each other steadily, smiling, their hands tightening together.

Then Mr. Lindsey said softly: "My dear, dear boy. How glad I am to see you again! Sit near me, please. I want to look at you."

Jerome looked about for a chair, then encountered the grave dark eyes of young Philip Lindsey, Alfred's son. He paused. "You're growing up, Phil," he said, forcing friendliness into his voice. He had no antagonism in him for the boy, but only an uneasy pity and aversion. Once, someone had told him that Philip resembled him, and he had been outraged. Where was the resemblance, in that white small face, so sunken, so attenuated, so spiritual and quiet of expression? Perhaps the eyes were similar, and Jerome egotistically conceded that, for they were large and black, and brilliant with intellect, quite overshadowing and minimizing the little delicate features below them, and shining steadfastly under an unusually high broad brow of extreme whiteness and strength Also, Philip's hair was thick and dark and curling, like Jerome's. But beyond these, surely, there was no resemblance! Who could look on that deformed little body in gray broadcloth without a shudder of repugnance? Jerome always resolutely averted his gaze from

35

the large hump on the boy's back, and, as if in careless apology, assumed a jocund affability when conversing with Philip.

"Thank you—Uncle Jerome," said Philip, with difficulty, and remembering that only the formality of the law made Jerome his uncle, and that, in reality, they were only second cousins. A film of color ran under the white skin of his cheeks. His small and fragile hands knotted together in his nervousness.

Jerome pulled a chair close to his father, and sat down, immediately forgetting the boy. Philip moved away, uncertainly, and sat down in the shadowy distance as unobtrusively as possible.

Mr. Lindsey studied his son's face, and sighed at its bad color and at the marks and stains of dissipation under the bold hard eyes. He said gently: "You are looking well, Jerome. Tell me you are well."

"Oh, I'm always well," replied Jerome, with lightness. "And you, sir?"

Mr. Lindsey looked down at his hands, knotted with arthritis, and glanced at his crippled legs. He said: "It does not bother me much or often. But it makes it difficult to get about. However, I do not complain."

He smiled at Jerome. There was no resemblance between the two. Mr. Lindsey had the spare pale countenance of the New Englander, and, indeed, his mother had been born in Boston. His was the lean and austere face of New England, intellectual and reserved, gently dignified, with large light-blue eyes full of astute gentleness and breeding. His white hair lay sleekly on his bony skull, above whittled temples and large, well-shaped ears. Once it had been quite yellow. His nose was thin and of Roman contour, and his wide straight mouth expressed compassion and shyness and humor. It had been his paternal grandmother who had given both to Jerome and Philip their almost Latin darkness. Not from this lady had come Mr. Lindsey's calm and fortitude, his quiet courage and objective temperament.

He held his son's restless and jewelled hand in his dry and paperlike fingers. He seemed unwilling to release it. "I am glad you are home, Jerome," he said softly.

Home. Jerome looked at the fire. How he had always hated the still peace and tranquillity of this high and isolated big house, the dim order that prevailed in it, the contemplation that filled this library and the parlors! It had suffocated him. He wondered at this vaguely, now. Just at this moment, at least, it was warm and secure for him, dignified and welcoming, a shelter and a refuge. His face tightened. This was his home, filled now with interlopers. This was to be the inheritance of an unimaginative and detestable man, and a low-born trollop, and a miserable cripple! It was not to be endured. He must end it, and quickly. Did he wish to live here, among these pines, on this long and lonely hillside with only the wind and the hearth fires for company? Did he wish to immure himself here, with only a wretched village to enliven him, gazing eternally on these books, walking daily about the desolate grim grounds, looking through the windows of the sun room, and dining endlessly in the lofty panelled dining-room a-glitter with dim silver? Did he want this timeless peace, this heavy and cultured formality and routine? Something contracted in him, with a familiar depression and revulsion. Yet—the three repellent strangers must not live here, either, after his father was dead! It was not to be borne. He felt a stir of ancient hatred within him, a sickness.

He looked up. His father was regarding him steadfastly, with the strangest look, as if reading his thoughts. The old boy had this disconcerting gift of divining the emotions of others. Mr. Lindsey's still, blue eyes had darkened as if with sadness.

He said: "How is the painting, Jerome?"

Jerome smiled with an effort. "Doing well. I don't sell any, as you know. I won't sell them. I give them to my friends, as always. By the way, I've brought two home; one for you and one for—for Alfred's wedding present." His smile became disagreeable. "I've brought back the miniature of my mother, from which I made the portrait. You'll see them all, later." He added absently: "I never liked that portrait of my mother, in the hall."

The door opened, and Alfred and Amalie entered. Alfred paused on the threshold and looked long and searchingly at his uncle and cousin near the fire. Then, as if thrusting back an uneasy and unworthy thought, he lifted his head and followed Miss Maxwell as she approached the two. Jerome rose, with deliberate hesitation, and offered her a chair. She sat down gracefully, acknowledging his politeness with an ironical bend of her head. But she did not look at him. She began to gaze pleasantly at the fire as if she were alone, leaving Jerome, fuming against her, standing at her side.

Alfred said: "I have just heard from your man, Johnson, that you've not dined, Jerome, so I've ordered a small collation to be brought here to you, by the fire."

"Thoughtful of you," commented Jerome, politely. "But I'd

37

prefer just a whiskey and soda."

Alfred ignored this. "You are certain you would not care to change before dining?"

"Do I look so disgracefully bedraggled, then?" asked Jerome. Alfred's pale mouth drew together. "No, no, certainly not."

Jerome sat down beside his father again. Alfred, slightly flushed, stirred up the fire. Amalie continued to regard it with pleasant abstraction. Mr. Lindsey, feeling the constraint, drew his watch from his pocket and glanced at it. "Almost nine," he commented.

Amalie said idly, without moving her head: "Philip, isn't it time for your bed?"

They had all forgotten Philip, lurking in the half-darkness at a distance. But at Amalie's voice and question, he rose and came courteously towards the group at the fire. He bowed to Mr. Lindsey and to Jerome, then to his father and Amalie.

"Good night—Grandfather. Good night—Uncle Jerome. Good night, Papa. Good night, Miss Maxwell." Jerome smiled irrepressibly at the order of the names, and looked at Philip with more interest. Did the poor humpback, then, resent this woman, also? But, to his surprise, Philip was gazing at Amalie with a curious expression, softened, eager. She lifted her hand and touched his thin arm, and instinctively he moved closer to her. Even when seated as she was, her strong purplish eyes were on a level with the boy's, and the look in them was oddly gentle and understanding.

"Good night, dear Philip," she said very gently.

She drew him to her then, with natural affection, and kissed his transparent cheek. He leaned against her shoulder for a brief shy moment; then, bowing again to them all, he drifted silently from the room. Amalie watched him go, with an unreadable thoughtfulness. But Alfred looked only at Amalie, and now his pale, amber-flecked eyes flared briefly but urgently with a terrible, suppressed passion. Seeing this, Jerome said to himself, with an inner grin: "Well, well, so that is how it is!"

He suddenly remembered someone else. "Where is my dear sister, Dorothea?"

Mr. Lindsey replied: "Dorothea is confined to her bed with a feverish cold, I am sorry to say. She insisted upon driving into town yesterday, and the weather was very bad. But, doubtless, she will be anxious to see you."

"I have sent word to Dorothea," said Alfred. "You are right, sir. She has asked to see Jerome, after he has dined."

With his new acuteness about his family, Jerome saw that

the look Alfred directed at Mr. Lindsey had no hypocrisy in its grave affection and gentleness, and that his propitiatory manner towards the older man was impelled by a genuine and solicitous regard, and a most profound respect. But Jerome was not touched by this. In earlier days, he had almost liked Alfred's tenderness for his father, and had been relieved by it. It had absolved him, then, from any responsibility, had permitted him to go his own way, assured that his father was in adequate and protecting hands. But now he was secretly enraged. Something like jealousy boiled in him, and unreasonable outrage. He had always prided himself on being "completely objective" in his attitude towards others, but like almost all others who so pride themselves he was invariably the victim of his shameful emotions.

He sneered inwardly at Alfred, who was shaking up the cushions behind Mr. Lindsey. He watched the other man with the alertness and jealousy of a dog. Feeling his master's reactions, Charlie, on Jerome's knee, set up a renewed snarling. Mr. Lindsey put out his hand and smoothed the dog's silken head, and murmured to him. Then the old man sank back, with a word of thanks to his nephew. He looked at them all with frank affection, letting his eyes wander from face to face, as if he felt security and continuity about him. Only when his glance touched Amalie did it shrink into reserve for a moment, and then, as she smiled at him, he smiled in answer.

A servant brought in a large silver tray on which were arrayed a silver pot of tea, sugar and thick cream, and a rich meat pie. Jerome spread a large white napkin on his knee, and began to eat with candid appetite, laughing and talking inconsequentially to his father as he did so.

"You might know I'd arrive in the worst snowstorm of the season," he said. "Damn those telegraph people, making that mistake!"

"They rarely make mistakes," Alfred said with dignity. "I can't understand it. I shall discuss it with them in a few days."

Jerome shrugged. "Give them my personal regards, and rebuke them properly," he said. Then he saw that Amalie was scrutinizing him ironically and with a cold smile. It was as if she understood all about him, his egotism, his brutal disregard for others, his carelessness, and all his follies and conceits and cruelties. He stopped eating to stare at her viciously. She was not quelled by his look. Languidly, she lifted her hand and touched the coral cameo at her throat with her long white fingers. We are two of a kind, she seemed to be saying to him, her eyes brilliant between her lashes. We understand each other.

He returned to the meat pie, hating her with fresh rage. Ah, my fine strumpet, he said to himself, we shall see what we shall see. So you enjoy the prospect of being mistress of my father's house, my house, do you? You will lady it over the household, and queen it over the servants, and direct and rule and advise, eh? We shall see, and very soon, I promise you.

Amalie smiled faintly, turned her beautiful face to the fire.

Satisfied at length, Jerome allowed the tray to be taken from him. He asked for whiskey, and Alfred, with no comment, ordered it brought. Jerome poured a small glassful from the decanter, whisked a very little soda into the amber fluid. Then he paused. "Will no one join me?"

To his incredulous surprise, Amalie said tranquilly: "I will, thank you." And stretched out her hand.

Jerome looked from her to Alfred, with an unpleasant grin. Alfred had colored, his dry skin suffused. Mr. Lindsey took Charlie upon his knee and began to stroke him. It was as if he had not heard.

"With pleasure," said Jerome. He filled another glass, waiting for Amalie to protest the quantity. But she gave no word until the glass was almost as full as his own. Then she murmured. He filled the glass with the soda. She took it from him then, with a polite acknowledgment, and put the glass to her red lips. She sipped appreciatively.

Then Jerome glanced up at Alfred, with a virulent smile. But Alfred, in his chair, did not move or speak. His face was averted. Jerome leaned back in his chair in an attitude of enjoyment. "Excellent whiskey," he commented. "You miss a great deal, Alfred, in your teetotalism."

"I miss many other things, too," replied Alfred, stiffly. His voice sounded muffled.

"And all of them pleasant," said Jerome. He paused. "Is that not so, Miss Maxwell?"

She looked at him directly. "Yes, indeed," she said.

Had she no discretion? Jerome asked himself. Had no one ever informed her that ladies did not drink whiskey, or any other spirits, in the presence of gentlemen, or at all? She was no fool: could she not at least pretend to some decorum, some gentility, if only for her own avaricious sake and prospects? Was she deliberately attempting to disillusion the fatuous Alfred, trying to alienate and disgust him? Or, did she know that her octopus hold on him was too secure to be shaken, and that she could with impunity flaunt her shamelesness in his Puritan face?

What sort of creature was this, utterly without refinement and decency? She was worse than an open trollop, for a trollop at least pretended to some manners and proper deportment when it was best for her. And, from the look of her, and her evident enjoyment, she was no stranger to whiskey, and this was no gesture of gauche bravado. She sipped her drink, relishing it like a man, brazenly, before his father.

"You find whiskey a stomachic, Miss Amalie?" he asked, with deep politeness. He felt, rather than saw, Alfred's sudden suppressed movement.

"A most efficacious one," she agreed.

"It makes life bearable," Jerome suggested.

"Almost endurable," she answered, in his own tone.

"But it must be taken regularly, for that salubrious effect," went on Jerome, malevolently.

She withdrew the glass from her lips, and turned the full purple blaze of her eyes upon him, and he saw understanding contempt in them.

"I don't know anything about that," she said quietly. "But doubtless you could tell me."

Mr. Lindsey raised his head and looked slowly from his son to the young woman. His gray thin brows drew together just slightly.

Jerome said: "Then, you do not need to escape from the exigencies of life very often, Miss Amalie?"

She regarded him in silence, and her lip curled. "I am no coward," she said. "But there are others who must escape constantly. Is that not so, Mr. Lindsey?"

Jerome did not answer. He turned the glass about in his fingers. Then he looked at Alfred, and meeting the latter's distressed eye, he laughed in open but silent mirth. Alfred pulled himself upright in his chair; his eye narrowed upon Jerome, and one suddenly saw that he could become coldly violent and ruthless when necessary. All his inherent dislike, his involuntary and suppressed hatred, for his cousin, shone like lightning for a moment on his face.

Damn you, thought Jerome, not shrinking from that look, but returning it with one of virulent disdain, I am not gratuitously insulting your love. I am only trying to reveal to your stupidity the full extent of her shamelessness.

Mr. Lindsey said quietly: "I have never subscribed to the foolish belief that females are different from the other half of

41

humanity. Woman begotten of man shares his proclivities. And man is born of woman. If Miss Amalie wishes a glass of whiskey, or of anything else, occasionally, that is entirely her own affair, and I wish her enjoyment. I have changed my mind, Jerome. I believe I will join you and Miss Amalie in a toast to the coming wedding."

His manner was stern and cold and imperative. He looked at Jerome fixedly, then slowly turned his full blue eyes upon Alfred, and his manner implied a certain aristocratic censoriousness. Jerome, in the sudden silence, filled a glass for his father, extended it to him with an elaborate bow. But Mr. Lindsey was not to be placated. His breath came a little faster. He held the glass high.

"To my dear son, Alfred, and to a very charming and understanding lady," he said. He inclined his head to Amalie, whose face had changed, becoming sad and tired.

"To a very happy marriage," said Jerome, gallantly, smiling full at the young woman, and then at his father. He and his father drank the whiskey.

Then Alfred said, in a strained voice: "Father—you know your physician has forbidden spirits——"

Mr. Lindsey replied composedly: "There are times when a man must drink for the sake of his soul, and for the sake of other equally important things."

Jerome rose and bowed deeply to all of them. "And now, if you will excuse me, I think I shall run up to see my sister. We have much to discuss." He paused. "After all, we have not seen each other for a long time."

Amalie held her glass near her lips. Her eyes were almost black in the lamplight. "Give her my regards, please," she said. "And tell her, please, that I wish her much pleasure—in your discussions."

CHAPTER FIVE

Jerome went up the great oaken staircase, whistling softly and abstractedly, stroking the head of the dog, which was tucked under his right arm. He had always despised the "stuffiness" of these somber halls, this massive stairway; but with his newly aware eyes he suddenly admired their Elizabethan atmosphere, their grave dignity and strength. His taste had always run more to the delicate and the airy, the ultrarefined and exquisite, and he had found the solidity of the old house, which his great-grandparents had built, oppressive and too heavy. But now the house felt secure in spite of its somberness, impregnable despite its darkness and massiveness. It was perversely dear to him, and his new jealousy and outrage made him glance about him, frowning and grim-eyed.

No! No stranger should live within these halls, and lord it over this household! He thought of the stony-lipped Alfred and his "trollop," and his face became ugly in the dim lamplight. Strangers, both; interlopers, both. So, they would fill his father's house with alien brats, would they? Not so long as he, Jerome Lindsey, had a claim here.

He paused on the second landing. Did he have a claim? But, surely to God, his father knew him, knew his volatile nature too well to have taken him seriously when he had declared that he wanted nothing of this house, and that nothing would ever induce him to live here! He, himself, distrusted the capriciousness of his own temperament, and he was always obscurely annoyed whenever anyone took him at his word, especially when it was later very inconvenient, or when he had changed his mind. Yet, he could not go to his father and say sheepishly: "I trust you did not take me seriously? After all, I spoke thoughtlessly, when I was young and stupid." It was damned embarrassing. And even now, he did not know exactly what he wanted! He only knew that instead of despising Alfred, and indulgently deriding him, he now loathed him, and felt in himself a dark and powerful repulsion and hatred. Though fond of analyzing others, and quite subtle and astute in estimating and dissecting their natures, he had never known anything, really, of himself.

He stood, now, on the top landing, and leaned against the strong oaken railing, looking down at the duskily lit hall below. It was very strange, but he was remembering a text from his old Sunday-school lessons: "He that hath no rule over his own spirit is like a city that is broken down and without walls." Odd that that phrase, so meaningless to his youth, should strike him now with malignant meaning. "The city without walls." Yes, he was like a gay and riotous and heedless city, open to attack, all its broad and colorful avenues vulnerable to the advance of an inexorable enemy.

Whenever he was disturbed, baffled or tormented in his thoughts, he was seized with an angry melancholy, and a kind of impotence. He felt these, now. He despised sentimentality, yet he found himself thinking: I've been like Esau. And those

43

two down there are going to gobble up the feast—unless I prevent them.

Then he remembered his sister, Dorothea, and he smiled. It was most amusing that he thought of Dorothea, in this hour, as an ally. For Dorothea had not only never been his ally; she had always been his worst critic, his indomitable enemy. But enemies, when they had a common foe, frequently joined together in mutual effort.

He began to whistle again. He walked down the vast oaken corridor, with its thick dark red carpet, and came to Dorothea's door. He paused a moment there, before knocking, in order to fix an amiable smile on his face. It was not a difficult thing to do, for he found it very easy to dissemble, and he could simulate, sometimes even to his own inner conviction, any emotion he desired.

Then his smile faded. He said to himself: Stop it, you fool, you actor. This is too serious. Why do I always have to place myself on a stage and stand back, fatuously admiring my own antics, as if they were too delicious for words? You confounded bore and idiot! Some day you will be the fine exquisite to your own undoing.

He knocked abruptly on the carved panels of Dorothea's door. He heard her voice, quiet, strong, but hoarse, now, telling him to enter. He opened the door and stepped across the threshold.

The great room was hot and almost dark, and only the red firelight and one feeble lamp made anything within it visible. The odors of vinegar and mustard and warm wool filled the stifling air. Massive dark mahogany and carved black walnut furniture lurked about on the heavy green carpet; green velvet draperies were drawn tightly across the four windows that looked out upon the front lawns. They made a glimmering rich green wall, closed against the stormy winter night. At right angles to them was Dorothea's large black walnut desk, neatly heaped with papers pertaining to the household affairs, for she was an excellent housekeeper. In the middle of the room stood her enormous canopied bed, all dark red comforters and pure white linen, the crimson curtains looped back to show her sitting high on her pillows. This had been her great-grandmother's bed, and she clung to it with a kind of desperate grimness, for she preferred the past to the present, which she hated.

"Well, Jerome," she said, in her domineering voice. How familiar it was, even to that old and automatically inimical note with its undertone of suspicion and wariness! "Do come

44

in and shut the door. There is such a draft." She began to cough, painfully and hoarsely, putting her white kerchief to her lips. "And do not sit too near me. It is nonsense, of course, but Dr. Hawley insists that feverish colds are infectious, and while I disagree, I must obey his orders. There, between me and the fire, please, so I can see you without strain."

Brother and sister had not seen each other for five years, but Dorothea's manner and voice would never have suggested it. He and she might have met only that morning. He sat down, arranged the dog on his knee. Dorothea said, with incredulous umbrage: "A dog? Impossible! You know I never allow dogs here, Jerome; it is most thoughtless of you, and he will have to go to the stables at once. I trust he does not bite? He has a most unpleasant growl."

Jerome answered amiably: "Oh, no, he'll not go to the stables, darling Dorothea. He doesn't bite, and he only growls because of that hideous cap he sees on your head. He is really a most agreeable little fellow. Shall I let him down, to explore?"

"Certainly not! Dogs are so filthy. Please to take him on your knee again, though doubtless he will cover you with his hairs."

Jerome lifted Charlie to his knees and stroked him fondly. He said: "I really don't care about dogs, but it is the fashion in New York. I detest the little brute, but he doesn't seem to know it. Do you, Charlie?"

The dog licked his cheek, then curled up on his lap, continuing, however, to regard Dorothea with a sharp and hostile and most bewildered bright gaze.

Certainly the woman in the bed was formidable enough in appearance. It was evident that she was tall, and imposing, for all her thinness. She wore a dressing gown of red wool over her ruffled linen nightdress, whose collar was tied high over her throat. A thick gray woolen shawl huddled in folds about her shoulders. On her dark straight masses of hair, threaded with coarse gray, was her ruffled high nightcap, tied under her chin with immaculate white strings. It was like a stiff crown, and was hardly different from the caps she invariably wore when going about her household duties.

Her complexion, like Jerome's, was dark, and her eyes were dark, also, but somewhat small, and very intimidating and harsh of expression. Her nose was long and thin, quite aquiline, with arrogant nostrils. Her mouth, intolerant and without the slightest feminine softness, had a rigorous look, and its thin pallor was drawn together in a stringent pucker. Everything about her was gaunt and repellent, yet she had a high dignity,

45

and always commanded fear and respect. One knew instantly that here was a woman of principle and integrity, without imagination or gentleness or much compassion. She even had a kind of handsomeness, and could be impressive by sheer force of her austere and excessively stern character. Jerome had always considered her very amusing, and was the only one who had ever dared to laugh in her very face. Even her father, to whom she was so devoted, lived in quiet awe of her, and though it was not possible for him to displease her (for she loved him so), he tried never to disagree with her but to appease her. He considered, regretfully, that Dorothea was almost always right.

She was the sort who never forgave nor forgot, and her opinions, once formed, were incapable of change. If other evidence was inexorably presented to her, she was personally affronted, and still retained her former judgment, certain that she was being deceived deliberately. If Dorothea had ever lied, neither she nor others were aware of it, and she considered a falsehood little better than a murder. Yet, like many of her kind, she could be ingenuous, and was susceptible to flattery. However, only Jerome knew this, and, without conscience, often took advantage of it. Once, when he had needed some money for a shameful debt, he had told her she was an "aristocrat," and, as she secretly believed this, she had disgorged a considerable sum for him from her own pocket.

She firmly believed that her way was best, and was relentless in imposing that way, for the "good" of others. As she was usually right, this did not endear her to her victims. Religious, creaking with probity, she could not endure the easy of character, the benign of judgment. She believed these things to be weaknesses. It was not hard to imagine, then, that the pastor of the village Episcopal church found her a very pillar of fortitude and support.

Jerome had always been her curse and her cross. From his earliest childhood he had opposed her, had laughed at her, with impunity. Her strictest punishments had made no impression on him at all. He slipped from her control, from her grasp, like a greased eel. She had never understood him, and because she had never been able to dominate or intimidate him, her bafflement had reached the heights of secret and unacknowledged hate.

They looked at each other across the dimly flickering path of red light from the fire, and thought of these things. Dorothea's stern eyes were pink of rim, and Jerome reflected that more than this "cold" had brought that betraying color to them.

Dorothea was suffering. She saw his faintly smiling scrutiny, and lifted her head with hauteur. She said: "You seem well, Jerome." She paused. "I am glad to see you home again."

"And I," he said gently, "am glad to be home."

She narrowed her eyes at him suspiciously. Then a flash of surprise appeared on her face, as she saw that he was not lying. She fumbled for her handkerchief, and blew her nose loudly and unaffectedly. Then she dropped her hands and stared down at them. All at once she appeared helpless and without defense, as if she were alone and could be herself.

She said, her voice catching as if her control had slipped: "You ought to have come home before. I—I've needed you."

Jerome regarded her in intent silence, and feeling it, she looked up quickly. He then said: "Yes. Yes, I know. You are right, Dotty."

Her features automatically winced at this hated nickname, and then, amazingly, she must have felt its casual affection, its implications of family solidarity, for she winked rapidly over and over, and averted her gaunt profile. She murmured: "I'm glad. Thank you, Jerome."

Jerome stood up and poked the fire to a higher blaze. His sister watched him; her lips worked, as if she were struggling to keep herself from weeping. Her long fingers twisted together convulsively.

Jerome sat down again. She forced herself to some measure of her usual calm. "You have dined, Jerome? Your old rooms are comfortable?"

"Yes. Yes. Thank you, Dotty." His tone was still gentle. He drew his chair a trifle closer to her.

They looked at each other again, in a long silence. Then Dorothea whispered hoarsely: "After all, you are my brother, and I am your sister. Who else is there, especially in time of trouble?"

Jerome said nothing. He took out his thin silver cheroot case. Dorothea watched him. Then she compelled herself to say: "Please smoke, Jerome, if it pleases you, but blow the smoke towards the fire." She sighed. He lit the cheroot with a "lucifer," and leaned back in his chair, smoking contentedly.

Poor old girl, he thought, with unusual understanding and pity. It surprised him that he could feel compassion for Dorothea. But, he reflected wryly, it is amazing how much sympathy and human emotion we can feel for an old enemy who is about to become an ally. Why such an enemy becomes actually flesh and blood, like one's self, actually a fellow creature!

47

There is nothing like a common threat, and a common hatred, to stimulate nice sentiments of brotherly love between foes.

But, he saw with shrewdness, she was not Alfred's enemy; at least, not yet. Alfred's blank unawareness of her passion for him, and her devotion, had not enraged or humiliated her, or inspired in her a hunger for revenge. He had taken her love and consecration for granted, and had given her strong affection in return, purely fraternal affection. Though they were almost the same age, Alfred considered her much his senior, and often felt for her a filial respect and attachment. His obtuseness was amusing to Jerome, saddening to Mr. Lindsey. Both knew that Dorothea had firmly believed that Alfred might come to love her, and both knew that she had lived for this. If, first, there had been the timid little Martha, and now this new and dreadful woman, Dorothea did not blame Alfred. He had only been the victim of designing women, had fallen helplessly before their "wiles." She felt for him, still, only a passionately burning protectiveness, fierce in its strength.

So, thought Jerome, eying his sister with deliberate friendliness and sympathy, we must still not attack that damned Alfred. He wondered, with amusement, why Alfred had never discerned that Dorothea was the perfect wife for him. They were a pair. Yet Alfred had gone skittering after innocent little Martha, from Saratoga. One could understand that, in a measure. Martha was an heiress, and Alfred loved money, in his religious and reverent fashion. Had he loved the small and fragile creature? Yes, it was very possible. Certainly, he had been stricken for years over her death, and had forgiven her the crippled Philip. But why this terrible and ruthless passion for that strumpet, a strumpet who was penniless, and of an unsavory reputation to boot? It was not consistent.

But Jerome had lived long enough to know that nothing in life is consistent, and that the impulses which drive men are inexplicable. Passion and lust and insane desire had come late to Alfred Lindsey, and, like late springs which release long-frozen rivers, they came tumultuously, and with devastating force. The frozen river which was Alfred's nature was in full and destroying spate. Jerome had seen that, less than an hour ago. Alfred's reason had been torn from its reluctantly thawing banks; his self-protectiveness and ancient caution were whirling in the foam of his furious infatuation. He wanted that woman, and his desire, raw and red and mad, was tearing at his cold flesh. Nothing could stop him now.

Jerome stroked his dog's head, as he waited for Dorothea to

speak again. And then, all at once, he was overwhelmed by a sudden and nameless desolation, by an ache like unappeased hunger. He was amazed at this. His hand slowed; he stared before him, forgetting his sister. What was wrong with him? He could feel his misery sharp within him, like an evil tooth. This was new in his experience. He had always lived lightly, and wretchedness was a new sensation and a sickening one. He said again, to himself: What is wrong with me? Am I tired of this place so soon? He moved as if to get to his feet, so urgent was this unfamiliar emotion.

Dorothea was speaking. "Have you seen that—that woman, Jerome?" Her voice was quiet, yet it rang with pain and loathing.

He said: "Yes."

She leaned towards him, quickly. "Am I right, Jerome? Was I unjust about her?"

He thought: Am I sickening with something? Was that damned ride in the wagon too much for me? He stood up, stood with his back to the fire, his head bent. He said: "You are right, Dotty. You weren't unjust, I'm sorry to say."

He fumbled absently at the seals on his watch-chain. He stared at the vague pattern of the carpet. A new sensation had him now, a kind of wild rage and hatred. He said, still looking at the carpet: "We've got to stop it."

She fell back against the pillows, and now she cried unashamedly, rubbing her eyes with her handkerchief. "But how, Jerome? What can we do?"

He said, in a loud and angry voice: "I don't know! Why haven't you and Papa done anything before this? You must have seen it coming. It didn't fall from the blue, did it?"

He pushed his chair rudely towards his sister, and sat down again. "I want to know all about it. How can I do anything, or suggest anything, unless I know? How did he meet her? You wrote me something about her appealing to him for money."

She had never seen him so concerned and so genuinely agitated, and though warmed by this, she was also made timid. She spoke, almost apologetically, as if pleading for his forgiveness in advance: "Jerome, you must not blame me too much. Perhaps I was a little obtuse. But how was I to dream? Whoever would have thought poor Alfred to be so flagrantly lacking in judgment? Certainly, Papa could not know, either."

She paused. "It was all so sudden. You know that Alfred is on the school board. He must have met that woman some time ago. But he never mentioned her."

49

"So, he's a sly devil, after all," Jerome interrupted, grimly.

"Oh, no, no! I beg of you, Jerome, to withhold your condemnation! It is unfair to Alfred. She must have made no impression on him at all, at first."

He watched her and was abstractedly surprised that she flushed suddenly. She looked away from him. She said lamely: "Perhaps I am being a little unjust. I must be just, even to her. You see, she didn't actually appeal to him for money, for herself." Her voice dropped, became hoarser, and she coughed. "It seems that she was boarding with a farmer. Their name is Hobson, or something equally odious. Very impecunious and worthless people, doubtless, for they could not meet the payments on the mortgage, which is held by our Bank. Hobson had appealed to poor Alfred before. There were so many children, he pleaded, as if those children were Alfred's fault."

At this, Jerome could not help smiling.

Dorothea continued, with gathering indignation: "Alfred tried to be just. But what could he do? Payments had fallen far behind. Alfred had a duty to his depositors, and he knew his duty. He informed the farmer, regretfully, that the Bank must foreclose. But he was generous, too. The Bank would not foreclose until the harvest was in——"

"My God," said Jerome. "So, the Bank 'would not foreclose until the harvest was in'! How very, very generous of dear Alfred!"

Dorothea's harsh face flushed, and she bridled. "I don't understand your tone, Jerome. After all, as I have said, Alfred had a duty to his depositors, and the harvest appeared very promising. In the meantime, of course, the farmer and his family had a roof over their heads, and it was only right that the abominable man should bring in the harvest and pay something on his indebtedness. He owed the Bank over three hundred dollars."

She waited for Jerome's comment, but his smile was dark and unpleasant. She continued, with rising heat: "The man had the effrontery to suggest to Alfred that he be allowed to remain, as a tenant, working the farm on a share basis. But Alfred already had a buyer for the farm. He saw his duty."

Jerome looked down at his cheroot, and watched the gray smoke coil away. "I see," he said softly. "So Miss Amalie came to Alfred and begged for mercy."

"How did you know?" asked Dorothea, with ingenuous surprise.

Jerome laughed. "Oh, I'm very astute. I was always a sub-

50

tle devil. So, that is how it was. What interests me now is this: Did Alfred thaw out and extend the mercy?"

Dorothea's face changed, became thinly violent. "Yes! You can see how he is in her power! How she flattered and deceived and influenced him! That is what is so terrible, so hard to understand. Defying his sense of duty, he permitted the farmer to remain, after her blandishments. Not only that—and I do not expect you to believe me, Jerome—he extended the mortgage; actually gave Hobson money for his sick wife and children, bought them a wagonload of clothing, filled their larder with food, and sent them a physician, one no less than our own Dr. Hawley! Does it seem incredible to you?"

"Yes," said Jerome, very quietly, and only after a long silence, "it does seem incredible to me."

Dorothea was more and more excited. "Not only that, Jerome! But it seems that that woman was very sly indeed. She informed Alfred that she was ill, that she had spent many nights in tending the farmer's disgustingly ailing family. What does the infatuated man do then, pray? I will tell you. As head of the school board, he ordered the creature to remain on the farm and to rest, and he forced the board to continue to pay her salary."

"Was she ill, really?"

Dorothea stared at him, frowning, evidently taken aback by this irrelevant question. She said, harshly: "That is what she told Alfred. I think she was merely indolent. After all, she is a strapping creature, full of the most odious health." She paused. "Alfred tried to interest me in the family, and to please him, I visited them." She coughed. "We found Amalie in bed. She must have had a slight cold; I must be just. She did appear ill, but doubtless it was affectation. The family seemed devoted to her, but you know how that class dissembles. They were tending her. It seemed quite enough, and I cannot understand why Alfred sent nurses to care for her."

"How long was she ill?"

"From Christmas until spring. She never returned to the school, except for the last month. She had become fashionably slender then, for, when I first saw her, a year ago in church, she had been of a most robust and hearty appearance."

Jerome stood up, and began to walk slowly up and down the room.

"She has forgotten her old Hobson family, I presume?"

Dorothea was again excited. "Indeed not, and that is another evidence of her low instincts! She visits them at least

51

once a week, with baskets. She has even tried to induce me to employ the older girl as housemaid! I need not tell you my reply." Dorothea tossed her head with grim triumph.

"So she and Alfred are now the guardian angels of the Hobsons?" Jerome's voice was bitterly amused, but curiously thoughtful.

"Yes! Is it not intolerable? You can see how infatuated he is. It is not in the least like Alfred."

"Why does he do it?"

"He claims he can never repay the Hobsons for their care of his dear Amalie! After all, he declares, had it not been for them, he might never have come to know her at all!" Dorothea burst into fresh tears.

But Jerome again began his slow yet restless pacing up and down the room. Dorothea watched him, twisting her damp handkerchief in her desperate fingers. Jerome began to talk aloud, meditatively. "We must look at this reasonably," he said, smoking as he walked. "The problem would not be settled by disposing of Miss Amalie. Alfred wants to marry. He has the urge for it. I doubt very much that we could disentangle him from this woman. But—if we did, he would find someone else."

"Yes," murmured Dorothea, and her gaunt cheeks flushed.

Jerome paused and regarded her levelly. "It might be you, eh, Dotty? Especially if you gave him a hint. Why hasn't someone hinted, anyway?"

Dorothea colored even deeper. She said, coldly: "Females do not 'hint,' as you say, Jerome."

"No? I've found them excellent hinters. You might try it, Dotty. Or, I might. I'm surprised at Papa; he understands everything, yet he has done nothing to influence Alfred. He might have said: 'See here, my boy, Dorothea will naturally be one of my heirs. I'd like to keep the money in the family.' Alfred may be insensitive to many things, but he is certainly not insensitive to money! So, I am surprised at Papa."

"You have no delicacy, Jerome!" cried Dorothea, moving vehemently on her pillows.

"Who was ever delicate about money? Only hypocrites, or those who have more than enough. And even they can be stirred to most gratifying activity when money is involved."

"You wouldn't be so presumptuous as to—interfere!" Dorothea's words and manner were indignant and denying, but Jerome detected the faintest pleading, the faintest hope, in her voice.

52

He laughed. "I might! I really might! After all, you are my sister."

"Oh, Jerome!" But again, Dorothea's protesting words were gilded with pleading.

"Really, Alfred's an abominable fool, Dotty. Why can't he see that you would be the best possible wife for him? Who else could do better, or be more congenial?"

Dorothea sobbed drily. "How excessively kind of you, Jerome! But doubtless you are prejudiced."

He replied, gallantly: "I am, perhaps, prejudiced against Alfred. He is not good enough for you, Dotty. I can't imagine why you are so fond of him."

Involuntarily, she extended her hand to him, and he went to her bedside and took it. It was hot and parched, and again he felt for her that unfamiliar compassion. She gazed up at him with eyes that swam in suffering liquid. "Is it you, indeed, Jerome, who address these words to me? I can hardly believe it." Her tone was actually penitent.

Her old-fashioned phraseology touched him. He pressed her hand. "Dotty, I'm afraid you've always underestimated me. I've really been very fond of you, in my own peculiar way." He dropped her hand. "But let's get down to business. Let us get at the root of the matter. We must first begin with Alfred, and dissect him neatly, and discover what activates that odd mind of his.

"Let us go back to the years when we were young. You remember Alfred's father, our Uncle Thomas, very well?"

"Certainly. After all, I was eighteen when he died!"

Jerome sat near his sister. "And I was fourteen. Alfred was about your age. Let us consider Uncle Thomas, our papa's brother. A dull and pious man, I remember. A somber failure, with no wit or mind at all. He adored Papa, but he also envied him. Papa, his senior, was, of course, the president of the Bank. Uncle Thomas was vice-president. But he was too stupid, too rigid, too lacking in imagination, to have retained any position at all with any other firm. His salary was really an annuity, granted him by Papa. We are being honest, now, so we must admit all these things.

"Papa took Alfred into the Bank. That was when I was away at school. Alfred, in many ways, resembles his father. But he had something else, too, and this we must admit also. He was dogged, and his devotion to Papa was complete, with good reason. Papa was powerful, and this influenced Alfred. The Puritan temperament worships potency, property, and power.

It worships money, for money, it believes, is 'God's reward' for a life of probity, piety and consecration to duty. So Papa, according to Alfred, wore a halo of Heaven's approval. To be just, however, Alfred accorded to Papa the love and service of a true son.

"Alfred soon demonstrated other qualities which appealed to Papa, who is hard-headed in spite of his gentleness and patrician ways. Alfred's love would have bored him, would have been distasteful to him, if Alfred had not had in addition a very acute mind, a natural leaning towards finance, and an impeccable and rigorous judgment. Alfred, in short, was the perfect banker, and Papa was becoming anxious. There was no other perfect banker in the family. Alfred might be a little narrow, as witness that railroad business. But he subscribed to the banker's creed: Justice without mercy or malice. Or, rather, money-lending or money-grasping, without attention to human values. To a banker, humanity operates in a sphere by itself, and never touches the rim of the orbit where banking circulates. As for myself, I confess that the cleavage between the two baffles me. But then, I've never considered money anything except a medium of exchange."

Dorothea listened, and then at Jerome's last words her features tightened, became forbidding. Her mouth automatically opened in reproof, then she closed it, and looked away.

"Money," continued Jerome, intrigued by his subject, "cannot possibly exist apart from humanity. It is humanity that gives significance to money. Nothing is valuable unless men give it value. To a banker, I realize, such sentiments are blasphemous. Money is a thing in itself, a value in itself. What an amusing and preposterous idea! But there it is. Alfred is the true banker. So is Papa.

"Papa has always had a strong family feeling. But family feeling needs progeny to feed upon. Papa and Uncle Thomas were the only children of their parents. The line is not prolific. Here are you, Dotty, still a vir——, still unmarried. Here am I, unmarried, and determined to remain unmarried, with the grace of God. Papa saw these things very clearly. His two children could not be depended upon to increase the line. It was natural that he looked to Alfred, of whom he was very fond, and who was a son after his own heart. Alfred was his nephew; he was as close as a son. Formal adoption followed, after Uncle Thomas's death." Jerome paused. "And so, Alfred shares with us equally." He paused again, and now the pause was significant. "Who knows? Perhaps he will have the greater share.

Certainly, when Alfred remarries, he will naturally live in this house, and fill it with his brats. You will remain as housekeeper, a kind of respected upper servant, but under the thumb of the new mistress."

Dorothea uttered a loud, despairing cry, and tears spurted from her eyes. "I cannot bear it, Jerome! I will not endure it! I will go away; I will hide myself in some quiet little village, far from my old home, and live out my days in grief and solitude! Oh, Jerome, to be subservient to that dreadful creature, to be servant of her whims, her coarseness, her low breeding!"

She covered her face with her hands, and sobbed: "How can Papa be so oblivious to what all this means to his children, to me, his daughter!"

Jerome moistened his lips. He waited until Dorothea was quiet again, weeping silently. Then, very softly, he asked: "You know nothing of Papa's will?"

In more guarded moments, Dorothea would have withdrawn indignantly, would have repelled her brother's curiosity, out of loyalty to her father. But now she had lost control of herself. Speaking from behind her trembling hands, she said: "Only a little. He was kind enough to discuss—certain things with me. I do not know everything. But Papa is just. Alfred is to have this house, all this property, and all that is in it, including Mama's and Grandmama's and Great-grand-mama's precious things—all, all, is to be his! As for myself, I am to have one-third of the income from the Bank, for life. If I marry, my husband will inherit upon my death—or my children, whoever survives. If I die unmarried and without children, then my income reverts to the estate, and to Alfred. Alfred, himself, is to become president of the Bank. It is very involved——"

"And I, darling Dotty?" asked Jerome, even more softly.

Dorothea wiped her eyes. "Papa knows it is useless to try to interest you in the Bank, Jerome. You have given him your unqualified refusal, and that you know. Oh, when he explained it to me, I believed it just! Why do I no longer believe it just?"

She gazed at Jerome wildly, and again extended her trembling hand to him. He took it, held it tightly. "Darling Dotty. Please tell me."

She said, her voice shaking hysterically: "Jerome, Papa spoke of the money Grandma left you, and you alone. Papa did not think that fair, I know. I was left nothing but her pearls. You were her favorite. Papa believed she was unduly under your influence. I do not believe it now. Papa said that with discre-

55

tion that money ought to have lasted you all your life, allowing you to live in moderate comfort. And Papa told me that you had spent it all—long ago."

Jerome stroked his sister's hand with his thumb. It was hypnotic in its influence upon the distraught woman, the loveless woman whose heart had burned in loneliness and hunger for thirty-eight years.

"Yes, dear Dotty?"

"You, Jerome, are to be paid three thousand dollars a year for life. That is all, Jerome. Upon your death, your income, too, will revert to Alfred."

Jerome stood up, abruptly. He looked down at his sister, and his eyes were fiery. "Three thousand dollars a year," he said, softly. "I spend more than five times that now." His dark face became narrow, and evil. "So, I am to have a loaf of bread, and a jug of cheap wine, and one or two stinking rooms on a back street. That is all."

Something in his manner affrighted his sister. She caught at his hand; it felt like cold iron in her feverish fingers. "Jerome! Do not look like that! Oh, what have I said? What have I done? Oh, Heaven forgive me! I ought not to have told you."

Her voice rose to a great cry, and Jerome, apprehensive, glanced at the door. He sat down, tried to soothe his sister. "There now, Dorothea, rest assured I shall not tell anyone what you have told me. Please. Here is my handkerchief. Wipe your eyes and your face. We must be sensible, Dotty. We must keep our wits about us if we are to accomplish anything at all."

My God, he thought, if she does not stop her idiot shrieking, we'll have all the house about our ears! He was shaking inwardly; he was filled with hatred. He wanted to kill. His hand tightened over his sister's hands. His voice was quiet and sedative as he murmured consoling words to her.

"We aren't lost yet, Dotty. We have things to do, together. Papa isn't dead yet." He paused. For the first time in his life, he hated his father, saw him as a malevolent and plotting devil ruining his children. "We have time, Dotty. We can do a great deal. The first step is to prevent Alfred's marriage to that strumpet."

"Oh, Jerome, is that possible?"

"We can do what we can, Dotty. I must think about it. When is the marriage to take place?"

"December twenty-eighth." Dorothea's swollen eyes fixed themselves upon her brother as upon a deliverer.

"There must be some way we can prevent it. I will think about it later. But we must remember that Alfred will look about again for a wife. We must direct his attention to you.

"As for myself——" He paused. He stared grimly before him. "I must have a talk with darling Papa. Tonight."

He stood up. He forced himself to smile. "I think I shall have that talk now, Dotty."

He bent over her and kissed her wet and wrinkled forehead. He touched her head lightly with his hand. "Dear Dotty. Trust me. Leave it all to me. Promise me that."

CHAPTER SIX

He first went to his own rooms, carrying his dog, whistling tonelessly. These were his old apartments, which he had occupied, when at home, from the day he had been graduated from the nursery on the third floor. (That nursery, designed for a dozen children, and occupied by only two! In a way, it was a judgment on the old devil.)

The apartments consisted of a snug warm sitting-room, somewhat small, adjoining a larger bedroom which looked out upon the side grounds. Next to it was a tiny lavatory, placed there upon his own insistence ten years ago.

He had chosen his own furniture from his grandmother's property, and he had displayed fastidious taste. He had been glad that the mantelpiece was delicately carved white marble, hearth and all. Here he had placed his grandmother's fire-tools of pale steel, handwrought, and polished to the patina and lustre and color of old silver. The walls were panelled in light wood, a circumstance which had annoyed Dorothea and had made her voluble on the subject of "fancifulness and pretension." A dim and exquisite Aubusson rug covered the floor, all its tints faded and soft. Not for Jerome the heavy black furniture of the other rooms: he must have light and lovely pieces, covered with rose, pale green and gold damask, all from his grandmother's impeccable store. The lamps were of crystal and old gilt, shimmering like jewels when lit. Against one wall was a bookcase of pale wood, filled with wonderfully tooled volumes in crimson and dark-blue leather.

Alfred had called all this "woman's rooms," and had indicated that Jerome must be lacking in virility. "I am not one that prefers a rhinoceros to a swan," Jerome had replied, touching the little crystal and enameled boxes on the delicate tables, and glancing at the priceless Dresden figurines and ivory articles which filled his buhl cabinet.

The bedroom was similar, in its furnishings, to the sitting-room. Even the draperies at the many wide windows were light and airy, of pale colors and lovely soft patterns. He had few pictures, and though Alfred found them decadent and disgusting, Jerome knew them to be charming and perfect and very valuable.

A warm and quiet fire burned on the marble hearth tonight. Jim was sleeping contentedly in a Louis XV chair before the fluttering coals, his mouth open, and snoring merrily. A single lamp had been lit on a table near the window. Jerome glanced into his bedroom. The satiny white linen had been folded back; his silk nightshirt was lying there in readiness. Charlie barked at Jim, and the valet stirred, groaned, then sat upright. Jerome dropped the dog, who ran to Jim and climbed upon his lap.

"Well, we seem comfortable," said Jerome. "Hope you enjoyed your nap."

Jim got to his feet. "I have that, sir. Just drowsed off, waitin'. Bed, sir?"

"No, not yet. Where are you sleeping, Jim?"

"On the third floor." The wizened little nut of a man winked. "A fine room next to a fine wench, beggin' your pardon, sir."

Jerome laughed. "Remember, we're virtuous in this house, Jim. No larking about. You may go to bed now, and take Charlie with you."

"You won't need me, Mr. Lindsey? I've done what I could; got everythin' settled."

"No, just go to bed. And thanks."

Jim carried the dog from the room, closed the door softly behind him. Jerome looked about his apartments. In the end, he had come to hate them as he did the rest of the house. They had been a prison for him, a prison of decorum and quietness and stately living. They had smothered him. The long and precise routine of the days had driven him frantic. Even his beloved books could not quell his restlessness, or give him contentment. Contentment. He had never been content. He had been a brazier of coals. He had carried that brazier away from this peaceful and somber house, and had never desired to return to it.

But now everything looked lovely and desirable to him.

With a kind of fierceness, he walked through the rooms. No doubt they would be occupied by that trollop. She would lie in that swan-shaped bed; she would look at her impudent interloper's face in that long pier-glass between the windows. She would touch these precious books, sit in that little gilt chair beside the bed. Her trumpery gowns would fill his wardrobe; she would draw aside those light and gleaming draperies at the windows and look down the majestic sloping grounds to that copse of pines which had been so dear to him.

He put his hand on the heaped white pillows of the bed, stroked the silky linen gently. Here her head would lie; her black hair would be spread out on this whiteness; her long pale arms would rest on this blue and puffy quilt. Her black lashes would lie on her cheeks; they were pale cheeks, and translucent, and the moon would shine on them and make them look like marble. Her mouth would look like a dark plum, in her sleeping face.

As if bewitched, Jerome stood motionless by his bed, staring down at it fixedly. He was very still, but now that strange and devouring pain had him once more, that inexplicable and bitter pain. He said to himself: I can't endure it. I won't endure it. But the words were mechanical. The pain grew stronger. He could actually see the dreaming woman in that bed; he could see, beneath filmy silk, the soft rising of her beautiful breast. He held his breath. He bent over the bed. His heart was beating with a curious and stifling wildness, and the pain was tearing him with iron teeth. He put his trembling hand on the phantom's breast, and so great was his enchantment that he could actually feel the warm round flesh under it.

He stood like that for a long time; he was frozen in his enchantment. Only his heart was alive, like a raging and hungry animal.

Then, as if shaking off a bewitchment, he pulled himself away from the bed. He drew out his handkerchief, and wiped his wet palms. He went back to the sitting-room and stood before the fire, looking blindly at the glowing grottos formed by the coals. He ran his fingers through his hair; a cold prickling followed their path. He said, aloud: "No. No."

He felt sick and shaken. The pain had subsided to a huge and pulsating ache, less sharp, but larger. Again he asked himself: What is wrong with me?

A hideous answer began to form in his mind. He shook his head, and turned away. He went down the stairs to the library.

CHAPTER SEVEN

The clock in the hall struck a long and sonorous series of notes as Jerome descended the stairway. Ten o'clock. The great warm house lay in complete and dusky quiet; the fire in the hall grate had fallen into glowing coals that palpitated a little. Somewhere, in the darkness, the gales were still screaming beyond the stone walls, increasing the atmosphere of security and strength within. The hall chimney boomed faintly; the coals flared into brilliance, then faded.

William Lindsey was alone in the library, his head bent over a book, his tortured feet stretched out to the fire.

Jerome paused on the threshold to study his father. And he thought: He's a stranger. Strange it was, indeed, that never before had he felt, under a surface kindliness and tolerance, this formidableness in the older man, this cold and patrician steelness, this relentless quiet. He saw his father's frail profile outlined by the bright fire, and now it seemed no longer to be full of wise composure and aristocratic gentleness and profound understanding. Rather, to Jerome, it appeared without pity, of a Roman sternness and austerity. There was a sad cynicism about the wide, reserved mouth, and its very serenity precluded any emotionalism.

Jerome had always smugly prided himself on his ability to discern even the subtlest hints of inner character. Now, he was singularly disturbed, and helpless, and even a little afraid. He remembered his childhood, his youth, his early manhood, in this house, and he wondered, with angry perplexity, how his father had ever deceived him so completely. Always, William Lindsey had exhibited only the most tolerant understanding of his children, and a deep quiet affection. Always, he had said: "Your life is your own. You must make your own judgments. Whatever I advise will appear old-fashioned and tiresome to you. Rochefoucauld once said: 'Old men are fond of giving good advice to console themselves for being no longer in a position to give a bad example.' Moreover, what was valid and proper for me might be a grave error on your part. You must conduct yourself according to your own interpretation of life, and according to your innate conscience." Whenever Jerome had been unusually stupid or flagrant, William would quote again from his beloved Rochefoucauld: " 'Scarcely any man is clever enough to know all the evil he does.' Jerome, I believe you are not so much reckless and absurd as you are conceited. 'Virtue or vice would not go so far if vanity did not keep her company.' And, my dear boy, I consider vanity the silliest of the vices." Then, he had once smiled as he said: "If I sound too unbending, I remember that 'he who lives without folly is not so wise as he thinks.' "

He had never, Jerome remembered, been inexorable in his precepts. He had never declared that black is black or white is white. He was flexible in his judgments. He argued from both sides, and ruefully admitted that no one actually knew which side was wrong and which side was right. Compromise, he had declared, was the watchword of the intelligent man. Nothing in life was clearly defined and immutable.

You were wrong, thought Jerome, with sudden confused anger. That is no way to bring up children. They are not intelligent men. They must, for their own safety, be guided by hard and fast rules. They have no experience by which to judge wisdom or folly. To set children adrift with the remark that perhaps their ignorant folly is right, after all, and the old teacher wrong, is to add bewilderment to their inexperience, and take from their horizon any firm landmarks which would guide them to safety and reasonable living. The iron hand, and not the benign and skeptical philosophy, is the need of the young.

He did not find his own unique thoughts strange, as he watched his father. Always, he had considered his father the most just and the wisest of men. Now, distrust was added to his furious resentment. He began to wonder whether it was indifference, rather than love, which made a man temperate towards his children.

His father had become a frightening enigma, but in view of what Dorothea had told Jerome, it was a consistent enigma. His children had never really known him. The mystery of him had remained undiscovered by them until now. If his will had seemed incredible to his children and not in accord with what they believed was his character, it was they who deceived themselves and not he who had deceived them. If he intended to humiliate his daughter, to set his son adrift with a beggarly pittance, the fault was theirs for egotistically believing that they thoroughly understood their father, and that he could do nothing that would be a surprise or an embarrassment to them. William Lindsey, then, had not changed; he had remained himself. His children had been self-deluded.

Jerome was suddenly afraid, as he stared at his father. He

felt impotence in himself, and this enraged him. He clenched his hands at his sides. The clock in the hall ticked loud in the stillness; a coal dropped; the wind drummed in the chimney.

Mr. Lindsey quietly turned a page. Then he glanced up, slowly, and saw his son in the doorway. He smiled. "Jerome," he said. "My dear boy, come in. I had been hoping we might have a little talk together, and that is why I have waited here for you."

It was his old tranquil voice, affectionate and calm, and a surge, as of nostalgia, rushed through Jerome. It was a stranger speaking in the voice of one who had never really existed except in Jerome's mind. He went towards the fire in silence, then stood on the hearth, looking down at the fire. His father watched him with smiling thoughtfulness.

"You have seen Dorothea?"

Jerome moved a little, but without looking away from the fire. "Yes, Father." He no longer used the childish "Papa," yet the "Father" was involuntary rather than deliberate, and he was not aware of the changed word. But Mr. Lindsey heard it, and his blue eyes quickened and darkened, and he laid aside his book.

"Sit down, Jerome," he said, very quietly.

Jerome sat down. Mr. Lindsey scrutinized his son. Jerome wore an unfamiliar expression, now, confused and surly. Mr. Lindsey could not recall having seen that look before, and his white brows drew together for an instant. But he said: "Dorothea is well tonight?"

Jerome shrugged slightly. "She seems so." He paused; he lifted the poker and turned over a few smoldering coals. "She is naturally upset about this—marriage."

"Ah," murmured Mr. Lindsey. He lay back in his chair, his long and elegant figure hardly bending the cushions, so slight it was. "Yes, she is inconsolable, poor girl. She always believed Alfred would marry her, eventually."

Jerome took a long time to light a cheroot; he clipped the end, studied it intently, stood up, lifted a wax taper from the vase on the mantelpiece, lit it, puffed at the cheroot experimentally, then sat down. It was evident that he had no wish to meet his father's level eyes. And Mr. Lindsey watched him, thinking: It is not like Jerome to beat about the bush. It is certainly more in his nature to rush in, violently and explosively, in spite of all his genteel affectations. Something has perturbed him; something has upset his usual indifference.

"Ah, well," sighed Mr. Lindsey, when he saw that Jerome

would not speak. "Man proposes, and then his passion disposes. We mustn't condemn Alfred, after all."

"No," said Jerome, and now he spoke in his old hard and cynical voice. "We must always remember that Alfred is a fool, in spite of that granite and reasonable exterior." He pointed at the book near his father's hand. "Rochefoucauld again? Well, I can quote from that, too, and it is pertinent, for Alfred. 'Some people of great merit are disgusting.' "

"You find Alfred disgusting?" Mr. Lindsey spoke calmly.

"Yes, I always have. But that isn't news to you, Father, is it? However, I confess that even I am surprised at this new folly of his. I never believed him fatuous; I always thought he had great self-protectiveness, and an eye out for what was prudent and safe for him."

Mr. Lindsey stirred in his chair. "Will you give me a small glass of sherry, Jerome?"

Jerome rose, went to a nearby table, and poured a glass of sherry for his father. Mr. Lindsey received it with an absent murmur of thanks. He put the glass to his lips. He said, looking inscrutably at the fire: "You do not think Miss Amalie a safe or prudent choice for Alfred? How can you tell? You have scarcely seen her."

Jerome laughed a little, and it was an ugly sound. "Father, I am not a child. I have seen hundreds of women of her kind. Paris, London, Rome, New York, are full of such women. I recognize the sort instantly."

Mr. Lindsey put aside the glass of sherry. He said: "Jerome, look at me. You've been avoiding that ever since you entered the room."

Jerome turned his eyes reluctantly to his father, and he flushed darkly. His black eyes were very strange to Mr. Lindsey: they were uncertain and full of vicious resentment and distrust. "Ah," murmured the other man, and passed a lean white finger over his lips.

He sat upright in his chair. "Jerome, you might be mistaken, you know." His tone was mild. "I have had occasion to study Miss Amalie for the past three weeks, since she came to live here with us, on my own invitation. After all," he added, "it was important to me who was marrying into the family."

"Yes." Jerome smiled nastily. "And, you are satisfied with your study? You approve of the marriage?"

When Mr. Lindsey did not immediately reply, Jerome exclaimed: "Are you going to be 'tolerant,' again? Are you going to 'compromise' again? Are you going to 'withhold your final

63

judgment'?" He paused: "I suppose you have never considered that such an attitude indicates vacillation, a dislike for facing issues squarely and realistically?"

Mr. Lindsey was about to say: "What is wrong with you, Jerome? This is not like you." But he held back the words. After all, he thought, what can one know of another? If Jerome seems strange tonight, it is perhaps because I have never really understood him. This saddened him, and he regarded Jerome with quiet earnestness.

"You would prefer that I make quick, even if erroneous, judgments?"

"No!" Jerome kicked at the hearthrug. "That would not be in accordance with your character, Father." His smile was more disagreeable than ever. "However, I cannot see how even you can 'compromise' with regard to this woman. Or, perhaps, you think a strumpet would enliven this genteel and refined atmosphere?"

Mr. Lindsey's voice was louder and clearer now, as he said: "It is ungentlemanly, and cruel, to use that abominable word. You know nothing of this young lady. Your indecent conclusions, doubtless from your own experience, might not apply to her. The appearance of virtue does not presuppose virtue, nor does the appearance of—lightness—presuppose a lack of virtue. I always believed that I had instilled in you some measure of respect for every woman."

"Not for strumpets." Jerome looked fully at his father now, and it was an alien and derisive look. "Nor do I enjoy the thought that a strumpet will live in this house and lady it over my sister, and fill these old rooms with her ambiguous brats." His voice thickened towards the last, for his heart had begun its inexplicable pounding again.

"Jerome!" Mr. Lindsey's tone was stern. "I must forbid you to apply that word to Miss Amalie again in this house, and in my hearing." He waited. But Jerome did not speak. He was breathing loud and unevenly, but his fixed and evil smile did not disappear as he stared at his father. At last he said softly: "I will not apply it again. Forgive me. But that does not change my opinion of her."

He stood up. "Do you actually believe this a love match on her side?"

To his surprise, his father responded evenly: "No. I do not. I have talked, alone, with Miss Amalie. She told me frankly that she has only the mildest fondness for Alfred, but considerable respect. She also told me that she was marrying him for what he represented: security, home, money, position, fine clothing, a carriage, jewels. She confessed, with a commendable lack of reticence, that were Alfred a poor man, without prospects, she would not look twice upon him. She also told me, and I believe her, that she had been equally frank with Alfred."

Jerome waited, for he saw that his father had not finished. Mr. Lindsey lifted the sherry to his lips and drank composedly. "From that moment on, I knew Miss Amalie to be an honest and fearless woman, without hypocrisy, and incapable of lies and deceit. That was when I accepted her, and consented to the marriage."

Jerome said: "You do not find her admissions repugnant, and repellent, and without decency and honor?"

Mr. Lindsey laughed softly. "I find them refreshing and reassuring. Thousands of refined and respectable young ladies make such marriages every day, but are less honest in their avowed reasons. I am also reassured that Miss Amalie will make Alfred an honest wife. Jerome," and he laughed again, "you are being sentimental, and you surprise me. Do you think all marriages should be, or are, love-matches? Dear me, I am afraid you are a romantic, and this surprises me excessively and disappoints me a little."

Jerome clenched his teeth. But he had nothing to say. Mr. Lindsey continued, as if mildly amused: "Surely you know that the most enduring and respectable marriages among the French are arranged marriages, into which sentiment does not enter? Marriages like that, I have discovered, are almost invariably sound, and as they are based on realism, they are very seldom disappointing. This marriage was 'arranged' between Alfred and Miss Amalie. Alfred wants the girl, and she accepts him for what he can offer her. I predict a very successful and solid marriage, without disillusionment or upheavals."

"In spite of her antecedents, low birth, lack of breeding and refinement?"

Mr. Lindsey turned the glass in his attenuated fingers. His face changed. He said reflectively: "I have considered that, also. As I wrote you, if I had to choose, I should not have chosen as Alfred did. I believe both partners to a marriage should bring equal gifts. I am not complaisant, Jerome, about Miss Amalie's background."

"Ah!" said Jerome. "Now we are getting somewhere, at last. Dotty has acquainted me with the lady's past history. So, it does revolt you. You are not democratic. You do not look upon the daughter of a drunkard and a charwoman as a proper mate for your adopted son." He paused. "And, may I ask, what do our friends think of the matter?"

Mr. Lindsey, disregarding Jerome's sneers, replied composedly: "Our friends are astounded, to say the least. Of course, their opinions are colored by the fact that they have eligible daughters who would make Alfred acceptable wives. That he chose a stranger, an obscure young woman who has had to earn her living, who has lived too freely for a female, who has no family, no money, no connections, no position, is naturally outrageous to them. Many, I have heard, have vowed not to accept her. However, I doubt that this antagonism will long continue." Nevertheless, he frowned.

"They are hostile to Alfred, as a result?" Jerome's smile was gleeful.

"No. On the contrary." A slight cynical smile touched Mr. Lindsey's lips. "They seem to share Dorothea's conviction that he has been seduced by Miss Amalie's face and 'wiles.' Which, I confess, is probably true. Well, I must admit that there is more sympathy for Alfred, and for us, than reproach. I hope, I pray, that the disagreeableness will not endure too long. Not that Miss Amalie would be devastated. The whole thing amuses her. And that causes me to recall that a sense of humor is very strong in her. And a most intelligent and discerning mind, and a surprising taste."

"You think these make up for all the other things."

Mr. Lindsey moved in his chair. He put his hand to his lips and gazed at the fire. Then he said, as if in wonderment: "Strange to confess, they do! I wondered why I was not more antagonistic, or disapproving. Now I know. Miss Amalie is not such a young female as I knew in my youth, or know even now. There is strength in her, and courage, and fearlessness, as well as honesty. She does not simper; she never has the vapors. There is a clarity and a forthrightness in her mind which is like an open wind. I have never heard a word of deliberate malice from her, nor gratuitous cruelty, nor any meanness." He was silent a moment, then said, softly: "If I were a young man, I could not resist her. She is a woman."

He looked up, seemed about to speak, then was silent. For the strangest look had appeared on Jerome's face, an indescribable look that suggested pain and restlessness and confusion.

The young man stood up and leaned against the mantelpiece, half turned from his father. He said, in an odd voice: "I hoped that you would be agreeable if I did all I could to prevent this marriage."

Mr. Lindsey was so perturbed by the glimpse he had had of his son's face that he did not immediately answer. Then his voice was obscurely disturbed and impatient: "What can you do, Jerome? There is nothing you can do. There are things which must be accepted."

Jerome did not turn. He said: "If you forbade the marriage, Alfred would obey you. You have means to compel his obedience."

Mr. Lindsey was silent. His fingers stroked each other, slowly, over and over. He said to himself: There is fear in this room, and danger. What is it? What has happened? Yes, I feel violence, too. Does it come from Jerome? What does he care whom Alfred marries? What is it to him? There is more here than I can understand. Is it money? Yes, perhaps, it is money.

He said: "I will not compel obedience. Alfred is not a young man. It is his life to live. I accord him that dignity. Jerome, will you please sit down?"

Jerome dropped into his chair again. He looked into the fire. His profile was dark and intent, and unreadable. Feeling his father's gaze, he put up his hand instinctively, and hid his face behind it.

Mr. Lindsey said: "I trust you are to remain with us for a while, after the wedding? It has been a long time since you were home, my boy."

Jerome did not move. He said, from behind the shelter of his hand: "Would you care if I remained—indefinitely?"

Mr. Lindsey sat upright in his chair. "Would I care? Jerome, are you serious?"

Jerome dropped his hand. He appeared quite calm. "Yes, I am serious." He hesitated. "I think I am a little tired of a foot-loose life——"

Mr. Lindsey smiled, and the smile was pleased and radiant. He put out his hand and touched Jerome's arm. But Jerome did not respond. His eyes fixed themselves, with a hard expression, on his father's face. "Jerome! If I could believe that! It is what I have always hoped for, but in the past years, since the war, I had given up hope."

Jerome watched his father. "I have considered asking you to place me in the Bank," he said, evenly.

Mr. Lindsey frankly stared. Then, all at once, his face slowly closed, withdrew. He lay back in his chair. He said: "Jerome. What is behind this?"

"I thought I was clear, Father. I'm tired of a footloose existence. I think I might like the Bank, if I tried it. Are you going to give me the opportunity?"

"Is that not a peculiar and sudden decision?"

Jerome smiled. "Perhaps, to you. But, on the way here, I did some thinking. Perhaps, unconsciously, I have been doing some thinking during the past year. Then, since I have been home, I have felt some contentment. It is probable that I have been homesick and never knew it." His eyes were candid on the surface, but Mr. Lindsey thought that something murky moved under all that clarity.

"You are not frank with me, Jerome."

"Damn it, sir, I am frank! Is it so strange that a prodigal wishes to return home?"

"But, you have not exactly eaten husks or lain with the swine and the oxen, to continue with the parable."

Jerome's smile grew wider. "How could you know, Father? My God, I think I am getting literary in my approaching old age!"

But Mr. Lindsey did not return that smile. Instead, he became stern and reflective, not removing his steadfast regard from Jerome.

He said: "Your decisions have always been volatile, Jerome. And banking is not a profession to be taken up lightly, and deserted as lightly. It demands discipline, study, clear judgment, application and much tedious thought. You will forgive me if I say that so far you have not demonstrated any of these qualities, which, tiresome though they might be at times, and offering no amusement, are necessary for banking."

"Why not try me?"

Mr. Lindsey said: "What do you know about banking?"

"Nothing, frankly. But, I can learn, under Alfred's excellent instruction. After all, I am not an imbecile, and I flatter myself I have a quick mind."

"Too quick, Jerome." But Mr. Lindsey's tone was abstracted.

"You never reproached me on that score before, sir."

Mr. Lindsey moved in his chair, as if seized with pains. He said: "Jerome, I have never reproached you for anything. Perhaps I was wrong. Perhaps, remembering my stern parents, I had decided that no child of mine should be restricted, or forced to fit any preconceived pattern in my own mind. Perhaps I was wrong in giving you your way at all times. Certainly, it has not proved eminently successful. You have no respect for money, and I am not speaking of its grosser values.

68

You have no respect for it as a symbol of man's time and effort and sweat and invention and life. To you, it is only a means of exchange for the purchase of pleasures and follies, and the gratifying of facile desires."

His voice was gentle, but his eyes were full of a blue sternness, and his mouth had taken on a relentless if saddened look.

"You have a low opinion of me, Father."

"Jerome, have you a better?"

Jerome was silent. Mr. Lindsey resumed, almost compassionately: "Jerome, you must remember what you did with your grandmother's money. Now, I have no quarrel with pleasure and joy, with travel and gaiety. I had too little in my own youth. I wanted you to see the world, and enjoy it. I did not believe that you would waste your entire fortune in the silliest of sensual pursuits and follies. I believed that you had some sense of proportion.

"Perhaps, though, I am wrong. Perhaps you will have something in your old age more joyous to remember than balanced ledgers. Perhaps it is the better part."

Oh, damn your "compromise," your "tolerance"! thought Jerome, somberly. He said: "I am coming to doubt it is 'the better part,' Father."

"But, you have enjoyed it?"

Jerome said: "Yes. I should be a sentimental fool to deny it. I should be even worse if I said the pleasures were 'empty.' They weren't. They gave me considerable satisfaction. However, even champagne and caviar and dancing can become tiresome, too. I'd like to try to be a solid citizen, for a change."

"You would revolt."

"I am not sure of that, Father. At least, let me try it."

"Your only excursion into the realms of banking, Jerome, was when you wisely induced me to help bring the railroad to Riversend. I must admit I was surprised and gratified at your vision."

"Oh, then try me with other visions!" His tone was light and facetious.

"Jerome, banking is not to be treated as a game. There is too much at stake, too many pulsing human lives are involved. It is not baccarat or roulette; it is not gambling, except in a conservative way, based on actual properties, values——"

"And on human character, and imponderables."

Mr. Lindsey smiled. "I see you remember my own remarks, Jerome. Well. But we must have some knowledge of the human character, and the imponderables, with which we deal.

Nothing is certain in this world; mistakes are made in banking. But not too many. Too many mistakes mean ruined lives, despair, death and misery. We cannot take that chance."

"Does Alfred understand these things?" asked Jerome, fixing his father with his hard, shrewd look.

Mr. Lindsey hesitated. "Not always," he admitted. "Alfred has a reverence for money, as a thing in itself. But it is a good quality, after all, a safeguard, a protection for those who depend upon us. It is better in banking to lack imagination than to have too much."

"And, I have too much?"

Mr. Lindsey looked at him steadily. "Yes, perhaps. And too much irresponsibility. You wished me to be frank?"

Jerome went to the silver tray where the decanter and whiskey glasses still remained. He poured himself a rather prodigal drink, and swallowed it quickly. He came back to the fire. "Yes," he said, "I adore frankness. It is no more deadly than the guillotine."

Mr. Lindsey smiled involuntarily. "I am afraid I am offending you, my son. But one must consider everything."

Jerome said: "Suppose you try 'withholding final judgment' with respect to me, sir? Suppose you give me a chance? After all, as a neophyte in the banking business I could not do much harm. Alfred probably keeps the keys on a chain around his neck."

Mr. Lindsey lay back in his chair and closed his eyes. He seemed to drowse, to have fallen into one of his interludes of weakness. The fire crackled, shot up flames. The gale no longer pounded the windows or shook the doors. The house was still, and the clock struck a melodious eleven, one slow and ponderous stroke after another.

Then Mr. Lindsey spoke, not moving, not opening his eyes: "You and Alfred have never been very congenial. That is your fault, Jerome. However, congeniality is not an absolute necessity in business. It is not that that worries me, nor doubt of your qualities. At least, they don't worry me as much as something else."

"Yes, Father?"

Mr. Lindsey still spoke as if out of a deep sleep: "I don't know what that something else is, what it is that lies behind this decision of yours. I do not fully believe it is homesickness, or weariness of sensuality and thoughtless living, though they perhaps have a share in your decision."

He opened his eyes. They were very wide, shining and blue.

"What is it, Jerome?"

It had always been a rare occasion when his father had looked at him like this, and always it had intimidated Jerome. It had made the heart in him shrink, it was something impelling shameful retreat, something which seemed to penetrate to every corner of him. He felt all these things now, and a dull and heavy flush moved over his features.

"Yes," said Mr. Lindsey, gently, "I was right. It is something else. What is it, Jerome? I am afraid. I have always used reason in my life, I believe. Yet, there are times when reason is not enough. The instinct is stronger, then, and more to be trusted. My instinct is disturbed, Jerome. For I do not believe that the powerful thing which impels you to this strange decision is a good thing. I think it is violent, dangerous, and terrible. Moreover, I think you are not completely aware of it, yourself. I am afraid, Jerome."

Jerome could not speak. His hand tapped slowly on the mantelpiece, for at his father's words he had stood up involuntarily. He could not look away from the inexorable blue shining of his father's eyes.

"Do you think to usurp Alfred's place?" asked Mr. Lindsey, almost pityingly.

Still, Jerome could not answer, though he realized the necessity of it.

"Then, in all honesty, Jerome, let me assure you that Alfred's position is impregnable. I have taken care of that matter, and nothing will induce me to change my—mind. You can do nothing to Alfred. But, what am I saying? Why should you wish to do anything? I do not believe that you have any active hatred for Alfred. Rather, it has been derision and contempt—petty things, both. No matter. You cannot hurt Alfred, Jerome. Reflect on that a moment."

Jerome said, in a muffled voice: "I don't think I want to hurt him. Why should I? Let him have what you, in your charity, have planned for him."

Mr. Lindsey's brows wrinkled. "I see. I believe you, Jerome. Then, what is it?"

Jerome's hands, suddenly cold and shaking, fastened themselves on the edge of the mantelpiece. "I don't know," he said, as if speaking without volition. "I don't know. I only know that I want to stay, that I wish to have a part in the Bank."

"You would not care to remain here—without a part in the Bank?"

"No. I must have occupation."

71

Mr. Lindsey closed his eyes again. "My instinct, against all my reason and my affection for you, urges me to ask you to go away, Jerome."

Jerome was silent again. His fingers felt stiff and aching when he lifted them from the mantelpiece. He flexed them. He saw the moist marks they had left on the marble. His knees were weak; the old wound began to throb in his leg, as if bleeding again.

He said, somewhat hoarsely: "If you wish me to leave, I will go. But, I'll never come back. Never again. I swear it. You will never see me after I leave."

"Why not? Have I offended you so, Jerome?" Mr. Lindsey's voice was very sad.

Jerome said: "I don't know why I should never return. I only know that I would not. I could not endure it."

There was a long silence in the room.

Then Jerome whispered: "Don't send me away, sir."

Mr. Lindsey stirred. He said: "Give me my cane, Jerome. Thank you. Your arm, please. I'm not what I used to be."

They faced each other on the hearth, eye to eye.

"Stay, Jerome," said Mr. Lindsey. "Stay. There is a place for you in the Bank."

Jerome forced himself to smile. "Thank you, sir. You won't regret it."

"Regret it," repeated Mr. Lindsey, musingly. He put his feeble hand to his forehead. "I am getting fanciful, perhaps, and a little feverish. But something tells me that I shall do more than regret it.

"No, please, do not go with me. I can find my way alone. Good night, Jerome."

Jerome was alone. The fire was dying down. He looked at his father's empty chair.

"Oh, my God," he said, aloud.

CHAPTER EIGHT

It was very late, but Jerome Lindsey could not go to bed. The profound silence which had followed the storm enhanced, rather than decreased, his tremendous and feverish restlessness. Yet his restlessness did not take the form of constant movement. It seemed to immobilize him, as a man is immobilized and rigid under the onslaught of long and intense pain.

He stood by the window and looked out blankly, his hand on the cord of the draperies. He fixed his mind on his inner suffering, resolutely, afraid to analyse it, to understand it.

He turned his head slowly and far to one side to see the faint golden lights below in the valley, faint golden stars here and there that flickered and shifted. Even as he watched, they went out, slowly, one by one. Finally, there was only darkness. He could hear the faint dropping of the coals in the fireplace, the musical boom of the clock below, the constant dim creakings and settlings of the old house.

Slowly, at last, his consciousness moved from himself and enlarged to take in the scene below his windows. They looked down upon a brilliant black-and-white world under a blazing moon flung at great speed like an enormous silver coin through the black sky. There was nothing static in this scene, in spite of the midnight silence and the lack of color. It was all white-and-black fire, furious with burning radiance. The stars crackled with it; the fleeting wisps of cloud that raced above and below the spinning moon were illuminated with flaming silver. The argent grounds flowed purely down a gentle slope to the black copse of pines below. A huge elm stood halfway down; its shadow lay like a stiff black web on the smooth snow, sharp and intricate and minutely detailed. Spruces were scattered about, each loaded with a weight of shining alabaster, each casting a vivid reflection of itself on the snow like deep black ink. The snow, itself, glittered and shimmered in its rounded swells, its long marble wastes.

The whole night was effulgent, leaping with scintillation, too dazzling for reality. It was not a night for sleep. Its splendor was too violent, with a kind of palpitating coruscation, its silence too intense, too wild with frozen rage. Yet, there was no wind, no movement of any kind. It was this that inflicted a sort of terror upon Jerome, in spite of his fascinated enjoyment of the spectacle—a sort of disorientation. It was as if he were deaf, and were witnessing a primordial scene of utter savagery, and yet could hear no sound. It was as if he had been transported to the moon, and were seeing an aspect of frightful beauty, tempestuous yet cold as death, never before discerned by the eye of man.

He thought: I should like to paint this! But what paint could possess that livingness of black and white, that violence? His thoughts ran over his inner depression like little rivulets over chaotic stone. He forced himself more strongly to be objective. But his restlessness increased. He felt a kind of panic. There

73

ought to be movement, there! Something should move, stir, give evidence of life. There was terror in lack of motion. The warm human heart repudiated it.

He, himself, moved. He saw a long thin shadow gliding over the snow below his window. Incredulous, he pressed his face to the cold window-pane. The shadow lengthened, became clearer. Someone was walking down there, soundlessly. That which cast the shadow came into view. It was Amalie Maxwell.

She wore a short jacket of fur, and her hands were in a muff. But her head was uncovered. She became part of the black-and-white brilliance of the world about her. Jerome could clearly see the black shadow of her hair falling down below her shoulders. Her face was pure and moonlit, her eyes caverns of darkness. She stood below his window, her profile towards him, and she gazed steadily at the moon. Now she, herself, was as still as all about her.

Jerome looked down at her, his fingers wound in the cord. The moon became ever more radiant. He could see the dark clarity of her mouth, and even its expression of mournfulness. Then she began to move again. She had turned away and was walking slowly down the gentle slope towards the pines. She paused in their black shadow, and now she could hardly be seen at all.

Without thinking, Jerome rushed to his wardrobe, pulled out his fur-lined coat, and flung it over his shoulders. He ran to his door, opened it with swift softness. He went down the dark warm well of the stairway. He passed the door of the library. He could see nothing except the faint crimson coals burning on the hearth. The bolt on the door had been drawn, and he opened the door without a single creak. He pulled it shut behind him.

Now the pure and sterile air of the snowy night flowed all about him. It was very cold, but exhilarating. He felt the bounding of his heart. At some time, during his haste, he had twisted his injured leg slightly. It was throbbing. Yet that very throbbing excited him. He was, he thought, in a delirium. He was in a wild world without reality.

The snow crunched crisply under his cautious feet as he moved away from the door, along the front of the house. He could see Amalie's footprints, small, firm, wide apart. They indicated a free stride, not a mince. Behind them was a faint brushing, which he knew was the mark of her skirts. She did not lift her garments, then. Jerome smiled.

Now he came to the angle of the house. He passed under the windows of his father's bedroom, and he paused, looking up at them. The draperies were closely drawn. He passed his sister's windows, and he saw the moonlight on the folds of the thick crimson velvet. He was under his own windows at last, where Amalie had stood and looked at the moon.

He had walked close to the house, but he knew that in spite of the caution of his steps, and his care to remain close to the wall, he was now clearly revealed to Amalie, in the shadow of the pines. He knew she was still there, facing him, that she had not moved. The moonlight poured down upon him; the radiance hid nothing of him. He felt singularly exposed, yet excited. He looked down at the copse of pines, and knew, instantly, that across that white and gleaming waste Amalie was watching him, though he could not see her.

It was curious and electrifying to know that, to feel the long and fixed pressure of her eyes upon him. Did she know he knew she was there? Or, did she think he had come out upon an impulse, as she had done? He could almost hear her thoughts. At any rate, she would not move, nor signify her presence. She would wait and see.

It was absurd of her to lurk there in that shadow, perhaps believing herself undiscovered. He thought: She must be smiling smugly, watching me exposed in this moonlight, like a butterfly on a pin, herself secure from my eyes. And then he knew that she was not smiling smugly at all. She was watching him as alertly as any wild animal come upon unexpectedly. She would not move until he went away.

The utter frozen silence of the night was unbroken. Not a twig cracked, not a tree groaned. The illumination grew brighter. Faint plumes of smoke from the chimneys turned to frail silver, floated over the house, cast ghost shadows on the snow. Time itself had ended on this world of the moon.

Across the snow the eyes of the man and the woman met in unwavering steadfastness. Now, he thought, she knows I know she is there. Why does she not move, if only to signify her indifference? It was absurdly obstinate of her, and ridiculous, to lurk there. Was she afraid? And, of what?

He moved at last, and followed her footprints down the slope. He walked leisurely, strolling. Yes, her stride was long.

He put his own feet into the prints. The throbbing was stronger in his leg; it had communicated itself to his chest.

Then he stopped, suddenly. Perhaps he was mistaken. Perhaps he would find her gone when he reached the pines. Perhaps she was meeting someone in those shadows, and was not aware of Jerome at all. Perhaps this was a midnight rendezvous. For the first time he was conscious of the bitter cold, of the empty and blazing sterility of the night.

Then, with less caution than before, and with more speed, he went down the slope. The pines appeared to move towards him, like a black and advancing wall. He stopped again. He could see the glimmer of Amalie's white face below the pines. She was facing him fully. The trees were no more still than she. She was alone.

He began to smile. His stride slowed. He glanced back at the house. It stood, square and strong and gray, against the illuminated sky, all its windows blind, and only the dim blowing silver above the chimneys testifying that any life existed in its core at all. No one had heard him and Amalie. Everyone was asleep. Only she and he himself were awake. Not a light twinkled in the valley below.

He took a few more steps. Now her face was a small silver shield in the darkness of the pines. He said, in a low voice: "Is it you, there?" His words were so quiet that they did not arouse a single echo.

For a long moment or two there was no reply. Was she going to be obdurately silent? Was she playing a silly game? Then her voice came to him, softly and coldly: "Yes. I am here."

He went on towards her. Now he, himself, was enveloped in the shadow of the pines. Let anyone look from those windows and he would see nothing. The moon struck the high glass with a white light. The snowy roof glittered.

Jerome was close to Amalie, almost within touching distance. She was standing straight and tall in the darkness, her face glimmering. He saw the diffused dark caverns which were her eyes, and the molded outlines of her lips.

"What on earth are you doing out here?" he said, keeping his voice low and hushed.

She said: "Why did you follow me?"

"Follow you?" He tried to make his tone light and incredulous. But she said, quickly and contemptuously: "You did, didn't you? How could you know I was here, unless you saw me from your windows?"

He said: "Perhaps I wanted a breath of fresh air, too. Perhaps I saw your footprints in the snow, when I came out."

"Perhaps," she replied. And then she laughed a little, disdainfully.

76

"What makes you think that I should care to follow you?" he asked. His throat had thickened with the salty swelling of anger.

He felt, rather than saw, that she shrugged. "That is what I am wondering, too," she said. "And so, perhaps you can enlighten me. I am very curious."

Now he saw a sparkle in the whiteness of her face, and he knew that her eyes were mocking him, dismissing him. A dozen replies came into his mind, and all of them were absurd. His anger was blurring his reason, his savoir faire. He knew that he could only rescue himself from this ludicrous situation by saying: "I was not sure it was you. I only wondered who would be out so late. And now, if you please, I shall leave you to undisturbed enjoyment of the night." And then, he had only to go.

But he could not say those words. He could not turn and leave her. He could only stand in silence, looking at her, forcing himself to meet the sparkle of her eyes with some semblance of composure.

He said, almost simply for the devious Jerome: "Yes. I admit I saw you. And followed you."

"Why?" The one word was clear and indifferent.

"Perhaps I wanted to talk to you."

"Why?"

He felt his face burning. "Is it odd that I might want that?"

She stirred. She was turning from him. Now she was moving through the dense thicket of the pines, towards the other side. He watched her go. His anger was mounting to rage. Again, he had only to return to the house. Instead, he followed her. He heard the whispering of the evergreens as she moved through them. Small plaques of snow dropped from them. Splintered fragments of silver broke through the twisted darkness. Finally, they emerged on the other side, and below them was only the continuation of the slope, steeper now, dropping down towards the valley. They stood in the shadow of the pines, side by side.

She looked down at the valley. She said, quietly: "Well, what have you to say to me?"

Snow from the fronds of the pines had fallen in silver stars on her bare head, and glittered on her shoulders. She stood, tall and straight, beside Jerome, her profile, calm and moonbright, turned towards him.

"You are not polite," he said, and knew his words were foolish. "After all, you are going to be a relative of mine, and

77

I might like to know you better."

She turned to him quickly, yet without agitation. "You have never wanted to know anyone 'better,' have you? You have only wanted to know others 'worse.' "

He kept his temper, though he felt the blood rush to his face. "I still maintain that you are not polite. Where did you learn your manners, Miss Amalie?"

"In a harder school than yours," she replied, scornfully.

"Doubtless," he said, with slow soft insult. "I do not question that in the least."

She drew a deep breath. He heard it clearly. "I, for myself, have nothing to say to you, Mr. Lindsey. I came out because I love such nights as this. You will be doing me a kindness, and be exhibiting your faultless manners, if you go away."

The rude and vulgar trollop! He said the words slowly and viciously in his mind. They gave him confidence, decreased his anger.

He said: "Manners and politeness are the prerequisite of those to the 'manor born,' " his voice was light. "I am not reproaching you, Miss Amalie. I am merely accepting a situation. Moreover, there is an obligation imposed on the members of a family such as ours."

She said, very quietly: "And what is that obligation, sir?"

"To see that any other member is not consciously, or unconsciously, guilty of destroying its prestige, its position."

She looked at him, steadily. And then she began to smile. Her white teeth shone in the moonlight. "Do go on, dear Mr. Lindsey. I find your conversation very amusing, even if it is disturbing my pleasure in my walk."

Again, he was beginning to lose control of himself. He felt in his pockets for a cheroot and his box of lucifers. He lit one with deliberation. The motions helped him. She watched him with exaggerated and assumed interest. He leaned against the trunk of a tall pine, and put his cheroot firmly between his teeth. He studied the sky contemplatively, bending his bad leg to relieve it.

"I am sorry to disturb your pleasure," he said, with mocking ponderousness. "It is indeed a lovely night. We are alone. What better opportunity for a talk?"

"I am all attention, Mr. Lindsey. The fact that my feet and knees are turning slowly to ice will not disturb you in the least, I know."

"Do ladies have knees, Miss Amalie?" His tone was very light, and bantering. "I did not think the subject of female knees was ever mentioned in conversation between ladies and gentlemen."

Again her teeth flashed brightly. "But you are not a gentleman, Mr. Lindsey, and I am not a lady." She paused. "I have very real knees, sir. And at the present time they are becoming quite numb. So, pray make your conversation brief and to the point."

"I shall, indeed," he said, seriously. "May I ask you a blunt question, especially now that it is settled that we are not genteel?"

"Do, sir." Her voice was as serious as his own.

"Why are you marrying my cousin, Alfred Lindsey?"

She was silent. She regarded him quietly. Then she said: "I could evade that question. I could tell you that you are a boor. I could leave you abruptly. That would reveal to you that I have some knowledge of proper conduct, and you might have a better opinion of me. But I am not concerned with your opinion. I do not care for it in the least. And so, I will answer your question. I am marrying your cousin for what he can give me."

He lifted his hand as if in shrinking protest. "Oh, Miss Amalie! How excessively crude! I did indeed believe that you might have acquired some slight polish, under the tutelage of my sister. I am mistaken, it seems. So the adage is true, that you——"

"Cannot make a silk purse out of a sow's ear," she interrupted tranquilly.

He bowed. "Thank you, Miss Amalie."

She began to laugh. It was a clear and sincerely amused laugh. "How ridiculous you are, sir! You believe you are quite charming, and irresistible? Not to me. I find you absurd. I do not know why you followed me, but it was certainly not to catechize me on my reasons for marrying Mr. Alfred Lindsey. And so, I am curious again. I am still waiting for enlightenment."

His cold fingers suddenly itched. It would give him pleasure to slap that bright and laughing face. At the thought, his heart leapt. He felt the sudden aroused drumming of his blood. He moved closer to her. Her smile faded, and he could see her expression, and it was, all at once, watchful and hard.

He said, thickly: "How much will you take to leave here, ma'am, and never return?"

He observed the widening of her eyes, and now he saw the vivid purple of them in the moonlight. He saw the palpitating pupil, and the shadow of her lashes on her white cheek. Her mouth was dark and full, and very still.

She said, softly: "You do not possess enough, Mr. Lindsey, to bribe me to leave."

The brilliant moonlit scene began to swing about him in wide circles. There was a strange roaring all about him. He thought, confusedly: The wind is rising. Now the brightness was diminishing, becoming duller. Her face was becoming diffused and uncertain.

He whispered: "I might be able to get enough."

He knew she was studying him calmly. She moved back a step. He followed her. The scene was darkening, dimming. She continued to retreat. Then she stopped abruptly, prevented from moving by the trunk of a pine. He could hear her breathe again, quickly, unevenly.

Then she cried out, in a shaken voice: "Go away! Let me alone!"

She lifted her large muff before her breast, like a shield. She shrank against the pine. He knew she was trembling. He put out his hand and caught her arm. His fingers pressed through the fur, and he felt the stiffening of her flesh, its quick tremors.

The moon had gone, suddenly. Clouds had mushroomed into the burning sky. The pines bent a little, quaking and groaning. All at once, the gale rushed out of space upon the earth. The quiet snow began to fume, to smoke, filling the air with stinging particles. But it was very still, as yet, among the pines.

The man and woman did not move. She did not attempt to pull her arm from his grasp. She felt him come nearer to her. She lifted her muff higher, as if to protect herself. Their breath mingled, rising in pale vapor between them.

Now he could feel the beating of her blood in the flesh under his fingers. The fur was thin; he felt its cheapness. His fingers clenched deeper, with a kind of fierce and inexplicable ecstasy. He pulled her roughly to him, so that her face was only a few inches from his own, and he could look into her eyes.

"Go away, Amalie," he said, with savage gentleness.

She was trembling violently. She lifted her muff higher still, so that it concealed the lower half of her face. He saw her do it. Then, with his free hand he dashed it out of her grasp. He pushed his hand into the masses of her thick black hair. He felt the soft warmth of it. He clenched it tighter, with fierce and twisting rapture. He pulled her face roughly to his own.

80

"Amalie," he whispered. She did not struggle. She seemed numb and without any volition. Even when he pressed his mouth to hers, his hand still tangled in her hair, she did not move. Her lips were cold and smooth under his.

He kissed her mouth again and again, with slow and delirious deliberation. It did not warm. He did not care. He held her to him, and felt the warmth of her tall and slender body, the pressure of her breasts under the cheap fur. Her eyes were closed.

Then a long shiver ran over her. With amazing strength, she pushed him from her. Her hair slipped from his fingers, as she flung back her head. Caught off balance, he fell back a step or two. She looked at him. The moon came briefly from behind a cloud, and he saw the sudden glaze of her eyes, the gleam of her teeth. Then she caught up her skirts and muff, swung about, and ran. He heard the crunching of the snow under her feet, the rustle of the evergreens as she rushed between them.

He followed her, pushing aside the weighted branches. He reached the other side in time to see her flying figure approaching the house. She ran along the wall, disappeared beyond its angle. He was alone, now, in the rising storm.

A curtain of snow fell abruptly. The wind was fiercer. It beat against his face. He felt the heavy pounding of his heart. He put his hand against a rough tree-trunk to steady himself. His injured leg was on fire.

The darkness increased. He was exhausted. He climbed towards the house, very slowly. The drifting snow was covering Amalie's footprints. He thought: By morning, there will be no trace of us. He became conscious of a slow and welling sickness, a heaviness, as if he were ill, and a hideous desolation.

His room was warm and dark, except for the dying fire on the hearth. Only a few coals remained alive. He stood before them, looking down at them. The desolation was becoming stronger, and the sickness. They were like the fulminating increase of disease.

He felt something about his fingers. Dully, he examined them. There was a black and gleaming strand of Amalie's hair still curling about his hand, a thin strand like torn silk. He stood and looked at it for a long time, until every coal had died on the hearth.

CHAPTER NINE

He awoke to the sound of faint laughter below his windows, and the shrill barking of the dog, Charlie. The sun was finding narrow entrances through the draperies. Long fingers of light lay on the carpet. Someone, during his sleep, had lit the fire again. It crackled cosily on the hearth.

The door opened and the gnomelike face of Jim pushed itself into the room. "Ah, sir, you are awake at last," said the hoarse, Cockney voice. The valet entered, a silver tray carried high in his hand. He beamed. "Coffee, sir, and muffins, and good eggs and bacon, the like I've never seed in the city."

He set down the tray, went briskly to the windows, and pulled aside the draperies. The windows were white with frost, forming scenes of valley and woods and branching firs. Charlie was barking almost hysterically. The laughter was louder. Jim smiled fondly. "A rare old time the dog's havin', sir, in the snow. Almost beside hisself. I've just come in. Nothin' like the country, after all."

Jerome pulled a pillow over his eyes. "Shut out that damned light a little!" he shouted. "And I don't want breakfast. I want a drink."

Jim subdued the light, regretfully. "Nothin' like country air and light, sir. Freshes up a man like nothin'. Makes him feel he's alive." He came to the bed, anxiously, and stood looking down at his master huddled under the silken quilts. "You don't want a drink, Mr. Jerome," he said, in a wheedling voice. "Doctor's orders, y'know. Thought we'd gone past that. Look at that coffee, steamin'. And the eggs——"

"I want a drink, damn you," said Jerome. He pushed aside the pillow. His face was gray and haggard. "Come on, be quick about it."

Jim's anxiety quickened. Had that ride in the snow brought on lung fever? He stretched out his hand and touched Jerome's forehead. He breathed more easily. There was no fever, after all. He said, coaxingly: "Just try that coffee, sir. Nothin' like it, in New York. And the bacon's heaven, like. Had five rashers, myself."

Jerome flung aside the bedclothes, and sat up, furiously. "I said a drink, blast you! Do I have to get it, myself?"

Jim said desperately: "Bad for you, sir. You wouldn't want

the old gentleman to smell it on you, so early in the mornin'?
And the ladies?"

Jerome stared at him, enraged at this disobedience. But before he could speak, Jim continued, hastily: "You're not lookin'
yerself, sir. Drink'll make it worse. Try the coffee, if nothin'
else. Then the drink. You don't want the old sickness back,
do you, sir? Thought all this might buck you up a little."

Jerome opened his mouth to swear. Then he began to smile.
"All right, I'll have the coffee." There were tremulous lines
about his mouth. "But I'll have a drink afterwards, damn your
impudence." He blinked his eyes; the rims felt raw and sore.
He yawned, winced away from even the subdued light.

Jim was delighted. He hastily brought a silver bowl and
towel to the bed. Jerome splashed his hands impatiently. He
looked with repugnance at the tray which Jim set upon his
knees. Babbling happily about the air and the sunshine, Jim
plumped up the pillows behind his master's lean back. He
poured the coffee into the fragile cup, deftly added cream and
sugar. "Look at that cream, sir! Like thick velvet. And the
eggs, shinin' like suns. Hot, too. Made certain of that." He
spoke as if to a sick and disagreeable child. He whisked away
the silver covers over the plates, and looked about him for a
place to lay them. He saw Jerome's coat, flung over a chair.
He frowned. He'd hung it up, he thought. He lifted the coat
uncertainly.

Jerome, thirstily drinking the coffee, paused. "I went out for
a walk last night," he said. "In the snow."

"Certainly, sir." Jim hung the coat up in the wardrobe. He
went to the fire and stirred up the coals. He straightened himself, after laying aside the poker. The clock on the mantelpiece chimed with a sweet light note. Jim smiled happily. Nothing like the country. All peace and quiet, like. He saw a thin
strand of black silk on the white marble of the mantelpiece,
and lifted it up curiously. He saw that it was not silk, after
all, but a slender length of a woman's black hair. It curled
about his fingers, as if alive. Even in the subdued light, it glimmered softly.

Instantly, Jim knew whose hair this was. He had seen the
masses of it only that morning, and had admired it greatly,
shining, as it had done, in the brilliant light.

Jerome spoke angrily behind him: "All right, I'm eating
your damned eggs and bacon. You'll have me as fat as a pig,
soon, you old woman."

Jim seized the poker again, stirring up the fire with violence.

Surreptitiously, he flung the strand of hair onto the glowing bed. It curled up, caught fire, disappeared. Jim turned back to the bed. "That's the ticket, sir," he said, jovially. "We'll soon have the roses in your cheeks. Long tramps in the snow, breathin' God's good air, and eatin' hearty, like."

But his little bead-like eyes were frightened. Then he thought: Might be this was the lass's room before he came. You can't rely on chambermaids. She might have left it about. Sloven.

Jim stood beside the bed. If "roses in the cheeks," depended on an excellent appetite, then they would be long in coming to Jerome's face. He had hardly touched the food. But he was drinking a second cup of coffee. Though inwardly warned, Jim could not help saying, with elaborate carelessness: "Found a piece of hair on the mantel, sir. Can't rely on servants, these days. Messin' about with a feather duster, and overlookin' things. The young lady must've had your room, before we came."

Jerome replaced his cup slowly. He looked up at his valet. He said: "Hair? Disgusting. What did you do with it, Jim?"

"Flung it in the fire. Girl needs a talkin' to. I'll remind her, this mornin'."

"Never mind. After all, we're only guests here." Jerome leaned back against the pillows. He motioned towards his silver case of cheroots. Jim leapt dexterously to the table. He struck a light for his master. Jerome did not meet his eyes. "Jim, how do you like the country?"

"Ah, sir, I loves it! All this air, and the snow. Not filthy, like. Never saw snow like this."

"It's better in the summer." Jerome looked at the fire. "How would you like to live here, Jim?"

Jim was astounded. "Here, sir? For good? Not goin' back? What'd you do here, sir? And all your friends in New York?"

Jerome smoked carefully. "Friends? Frankly, now, Jim, what friends have I? None at all, to be candid. I'm tired of the city, anyway. Yes, I'm thinking of staying here for good. I'm thinking of going into my father's Bank. Do you think you could stand it?"

Jim was silent. His face was more monkeylike than ever. His eyes were sharp and searching, and he felt a little sick. He glanced involuntarily at the fire.

"It's not like you, sir," he said, vaguely. Then his voice quickened, and he shook his head. "You're not serious, Mr. Jerome. You couldn't abide it, after awhile. After all, there's a lot to be said for New York." He became falsely enthusiastic. "The theatre. The opera. The musicals. The ladies. All the excitement, and such. You'd miss it, sir. You couldn't abide bein' away."

Jerome said: "I think I could. At least, I'm going to try it. Jim, if you feel you couldn't stand it, please be frank. I'll miss you, but I won't insist that you stay here and die of boredom. It's very quiet. And the servants aren't your sort." He smiled. But he waited for Jim to answer, with more anxiety than he would have thought possible.

Jim was still incredulous. The two regarded each other intently. It'll be bad, this, thought the valet. No good'll come of it. He's up to his old tricks. I'd'a' thought he'd not mess up, like, with his connection's lady.

Jerome spoke again: "Try it, Jim. Please try it. We can always leave if we get tired of the quietness. After all, haven't you just sung rhapsodies about the air and the sun and the roses in my cheeks? You remember, I haven't been well for a long time. This might do the trick for me. You see, Jim, I'm almost begging you."

He drew his leg out from under the sheets, and rubbed it with ostentatious tenderness. He said: "Well, Jim, what's your answer?"

Jim drew a deep breath, though his alarm was increasing. "I'll not leave you, sir. How could I, after what you've done for me? We've been together a long time, ever since the army. Though I'm not a chap as bets, I think we won't be stayin' long."

Jerome smiled. "I shouldn't wonder if you were right, Jim. But even a few weeks might set me up as well as ever. And now, tell me how everything is. Have you seen my father, Mr. Lindsey, this morning?"

"No, sir. He wasn't up and abaht. Had his breakfast in his room. And Miss Lindsey is still in bed, they say, with her feverish cold. I didn't even see Mr. Alfred. He was gone early, to the Bank. But Master Philip," he added, slowly, "and Miss Maxwell—they're up and abaht, with the dog. Charlie's off his head, like, with the snow."

Jerome lifted his watch from the table, and exclaimed. "Eleven o'clock! That's country air, for you, Jim. Slept like the proverbial log. Now, then, please bring me my clothes."

Jim chattered amiably through the dressing. He shaved Jerome neatly. He rubbed his hair with tonic, and brushed it vigorously. "No new gray hairs, sir, and that's a blessin'. Your black cravat, sir, or one of the new French ones? Subdued, like, for the mornin'. What abaht this?" And he held up a rich Paisley design for Jerome's inspection. "Go well with the brown broadcloth. Just the thing for mornin'."

Jerome studied the proffered garments critically. Then he shrugged. "Your taste is better than mine, Jim. We don't dress much, in the country."

"I heard abaht the Christmas eve party, sir. Carols and such. Like the old country." Jim sighed. "Reminds me of the old country, this. Solid, like. New York's nothin' to it. All the hustle and bustle, and no one rooted down. I'm to go into the woods with the coachmen and the stableboys, and look for mistletoe, and a tree."

Jerome laughed. "I can imagine you looking for mistletoe, Jim! Well, don't mind me. Go rustic. Climb about, like the monkey you are. Do you good."

He fastened his watch-chain across his brown silk waistcoat. He looked in the mirror. He rubbed his sunken cheeks with the palms of his hands. Jim sprayed a little eau de cologne on a linen kerchief, and neatly folded it into his master's pocket. He held the coat and carefully smoothed the shoulders after Jerome had slipped his arms into the sleeves. "Bright you are, sir!" said Jim. "Fresh as the mornin', itself. Will you be going for a walk, sir?"

"Shortly. First I must visit Mr. Lindsey."

He still regarded himself critically in the mirror. Then he paused. He saw Jim's anxious face, all the wizened features screwed together. He turned from the mirror. "What is it, Jim? Something's wrong. Come on, you've never kept anything from me before. What is troubling you?"

Jim was frightened again. He said, hurriedly: "Nothin', sir. I beg your pardon." Then, as Jerome scowled, he went on, almost incoherently: "It's a feelin' I have, sir. That nothin' good'll come of us stayin'. Stayin' long."

Jerome glanced at the fire. The strand of hair was gone. But he seemed to see it there still. Then he smiled easily, and laid his hand on Jim's shoulder. "Nonsense. Haven't you always been at me to settle down and accomplish something? See here, Jim, I'll take up my painting again, seriously this time. After banking hours, and during week-ends. I'll become the country gentleman, and you won't know me."

Jim sighed. "Yes, sir," he said, in a subdued voice.

Whistling softly, Jerome went down the warm corridor to his father's room.

He found Mr. Lindsey in scarlet dressing gown, gray shawl and woolen nightcap before the fire, slowly inspecting the contents of a silvery tray laid at his elbow on the round mahogany table. He appeared very wan and tired in the blazing noon light, and the fire, too, was pale and fugitive. His room resembled himself, for it was austere, the draperies grave in coloring, the bare floor polished, and relieved only by scattered Oriental rugs. The walls were lined with his cherished favorite books, as if the library below were not enough. His prim tester bed was neatly made. Jerome had often remarked that his father's room smelled of New England, and that it had a frosty and rebuking odor, fresh, but chilling.

"Ah ha," said Jerome, stepping briskly into the room. "A slug-a-bed, I see. Just beginning breakfast."

Mr. Lindsey laid down a silver cover over the contents of a dish. "This might possibly be luncheon, you know," he remarked, thoughtfully. He lifted the dish-cover again. "In fact, it is." He looked at his son, and smiled, and his pale face, wrinkled and dry as parchment, brightened. "Good morning, my dear boy."

Jerome laid his hand for a moment on his father's shoulder, and after an instant or two, Mr. Lindsey touched that hand with his cool fingers. Jerome sat down. In spite of his air of gaiety and affection, he felt that new constraint with his father, that strange uncertainty and wariness. But if Mr. Lindsey, himself, discerned his son's constraint he did not betray the fact. He regarded Jerome with affection.

"Well, if that is luncheon, then I am reproached," said Jerome. "Please do not delay—Father. It smells very appetizing."

But Mr. Lindsey lay back in his chair. "It can wait. I never did like fish, anyway. But Dorothea insists it does something for the brain. She must think I am getting senile."

They laughed together, and for a brief few seconds the constraint was entirely gone and they gazed at each other with the old fondness and understanding, complete and intimate.

Still smiling, Mr. Lindsey said: "At eight this morning, I had a talk with Alfred. I told him of your—decision. He was much interested. He waited to discuss the matter with you. He waited until nine o'clock."

"Did he expect me to be up then?" asked Jerome, with light derision.

Mr. Lindsey rubbed his lip reflectively with his index finger. "Banks have not changed their custom. They open at half-past eight still, I believe. Or were you under the impression you might stroll in at noon?"

Jerome winced elaborately. "Then, it seems, I must crack the dawn every morning after this?"

"No, but I fear you will have to meet it face to face." Mr. Lindsey paused, as Jerome pretended, with ruefulness, to consider the unattractive idea. "I repeat, my dear boy, that Alfred was much interested. And pleased."

"Oh, certainly. He would express his pleasure. Especially when you indicated that you were already partial to the thought."

"You do Alfred an injustice. Do you mean to imply he is a hypocrite?"

Jerome's eyes were unpleasant. "No, he hasn't the imagination. Don't frown. I grant that he, after judicious and conscientious reflection, decided that justice, and fealty, demanded that he be pleased. So—he was pleased. He manufactures his reactions, with the highest motives."

"That is very encouraging. It leads me to hope that mankind, after due consideration, might be able to manufacture lofty sentiments at will, however base the initial emotion. Aren't you a little too sanguine, Jerome?"

"Oh, I have the utmost faith in human nature, Father." Jerome glanced at the fire, then stirred it up vigorously. "I believe in everybody. I am full of brotherly love. Sweetness and light originated in me. But, in the name of God, did Alfred actually believe that I would be up carolling at the dawn, my first morning home?"

"He might have believed that a gentleman, suddenly inspired by auspicious ambition, would not be able to sleep for excitement and resolution, and so rise early."

"I was busy putting the roses in my cheeks, among the pillows," said Jerome. "I am quoting Jim, my valet."

Mr. Lindsey again rubbed his lip. "That brings me to another thought. Don't you think it slightly pretentious of you to retain a valet, here in the country?"

"No, I don't. I'm used to being waited upon. Besides, Jim can do other things. He is an excellent cook. Not English cooking. French. He has imagination. Then, he is marvelous with horses. He used to be a jockey. He is good at mending, too. He is full of virtues, and conveniences. You, yourself, will soon find him indispensable. He serves beautifully. In fact, you could discharge half the staff here and never miss them. Not that I recommend that, however. Jim is bent on going rustic, so he will probably be out in the stables most of the time, doing things with the horses, if you 'do things' with them. He shoots, among other things. I expect to do some hunting again."

"Remarkable," murmured Mr. Lindsey. "Where did this estimable man learn all this?"

"Some talents he acquired in gaol."

"Gaol!" exclaimed Mr. Lindsey.

"Yes. I forgot. He has a talent for pickpocketing. Don't look so dismayed. He has reformed. Like me. He doesn't pick pockets now. He has sublimated that genius into a knack with magic. He will keep the other servants endlessly amused, and satisfied."

"That is a consideration," said Mr. Lindsey, ironically. "We ought to keep the rabbit hutch well-filled, then."

But he was not displeased. He felt quite invigorated. Jerome had that effect on him, always. His eye was even bright, as it had not been bright in months, or years.

"With your arduous work at the Bank, and your hunting, you will be very busy, my boy. Do you intend to give up your painting?"

"No. I expect to have time for everything. You have no idea how energetic I can be, when I wish. I have only one failing: I cannot endure to be bored. Is banking exciting?"

"I imagine you will make it exciting. I think that worries Alfred. He believes banking is sacrosanct, and that any levity with regard to it is blasphemy. But, seriously, you must not expect to discover a circus within the confines of that august institution. There is much dreary detail, there, and much dryness. And you were never one to love detail and exactitude. I fear you are indeed going to be bored at times."

They gazed at each other in a little silence. Jerome's eyes narrowed, though he still smiled. "My decision has not changed," he said, finally.

Mr. Lindsey sighed. "I know. I only hope you will not regret it. I have always feared that you like to add experiences to your garden of adventure. I trust you will not regard this as just another experience, something to be collected for future merriment. That was always your way, was it not, Jerome?"

"I like to live." Jerome's voice was hard, if still light.

Mr. Lindsey raised himself in his chair. He no longer

smiled. He said: "Under that pretty heading you have inscribed a number of foolish things. Forgive me if I seem to harp, or complain. I am only warning you. You have thought yourself very unique taking that motto as your own: 'I love to live.' As if everyone else detested life, and grimly replaced joy with duty, out of sheer perversity! No, my dear boy, there are many happy men who know duty and fulfil it with pleasure, and still continue to love life. The foolish man, prating of his love of life, believes that only vice is enjoyable."

He pushed aside the silver tray, and picked up a book. Jerome closed his eyes. "Not your old favorite, Father! Again!"

Mr. Lindsey could not help smiling. "No, another. Joseph Addison this time '——that vice and ignorance, imperfection . . . should contend for praise, and endeavor as much as possible to make themselves objects of admiration.' "

Jerome colored. "I am not contending for praise, nor do I wish to make myself an object of admiration, in desiring to enter the Bank. I care only for my own opinion of myself." He indicated the book. "Addison's essay On the Wise and the Foolish? Well, I know that, too. 'The wise man is happy when he gains his own approbation and the fool when he recommends himself to the applause of those about him.' " He paused, then said in a soft and ugly tone: "Alfred adores your applause, Father. And, doubtless, you have been lavish with it."

Mr. Lindsey closed the book slowly, and replaced it on the table. He fixed his pale-blue eyes with a level look upon his son. "You have always hated Alfred. But you never resented him before. Are you jealous of Alfred now, Jerome?"

Jerome shrugged. "Jealous? I was never jealous of anyone. Perhaps it is because I am an egotist. But, candidly, I have always found Alfred tiresome. He bores me to death. He has no conversation. I can forgive a man anything, if he has conversation. You might deny it, Father, but I know he bores you also. What can he discuss, beyond the Bank? During these long winter nights, with what talk has he enlivened you? Philosophy, politics, taste, religion? If he has any ideas whatsoever about them, they are bound to be as dreary as death, and as vital. I think he has acquired them too from the Bank ledgers. What gay evenings you must have together!"

Mr. Lindsey compressed his lips to prevent an involuntary smile which he felt was unjust and unkind.

"On the contrary, Alfred and I have had many interesting talks."

"Oh, what a gentleman you are, sir! What tolerance! On what subject can you and Alfred possibly agree, or even disagree? You can't use intellectual reason on Alfred. You must admit that, yourself. And now, a little quotation from a pet of mine, Samuel Taylor Coleridge. You remember Coleridge? He speaks of men afflicted with inward blindness, and I apply that to Alfred, with no reservations. With such men, he says, 'nothing is possible but a naked dissent, which implies a sort of unsocial contempt: or—what a man of kind disposition is very likely to fall into—a heartless tacit acquiescence, which borders too nearly on duplicity.' I cannot accuse you, Father, of having contempt for any man. I can only accuse you of your 'kind disposition.' "

"And of duplicity," added Mr. Lindsey. He could not repress his smile now.

Jerome made a deprecating gesture. "How can a gentleman of intellect and reason talk for five minutes with Alfred and not be guilty of duplicity, of the violation of his deepest convictions, especially if he be a kind man?"

"He might be charitable," said Mr. Lindsey. "He might be tolerant, as well as guilty of dissimulation. Men like you often turn the world into a bloody battleground. I prefer peace. Especially in my own household." His tone was tranquil. But Jerome smiled at him disagreeably.

"You are warning me again," he said, thoughtfully.

Mr. Lindsey lifted the silver covers from his dishes. He began to eat, with real and new relish. "At any rate, I never accused you of being obtuse, Jerome."

Jerome stood up, thrust his hands into his trouser pockets, and began to walk restlessly up and down the room, staring at the rug. "I think I have made it clear that my nature is inclined to sweetness and light. I shall shed beams on Alfred. I shall be guilty of duplicity. Not a tone of my voice shall disturb the holy and placid atmosphere of this house. Even if I choke to death."

Mr. Lindsey began to laugh. "Really, I see many happy months ahead!" he exclaimed.

Jerome stopped his pacing to pour his father's tea. He did it with an air of real affection and care. He dropped three lumps of sugar into the steaming liquid; he added cream. Mr. Lindsey watched him, with open fondness. "Thank you, my dear boy. You have not forgotten how much sugar I take. Dorothea thinks it bad for me. I often feel guilty."

"Dutiful people have that effect on the civilized," remarked Jerome.

Mr. Lindsey sipped his tea, and sighed contentedly. "I have the oddest feeling that this conversation of ours is very unkind. Even treacherous. My mother used to say that no conversation was worthy of the truly elegant man if it could not be heard without reproach or embarrassment by any eavesdropper."

They looked at each other, then burst out laughing. Jerome added an obscene remark, and the laughter became uncontrollable.

So happy had Mr. Lindsey then become that he, himself, suggested that Jerome postpone his labors at the Bank until after the Christmas holidays. Jerome's objections were faint. They parted, feeling soothed and most agreeable.

Jerome then went to visit his sister, who was still in bed with her cold.

The draperies were barely drawn from the windows, and by the dim light Dorothea was sitting up in bed reading the last pious issue of the "Gospel Trumpet," an organ published by a missionary society for which she had much esteem. The smell of camphor, lavender and vinegar was even stronger in the room, and Jerome's nostrils contracted. He no longer felt soothed and agreeable, but he greeted his sister with a grave question about her illness. She put aside the paper and looked at him with her old impatient imperiousness, touched with an eager hope.

"Well?" she demanded, brushing away his query about her health. "Have you talked to Papa about that—woman? What have you done, Jerome? Please stop staring at the fire. It is quite hot enough!" For Jerome had shown indications that he intended to stir up the coals. "Do sit down, Jerome. I am all impatience."

Jerome sat down and regarded his sister somberly. "I am sorry, my dear. It is hopeless. I harangued Father for hours." He fingered his watch-chain. "I even offered the lady in question a—a consideration if she would give up her obdurate and greedy plans. It is hopeless. We must reconcile ourselves to the inevitable."

Dorothea's grim gray face immediately became pinched and desperate. Her hands trembled as they fumbled with her handkerchief. She tried to speak, then was silent. Her lips shook. Jerome watched her with an unusual pity, in spite of his first mean pleasure in her bitter disappointment and misery. He saw how she blinked her eyes to restrain her tears, how she swallowed convulsively. He felt a sudden admiration for her when she threw up her graying head with such resolution that her frilled cap was strongly agitated.

"But you have not talked to Alfred," she said, and her harsh voice was quite firm.

"My dear! That is asking too much. As well ask a dog to give up a juicy piece of meat!" And he made a slight smacking sound.

She colored violently at his words, and the sound that had followed them. "Jerome! How disgusting of you! Give me my salts, if you please."

He brought them to her, and she held the pungent bottle firmly to her nostrils, and sniffed urgently. When she withdrew it, the water was thick in her eyes. It formed into tears, which spilled over her cheeks. "Really, too strong," she murmured. "But everything has deteriorated, since the war." She replaced the bottle on the table. The tears would not stop. She was, all at once, a shrunken if still indomitable woman, on her pillows.

"I have only one last resource: to make things so unpleasant for the slut that she will leave voluntarily," said Jerome. "Of course, that will not make Alfred love me more than he already does. Or, I might contrive to reveal her to him as she is. I have already made a good beginning in that direction, I think. But, you must not depend on this too much. A man who is determined to sl——, to marry a certain woman, is a man shut out from all reason. She has hypnotized him. She watched my efforts against her, and smiled like a smug and very replete cat. No, I cannot promise too much in that direction."

"He is bewitched!" cried Dorothea, hoarsely. She wiped her eyes again. "Oh, dear, those salts!"

"Of course," said Jerome, thoughtfully, "he might find out after marriage."

"But that would be too late."

Jerome pursued his thought. "Sometimes a jam pot is revealed to have turned sour. But that is only after it is sampled. And Alfred is determined to sample."

"Jerome!"

"As for Father, he is inclined to find her refreshing." He grinned, "I am happy that dear Papa has his arthritis, or we might discover ourselves with a stepmama considerably younger than ourselves, and equally rapacious."

Dorothea was aghast. "Jerome! How can you be so unspeakable, so shameless!"

Jerome shrugged. "Well, dear Papa is still a man, and he always was. Or do you believe we were begotten while he elegantly held Mama's hand, and conversed of edifying matters? No, my dear Dotty, we must consider that things might be worse. Many a man has forgotten his children while he dallied behind the bed-curtains with a strumpet."

Dorothea's color became dark crimson. "You are not only odious, you are loathsome." She shuddered involuntarily. "How can you speak so of Papa? But you never had any respect for him, or any decency."

Jerome rose, happy to escape. "Then I shall remove my contemptible presence from your room, darling Dotty, if you find it so insupportable."

Dorothea lifted her hand. "Wait! Are you confessing, now, that you can find no solution, you who were so assured last night?" She was still crimson, and she could not look at him without shame, but her urgency made her temporarily forget her emotions.

"I said, the situation seems hopeless, but I have not entirely given up. I am merely warning you not to expect too much. That is only reasonable. There is another thing: we are having a Christmas party, I believe. Perhaps when Alfred sees her among his stuffed-duck and respectable friends, with their breeding and gentility and manners, the woman will suddenly seem impossible to him. Doubtless, too, those friends will convey to him their disapproval of the marriage, and their shock and outrage, and Alfred, who is always so sensitive to the opinions of others, might be impressed."

Dorothea was silent, pondering this. The gloom lifted slightly from her face. "Yes," she murmured, at last. "There is some hope in that. Yes, I am inclined to think there is." She sank deeper into thought. She saw all the elegant young ladies of her acquaintance, and their irreproachable mamas, and their solid papas. And she saw them staring haughtily at Amalie Maxwell, and listening to her shocking conversation.

"As for the money," said Jerome, "we have reason to hope substantially there. I am going to safeguard our interests. I am going into the Bank."

"Interesting," murmured Dorothea, abstractedly, her busy thoughts continuing. Jerome moved towards the door. Then suddenly the impact of what he had said reached her. "What!" she exclaimed, galvanized. "What did you say about the Bank,

Jerome? Did I hear aright? You are going into the Bank?"

"That is what I said," he agreed.

She stared at him, overcome with amazement and incredulity. She blinked her eyes at him. Her mouth opened blankly.

When she spoke, she stuttered: "I—I can't believe it! Why should you go into the Bank, Jerome? You?"

"I can't see why it should stun you so," said Jerome, disagreeably. "Our money is there, isn't it? And where the mouse is, the cat hangs about."

"But you would be impossible in the Bank! It is not to be thought of!"

"Thank you for the compliment, so gracefully and tactfully made."

"But you couldn't go into the Bank! Papa and Alfred wouldn't let you!" She was overcome, shocked at the very thought.

"Papa will not only let me, he has already agreed. And Alfred is 'pleased.' "

She still stared at him, as though he were an incredible and appalling creature dropped from another sphere.

"But you would be absolutely—impossible—in a bank! Our Bank. I cannot see you in the Bank!"

"You will," Jerome assured her, his hand on the door. "You will see my handsome countenance bent over the ledgers, and my graceful legs curled around a stool. It will be an uplifting sight, one to cheer the heart in your bosom. I shall sit next to the safes."

The idea stunned her more and more. If he had expressed his determination to occupy the pulpit of her favorite minister she could not have been more horrified and disbelieving. Even her misery was dissolved in her stupefaction.

"If you are thinking that I shall probably make off with the money-bags, disabuse yourself of the idea, my love," he said. "For, while on the surface it appears to have its certain attractions, I have no doubt that Alfred would have me pursued and thrown into gaol. All in a spirit of impartial justice and disinterested integrity."

"But, what would you do in the Bank?" She fell back against her pillows, weak with shock.

"I told you: watch the money. Make myself such an infernally good banker that Papa will be impressed, and revise his will, and such. I'm a reformed character, Dotty. I itch for the ledgers. I pant for the cash. I'll watch it as a vestal virgin watched the sacred flame. I'll out-bank Alfred. You'll see."

"The very idea is ludicrous! I shall speak to Papa——"

"Thank you for the flattery. And, do speak to Papa. He is entranced with the idea. He drools with joy at the very thought of it. If he has any misgivings at all, your objections will dispel them. Damn it, I thought you'd be delighted."

"Don't swear," she said, faintly and mechanically, as usual. She lay back on the pillows and brought her distracted thoughts to play on the impossible thought of Jerome in the Bank. His arguments, however, impressed her. But she shook her head numbly. "You, in the Bank," she murmured feebly. "No one would feel safe—if you were there."

Jerome threw back his head and shouted with laughter.

She was suddenly overcome with alarm. "You will ruin the Bank! You will destroy its prestige, the people's faith in it! They will take out their money! Oh, you are doing this to crush Alfred, to wreck him! You wicked, wicked man! To injure him so, to cover him with shame and ruination!"

He grinned broadly. "All right, then, I'll withdraw my offer. I shall return to New York. Then the strumpet will have everything, and you may meekly accede to being her upper servant, and then dear Papa will die, and you and I will be practically penniless. Does that attract you more, my pet?"

She was dumfounded, completely shaken. He watched her mind digest this. He waited. He saw the struggle between her native rapacity and her love for Alfred, her bitter grief and disappointment, and her terror of what Jerome might do in the Bank. He nodded his head, as if delighted. Then, assured now of the outcome, he bowed ironically, and left the room.

For sheer amusement for the spectators, he thought happily, there's nothing like having a conscience and being a woman scorned.

Quite exhilarated, he returned to his room, brought out his coat and swung it over his shoulders. The laughter and voices were still gay outside.

CHAPTER TEN

The air sparkled and glittered with sunlight. Chimney smoke arched and danced under a sky like a blue diamond. The large square old house, impregnably built of its heavy gray stone, was festooned with icicles, all incandescent. It stood on its hilltop, surveying the far valley below with amiable dignity and pride, and commanding its snowy slopes serenely. The firs still carried burdens of scalloped white on their black branches.

It was a most exciting day, hinting of gay festivity, comfort and security. The stableboys had been busy in the early morning, and had shovelled the flagged walks free of snow, so that flashes of dull blue and terra-cotta red appeared regularly in the surrounding whiteness. The red brick wall which fenced off the garden in the rear of the house was cushioned with soft purity, and the branches of the fruit trees were alive with chattering and scolding sparrows. The runners of the sleigh which had conveyed Alfred to the town below had carved sharp tracks in the shining virginity of the circling drive, and here the boys were again busy with their shovels, their voices clear and imperative in the shining silence. Beyond the gardens, and the other grounds of the house, the dark woods blurred themselves massively against the sky, their tangled branches outlined with snow. From the stable came the neighing of horses, and from behind them, the clucking of fowl. Mr. Lindsey's conservatory, adjoining the house, blazed from its glass walls and roof. Every sound echoed like music, bounding back from the hillside in bell-like notes.

So incandescent was the air, so pristine, that the town below was distinct in all its detail, as were its paths and streets, irregular black veins between the houses and the other buildings. One could see the chimneys smoking, and even the minute crawling of sleds and wagons and carriages.

Jerome stood just outside the front entrance of the house and sniffed the bitter pure air, so sterile and so fresh. His childhood and boyhood came back to him vividly. He wondered if his sleds and snowshoes still hung in one of the barns, and he had a sudden and pleasurable desire to coast down the gentle hill behind the house to the terraced level below. Was the fishpond still in the gardens, forming a glittering blue shield of ice, and excellent for skating? His skates must be rusty now.

As for the hill stream which wound its way from some spring near the house: was it black and frozen now, stilled on its mossy rocks? He wanted to see all these things.

He heard a fresh burst of laughter, and walked casually around the side of the house. Miss Maxwell and Philip were still playing with Charlie, who was beside himself with this new freedom and this strange white stuff that was so soft and yielding and cold. He kept hurling his taffy-colored body into the drifts headfirst, then, after some frenetic and subterranean churning, reappearing with a look of amazed bewilderment, his nose crowned with snow. He would bark wildly, pull himself from the drift, and leap upon his new and fascinating friends, who received him with laughing affection.

He was the first to detect Jerome. Barking excitedly, he scrambled along the cleared flagstones, and flung himself upon his master, as if calling the latter's attention to this enexplicable wonder. Jerome picked him up; the little dog was trembling with joy.

The two others turned to him smilingly. "Uncle Jerome!" exclaimed Philip, shyly. He was a shrunken and misshapen gnome in his long brown coat and tall hat. But his pale face had acquired some color, and his eyes, so like Jerome's, were sparkling and dancing.

The flashing smile on Amalie's face changed very subtly. It hardened, became frozen. She stood silently, looking at her enemy with full and inscrutable steadfastness. She had tied a shawl over her head, and it hid all but a wing of her black hair, which lay on her white forehead. She was more beautiful in this sharp and brilliant light than she had been the night before, and an immense vitality, an inner and healthy vibrancy, flowed from her. The cold had flushed her pale face, brightened her lips to pulsing color.

"Good morning," said Jerome, affably, stroking his dog and advancing upon Philip and Amalie. "A glorious morning. I think Charlie is drunk with it."

Philip offered shyly: "He's such a nice little dog, so friendly."

"Is he? Hasn't he nipped you yet? He has a bad temper." Jerome smiled down at the poor boy. He could not quell his familiar repugnance for Philip's deformity, but as he had also an easy and indifferent pity for Alfred's son he did not find it difficult to be kind to him. He pulled Charlie's ears. "Charlie, like his master, is famous for his temperamental ugliness."

Amalie's face changed. It became faintly derisive, and she bit her lip as if to keep from bursting out laughing. Jerome, who had glanced at her blandly, saw this, and his eyebrows drew together. But Philip did not find Jerome absurd. He looked up at the man with the gentle seriousness that so distinguished him. "Oh, no, Uncle Jerome. There is nothing ugly about you. Or Charlie." He had spoken impulsively, and now he colored with embarrassment. He turned to the woman. "We've been having such a nice time, haven't we, Miss Amalie?"

"We have been," she said pointedly. She picked up her skirts.

Philip's acute sensitiveness caught something wrong in this situation. He looked timidly from Jerome to Amalie, and then back to Jerome.

"Are you going in, Miss Amalie?" he asked, in a pleading voice. "You remember, you promised to walk down to the pines with me, and throw some corn for the birds." He fumbled in his pockets, brought out a striped bag of grain, and looked at it uncertainly.

"Shall we go, then?" asked Amalie, lifting her skirts a trifle higher.

Again, Philip glanced from one to the other.

"Will you go with us, Uncle Jerome?"

Jerome hesitated. He began to grin. "Thank you. I will."

Amalie stiffened. The color dimmed in her cheeks. But she smiled at Philip. "I have just remembered, my love. I have some small tasks to do, and so, I know, you will excuse me. You have your Uncle Jerome, now." She paused, watching the pleasure fade from the boy's large dark eyes. She sighed. "Tell me you do not mind, dear Philip," she pleaded.

"Oh, no," he replied quickly, always eager not to hurt or offend. "I am only sorry for myself. But you have spent hours with me, and I must not be selfish." He made himself smile, and now he went to her, as if irresistibly drawn, and timidly touched her arm. She bent and kissed his cheek and, without another glance at Jerome, walked swiftly away around the angle of the house, to the rear.

Jerome bowed to her retreating back, but she did not see the gesture. Then Jerome and the boy walked slowly down the slope towards the pines. Philip began to scatter the corn, in silence. Charlie struggled in Jerome's arms, and Jerome put him down. Charlie floundered ahead of them, with renewed excitement, wondering what new game was about to be played.

They reached the pines. They stood all about them now, tall and black, furred with snow, casting their clear black shadows on the smooth whiteness. Philip cleared a spot or two with his foot, stamped it down, and put the corn upon it. Charlie went to sniff, barked, retreated with disappointment.

The man and boy then stood side by side, looking down at the valley which curved below. They could hear the faint barking of a dog, disembodied and clear. Charlie pricked up his ears, then began to bark wildly, darting and retreating with the most furious ebullition, challenging the distant intruder to combat, inviting him to come up and share this wondrous experience. Jerome watched him and laughed.

"Charlie's such a fool," he commented. "He is delirious at discovering that there are others like himself in the world."

"I think it makes all of us delirious, when we find that out," said Philip, in a low voice.

"What?" said Jerome. He looked at Philip with sharp interest. What an odd thing for a boy of fourteen to say! He was incredulous and pleased. "Who told you that, Philip?"

"Well, Miss Amalie and I have talked." Philip's sensitive color rose in his thin face, which was marked by introspection and patient suffering. His eyes lighted at the mention of Amalie's name. "We have such fine talks. She helps me with my music, too, for hours at a time."

"Indeed. Is she a wonderful musician, too?"

Philip dug his foot in the snow. "She can't read a note, she tells me. But she plays marvelously, and has the most excellent ear. Her criticisms are far better than Mr. Baxter's. Mr. Baxter is my teacher, you know. He comes for a week, every two months, and stays with us. He is from Philadelphia. Grandpapa is very kind. He loves music, and he says that he is determined that I shall be a fine musician, for his own enjoyment."

"So you quite approve of Miss Amalie as a new stepmamma, eh?"

Philip turned to him quickly, and again his eyes were alight. "Oh, so much, Uncle Jerome! I am so happy. Sometimes, at night, I dream she has gone away and left me forever, and then I am quite ill the next day. I couldn't bear it if she ever left me," he added, with profound and touching simplicity.

The clever slut! She had taken pains, then, to ingratiate herself with this poor lad, and fasten him to her side as an ally. Jerome looked down at his cousin's son and frowned. But he had nothing to say.

"She helps me with everything," Philip went on. "She is a teacher, you know. When my tutor left, Miss Amalie volunteered to take his place. Long before she came up here to live, she used to climb the hill, afternoons, until Papa began to send the carriage for her. She is so kind. So very, very kind. I—I love her." His face turned scarlet, but his eyes did not waver away. They gazed at Jerome proudly.

"Kind," thought Jerome. The poor deformed creature has had little experience with kindness, apparently. Alfred would be scrupulously just and attentive to his son, of course. Dorothea would consider it her "duty" to care for Philip. Mr. Lindsey, who had often openly confessed that he did not enjoy the young, might be languidly amiable and benign to the boy, provided that Philip did not too often intrude upon his meditations. But tenderness—that would be too much for any of them. Yes, the baggage was shrewd, thought Jerome, admiringly. She had found the chink in the armor of all her potential enemies. But she had not found any chink in the armor of Dorothea or of Jerome.

Philip was sighing. "Soon, I must go away to school. That will be in September, I am afraid. I hated the thought. I did not want to go away. But Miss Amalie has persuaded me that I must. And she has promised that I shall come home on all the holidays, and that she will visit me often. It is Mr. Van Goort's school, in Philadelphia, and Philadelphia is not too far away."

"Of course not," said Jerome, absently. "It will really be pleasant for you, Philip."

He stared attentively at the boy, and now he experienced a faint pang. The poor, poor little devil. He saw Philip's profile, sensitive and delicate, and with such an expression of purity and patience and gentleness. Yet, there was strength there, too, in spite of the evidences of prolonged meditation and thought and intellect. And there was more than a hint of passion in the flared nostrils and about the firm mouth. Jerome suddenly felt drawn to him, and wondered.

"Tell me more about Miss Amalie," he said kindly. "You see, I know so little about her, and no one tells me anything."

Philip gazed down the valley. He said, in a low voice: "She was very poor, you know. She had to work very hard. Miss Amalie has great courage. She laughs a great deal, and when I asked her why, she told me that a man has only two choices: to laugh or to die. She says she prefers to laugh. I am afraid that I used to be—very drawn in on myself. She taught me how to laugh." He drew a deep breath. "Miss Amalie is the most wonderful thing that ever happened to me. Sometimes, I can't believe it. We play together, and walk and ride together, and she tells me the strangest tales about the people she has known and about her work. But she doesn't hate anyone, and that is so odd. I think that, in her place, I must have hated many people."

Oh, the clever, clever strumpet! He could see her now, playing upon the sympathies of this naïve and cloistered boy, and displaying such courage and high-heartedness! He, Jerome, had underestimated her. She was formidable. He felt his blood

101

quicken and his breath come a little faster.

"Miss Amalie has been to Philadelphia," Philip was saying. "She has heard the operas, and seen the plays. Of course, she sat, she says, in the last row, but that did not matter. She tells me that those who sit in the last rows in the balcony are the only ones who really appreciate operas and plays. They are willing to be uncomfortable and cold, if only they can go."

"What a remarkable lady this is!" exclaimed Jerome, laughing.

But Philip had not heard him. His mouth was tense with passion, his eyes ablaze with it. "She reads to me. We have developed a story of our own, and sometimes she tells me a chapter, and the next night I invent another. It is very amusing and exciting. She came to my room last night, and had a new chapter. It was all about a new hero who has come into the story. He is a very blasé and worldly man, and thinks himself charming and so very witty, and all the time he is very comical. We laughed a great deal about it. He is so very pretentious, and thinks himself very wicked."

He had begun to laugh. His whole meagre little face was alight with mirth. He was so engrossed in his recital that he did not see how ugly and flushed Jerome had become.

"Oh, it was so amusing, Uncle Jerome! We invented witticisms, and each one was funnier than the last. I ached as if I had been bruised, when she finally said good night. And then I kept waking up in the night, and had to cover my face with the pillow, so that no one would hear me laughing."

Jerome whistled for Charlie, and the little dog came to him reluctantly, still ferociously growling at his distant enemy. Jerome picked him up.

"So, we have a wit in the house, also," he said.

"It is better than a play, to talk to Miss Amalie," Philip assured him artlessly, his eyes bright with reminiscence.

The sparrows, now that the two had considerably withdrawn, had discovered the grain. They swarmed down in shrilling droves, and pecked and whirred about. The man and the boy watched them. Philip was delighted. Jerome did not see the birds. His temples were pounding with fury and mortification and hatred.

"I am afraid," he said indulgently, "that Miss Amalie is a poor judge of character."

Philip was baffled at this. Jerome turned to climb the slope again, and Philip followed. But now the boy was silent. There was something wrong again. He admired Jerome deeply, but

102

was slightly afraid of him. Jerome, too, was often very "kind." Philip distressedly hoped that he had not offended him in some way.

Upon reaching the house, Philip apologetically explained that he must now take his afternoon nap. Miss Amalie insisted upon it, and it had done him much good. Jerome dismissed him agreeably. He stood alone in the sun-filled warm hall, stroking his dog. Then he lifted his head alertly.

The doors of the music room were folded shut. But from behind them flowed strong and passionate music, subdued yet intense. His trained ear immediately caught all the flaws in it, all the errors in technique. But it was music played by the hands of discerning strength and vitality, and what it lacked in technique and finish was more than compensated for by vitality and truth and unconventional beauty.

He silently folded back the doors. Now the music rushed out at him like a great wind of unrestrained vehemence and emotion. The pianist knew nothing of measure and flow, that was certain. But that did not matter. Jerome was overwhelmed by the grandeur and loveliness of the sounds that beat upon him.

The music room was austere and chill, despite the fire that burned on the black marble hearth. The dark floor was bright and polished, and completely uncovered, so that its great width and length glimmered in the light that streamed through the high and narrow windows, which were framed in dull blue brocade tied back with golden cords. A few dim chairs of frail carved mahogany and blue and rose brocade stood in their own gleaming reflections on the floor, and against the walls were ranged ranks of small gilt chairs ready for any musicale which Mr. Lindsey might arrange for his friends. The walls near the windows were banked with ferns and small palms and rubber plants in big majolica pots, and they filled the cool air with a fresh smell. Dorothea's harp, all gilt and marble, stood to Jerome's left, near the windows. In the far corner, at a distance from the wall, stood the great pianoforte with its covering of French shawl and silver fringe. There was a dais, empty now, on which paid musicians performed, upon engagement from Philadelphia, or even from New York. Mr. Lindsey loved music, and Jerome remembered many musicales from his childhood and boyhood. He remembered, too, the dances Mr. Lindsey used to give, when Jerome was at home, and he was suddenly transported back to those bright and festive evenings when he and his young friends had waltzed and bowed in grave measures to entrancing tunes. He could hear, again, young laughter and gay voices, and could see the swaying hoops of the girls, and their shining faces, and the ruffles of the local young bloods who squired them.

The music room was empty, now, except for the young woman at the piano. Her plain brown dress was innocent of bustle, and fitted her wonderful figure superbly as she sat upon the stool. The afternoon light lay on her shining black hair, which fell in a ringletted mass on her shoulders. Her back, which was straight and held in a natural and perfect posture, leaned slowly from side to side with the motions of her white hands. Her profile was rapt and withdrawn, her lips parted, her eyes raised and glowing with purple lights. From beneath her fingers poured the cataract of bewitching sound. She was happy. She was alone. She was entranced with her own music.

Jerome sat down upon one of the brocaded chairs. He quelled the restless Charlie with a warning pressure of his hand. He leaned back in the chair and crossed his legs. He stared intently at Amalie, who was oblivious of him and of everything else.

So, this is what she was! All that "high-heartedness" and "courage" were only assumed, for effect. All that mean and vicious wit, which passed as harmless gaiety! She was here, revealed in all her innate turbulence and discord and infuriated passion, all her uncontrolled strength and indomitable defiance of anyone who dared to challenge her ruthlessness and will. The music was powerful still, but now the discord was stronger, the chords were more inexorable. It was beautiful, yes, but primitive, even savage. Jerome smiled and idly stroked one of Charlie's silken ears. He caught a melody, heard it repeated, understood it was the theme. It had a primordial intensity and insistence. He no longer smiled. His pulses, against all his will and desire, followed the relentless rhythm, so that they sounded, to him, like accompanying and helpless drums, drawn into a vortex of mounting frenzy.

There was something coarse and riotous in the music, thought Jerome, something unbridled and even violent, for all its heroic undertones. But his hand became still, motionless, on the dog's head, and he saw, for a vivid moment, a mountain peak outlined in lightning, and heard, from its caverns and its chasms, the roaring echo of the thunder, the screaming defiance that gushed from the lower crags.

Then the Gothic insurgence suddenly ended on a great swell, like a shout, and the silence that followed reverberated with remembered sound.

Amalie still sat at the piano, in the posture of playing, but her hands moved over the keys slowly, without evoking a whisper. Then she started uncontrollably, for Jerome had begun to clap, loudly and slowly.

She swung about on the bench and looked at him, and he saw her startled affront, her anger.

"Really, that was remarkable, even singular," he said. "I congratulate you on your teachers, Miss Amalie."

She did not speak, but only looked at him. Then, very quietly, she stood up and closed the piano.

"Something by Wagner, perhaps, or Beethoven?" he suggested, idly beginning to stroke the dog again.

She turned to him and said softly: "Why can't you let me alone?"

He smiled at her meditatively. "Now, that is a question I have been asking myself," he answered, with a great air of candor. "Is it your wit, perhaps? Or your charm? Or your great gifts? Or your delectable conversation? Or your exquisite manners which so fascinate me? Doubtless, it must be your manners. They are so—so extraordinary."

All at once, her face turned scarlet with some suppressed emotion. "Why can't you let me alone?" she asked, and her voice was low and hoarse. "What have I done to you? What enmity have I expressed for you? What malice have I inflicted upon you?"

"You can do, and have done, nothing to me, gracious lady," he said, looking up at her amiably. "But, now that we are so frank, let me say that perhaps I resent you here. I resent you on the stairway where my mother walked. I resent you at her piano. I resent you at her table. I find the idea insupportable, that you will sit in her place at her table. You will forgive me, I know, for these ridiculous sentiments."

She had become quite white, while he had been speaking. And now she smiled, and the smile was not beautiful.

"I think," she said, "that you might mention all these things to Alfred."

He cocked an eyebrow. "Oh, no, indeed! A dog will not be persuaded to give up his luscious bone. Have you ever attempted to withdraw such a bone from a dog? One gets one's fingers nipped, quite properly."

She ran her hand over the closed piano. "Let me warn you,

105

dear Mr. Lindsey. You will indeed get your fingers nipped, if you continue. But, again, I suggest you discuss these interesting matters with Alfred. Or have you tried?"

But he did not answer, continuing only to stroke the dog and smile up at her with deliberate and knowing insult.

Now her voice and breath became hurried. "You say you resent me here. Why? Let us come out with it. Because I am poor, and not genteel? Because I have had to work for a living? Because I have no background? Because what I have I have gotten with my bare hands? Because I have asked no quarter, and no pity? Then, Mr. Lindsey, you must hate most Americans. You must resent nearly all of them."

He lifted an elegant hand languidly. "My dear Miss Amalie," he protested, "you are accusing me of most undemocratic sentiments, and that is unfair! Hasn't democracy been the most edifying way of life, since our noble Mr. Lincoln? Who am I to disagree with him? No, you are quite wrong. I do not resent you for your poverty, your lack of gentility, your arduous fight for a living, your ambiguous background. No, no, a thousand times no! Let us say that I resent you for what you are, what I know you to be."

She looked at him silently, and he saw the bitter violet flash of her eyes. Then, with great quietness, she asked: "What am I?"

He shrugged. He sat up in his chair with an air of purpose. "Miss Amalie. You are not talking to a naïve buffoon like Alfred. You are not talking to a secluded country squire, like my father. You are not talking to a trusting boy, like Philip. You are talking to a man who may be pardoned when he says that he knows something of the world, and something of the men and the women who inhabit it."

She did not speak. Her smile was even less attractive.

"Now," he said reasonably, "I always was an admirer of the Cinderella theme. I find it charming. But I look at your feet, Miss Amalie. I do not see a slipper of pure and innocent glass. I see a slipper of——"

"Of what?" she asked, when he paused.

He shrugged again. "Now, you would compel me to be unkind, and that you shall never succeed in. I am only advising you."

She deliberately lifted her skirts, and revealed beautiful ankles and fine narrow feet. "My heels," she said, "are not worn down by trampling them on the necks of the defenseless. The toes are not scarred by kicking those who cannot kick back."

Jerome leaned forward. "Very pretty, very pretty indeed. I have not seen handsomer ankles even on the stages of New York. Thank you for the charming view."

She dropped her skirts, slowly. She stood straight and composed before him.

"Mr. Lindsey," she said, "I am not going to waste any more time discussing myself with you. I am not going to quarrel with you. You are not worth my efforts. I could say you are a vulgarian, and a boor, and a fool. But you wouldn't believe it. So, for the last time, I warn you. Let me alone. Stay out of my way. Don't address me except in the most casual manner, and then only when amongst others. For, my witty and debonair Mr. Lindsey, if you continue to annoy me I shall have recourse to Alfred. I shall tell him that you follow and hound me. I shall tell him that last night you pursued me into the pine woods, and there forced your repulsive attentions upon me."

Again, there was silence. Then Jerome smiled gently, and said: "You would not dare."

"I would dare, Mr. Lindsey! In fact, only native charity, and a regard for your father and your cousin, have prevented me from telling Alfred this, this morning. I am a woman of peace, sir. I prefer to remain at peace. You disturb my resolution at your own peril."

He stood up now, and dropped the little dog, who ran eagerly to the girl. Jerome and Amalie faced each other. He took a step closer to her. She did not retreat. He could see the pounding pulse in her white throat, but she met him eye to eye.

"The words of an adventuress," he said.

Her face changed, and then she smiled involuntarily. "Perhaps, Mr. Lindsey."

"I can't have an adventuress in my mother's place."

With immense courtesy, she said: "I do not see how you are going to prevent it, dear sir." Then she added: "But do not forget what I have told you. You will not find me a weak enemy."

He leaned his hand on his chair, negligently, and surveyed her with open insolence. "I admire you, Miss Amalie. I admire your courage. I admire your fighting spirit. You ought to have been a man. I think I'd have loved you, then."

She opened her mouth to speak, then closed it. Now her expression was grave and searching.

"Yes," he said, with a considering air, "I think I'd have

loved you, then. I might have been your friend, for I admire ruthless creatures."

"I am ruthless because I have had to be ruthless," she said reflectively. "I did not choose my parents, my poverty, my life. But I surmounted all of them. And I shall not give up what I have attained. Nor shall I be compelled to."

She took a step to the side and prepared to pass him. He caught her arm with a sudden rough movement. He expected her to struggle. But she did not. She merely looked at him contemptuously.

"Damn you," he said softly, "I can't let you alone. Why? I don't know. I really hate you and despise you. But there is something about you——"

She smiled.

"Mr. Lindsey," she asked, "will you be content never to see me again? If I should leave, would you refrain from following me?"

Slowly, he removed his hand from her arm. He stared at her.

"No," he murmured. "No. I think not."

She nodded her head. "Thank you."

He said: "I don't know why, but you fascinate me. You are a handsome woman. There is something about you. Under other circumstances, my love, I could make a fool of myself over you."

He stopped speaking, and a dark stain of color washed up to his brows. "I might make you an interesting offer, Miss Amalie."

Her face changed, turned extremely pale. Then, as Charlie churned insistently at her feet, she bent and lifted him, and every motion was full of grace. She held the little dog in her arms, and he nestled his head under her chin.

"Mr. Lindsey," she said, after a prolonged moment of silence, "all this is very interesting, I admit. But I ask you to remember my warning."

She held out the dog to him, and he took it. They regarded each other intently.

"I shall never let you alone," he said, and his voice was thick. "I don't know whether I hate you, or— I'll find out, eventually. For, you see, I am not going away again."

"But you cannot remain here!" she said, in a low and shaken tone.

"And why not? This is my home, please remember."

She drew a deep breath, and now the despair was brighter on her face.

"It is impossible for you to remain here!"

"Why?" He drew closer to her. She flung back her head. They looked into each other's eyes.

"I couldn't endure it," she whispered.

He put his hand behind the back of her neck. He began to draw her to him. But, recovering herself, she flung him off, turned from him with a faint cry, gathered up her skirts, and fled to the door.

On the threshold, she stopped abruptly. Jerome had neglected to close the doors behind him. Dorothea, ghastly and grim in her black bombazine, stood there, in rigid silence.

Amalie retreated a step, Jerome, turning to follow her, stopped also. He looked at his sister, and she stared back at him, and her eyes were like stone.

Amalie had recovered herself. She stepped aside, then passed Dorothea without a word. They heard her steps running lightly up the stairs.

"Good evening, Dorothea," said Jerome.

"I heard everything," she replied, and her voice was loud and harsh, "everything."

"Good," he said easily. "You see I am doing what I can."

She stirred, then. "You wicked, you most abominable man."

"Oh, come now, that is ungrateful! You are drawing wrong conclusions." He smiled at her sardonically. "I thought all this was understood between us."

She drew a rough and tearing breath. "So she has you, too. I might have suspected it."

Her Gothic features became convulsed. She lifted her hand and pointed a lean finger at him. "Stay away from that woman. If you do not, I shall tell Alfred and our father."

Then she turned about, like a figure of black granite, and left him.

But he followed her indolently into the library and closed the door behind him. Hearing his step, she swung stiffly about, her black silk rustling with strident sound, and her gaunt face denied and repudiated him with detestation.

"Don't be a fool, Dotty," he said. But he was inwardly alarmed and nonplused. "Let us be reasonable. Do you wish me to desist from my arduous labors in inducing the woman to leave?"

He leaned negligently against the doorway and stroked his dog.

She shivered, and he saw he could not longer deceive her. He shrugged.

"Bad man," she said, in a loud whisper. "Unscrupulous, dishonorable man! You are a liar, sir, a blackguard." She put her veined hand to her breast, as if her heart pained her, and a grayish shadow deepened on her face. "I see now what you are trying to do. You not only would ruin Alfred in the Bank, and undermine his position, but you would destroy what he believes is his happiness.

"And now," she continued, with bitter resolution, "I understand much. I know what I must do. If Alfred wishes to marry —her—then I shall not oppose the match further. Moreover, I will safeguard him. I shall watch you constantly. You shall never injure him, or attempt to injure him, again."

"Threats," he murmured abstractedly. "It seems to me I have heard nothing but threats since I returned to this house."

"Then go! Leave us in peace. Something urges me to prevent your staying——"

Jerome laughed, and his white teeth flashed in the quiet gloom of the library. "This house is positively psychic! I shall be looking for ghosts, trying to hear their mutters. It is very odd. I feel quite perplexed. I am really a harmless person. I wish everyone good. I desire only to be enfolded to everyone's bosom."

Then his mood changed, and he gazed at his sister with ruthless contempt.

"You are a fool, Dotty," he said. "Don't believe you can frighten me. I intend to stay here. I shall be very circumspect. But I shall stay."

It was she who was frightened now. She retreated from him, backwards. She watched him go, and she thought to herself, fearfully: He is evil. There is something terrible about him, in spite of his smiles.

CHAPTER ELEVEN

Jerome came down to dinner, whistling abstractedly, two small canvases under his arm. He found his father before the library fire with Alfred, Amalie and Dorothea. Before entering the room, Jerome paused on the threshold. Alfred's low monotonous voice, as calm and persistent as a quiet stream, had been enlarging on the business of the day. Mr. Lindsey had been listening with attentive courtesy, but now he lay in the depths of his library chair with every evidence of weariness, and his eye had begun to wander. Dorothea, straight and stiff upon her own chair, embroidered with a swift grim resolution, as she did everything, whatever its importance. Clad in her somewhat old-fashioned dull purple silk, her matronly fluted cap upon her gray-black hair, she had an inexorable air of no-nonsense about her. Amalie was frankly not heeding anyone. Her face was quite pale; she ran her hand constantly over the smooth leather of her chair, her feet stretched out and crossed at the ankle. She seemed to have fallen into a deep study, and her breath hardly stirred the dark green wool of her bodice. She had dressed her hair severely, and it was drawn back from her temples and brow into a heavy knot at the nape of her neck.

They all glanced up as Jerome entered with a cheery "good evening." Mr. Lindsey's tired countenance brightened perceptibly, and he lifted himself a few inches higher on his seat. Dorothea glanced at him; she looked away, without speaking, and blew her nose on a kerchief she withdrew from her sleeve. Amalie studied him briefly, then returned to her contemplation of the fire, and her hand continued to stroke the arm of her chair. But Alfred rose, all restrained pleasure and open friendliness.

"Well," he said. "I've been hearing good, and extraordinary, news of you, Jerome."

Jerome regarded him easily. His eyes narrowed, though he smiled. Yes, Alfred was "pleased," that was evident. Jerome was vaguely baffled, in spite of his previous analysis of Alfred that afternoon. There was no hypocrisy in Alfred's pleasure. He was doing his damn duty, as usual, and quelling any natural and human apprehension or dismay which a less virtuous man might have felt.

"Good of you, Alfred," said Jerome, politely.

"Good of me?" repeated Alfred, a trifle perplexed. "What do you mean, Jerome?"

Mr. Lindsey's tired eye twinkled briefly. He put his hand on Alfred's arm. "Jerome is merely felicitating you, my boy, on displaying Christian fortitude."

Amalie turned her head slowly, and the very shadow of a smile touched her lips. Dorothea continued to embroider with new energy. But Alfred was now completely puzzled. "Eh?" he said, giving his uncle a fond and honest glance. "What forti-

111

tude? Do you think I shall need fortitude?"

"Doubtless. Oh, doubtless," said Mr. Lindsey.

"I think not," said Alfred, resolutely. But he was still perplexed. Seeing nothing better to do, he sat down again. Jerome approached his father's chair and leaned against it. Alfred contemplated him. He said: "Why should I need fortitude?"

"You might find me an exasperating pupil," replied Jerome. He tried to meet Mr. Lindsey's eye for a private exchange of subtleties, but Mr. Lindsey refused to oblige him.

"Well, I admit that banking is not a profession that is learned in a day," confessed Alfred, a trifle pompously. "However, any man of intelligence, and with any desire at all to learn, can soon compass the mysteries of banking."

"Then, there is something exotic about it?" remarked Jerome, turning his head idly towards his cousin.

"Exotic?" Alfred frowned carefully, and considered the matter. He then laughed awkwardly. " 'Exotic' is not exactly the word for banking, I am afraid."

Jerome gave him a cherubic smile. "But you did speak of 'mysteries,' my dear Alfred. Perhaps the word 'esoteric' best describes your labors?"

Alfred was bewildered.

"You did say 'mysteries,' " Jerome added, gently.

Mr. Lindsey cleared his throat. Alfred stared at Jerome, and now a tinge of color came into his usually colorless face.

Jerome pursed up his lips and looked into the air. "Do you do it by divination, then?" he asked.

Alfred did not answer, but his right hand clenched involuntarily on his knee. Jerome assumed an expression of enjoyment. "Well," he exclaimed, "I'll not be bored, after all! Evidently the psychic element enters into banking! How very titillating! One opens a ledger, and goes into a trance, and experiences all sorts of exciting emotions. I think I've neglected the subject of banking too long."

Alfred stiffened. "I don't understand," he said bluntly, and his voice was a trifle thick. "Banking is an exact science. It is as exact, and as prosaic, as any sum in mathematics." His voice rose a little, and it shook faintly, as if with outrage and dim panic. "One does not divine, as you call it, Jerome. It is an utterly unemotional profession. I can think of no other business which is so devoid of the human element, so aloof from passion or whimsy, so intellectually absorbing!"

Jerome murmured: " 'Sir, you are speaking of the lady I love.' "

112

Mr. Lindsey bit his lip and gazed steadfastly at the toe of his boot. Dorothea's needle flashed, and her withered mouth tightened. Amalie averted her face abruptly.

"What did you say, Jerome?" asked Alfred.

Jerome straightened up. "Nothing, really." His tone was bland. He gave Alfred a brilliant smile. "I do hope you will not find me too obtuse, Alfred."

Alfred recovered himself. "I'm sure I won't," he said. "You are a clever man, Jerome. I've always told Uncle William that you have wasted your talents. You will not find the business hard to grasp. It is not in the least dangerous," he added, with his usual heavy attempt at a joke.

"Indeed?" Jerome pondered the thought, then said: "Frankly, I always regarded banking as twin sister to Medusa."

"Medusa?" repeated Alfred, completely baffled now.

"Jerome fancies himself as a Perseus, perhaps," Mr. Lindsey could not refrain from saying.

Jerome cast him a chiding look. "We are unfair, Papa. Alfred is not, perhaps, too well acquainted with classical lore. He has never wasted his time on the Greeks."

Alfred felt all this was beyond him. "I had two years of Greek," he said. "A waste of time, for a professional man." He sank into thought, trying to puzzle out Jerome's words. After a long moment or two, an unhealthy color appeared on his flat strong cheeks, and he gave Jerome a glance which had something brutal in it. "Medusa?" he said, in a low voice. "Yes, Medusa. I follow your allusion now."

Mr. Lindsey began to perceive that the situation was taking on a certain element of strain, and he said hastily: "Are those your paintings, Jerome?"

"Yes. The portrait of Mama, as I told you, and the wedding gift for our Alfred." He laid the small canvases on his father's knee.

"So," said Alfred, "you think banking might turn you into stone?"

Jerome flung up his head assuming an actor's exaggerated attitude of heroic resolution. "I shall not let it, sir, I shall not let it! I shall infuse life into the da———, into the Apollonian science, and it will embrace me, as Galatea embraced Pygmalion!"

Mr. Lindsey picked up a canvas, and said, in quite a loud voice: "Your mother, Jerome! From the miniature she left you." And now he was silent, looking at the portrait, which smiled at him with a kind of secret and shining tenderness.

"Lovely, lovely," he whispered, and to himself he said: "My darling."

Dorothea embroidered more swiftly than before. Amalie turned her face to Mr. Lindsey. She saw his thin hands trembling, and leaned forward a little to see the portrait. The young face and sweet young eyes gazed back at her. Amalie was astonished. The execution of the work amazed her. The blackguard, then, had real genius. She could not help glancing at him furtively, and an expression of involuntary pain darkened her own eyes.

But Alfred did not rise to examine the portrait of his aunt. He felt coldly infuriated. He did not know at whom to look. His pale and wandering eye encountered Dorothea's. Slowly, then, her strong and sinewy hands faltered, were still. She regarded him with bitter yearning and understanding. His large and colorless lips jerked, and then he turned away.

Mr. Lindsey extended the portrait to his daughter. "Your mother, my dear," he said a little hoarsely. Dorothea stared at the portrait. "Very like," she muttered. "But too frivolous of expression. Dear Mama was never frivolous."

"She loved everything," said Mr. Lindsey, not hearing her. "She was gay, gay as a butterfly, gay as a little spring cloud. There was something too fair about her, too delicate, too delightful. When she died, all the color went out of the sky, and out of this house, and never returned."

He held the canvas as one holds something dearly beloved. He said to his son: "My dear boy. My dear boy. Thank you." He cleared his throat. "But you were so young. How could you have remembered her so? How could you have captured what she was?"

"He could not," said Dorothea, in a loud and hectoring tone. "He imagines it all. And I still think it very frivolous. I think it insulting."

Mr. Lindsey's brows knotted, and his features became stern. But he said, controlling himself, forcing himself to speak gently: "My dear, you and your mother were not very congenial."

"I adored her!" cried Dorothea, and now something long buried in her memory rose up to choke and embitter her with its unfairness. "But she never understood me! I tried so hard; I was as dutiful as one can be. I took every task from her. But she was never grateful. She only laughed. But I loved her so!"

Mr. Lindsey's heart contracted with pity. "And she loved you too, my dear. When she—when she was dying, it was you to whom she turned, to your strength and goodness."

114

Dorothea reached for her kerchief, and buried her face abruptly in its depths.

Mr. Lindsey sighed. Then, hesitatingly, he stretched out his hand and patted his daughter's arm. "There, there, my love, we all know your worth, and we are not ungrateful."

"Indeed not," said Jerome, promptly. He was beginning to be bored, and he was alarmed. Good God, if he was to be bored like this, constantly, it would be unendurable. He lifted the other canvas from his father's knee, gazed at it, then extended it for general view. "The wedding present," he said, with an open and smiling look.

Mr. Lindsey was too shaken, at first, to grasp the subject of the canvas, and then when he did so, he uttered a small and uncertain exclamation.

The subject was a stereotyped one, but the execution was original, to say the least. It was the Expulsion from the Garden of Eden, and though in miniature, every detail was worked out vividly, and with a sardonic and even licentious deliberation. The Garden, in the background, swam in too languid and banal a light, every distant tree too perfect, too conventional, too dull. The figures of Adam and Eve were as white and gleaming as porcelain, exquisitely beautiful and graceful, shining out from the tangled darkness which surrounded them like bright new ivory. Adam walked briskly ahead, his face frightened yet curious, his hand grasping the hand of his lagging spouse. He seemed in considerable of a hurry, as a man does who has something on his mind. He wore a series of decorous fig-leaves, tactfully disposed. He appeared to be saying: "Now, then, all that nonsense is over, so let us get down to common sense immediately." His grasp was very tight and purposeful on Eve's little hand. One could see that the problem obsessing him at the moment was to find shelter and establish a business as soon as possible.

But the reluctant Eve trailed behind, despite the firm grasp on her hand. She was delicately painted, all silver faintly flushed with rose, and was apparently very young. But it was a knowing and sly sort of youth, and a coquettishly libidinous one. Her golden hair floated about her, but was so arranged as not to conceal one swelling breast, rise of hip or curve of seductive thigh. One saw her smiling profile, the red underlip thrust out invitingly. Her face was directed backwards at the very manly, very handsome, and very interested angel who guarded the gate. She did not wear fig-leaves, nor any leaves at all. Where the fig-leaves ought decorously to have been disposed, her hand lay instead, and with a definitely wanton gesture.

The angel, instead of standing upright, holding his flaming sword high above him and wearing a most stern and casting-out expression, was decidedly taken by Eve. His sword was a fierce affair, but he had thrust its point into the ground, and he was leaning on its hilt with an air of engrossment. He was smiling; one almost suspected he was about to wink. He was much more enchanting than Adam. He was taller, darker, and ever so much more muscular, and had the alert grace of a soldier at ease. His black locks framed an excessively masculine and vital face, and his smiling mouth was sensual and full. His wings were not feathery and pure; rather, they were mere bright outlines of light. The hands that leaned on the sword were strong and hard. His garments, though shining, were the garments of a vibrant warrior.

The whole painting made one wonder whether it was, perhaps, the angel who had had that interesting conversation with Eve under the apple tree, rather than the serpent. For there was a most promising look about the angel, as though he were murmuring: "We shall meet again, my pet, when I am off duty, if you can get rid of him."

There was something about Mr. Lindsey's attitude, too silent, too prolonged, which aroused the curiosity of Dorothea and Alfred. They strained forward to see the painting. Amalie leaned over the arm of her chair. Jerome, with the shy and bashful air of a boy who displays his first "masterpiece," stood among them, smiling diffidently, eagerly and touchingly awaiting applause.

Then, all at once, Mr. Lindsey's dry and sunken face broke into a hundred wrinkles of sparkling laughter. "Good heavens!" he murmured, and rubbed his nose.

He looked at Amalie Maxwell. Her mouth was repressed. But a dozen heretofore unsuspected dimples had spilled out all about it, and her eyes were dancing like violet lights. She was biting her lower lip very hard; her breast was convulsed with little fine tremors.

Alfred stared doggedly at the beautiful and enthralling painting. He said frigidly: "I see. The Garden of Eden. I didn't think you went in for Biblical subjects, Jerome." Then he colored, embarrassed, eyeing Eve's unchaste nakedness, and unable to look away. He cleared his throat. "Hardly a picture for ladies," he muttered. "Too—er—too——"

Dorothea recoiled in her chair, her face quite crimson.

Jerome regarded Alfred seriously. "Do you think so?" he said, in an anxious tone. "I thought everything in the Bible was only too fit for females."

Mr. Lindsey could control himself no longer. He burst into violent and delighted laughter. Helpless, he lay back in his chair, and there was a suspicion of moisture about his eyelids. He tried to inhibit himself, but, at each glance at Alfred, he went into fresh convulsions. These increased when Alfred began to stare at him in utter bewilderment and offense. For Alfred had the picture on his knee, now, and did not quite know what to do with it.

Then Alfred spoke awkwardly: "Thank you, Jerome. It is —is very edifying. I never cared for religious subjects, myself, and I repeat that it is surprising to me that you have painted this one."

Jerome inclined his head gravely. "I hope you will enjoy it," he said, in the humble voice of an inferior gratified at the praise of a superior. "You could hang it on your bedroom wall."

Mr. Lindsey was still laughing, but with the strained and gasping sound of one who is suffering pain from his mirth. At Jerome's words, he put his hand over his eyes and said, simply: "Merciful Lord!"

Alfred judiciously considered what Jerome had said. He remarked, finally: "Well, it is hardly the thing for——"

"Oh, most appropriate," said Jerome, enthusiastically.

Alfred cast his eye painfully on the library walls. "Perhaps here," he said, with uncertainty.

"Indeed, by all means," agreed Mr. Lindsey, in the weak voice of one spent with laughter.

Jerome removed the canvas from Alfred's stony knee and laid it on a table. For the first time he looked at Amalie.

She met his eyes fully, then turned her head aside abruptly, but not before he saw her secret laughter and complete, if unwilling, enjoyment.

CHAPTER TWELVE

Even Jerome's natural and cardinal, if apparently languid, awareness of living sagged noticeably during the last few days before Christmas. At first he believed it was because Hilltop had subsided into its usual tranquil routine. But later, and not too much later, he began to suspect that it was being over-played. Quite subtly, he was being shown what life at Hilltop was in its essence, and the lesson was pointed. In the beginning, he had thought: How had I forgotten how unbearably tedious it is? In three days, he thought: So, they are showing me, and they are watching me, to see how I will respond to this rigid beatitude, this timelessness, this studied peace.

He was amused, maliciously and without anger. He noticed that he slept better, and without the sedatives which his physi-cian in New York had prescribed. He found more enjoyment in drinking, however, and it no longer had that deleterious ef-fect on him which he had stoically begun to accept as the price of his brief enhancement of consciousness. He explored the countryside, on foot and by sleigh, feeling a faint but pleasant nostalgia as he recalled his boyhood and youth. He was not overly fond of horses, but, as Jim could often be found in the stables vehemently agreeing or disagreeing with the stable-boys about the care of the animals, Jerome would join him there to listen to the pungent conversations and to add asinine opinions of his own. This would result in Jim and the lads stop-ping to stare at him pityingly.

Jerome rediscovered his father's library, and spent many solid hours of pleasure in reading by the fire. It had been a long time since he had been able to sit quietly for more than half an hour, and for months it had been impossible for him to focus his attention upon a book. He was delighted to find that Mr. Lindsey had kept abreast of all current literature, and that the volumes were not covered with moss, as he had suspected. Here were Mr. Charles Darwin's *Origin of Species,* and Mr. Thomas Huxley's essays, both daring examples of the new fer-ment which was foaming through scientific and politely reli-gious society. Jerome had heard much of Mr. Darwin's sacrile-gious theories, and he knew that Mr. Huxley was being damned thoroughly in the more intellectual pulpits, but he had not bothered to enlighten himself in the matter. When he had so attempted, once or twice, his exhausted yet feverish mind had conjured up the most distracting and sickening thoughts, or had simply thrown up its hands in complete numb-ness. Now he settled down to reading the two blasphemous gentlemen, and though he found it heavy going at first, he was soon caught up in the excitement and the implications which they communicated to him. Mr. Lindsey, with his careful habit of compromise and his tiresome habit of "hearing both sides," had included a report of the controversy between Mr. Huxley and Bishop Wilberforce at the British Association of Oxford, in 1860. All through the latter volume, which included the opinions of many other gentlemen of the bishop's cloth and bent of mind, Mr. Lindsey had made his neat and spidery comments in blacklead, which ended up like this: "Note: Page 47, Origin." Jerome enjoyed himself skipping back and forth between Bishop Wilberforce and Mr. Darwin, ending up with the clinching of the argument by Mr. Huxley. All in all, however (and he felt quite irritated with his father) it seemed to sum up that no one was right, or that much could be said for both sides. Damn these compromisers, anyway! They took all the life out of a thesis, so that the bystander became wearily convinced that no one should do anything about anything, but should only sit back in a genteel inertia and sip port wine. Mr. Lindsey did not reproach or criticize; he merely presided as an aristocratic referee and let the boys argue, and was quite impartial, and most exasperating, and entirely noncommittal.

Compromise, thought Jerome, is the senility of the mind, the arteriosclerosis of the soul. Compromise was the spiritual arthritis which eventually afflicted those who had murdered all private opinion. Judges inevitably became stiff of joint and fossilized. Only the plaintiffs and the defendants remained young and vigorous. I'd rather be wrong, and in the fight, he thought, than sit back and say, "There are always two sides, you know." When he became too irritated, he went in search of his father, to argue it out with him, his finger tucked in a particularly provocative section of Mr. Darwin or Mr. Huxley.

It was then that it dawned on him that something peculiar was afoot. He rarely found his father. Mr. Lindsey was "out for a short drive, sir," or "Mr. Lindsey is resting, according to doctor's orders, sir," or, simply, Mr. Lindsey was incommunicado. Jerome accepted this artlessly for the first day or two, then he began to have his suspicions. His father was avoiding him. He was demonstrating very subtly to his son that the latter must not depend on him for companionship and amusement, and that the day of stimulating conversation (which had been part of Jerome's rare visits home) was gone and past, and the amenities and entertainment accorded a visitor could not be indefinitely offered to a permanent resident.

Even on the fifth day, Jerome was still amused, but slowly he began to be exasperated and affronted. He saw his father, now, only in the evenings, in company with the others. Then Mr. Lindsey would greet his son with bland affection which Jerome found faintly infuriating.

Young Philip, with his intense dark eyes, was not available, even if Jerome had been reduced to seeking his companionship. Philip was engaged in concentrated study, in preparation for his school in the autumn. Sometimes Jerome heard him practicing in the music room, and once or twice he had heard Amalie's clear deep voice praising or criticizing the rendition of a particular passage, but the door of the room was firmly closed and there was a look of denial about it that Jerome could not overcome.

As for Dorothea, Jerome had only remote glimpses of her on the business of the household, her keys jingling at her waist, and very often she was in the company of Amalie, whom she was instructing in housewifely duties. Jerome caught fleeting whisks of their skirts along the corridors, heard them discussing the contents of the linen room and the blanket closets, heard their busy and absorbed steps on the back stairs. Dorothea, who had apparently, and inflexibly, accepted the inevitable, was coaching Amalie with grim and intense energy. Once, when passing Dorothea's apartments, Jerome had discovered that the door was open, and he saw the two women with their heads together over Dorothea's ledgers and accounts. He found the vision dreary.

He tried to waylay Amalie several times, but desisted when he saw that a servant, or Dorothea, or Philip, was usually only a foot or two behind her. She was never going to be caught alone, he saw. When she passed him, on these busy excursions, he would lift his hand to his forehead in an ironic salute, but she would go by with only the briefest glance or the coldest word of greeting.

However, these glimpses of her increased his restlessness and inner ferment. It became a necessity for him to see her; he haunted halls and stairways; he listened for the rustle of her skirts, the sound of her step. He rarely heard them. He said to himself: Damn the trollop! And plotted her discomfiture. When he finally discovered that too much of his waking thoughts, and even his sleeping ones, were engrossed with her, his fury became a definite if torturing hatred. She had told him that he could not hurt her, that she would not allow him to hurt her, that she had planned what she wanted, and that he was impotent. He believed he saw a contemptuous and triumphant gleam in her eye on the few occasions when they passed each other in the corridors, Amalie always with her bodyguard.

Yes, he was impotent. He could do nothing. He was confronted with one as ruthless as himself, and she had won. But he consoled himself malevolently with the reflection that though the first round in the battle had gone to her, there were other rounds, extending into the coming years, when he would have his own day. He spent hours on his plots, and they gave him comfort.

His only pleasure was in the evenings, when, for a short while before dinner, and an hour or less afterwards, he could bait Alfred. But Alfred, whether particularly obtuse, or whether he had come in his stony mind to some compromise with regard to Jerome, did not rise to the goad. He turned aside even the most outrageous of Jerome's sallies with a blank steadfastness, or a heavy change of subject. It did not amuse Jerome on these occasions to see that Mr. Lindsey was smiling faintly, or that Amalie was openly enjoying herself, or that Dorothea regarded him with weary scorn. Worst of all was when Alfred attempted to instruct Jerome informally about the Bank, at the dinner table or in the library. At these times, Jerome was seized with such a powerful ennui as to feel that in some way he had inadvertently swallowed one of his forgotten sedatives.

All in all, then, he came to the conclusion that the family had placed him in a neat niche in the house, and were determined that he fit in there, and be damned to him. He was a member of the household, now; he had his place. He could not disturb it unless by taking his departure or making a general fool of himself. He was prepared to do neither.

In sheer desperate self-defense, he began to paint again, but he found his inspiration sluggish, his hand without creativeness. The weight of the house, its tranquillity, silent warmth, individual concerns, routine and pleasant order, bore down upon him. I'm the damned speck of grit that got into the shell of the oyster, he thought, and the whole infernal house is busy covering me with solidifying slime. I'm to work myself out, if I can, or consent to become one of the pearls, with layer upon layer of polite opalescence hardening around me.

He found the prospect horrendous. He was enraged. But his own reason wryly assured him that he had made his choice, and he must conform or leave. He was the insurgent minority, and minorities who attempted to create disturbances and who pricked the complacency of the established majority, had a rough time of it. This is how I am, said the house and the occupants, with smooth smiles, and you may take me or leave me. In any event, I am too busy to concern myself with you.

He was accustomed to taking his meals whenever he desired. But in this house, if he did not appear decorously for breakfast at eight o'clock, he was served by tray through the medium of Jim, who had dismayingly become a part of the household and who was very enthusiastic about it. (Jerome found this defection quite infuriating, but could do nothing.) Jerome had his tray. And then the house settled about him in its self-sufficient and impersonal business, and he had nothing to do. Worst of all, his late breakfasts and lunches unfitted him for dinner, not to speak of the fact that he could not compass tea. As Mr. Lindsey had an excellent cook, and the dinners were really quite remarkable, Jerome was faced with the unpleasant prospect of either giving up lunch, and thus arriving too faint at the table to enjoy the dinner, or of eating meals at the regular time. He was reduced to the latter. This made the day longer and emptier than ever, and the morning light was not agreeable to his eyes. His health improved in consequence, but his ennui of spirit was like a drug, and he began to feel slothful.

He read, he played the piano, he brooded, he wandered through the warm and quiet house, he tried to paint. And he yawned constantly. I'm like a damned ghost around here, he would think, vaguely moving from room to room. I might as well not be present at all.

He was temporarily enlivened by the preparations that were afoot for the Christmas Eve party and the wedding, which was to take place on December 28th. He lounged in the doorways of the two great drawing-rooms, which were not used by the family except at holidays and when guests in any number were present. He watched the servants sweeping, dusting, polishing, making the floors gleam, the furniture shine. He watched the hearths being garnished, logs laid, mistletoe being fastened over the doorways, holly being distributed here and yon. The tree already stood in the east windows, green and dark and cold, but still naked of ornament. It filled the active air with the scent of pine and wild loneliness. Jerome offered to trim the tree, and the servants turned rebuking and shocked eyes on him, or furtively disdainful ones. He was not to be allowed to do anything, apparently. So he lounged in the doorways, and yawned, and watched, and sipped a tall glass of whiskey and soda, which the servants apparently found reprehensible during full daylight.

He saw big boxes and trunks being brought down from the attics and carried briskly into Alfred's and Amalie's rooms.

122

Activity was all about him, more and more, and he was increasingly left on the high beach in a state that closely resembled rotting flotsam. I'm growing mold, he thought. I'll soon be plucking fungi off myself. He drank more and more, to keep from falling asleep. So, finally, he moved in a mist through the house, but it was an abandoned mist.

At last, he became aware that the very walls, the servants, the portraits, the furniture, the thick Aubusson carpets on the floors, the books in the library, the shining daylight outside thoroughly disapproved of him. It was a courteous, and slightly wounded, disapproval, like the manner of a solid relative who did not like the conversation of a spoiled and useless little boy. The house was telling him that it had no tolerance of useless gentlemen who had no reason for living, that "there was work to do," and that if he had any sense at all he would be out doing it. The house was no place, during the day, for creatures of the masculine persuasion. Jerome, in angry self-defense, conducted long arguments with the house. Curse it, Europeans did not believe that the sole end of the masculine creature was to spend his life bending over ledgers or shop counters or in offices. Rather, Europe was all for gracious and stimulating leisure, the enjoyment of the arts, gay conversation and the love of living, for itself alone. It was all for happy companionship at prolonged luncheon tables, over bottles of brandy or good wine. What was wrong with America?

But this is not Europe, said the house, with inexorable gentleness. This is America, and we have work to do. What work? queried Jerome, contemptuously. Work, replied the house, blandly. What else is there for a human creature to do? Work! swore Jerome, with loathing. He had never found work his enemy before; it was just something unpleasant that was avoided by the true aristocrat, the truly civilized man. But now work was his active foe, and he smelled it all about him, and was appalled by its presence.

There was no place for enlightened men in America, and that was very sad. Something most valuable was being lost, in all this welter of activity. He thought of the whole of his country as a bustling hive of ants, sexless and absorbed, busy bringing more and more food for more and more ants, who would then emerge as full adults and start bringing in food for other generations of automatic insects, *ad nauseam*. What was the end result of ant-activity, anyway? The flourishing of more ants, who never noticed the sun or the moon, or the smell of the earth and the mystery of the night, who never knew God, and merely crumbled into fragments when their business was done.

The house apparently found this argument too subtle for its stolid realism. It blandly forsook Jerome. He argued in a vacuum. The house went about its affairs.

At times, he could not endure it. He often began to pack his clothing, while the constantly absent Jim was in the stables or down teasing the girls in the kitchens. And then he would remember and, setting his jaw, unpack again. He would go out into the blazing sterility of the winter days, alone except for his dog, who showed a wistful propensity for the stables, and who stayed with Jerome only out of a sense of duty. At last he sent the dog away, and watched the little beast scuttle off to the stables, and he would laugh and swear to himself.

He would listen to the shining white silence all about him. He would resume his wandering through the house, his reading, his attempts to paint. He walked a great deal, sometimes wading through snow to his knees. His color improved. His ennui became unendurable. He must escape this accursed house, or die on one last yawn.

So it was that, at dinner one night, he announced to Alfred that he "thought he might as well make himself a little familiar with the Bank, before the holidays," and before Alfred went away to Saratoga on his honeymoon.

CHAPTER THIRTEEN

Jerome looked back at Hilltop. "I never noticed it before," he remarked to Alfred, "but the house has a smug look, as if it had just won a point."

Alfred followed his cousin's eyes. "Smug look? I think it is very substantial, and has an air of security and strength not to be found in other houses of the township. I never cared for the bizarre or rococo in architecture."

Jerome smiled, but made no other comment. He began to shiver, and pulled the fur robes closer towards his chin and chest. The blaze of light on the snow made his eyes sting and a vague ache start through his temples. Most definitely, early morning did not agree with his constitution. Nevertheless, it would have to submit to such outrages.

The cutter, driven smartly by the strong and competent Alfred, carved the bright snow with a razor's edge as it wound smoothly down the long and rambling slope to the valley. The horse, young and coal-black, had a hide like watered silk, and his warm breath floated over his shoulders in a cloud of vapor. He flung up his maned head, almost prancing with pleasure at the pure and stimulating air, and apparently enjoying the musical jingling of the bells on his harness. White spume flew backwards from his hooves, from the runners of the cutter, and Jerome winced as the sharp and tinsel spray stung his face. His cheeks felt numb and thick from the lashing of the thin and radiant wind, and despite the robes his toes were beginning to acquire an unpleasant lack of sensation. I am certainly effete, he thought, and glanced at Alfred.

He was much annoyed by what he saw. Alfred wore a thick gray greatcoat with a fur collar. Dorothea had knitted him a sober dark blue scarf, which, wound about his neck, doubtless was very comfortable though it did not add a fashionable note to his costume. Alfred also wore a round warm cap of silver fur, with ear-laps, and his big hands were enclosed in mittens of the same fur. Alfred was too obviously enjoying the air and the burning sun; his shoulders were as hard and firm as rock under the coat. The young horse might prance, and wish to cavort, but Alfred controlled him expertly, and with such evident satisfaction as to make Jerome stare at him disagreeably and think: Why, he likes to control, to impose his will! It gives him a sense of puerile power, the ass! So it isn't always 'duty' and righteousness with him, but something much more obscene and dangerous. Jerome understood the lust for power that lies in men, and shrewdly guessed that his own elegant languor and pretence of civilized nonchalance came from his belief that he could not excel spectacularly in any particular field and thus acquire overwhelming power of his own. But he felt only a disgust for those so malformed of soul that they experienced a sadistic pleasure in the imposition of their will on even so lowly a creature as a dog or a horse, as well as on more potent and human personalities.

I've both underestimated and overestimated him, he thought, looking sideways at his cousin. And that is sinister. Yes, there is something ominous about him, and menacing. But he'll not subjugate me, now that I understand.

To the casual observer, Alfred did not appear either ominous or menacing this morning. His profile was somewhat rocklike, blunt and harsh of outline, it is true, and his pale skin and pale eyes gave him an aspect of brutal strength and a lack of warm and human sensibility. But to the casual observer

125

these were only the marks of a strong and healthy man in early middle age, who had been guilty of no excesses and no profligacy. He was all well-preserved and weighty virility, all big and masculine angles. However, Jerome's new or reawakened sensitivity saw something implacable under all this, something threateningly self-centered and dull and malignant. Again Jerome said to himself: He is dangerous.

At this thought, he felt an unfamiliar tingling in himself, an excitement. He stared at Alfred with furtive curiosity and intent wonder.

The valley road, full of ruts of black ice, powdered with snow, wound down to Riversend. The town rose up to meet them. They passed a straggling settlement of workmen's shacks, indecently ugly in the morning's pure and radiant light. They were built of gray clapboards, and leaned at discouraged angles, their windows tired and dirty, their broken eaves trailing scarves of smoke. All about them, the snow had become dingy and trampled. Jerome saw a group of slatternly shawled women waiting patiently at the communal pump, while two other women attempted to work the frozen apparatus. Wan and ragged children surrounded the women; they were silent and still, possessed of none of that robust and noisy vitality which marks the lucky children who are well-fed and warmly housed. These were the families of the soiled and half-starved men who worked on the local railroad and in the local brewery.

The women did not chatter or laugh; they stood like so many exhausted and dazed animals in the snow, their gaunt bodies whipped by the wind. Jerome saw their pallid faces, their hungry and hopeless eyes, as they turned to look at the passing cutter.

Jerome closed his own eyes briefly. "My God, haven't they done anything about these people yet?" he asked. "Increased their pay or mended their houses?"

Alfred looked back at the shacks and the women and children, and his harsh face became ugly with repulsion and disgust. "They never save a penny," he said. After a moment, he added: "Besides, the houses are surrounded by fields of wildflowers, in the summer. It's quite pretty, then."

Jerome was acridly delighted. He laughed. Alfred stared at him briefly, then shrugged his massive shoulders slightly.

Jerome had what he considered a very brilliant and revolutionary idea. He even pushed aside the robes a trifle. "Look here, something could be done. For instance, if the railroads

126

paid their men decently, and the other local industries, and the owners of the big estates, and what not, these people could buy houses! The Bank could finance them, on long-term mortgages! Architects could be engaged to draft plans for small but neat buildings, with some air of originality and quaintness. Something appetizing, and pleasant to the eye, agreeable as English village homes, but with more soundness of roof and more windows. The grounds could be landscaped prettily. Give the poor devils some self-respect, some pride in their community, some hope for the future——"

Alfred reined in the gay young horse with an almost vicious strength, so that the animal, frightened and hurt, reared, then pursued his way at a slower pace. Jerome wiped the white spume from his face automatically and turned hopefully to his cousin. Alfred was regarding him with dark and somber repudiation.

"Jerome, that is a mad idea. Please do not give voice to such ideas among our friends, and depositors. It might annoy, or even alarm, them. I should not dare to prophesy the consequences." He paused. "But, of course, you were only joking."

Jerome was silent. He turned his head over his shoulder to look back at the shacks, which were like a broken ulcer on the long white slope of the foot of the hill. His eyes narrowed in his thin brown face.

"Yes," he said slowly, "I was only joking."

Alfred was visibly relieved, but still affronted. He flicked his whip cuttingly at the horse's flanks. "You don't understand these people, I am afraid. Idealists speak of slums as if they were an act of God. They aren't. Slums do not make the misery of these people; it is the people who make the slums, and create an ugly and repellent atmosphere about them. If they had any spirit, or the slightest decency, they would mend their houses, clear the weed-infested and filthy grounds, and generally improve themselves."

"Nevertheless," said Jerome, gently, "if a man is constantly conscious of his unfilled belly, his coldness and hopelessness, his poverty and despair, he cannot force himself to plant roses and vines and put little flower plots about his hovel. One must first give the poor adequate pay."

"A dangerous idea!" exclaimed Alfred, with cold violence, and now his big features were congested with outrage. "A nihilistic idea! Once give these wretches more money and the taverns will only become more prosperous! As it is, they spend much of their wages on drink. Moreover, if the poor receive 'adequate pay,' as you so heedlessly call it, they would become boastful and uncontrollable and increasingly arrogant. They would attempt to rise above their stations, and society would become chaotic and disorganized. They would lose that proper respect for their superiors so commended in the Bible, and what little piety they now possess, and they would demand a larger and larger share in the business of government, thus rendering precarious the position of those who were born to rule and guide them."

Jerome regarded the horse's back reflectively. "Dear me, I always thought America was a republic. It seems I am mistaken. And Mr. Lincoln was mistaken, also. If I remember, he ill-advisedly mentioned something about democracy——"

"He, too, was a revolutionary, and a most dangerous one." Alfred's voice was pent, more than a little stifled. "Heaven alone knows what might have happened to America, had he lived. You will find nothing about democracy in the Constitution, Jerome."

Jerome's expression became dreamy. " 'We hold these truths to be self-evident—' " he murmured. He said more audibly: "It appears that the pursuit of happiness is the prerogative of those who can afford to pay for it."

"Rather, of those who are worthy of it," said Alfred vigorously.

He whipped the horse again. His face steadily darkened. "Jerome, what you say is mischievous. It can cause untold damage. Again, I must remind you to keep your perilous ideas to yourself. Besides, I do not believe your emotions are involved in the least. You cannot convince me that the 'plight' of the poor touches your heart. I know you too well. You merely love mischief for its own sake."

He spoke coldly, even malignantly, and the glance he gave his cousin was both warning and full of open dislike.

Again, Jerome felt that unfamiliar and dangerous tingling through his flesh. He thought: I was a fool. He is not in the least stupid. He is really deadly. He hates me, though he would never admit it even to himself.

Now Jerome was wide awake, all his genteel languor gone. His blood tingled and fumed. He felt alive, as if all his muscles were hardening, flexing.

"I feel something in the air, in America," he said thoughtfully. "I felt it in Europe, too, only in a heavier and more sluggish fashion. I think we are inevitably passing from the 'rule of the superior,' the 'God-appointed.' I think the dream of the Greek philosophers is fermenting under the misery and the hopelessness of the world. Socrates walks the earth like a brightening ghost. The Parthenon is full of strong and spectral voices. And there is nothing you can do about it, my dear Alfred. It is your kind of idea which is perishing."

Alfred smiled grimly. "You truly surprise me, Jerome. And so, will you kindly tell me what you have been doing all these years in New York and in Europe? What heroic movement have you set afoot? To what cause have you donated your efforts and your money? It seems I have underestimated you."

Jerome burst out laughing, but did not answer.

Alfred's smile was even more grim. "I like to think of you following the ghost of Socrates, perhaps carrying a banner. The thought is edifying."

Jerome only laughed.

"I still believe, Jerome, that you are only mischievous. You delight in being provocative, out of sheer malice. I am both alarmed and assuaged by the thought. And so I can only warn you again: Do not speak of things, in which you, yourself, do not truly believe, to those who might misunderstand."

He added, in a lower and more threatening tone: "I have determined to guard what your father, my uncle, has built in wisdom and prudence."

"Doubtless," said Jerome, agreeably.

They were approaching the gates of a beautiful estate. A mansion of rosy brick stood nobly in the snow, its great chimneys smoldering against the sparkling blue sky. Spruces and firs, heavy with whiteness, were scattered about the grounds. The wall about them was low, built of brick, cushioned with snow. A very tall and lean gentleman, several inches above six feet in height, was standing outside the iron gates with a brace of formidable dogs, who now set up a wild barking at the approach of the cutter.

"Why, isn't that old General Tayntor?" asked Jerome, with pleasure. "I haven't seen the old devil since the war."

"I believe it is Brigadier General Tayntor, yes," said Alfred, stiffly. He began to rein in the horse. "I told him a few days ago that you were here, and that you intended to go into the Bank. He was much interested and pleased."

But Jerome was smiling broadly at the sight of his old friend. His teeth flashed in the bright sun. He began to wave. The cutter drew up at the gates of the estate. "I ought to have visited the old bastard before this," said Jerome, forgetting that in the country one does not visit regularly, but only upon stated, and stately, invitation.

"Your language, sir," said Alfred, angrily, then touched his cap as the elderly gentleman, recognizing them, came briskly towards the cutter, waving, and pushing his way through the barking and leaping dogs.

Brigadier General Wainwright Tayntor was a very alert soldier whose movements denied his sixty-five years. He was as tall and lithe and thin as a vigorous sapling. His black fur-lined cloak blew about him in youthful lines, revealing the gloved hand and the strong right arm that held the dogs' leashes firmly, and the empty sleeve of his left arm. He walked briskly, with long and purposeful strides. His tall hat was set at a rakish angle on his smoothly clipped white hair. He smiled broadly, with delight.

"Well, well!" he exclaimed, reaching the cutter. "Jerome, my dear, dear boy! How delicious to see you again! Damn these dogs! I cannot shake hands with you, dear boy, in this predicament. Let me look at you. Damn you, my boy, you give me pleasure just to see you! Ho, ho!" said the General.

"And it gives me pleasure to see you, sir," said Jerome, leaning out of the cutter to grasp his old friend's shoulder. He pushed aside the robes, and got out, courteously, his hand still in place. He was tall, but the General topped him by at least three inches. They stood and beamed at each other, fondly.

"Good morning, General," said Alfred, formally.

At the sound of his voice, the General started. "Eh? Oh, yes, Alfred. How are you, Alfred? Bright morning, eh? But cold as hell." He dismissed Alfred and returned to Jerome. "What is this I hear about you, you rascal? Going into the Bank. You, in the Bank. Ho, ho, ho!" said the General, turning quite crimson, and going off into a spasm of ribald chuckles.

Brigadier General Wainwright Tayntor had a wicked and satanic face, gaunt and ruddy and mobile, all sharp points and quirking angles and licentious wrinkles. His white eyebrows slanted upwards, as if he were full of constant and sinister amusement, which was very possible. He had very small and very bright blue eyes, flashing and knowing, and completely disingenuous, and extremely witty and subtle. He also possessed a long thin nose, which dipped over his wide thin mouth, when he grinned, like a sardonic beak. His color was usually very high, for he was happily addicted to whiskey, which he consumed in great and lighthearted quantities, and his expression was alert and openly bawdy. Whiskey was not his only

130

reprehensible addiction; he was also addicted to women, the younger the better. Had he not been a rich man, and a power in the community, he would have been regarded with horror and ostracized from all decent society.

Alfred Lindsey was afraid of the General, and disgusted by him. But the General was powerful, and believed in his community, and was a heavy depositor in the Bank. He owned the local railroad, the land on which the workers' shacks stood, and held many secret, and juicy, mortgages over the heads of the local gentry. So Alfred climbed out of the cutter, also, and stood uneasily against it, while Jerome and the old soldier slapped each other's shoulders and exchanged improper and insulting remarks.

"Come in, come in, and see the girls!" cried the General. "They are pining to see you, you scoundrel. Sally, especially. As for Josephine, she languishes daily, and sits at the window, though she is too modest to say anything."

Jerome was intrigued by the idea. But Alfred cleared his throat politely. "We are already late, sir. I understand, however, that the young ladies and yourself are to be present at our reception on Christmas Eve. We shall all meet again, at that time."

The General scowled at him. "Yes, yes, of course." And then he laughed loudly, and struck Jerome on the arm with such force that Jerome staggered. "Ho, ho! You, at the Bank! It is delicious, incredible. Have you been reduced to that, at last?" He glanced at Alfred. "Watch the safes, sir, watch the safes! I know this rascal!"

Alfred smiled painfully. He put his hand tentatively on the cutter, and gave Jerome a beckoning glance.

"I've some investments I am considering," said the General to Jerome. "I want your opinion. Oh, this is delightful! New York investments. Know the Vanderbilts well, the—! They've been after me. Might make a deal with 'em, on the railroad. For a luscious consideration. Coal, too, in Pennsylvania. Need new life about here, with vision and daring," and he threw Alfred a mocking sparkle.

"Safety—" began Alfred. But the General had forgotten him, and was again shaking the younger man by the right shoulder. "Damn it," said the General, "you fill my eyes like the sunset. How's your leg?"

"It gives me little trouble, sir."

They beamed fatuously upon each other again. Alfred began to find it tiresome. He could not fully understand the General's infatuation for Jerome, though he had the suspicion that they were much of a kind. He caught himself abruptly, conscious of impudence and impropriety. He sternly reminded himself of the General's position.

The General had an inspiring and agreeable thought, and remembered Alfred. "And how is our exquisite Miss Maxwell?" he demanded, with a wink. He rolled up his eyes with a sprightly expression. "What charm! What grace! What—" He halted, looked at Jerome, grinned, winked again.

"Miss Maxwell is in excellent health, sir," said Alfred, coloring. His hand clenched on his whip.

"I love that lady!" exclaimed the General, with enthusiasm. He wagged an arch finger at Alfred. "Ah, sir, had I seen her first!"

He pushed his tall hat far back on his head, touched his lips with gathered fingers, and threw a kiss into the air. "You lucky devil, sir," he said, with a romantic sigh. "And now, if the contents of the package but live up to the label, ah, what a treat is in store for you!"

Alfred's color deepened with suppressed fury. But Jerome laughed loudly, looking from his old friend to his cousin.

"There are times," said the General, "when I become quite addicted to the Cinderella theme." He thought of something which pleased him, and said to Jerome: "Did I ever tell you, my dear boy, about my great-grandfather, who lived in Virginia?"

Alfred suspected that the story would be very bawdy, and that in some way it would cast an oblique reflection upon Amalie, so, in spite of his respect for the General, he sprang into the cutter and gathered up the reins. He was shaking with inexplicable anger. Unable to control himself, he cried: "Jerome, it is almost nine o'clock, if you please!"

Jerome reluctantly tore himself away from his old friend, and Alfred involuntarily struck the horse a savage blow. The cutter leaped forward, and Jerome, only half in the vehicle, was flung back into the seat. Recovering himself, he waved his hat at the General, who watched the flight with a wide and knowing grin. The General kissed his hand; the dogs barked; the cutter rushed forward, spume spurting up from its runners.

132

CHAPTER FOURTEEN

Riversend, township and county seat, was precise and clean amid its snow. But, then, it always was rather immaculate, due to the efforts of its "best families," who could invariably procure cheap labor for the streets.

The snow had been well cleared; the red-brick streets were wet and shining in the sun. To the north, were those sections inhabited by the imperious holders of wealth: the three physicians and surgeons; a few buxom widows; the Sheriff of the county (a fat little man who was "independent"); Judge Barlowe and his family; rich retired farmers; Mr. Burt Shrewsbury, owner of the beer and ale brewery; Mr. Seth Brogan, owner and proprietor of the very well equipped and flourishing boot, saddle and harness works; Mr. Ezekiel Sewell, owner of the four local taverns and breeder of race horses for the Saratoga events; the Reverend Adam Gordon, pastor of the Riversend Episcopal Church; Mr. Horville Danton, of the big lumber mills located in the nearby village of Milton, and Mr. Endicott Spinell, of the law firm of Spinell, Bertram & Sinclair, Inc. There were several other families, also, most genteel, who were not in trade at all, and so were much emulated and admired and respected.

About five or six streets composed this section, which was farthest away from the railroad tracks. They rose and fell gently through arches of trees. The houses were all of gray stone or red brick, with vast and dignified lawns and great gardens in the rear. No touch of commerce violated the calm and dignity which rigorously prevailed; no brewers' wagons polluted the delicate air. There was little noise, even in the summer, for the immense piazzas were shrouded in vines and rattan curtains, and shaded by thick, well-groomed trees. At the end of West North Street stood the Episcopal church, properly decorous, and impressed by its association with the genteel. The lesser churches, of course, lived timidly in the streets occupied by a very struggling, and very refined, small middle class, who, naturally, were far more exclusive than their betters and far more overbearing and oppressive to their employees. Ignored or patronized by the local aristocracy, feared and hated by their inferiors, they lived in chronic consciousness of their respectability.

The middle-class section, closer to the main street of River-send than was the wealthy section, stopped abruptly at the end of East River Street. There began the sections of the poor, the workers in the brewery, the tannery, the big lumber mills, the taverns, and the stables of Mr. Sewell. They also supplied a number of the servants of the county, the laundresses and the railroad workers, though most of the latter lived on the slope of the hill. Their little houses and shacks were execrable, but, belabored by their masters, they were forced to keep their streets in some semblance of cleanliness. However, the dirt of commerce could not always be held at bay, and here the snow was soot-grimed, trampled and muddy.

The town's edges were sharply defined. The last houses stopped at the very edge of fields and meadows and the rising slopes of surrounding white hills.

The Bank of Riversend (the only bank in the township), built of smooth and shiny gray granite, stood in its own impeccable dignity on East River Street. It lay on the top of the very slightest rise of ground, surrounded by virgin snow in the winter, and smooth green lawns in the summer. Very unnecessary, but very impressive, stone stairs approached it from the street, and though the rise was almost imperceptible, the stairs were so ingeniously shallow that it was possible to mount them from the sidewalk and reach the very door without a single blank space. This gray stone stairway had been well cleared and sprinkled with rock salt against ice, and it sparkled with gray diamonds in the early sun.

The Bank repudiated the surrounding evidences of trade: the shops and the taverns, the markets and the blacksmithies. It stood alone in its austerity and polished severity, its big glass windows glittering in the light. No speck of dust ever marred that pristine radiance, this temple to flourishing commerce, and depository of the county funds. It denied that it financed mortgages on obscure farms, lent money on future crops, or had anything to do with anything so humble as chickens and stock and truck-farm business. Nevertheless, this was the bulk of its business.

The great bronze door (Alfred's joy and pride) stood squarely between two plate-glass windows. At the bottom of the window to the right were inscribed, in neat gold letters, not too obtrusive: "William Cherville Lindsey, President. Alfred D. Lindsey, Vice-President." Then, in even smaller letters, but the more pretentious for that: "Associate: House of Regan, Wall Street, New York." Jerome maliciously sus-

134

pected that the last phrase was more brilliantly and sedulously polished than the others, for all its genteel modesty.

The interior of the Bank lived up to its exterior. The floor was of polished gray granite and black granite squares, while squat and solid black granite pillars suported a white plaster roof. The light poured in the windows, gleamed on floor and pillar, with a religious and subdued intensity. To the rear, were the cages of the three cashiers, all shining brass bars, very impressive. Approaching them was like creeping down a glimmering nave to the altar, and the pale and waxen faces of the young men behind the bars added to this atmosphere. Two guards, in dark blue uniforms, and with conspicuously displayed lethal hardware, marched slowly up and down, passing each other with a soldierly lack of recognition. ("Muskets over the shoulder would be very appropriate," Jerome had once remarked, and had been properly ignored by Alfred.) To the left, on entering the solemn hush of the nave, were two carved wooden doors, bearing brass plaques: "President." "Vice-President." Alfred now occupied the first office, by courtesy of Mr. Lindsey, and his own was occupied by his assistant, a Mr. Frederick Jamison.

Behind the cages were the offices, dark and cold and grim, where the three bookkeepers and two clerks labored at high desks and kept their mufflers and greatcoats on in the winter.

Jerome always smiled when he entered the Bank, and invariably always shivered, for effect, irreverent manifestations ignored by Alfred. Today, Jerome looked about him with more interest, and despite his amusement, his heart sank. How was it possible for a man to spend his days in these precincts and not expire of chill and gloom?

Alfred, suddenly ceremonious and full of hard pomposity, responded to the trembling greetings of his cashiers and led Jerome into his own office. Here a fire burned on the black hearth, a fact which Jerome noted appreciatively. Alfred had put a crimson rug on the polished stone floor and a few excellent prints on the panelled walls. The furniture was all old and massive oak, gleaming with a careful patina. His desk, like himself, was immaculate, the silver inkwell shining, the pens and pencils laid out in a row. He had a bookcase containing volumes on banking, both national and international. Over the fireplace hung a portrait of a stout and massive gentleman with a thick gray moustache, very well executed. The little pale eyes gleamed under enormous gray eyebrows which accentuated the immense expanse of bald head above. The gentleman was the high priest of the banking profession: Mr. Jay Regan of New York, personal friend of Mr. William Lindsey.

"Very good of him," said Jerome, pleased, for the portrait of Mr. Regan had not been there on his last visit. "I know the old bandit. When did he give you the holy canvas?"

He stood beneath the portrait and critically examined the execution. "Oh, yes, Thompson. A very good artist. This is really quite excellent. Did Regan give you this, or did you have to pay for it yourself?"

Alfred was standing by his closet door and was removing his greatcoat and hat and gloves. He shot Jerome a cold glance, which was lost on the younger man, whose back was to his cousin.

"Levity," said Alfred, with disapproval. "Mr. Regan sent this to Uncle William on his last birthday. 'Pay for it,' indeed!"

"Well, I was only asking. I know Regan. So it surprises me that he'd give anything away, even an old shoe. Good old bastard, though."

Alfred paused. "You know Mr. Regan? I wasn't aware of that."

At his somewhat tentative tone, with its hint of uneasiness, Jerome turned and eyed his cousin curiously. "Well, I do. He wanted me to paint him and his daughter, Alice. Free of charge, of course. All in the name of friendship. But I wasn't interested, free or otherwise."

"It would have been a great honor," said Alfred, censoriously, with some shock.

Jerome bowed. "Yes, I know. But I didn't wish to extend him the honor."

Alfred opened his thin colorless mouth and then closed it firmly. He pushed the door of his closet into place, moved to the fire, and began to rub his cold hands. Not looking at his cousin, he said, with dignity: "I haven't yet had the honor of meeting Mr. Regan." He paused. "Is he as impressive as his portrait? Did you find him inspiring?"

Jerome drew out his silver case and thoughtfully lit a cheroot with a taper which he lighted at the fire. "Inspiring? I don't know whether that is the word. He's a very solid patron of the arts in New York, that I know. Box at the opera. Patron saint of worthy artists. A rounder. Yes, I should say he was a rounder. Did you know of Miss Mary DeVere, the variety actress? Well, he was exceptionally generous to her. But then, she is a very exclusive whore, and has half of New York's fashionable gentlemen after her."

136

Alfred was stunned at this sacrilege. He stared blankly at Jerome's dark and serene profile, which was lifted with a knowing smile to the portrait. Then he slowly turned crimson.

Jerome inclined his head modestly. "She seemed to prefer me, though I am no man to poach on another's—temporary—property. Good old Regan. He lent me five thousand dollars once."

"Five thousand dollars!" cried Alfred. He was terribly agitated. "You owe Mr. Jay Regan five thousand dollars?"

"My dear cousin," said Jerome mildly, "you have your tenses mixed. It is 'owed' not 'owe.' I paid him back, eventually. He only charged me two per cent interest. It was a struggle for him. I could see he wished to charge me no interest at all, but once a banker always a banker. He gave me a huge party when the last note was paid, and I imagine it cost him all of the five thousand dollars." He smiled, reminiscently. "Miss DeVere performed very creditably that night."

There was a timid knock on the door which separated the two offices, and in an unnecessarily loud and infuriated voice Alfred commanded the knocker to enter. It was Mr. Jamison, Alfred's assistant, a tiny meager little man with enormous moustaches and timid-blinking eyes. He started to speak, then recognizing Jerome, he bowed, overcome.

"Jamison!" cried Jerome, advancing and extending his hand with complete bonhomie. "I thought you'd retired long ago!"

Mr. Jamison looked at Jerome's ringed hand for a long moment before taking it, and then only after a beseeching glance at Alfred, which implored forgiveness in advance. He whispered breathlessly: "I'm delighted to see you, Mr. Jerome. Yes, delighted. No, I have not retired."

But his eyes glowed upon Jerome with spaniel passion.

"Well, now, I am very pleased," said Jerome. "How is Mrs. Jamison? And the boy?"

The little man colored with pride. "Brewster is at law school, in Syracuse, sir, and doing excellently. He may establish himself there." Then he sighed. "Mrs. Jamison is not very well, I am sorry to say. But not complaining."

Alfred cleared his throat. "Jamison, you remember that I told you yesterday that Mr. Lindsey is joining us? I am wondering if you have time this morning to instruct him in procedure?"

Jerome made a wry face, but Mr. Jamison shook with startled pleasure. "Indeed, indeed, Mr. Lindsey, sir! Most delighted." His hands trembled as he laid a sheaf of papers on Al-

137

fred's desk. "The report on the Hobson farm, sir. Doing quite well this year. Winter wheat in. You will be gratified."

Jerome pricked up his ears. Hobson? Hobson? Where had he heard the name before? But Alfred was already seating himself at the desk and indicating severely that he was about to get to work. So Jerome followed Mr. Jamison into the back office.

The room was smaller and much darker than Alfred's, and there was only the barest glimmer of a fire on the hearth. Jerome shivered elaborately, stirred up the coals, flung another scuttleful on the feeble blaze. Mr. Jamison was alarmed and made a timid sound. "If he thinks I'm going to freeze, he is mistaken," said Jerome. "Order some more coal for this mausoleum, Jamison. I don't cherish the thought of lung fever."

He looked about him with disfavor and was depressed. There was no rug on the granite floor. Two dull oaken desks stood side by side. No crimson curtains hung at the windows, as they did in Alfred's office. No etching brightened the panelled walls. Jerome said: "I'll order a rug, and put up a couple of my sprightlier canvases. They ought to add interest to this tomb. And a clock for the mantel, something bright and rococo. And, let me see: no, I don't think I'd care for crimson draperies. Something with a touch of dim gold, perhaps."

Mr. Jamison listened to this heresy, and was terrified. He whispered: "Mr. Alfred Lindsey might not—care—for that, Mr. Jerome."

"The hell with Mr. Alfred," said Jerome, in a genial voice. "I am the one who must endure this damned place, not he. Who the devil does he think he is? He's only my father's nephew and adopted son, after all. I am of the blood royal. Jamison, I think we can do something gay for this room."

Mr. Jamison regarded him with adoration. He stood at the hearth beside Jerome and rubbed his cold veined hands. Jerome looked at him affectionately. "Good old Jamison. We ought to be happy together, comforting each other under the Pyramids."

He hung up his greatcoat and hat in the wardrobe and then from the pocket of his coat he extracted a beautifully traced silver flask. "Glasses, Jamison, two," he ordered, grandly. "We'll drink to my initiation among the dead."

"Oh, Mr. Jerome! I am sorry. I cannot. What would——"

"Glasses, Jamison," said Jerome, with inexorable gentleness.

Mr. Jamison, quite white now, produced the glasses. Jerome poured a quantity of golden liquid into them, added a dash of

138

water from the battered carafe on Mr. Jamison's desk. Mr. Jamison held his glass as if it contained hemlock; his hand shook.

"It won't poison you, Jamison," Jerome promised. "Down with it. I command it."

They drank. A spot of color appeared on Mr. Jamison's meager cheekbones. He giggled tremulously and wiped his mouth neatly with his kerchief. "Oh, Mr. Jerome!" he whispered, with a glance at Alfred's door.

They settled down at the two desks, side by side, and Jerome began to receive his instructions. He forced himself to listen attentively, but eventually his face became quite grim with his suppressed yawns. Mr. Jamison brought out ledgers, and Jerome scanned them. Rows upon rows of figures, without the slightest vitality. Jerome glanced at his watch. It ought to be noon now. It was only ten. He took another drink.

"Banking is really very interesting, sir," said Mr. Jamison, hopelessly.

"It could be, old feller, it could be. But not in here. What this community needs is a little sparkle and enterprise. Investments, necessitating long business trips to New York. Mines, a little precarious, but exciting. Industries to finance, with smooth exploiters. Visits to mining sections, manufacturing sections, in private railroad cars, with a battery of young and enthusiastic investigators. Finance. This business here had nothing to do with finance. Wheat, chickens, oats, cattle, vegetables, by God!"

"This is a farming section, sir."

"Yes, I know. But does one need to limit one's activities to farms?"

At half-past eleven Jerome put on his coat and hat and announced that he intended to visit the shops for a suitable rug and draperies. He ordered Jamison to bring in more coal. He took another drink. But he was careful to leave the office inconspicuously by a back door. Once out in the lively air of the street, he felt renovated and happy.

He did not return until nearly one, and then only had time to replace his hat and coat before Alfred entered.

"Good afternoon!" cried Jerome, briskly returning to his desk.

"It is not yet one," said Alfred severely. He looked at the two desks. "I trust the instruction is proceeding?"

"Oh, excellently. Jamison is a fine teacher." Jerome beamed at his cousin.

"Will you dine with me at Riversend House?" asked Alfred, frigidly. "There are some matters we might discuss, about your instruction this morning."

"Has the cuisine improved there?" said Jerome, returning to the wardrobe for his garments, and furtively inspecting them for snowflakes and dampness. "Or is it still watery roast beef, or chicken which has died of old age?"

Alfred did not reply. They went out for lunch.

CHAPTER FIFTEEN

Hilltop blazed on its heights. Every window threw golden reflections on the snow, mingled with firelight. The great drawing-rooms stood open; the tree twinkled with scores of candles, which were carefully and unobtrusively watched by a servant with a pail of water nearby. Every hearth roared with logs; every lamp was mellow. The crystal chandeliers, lit only on these occasions, were stalactites of glittering radiance; the polished floors reflected back lights and color. The musicians were already tuning up in the music room, which was to be used for dancing; the potted plants were grouped strategically in miniature grottoes. The servants, augmented by "help" from Riversend, were putting the last touches to the collation in the dining-room, where hams, turkeys, beef and sundry other edibles were already waiting on the sideboards.

The forty invited guests were arriving now, and the grounds were musical with sleigh bells, the shouts of stableboys, the laughter of women and the gay voices of men. Some were singing carols; the bells jingled; a night of brilliant stars drowned out the waning moon. Servants stood to relieve the guests of greatcoats and cloaks, of canes and bonnets and gloves and furs, and the big hall seethed with the rich gowns of the ladies and their bright and festive faces.

Dorothea, Jerome and Alfred waited to receive their guests, while Mr. Lindsey sat in the first drawing-room, his cane beside him, greeting those who surged in. Young Philip, pale with excitement and shyness, stood near him. But Miss Amalie Maxwell had not yet appeared, and from his station Alfred kept glancing impatiently over his shoulder at the stairway, his face suffused with embarrassment. In a slight lull, he managed to whisper to Dorothea: "Did not Amalie understand that she was to be here with us to receive the guests?"

Dorothea, in a severe black satin dress with the slightest bustle, whispered back grimly: "I am certain she did. I told her only this afternoon. Perhaps she mistook the time."

"She cannot help hearing what is going on below," said Alfred, exasperated, and feeling more humiliated every moment. None of the guests had mentioned the absent lady, but their tactfulness, in the face of absence, did nothing to relieve him.

Dorothea tossed her head; her gold chains and bangles rattled. More guests arrived, and the three received them.

An incredibly ugly old woman was entering, in purple velvet and pearls, her train sweeping behind her. She was very short, very fat, and had a face resembling a huge and less good-natured bulldog. Her hair, a mass of bright black bangs, curls and chignon, was frankly false. Her color was ruddy, her jowls magenta. She had a short gross nose and vicious little black eyes, darting and bawdy. Her heavy and sensual mouth was both arrogant and humorous. Thick clusters of rings sparkled on her hands, which resembled the hands of a washwoman rather than those of a powerful aristocrat. The scent of musk surrounded her like a visible aura.

This was the Widow Kingsley, or Mehitabel, as she was known to her intimates. Like her great friend and fellow-raconteur, General Tayntor, she was extremely "unconventional" and "quite a character." Thrice married, thrice widowed, she had added to a very considerable fortune by her shrewdly plotted marriages, and her income was only less than the General's. She was famous for her loud and raucous voice, her indecent language, her malice, her deliberate insults, and her rapacity, not to mention her extraordinary toilettes, her lavish and luxurious mansion, her stable of excellent horses, her many cats, and her insatiable appetite for food and drink. Her enemies were legion, especially among women, and her friends devoted. She feared no one, and her scalding tongue spared few.

She came in on the wave of her own shouted execrations. She walked with a wallow and carried a gold-headed ebony cane. She was exuberant. Dorothea, wincing, came forward primly, followed by Alfred and Jerome. The widow's eyes swept over them; she paused, and her expression was deliberately contemptuous, though she merely exclaimed: "Those boys of yours are impossible, Alfred! I'd——" And then she caught sight of Jerome, lurking behind his cousin. Her coarse face changed, became delighted. "Jerome!" she bellowed. "You dog! Come here at once and kiss me!" And she flung out her arms to him and caught him to her in a pungent embrace.

He hugged her affectionately and patted her back. "Metty," he said, "I've come all the way from New York just to see you again, you darling rascal."

"Liar!" she screamed, with a knowing grin, releasing him. "I wager I know why you came," and she winked and took his arm in a strong grip. She snorted happily. "Never mind. It is enough for me to see you. My God, but you're beautiful, Jerome! Kiss me again."

She had another thought and scowled at him. "Like animals any better, eh? Know the front end of a horse from the back, yet? Heard you were in Saratoga last year, betting, so you ought to know now."

"I have a dog, a spaniel," he admitted.

Her scowl deepened. "A dog? You never liked dogs. French. That was Louis XIV. Spaniels. Do you mean to tell me you like dogs now?" she demanded, outraged.

"Not very much," he admitted. "In a way, I inherited Charlie. The lady went abroad."

She laughed boisterously and struck his arm with her free hand. "Oh, in that case." She literally howled with laughter now. "What is this about you and the Bank? I don't believe it! You've got to tell me it isn't true!"

"It is," he said, smiling. "I am to be a business man now. I am settling down, and beginning to grow moss and roots."

Alfred came forward now, clearing his throat. "Good evening. Merry Christmas, Mrs. Kingsley," he said, with a cold glance at Jerome. The old lady swung on him, frowning. "Eh? Thank you, Alfred. What is so merry about tonight, please tell me? All this damned snow, and my rheumatism." And she regarded him with umbrage, as if he were personally responsible for the weather. She took Jerome's arm and said: "Take me to your papa, sir, at once."

The two turned away. She suddenly halted and looked over her bulky shoulder at the discomfited Alfred and the shocked Dorothea. "By the way, Alfred, where is that girl of yours, that dressmaker, or something?"

"Miss Maxwell has not yet appeared," said Alfred, and his pale eyes flashed dangerously as he forgot the power of the widow. "She will be down very shortly, now." He turned to Dorothea. "My dear, would you please——"

"I shall go up for her at once," said Dorothea, turning away with a stately swish of her skirts and beginning to climb the stairway.

The widow grinned, and chuckled hoarsely. "Let us wait a moment, Jerome. I have a fancy to see the wench immediately. I hear she has a handsome face."

A pulse began to beat in Alfred's forehead, but he controlled himself. A few more guests arrived. A pleasant confusion ensued.

A figure began to move down the stairway, very slowly and haughtily. The guests, including the widow, glanced up with polite smiles. Then the smiles disappeared, and the faces were startled masks, and a silence fell over them.

Against the dark shadow of the stairwell, Amalie was descending with indifferent poise and erect head. The blaze of the chandelier struck her. She wore a gown of vivid scarlet velvet, exceptionally daring. Her white shoulders were entirely bare and glimmered like snow under the moon. The tight bodice was moulded over her high and pointed breasts and slender waist, falling away from the latter in folds of glowing ruby-like color, which were caught up at the rear in a cascading bustle. Rubies sparkled in the masses of her severely coiffed black hair and low chignon, and in her small ears. Her beautiful face was luminously white, her eyes deep and purple, her mouth as scarlet as her gown. Her large and lovely hand moved along the balustrade, and it, too, sparkled with fiery gems. My mother's, thought Jerome, through the strange humming in his ears, and the stranger pounding of his heart.

Now she was fully in the light, almost on the last step. She paused. All the strong carved planes of her face were revealed, the molding of her firm chin.

The petrified silence deepened in the hall. It enveloped everything.

"My God!" screamed the widow, staring.

Everyone started violently. Some of the ladies then lifted their fans to cover the lower half of their faces. The gentlemen stared at Amalie, completely fascinated. And now behind Amalie appeared the spectral figure of Dorothea, who was paler than any ghost and apparently quite numb.

Jerome looked at the pulsating vision on the last step, and there he stood in silence, his arm falling to his side.

Alfred, recovering from his stupefaction, stirred. His color was quite ghastly. But he lifted his head and advanced firmly to the stairway. He extended his hand to Amalie, and she took it. He led her down, and forward. He said, very clearly and

143

quietly: "Amalie, my love, our guests." And proceeded to introduce her.

The ladies tried to acknowledge the introductions, but could only whisper, their eyes huge in their appalled and genteel faces. Amalie was quite composed. She acknowledged each introduction with cool politeness and calm. She looked openly and steadily at each bowing gentleman, who stammered her name. She arrived at the Widow Kingsley, smiled a little, and gave the older woman the brief curtsy of youth being presented to age. Every eye rotated to her as if bewitched, noting every fold of scarlet drapery, every gleam from her white shoulders and throat and only half-concealed breast.

"Well!" shouted Mrs. Kingsley, deliberately inspecting the girl through a raised lorgnette. "So this is our great beauty, eh? My God! Alfred, you've done yourself proud now. A handsome wench, if I ever saw one, and a hard filly to handle, I wager." She fixed her eyes shrewdly upon Amalie's face. Amalie smiled. The widow began to grin, her thick underlip curling out. "I like you, my dear," she announced. "Even if you are a dressmaker, or something." She added: "You may kiss me, if you like."

Amalie bent her head and kissed the old woman, who patted her cheek during the embrace. The widow sighed. "And to think this lived in Riversend, and I never knew. Tell me, my love, did you design that gown yourself?"

"Yes," said Amalie, with a deeper smile. "But I'm not a dressmaker. I am a teacher, ma'am."

"Who cares?" demanded the widow, recklessly. She studied Amalie again, and again she grinned. "I like you, my child," she repeated, and took Amalie's hand. Then she snickered. "But why are you marrying Alfred, when you can marry my beautiful Jerome? Two handsome rascals together. For you are a rascal, aren't you, my pet? Yes, I was never mistaken in my life, and I am not mistaken now. Why are you marrying Alfred?" she demanded, stridently. "It's his money, of course." She paused, beetling her brows as she glanced at the unhappy man. "I never liked Esau," she commented, witheringly.

The guests looked at each other, and again the ladies covered their faces with their fans and their eyes danced maliciously. The gentlemen smiled, but considerately turned their regard away from Alfred.

The widow glanced up with a hard chiding look at Jerome. "Well," she said, "speak up, can't you? Why aren't you marrying this delightful creature yourself? It isn't too late, you know."

Jerome bowed. "Why, ma'am, the lady has not asked me," he said. He turned to Amalie: "Have you?"

Amalie gazed at him with cool consideration. "I believe I have not. Doubtless an oversight on my part, for which I hope you will forgive me."

The widow chuckled. She took their arms, drew them on each side of her. "Let us go in to Papa," she said. "We can leave Alfred to do the stupid honors."

And she drew them away with her towards the doorway of the drawing-rooms.

Slowly, one by one, the guests considerately removed their embarrassing presence from Alfred and Dorothea, and talking and laughing more ostentatiously than necessary, followed the remarkable trio.

Dorothea and Alfred were alone in the warm but still palpitating silence of the hall. Alfred was visibly shaken. He drew out his kerchief and wiped his brow. His features were rigid. His temples throbbed, the veins thickened. Dorothea regarded him with bitter compassion and understanding.

He said, not looking at her: "Please, Dorothea. Say nothing. I do not believe I——" And his voice broke, and he turned away.

Dorothea's hands moved up in a slight arch, and then she clasped them together. She said, very quietly: "I believe all our guests have arrived, Alfred. Shall we join the others?"

She took his arm. At least, she thought, he has been spared the ordeal of seeing the faces of the others in the drawing-rooms when they first encounter that woman. Oh, the despicable creature. Oh, Alfred, Alfred!

CHAPTER SIXTEEN

Amalie was a distinct sensation, to say the least. But if she was aware of it she gave no indication. Completely composed, gracious and affable, she whirled about the music room in the arms of fascinated gentlemen, who awaited their turn with every indication of most ungenteel impatience. Her flashing scarlet figure twirled and glided among the dim grays, blacks, browns and purples like a tongue of flame through sluggishly flowing lava rocks. Even those very young ladies who wore soft blouses and pinks and lavender were instantly robbed of color by her swift proximity, and after her passing they seemed not to regain it, but to remain ghosts of themselves. This did not, in the least, endear her to the ladies, who watched her passage with un-Christian sentiments in their hearts. "The men are making perfect fools of themselves over you, my love," said the Widow Kingsley, with a delighted grin.

The musicians, as if becoming infected by her resplendent presence, played with heightened tempo and vitality, so that even the most decorous found themselves whirling about at a tempestuous pace, quite breathless and quite flushed. Mr. Lindsey watched from his chair, and young Philip, pleading for an extra half hour, watched also, his dark eyes blazing with pleasure as they followed Amalie.

The young ladies, panting, fanning themselves vigorously, were deposited near Mrs. Kingsley for a few moments of rest. "I will say her costume is indecent, more unrefined!" exclaimed one, gasping, her soft voice unusually shrill. "Those bare shoulders—really, almost nude," and she blushed furiously. "Doubtless, the gentlemen are most embarrassed."

"Doubtless," said Mehitabel wryly. "They are so embarrassed that they cannot get rid of you girls fast enough, so that they can be embarrassed some more." For the swains of the two young ladies, after a brief and polite word or two, were out looking for Amalie again and skirting the fringes of the dancers with intent and delirious impatience. They were not alone. Many others were dogging Amalie. During interludes, they besieged her, glaring at her dance program, insisting an error had been made and that the next dance was theirs. Amalie's voice, low, clear and amused, could be heard over the elegant murmuring of the ladies.

"She has danced only once with Mr. Alfred Lindsey," said the other of the two girls near Mrs. Kingsley. "And that was the opening dance. I call that most—irregular. But then, they say, it is impossible for her to have manners."

"With that face and that figure, no woman needs manners," said Mehitabel. "She needs a bodyguard."

"There she goes now, with Mr. Jerome," said the smaller and darker of the two. She added reluctantly: "What a handsome couple they make. But, dear me, how high she lifts her skirts! I can actually see her ankles."

"Is that why all the men are staring so rapt at the floor?" asked Mehitabel. "I wondered what caused all those downcast eyes."

She grinned widely, fanned herself with her huge fan of black ostrich plumes. She was sitting on a little gilt chair in the shelter of palm fronds. The two girls sat near her, one on each side. They knew Mrs. Kingsley very well, and went to her "as to a mother," for she was kind to them in her way, and they had no living maternal parent. She was fond of them, in her rough fashion. She hoped that local gossip had not yet informed them that she and their father, General Tayntor, had been lovers between Mehitabel's husbands. Of course, that was over and done with years ago. "There comes a time in a woman's life when she is finished with all that," Mehitabel would say, "and she breathes a hearty 'Thank God!' for it. Though, it seems, no one believes her."

The older of the girls, Sally, was small and dark and dainty, with a dimpled rosy face flushed with intelligence and verve. She had a high and full little breast, and the tiniest of waists, and considerable style. "With a little encouragement," the Widow Kingsley would say, "she could develop into quite a knowing and interesting woman. But who will encourage her in Riversend?"

Miss Sally had lively big black eyes and a mass of black ringlets and a mouth like a pudgy red rosebud, in addition to her pretty little figure. She wore a gown of deep pink faille and creamy lace, draped exquisitely. She was naturally mischievous and gay of temperament, and a great belle. It did not please her to find herself deserted by those gentlemen whose names were inscribed in her program as next in line for her dancing favors. She pouted.

Her sister Josephine (whom no one ever called "Josie," for obvious reasons) was taller and more graceful than the bouncing Sally. She was also much fairer. Her skin was pale and delicate, only slightly flushed at the cheekbones, and her eyes were a soft and gentle blue. Her hair, decorously without curl or twist, was of a very fragile texture, and only missed being golden by a slight margin. But its gleaming pale brown was still very attractive, and rested in a huge chignon on the nape of her long white neck. Many professed to find her prettier than her nimble sister. Miss Josephine's features were always reserved and modest and sweet in expression. If she lacked Sally's animation, she possessed a purity of brow, a slender length of nose, a tenderness of quiet rosy mouth, which gave her a classical look. Every movement, every lift of her head, was imbued with serene aristocracy, and her voice was soft and musical. She wore a simple rich gown of blue satin, very styl-

147

ish and very elegant, her bustle caught up with pink rosebuds.

Mrs. Kingsley found the girl dull, though she loved her more than she did the knowing Sally, who had a sharp tongue on occasion and a reckless way of using it. "For conversation," Mehitabel would say, "give me Sally. She never bores me. But for restfulness, give me Josephine. She quite soothes me, and I find her presence a perfect cure for insomnia."

Josephine was only nineteen, Sally's junior by two years. Neither of them was as yet betrothed. Sally could find no one to please her in Riversend, which she hated. As for Josephine, she had had her hopes. Amalie had blasted them. The poor girl had quite resigned herself to the prospect of fading into gentle spinsterhood and devoting herself to church work and visiting the poor and being a comfort to her father. Of this last nefarious design, the General was still happily ignorant. He fretted considerably over his daughters and urged them, in quite vulgar language, to acquire husbands. He'd not have any damned old maids about him, he would say, pulling their hair and kissing them heartily.

No one knew of Josephine's secret pale passion for Alfred and her fanatical devotion to him. She was nearly twenty years his junior, but since her childhood she had fastened all her silent but tenacious hopes upon his oblivious person. He was always very kind to her and found her company a relief from Sally's. It was necessary for him to visit the General often, on business matters, for the General genially but obdurately refused to go to the Bank. Sally hardly liked him, and when forced into his presence would torment him with witty remarks. But Josephine was like a waft of attar of refined roses on air too brisk and windy. She was content to sit and embroider near him, her slender ankles crossed on a low stool, while her father and Alfred conversed of finance and mortgages and crops and investments. From time to time she would lift her lovely head and fix her sweet blue eyes upon the visitor, and a brighter flush would appear on her cheek.

For Amalie, she had a most dismaying and desperate hatred which she did not confess even to herself. But her young and inexperienced heart was lacerated with pain and a quite violent grief. This most odious creature was not good enough for dear Alfred; she was most unrefined, a nobody, of low birth and no breeding whatsoever. She would make Alfred miserable, ruin his life, with her flaunting ways. She had a greedy mouth, and her eyes were hard. Josephine indulged herself in the ancient wonder of neglected and heart-sick women: "What does he see in her?" She was too tall for a woman, and she was bold and coarse, with no gentility. A woman who had had to earn her own living! That was shameful enough in itself. Who, in his right mind, could endure such a creature? Alfred was not in his right mind. Amalie was not even the daughter of one of those disgusting new-rich who had exploited a prostrate South after the war. She had no money, no distinction, no background, no tradition, to bring to Alfred in lieu of cash. Josephine was vaguely aware that her sentiments were un-Christian, but between tears and prayers for forgiveness and supplications that she would be given courage and resignation, she hated Amalie with an overwhelming fury that would have amazed those who knew her.

Besides, she would think despairingly, from her vantage point of nineteen years, she is so old! She is almost twenty-three, they say. An old maid.

Her secret thoughts were being vehemently echoed, but vocally, among a number of other ladies who languished in corners and against the walls, while their gentlemen pursued Amalie, completely oblivious of the fact that their names were inscribed in the ladies' programs. A malignant little breeze of voices blew along the neglected walls, accompanied by nasty titters behind fans, and virulent looks.

If Amalie was aware of all this (and it was impossible for her not to be) she did not mind it in the least. She despised these genteel and foolish women who did nothing but breed, whine and complain gently at the breakfast table, and manage their large households. She was enjoying herself. At least, she *had* been enjoying herself until Jerome had become her partner. She could not have refused him, for he had made his request in the presence of others. To have denied him would have created a scene, for she was well aware that he could make scenes, shamelessly, if he so desired.

The music soared and lilted and swung. Jerome whirled Amalie about in a rapid waltz. She danced beautifully, but she was rigid in Jerome's arms. Her face was white and withdrawn; she looked steadfastly over his shoulder, as if she had forgotten him. He tried to draw her closer; she resisted. Again he was surprised at her strength. Couples flew by them, the women's eyes malevolent, the men's envious. Light poured down from the great chandeliers that hung from the vaulted ceiling. It was all very gay and delightful.

"I must talk to you," whispered Jerome.

Amalie smiled faintly, but did not reply. She glanced hopefully at the musicians. This waltz was almost over.

He looked at her beautiful white shoulders and the swell of her white breast. He said, softly: "Come away with me. To-night. We'll go to New York."

She turned her eyes to him then, for the first time, and her smile was wider. "Mr. Lindsey, sir, is this a proposal?"

He laughed. He pulled her to him unexpectedly, and they danced now in quite ungenteel proximity. "In a way," he murmured.

"An unconventional way," she reflected, "but with no book, I presume."

"No book," he agreed. "But who cares for books?"

She did not smile now. But she looked at him long and contemptuously. "And on what, may I inquire, should we live in New York?"

He frowned slightly. "Live on? We'd live as I've always lived, I imagine."

"On your father's money?" She paused. "But I seriously doubt that your father would be a source of revenue, under your proposed change of circumstances. You would have to work, Mr. Lindsey, and I wonder if your constitution would endure it."

"You do speak of the most disagreeable contingencies," he said, lightly. But it was evident he was thinking. "Damn it, I'm an excellent artist. I'd paint portraits, or something. Besides, after five days, I understand banking astonishingly."

"In short, you'd have practically no money," she said. She pulled herself away from his shining bosom. "And money, sir, is what I am after. Of course, there are your irresistible charms. But I doubt very much that they would be a substantial substitute for what I have already been offered."

Her tone had been consistently light and cool and mocking throughout the conversation. But she was trembling, and her mouth was rigid.

"You are mercenary," he chided. Then his face changed. He bent his head. "Amalie, Amalie. I love you, Amalie."

She jerked back her head to look at him piercingly. He was smiling. But she saw his eyes, and her trembling became quite violent. At that moment the music ended on a wild and exuberant flourish, and the dancers halted, clapping restrainedly. Several gentlemen, with purposeful gleams in their eyes, were coming towards Amalie, trying to outdistance each other without actually running.

"Oh, go away, go away!" she murmured. "For God's sake, let me alone!"

Jerome saw nothing but this woman. He was heavily flushed, and his breath was thick. He still gripped her hand. Several of the dancers, preparing to leave the floor, eyed them with avid curiosity. Amalie tried to withdraw her hand. He held it more tightly.

"You can't marry him," he said, almost inaudibly. "I want you, Amalie. We belong together. Some way, somehow, I will manage things, for you and me."

He saw tears in her eyes for the first time, thick clustering tears that tangled her eyelashes and made the color between them a more vivid but wavering purple. Her mouth had deepened in tint, had become more intense, and softer. But she whispered: "Please. Please." And turned away from him.

He had to drop her hand now, for he saw that in the forefront of the pursuing gentlemen Alfred had quite an edge over the others. And there was a dangerous look about Alfred. He favored his cousin with an almost malignant glance, bowed to Amalie, and said: "My love, I believe the next waltz is mine."

Jerome retreated slowly towards the wall. He passed Dorothea, in the arms of an elderly gentleman with a white beard. Dorothea stared at him grimly. He did not see her. He reached the Widow Kingsley, who was sitting alone with Sally of the dimples and the bouncing black curls.

Mehitabel gave him a long and penetrating look. "Well?" she demanded loudly, putting aside her fan.

He smiled down at her. "Well—nothing," he said, pleasantly.

She considered him. "It is hard work, dancing," she remarked. "Your face is very red and hot. Wipe it." She paused. "You are a fool, Jerome."

But he turned to Sally. "Miss Sally, may I have the honor?"

She bounded up happily and rolled her huge black eyes at him most coquettishly. "Indeed, sir, it is a pleasure," she said saucily. "I refused all others for this!"

He whirled Sally away to the tune of a rollicking waltz. She was a lovely little dancer. She exhaled the odor of sweet lilacs. Her pretty bosom bounced decorously. She threw back her head to laugh at him and tease him. To his surprise, he found her delicious. The strong sickness was still in him, like something festering and devouring, something bleeding and oozing. He still tried to catch glimpses of Amalie's scarlet gown flying among the dancers. But Sally interested him in spite of himself, for he was always vulnerable to pretty women. How her black eyes danced and glittered! How her little white teeth shone and flashed! She was all warmth and voluptuousness. Involuntarily, his arm tightened about her, and she did not resist. In fact, she actually cuddled. He found it delightful.

"You have quite grown up since I last saw you, Miss Sally," he said.

"The effect is not too disagreeable?" she asked pertly, but her breath came faster.

"On the contrary, it is dazzling," he replied, and meant it. "I am enchanted."

Her firm and rounded breasts leaned more intimately against him. "How kind of you, sir!" she exclaimed, and tossed her head so that her curls rioted briefly against his lips. She was a natural coquette, was Sally, and her heart was misbehaving in a most unusual fashion, and her blood felt hot and foaming in her veins.

"I understand that you are not leaving us again," she said, laughing, but with an intent and suddenly serious look.

"No. Never again." He hesitated and looked for Amalie. "How could I?"

He danced twice with Sally after that, and each time he found the occasion more pleasant. It was impossible to claim Amalie again. Alfred remained with her, doggedly and grimly.

At eleven o'clock he discovered that the old wound in his leg had begun to cripple him, and he could dance no more. Instantly, a most horrible restlessness and depression fell over him. He looked about the animated music room. Mehitabel was dancing with the gallant General. Everyone was dancing. Amalie and Alfred had unaccountably disappeared. Mr. Lindsey had excused himself and had gone to bed.

He left the room unobtrusively, his departure noticed by no one but Sally Tayntor, who immediately drooped in her partner's arms. He went through the warm and silent hall, where the fire had burned low and the lamp was dim. The clock struck a long and sonorous series of notes. The sounds and music from the distant room were subdued here, like fairy revelry.

Jerome wandered through a door, entered a dark passage, continued down it. He opened another door and found himself in his father's small but complete conservatory. It was very dark here, and silent, filled with the pungent smell of earth and growing things. He closed the door behind him. The air was cool and moist in the conservatory, and there was a hint of moss and mould. The light of the moon came through the glass roof, blurred and doubled, like a moon in a nightmare.

Jerome could smell the hothouse roses and geraniums and lilies, but he could see only the long earthy stalls. The wooden floor was gritty under his feet.

He leaned against a stall and slowly and abstractedly began to pull a rose apart.

CHAPTER SEVENTEEN

The "death-dews," as Jerome winningly called it, had settled over Hilltop. The long quiet of a country winter Sunday had engulfed not only Hilltop but the entire community in that death-in-life atmosphere. Even the horses and the fowl and the sparrows seemed to understand that this was the Sabbath, and they disturbed the empty peace at their own peril. Another storm had raged the day before, but understanding, with commendable intelligence, that this was Sunday, it had subsided precisely at midnight. The only sound at all was that of the churchbells in the valley, and they reached Hilltop's clarified heights with faint tremblings of airy music. But they only enhanced the "encompassing gloom" and the white and religious vacuity.

In the morning the servants and Dorothea dutifully descended to the valley for services. This was impossible for Mr. Lindsey. It was incredible for Jerome, so no one suggested it. Jerome had heard the sleigh bells retreating and had eventually heard them return. Then dinner had decorously been announced, had been eaten. Mr. Lindsey had then retired to his room for a rest, and Dorothea had followed suit, and the servants. Everything had died. Jerome sat before the library fire, with an unread book on his knees and stared at the silently glowing coals.

Jim was apparently in the stables, as usual, with Charlie and Philip. Jerome listened to the loud ticking of the clock in the hall. The white silence deepened. He tried to drowse, but all his muscles began to twitch, his flesh to ache. This was the pattern of all the Sundays of his youth, and he wondered, for the hundredth time, how he had ever endured it, would ever endure it in the long future. He knew that in the valley people paid calls, but last night's storm had quelled the enthusiasm of even the hardiest who might wish to visit Hilltop. He listened to the clock striking three. Still, some callers might come and relieve this appalling tedium, this motionless silence.

He contemplated tea, at six. But that was three hours away. He closed his eyes, and immediately he was assailed by his terrible and chronic illness of mind, his insupportable misery.

Amalie and Alfred had been on their honeymoon for the past four days. Every evidence of the intimate wedding had been removed from the house: the flowers, the ferns, the festoons of white ribbon, the litter, the loaded tables. There was nothing left of it all for Jerome but the increasingly poignant memory of Amalie's face under her veil and wreath of fresh orange blossoms. He could see it now, in the center of the fire: pale, quiet, utterly without expression, only her lips moving in the responses. He saw the marble flash of her hand as it emerged from under the veil, extended for the gold wedding ring. It had been the movement of a statue, briefly coming to life. Then he had seen Alfred bend his head and kiss Amalie on the lips. When Jerome could see her face again, it was unchanged. The kiss had touched snow.

He stirred in his chair, as if struck violently with a sudden pain. He sat up, pressed his hand over his eyes, his face, dropped them upon his knee. Finally he lit a cheroot and knew that one of his abhorred moods was coming over him again and that there was no way to escape it. For now suffering was part of it, suffering for which there was no hope at all.

He told himself: She will return. In two or three weeks, she will be back in this house. This is not the end. For me it will, in a way, be only a beginning. I shall be here. It is not the end.

And then he thought of Alfred and Amalie in their own apartments, and he was ill again, even more ill than he had been before. I ought to have stopped it; I ought to have found a way, he said to himself, in the most urgent despair of his life. What had happened to her, that she was so realistic, so appallingly open-eyed and grim? What had the years of her life done to her that she was without sentimentality, without softness, without gentle femininity? Another woman would have preferred passion to security. But not Amalie Maxwell, who knew so much of life and its murderous fury against those who had no strong city of money in which to dwell.

She had bought money and security, openly, without dissimulation. Alfred had not been deceived that she loved him. She had been honest. Yet, when Jerome thought of this, he hated her, hated her with such savagery that his face became wet and his throat thick with wild misery.

154

He stood up, paced up and down the room. If only he had something to do! Something to distract him, or interest him! Something to help him forget. He went into the dusky cave of the dining-room, where the silver on the sideboards winked at him faintly, and the wan rectangles which were the windows stood in the gloom like pale paintings of snow and twisted bough and glimmering white slope. He found a decanter of whiskey and a glass and returned with them to the library. He poured himself a generous portion of the amber fluid and began to sip it, standing as he was near the fire. Long bars of flickering and rosy light darted from the coals. A flutter of sparks beat against the fire-screen like vehement fireflies, hissing. Flames burst up, shone upon the glass, upon the rings which sparkled on Jerome's fingers. He thought of Aristotle's wry comment: "Anaxagoras says that man is the wisest of animals because he has hands." He burst out laughing and sat down.

The wisest of animals! Whoever would have thought that the old boy had such a sense of humor? Jerome could see Aristotle very plainly, seated in his ivory chair, a white monolith of a man with his majestic white beard. He could see his strange and twinkling smile, and hear his voice. "——because he has hands." How the solemn sentimentalists, and now the humorless scientists, had indulged in learned discussions over that comment! But none had ever seen Aristotle's smile; they had only the fleshless bones of his words to gnash their noisy teeth upon.

Jerome turned the glass slowly in his hands. He did not like to think. He had always evaded the hard and bitter discipline of thought. It was so tedious. It was unsettling. It gave a man no real pleasure, unless he confined himself to the abstract, and that was like playing the childish game of battledore and shuttlecock, keeping a bird of feathers in the air, uselessly, with light battings of a stringed oval of wood. Even then, the silly bird of feathers inevitably must strike ground. It must come back to the fundamentals, and the fundamentals had always sedulously been avoided by Jerome. He had the well-founded idea that not only would they be unpleasant, but that they would be futile, as well as painful. It was wearying to think of all the wise men who had struggled with thought, like pigmies struggling with Titans who always became stronger the moment they hit the earth. Abstracts, inexorably, became pertinent thoughts, with a disagreeable tendency to revert to the particular.

He thought banally: What have I done with my life? I am not young. I have done nothing. He smiled to himself ironically. I have had a fine time. I have enjoyed myself. I have always preferred the hedonists, who seem to me very wise old fellows, indeed. What more can a man ask than that he enjoy good food, hear the best music, look on the finest paintings, love the prettiest women, sleep in the softest beds—and all without much exertion on his own part? What devil is it in a man that urges him to "accomplish something"? God knows, I have never been such an egotist, such a colossal bore. I never desired to accomplish anything, for what can any man accomplish which will not eventually overcome him with tedium? Does he desire accomplishment for the satisfaction of his own ego? Or does he believe that he is changing the face of the world, which would much prefer not to be changed? In either event, he is affirming his belief in a personal immortality, and that is a shameful impudence.

He thought, suddenly, of his years in the war. Why had he enlisted? He could easily have bought an alternate. The streets of New York had seethed with men anxious to risk their lives for a few dollars. But he had not bought an alternate. He had waited for no draft. He had become a commissioned officer.

He yawned. It was very tiresome, this thinking. What had he believed he might "accomplish"? He had not particularly desired to "save the Union." If the South wished to secede, that was their privilege, their right, he had thought. He had thought it very silly for white men to die to give Negroes their freedom. Eventually, and quite bloodlessly, the Negroes would have been freed, anyway. A few years longer, perhaps, and it would have been done, leaving no residue of hatred and terror and rage such as now afflicted the nation, and would continue to afflict it for generations to come. After all, even the South had been coming to the conclusion that slavery was ridiculous.

Had he wanted adventure, then? It was a strange adventure, if that had been the motive. He was definitely not the sort of which soldiers are made. He had no propensity for blood and mud, for death and suffering, for murder. He frowned. Why, then, had he gone, when he might just as well have stayed cosily in New York, and jeered at the battle?

Restless, he got up and went to the windows, and looked out at the white and motionless landscape beyond them. He thought: I was not patriotic. In a way, I was never an American. I do not love Americans; but then, I do not love anyone, really.

He drummed on the windowpane with one hand, while he held his glass to his lips with the other. This thinking was a very dreary matter, and he had been wise to avoid it in the past. Why could he not avoid it now?

It seemed that a man must "do something," however absurd. It was not enough for him merely to earn enough to shelter himself and to provide bread for his belly. He must "do something," whether that doing meant the forcible conversion of the obstinate to his particular brand of theology, or piling up a useless fortune, or writing books that would be crumbling dust in a few years, or painting pictures which would hang in empty galleries, or inventing a new philosophy. And always, he must talk. Endlessly, he must talk, about what he had done or what he intended to do. He could not help it, poor devil. He was caught up in some impotent and dreadful inertia, and he could not prevent himself from spinning like a top, and humming constantly as he did so. "Vanity, vanity." But man could not stop himself from loving this vanity and serving it until he dropped dead of sheer exhaustion.

But there was an immutable law behind the phenomenon of inertia. The most callow of mathematicians understood that. What the hell was the immutable law about? What was its design, its object? And could it produce nothing of greater grandeur than the futile whirling of a human top, which was the ultimate degradation of what was amusingly called "human dignity"?

Perhaps it had an inscrutable purpose. But that field was best left to the metaphysicians. He, Jerome, was no mystic. He rubbed away a fern of frost on the window. Beautiful and exact creation! Minutely and lovingly established by another immutable law, destined only to be obliterated by one hot and idle finger! What magnificent purpose had been behind that destiny? To give one man a few moments of most uncomfortable soul-searching and misery? It seems, he thought, we can bring anthropomorphic theories to bear even on the subject of the destruction of an ice crystal. A little more, and I could be a thumping egotist myself.

He was amused by the foolish drift of his thoughts, but he clung to the folly as a man clamors for drugs to ease his pain, which he dare not face. He saw the valley below, snowbound and silent and very still. The drift of his thoughts changed. The population of the valley was not increasing, and those who remained were miserable and stagnant. Why? Because a few men, such as Alfred, preferred the status quo, even if it meant

157

dull wretchedness forever for the many. No, no, we must not have the nasty factories here; it would ruin dear old, nice old, Riversend. Besides, it would give men too much money to spend unwisely, on drink and carousing, or, even worse, on better homes and better food. That would make them arrogant, and life, accordingly, would be much less comfortable for their betters. No, we must not bring commerce here, and liveliness, nor expand our darling little town. We are satisfied, are we not? If a carper might complain that the people were daily sinking deeper into the mud of despair, or that other cities were expanding all about the village, or that the youth and brightness of the new generation were leaving the vicinity in droves, and the farmers struggled hopelessly to keep their little land and their homes—why, that was all the troublesome imagination of a man who liked to stir up mischief.

It was useless to point out to such fools that expansion meant the very life of America. They had a stock and smug reply: America had stopped growing; it was now in the process of conserving, maturing. What of the wild territories to the West? Oh, they would forever remain the playground of Indians, and the pioneers were merely restless men who had failed at home. The dream of America? It had become a reality, and it was the duty of the responsible to preserve that reality in the form of banks and mortgages and pleasant interest.

The finger which had slowly been rubbing away the ice crystals was still now. The immutable purpose behind the inertia. Was that purpose the growing, and the expanding, and the passionate life of America? If so, why? The immutable purpose was silent. But Jerome, strangely enough, could feel it expanding and swelling behind him like an approaching power, like a terrible and sonorous insistence.

No, he thought, I am a fool. What does it matter to me, anyway?

But the power swelled behind him, and he felt it in spite of his amusement at himself.

He wandered away from the window restlessly and sat down again. But he still felt the vibrancy of the power. Besides, he thought, assisting such power would be an attack on Alfred, and Alfred was a dangerous man. He could not see, at this moment, just how it could be done, but surely it could be done.

Well, it seemed that if a man was not to die of sheer boredom, he must "accomplish something." And that was reason enough in itself. He had only not to think too much. He recalled a conversation he had once had with Mr. Jay Regan. He had expatiated quite fully on Mr. Regan's vast financial empire and had said: "But why? What is the use of it? Why do you want it?" And Mr. Regan had replied: "Because I wish it." The answer did not seem so silly now, though Jerome had laughed at that time. If a man wished a thing, and did not waste any time on speculating why, he could accomplish wonders. The only snag was the "why?" But that could easily be avoided. The greater part of wisdom was in not being too wise. A man could think himself into petrifaction, a most undesirable state of affairs. Be a trifle more primitive, Jerome urged himself, sardonically. Not only fools live on the surface.

To his amused astonishment he found himself wishing that it were Monday morning and that he were on his way to the Bank. The Bank was a potential, in spite of the barnacles that were fast growing over it and obliterating it. Something could be done with it, something vital and exciting, rough and exuberant. The secret was locked in its barren safes and tight little drawers. I'd like to talk it over with Jay, he thought.

The clock struck a deep and fateful four. Jerome was surprised. For an hour, now, he had not thought of Amalie at all, and the pain and hate and rage had subsided to a quite endurable ache. It was then that he heard the musical chiming of sleigh bells, the sound of voices. The knocker was struck briskly, and Jerome sensed the sleepy descent of a maid on the backstairs, the opening of a number of doors, and the increased nearness of the voices. He stood up, quite pleased. If he was not mistaken, that was the General and his pretty daughters.

He went into the hall to greet them. "Ho!" cried the General, in the process of being relieved of his coat. "There you are! I thought you had all been buried in the snow, and we came up in Christian charity to rescue you. Didn't we, loves?" he asked of Josephine and Sally, who were smoothing their ringlets and shaking out their ruffles and discreetly plumping their bustles.

"I'm mighty glad to see you, sir," said Jerome, with genuine pleasure, and he and the General clasped hands together firmly and smiled at each other. Jerome bowed to the ladies. Sally tossed her ringlets, rolled her big black eyes at him, blushed, cast her eyes demurely in the direction of her toes. Josephine smiled at him only faintly, and his automatically observant glance told him that the smile was an effort. The girl, as usual, was silent, grave and reserved, but her gentle and classical face was very pale and lifeless.

The General noted Jerome's look and said: "Thought it would cheer the girls to bring them into your sprightly com-

159

pany, you rascal. Josephine, especially. She has the vapors, haven't you, my love?" And he put his one arm about the girl. But as he looked down at her, there was anxiety in his face.

She withdrew from the circle of his arm, but with a swift glance of affection at him. "The winter, Papa," she murmured. "I do not like the winter."

"Ho, it always was a hothouse flower!" exclaimed the General, drawing the girls with him into the library. "But my little Sally, here, is a robust little baggage. She flies about on ice skates. She flounders on snowshoes. She glides about most indecorously on sleds. Why don't you marry her, eh, Jerome?" asked the General, standing with his darlings on the hearth. "One hundred thousand dollars goes with the filly, 'paid on delivery.'"

Sally blushed furiously; her eyes sparkled beneath her lowered lashes. Jerome laughed. He regarded Sally with interest. She was a most engaging vision, in her crimson wool and velvet, and braided bodice. He saw her bright rosy cheek, firm as an apple, and as shining.

"Miss Sally may have plans of her own," he said lightly. "After all, she is very young, and I am an old man."

"Nonsense," said the General vigorously. "Thirteen—fourteen—years. What is that? I was eighteen years older than my Jerusha. And she was much older than I, really. Ho! Ho!"

He seated his daughters with old-fashioned courtesy. Josephine, sighing slightly, relaxed in her chair and gazed at the fire. But the rosy light could not brighten her cheek nor bring a sparkle to her sad and heavy eyes, though it made her light-brown hair to shine like burnished gold.

The General stood with Jerome on the hearth, his long soldier's legs spread firmly. He added, beaming on Sally: "Yes, one hundred thousand, on delivery. And half my estate, when I kick the bucket. What a morsel for any man, not to speak of her——"

Jerome interrupted swiftly, in order to spare Sally's blushes, though, to tell the truth, the young lady did not apparently find the conversation distasteful: "Miss Sally and I have much in common, and I look forward to making our acquaintance much stronger in the future. If I have her consent?" and he bowed to the girl again. She looked up from the depths of her chair, like a sleek little kitten, blushed again, simpered. It was an intelligent face, he observed, and a damned pretty one, and one hundred thousand immediate dollars were not to be despised. Moreover, if he understood women at all, there was

160

promise of excitement in that dainty little body. No prude, Sally. She had life and gaiety and verve. A man could do much worse.

He sat down near her, a circumstance which did not annoy her in the least. The General remained on the hearth. He accepted one of Jerome's cheroots and looked on the whiskey decanter with pleasure. He helped himself to a large swig, drinking with prodigious enjoyment.

"Where's William?" he demanded, smacking his lips. "Good whiskey, that. Where's William, eh?"

"My father is resting in his room. Shall I call him? And my sister, who will be glad to see the young ladies?"

"Never mind. Let us have a few moments to ourselves. I never see you alone," complained the General. "I even thought of going to the Bank to see you. And I haven't been in the infernal place for ten years! Ho!" and he burst into raucous laughter. " 'Give him a day, three days,' I said to the girls, 'and he'll be hot-footing it back to New York with his tail between his legs!' But instead, there you are, sticking it out. What's the attraction, eh?" and his wicked blue eyes fixed themselves with shrewd mirth upon Jerome.

Jerome smiled. "A number of things, all very boring, I presume. Besides, I really have no place else to go."

He rose, went into the dining-room, and brought a crystal decanter of sherry and two small wineglasses for the young ladies. Josephine declined with a listless smile, but Sally accepted eagerly. The two men refilled their glasses, drank a toast to the ladies. Sally lifted her arm high, and the crimson ruffles fell back from its smooth white contour, as dainty as a piece of Dresden china. Jerome noted the dimples in the elbow, and was seized with quite an urge to kiss them. Sally must have felt his thought, for she held her glass demurely to her lips and fluttered her eyes at him.

"What've you been doing with yourself, while the house slept?" asked the General, feeling the warm and silent weight of all the rooms closing in about him. "Funny life, for a scoundrel as active as yourself."

"I've been thinking," said Jerome, and now he narrowed his attention on the General and felt a sudden leap of excitement. "I should like to tell you, sir, what I have been thinking. Perhaps later."

"Why not now?" asked the General robustly. "Before the others come trooping down the stairs to press genteel tea on us? Did I tell you we are staying for tea? Out with it."

161

Jerome smiled down into his glass. "I might say that I, too, have had the vapors, General. I have been thinking——" he paused.

"Bad business, thinking," said the General. "Gave it up years ago. Rotten for the digestion. Binding to the bowels. If you think too long, you end up by cutting your throat or becoming a damned parson. Only sensible to avoid that. Well, what were you thinking?" he demanded loudly. He lifted the long gray tails of his coat, sat down, crossed his legs, and raised his wicked white brows.

Jerome hesitated. "It seems very nebulous, now, in restrospect, but it was very vivid and pertinent while it was going on. Like a dream. But there is a residue." He leaned towards the General, who was studying him with a kind of ribald interest. "It started with the war—my thinking. Of course, I never believed in the brave new world which had been promised us, afterwards. My world, my own private world, was still brave and new in itself, and I preferred not to change it. However, millions believed in it. Freedom, new opportunities for all men, a new birth of life and hope. The younger generation, it was said, would revolutionize the world. They had courage and strength and determination. Their elders had erred, in their middle-aged or senile stupidity. But the young would bring about a blazing regeneration."

He paused, and smiled with embarrassment. "And now, what have we? We have the evils of Reconstruction. We have panics and fear and poverty and hopelessness. The brave new world has failed to arrive. Worse, the old one is falling apart."

There was a silence. The General pulled at his long nose, thoughtfully, and regarded the fire. Finally, he began to speak, in a reflective voice: "When I was young, there was a war. There was always a war going on somewhere, either against the British, or the Indians. And, each time, we were promised that things were going to be very different, afterwards, and very glorious. Who promised us this? I do not think it was our government, or our leaders. I think it was ourselves. But we always blamed the government, and the leaders, afterwards, when the world jogged on much the same as it had been before."

He drank again. He began to grin. "I remember that I said to my father: 'You oldsters, sir, have made a muddle of the world. We, the young, shall change that. We shall set things to rights, and no interference, if you please. We are young and strong, and we have courage, and there is a dream to be fulfilled.' " He pulled his nose again and smiled wryly. "Damn me, if the dream didn't seem real to me then. But I've forgotten what it was."

He went on, after a moment: "I do remember very clearly, however, saying those ridiculous things to my father, who was a very dignified gentleman and rarely smiled. But he did smile, then. He said: 'It is good to have a dream. I had them, also, when I was young. And I remember most particularly that I said these very things you are saying now, to my own father. Doubtless, too, he had said them to his father. The young complain incessantly to their elders, who complained, in their turn, to their elders. No one accepts responsibility for himself. No one realizes that revolutions in human affairs do not come with a single war, or a single convulsion, or a single man. It is impossible. But then, we have not grown out of our silly propensity for expecting miracles.' "

The General laughed gently. But his lewd and vigorous face was unusually thoughtful. He rubbed his chin. "The worst of it is, I cannot remember what the dream was all about—the dream I had. But, sir, it was a good one. It must have been, for it sustained me in battle. Yes, my father mentioned his dream, too. He was with Washington at Valley Forge. He lost an arm. But I do not remember him ever saying that the new nation was, in its essentials, much different from its condition under old German George. The same old abuses of power, the same old oppression of nonconformists, the same old greed, the same old intrigues."

His eyes became lively now, and he sat up. "Damn me, sir, it is a strange thing, though! To a worm's-eye view, it does not appear that man has ever changed, or even his dreams! His dreams of freedom and plenty and peace. No, says the worm, man remains the same. But so do his dreams! A very, very odd thing. Who gave him his dreams? How were they conceived, in his state of original sin, his wickedness, his voracity, his cruelty, and his madness? Damn me, sir, I am becoming a mystic, I am becoming a parson! I shall soon be singing hymns!"

He allowed Jerome to refill his glass, and drank it down with one gulp. Sally played with her ruffles; Josephine still gazed at the fire in her trance of mute sadness. It was evident that Sally was impatient at this most unusual conversation. But Jerome was leaning towards the General, completely absorbed.

"Our view," said the General, quite inspired, "is a worm's-eye view. We expect the landscape to change overnight. It never does, and so it appears to the worm-man that it remains forever the same. But it does not. Over a period of one hundred, two hundred, years, the pattern has shifted. The sunken plateau of human misery and despair has lifted an inch or so. We see that, in restrospect; we see that, over the century-miles we have come. But the ground on which we stand now seems fixed forever, incapable of change. Our children will laugh at us. Our grandchildren will say, with truth: "We have come a long way, since the nineteenth century.' And their grandchildren will say: "We have changed the world since the twentieth century.'

"It is only the worm who maintains that nothing transpires, nothing changes, nothing becomes better. But then, the worm has such a short life, and his point in time and space is so infinitesimal. Change takes time, and the tides cannot be hurried, however much the worm prays and complains and denounces and accuses his parents of laxity and blindness and stupidity."

He lay back in his chair and smiled maliciously at Jerome. "And have you been complaining, sir, you worm-man?"

Jerome laughed. "In a way. But my complaint is that nothing is worth while, whether it changes or not. I have been trying to persuade myself not to think of it. I have been trying to believe that I must live on the surface of things, and not meditate too much."

"An excellent thought. Once look back, once reflect that all is wariness and dustiness, and one turns to salt. For instance, you have been having some thoughts—have you not?—how you, personally, might help things to change?"

Jerome glanced up in surprise. The General chuckled. "I thought so. Well, help to change them, then. There is a certain satisfaction in flexing the muscles, whether they are of the brain or of the body. You have only to avoid one murdering thought: 'Who cares? And why?' "

"You mean, sir," said Jerome, quite astonished, but passionately interested, "that we should take an anthropomorphic view of everything?"

"And why not?" asked the General vigorously. "That is a pattern in itself. Doubtless the bird has its bird-view, the chipmunk is convinced that the world revolves around chipmunks, and the cattle in the stables believe that creation was conceived for their especial benefit. Perhaps we are all of us right. There are a thousand worlds within a world, wheels within wheels. And every one is essential."

The General asked abruptly: "What is it you wish to change?"

Sally was yawning, plucking discontentedly at her ruffles.

Josephine sat in her trance of sorrow; a tear was stealing down her cheek. The two men saw neither of the young ladies.

Jerome said cautiously, staring at the General: "There are times when a man is impelled to instigate change to keep from dying of ennui."

The General considered this. Then he began to smile. He laid his finger against the side of his nose and looked fixedly at the younger man.

"I," he said, at last, "have felt matters were tedious for a very long time. They also did not bring in enough interest."

There were sounds on the staircase. Dorothea entered, in her grim black bombazine. The men sprang to their feet. She ignored Jerome, but favored the General with a stately smile, and accepted the kisses of the young ladies. The General led her gallantly to a chair.

"My dear, dear Dorothea!" he exclaimed, "I trust we did not disturb you with our conversation?"

"Not at all, dear General. I heard nothing until I came down." She sighed and glanced pensively at the young ladies. "How constrained you must feel, my dears, by this weather."

"Sally," said the General, "is having a splendid time. She flounces about most gayly. She skates like the wind. But then, she has excellent legs, and wishes to titillate the young gentlemen."

"Papa!" cried Sally, blushing, but most indecorously pleased.

Josephine smiled languidly, and put her kerchief to her lips. Dorothea's withered mouth set primly. She turned majestically to Josephine. "You are rather pale, my love."

"Josephine found the wedding festivities a little too arduous," explained the General. "She is of a delicate constitution. I intend to take her to Saratoga, for the waters."

"No!" cried Josephine, with involuntary vehemence. Then she cowered in her chair. "I do not wish to leave home, Papa. I told you that last night."

The General studied her reflectively. "The girl seems love-sick, does she not? Who, among our friends, spurns her affections?"

Josephine colored feverishly. Tears thickened in her eyes. She half-rose from her chair, then fell back in it.

"It could not be Jerome, could it?" asked the General, with interest. "If so, that is all nonsense. I intend him for Sally. Besides, Sally is the older, and must be married first."

"Papa!" cried Sally.

But Josephine had become listless again, had lost touch with the conversation.

Dorothea looked at Sally attentively, and for the first time an expression of hopeful relief passed over her gaunt features. Her furtive glance touched Jerome. He was smiling at Sally, his head bent towards her. He had begun to murmur a few inaudible words, and Sally was listening with downcast eyes and bright cheeks.

Dorothea said, in a voice almost lively for her: "Papa will be down shortly. You will remain for tea, General?"

"That is my plan," he answered.

Dorothea turned to Jerome, and her voice was quite amiable: "Jerome, will you ring the bell? And I shall inform Papa at once that the dear General is here, and the young ladies."

In a short while Mr. Lindsey came down, accompanied by Philip, who held his arm. In the ensuing confusion of greetings and amenities, the General whispered to Jerome:

"That change of yours, sir: nothing is impossible, if not too illegitimate, and if the mare is more or less respectable."

He said, in a loud voice: "William, I am pleased with your son. Did you know he is going to marry my daughter, Sally?"

CHAPTER EIGHTEEN

Jerome remembered that Carlyle had once said: "Gunpowder has made men all of one height."

But Jerome added, from his present illuminating experiences: "Uniformity, however, reduces men to pygmies."

As he distrusted himself almost as much as he distrusted others, and had a skeptical eye out for his own epigrams and impulsive conclusions, he was very cautious in allowing himself to believe that uniformity was settling over America. It was only when he was beginning to collect a nice set of bruises on his mental body that he realized that there seemed to be a grim and collective effort to reduce American life to a gray and drab uniformity, not only in thinking, but in economics, industry and social life, as well as in politics and mores. Men were not only expected to be of the same height, but their stature was being reduced.

He, who rarely allowed his emotions to become involved in anything, and who loved trivia in a kind of obscure self-defense, found himself emotionally and furiously in revolt.

(Sometimes he paused, cynically, long enough to reflect that this was a unique and effervescent experience for him, and not at all unpleasant.) There seemed a universal plot against the former diversity and variety of American life. It was like a stream of sluggish but relentless gray lava pouring over the fertile and teeming vineyards and colorful villages of the American world. The boisterousness and color, the crude grandeur and swashbuckling vitality, the gay and riotous unpredictability and exuberance of the American people were being obliterated, as the sun is obliterated by a smothering fog. Worst of all, it seemed deliberate. Why was this? What had happened to the happy brigands, the adventurers, the living, sun-browned faces, the laughing men who had moved mountains with their hands and their mirth and their courage, who had exploded frontiers and crowned a new world with their vigorous splendor? Like warriors, they had stood with their sunlit shields on the crest of the wilderness, and had shouted to the morning. But now the fogs were rolling over the crests and the warrior was only a ghost in the gathering and crepuscular gloom.

Jerome, though incredulous at first, saw that it was indeed deliberately planned. And he began to see by whom, and why.

An army conquered and laid open new territory. But, inevitably, it seemed, the army was followed by the dun-colored ranks of the ant exploiters, the ant stabilizers, the ant lovers of the status quo, the insects who instinctively hated vitality and noise and adventure and excitement. Some there were who called them the "builders." Yes, to some necessary extent, they were indeed builders. But they, most of them, lacked imagination. It was their predetermined intention to reduce life to mechanics. There must be order, they said. There must be order and stability, for the sake of the profits of the ant men. Civilization demanded a regulated society, administered, not by joy and hope and enthusiasm, but by drab laws. The living cities must be surrounded by walls. The wild gardens must be replaced by heaps of slag. Man must not be governed by the sun in his course, but by the clock. Laughter and delight, passion and adventure were immoral, because they contributed little to factories, banks, the building of stony and lightless cities, and profits.

Why were they so potent? How could they so easily reduce the joyous free human animal to a blind slave willingly wearing his chains? Was it because they wore such pious livery and were so persistent? Was it because they had such a knack of making money from the bright chaos of living men, and money was so powerful? Was it because they had succeeded in making money powerful and quietly and murderously created a society, in the dark of the moon, wherein only the dun man of wealth could survive—right behind the backs of men who were wiser but less ruthless, and who stood in the sun?

Jerome saw that an unending battle raged always between the gray man who lusted only for dark and lifeless power and the man who lusted only for life. He was fair enough to concede that the gray men had their necessary place in society. But they were not the only ones who counted. Just as wild and clamorous chaos was the inevitable atmosphere of the unrestrained adventurer, so death-in-life and oppressive misery and exploitation was the inevitable atmosphere of the unrestrained "builder." They each had a place in the world. But it was necessary that neither entirely usurp the place of the other. A balance was necessary. A middle-of-the-way was imperative, lest man become either a ranging beast or a shadowy evil plotting behind the doors of banks.

I am becoming quite enchanted with moderation, he thought to himself, with amusement. But it was without amusement that he hated the ant man, who had a ledger for a brain and was without joy or mercy or passion.

If the ant man had any passion at all, it was the passion for uniformity. If he could impose uniformity and its sister, docility, on other men, his own position was secure, and, in peace and quiet, he could go about filling his next-cells with profits. He knew he was no match for beauty and glory, and so he systematically set out to destroy them. In their presence, he was impotent and revealed in his ugliness, in his gelid mediocrity.

America, Jerome saw, had arrived at the age of machines.

He had not come to this almost psychic conclusion of himself, for he had never been aware of the intrusion of the machine either into his own life or into the lives of his friends. His social companions were singularly free from any suspicion that the pleasant handwrought world about them was threatened by any conglomeration of mechanics. If some new machine was heralded in the public press as guaranteed to do the work of one hundred men while guided by only one man, they would murmur: "How dull." One of Jerome's friends, however, blessed or cursed by a greater imagination than the others, had remarked, with concern: "If machines make many things quickly, then they will be able to make them cheaper,

168

and neither in wardrobe nor conveyance, in books nor furniture, will it be possible to distinguish between the gentleman and the plebeian."

The idea had struck Jerome, for no discernible reason. It stayed with him, and he found himself discussing it one agreeable evening with his friend, Mr. Jay Regan. Jerome had ridiculed the thought, but Mr. Regan's ambushed eyes had begun to sparkle. He had nodded his head.

He had said: "The complete industrialization of America has begun. The war has given it impetus. There may be some mysterious design in this. If America is to grow, to expand, over her vast territories, then the hand must be implemented by the machine, most enormously. It is a matter of life or death, for America. The machine is her private messiah; without it, she will remain a little spot of civilization in a mighty wilderness. Necessity is always the mother of invention, and the machine is America's necessity, and mechanics will, and must, become the very life of this country."

Jerome sardonically murmured his friends' remark: "How dull."

"Not dull!" Mr. Regan had exclaimed. "Most exciting! Think of the huge production of commodities, the cornering of world markets, the expansion, the wealth! We shall pass from an almost defenseless and ridiculous position in the family of nations to that of the most powerful, the leader, the dictator of policies. Through the machine."

Jerome had become much interested, in spite of himself. He had an inspiration. "But mechanics superimposed on life will murder the importance of the individual. He will be ruled by the clock, and I have always had a singular aversion to clocks."

Mr. Regan had considered it, with a deep brooding gleam in those hypnotic eyes of his. Then he had said, slowly: "Yes. I can see that. Subordinated to the machine, Americans may become lifeless and mechanical, servants, not masters, of mechanics. That must be combated by those with vision. Mankind tends to dullness, for it is easier than activity. Inertia is the natural state of all things, and is only disturbed by outer or inner convulsions or compulsions, mostly violent. It will be wise for future generations not to set up the golden machine and worship it, but to control it. It will be necessary to declare war on any system of life which subordinates the individual to the service of any one thing, or of any one idea, however seductive and easy it may seem. Uniformity in anything is death-dealing. There is nothing so uniform as a cemetery."

Old Jay was right, Jerome reflected. Mankind tended to uniformity. It saved individual effort and ardor. The masters took advantage of this natural trend in the nature of men. Man preferred to subordinate rather than to sublimate. For instance, the old Pilgrim religion of service to God had been superseded by the service to money, and it served the latter with equal, if not greater, dedication. The expansion of the morals and the dignity of men, so dearly beloved of the Founding Fathers, had been reduced to the expansion of individual power and the degradation of vast masses of mankind to the service of that power.

Jerome was filled with violent hatred. He saw Alfred's face before him. It was not that he cared so much about the degradation of his fellowmen to the service of the deathly lust of a few. But he felt his own dignity and potency as an individual man threatened by that lust. He felt himself thrown upon an anvil, to be beaten by the iron hammers and ruthlessness into a shape which would best serve those who were stronger than himself.

He marvelled at the ancient paradox that if a man is to save himself he must first save others. If he is to protect himself, he must build armor for his fellows.

In microcosm, then, what was happening in Riversend was happening all over America. Jerome enjoyed his hatred passionately, for the thing he hated had always been his hatred: uniformity, lightlessness, hopelessness, and the dull march of days. He had always avoided them, making his individual escape, and believing that his derision could keep the horror at bay. But now he saw that the horror was a spreading gray fog over America, and that he could not escape it. It was everywhere.

The three or four weeks during which Alfred was away became to Jerome a time of feverish activity and thought. He was at the Bank at eight in the morning. He demanded that all books be opened to him. He read ledger after ledger, report after report, endless files of correspondence. He now saw clearly that Alfred and many of his friends had refused to allow a manufacturer of farm implements to buy a stretch of farmland, on which they held mortgages, or owned outright, near the outskirts of Riversend, whereon the manufacturer had desired to build a factory. After Alfred's first refusal, the manufacturer had become eloquent in his pleading. The whole community would prosper, he had pointed out, beguilingly, not understanding his Alfred Lindsey in the least. The necessary raw materials were to be found in the country near Riversend, or in nearby Pennsylvania. The manufacturer outlined his plans to induce new workers to swell the population of the town; he would build a community of hideous shacks near the factory, which would give local carpenters and others considerable employment. (Jerome could see the shacks, in his mind: a mass of hideous ulcers on the faces of the lower slopes of the hills. Expansion, he had heard somewhere, inevitably resulted in such scars. He was wondering if this were true.)

Alfred, however, had permitted himself to foreclose a small farm on which the local railroad proposed to build its shops. But this did not account for the fact that the Widow Kingsley, General Tayntor, and a few others, had bought considerable land about the coveted acres desired by the manufacturer. Jerome read Alfred's bewildered queries to his friends, and their evasive answers. Jerome also read Alfred's grim and obscure reminder to all of them (couched in somewhat ambiguous phrases) that he, personally, owned the land on which the railroad *might* build a spur at some vague time. The ladies and gentlemen to whom these remarks had been addressed had replied very sweetly, and in phrases that imparted some innocent bewilderment. Why should they be interested in a railroad spur?

It was often that Jerome hardly arrived home in time for dinner. Even then, he brought along ledgers and records to read over in his own room. Mr. Jamison, in terror, had aided and abetted him. Mr. Jamison did not know what Mr. Jerome "was after." But he had a foreboding that it did not tend to peace and comfort in the Bank.

Dorothea, observing this incredible manifestation of energy on the part of her brother, only thought to herself, with sour and passionate indignation: "He is trying to undermine Alfred. He is trying to be important, to make a name for himself. He is trying to influence Papa, hypocritically, for really, he can have no genuine interest in the Bank." She could not know that, as usual, Jerome's interest was in himself.

Mr. Lindsey, for all his weariness and illness and retirement, knew that something was going on, but he did not speak of it to his son. He had long ago withdrawn from any active participation in the Bank, and often declared that he had no further interest in it. But he felt radiations of intense energy in the house, all emanating from Jerome, and while he was amazed and delighted, he was also uneasy. He wished Jerome would tell him what was on his mind. But he was both afraid and vaguely aware that Jerome would be uncommunicative. However, an idea of his own was forming in his own thoughts, for he, too, had begun to ask himself: "Is it really possible that Jerome is taking an interest? Has it really captured his imagination? If so, then I must consult——"

But the man he intended to consult was not Alfred.

In the meantime, he was entirely aware of the ledgers and books under Jerome's arm, and the fact that his son was gone all day.

Jim, Jerome's valet, was thunderstruck at the change in his master. Jerome was often gone when the little man arrived with the breakfast tray. Jerome was often gone before the household was astir. Jerome was becoming careless of the finer niceties of his dress. Jerome was drinking more than ever, and eating a great deal. He could be seen, at night, pacing the snowy walks around Hilltop, his head bent, brooding, little Charlie yapping unheeded at his heels. Jerome's color was rapidly improving, in spite of all these incredible goings-on, and he looked less fleshless. Moreover, there was a buoyancy about him now, a physical energy, quite different from the elegant languor and cynical detachment which had been his affectations.

When Jerome met his father at dinner, his conversation was always sprightly, but superficial. And Mr. Lindsey, as usual, was delighted and amused. He had a natural and cynical pessimism of his own, and this was echoed in Jerome's conversation. But now Mr. Lindsey saw that all this sprightliness had become but bright sparkles on deep water. He preferred, just now, that the water be not explored.

One evening, as they sat over their port near the library fire, Jerome said casually to his father: "Did you know that a feller by the name of King Munsey wants to build a factory in Riversend, to manufacture farm implements?"

Mr. Lindsey aroused himself feebly, frowned a little, and murmured: "Alfred did not—er—agree?"

"He did not. I gathered, from the correspondence, that he considered Mr. Munsey's offer to be compounded of rape, mayhem, the refutation of Alfred's belief in the divine right of the poor to starve peacefully, and a sinister desire on the manufacturer's part to paint the façades of the landed gentry's houses with soot. There was a great deal of real poesy in Alfred's lyrical prose to the unhappy industrialist. Riversend would remain 'unspoiled and undespoiled,' a 'tranquil spot in a turbulent State,' or Alfred would die gallantly in the attempt. In his noble excitement, he committed a few gross errors in grammar, and I detected a split infinitive or two. Which reveals his state of mind."

Mr. Lindsey sternly prevented himself from smiling. But he gazed at his son attentively. "How did you discover all this, my dear boy?"

"Curiosity, as well as love, laughs at locksmiths."

Mr. Lindsey was shocked. "You ought not to have done that to Alfred, Jerome! You had only to ask him——"

"How could I," Jerome pointed out, reasonably, "when I had no idea what I was looking for?"

But Mr. Lindsey was really perturbed. His New England conscience grumbled alarmingly. How unscrupulous Jerome was! And what an unpardonable thing to do! He said: "Well. What else did you discover, while you were laughing at locksmiths?"

CHAPTER NINETEEN

Mercifully unaware of what was transpiring during his absence, Alfred had quite recklessly extended his honeymoon from three to four weeks. Though he had a stern belief in the sanctity of the Sabbath, he unavoidably was compelled to violate the holy day and arrive home on the last Sunday in January.

A January thaw had set in, and all the countryside was awash with slush and sleet, howling with boisterous winds, and robbed of all color by the ashen skies. Dorothea was "indisposed," and young Philip was abed with influenza, and it was impossible for Mr. Lindsey to accompany the carriage down to the depot to gather up the bridal pair. Alfred believed that Jerome, at least, would be at the depot to greet him, and welcome him home. But Jerome was not there. As usual, he had blithely ignored all amenities which might cause him any inconvenience.

Besides (and of this Alfred was also mercifully ignorant) Jerome was working against time. He was completing his impertinent investigations into Alfred's affairs. He closed, and hid, the last ledgers just as the carriage, wallowing in slush, climbed up the winding driveway to the door. He looked down from his windows, passed his hands over his ruffled hair, and then, humming lightly, descended to the hall below.

There was quite a bustle going on. Jim, who had appointed himself overseer of the servants, was assisting in the disembarking of the luggage. It stood in the hallway in heaps, running with drops of water. Alfred and Amalie were standing before the fire, removing their gloves, while a maid gathered up their cloaks Alfred was murmuring something to his wife, and she had turned to him, smiling politely. It was her face that Jerome saw first, lit by the leaping firelight in the early afternoon gloom that filled the hall.

He saw that she was rather pale and quiet and abstracted, in her dark gray traveling dress with the black fur collar, dark gray bonnet and veil, and fur muff. She was very composed, and very still. So, thought Jerome, before revealing himself, the money has not been enough, then.

She discovered him first, glancing up as he descended the last stairs. She did not move, or smile. But he felt her strange alertness, her withdrawal.

Jerome greeted them affably, shook hands heartily with Alfred, then turned to Amalie. "Would it be in order," he asked, "to kiss the returning bride?"

She looked bored. "It would not be in order," she responded, and looked at the fire indifferently.

Alfred appeared smug and satisfied. He laid his hand possessively on Amalie's arm, as he asked Jerome about the family. He was genuinely concerned at the report of his uncle's increased illness, Dorothea's indisposition, and Philip's influenza. At the mention of Philip, Amalie looked up, alarmed, and addressed herself directly to Jerome.

"Is he very ill? I must go to him at once."

Alfred was pleased. "My love, I understand influenza is infectious. And from Jerome's report, the boy is being well cared for."

She moved impatiently. "How lonely he must be. Really, I must go to him. Besides, I have something for him which he especially wanted."

Alfred was more pleased than ever at this evidence of Amalie's genuine fondness for his poor son. "We shall both go up, my dear, after we have had tea."

But Amalie glanced at her reticule, and said: "If you will please excuse me, Alfred, I will go now. Do not wait tea for me, if it is inconvenient."

She turned away abruptly, and ran lightly up the stairs. Alfred watched her go, smiling, according to Jerome, quite fatuously. Jerome, in turn, watched his cousin with cynicism. "Let

174

us have tea in my father's room, Alfred," he said. "He suggested it himself. Dorothea will join us."

Amalie discovered that her breath was short and her heart beating heavily as she arrived at the upper landing. She also felt extremely ill, and had to pause in the warm dusk for a few moments. She heard her husband and Jerome giving last directions about the luggage below. The long hall before her was quiet in the Sunday gloom. She bit her lip and clenched her hands about her reticule. No, she thought, one mustn't think. Ever. She went down the hall to Philip's room, knocked gently, then entered.

Philip was lying on his pillows, coughing feebly. A book lay near his hand, but he had abandoned it in his sick weakness, and his face was turned away from the lighted lamp. He thought it was some maid bringing him his tea, and he lifted his head listlessly. But when he saw it was Amalie, he rasied himself on his pillows, his eyes sparkling with delight, and stretched out his hands to her with a cry.

She came to him at once, smiling, and took both his hands. She felt their tremulous heat and throb. She searched his feverish face, sighed, smiled again, and kissed him warmly. She sat beside him, still holding one of his hands. His fingers clung to hers almost desperately.

"Oh, Miss Amalie!" he exclaimed, hoarsely. "I have missed you so much. It was almost more than I could bear."

"And I have missed you, too, my darling," she said, in her full strong voice. "You received all my letters?"

"Yes. I have saved them all," he said, unable to look away from her. He laughed a little, feebly. "They were so amusing. Especially the stories about the fat old ladies who sat in the lobby of the hotel, and gossipped. Did they really say all those things?"

"Oh, and much more." They smiled into each other's eyes. Amalie gently straightened the boy's pillows after a moment, brought him a cool glass of water, and pushed the lamp a little farther away on the table. He submitted to her ministrations with a sigh of satisfaction.

"Do have tea with me here, Miss Amalie," he pleaded.

"If you wish it, darling," she said, sitting beside him once more. She sat and smiled while his wise young eyes studied her. "What is it, Philip?" she asked, after a long moment or two, when she saw that his thin face had clouded.

"You have changed, Miss Amalie," he murmured, and his

175

flush deepened. "You seem so tired, and pale."

She rubbed his hand strongly, and her smile was forced. "Well, it was a dreary journey home. And our four weeks were very festive. I am really just a country girl at heart."

He said an odd thing then, on strange impulse: "Miss Amalie, I do hope Papa understands you!"

She stared at him, and was silent. Then she laughed. "How curious of you to say that, Philip! Your papa is very good to me, and is the best possible husband."

But he murmured: "Miss Amalie, tell me you are happy."

She laughed again. "Philip, don't you know that happiness means getting what you want? I have what I have always wanted. So, I must be happy." She paused. "Except for one thing, dear. Will you call me Mama, now?"

He gazed at her with such incredible love that she had to kiss him again. She laid her head beside him on the pillows. Her hands clung to his. The boy turned to her as one turns to deep rest and surcease from pain.

She lifted her head finally. Her eyes were moist with tears. But with much briskness and archness she opened her bag and produced a small box covered with gold-colored velvet. She held it high for Philip to see. "You have no idea what this is!" she cried. "But you must guess. I will allow you three guesses, only."

His eyes sparkled with young anticipation. "A ring! A set of cufflinks! Oh—Mama, I can't think! Please let me see it!"

She put the box into his hands, and he raised himself on his pillows. His fingers shook as he opened the box, while she watched him, smiling. Then he gave a loud cry of delight. Revealed on white velvet was a beautiful gold watch, a repeater. Moreover, the face showed the phases of the moon, the days of the week, the months of the year. While he held it, dazed and awed, the tiny golden bell inside sounded the quarter hour on a series of fairy notes. He could not speak. He could only raise his eyes slowly and look at Amalie with an expression of ecstasy.

"Look at the back, Philip," she whispered.

He turned it over, almost stupidly, so great was his joy. There was some elegant engraving on the smooth gold: "To Philip from his loving mother, January 29, 1869."

The boy read the inscription; then, with touching simplicity, he put his parched lips to it. He trembled. Tears ran down his cheeks. Amalie felt a quivering pang in her breast. She caught Philip in her arms and held him to her, her face pressed strongly to the top of his head. "My dear, my love, my darling," she whispered.

When the maid brought Philip's tea, she informed Amalie that the gentlemen were awaiting her. But Amalie, expressing her regrets, ordered that tea be brought for her in Philip's room.

Amalie fastened the emerald earrings carefully in her ears. She looked into her mirror. She saw her pale face, framed in its glistening waves of black hair, her long pale neck rising from the lace collar of her green velvet gown. She reached into the depths of a drawer, withdrew a scrap of red flannel, moistened it at her lips, and rubbed the flannel quickly and deftly on her cheeks. She was rewarded by a faint glow, which, however, only increased the dark hollowness of her violet eyes. She then rubbed her lips quickly, replaced the flannel in her drawer. She stood away from the candle-lighted mirror and carefully studied her slender firm figure. Her gown, with its heavy drapes and folds, was becoming and demure, yet she mysteriously imparted to it a kind of drama and excitement.

The dim, fire-lit room behind her was warm and still. Alfred was completing his evening dressing in the small room adjoining. Amalie turned from the mirror and looked long and slowly at the room. It was large, and had been Alfred's alone. The great four-poster bed lay smoothly under its white silk quilt. The Turkey-red carpet was thick and deep. The large mahogany chairs, covered with dark blue or red plush or damask, were touched fretfully but quietly by the rosy streamers from the hearth. A desk of rosewood stood between the windows, which were framed in crimson velvet, heavy with gold fringe. Two chairs, covered with dull tapestry, and garnished with footstools, stood on each side of the marble fireplace. The mirrored wardrobe flung back firelight and candlelight in cosy gleams. Amalie's dressing-table, which had been Jerome's mother's, sparkled with cut glass and gilt. Amalie's perfume mingled with the warm fresh smell of the room, which was compounded of wax and soap and fire. There was a bouquet of roses on a table near one of the chairs by the hearth, and it added its lovely and languorous fragrance to the others.

Alfred was humming tonelessly behind the closed door of the dressing-room. The sleet had turned to a lashing rain. Amalie went to the windows and pushed aside the draperies. She could see nothing, not even a twinkling light from the valley. She saw only the reflection of her tired still face on the dark glass. She started back, suddenly, then smiled at her nervousness. There had been a thin tapping at the window, but now she identified it as the bare twigs of a tree which stood just outside. She stood and listened to the tapping and the restless wind and rain. She heard nothing else but these, and Alfred's humming. The house had settled down to a pre-dinner hush.

This is how it would always be, these quiet relentless evenings, the long dull relentless days. But she had known it before, for weeks. However, that had been prior to the wedding, when a certain excitement had pervaded the house. Now she was part of this house, its massive stillness, its inexorable routine, its changelessness. She would watch the changing seasons, but she, herself, would not change, except to grow older, more quiet, like the others. Yes, she was part of this house. She was part of—Alfred.

Her hands tightened on the draperies, and a sick wave of heat ran over her flesh. Memories of the last four weeks flashed through her mind. She had been everything that Alfred had desired; she had been much admired at the fine hotel at which they had stayed. She thought of the nights she had endured. Endured. She could not free herself from the thought. She said to herself: What a fool I was, to deceive myself that his solid quiet and composure extended to—all things! How jejune she had been, she who had prided herself on not possessing any illusions at all, who had congratulated herself that she was immune to shock, disgust, fear, dread. She had told herself, in her fatuous ignorance, that she was a worldly woman who had made a bargain, and that passion was the least important of the things she would have to endure to gain that which was so vastly more important.

I knew everything, and I knew nothing, she thought, with profound and loathing ridicule of herself. She looked back at the self before the marriage, and laughed aloud at the spectacle of the disingenuous and open-eyed girl she had believed that self to be. What a smirking and odious imbecile, making her "bargain"! She would give so-and-so for so-and-so, all extremely matter-of-fact, and undeluded.

But she had known nothing of Alfred. She had known nothing of passion. For all her boldness and her cynical conversation, she had been as inexperienced and as innocent as any of the simpering young ladies she had despised. She had looked at men openly, had laughed and joked with them, had flirted with them outrageously, and without reticence—and had known nothing whatsoever about them.

Her sick terror and loathing increased. But she fixed her thoughts decisively on Alfred's virtues, his truly deep love for her, the comfort and security he had given her with his name. And that name, she reminded herself, was an honorable and a good one. He had given her sanctuary and peace, the strong walls of this house, a lofty position. She glanced at the emeralds in the bracelet on her wrist, the flashing diamond on her finger.

She was a wife, protected and unthreatened. Never again for her terror of hunger, the constant threat of miserable and ugly days, the hideous existence of the poor and the undefended. No longer, for her, that precarious life of the unprotected woman, the dread of the years, the cold stark bedrooms of the moneyless, the dirt of the hopeless. The menace had retreated from her forever, and all the ugliness and pain and uncertainty. Fortune had given her this face, and this figure, and with them she had purchased all the enviable things she had dreamed of, and had desired, while she had lain under ragged blankets or had eaten the drab meals of poverty.

She thought: It ought not to be so for women, who are human beings in a world of humanity. We ought not to be so undefended, so helpless. We ought not to have to wonder if our faces and our bodies are of sufficient pleasantness to attract security and food and shelter to us, in the form of a man. This is a refutation of our dignity as part of humanity, a degradation of our deepest instincts, a denial of our right to live. Have we not hearts that beat, and blood that flows, and emotions that are subject to the same laws and the same tides and instincts that govern men? Women are the daughters of men; they share the identical passions and longings and hopes that are a part of their fathers. Yet, we are debased to mere chattels, relegated to the ranks of the sub-human, dependent on the whims of the masters, denied the right to dispose of our own lives and climb to any heights we desire, to live and laugh in self-made security and dignity. We must please—or we do not eat, or, if we eat, we eat the bread of charity or of menial work. We cannot choose the men with whom we must lie, and to whom we must submit, whether in indifference or in loathing or in terror.

A sudden hot rage engulfed her. She closed her hand about her bracelet, as if to wrench it off. And then she said to herself: He is good, he is kind, he is almost always gentle, except—— I can offer him no reproach. It is I who am the fool. But there is no choice for women but folly.

She looked at herself in the mirror again, and deliberately

stroked the velvet of her gown. She began to smile. I am being dramatic, she thought, over her tumultuous misery. I have made a most excellent bargain. I am even fond of him. I have gained more than he has, and must make the greater concession. For what he has given me, I have only to please. Her smile became bitter.

She heard soft footsteps in the hall outside, passing her door. And then, without any warning at all, her heart bounded up in her breast and all her flesh trembled and quaked. She stood rigid, while the footsteps retreated. Even after they had gone completely, she stood like that, one hand pressed hard on her dressing table, her face turned to the door.

So Alfred found her, coming out of the dressing-room. He thought she was listening. He stopped, and listened, too. But he heard nothing. He saw her green-clad figure leaning against the dressing-table, her white and beautiful profile. He smiled contentedly. Then he frowned a little.

"My love," he said, "is not that dress just a trifle—extreme?"

She started, then turned slowly towards him. But she made herself smile. "Extreme?" she asked, glancing at the mirror. "I think not. It has such a high neck, and long sleeves." Her own words wearied her; she had had to repeat them so often these past weeks.

Alfred considered her acutely. The gown was indeed quite respectable, with its conservative bodice trimmed with crystal buttons, its modest bustle and flowing lines and white lace collar and cuffs. He was puzzled, as usual. Such a gown on Dorothea would have appeared drab and refined and nondescript. Yet, his wife gave it a most curious air, almost theatrical. It was unfortunate that Alfred did not recognize style when he saw it. He thought it "unrefined."

He studied her face and her hair. A faint sharp thrill ran through him. But he held his mind sternly to his consideration of her. Her hair was not twirled and curled and twisted in an extreme dress. Its bright black waves were very sleek, the chignon neat and controlled. But still, that hair was not demure and meek and matronly. And her face was too vivid, perhaps, too seeking, too alive. He did not think of it in these terms; he thought only that it lacked reticence and decorousness.

"You are charming, my love," he said, and drew her to him and kissed her cheek with a properly husbandlike dignity. "But those emerald earrings: I confess they give you a rather bold air. Would you please me, and remove them?"

She withdrew herself from his arms, trying to control the

180

rigidity of her flesh. Without a word, she removed the jewelry. Alfred watched, pleased. "There, that is much better. We have a certain decorum to uphold, in Riversend."

"Are we to have guests tonight?" she asked indifferently, putting the jewlery in its padded box.

"No. I think not. There will be only Uncle William and ourselves for late dinner. The weather is too inclement for Sunday visitors." He examined his tall strong figure in the wardrobe mirrors. "Jerome, I understand, will not be here. He is dining with General Tayntor tonight." He smiled. "I was given more than a hint by Dorothea that a match is in the making there. With Miss Sally."

He did not see how still Amalie's hands had become on the jewelry box. He did not see the whiteness of her knuckles, the sudden dropping of her head. He only heard her voice: "Miss Sally? The little girl with the big black eyes?"

"Yes. A lovely child, and very lively. A trifle too lively, perhaps. But with a considerable fortune. If it is true, and I pray it is, Jerome has done excellently for himself."

Amalie closed the drawer. She said, in her strangely dull voice: "Will they live here, also?"

Alfred adjusted his cravat. His face was serious. "Yes. I believe so. The house is large enough. Besides, I always remember that he is, after all, Uncle William's son, and has prior claims." He paused. "Though I am given to understand that the house will be mine, eventually. However, even under those conditions, Jerome's wishes must be considered."

Amalie said, almost inaudibly: "Alfred, cannot we leave here? Cannot we have a home of our own, alone? Just you, and I, and Philip? I should not care if it were less grand. Only so we can be alone."

Alfred was startled, then tremendously pleased. He came to his wife and took her in his arms again, and kissed her on the mouth with sudden passion. Then he held her off from him and regarded her with delight. Her lips were parched and white, even under the stain of the flannel. He said: "Would you really like that, my darling?"

"Yes," she said, faintly.

He put his hand on the back of her head and pressed her face into his shoulder. He said, in a low voice: "It would please me more than anything else, my dearest. But we must subordinate our own wishes. There is Uncle William to consider."

She stood quietly in the circle of his big arms and tried to restrain the violence of her old repulsion at the sound of his

181

"sanctimonious" and "consciously upright sentiments." With what derision she had heard them so often before, and with what cynical contempt! She had detested them as hypocrisy, the righteous dissimulation of complete egotism.

And then, in the very midst of her derision and scorn, it came to her with passionate amazement and self-hatred and humility that she had been wrong. Alfred had spoken honestly, partly out of a narrow but profound depth of honor and partly out of stern justice. If he saw that injustice might be closing in upon him, he was reminding himself resolutely that he had been accorded a great deal and had no right to ask more. If his natural human bitterness taunted him, he told himself that it was only fair that Mr. Lindsey's real son should be first in his favor. Alfred was a realist, then, even against himself, and he accepted the inevitable, if not without heart-burnings, at least with understanding. If he lacked flamboyant imagination and subtlety, and lived inexorably in the small tight house of his nature, that house was clean and bright with integrity.

Amalie stood within his arms, and hated herself, and felt herself to be soiled and mean and sordid beyond the endurance of her vanity. She lifted her head and said, with involuntary vehemence: "It is not fair! No one considers you! You are so good, Alfred, so very, very good! Yet that goodness means nothing, now that a dissolute and dishonorable man has returned to the house you have earned, and to enjoy the work that you have done!"

He looked down at her, dumfounded, and saw the purplish blaze of her infuriated eyes. For an instant, and an instant only, she in turn saw the pale hazel of his own eyes flash with uncontrollable and responsive anger and human revolt. She felt the tightening of his arms about her, as if in wrathful gratitude and despairing acknowledgment of her sympathy.

Then he was putting her aside quietly, and saying, even more quietly: "Amalie, my dear, you do not understand. Whatever I have done is only a fair exchange for what Uncle William has done for me. He took me in when there was no hope for me, and gave me his fatherhood in adoption and opened doors for me which I might never have entered by myself. My father was not fond of me, but Uncle William has given me affection and consideration and a home. I can never repay him.

"I cannot see that a reasonable man is justified in demanding more when so much has been given him." He paused. He fixed his eyes steadily upon hers with grave penetration. "I am no hypocrite, and I will not say that Jerome's return, and his expressed desire to enter the Bank, has not been a shock to me. For several days I was considerably—tormented. For several days I hoped it was only a whim. When I saw it was not, I hated him."

Now Alfred smiled, but it was a sad and curiously defenseless smile, and she knew, instinctively, that he was telling her things he would never have told another, and with a sense of release and loving gratitude to her that he could so tell them.

"You see, I am not so good. I am really not good at all. I hate Jerome. I hate him, in spite of the fact that I know Uncle William could not really do anything but what he is doing. I think, in my heart, that I have always hated Jerome, because he is so much cleverer than I, and inspires so much more admiration and affection. There is something about him which draws others to him. You see, my darling, I have always been so lonely."

He took her hand, and she saw him through a haze of tears. He led her to the bed, and he sat down beside her, still holding her hand. But he did not look at her; he looked into space, and his expression was very sad and heavy and quite bitter.

"They say such men as Jerome are 'enchanting' or 'fascinating,' and imply that these men deserve the fondness or admiration they excite, by reason of some peculiar inherent virtue. They believe that fondness and admiration are only the just dues of such as Jerome. Perversely, they believe that such as I neither desire affection, nor miss it. We are 'remote' or 'uninteresting' to our lukewarm friends, or repellent to our enemies. They do not know how lonely we are, and how we long, with real passion, for gentleness and understanding."

He glanced at her now and smiled ruefully. "I am afraid I am speaking in quite detestable self-pity or sentimentality, and I know you despise such things."

Her tears were thicker, and she gazed at him with speechless astonishment and deeper humility. He was not so unimaginative then, not so insensitive as she had thought, and she hated herself afresh. He understood so many things with silent perception, like life stirring unseen and unsuspected in the deep earth. Her hand tightened about his.

"Do not have any illusions about me, Amalie," he was saying, with extreme quietness. "I am not a resigned man by nature, nor really a good one. My thoughts are uncharitable and I am ambitious. And is there not a saying that ambitious men are dangerous? Yes. I am dangerous. And I hate Jerome. I have always hated him. Perhaps I am envious, though I see nothing attractive in the life he has led, or in what he is. Perhaps my envy springs from my own realization that there is nothing in me which inspires the admiration and fondness which follow him naturally. But do not believe I am humble. I know I am the better man, and I intend that others shall recognize that also. You see, now, that I am not kind or forbearing, though I try to understand and try to be just."

He laughed abruptly. "It is hard to reconcile instinct with reason."

She thought to herself: "He is speaking to me as he has never spoken to anyone else, because he trusts me and loves me. Perhaps he has never spoken so, even to himself.

And again she was passionately humble, overwhelmingly touched with anger for him, and compassion. So strong were her feelings that she felt that she loved him, and her loyalty, awakened now, sprang up in full and vigorous armor.

She said, and her voice shook: "I never really knew you, Alfred."

He raised her hand to his lips, and she looked at his strong round head, and smiled through her tears. She said to herself: I will do all I can. I will make myself what he wishes. I will devote myself to him. He must never know what I have been thinking these past weeks. How was it possible that I was so blind and so stupid and so greedy? How can I ever repay him?

She felt his lips on her hand, and they did not make her flesh grow rigid as they had done before. Her compassion and tenderness were like a warm fire in her heart. His narrowness of concept, his lack of imagination, his inflexibility, his obtuseness now seemed to her the admirable marks of a man of extreme integrity and strength.

The bell sounded softly through the warm stillness of the house, and they rose together, and went down the stairway, hand in hand, as they had never gone before.

CHAPTER TWENTY

"You are a dog, sir!" cried Mehitabel Kingsley, with an uproarious laugh, after Jerome's somewhat lewd remark.

They had been conversing, with regrettable candor, of Alfred and Amalie. Mehitabel had expressed her opinion of the inability of a fascinating gentleman such as Jerome to seduce his cousin's wife. The widow belonged to a lustier generation, when the influence of Queen Victoria had not been so insistently felt in England and America, and her conversation had an old-fashioned bawdiness about it which entranced and amused Jerome, and did not deceive him in the least.

For, paradoxically, he understood that both male and female rakes had a deep underlying Puritanism in them, and that, contrary to opinion, they were much less tolerant of infractions of the moral code than those whose boots had never been muddied. So he was well aware that Mehitabel was talking shockingly for her own amusement and his own diversion. It was one thing for a man to seduce a virgin, and quite another thing for him to seduce a matron, especially in his own house. Perhaps it was a perverted sense of honor in them, or a robust health. Therefore, even while Mehitabel bawdily outlined possible strategy for him in the seduction of Amalie, no one, he suspected, would have been more censorious and more merciless than Mehitabel if he had acted upon that strategy.

He could not refrain from saying, with a smile: "Metty, you are talking through your bonnet."

This made her laugh more raucously than ever, her merriment booming through her house. With one of her old-fashioned gestures, she rapped him smartly on the knuckles and leered at him. She ordered him to pour fresh whiskey and soda for them both.

"But seriously," she said, "I am disappointed in you. I had hoped you and that glorious wench would have eloped on the wedding night. I had my pastor in readiness. Have you lost your magic, Jerome?"

"I am afraid I have. The lady would have nothing of me."

They were sitting in the parlor of Mehitabel's huge, ugly and old-fashioned house in the suburbs of Riversend. Mehitabel's "love" for humanity did not extend to any desire to have neighbors. "I'll choose my own times to love 'em," she often said. So her six acres of land were firmly enclosed in a tall red-brick wall, lavishly sprinkled, at the top, with murderous broken glass. She also had three savage dogs who ranged constantly through the grounds, though she would not allow them near the house, or in her presence, for she had an aversion to the species. (Her love was cats, of which she had many. "They are so damned evil, and hate everybody," she would remark.) In the very center of her grounds, her house had been built fifty years ago, when she had been a bride. Tall, frowning, gloomy, it was of red brick, with deep piazzas and thin, high windows heavily draped. She had not cared for the wide expansiveness of Georgian architecture. "Too exposed," she had said. So her house was built like a fortress, with round turrets like battlements, behind which it was easy to imagine alert marksmen. Further, she had surrounded it with heavy dark trees, so that a watery green gloom invaded all the rooms even on the brightest day.

But she had immense fireplaces, filled with huge burning logs. She did not like lamps, but preferred candlelight, so heavy brass and silver candelabra stood on every table, and there were sconces on the panelled walls. All the floors, even those in the bedrooms, were of tile, partially covered with Aubusson rugs, and her furniture, inherited from her ancestors, was of beautiful proportions and dark shining finish. Her own tester bed, she alleged, had once been occupied by George Washington. "Quite alone," she had added, ruefully. She paid her servants well; otherwise, because of her humors, she would have been left servantless. However, though quite well aware of this, she often denounced those who paid their servants much less. "No wonder the poor devils steal," she would say, vigorously, carefully locking up her own valuables.

She listened avidly, today, to Jerome's account of the apparent devotion which Amalie lavished on Alfred. She was incredulous. "How could she? The man is a fool, an ox!" Mehitabel exclaimed. Jerome smiled.

He said, casually, sipping his whiskey: "When the children begin to appear, it might be time for me to leave my father's house. Especially if I desire to marry, myself. I have thought of buying some land beyond the east road."

He watched her closely, while not appearing to do so. He saw furtive surprise, rumination, uncertainty, on her huge and wickedly ugly face. He saw her thrust out her bulldog's jaw reflectively, and knew that her tiny black eyes were fixed sharply upon him. He saw the struggle between her own voracity and her fondness for him.

She said, with hypocritical thoughtfulness: "I don't know. That is not the best of sections." She was silent, staring at him. Apparently, however, her fondness for him won over her own greed. "I've thought of buying some land there, myself." She paused. He regarded her fondly, turning upon her his strongest measure of filial charm and interest. That apparently settled her, overcame her rapacity. She leaned forward and again tapped his hand with her black-lace fan and assumed a mysterious expression. "On second thought, my love, buy that land, and buy it quickly. Do not delay."

186

"No?" he said artlessly. "Why not?"

A sluggish color spread over her coarse skin. "Trust me, Jerome. Buy that land. Tomorrow, if possible. I have my reasons, of which I cannot tell you now. You want money, eh? Who doesn't? So, buy that land. Let it—lie fallow for a while."

Now that her greed was entirely thrust into the background by her affection for him, she was all animation.

"I have very little money," he said, regretfully. "Two thousand dollars in all. Of course, I could take an option on the land—— However, as you have said, that is not the best of sections on which to build."

But her determination made her quite excited. "Damn building! Take my advice. Buy that land. Two thousand dollars?" She plucked at her enormous fat underlip, frowned, again engaged in a struggle. "Enough for an option. For about six months." She nodded her head. "Who knows what might happen in six months?" She sighed. "If they will not permit an option, come to me. I will advance you the money, without interest."

She brightened. "Perhaps you will not need it. When are you going to marry Sally Tayntor?"

He put down his glass carefully. "Isn't that a little sudden?"

"Fiddlesticks. The girl is dying to sleep with you. But marry her first. The General is all for it; he has told me so himself. In fact, he has persuaded himself that you have already spoken for her. That is what you get for being so charmingly evasive and compliant. If you don't speak for the girl, the General is not going to love you any more."

"I am not a fortune hunter," said Jerome, with a stern air. "When I have some money of my own, that will be the time to speak of marrying."

"Oh——!" cried the widow. "Do not try to come over me with your sanctimonious lies, Jerome Lindsey! The girl, and her father, would snap you up in a moment, and you know it. And you are no fine gentleman of honor, and you need not pretend you are. One hundred thousand dollars as a dowry does not make you recoil delicately. There is something else. It ain't your cousin's wife, is it, eh?" She spoke the last with unexpected loud sharpness.

So, thought Jerome, the darling old hag can be very dangerous. He regarded her with eyes that deliberately danced. But she was not amused.

"That's all nonsense!" she ejaculated. "No use pursuing a fox that's already been caught. No profit in that, for you. Besides, it's nasty, and nastiness never advanced a man's fortunes. You want to advance your fortunes?" She stared at him bellicosely. He nodded. She pushed herself back in her chair, her great black belly glimmering in the candlelight. "Good. Time for you to mend your fences. No use using black dye on those gray hairs of yours. People always know. Go after Sally."

"Yet, you were just advising me how I could induce Amalie to sleep with me," he said, laughing.

"Oh, that was just an exercise in ribaldry! If you were a rich man, it would be different. But naughtiness is the province of the economically independent. It is no diversion for an insecure man."

He nodded in serious agreement, and her alarm subsided. She made him promise to take an option on the discussed land, and exhorted him again to come to her for any other money. "Without interest," she repeated sadly. She became interested in the Bank, and showed gratification when she saw his enthusiasm.

"It ain't all hypocrisy with you," she observed, shrewdly. "You like the damn place. It ain't just a scheme to induce your papa to look speculatively at you, is it? No, I thought so. We need new blood in Riversend."

The widow fanned herself vigorously. "Remember, don't forget about that option. Tomorrow. Do it secret. Don't tell a soul. Not even the General. Keep your mouth shut. Don't let anybody guess what you're about. It can be done. I know."

She added: "And leave that wench alone. You say, yourself, she is all devotion to Alfred. Let them be. All women are the same in the dark anyway. And from what I've seen of the girl lately, she's lost her style. Drab clothes. Creeps about like a shadow. She's Mrs. Alfred Lindsey now, and she's bright enough to remember it. Look at Sally: there's a girl with vivacity and distinction. Devoted to you, too. One hundred thousand dollars. If you knew what I know, you would realize that that money will come in handy." She hesitated, then grinned. "I'll give you my George Washington bed. About time it was slept in, double."

PART TWO

CHAPTER TWENTY-ONE

In February, Mr. Lindsey suffered a heart seizure which almost ended his life. He survived, but so painfully, and with such exhaustion, that those who loved him could not consider his escape from death merciful.

Dorothea and Amalie, assisted by one intelligent maid, nursed him. For several days after the attack, his son and nephew did not go to the Bank even for an hour or two, as the physician had warned them that the patient might die at any moment. If he survived the first week, the physician informed them, his chances for life were increased enormously.

A desperate and aching quiet settled over Hilltop. Jim, lest Charlie, the dog, might disturb that quiet by a single bark, kept the little animal with him on the third floor, or in the stables. Philip ceased his piano practice and stole about the house like a small deformed ghost with a white and suffering face. Even Amalie seemed to have forgotten the boy. He understood, but the loss of his two friends, Mr. Lindsey, and his new stepmother, filled him with grief and overpowering loneliness. He haunted the stables, where Jim and the other men were kind to him, but he did not find their conversation amusing or informative. He did not care for horses, and most of the talk centered about those uninteresting animals. Jim was certain that one of the mares had foaled a prospect for the racetrack, and he vehemently argued on the subject with the more cynical stableboys, pointing out the foal's amazing features. Philip's presence made them uneasy, though they tried to be deferentially kind to him. But Philip, whose life had been spent with books and music, and in a large unchanging solitude, finally found Jim and the others insupportable.

His father had always been affectionate with him, but the sensitive boy had early understood that he was a profound disappointment to Alfred, and he did not blame his father in the least. In fact, he was sorry for Alfred, and painfully sympathetic. He knew that Alfred cared little for books, and knew nothing of music, in spite of his labored efforts to appear intelligent when either was timidly discussed by Philip.

Mr. Lindsey had always been the boy's friend, in a gentle and tender fashion, but Philip had known, even from early childhood, that Mr. Lindsey did not particularly care for the young, and that he found their presence tedious in spite of his kindness and air of interest. Only in Amalie had Philip discovered a true and interested friend, and she was now temporarily lost to him. As for Jerome, that gentleman was so stricken by the illness of his father that it appeared he was not conscious of the existence of anyone else. He passed Philip in the rooms and corridors as if the boy were made of air and had no reality. This was true of Alfred, also, whose pallor gleamed in the dusk whenever Philip encountered him.

The whole household was disordered. Dorothea, who out of duty and some fondness had always seen to the comfort of Philip, was now engrossed in her ministrations to her father. To make less work for the servants in these days, few of the family appeared at meals, and it was finally decided that trays in their rooms would be less arduous than the elaborate setting of the dining-room table. So Philip ate his solitary dinners and breakfast in his room, with only his loneliness for company, and his books. His tutor arrived in the morning, and they went together to the library, and then, after the tutor's departure, the long and empty day followed. The boy tried to enliven his life by walks, but the month was raging with sleet and wind, and he dared not exert himself or expose himself after his influenza. So he sat alone, in silence, listening to the muffled striking of the clock in the hall, hearing the whispers of the servants, catching a muted footstep going in or out of the sickroom.

Dorothea acquired a reluctant respect for her sister-in-law in these sad days. For Amalie had devoted herself almost with fanaticism to the care of Mr. Lindsey. Nothing was too hard, too laborious, too unpleasant, to do for him. It was she who lifted his tormented body in her arms while Dorothea or a maid adjusted his bedding. It was she who seemed tireless and insisted upon the night vigil. The dim light in the window was like a faint yellow moon through the dark hours, expiring only when the red and angry sun stared sullenly and briefly through the rolling clouds.

Jerome, unable to sleep, often walked about the grounds. Very often, he would stand for a long time beneath his father's window and watch the silent shadow of Amalie moving between him and the lamp. He waited for that shadow; he saw the blurred outline of her head, her firm breasts, her slender waist. Sometimes, when the dawn came up, he saw her pale face, briefly, staring through the window at the sky, just before she pulled the draperies closed. She never glanced down, but stood only for a moment or two, the dull red light of the rising sun glowing in the sockets of her sunken eyes, or lying, an instant or two, on her white cheek. But long after she had disappeared, Jerome stood there, huddled in his greatcoat, watching the windows.

After ten o'clock, Jerome and Alfred were permitted to enter the sickroom for a silent few minutes with Mr. Lindsey. Dorothea would be in charge then, gaunt and more grim than ever, rocking by the fire over her knitting, or adjusting something in the room. Mr. Lindsey, sleeping or only half-conscious, would lie high on his pillows, breathing with choking and sighing sounds. He gave no sign that he was aware of the two men standing at the foot of his bed. Amalie had retired to her room, to sleep fitfully until evening.

Alfred often stole into the bedroom he shared with his wife, creeping in soundlessly. He would stand beside the bed, looking down at Amalie's exhausted and haggard face, lost in sleep, and all the passion and love he had for her stood reverently and gratefully in his tired eyes. Sometimes she would murmur faintly and he would bend over her hopefully, wishing that she might speak his name. But the sound was blurred, full of weariness. When she would awaken at evening, on the entry of a maid with a tray for herself and Alfred, she would find that he had filled a vase on the bed table with fresh roses. She was so weary that she could not keep the tears from her eyes, and when he entered the room she would hold out her arms to him speechlessly and sigh when he held her strongly to him, as if seeking a measure of his own reassuring

191

strength to sustain her. That short hour or two they had alone was infinitely sweet to both of them, though they could speak of nothing but the sick man. Then Amalie must dress and take up her duties again, and Alfred would not be able to talk to her until the next night.

In later years he never forgot those hours, and never was he able to quell the leaping of his heart and the mingled sorrow and suffering that came with remembrance.

Mr. Lindsey survived the crucial week. On the tenth day, he smiled at Amalie during the night and whispered a word of gratitude. On the eleventh day, Alfred and Jerome returned to the Bank. For the first, and the last, time in many years they felt a friendship for each other, born of their mutual anxiety and fear. They talked together with more ease and understanding, and briefly, at least, there was accord between them.

After two weeks, visitors were allowed to come to Hilltop and drink tea while they inquired after Mr. Lindsey's health. After three weeks, the General and Mrs. Kingsley were permitted to see the sick man, smile at him, and say a word or two. But it was not until six weeks had passed that Amalie felt that she need not spend the night with Mr. Lindsey, and she and Dorothea divided between them the daylight hours of care.

Dorothea, her brother, Philip, Amalie and Alfred now met at dinner. But their conversation was desultory, rising out of deep pits of weariness, and was punctuated by long and brooding silences. Alfred began to inquire kindly of his son what he was doing these days, and Philip's soft and timid voice would answer. Amalie began to look at Philip with her old tenderness and concern and expressed her regret that he had had to abandon his music. Dorothea questioned him rigorously about his meals, his walks, and his lessons. He knew they were all being kind, but that he was really far from their thoughts. Even Jerome was abstracted, eating in preoccupation. No one, not even Dorothea, saw how he glanced at Amalie, and what tight lines sprang out about his pale mouth as he studied her furtively.

Mr. Lindsey grew stronger as March came in with its traditional roar. But a dark apathy had fallen on his family, the aftermath of terror and devotion and work. He became quite cheerful and joked about his indestructibility, but their responding cheer was forced. He felt something exhaustedly restless and depressed in the house, but convinced himself that this was his imagination.

Dorothea read to him, but he soon put a stop to this. Her harsh and monotonous voice tired him. But Amalie's voice, deep and clear and flexible, soothed him, and he would listen to her for hours. He would watch her with deep fondness, the sight of her face in the firelight soothing and sweet to him.

One day he said: "My dear, do come here for a moment." She put aside the book and smilingly approached the bed. He looked up at her with understanding silence and regret. "You are very thin and pale, my love," he said. "I have been too much for you, I am afraid."

"No, Uncle William. You are never too much for anyone," she answered gently. She saw his hand groping for hers, and took it. Her fingers were warm and strong.

"Tell me," he said, "that you are happy, love."

She smiled down at him. "Indeed I am, now that you are getting so well."

But he sighed and released her hand. Still looking at her, he said: "You must promise me to walk in the air, now, and take rides. Otherwise I shall reproach myself that you are so thin and pale. You look quite haunted, my poor child."

"I promise," she said, comfortingly.

It was a Sunday afternoon, and upon Mr. Lindsey's insistence, she left him for an hour or two. She did not wish to speak to anyone, for a deep melancholy had come over her. She put on the sealskin jacket which Alfred had bought for her in Saratoga, and her heavy gown of brown wool, and her fur-trimmed bonnet. She thrust her hands into her muff and stole downstairs.

She passed the library. Alfred, overcome with weariness, had fallen asleep in a chair before the fire. Philip was doing his lessons silently under the light of one lamp nearby. Dorothea was sleeping in her room. Jerome was nowhere to be seen. Amalie, not wishing to speak to anyone, crept out of the house, closing the door noiselessly behind her.

It was five o'clock. The snow had retreated to a white line against the brick walls of the garden, and lay in leprous patches on the hillside. The trees were still bare, massed together in a tangled thicket about the house. But the sky was a pure ultramarine, profound and deep, and the evening star rose in it like a point of silver flame.

Amalie walked slowly down the slope to the copse of pines where she had stood with Jerome on that December night before her marriage. She could see the countryside lying below her, cupped in dark hills. She saw the glint of a distant dark-blue stream, winding down one of the western hills. Above those hills burned a lake of dull crimson fire, streaked with sea-green and dimmed gold. The earth was profoundly still, but a strange, strong promise exhaled from it, like a wide and welling breath. For the first time she heard the far twittering of birds, restlessly flying from one bare tree to another. Nothing revealed the promise that stirred deep in the ground and in the pure chill air, but Amalie felt it like a tide rising from the wet and muddy land, still devoid of color and movement. The earth was murmuring in its heart. Amalie saw the huge lacework of a distant poplar outlined against the poignant clarity of the ultramarine sky, and she stood for a moment and looked at it with tears in her eyes.

She reached the copse of pines. They dripped with moisture. The tips of their fronds were turning a brighter green. She pushed through them, and they whispered to her in her passage, and she felt the water on her cheek, like rain. They had an odor now, pungent and fresh. Her feet sank into the earth, over the softness of the needles.

She reached the other side, then stopped abruptly. For there, smoking and looking at the sky, stood Jerome.

CHAPTER TWENTY-TWO

Amalie did not move. But Jerome said, quietly and casually, not turning to her with even the slightest motion of his head: "Good evening."

Instinctively, she half turned away, then halted, feeling ridiculous, and understanding that for a moment her memory of another night in this spot had overpowered her reason, had spurred her on to irrational absurdity. She had eaten many dinners with Jerome these past weeks, had discussed his father's condition with him in the mornings, had asked his advice on homely problems, had smiled at him in hallways, had conversed with him about Philip. Their relationship had been coolly friendly and casual, and they had rarely been alone. Yet, her first instinct now was to run away, and she despised herself for the impulse.

She emerged fully from the copse of trees and said indifferently: "Good evening. The air is nice, isn't it, after the winter?"

He turned to her and smiled courteously. "You ought to feel it is nice. You have not had much opportunity to enjoy it."

She laughed a little. "Everyone seems intent on making me feel myself a martyr. I am not, really."

He still smiled at her. In the pellucid air of the evening she could see him clearly now. He had become thinner, his face had a grayish pallor and tenseness and his eyes were tired. She realized then that she had not, in fact, looked at him directly for a long time, that he had not impinged on her awareness but had been only a shadowy figure in that house of terror and grief and anxiety. But now he seemed imminent, too close, too sharp, to her, alone with her as he was on this long quiet hillside and in this thin palely bright air of early evening. Solitude, prolonged and hushed, surrounded them; the pines whispered faintly but eagerly of new life. From the valley below came the thin, far barking of a dog.

Then, all at once, as he stood beside her, with that polite smile and with those aloof eyes, she became conscious that her heart was beating with strong and painful rapidity, that her breath felt like a surge of suffocating air in her constricted throat, and that there was a spinning sound in her ears and the most unbearable tearing anguish in her breast.

Worst of all, there was a most curious consciousness in her of her very self, her flesh, the outlines of her face, the spasmodic clenching of her hands in her muff. And that consciousness extended to him so that he momentarily became more imminent, more intense in her awareness, until the only reality in the transparent and echoing silence was this man himself.

His voice came to her dimly, and with gravity: "I have not thanked you before, for your care of my father. But I cannot thank you fully. That would be impossible."

She spoke huskily through her constricted throat: "It was nothing. I am so very fond of him. He is so good."

"And he is very fond of you," he said, and she had never heard his voice so gentle and so kind.

She looked down at the valley and did not answer. But she saw nothing of the delicate lights which had begun to twinkle below. The earth appeared to move in long undulations under her feet; the sky, now amethystine and purely cold, appeared to widen, to extend into limitless horizons. Her lips were numb, for her heart had subsided into tremendous slow beats as if it were stifling, and the sickening anguish which filled her

195

had become a physical and crushing thing.

Jerome regarded her profile, which revealed nothing at all except the sunken expression about her pale lips. A light and frigid wind stirred the pines, and a tendril of her black hair played against her cheek. She stood motionless, her hands in her muff, her eyes fixed on the valley below.

"He will live, now, they think," he said.

"Yes."

"And you will have your well-deserved rest."

She lifted her eyes and looked at him fully, and he saw how dilated they were and full of some strange and involuntary emotion like terror or torment. But she saw only that he was smiling at her with brotherly regard and friendly interest. She moistened her dry lips, and murmured: "I am not very tired at all." And the sickness increased in her until she felt faint and exhausted and overcome with some mysterious and listless grief, so heavy, now, that she had a vague but poignant fear of falling.

He looked away from her, and his face was more gray in the gathering dusk. "It is almost spring, and we can forget what has happened," he said.

We can forget, she said to herself.

"There was a time," he said, musingly, "when I was afraid that time itself had stood still and we were all imprisoned forever in winter, and should never escape. When I came out here tonight it was with the sensation that I had been released and was free again. I was quite surprised to realize that spring is actually here and that I am alive."

"Yes," she said dully.

"Soon," he continued, "the valley will be hidden in trees, and the grass will be green on these hills, and the sun will be warm. I haven't seen our garden in the summer, for some years. I have pleasant anticipations of it. I never thought the idea of a garden could be so pleasant. But after one has left pain and dread behind, he becomes aware of how real life is, and how beautiful it can be."

But never again, for me, she thought. Never, never again. And now she had the sensation that she had been buried under great stones, forever shut from the light of the new sun and the sound and sights of the new earth.

"It is agreeable to think that we can now talk of other things besides my father's illness, and can make plans," he was saying. She knew that he was smiling, but could only wonder if the darkness which was deepening slowly about her was real or imagined.

He said: "It is fairly settled that Sally Tayntor and I are to be married in September."

She opened her mouth, but the thickness of her throat kept back her voice. She thought: I must go back. If I do not, I shall cry out, or scream, or die in this place. She drew in a deep breath, as if a smothering weight had been partially removed from her lips. She found that she could speak again:

"That will please your father, I know." Her voice sounded in her own ears as if it came from a great distance, and from another throat.

"It will please everyone, especially me," he said lightly. "Sally is a very dear girl."

He flicked with his cane at a black and sodden leaf on the wet earth. Amalie could not take her eyes from it. It seemed part of herself.

Jerome glanced back at the house. He could see only the red roof glimmering against a sky which was now darkly blue, broken with the points of new stars.

"The house will be filled again," he said, and his tone was pleasant and light. "You and Alfred, I and Sally. It has been quiet too long, I suspect."

"Yes."

He looked at her bent head and white profile, glimmering now in the pure and solitary dusk. His mouth opened a little, drew back on his teeth in a spasmodic grimace of pain, and the muscles contracted along his jaw. They stood in silence, not moving, though the air about them was pregnant and charged, and full of bitter misery.

Then Jerome moved a step closer to her. She felt his approach, rather than saw it, and started. She raised her eyes, and again he saw her stark anguish and motionless despair.

"I am sorry, Amalie," he said, softly. "I hope you have long pardoned my insolence to you."

She did not answer. She only gazed at him in her speechless suffering, and he knew she could not speak.

"It was vicious and unpardonable of me," he said. "I can only say, in self-extenuation, that I was a fool. I'd like to know that you do not think too harshly of me."

"No," she whispered. And then: "Oh, no."

"You are very good," he said gravely. "I never knew how kind and how good you are. But now I know. You have forgiven me, then?"

Her lips moved, but he heard only a rustle. He held out his hand to her. She stared at it dully for a moment, then withdrew her hand from her muff, and gave it to him. It was as cold and stiff as ice.

"Shall we go back, now?" he asked, very gently. "I thought I just heard the dinner bell."

They moved through the pines, and the drops of moisture fell thickly on their faces. Lights glowed from the windows of the house. Smoke plumed along the dark eaves. They climbed the slope together. They entered the warm hall, and Amalie went up the stairs alone. Jerome watched her go, and his face was closed and inscrutable.

Someone had lighted the lamp in her bedroom. It threw its soft light on the carpet, on the quiet furniture. A fire crackled in the grate.

Amalie sat down on the bed. Her whole body was trembling, as if it had been struck a savage blow. She stared at the fire, and the red light lay in the sockets of her eyes. Then she turned on her side and lay down, fully clad as she was.

"O God," she said aloud, in a strange sharp voice. "O God, God."

CHAPTER TWENTY-THREE

It was on April 2nd that Brigadier General Wainwright Tayntor celebrated the betrothal of his daughter, Miss Sally Atchison Tayntor, to Mr. Jerome Lindsey, the marriage to take place on September 15th, 1869.

Miss Sally's father was jubilant; Miss Sally, herself, a constant glow of blushes and delight; Riversend, amazed. The General and his daughters went to New York to look over the latest Parisian concoctions, both for the celebration of the betrothal and for Miss Sally's trousseau.

The day of the great celebration was particularly felicitous. There had been a heavy fall of snow a day or two before, but this had disappeared with promptitude. The pale gray sky of the morning had by five o'clock given way to the most delicate blue, and the countryside was vivid with new green, the air fresh and fragrant. By half past six, when the guests began to arrive, the General's mansion was lit from top to bottom. Relatives from Boston, Philadelphia and New York were already snugly quartered in guest bedchambers, and the local conservatories had been stripped to fill all the rooms, so that they resembled summer bowers. Extra servants had been engaged; one of the great drawing-rooms had been pressed into service as an auxiliary dining-room, and though the guests would not dine until eight, the five immense tables were already aglitter with silver, gold-decorated crystal and candles, and enormous platters loaded with hams and cold beef and fowl.

All agreed that for lavishness of entertainment, for food, for music, for the splendor of women's gowns, for hilarity and wine and handsomeness, the reception was unsurpassed in the history of Riversend. As for the bride, in her pale-blue Worth gown, looped with pink velvet rosebuds, her beauty, it was admitted, was dazzling. She seemed to be surrounded by an aura of radiance, her impudent liveliness somewhat subdued under the dazing impact of happiness. The bridegroom-to-be was according to the ladies, devastating. There were some carpers who said all this display and jollity was "unrefined" and not at all "elegant," for restraint was conspicuously lacking. But then, that was probably envy.

Never, the ladies sighed, was there so devoted a gentleman as Mr. Lindsey. He hung upon the steps of Miss Sally with ardor. And how handsome he was! There was no false note in the whole evening. Even Miss Dorothea Lindsey, noted and disliked and avoided in the past for her grimness and silent disapproval of everything, appeared almost gay. She had actually emerged from her constant grays and blacks, and wore a gown of deep purple foulard, enlivened by gold buttons on the basque, and quite extremely bustled. Many ladies exclaimed, behind their fans, that they had had no idea that she was so presentable a creature. Of course, they said, it was unthinkable that Miss Dorothea might have resorted to shameful art to give color to her usually pallid complexion, but her color was really remarkable! It was true that she was very old, almost forty, in fact, but there was such an air about her now that to a casual eye she might have appeared much younger. Her dark hair, only slightly threaded with gray, had been expertly dressed, and curled bangs were arranged over that austere forehead. Several bachelors became interested. After all, it was quite a handsome creature, and there was no inconsiderable fortune in the background.

Few had ever heard Miss Dorothea laugh, and when she did so now, somewhat heavily and reluctantly, many of those who had known her almost all her life turned their heads to discover who was the stranger in their midst. They were quite amazed to discover that the merriment emanated from Miss Dorothea.

Mr. Lindsey had insisted upon being present. Emaciated, weak and exhausted though he was, he sat and smiled and conversed with his old friend the General, and kissed Miss Sally whenever she halted prettily beside him. His white face glowed; it was as if some pressure and fear had been removed from him. When he was alone with the General again, he imparted to his friend some information which made the old soldier beam with pleasure and satisfaction.

All had been maliciously expecting some flamboyant display of toilette from Mrs. Alfred Lindsey, and all were disappointed. It was grudgingly conceded that she had finally, and sensibly, decided to subside into the rôle of the serious and responsible matron. Her gown of dim rose velvet and demure lace was cut on the most conservative and proper lines, and was relieved by no jewels. Her manner was abstracted, even dull. Doubtless, the once strong red of her mouth had been pure artifice, for now her lips were almost bluish, and even the purple of her eyes had dimmed. No one heard her laugh, and she had not danced, but had remained near her husband, who did not care for that exercise. It was noted, also, that she had lost much flesh and that she appeared to be very weary and distrait. Was it possible, whispered the ladies, that young Mrs. Lindsey was already ——? They scrutinized her figure closely. Of course, she had been married hardly four months, and stays were very tight. However, it would be an excellent thing for Alfred, poor gentleman, who had only that miserable little cripple as evidence of his first marriage. They noticed that Alfred seemed somewhat preoccupied and tired; perhaps he was concerned with his wife's "interesting condition." When called from her side, it was with a sort of ponderous impatience, and he soon returned. Such devotion! sighed the ladies.

The Widow Kingsley decided to investigate. She found Amalie alone, lurking against the wall, and hidden by a grove of rubber plants. She kissed the young woman heartily; then, after an exchange of somewhat listless amenities, the widow asked abruptly: "My dear, are you going to have a baby? Everyone is curious. You seem so languid."

Amalie did not blush or start. "No," she said, very quietly. "No. At least, not yet."

The widow eyed the other woman cunningly over her vigorously waving fan. "Nothing so settling for a wife as having babies, my love. I understand they are very satisfying." She chortled. "At least, the preliminaries. You must have half a dozen."

Amalie smiled slightly. "I shall remember your advice, dear Mrs. Kingsley. It is so very kind of you."

"Never had any, myself," confided the widow. "Never liked 'em. Of course, that is very unnatural of me. I am a most unnatural woman. Prefer cats. But in a world so hell-bent, always, on being natural and dull, it is very pleasant to be unnatural."

Amalie's smile was a little less forced. "I understand that it is the unnatural people who make history. Moreover, they have a hypnotic effect on the natural."

The other woman chuckled. "I suspect you are right, my pet. I have hypnotized three men into marrying me. Gentlemen of substance. Look at me: I am not in the least dazzling or alluring. Yet, three gentlemen of fortune have married me, and adored me. That is hypnotic. Do you blame 'em?" she demanded, grinning.

Amalie gave her her full attention for the first time. "No," she said thoughtfully, "I do not blame them. They must have found you exciting after association with so many insipid women."

The widow, pleased, tapped the girl smartly on the arm with her fan. "I love you, my child. Not once have you said: 'You must have been handsome, or charming.' You have a good eye. I was always very ugly, but I was always very entertaining. A man may tire of a pretty face and a beautiful figure (which he immediately sets out to ruin) but he never tires of a woman who entertains him. I always admonish a bride to be amusing. Garner gossip, I say, the more malicious the better. Invent it, if you are short of facts. Use your imagination. Read extensively, but privately, and remember jokes and exciting incidents in what you read. Do not set out to be learned; gentlemen do not admire sensible comments from their wives. Make the devils laugh; they will tell you that they do not approve of scandal, but the male of the species laps up scandal as a cat laps up cream. I have never known a wife with a talent for the scandalous who ever lost her husband to another woman. A shocking tale about a friend or acquaintance is worth any amount of wifely duty and virtue, and far surpasses French lingerie."

For the first time that evening, and even for weeks, Amalie laughed. The widow was gratified. She had not liked the gray color of Amalie's face, the dull and lightless despair in her eyes.

"If," she added, "one can add a shapely leg in a silk stocking, and a nice thigh, to a spicy tale, then you have the rascals enslaved for live. However, I had no shapely leg, but still I entranced 'em. That is because I have imagination."

The widow shook her head. "Men are such irresponsible and inconsistent creatures. They have imposed the most tiresome virtues on us, and have called those virtues 'natural' to us. But really, we are the most reckless and violent rakes, under our stays and our demure manners. And, strange to say, it is this quality in us, when used with taste and piquancy in the marriage state, which keeps our husbands at our sides. But if we take men seriously, and attempt to live up to the picture of the virtues they have held up for our guidance, then they weary of us and go off after the first pair of flashing ankles."

But Amalie was not listening. Jerome had just danced by with Miss Sally, in the measures of a most lilting and exciting waltz. Sally's curls had been most indecorously close to Jerome's lips; her face had been the face of a young sleeper caught in an intoxicating dream. Jerome had been smiling down at her tenderly, and his arm had been close. Amalie's eyes closed spasmodically.

The Widow Kingsley, with her astuteness, saw all this. She rose, waited a moment, then tapped Amalie firmly and sharply on the arm. Amalie turned to her, faint and sick of expression. The widow was quiet, but her regard was both stern and piercing.

"Have you ever played the Market, my dear? No? There is a saying that one must 'average his losses' occasionally. That you must do. Take my advice, for I am an old woman, and I have learned common sense."

Amalie stared at her. Mrs. Kingsley nodded grimly. "Yes, my love. It is a sad day when a woman is less wise than a man."

She rustled away then, shouting to an acquaintance.

Amalie stared at herself in the mirror over her dressing table. She said: I am not wise. I never was wise. She could not move; she had sat like this for over fifteen minutes, making no effort to undress, her hands lying numbly among the crystal and gilt bottles that littered the lace which covered the table.

How was it possible to know whether one were wise or unwise? The exigencies of the moment compelled one to decision, and one smugly assured oneself that the decision was

202

either inevitable or clever.

She thought of her childhood and her young girlhood, and now the whole flavor of them, the whole intensity and sordidness and hunger and fear came back to her overwhelmingly. She saw the shack in which she had lived with her dying mother and her drunken father. She saw the face of her mother, after her labors in the kitchens of others. She heard her father's oaths, breathed the acrid smell of his breath. She saw her own young face in the cracked mirror of the filthy kitchen, and heard her own voice: "Never. Never. There is something else for me, if I can find it. And I will find it."

She saw the snow that had seemed endless about the shack and felt the sharp wind on her thin body as she went to the pump for water. She had looked at the stars and had repeated over and over: "Never! Never!" She had felt the strength in her brain and in her will, and the beauty in her face. She had been only fourteen then, but the strength had always been there, like a weapon.

She had had this weapon of her will, and of her beauty. They were no small things, she had known very early. She had asked no help, no pity, no compassion. What she had done, she had done herself. A cool wind of pride momentarily blew upon the smart of her fiery suffering.

She could see the bedroom reflected in her mirror. She was safe; she was free. She must "average her losses." What, in reality, had she lost? "Nothing," she said, aloud. What was this silly thing that bedevilled her compared with what she had escaped and endured? If she had had greater strength, in the past, she need only exercise a lesser strength now, and then she would have peace.

She covered her eyes with one hand and called upon that strength, harshly and commandingly.

She did not hear the dressing-room door open and close. And so it was that she started violently when she heard Alfred's kind but reproving voice: "My dear, you are not undressed. Do you know it is long after midnight?"

She dropped her hand and looked at her husband in the mirror. She said, in a dull and mechanical tone: "I am sorry. I am so tired. I was just resting, Alfred."

She stood up. He stood near her, in his crimson dressing gown. He was hesitating, and his smile was awkward. But there was a heavy flush on his face. He drew her into his arms and kissed her lips, lingeringly. He whispered: "Darling, do you know it has been long over two months——?"

He felt her grow hard as stone in his arms. But he did not hear her sudden wild and terrified thought: "But that would be adultery!"

He released her gently and looked down at her in surprise. He exclaimed: "What is it, Amalie? Are you ill?"

But she was overcome with the horror of her involuntary thought, her monstrous and appalling thought. Frightened, he caught her hand and cried: "Amalie, are you ill?"

He chafed her cold fingers in his warm palms. Frantically, he looked at her table. He found her smelling salts, uncorked the bottle, held it to her nose, murmuring incoherent and distracted words. He lowered her to the chair. Her head fell forward. He knelt beside her, shook her beseechingly.

"What is it, Amalie, my darling?" He put his hand to her forehead and lifted her face. What he saw frightened him even more. He stood up, glanced wildly at the door, as if for help.

She was pressing her hands to her face now, and shivering. Alfred pulled out his own handkerchief, wet it thoroughly, and messily, with eau de cologne, and rubbed it over Amalie's brow and cheeks. "My God, what is it, Amalie? Tell me. I cannot bear it. Are you ill?"

The pungent smell and sting of the cologne steadied her broken self-control. She leaned against him, drawing deep breaths. But she did not look at him as she murmured, catching her breath between words: "I am only tired. It has been a long evening." She paused. Her murmur was lower but firmer. "Yes, I am tired. There was the nursing of your uncle. I am tired enough to die. You—you must give me a little while, Alfred." She raised her head and tried to meet his eyes. "You do understand?"

"Certainly!" he cried. But he did not. It was enough for him, then, to see that she had recovered somewhat. His heart slowed its frantic beating. He thought: There is no understanding women. It is true that she told me she did not love me, but was fond of me, and would try to make me a good wife. I knew all that before. But she did not shrink from me when I took her as my wife; she was gentle and compliant. I expected nothing else; I understood that well-bred women, or women with even a slight pretension to gentility, had no response in them. That is left for sluts and unnatural women. He drew a deep and reassuring breath of his own. One must remember that they are delicate creatures, at best, and inexplicable. One has only to be patient.

And then he had a most electric thought, powerful and

204

thrilling. He knelt beside her, held her to him; she dropped her head upon his shoulder, as if unutterably exhausted.

He finally whispered: "Is it possible, Amalie, that—that——"

She was silent in his arms. She was not acquainted with duplicity, with treachery. She had never struck a blow at one who had trusted her, or even against her enemies. But now, in her extremity, she whispered in return: "I—do not—know—yet."

He laughed aloud, but softly, in the access of his delight and wonder. "You must go to our Dr. Hawley, Amalie! Tomorrow! My darling, if it is only true!"

If this marvelous, this glorious thing were true, then all was explained, her shrinking from him, her avoidance of him. It explained it fully, even more than her "tiredness" and her reaction from the strain of long weeks of nursing his uncle. He was content; he would understand, he promised himself exultantly. He thought of young Philip, whom he loved in spite of his disappointment. It would be excellent for Philip to have a brother. Philip, then, need not go, in September, to the school he dreaded, in order to fit himself for his position as a banker's son. Philip, poor lad, could remain at home. There would be a sturdier boy, a whole boy, to take up the burden.

He helped her to her feet. She was flaccid, in his hands and arms. Very tenderly, then, he helped her undress. While he did so, he talked lightly and lovingly, and with hushed laughter.

CHAPTER TWENTY-FOUR

Mr. Lindsey, Philip and Amalie sat in the warm sun of early May.

To Mr. Lindsey, at least, the hills had never been so green, so softly rimmed with mauve, so tender. Never had there been a sky so lucid, so passionately blue and filled with the cry of life. Never had he so felt the poignancy of living, the tranquillity and joy of mere being, the ardent and ecstatic sorrow of awareness.

He had never been a religious man. He was the gentle skeptic, who had built his house upon reason and logic. But now he was old, and had come to suspect all reason. Logic, he thought, is the great conservative, the great sneerer. It is the blind procrastinator. Had man, through the ages, listened to logic what little progress he has made would never have come into being. But man, fortunately, has listened to his instinct, that mighty enemy of reason. We shall never, he thought, solve the riddle of man by the application of scientific instruments. We shall know ourselves only through our instincts. In the dark desert of those instincts stands God, a burning bush, lighting the whole chaotic landscape.

He had always believed that only the young are instinctive, aware of mysterious powers and forces in the universe. But now he knew that the old, sitting in the sunshine, done with so many things, feel the full power of instinct. The old, then, come to a time when they suspect reason and logic, for they have emerged from the hard dark prison of the struggle for existence, or the dim cloister of philosophy. It is significant, he thought, that logic has always been most admired by the secluded dialecticians, and by them has been developed to its ultimate absurdity. Logic is any man's servant. He can rise up to his grotesque private universes on the sedate ladder of a perfectly valid and logical syllogism. By sincerely logical reasoning, he can persuade himself to commit enormities, or suicide. Mr. Lindsey suspected that most men commit suicide. Someone had once said of a certain man: "Died at fifteen; buried at seventy-five."

When had *he* died? That was more important to him now than the question as to when he would be buried. But no, it was no longer important, after all, for he was alive again, completely alive, on the very edge of his grave.

It was sad, it was even terrible, that a man only knew the value and the loveliness and the grandeur of life when he was about to depart from it, just as one, forever departing from his old and familiar home, suddenly becomes aware of its dearness and meaning for him. He sees every tree in its clarity, as he has never seen it before. He sees the light on the windows of rooms he shall never enter again; he sees the tender ivy on the stones, the bloom of the old gardens, the familiar walks and the sun-warmed walls. He sees his house, not as a mere building, a mere place of habitation, a mere enclosure for his body and a protection from the terrors of the night, but as part of himself, part of all the pain he has endured and part of all the things he has loved and the passions he has experienced. When he turns finally from the door, twists the key in its lock, he goes forth an exile, full of grief.

We learn to live, to understand, when it is too late, he thought. Then he began to wonder. Time was nothing. Perhaps the few hours given to the old, to the departing, when they may look back with full awareness, are the only hours of significance in a man's life.

He looked at the sky, and suddenly he was full of a calm ecstasy, a kind of rapturous realization. It was not faith. It was something much deeper, much tenderer, much more profound. It is enough, he thought, and it is enough to compensate for a lifetime of suffering and sadness and struggle, that we have had that moment or two of ecstasy which accompanies the knowledge of the being of God, and of the meaning of man, and the peace that comes with them, the light that "never was on sea or land."

He was sitting in the sun, with his Cashmere shawl over his crippled knees, his long white head bare to the gentle wind. Amalie was sitting near him, and Philip, in the chairs they had drawn up to him. Amalie, at his and Philip's request, had been reading Plato's *Phaedo*. But now Mr. Lindsey touched her shoulder gently.

"Please, my love, that is enough," he said. "Even Plato can become tiresome. He was always so logical."

Amalie glanced up in surprise. Then she saw Mr. Lindsey's face, and was silent. She closed the book.

Mr. Lindsey looked reflectively at Philip. "What do you think of Plato, my boy?"

Philip blushed. He looked down at his beautiful white hands, so thin and twisted together now. He almost whispered: "I—I think almost all philosophers make—things—so wearisome."

Mr. Lindsey did not speak, but he was intensely moved. Yes, his instinct, then, had been right. Only the very young and the old understood. He put out his hand and rested it on Philip's deformed shoulder.

"And our new scientists," said Mr. Lindsey, in a murmuring voice, "and our new materialism—they make things 'so wearisome.' Yes, our scientists, intoxicated now with Darwin and Huxley and so many others, will one day emerge from their darling materialism, their adoration of 'natural laws,' and rediscover God. Perhaps in the test tube, or the atom, in the star, or in geological strata, or in chemicals. What a shock it will be to them!"

Amalie looked from Philip to Mr. Lindsey. How alike they are! she thought, in spite of the pale Puritanism of the New Englander, and the dark, almost Latin, coloring of Philip. There was a certain vividness about them, in spite of their silences and their self-repressions. There was a frail but steel-like vitality in them, thinly shining but intensely strong. She sighed, rested her hands on her book, and looked down at the valley.

Mr. Lindsey heard the sigh. He regarded Amalie with sudden concentration. How had it escaped him, consciously, that she was so pale and thin, so subdued and listless these days? He was startled into deep anxiety by what he saw. Where had the splendor and power of Amalie gone? He had always thought of her as a wild young mare, standing on a hilltop, wise but passionate, trembling with a sense of delicious adventure, confident and dauntless. He recalled now that he never heard her laugh; that she had become a ghostlike presence in his house, her voice low and without accent. He remembered, vaguely, that Dorothea had reluctantly praised Amalie's devotion to household duties, her new "common sense." (Dorothea had discovered that Amalie did not attempt to replace her, that she was content to be an industrious and younger inferior, and for this Dorothea had been immeasurably grateful. She, Dorothea, had unbent so far as to complain, apprehensively, of the addition of Miss Sally Tayntor to the household, Sally who would most probably not be so amenable and so "sensible.")

Mr. Lindsey knew that Amalie was not in the least popular with the matrons of Riversend, but she had failed to arouse in them the antagonism and dislike they had so vigorously expected. They had armed themselves against her, and then had found that she carried no arms of her own, and made no hostile gestures. They were beginning to accept her in the pattern of their quiet days, and even to patronize her with some kindness. All her flamboyance, her defiant laughter, her sharp comments, had gone. She was "settling down," and a good thing, too. In time, they said, she might be quite acceptable, for she was probably realizing, now, her good fortune and the full extent of her base background and lack of advantages.

Mr. Lindsey, recalling all this with a kind of angry alarm, said to himself: What has happened to Amalie? Has she discovered that her bargain was too much for her? But no, Amalie, he knew, was not ingenuous. She had long known the full extent of her bargain. When with Alfred, she was all gentleness and compliance, and her few smiles were reserved for him. If he was in her vicinity, she always managed to be near him, putting her hand into his, as if for protection. It was evident that she had no distaste for him, but a kind of touching fondness. But Mr. Lindsey had often caught her expression as she looked at her husband. He had seen a kind of fear there, a humility, a vague despair. However, all these things had been observed by him subconsciously; only now did they rush strongly to his conscious mind.

Was she bored by her quiet life in this backwater? It was more than that. Did she find existence without vitality and excitement? There had always been a subdued vivacity about her, a suppressed ardor, as if she were too filled with an awareness of being. But now this terrible melancholy had fallen on her like a flat and crushing tombstone, and she moved faintly and sluggishly under it in blind and mechanical helplessness.

He knew Amalie too well to be deluded that she wished she had not made this bargain, or that she had a longing to return to the perilous and miserable existence which had been hers before she had married Alfred. It was something else which had taken the light and brilliance from her face, which had taken the color from her eyes, and made her lips white and languid, her step slow and heavy, her voice almost feeble.

For a moment he had a certain thought. But no, women in that "condition" involuntarily bloomed, became rosier and rounder. It was some sickness of soul that possessed Amalie, some hidden but murdering grief.

His alarm grew. Something had happened to this girl, whom he loved more than he had ever loved his daughter. Something had taken life from her, had replaced it with a silent and soft-footed deadness. Perhaps some relative had died, whom she had loved? But no, she had none; this he knew. What could have happened to her in this quiet and orderly house, where even Dorothea had become her harsh and reticent friend, where he and Alfred and Philip adored her, where Jerome treated her with the casual fondness of a relative? What had someone, something, done to her?

He said: "Amalie. Is there something wrong? You do not look well. How stupid of me not to have seen it before!"

He noticed, with his sharpened awareness, how slowly and heavily she lifted her head, on which the black thick hair had lost its brightness. She was smiling at him now, but his tired heart quickened with concern when he saw that her eyes were only full of dull pain. "Please do not alarm yourself, dear Uncle William," she said softly. "It is just that—that the spring weather, so warm, is tiring me."

"You have not been well since I was ill!" he exclaimed remorsefully. "It was too much for you." But he did not believe it.

"I was so very anxious about you," she said, and his quick ear caught her evasiveness.

He leaned back in his chair and was silent. Philip, in his turn, regarded his stepmother with loving concern. His hand stole involuntarily to her, and she took it, pressing it, smiling reassuringly at him.

Mr. Lindsey said: "Nothing ever happens here. You need young people, young women, Amalie. It will be good for you when Jerome marries Sally, and brings her here. You are almost of an age." He smiled, momentarily forgetting his anxiety. "It will be pleasant to hear children running about these quiet rooms of ours."

Amalie's thin fingers tightened about the book. The pinched look deepened about her mouth.

Mr. Lindsey returned his attention to her. "Is it not possible that you could accompany Philip and me to Saratoga, Amalie? Of course, you do not have arthritis, like us old people," and he gave Philip a gentle smile. "But the waters might do you good."

"No, it would not be fair to Dorothea, to leave her with—everything," said Amalie, in her dull voice. "Besides," and she smiled, herself, "I have already suggested it to Alfred. I have pointed out to him that when he leaves you and Philip in Saratoga, and goes on to his business in New York, I should love to go with him. But he believes, and wisely, that I should remain here." And now a dim flush crept over her face, rose to her forehead, and she thought to herself: When he returns, I will end the farce. When he returns, I shall have recovered a little of my strength and my reason, please God. I shall have had time for perspective.

Mr. Lindsey saw the flush, and he thought it natural resentment against a domineering husband. But he wisely said nothing, only gazed at Amalie with increasing concern.

The radiant sun sloped towards the western hills, and a more mellow light, faintly misted, blew over the valley below. The three on the terrace could hear the gardeners, clipping and pruning. They could smell the lilacs, the wild cherry and apple blossoms, the scent of the rich green earth. The upper windows of the house turned slowly to fire.

They heard carriage wheels on the gravelled drive, the sound of Alfred's and Jerome's voices. Then the two gentlemen came around the side of the house and greeted them pleasantly.

"A lovely day," said Alfred, taking off his hat and lifting his head to the quickening breeze.

"I have just been saying to Alfred that work is a crime when the weather is good," said Jerome, glancing casually at the three with an affable smile.

Alfred, the humorless, suddenly became censorious. "A man must work to live," he said sententiously. And frowned. He and Jerome had reached quite an accord since Mr. Lindsey's illness, and he earnestly hoped that his cousin was not about to relapse into incorrigibility and his old unpredictable heresies.

Jerome laughed. "But if a man works constantly to live, then his life is worth nothing." He threw himself down on the grass and stared agreeably at the sky. "We need a new educating influence in America. Americans should be taught that man cannot live by bread alone. They should be taught that work is a thing to be done in as few hours as possible, and that the world is full of amazing wonders and joys to be savored only in long periods of leisure, that the universe of the mind cannot be invaded by an exhausted man who has wasted the substance of his life over a machine or a desk."

He looked, with his dark and mocking smile, at the others. His eye touched Amalie, lingered a moment, turned away. Mr. Lindsey smiled in return. "I almost agree with you, Jerome."

But Alfred said sternly: "Man was made for work. Civilization is the result of work. Do you suggest we return to barbarism, Jerome?" He did not sit down, but stood stiffly near his wife.

Jerome said meditatively: "The Spartans, who were all for work, and who labored from sunrise to sunup, never created a noble statue or wrote a poem or founded a religion of love and beauty and joy. They produced only soldiers. It was the Athenians, who gathered for hours in the shade of colonnades, and in the porticos of temples, who founded life-giving philosophies, who wrote immortal poems and plays, and who built the altar to the Unknown God."

He glanced up at his father, who returned his look gravely and eagerly. Jerome touched the shawl that covered his father's knee.

"All nonsense," said Alfred, frowning. "I do not know about the past, but I do know that if America is to be built up to her proper position as a leader among nations, we must all work, and work hard. After all, work is the salvation of man," he added.

"Sparta," said Jerome softly, "is forgotten, and her soldiers, too. But Athens lives forever."

He got to his feet, lightly and restlessly. He hardly limped any more. There was a kind of feverish buoyancy about him these days. Mr. Lindsey found himself studying his son with his new acuteness. Was he imagining things about Jerome also? Was it really true that Jerome had aged much, had become haggard and febrile? He said: "Are you tired, Jerome?"

"Oh, I think I was born tired," laughed his son. "I am especially weary when I waste my time working. Not," he added, "that I do not understand the importance of work!" And he glanced at Alfred maliciously.

"How is the Bank?" asked Mr. Lindsey.

"Splendid." It was Alfred who replied, and now his pale strong face lighted. He hesitated, then continued: "Jerome is doing remarkably well. I feel I shall leave the Bank in good hands, when I go to New York tomorrow." His voice became warmer, and he gave his cousin a reserved smile, to which Jerome responded with a deep bow.

"We are all packed, Papa," said Philip timidly.

Alfred turned his attention to his son. "Are you, Philip?" he asked, in a kindly tone, and with his usual shadowed but affectionate look. "I do hope you and your—your grandpa will benefit from the waters. I will return for you in two weeks, and I hope to see both of you very rosy and fat."

He held out his hand to his wife, and she took it. She stood beside him for a moment, as he put his arm about her. Her head was bent. Jerome studied them intently, from the background, and his face was impassive.

CHAPTER TWENTY-FIVE

It had been very warm during the day. But at noon the sun became curiously brazen yet dull. A little later the sky turned saffron, and a yellowish light, ominous and appallingly silent, lay over the hills and the valley.

That silence had swallowed up in a yellow vortex even the smallest sound. It was Sunday, but the bells from the valley churches were not heard at Hilltop. Everything was muffled. By two o'clock the last servant had gone, Dorothea graciously allowing them an extra holiday (which she rigorously hoped would be devoted to pious pursuits in the valley churches and Sunday schools) because of the absence of three members of the family. Shortly after two, in the wake of the servants, she called for the family carriage for herself. Her best friend, the wife of one of the local lawyers, had been taken seriously ill, and Dorothea intended to spend the rest of the day, and possibly the whole evening, with her. As she prepared to leave, anxiously glancing at the saffron sky, she complained of Jerome's inconsiderateness. He might have waited for her in the small buggy, and thus have given Joe, the coachman, an earlier start on his unexpected holiday. But no, he must be off to see that young minx, Sally Tayntor, at a very early hour, and she, Dorothea, must lumber down into the valley in this heavy and stately vehicle. Now Joe must wait for her, within call, unless Jerome could be induced to bring his sister back when she desired.

"I shall send a message to him," she said, threateningly, to Amalie. "I do wish, my dear, that you would come with me. It would be a change for you."

"No, please," said Amalie. "I—I have a headache. It must be the weather." At the very thought of any exertion, a hideous apathy would come over her, and she would feel exhausted. "I intend to nap this afternoon. Will you return in time for late supper?"

"I am afraid not." Dorothea irritably adjusted her bonnet with a mittened hand. "But I understand that a cold luncheon has been set out for you." She paused. "I do not quite like it that you will be here all alone, with not even a single servant, unless you can call old Hiram in the barns any protection."

"I do not need protection," said Amalie, smiling faintly. "Please do not concern yourself with me, Dorothea. I shall be asleep in half an hour."

Dorothea considered, staring at the girl fixedly. She certainly seemed vaporous. Dorothea's sense of duty stirred uneasily. If only Jerome were here, he might be some slight protection. Dorothea lived in a world where everyone needed "protecting," in one form or another, from the vague terrors which stalked life incessantly. She regretted that she had given the servants a holiday. Perhaps it might be possible to find one below, and send him or her back immediately. That was hardly possible, however, she thought, ruefully. Servants had a way of disappearing, and she suspected that the disappearances boded no good. She looked at the sky again. It had a very

213

strange look, indeed. "There will be a storm," she said hesitatingly. "I almost feel I ought not to go."

But at that moment the sun came out from behind the yellow vapor and threw a cataract of strong and golden light over the whole landscape. That decided Dorothea. She said: "I will try to return as soon as possible. Rest, if you can. You are not looking very well."

She hesitated again. Then she kissed Amalie's cheek with her dry lips. With her usual good sense, she had become reconciled to the thought of Amalie as Alfred's wife. She wasted no time in weak repinings or sadnesses. The fact accomplished demanded readjustment in one's mind, and she had made the readjustment. She saw only that Alfred was happy, that Amalie was amenable and gave no trouble, that she had "settled" into a pattern of wifely duty, that she was beloved of Mr. Lindsey and Philip, and that she had removed considerable of the burden of the household from Dorothea's shoulders. It was far more than she could ever have expected, thought Dorothea, and she was not ungrateful.

She drove off in the carriage. The top was down, but Dorothea hoisted her black parasol over her head. Amalie watched her go.

She went outside and stood on the terrace near the front door. She saw the sinister golden light on the hills, whose very May greenness had been dimmed. She saw the brazen shadow of the sun through the citron-colored clouds. The valley floated in an ochre mist. The grass at her feet had a tawny overtone; the shadows under the spruces and the pines and the elms were jaundiced. The gray stone walls reflected amber, as did the windows. The strangeness of the spectacle awed Amalie, increased, as it was, by the overpowering silence, the absence of the slightest wind. The trees and shrubs stood in lemonish passivity. No sound came from the horses in the stables, or from the fowl. It was as if life had retreated, flying from something ominous which was about to occur.

She felt the heat of the oppressive air heavy on her flesh. She took a languid step or two, then halted. Her instincts stirred apprehensively. It was cooler in the house, she remembered. She went in, closed the oaken door behind her, stood in the dusk of the hall. At least the horrible yellow tint was absent here. She wandered into the music room, then shivered. Every window was a painting of ochre desolation hung upon the dim walls. How terrible it is, she thought vaguely. We shall have a storm. The weather is unseasonable.

The old familiar lassitude was creeping over her again, the old dreadful weight dragging at her heart. She could hardly move over the polished floor of the music room; it was as if she were carrying an immense burden on her shoulders. Her sprigged voile dress scratched her shoulders and arms; her hair felt too ponderous on her aching neck. Her feet shuffled in their passage. She pushed a lock of hair from her forehead, and said aloud: "I am so tired."

She stood beside the piano and looked down at the keys glimmering with pale ivory in the deepening dusk of the lonely room. She sat down; her hands lay on the piano soundlessly. She stared before her.

I cannot endure it, she thought simply. I shall have to go away. Forever. Oh, Alfred, Alfred. What have I done to you? You never deserved this. Where shall I go? What shall I do? Where can I hide? If only I could die. I am a coward, because I can never forget. It is always with me.

She put her hands suddenly over her eyes. She heard the sound of her own weeping, desolate and abandoned. She leaned her head against the piano and her tears rolled over the dark wood. She felt the silence and the immensity of the house closing in about her, and in her weeping there was the sound of helpless chained terror, the sound of nightmare.

After a little she was quiet, but the tears still gushed from her eyes in the silence of an unutterable grief. She knew there was no escape; she could not leave Alfred, who loved her, and his uncle, and his son, who trusted her, and loved her also. She had nowhere to go; there was none who would give her shelter. She had no money, save what Alfred gave her. She trembled with the urge for flight, but there was no spot on earth where she could live in peace, or hide.

She thought of the long life before her, and knew no hope that her present agony would subside in those years to come. How could she endure it, to see him every day, to see him with Sally, to hear his voice, catch his disinterested eye, listen to his laugh and the sound of his footsteps which would never come to her? How could she endure to be Alfred's wife, Alfred who had no fault and no folly, except the fault and the folly of having wanted her? She tried, as she had tried so often before, to picture the kindness in his eyes for her, the tenderness, the thoughtfulness. And then she could only shiver and cry out feebly, as if sick with torment.

It was a long time before she became aware that it was quite dark in the room. Lifting her swollen eyes, she looked at the windows. They were rectangles of ashen shadow. Suddenly that shadow was torn by fiery lightning which blazed into the room like the flash of an explosion. As if indeed it had been the blaze of an explosive charge, it was followed by the most stunning crash, which caused a curious subdued rattling all over the house. The floor trembled under Amalie's feet; boards creaked; there was a faint but terrible groaning in the assaulted air after the last reverberation had died away in hollow echoes on the hills.

Instinctively terrified, Amalie started to her feet, leaning against the piano. She could see little but vague forms of furniture in the room. And now she heard the sudden screaming of the awakened gale, tearing and pounding at the windows, the moaning of the trees, the prolonged rustling of grass. With it, after a moment or two, came the rain, like a wall of glistening water illuminated, at intervals, by fresh explosive flashes, fresh and stupefying cannonading. All the world had been swallowed up in fire and fury. The strong old house shivered. A tree nearby was struck, and immediately the air was permeated with a smell of brimstone.

Amalie was overwhelmed by sheer primitive fright. She was alone in the house. If it were struck, thrown down about her, there was no one to help. She sank upon the piano stool, cowered upon it, covering her ears with her hands, closing her eyes. Then, in a moment's comparative quiet, broken only by the wind and the rushing rain, she heard a sound, even through her hands.

It was a sound as if a door had opened and closed hastily. She started up, and her voice was wild with hope as she called out. But no one replied. It was only the banging of a shutter, she thought.

The fire and the fury were resumed, with more intensity. She could not stay alone in this vast room. In her own room, in her bed, there was at least a spurious protection. She could draw the curtains; she could cover her ears with the pillows.

She ran towards the doorway, wincing away from the lightning, her heart beating with pure terror, her gown streaming behind her, her hands thrown before her as if she were blind and seeking.

It was not until she reached the doorway that she saw that Jerome stood there, watching her.

She stopped in the very midst of her headlong flight, her arms flung out instinctively to balance herself, her face gleaming frantically in the semi-darkness. And then she was motionless, her breathing loud and irregular in the room, during the momentary pause in the storm.

He held out his arms to her and came slowly towards her. She watched him come. Her own arms dropped. She waited numbly. He reached her, and took her in his arms and held her to him gently.

And then she was clinging to him, sobbing wildly, clutching the wet cloth of his sleeves, pressing her face into his neck, crying out the most incoherent, the most heart-breaking words, as if her last control were gone. She felt his lips on hers, his tender and soothing reassurance, the pressure of his arms, the devouring and leaping hunger in her heart, and, finally, a terrible and soaring joy that seemed part of the lightning and the thunder.

CHAPTER TWENTY-SIX

The storm raged almost without pause until sunset. By that time the last of the thunder bounded off the hills in one final sullen echo, the lightning retreated to the east where it occasionally lit up some dark hilltop with pale fire. But the rain continued to fall in sheets of glimmering steel even though the wind had lessened.

By nightfall, the rain began to slacken, and at eight o'clock it stopped. A dim lavender light ran over the valley and the hills; a fugitive pink glow shone through the trunks of the evergreens on the slope. Trees dripped audibly in the exhausted silence; the earth sent up a strong sweet fragrance as of crushed grass and flowers and pine. Finally, the birds faintly discussed the storm with last tired chirpings, and went to sleep under a darkening heliotrope sky.

Wheels grated only slightly on the wet gravel. Dorothea sat in her carriage, stiff with anxiety, and looked up at the silent, unlighted house. She tried to reassure herself that Amalie was a strong and dauntless woman, but she remembered, with some misgivings, her father's remarks about Amalie's failing health. At that time, Dorothea had cried: "Nonsense!" But she recalled, very clearly now, that Amalie had apparently been going into a "decline" since Mr. Lindsey's illness, and her conscience assaulted her sharply. The storm had been fierce enough, indeed, to intimidate anyone. Dorothea had seen quite a number of stricken trees on the way home, and one smoldering barn. She had no particular nervousness about storms herself, but this one had quite frightened her.

Amalie's window was unlighted, and this increased Dorothea's anxiety. But just as the carriage rolled under Jerome's window, she saw the golden bloom of a lamp suddenly lit. He had not drawn the curtains. Dorothea heaved a sigh of relief. Amalie, then, had perhaps not been alone in the storm.

Dorothea alighted from the carriage and it went on to the stables. She glanced up again at Jerome's window. And then she became rigid. The parasol fell from her hand, clattered to her feet. Her face, in the last wandering light of the evening, turned a frightful color.

Quite distinctly she saw that Jerome was not alone, and she saw that the one with him was Amalie. She could see little of them, only their shoulders and their heads, and they were held together in an embrace which even Dorothea instinctively recognized as passionate. She saw their faces merge; she saw the gleam of Amalie's arms about Jerome's neck.

Dorothea never recalled moving a single step consciously, but she next remembered that she had reached the wall of the house under the window, and that she had flattened herself against it, as if seeking shelter. She heard a raucous and uneven sound in the quiet evening, and it was some dazed moments before she identified it as her own shocked breathing. Flashes and flecks of light soared and danced before her distended eyes; she was shaking to her very bones, and had to spread her arms on both sides of her body against the stones of the house in order to keep from falling. She had no conscious thought at all; she was aware only that she felt most frightfully ill, and that she might collapse on the wet earth at her feet.

All at once she longed, with a piteous hunger, for her room, for her bed. She mumbled to herself: "It is getting cold. I must go in." And then she began to whimper. She put her hand over her mouth, but from behind it the whimpering sounds came muffled and feebly frantic.

She never knew how long she stood there, but her next awareness was that it was dark and that a delicate crescent hung in the purple sky of night, and that she was thoroughly chilled. Her whole body appeared to be numb and bruised. She had heard no footsteps, but, as she pulled herself heavily away from the side of the house, she saw that the third floor was lighting up, room by room. The servants had returned.

The front door was unlocked. She crept up the stairs in

darkness. Someone had lit the fire in the hall, and it was like a crimson heart pulsing in the dusky gloom. She reached her room, having approached it slow step by step, as if she had turned old in an hour. Once behind her closed door, she dropped parasol, reticule, bonnet and shawl upon a chair and went to her bed. Very dimly, she recalled that she had seen a glimmer of light under the door of Amalie's room, but the very sight of it had sickened her, made her avert her head.

She lay on her pillows, her arms flung out on each side of her, her face stony in the dimness. There was a deep weak sensation in the region of her heart; the slightest movement of her body set up a wild trembling in her flesh. She held herself quiet, unthinking, for even a thought threw her into a disordered frenzy.

Perhaps she had slept, or perhaps fallen into some unconsciousness, for she was next aware that a wavering light was shining in her face. A servant was entering with a lighted candle. The girl recoiled at the sight of Dorothea's black gaunt figure on the white bed.

"Oh, Miss Dorothea!" she exclaimed. "I did not know you were here! Mr. Jerome said you were probably staying the night in the village, but I thought I would turn down your bed in case——"

Dorothea raised herself slowly on her elbow; it appeared to her that this small movement took all her strength. She pushed back her hair. She heard her own voice, calm and neutral: "I just returned, Nancy, and I am feeling very tired."

The girl set down her candle, nodded her head sympathetically, and lit the lamp on the table near the window. "It was a right bad storm, wasn't it, Miss? We thought we'd never get home."

Dorothea sat up; she tried to conceal the trembling of her body. She coughed and sighed. "May I have a cup of tea, and some of that fruitcake, Nancy? Here, in my room?" She must get rid of the girl at once, before she saw——

"Oh, yes, ma'am! At once!" The girl threw her a curious glance, then went out hastily.

Dorothea pushed herself to her feet. She said, aloud: "I must control myself. I must think. I must not give way."

She refused to think just now. She put away her parasol, reticule, bonnet and shawl. She washed her hands, threw cold water on her face. She smoothed her hair. Her muscles were quieter now, though at intervals they trembled violently and briefly. She sat down before her unlighted hearth and shivered.

She knew that the shivering was the result of shock, for the temperature was mild from the stored heat within the house.

Nancy found her sitting quietly there, her hands in her black silk lap. Dorothea thanked her, glanced with concealed loathing at the steaming tea and the cake.

But she finally forced herself to drink a hot and revivifying cup and to eat a little of the cake. One must never give way. Only fools did that. They invited chaos. One's mind must be clear and calm, or one might make an irreparable mistake, inviting the most terrible disasters. She drank a second cup. When Nancy returned for the tray, she found her mistress quite composed. Dorothea requested a small fire. The girl drew the draperies, knelt at the hearth, and soon had a fire sparking and crackling in its grate. Dorothea watched her. She could even inquire whether the girl had had a pleasant day in the village. She listened to Nancy's demure account with an air of kind if distant interest. They discussed the storm briefly, and then the girl departed with a cheerful "good night, ma'am."

But just as Nancy reached the door, Dorothea halted her with a word. "Are there any others home, Nancy?"

"Oh, yes, ma'am, I took a tray to Mr. Jerome, and to Mrs. Lindsey, in their rooms, about an hour ago. Mr. Jerome returned just before we did."

"I see." Dorothea's harsh voice was almost pleasant. Then no one knew or suspected but herself. She dismissed the girl again.

And now she could think, think without fury or horror, but only with detestation and hatred, both as cold as winter snow, and as relentless. She could think with one part of her mind, and that part was detached, unhurried, quite calm, and almost completely unemotional.

What was she to do? She asked herself this question without hysteria, or the slightest grief, or even outrage. Should she go to Jerome, and say: "I know what there is to know?" Should she go to Amalie, and denounce her? Should she inform Alfred, upon his return?

She knew, or thought she knew, Jerome. He was a blackguard and a villain, without conscience or scruple. It was quite possible that he would laugh in her face, defy her, lie to her. It was quite possible for him to say: "Then, my position here is untenable. I will leave at once." If he left (and here Dorothea drew a deep breath such as one might inhale at the sight of a dark door opening upon peace), what then, after his leaving? Would the wrong done to a good and just man be rectified?

Would the crime committed against him be obliterated? No. Moreover, it was even possible that Jerome might, knowing he had been discovered, decide to tell Alfred himself, or run away with Amalie, though Dorothea had her doubts about this. Jerome was a reckless man, but he was not a coward, and his sister coldly considered this. What of the honor of the family? What of Mr. Lindsey, who loved the drab? Would his health survive the shock of a shameful disclosure? Dorothea shivered again, involuntarily, and it took all the stern admonition of her inexorable mind to regain her control. Jerome, she told herself, burning with the acrid fire of bitterness, was his father's darling, after all. She had rediscovered this painful fact in the past few months.

No, she could not tell Jerome that she knew of his crime.

Could she denounce Amalie? What if Amalie went at once to Jerome, and informed him of the denunciation? The same results would accrue as if Jerome, and not his partner in adultery, had been told.

For a few moments Dorothea partially lost control of herself, and all her emotions of fierce hatred and shamed loathing and repulsion smote like battering fists on the door of reason. Oh, the hideous and shameless creatures, the criminals, the traitors, the defilers! How could they have done this thing, this baseness, to such as Alfred, who loved and trusted his wife and had no evil thought against anyone? How could they have done it to such a noble man of integrity and decency and kindness? He had given that strumpet his whole heart and all his life, and she had flung them aside with derision, careless of his suffering. He had extended friendship to his cousin, and had received a mortal wound in return. They had sought out a proper opportunity for their baseness, for the dishonoring of this house, and the deceiving of a gentle husband. Dorothea was certain that she saw it all clearly: the occasion had been plotted, carefully planned. Jerome had deliberately gone to the village alone, so that he could return alone. Amalie had refused to accompany Dorothea, had waited for the return of her lover. How they must have laughed together, in their vileness!

Dorothea, for the first time in her austere life, felt the urge to kill, to crush, to stamp down, and the urge was so compelling that she actually sprang to her feet, hands clenched, eyes flaming. Her thought raced like a thread of consuming fire to those two, smug in their rooms, confident that their foulness was undiscovered. She ran to the door, intent only on confronting them, on screaming out against them so that the whole house, the whole world, might know of what they had done.

She was actually out in the corridor, gasping aloud, before she came to her senses, and when she did so her trembling had returned so violently that she had to grope her way back to her chair, and she was again whimpering deep in her throat. She collapsed in her chair, covered her face with her hands, rocking back and forth in a fit of anguish.

What had she almost done? She had almost destroyed Alfred. She had most certainly almost destroyed her father. She had been on the verge of bringing even greater calamity to this house, this house where she had been born. Shame that is known only to one, and held fast and still in the heart of that one, does no harm, exposes no innocents to the contemptuous pity or hateful laughter of the hostile world. She knew Alfred well; she knew there would be no forgiveness in him for his betrayers. He might even kill them; certainly, he would drive the woman away, and Jerome also. But the hurt that had been dealt him would be mortal; he would never again recover his prestige among his friends, his associates. He would be a poor thing, whose wife had incontinently betrayed him behind his back for a lesser man. His pride could not endure such a thing. He would be utterly destroyed. Her father, too, would suffer enormously. It was possible that he would even die under the blow.

She stopped rocking in her chair and stared before her with parched eyes which strained in their sockets. Were the guilty to be free, never to be reproached, and always seeking an opportunity to repeat their crime? It seemed so. There was no solution. There was no solution but one of silence. The guilty escaped, in order that their victims might be saved.

But how could she, Dorothea, endure the endless days when she must see them frequently, look upon their false faces? Would they not guess, merely by glancing at her, that she knew? If she refrained from speaking to them, or could not control the loathing in her eyes, they would know. Then the final calamity would fall upon this house. It was not something they dared share with her. They would be precipitated into committing even greater enormities.

She must be an actress, then. She must remember how she had spoken to Amalie yesterday, and to Jerome. She must guard every inflection of her voice. She must veil any flash of her eyes. She must curb any shrinking. She must play the bland, deceived fool, the old spinster sister who would never suspect

222

anything. She must do this terrible, this revolting, thing, for the sake of her father, and for Alfred. How was it possible for human flesh to exercise such restraint, such awful self-control?

It never occurred to her that perhaps Jerome and Amalie had plans of their own. She was completely certain that they intended to retain the status quo of their lives and would only seek opportunities for fresh betrayals of Alfred. Amalie would not relinquish what she had gained, and neither would Jerome. The thought never even came to Dorothea that perhaps there was something more than derisive contempt for Alfred, or mere foul passion, between Amalie and Jerome.

She said aloud, in a harsh, strange voice: "I have only to watch them, to guard them, and prevent them from doing this again. I will watch her, and him, during the day. When Alfred returns, he will be adequate for the night. In the meantime, what shall I do about the nights?"

Dorothea rose and went to her mirror and studied her blanched face intently. Yes, she looked extremely ill. She would take to her bed; she would confess weaknesses and night terrors. She would implore Amalie to sleep with her, declaring that she dared not be alone. Amalie could not refuse.

But at the very thought of sharing her virgin bed with that vile creature Dorothea turned violently sick. This was the most dreadful part of all.

But Dorothea did not have iron in her soul for nothing. It took her only five minutes of desperate struggle with herself to master her sickness. It was for Alfred, she told herself, with cold despair. It was for her father. Alfred would be home in two weeks. Two weeks of horror would be little enough to endure for the sake of the peace of this house.

Once her mind was made up, she, as usual, dismissed all qualms, all quailings. She could even undress with firm hands and go to bed quietly. Then she rang for a maid and asked that Amalie be sent in to her at once.

The first frightful step taken, she could fix her eyes calmly upon the door and wait for the other woman, her heart quite steady.

CHAPTER TWENTY-SEVEN

Dorothea was compelled to draw heavily on her capital reserves of faith, courage, strength and determination during the next two weeks. She must never leave Amalie "unguarded." But she must not make this obvious. She was naturally robust of constitution, and she must pretend to be afflicted by vapors, sufficiently disabling to demand Amalie's presence at night but not enough so to make her keep to her bed during the day. So she moved from chair to chair and from room to room, directing Amalie in the household management, and needing various cups of tea and her smelling salts. She was merciless in her constant demands. It meant nothing to her that Amalie became more quiet, more stern-lipped, more ghost-like, as the days passed. (Was it possible that the drab had a conscience? But no, it was apparent that she was merely restive under restraint, and wished to be gone.)

It was easier to deceive Amalie than Jerome. This, Dorothea knew. So she, almost at once, stirred up an hysterical quarrel with Jerome over some triviality connected with his dog, and pretended such elaborate hostility (due to her "unnerved state"), that it was not hard to affect an unforgiving and petulant attitude which prevented any exchange of amenities with him. As Dorothea had always expressed her disapproval of little Charlie, Jerome did not find her present attitude inconsistent, and as he cared little for his sister's company, he shrugged away the matter and avoided her.

It was with Amalie, then, that Dorothea had to be most dissembling, but here again her "unnerved state" came to her rescue. The family physician assured Amalie that Miss Dorothea was suffering from certain delicate nervous and physical symptoms common to women of her age, and Dorothea took full advantage of this diagnosis. So Amalie could not be puzzled by Dorothea's bitter silences, her hard words, her criticisms, her cold mute glances of aversion. Amalie endured it all with stoical compassion and abstracted courtesy. Perhaps, too, her own misery and desperate state of mind made her overlook unguarded looks and intemperately vicious remarks. She moved, spoke, dressed and did her work in a removed and mechanical state that suggested the actions and voice of a sleepwalker.

Jerome never saw her alone for an instant. But he did see

her bemused white face and hear her neutral voice at the dinner table. She did not turn her eyes his way; he had no method of communication, silent or otherwise, in Dorothea's constant presence.

A gloom, reminiscent of the dark days of February when Mr. Lindsey had been ill, fell over the house, with the sole distinction that there was now no anxiety, no terror, no lamps that burned all night. But the heaviness was there, the silence, the sense of imprisonment. "Damn the woman," said Jerome to himself, "she fills the whole place with dank melancholy and somberness with her humors and her hysterias and her demands."

When he would emerge from the house into the bright May weather and feel the nimble air on his face, and the dancing light of the sun, it all seemed incredible to him, and he began to hate the confining walls, the dark rooms unenlivened by firelight, and the hushed voices of the servants. He wanted to cry out to Amalie: "Come here with me, into this gay weather, into this air of hope and life!" But Amalie was a prisoner in that house, and he hated it for her imprisonment. He thought of her almost constantly, with tenderness and anger and impatience, and he tried to convey these things to her with his eyes, with a subtle intonation of his voice, under Dorothea's very nose. He did not know whether she understood, for her head was always bent wearily, her face averted.

Finally he could stand it no longer. He wrote a note to Amalie, sealed it, gave it to Jim. "It is a matter of some importance," he informed the little Cockney. "And it is necessary that Miss Dorothea be unaware of it."

Jim's gnomelike features darkened apprehensively, but Jerome, whistling, had gone out in the trap on his way to the Bank. Jim turned the note over and over in his hands, pursing his lips, and sighing. He would give it to the young lady at once.

But he found this unexpectedly difficult. It was hard to find Amalie alone. Jim began to hope, foolishly, that he would be compelled to return the note to its writer that night. However, shortly before luncheon, Amalie came downstairs to arrange some garden flowers for the table, and here Jim found her, all her movements listless and tired and abstracted. He glanced about the dusky dining-room, warily. He heard Miss Dorothea descending, and her petulant voice: "Are you down there, Amalie?"

Amalie lifted her head, looked at the doorway, and replied in the affirmative. Jim approached her hastily, the note in the hollow of his palm. He whispered: "I was to give you this, ma'am." He pressed the note into Amalie's hand, and for a moment he was surprised at the coldness of her fingers. Her expression was mute, her lips pale. Jim fled, for Dorothea was in the hall. The kitchen door swung to behind him.

Amalie had hardly sufficient time to thrust the note into the bosom of her dress before Dorothea entered, all rustling bombazine, harsh face, hair severely coiffed under her cap, and jingling household keys. She stopped on the threshold of the room and stared about her suspiciously.

"Was someone just here?" she demanded, in the loud contemptuous tone she unconsciously reserved for Amalie.

Amalie pushed the last flower into its bowl. Now something within her began to burn with a sharp fire, and her breath came quickly. She said, and her own voice was loud, also: "Did you expect to find someone?"

Dorothea stiffened, was silent, regarding the other woman intently. She was suddenly frightened. Had she betrayed herself, put this wretch on dangerous guard? But before she could speak, Amalie was saying, in a gentler tone: "Forgive me. I am afraid I am somewhat nervous myself."

Dorothea slowly approached the table. She found it odd that she was trembling. The two women sat down to their silent meal. A maid tiptoed in and out through the baize door. Then Amalie said, as if stifling: "It is so bright outside. Would it not be possible for us to go out for a short walk or a ride?"

Dorothea fished grimly for her smelling salts, which she carried in the pocket of her black alpaca apron. She sniffed at them elaborately, and then in a pent and melancholy voice, she replied: "I am afraid that you have not understood Dr. Hawley, Amalie. Have you forgotten that he said I must rest constantly, no exertion, no disturbing—conditions?"

The new fire in Amalie glowed and quickened. She said, steadfastly, looking up at Dorothea with her large purplish eyes: "No, I have not forgotten. But you seem quite strong, and the mild weather might do you good." She turned her head to glance with bitter longing at the bright panorama which made every window in the room seem a painted picture of Paradise.

"I feel exceptionally weak, today," said Dorothea, leaning back in her chair, and staring heavily before her. "I shall have to ask you to come to my room with me, Amalie, and go over the household accounts while I rest in bed."

You selfish, inconsiderate wretch! thought Amalie, follow-

226

ing Dorothea to the latter's bedroom. All her listlessness was gone. It was as if Jerome's note, which lay in the hollow between her breasts, had given her renewed and febrile life. Her heart was beating with painful strength; there was moisture along the line of black hair which ran above her forehead. She helped Dorothea remove her boots, assisted her into bed. Then she announced that she would bring her knitting into the room, for work when the accounts were finished and Dorothea napped. She ran into her own room, shut the door, locked it, though her first thought was that she was behaving ridiculously. Then she took out Jerome's note and read it.

It was quite brief: "Can you escape the Gorgon today for a few minutes? Or, in the evening, perhaps? There is much to discuss, as you know." It bore neither salutation nor signature.

Amalie crushed the note in her hand. Her face had come alive, brilliant, tremulous. She ran to the window, thrust aside the draperies to their limit. She opened the window and leaned out, breathing deeply of the soft, warm air. She felt the sun on her head; it was too bright for her cloistered eyes, and she blinked. She said aloud: "O God!" And laughed, tears thick on her lashes. The fever was strong in her now; her whole body was tingling.

She left the window, opened a drawer in her bureau, and hid the note deep under piles of silk and cambric garments. She saw her flushed cheeks in the mirror. She dashed cold water over them, and over her hands, in the wrists of which she felt the drumming blood. She smoothed her hair, took up her knitting bag, and returned to Dorothea's room.

The room was already darkened, but there was an alert tenseness about Dorothea's reclining figure which Amalie at once detected. She seated herself tranquilly. She was aware of the sun beating on the drawn curtains, the smothering warmth in the room, the close smell of wax and furniture and carpet. But she rocked, and discussed household accounts with Dorothea. Her voice was soothing and low. The heat thickened in the room. The house was silent; birds murmured drowsily in the newly leafed trees. Finally Amalie was quiet, her needles clicking sleepily. Dorothea, who always napped briefly in the afternoon, let her eyelids fall. She knew that she would find Amalie there when she awakened, still knitting, still rocking, or perhaps drowsing herself. This was the usual procedure every day. Dorothea fell away into an uneasy sleep. She heard the needles; the faint sound followed her down into the pits of unconsciousness.

Amalie stopped both knitting and rocking. She rose and tip-toed to the bed. Dorothea lay motionless, her long gray face relaxed in slumber. Her mouth was slightly open; she snored restlessly. Amalie crept soundlessly from the room, closing the door inch by inch behind her. Once it creaked, and she shivered, almost with terror. Dorothea stirred on the bed, muttered, then snored again.

Once safe in the hall, Amalie ran to her room again, hastily threw a shawl over the shoulders of her blue foulard frock, tied on a bonnet with fingers that shook absurdly. Damp tendrils of her hair clung to her cheeks. She caught up her reticule, fled silently down the stairway. She found a servant dusting the dining-room. She forced her voice to composure: "I need the buggy, Elsie. And please peep in at Miss Dorothea occasionally, and when she awakens tell her that I have gone to see Dr. Hawley, as I am feeling unwell myself."

Elsie, startled, could only gaze curiously at Amalie's excited face and shaking lips. She murmured something, watched Amalie retreat towards the door. "Never mind calling for the buggy, Elsie," said Amalie. "I am in a hurry, so I will go to the stables myself and get it."

She went through the baize door in a blue flurry of dress and shawl and bonnet, stopped for a moment to inspect the roast the cook was preparing for the evening meal, then let herself out through the back door. She ran to the barn. All her blood was crying: "Escape! Escape!"

The barn had a hot and fecund smell; the golden light streamed through the broad doorway and the small windows, and motes of drifting gilt danced in it. The carriage horses stamped restlessly, turning their heads to stare at Amalie with round and impatient eyes. Two of the stableboys came towards her, pulling on their caps.

She regarded them in silence. She felt quite delirious; her face was damp. Then she said: "I'd like to have the buggy, please."

One of the boys hesitated. "You'll be driving alone, ma'am?"

"Yes." She moved towards the door, her excitement growing, her hands clenched together under the fringes of her shawl. She glanced at the house, serene and dreaming in the warm sunlight. Dorothea's draperies were still drawn. Amalie's breath came fast.

She winced fearfully as the buggy was driven from the barn. What a fearful clatter the wheels made on the caked earth! The horse's back shone like brown watered silk. The nickel

228

trimming on the harness winked in the sun. The boy helped Amalie climb into the buggy. She settled herself on the seat. It was more the sight of her pale set face and feverish eyes than anything else that made him say, dubiously: "You'll be all right, ma'am? You know how to drive? Burney's a frisky mare."

Amalie gathered up the reins in her gloved hands and said, with a smile: "I can drive, Tom. I think I can control Burney."

She slapped the reins on the mare's back, and the animal, happy to be at liberty, jumped forward, throwing Amalie against the back of the seat. She recovered herself, tightened the reins, uttered an angry word of remonstrance, then turned the horse more sedately onto the gravelled driveway. Again, she winced as the wheels grated on the small stones and threw them aside. She loosened the reins, let the horse go swiftly in spite of the hazard of the downhill grade; she leaned forward on her seat as if in flight, not looking back.

Then the shining silence flooded all about her. The horse had found the clay roadway; the wheels rolled with a gentle swaying motion. Sunlight, silent and calm, glittered on the trees, on the brown earth, on the green grass. Amalie passed from light into shadow, from shadow into light. She heard the birds, the whisper of tall grasses, the scurrying of animals in the brush. The valley stood clearly and distinctly below her. The roadway bent, straightened, flowed past woods, past blue and running streams, past abandoned old barns. Now she had reached the road to the village, and the round hill lay behind her. Hilltop was a toy mansion among its trees.

She was acutely sensible of everything about her, and she fixed her attention on the road, on the back of the horse. But her mind was empty. She kept it deliberately so, sternly controlled the sudden sharp tremblings that ran over her flesh. She passed the General's house. Josephine and Sally were daintily working in the garden. Amalie lay back in her seat, so that the curtain of the buggy concealed her face. She thought she heard a call, and slapped the reins briskly on the horse's back, her heart pounding. The wheels skimmed and bounced on the road: the mare threw up her head, her mane flowing.

It was fortunate that the village streets were unusually deserted this warm afternoon. Amalie moved to a corner of the leather seat and lowered her head. The Bank rose before her, sturdy and smug on its low green slopes, every window gleaming. It had a solid arrogance which normally irritated Amalie, and made her smile, for its self-importance was too much for her sense of humor. But now she reached out for it, mentally, as for a refuge against the peril and gossip of the town streets.

The buggy drew up at a carriage block and hitching post, and Amalie sprang out, stumbling on her heavy skirts and petticoats. She tied up the horse, bent her head, and with as much decorum as possible walked swiftly up the long low stairway. It was after banking hours, she reflected thankfully. There would be no customers about to stare at her curiously. She adjusted her bonnet, smoothed her shawl, and entered the cool dim interior of the Bank with a tranquil air. The clerks lurked behind their gratings; she pretended not to see them. She put her hand on the door of Alfred's office, and entered quickly, closing the door behind her.

The office was empty. All at once, Amalie's controlled calm left her. She fell into a chair and began to tremble. She looked at the door which led to Jerome's office. She wanted to rise and go to it, but her legs had become too feeble. She loosened her bonnet ribbons, passed her kerchief over her wet face, fumbled at the strings of her reticule. How terribly indiscreet she had been! What were the clerks saying in their cages, probably smirking all over their pallid faces? Then she whispered, aloud: "I am ridiculous. It is perfectly proper for me to visit the Bank."

The office was as quiet as a cemetery. She heard the ticking of the clock on the mantelpiece. She forced herself to stare at the engravings on the walls. And now everything reminded her of her husband: the neat row of pens on the desk, the heaped closed ledgers, the big mahogany chair standing silent and empty, the green vase waiting for flowers, the streaks of sunlight on the dark carpet and on the draperies.

Sick terror and misery made her start to her feet, run swiftly towards the door of Jerome's office. She flung it open. Jerome was at the windows, smoking, his hands clasped behind his back.

He heard her enter. He said: "Well, Jamison, did you find those letters?"

Then he turned. They looked at each other across the width of the room in an alert and intense silence. Jerome removed the cheroot from his mouth; his eyes narrowed.

But he said nothing at all. With a sense of sickness, Amalie saw that he glanced at the doorway which led to Alfred's office, and then at the doorway which led to the Bank proper. He came away from the windows with a step that sounded furtive in Amalie's sharpened ears. His eyes narrowed still more.

"Well," he said, softly.

"There was no other way—to see you," she said huskily. And now shame and exhaustion welled over her, made her feel actually ill. She felt the wretched blood in her cheeks. She said: "Was it indiscreet?"

He hesitated, then replied quietly: "It was not exactly the most discreet thing in the world." He hesitated again. Then he drew out one of the chairs which stood against the wall, and said, more gently now: "Sit down, Amalie."

She sat down, clutching her reticule, her lips dry and thick with her increasing shame and ignominy. As clearly as if she saw herself in a mirror, she was aware of her country blue dress, her shawl, her dowdy bonnet, her pale and lifeless face and heavy eyes. The gloved hands on her knee appeared to her to be too large, too awkward. There was a sudden and desperate urge in her to rise, to fly from the Bank, to go home, to forget. How contemptible she must appear to him, how disgusting, how unwanted!

To her horror and mortification, she heard herself repeating dully: "There was no other way."

"Yes," he said. "I understand." He put down his cheroot in a metal tray and sat down behind the desk. She glanced up at him, sitting there so unperturbed, so immaculate, so contained. And then she hated him. Her despair was a salt taste in her mouth. How could he regard her like this, with such a dispassionate look, and with such cool and thoughtful eyes? Then he was glancing at the doors again.

Her hands clenched. Through the clamoring of her misery, she said to herself: But what did I expect? Did I expect he would embrace me vehemently, make a hideous display of himself, and of me, within doors that might open at any moment? She pressed her colorless lips together and gazed at him with courageous steadfastness. She could not know how pathetic and weary her violet eyes were in the shadow of her bonnet, and how sad. But Jerome saw. He took up his cheroot again, and puffed at it with determination.

"We must be quick," he said, almost in a whisper. "Jamison, or one of the clerks, may come in at any moment. We must settle things—now."

"Yes." Her lips formed the word soundlessly.

"We must go away. Very soon. Before Alfred returns on Saturday."

She could not speak. Her hands fell, slackened, on her knees. Her face glimmered whitely.

"He must divorce you," Jerome was saying. "We'll leave him

231

letters. This is Wednesday. We must leave tomorrow night, or Friday morning, at the latest."

He spoke without emotion. He flicked the ash from his cheroot. He was looking at her with straight hard eyes, without passion.

Then she said, her voice quite loud and clear in the silence: "No."

He paused in the very act of putting the cheroot into his mouth. Now all the lines of his face tightened. "Yes," he said.

She pushed back her bonnet with a distracted hand. "No," she repeated.

"Why not?" There was no anger in his words, and only the slightest impatience.

"We cannot do that." She moistened her lips. He saw that she was trembling. "We cannot do so cowardly a thing, so disgraceful a thing."

He smiled, and the smile was ugly. "And may I ask you, my dear, what you propose as an alternative?"

She tried to speak; she swallowed thickly. But she still gazed at him fixedly. "We must wait until Alfred returns. We must wait—a little. Perhaps a few weeks. We cannot do this to your —father." Her voice shook. "You must remember that he has been ill, that he is ill. We cannot run away, like criminals. We —owe it to all of them to be honest, to discuss it, to make plans that have dignity and decency."

He smiled again, even more unpleasantly, as if something she had said amused him. Seeing this, she cried out wildly: "You must understand! Surely you understand? Jerome!"

He leaned back in his chair. She could not know how the crying of his name disturbed him. He spoke firmly: "Please, Amalie. You'll have the whole damn Bank running in here. Let us be sensible. If we do as you so sentimentally suggest, all hell will break loose in that house. 'Dignity'? 'Decency'? Let your imagination dwell on the subject, just for a little. Do you imagine that Alfred and my father will sit down with us in a very civilized manner and discuss our——"

She put up her hand in a wild and defensive gesture, as if to avert a blow. Her expression was sick.

Jerome said, with sudden gentleness: "My darling. You see, yourself, how impossible that is."

She was silent. For now the whole enormity of the situation struck her as it had not struck her before. She had come as a calamity to that house on the hill. She had come as a pestilence, poisoning the air, disrupting the peace, striking mortally

232

at a dying old gentleman, a crippled, loving boy, an honorable man. She had betrayed them all. In a measure, she had even betrayed Jerome. Had none of them known her, that house would still be tranquil: Mr. Lindsey living out his last days in quietness, Philip continuing his music in undisturbed happiness, Alfred retaining his name with pride and respect. Life would flow in and about them, without horror and shame. Jerome would live there, placidly awaiting his marriage with Sally Tayntor, planning his life.

But now, because of her, they were about to be thrown into everlasting disgrace and misery. It would kill Mr. Lindsey, who trusted and loved her. It would leave an eternal mark on Philip. Alfred would never recover from his humiliation and despair. Jerome's life was ruined.

She said, in a strange, strained voice, her eyes darkened: "I think it would be best if I went away. Alone."

Jerome tapped the desk with slow fingers. "You mean, I should follow later?"

She shook her head. "No. I—I could leave a letter for Alfred, saying—" She could not continue. She put her kerchief to her mouth. Then she withdrew it and went on with increasing steadiness: "I could say I had decided to go away, and beg him not to try to find me. It would—hurt him, immeasurably. But it would not injure him as much as if——"

He got up and came to her and took her cold and flaccid hand. Now she saw his face, moved and compassionate. "My dear," he said, and for the first time there was emotion in his voice, "you don't know what you are saying. Do you think I wouldn't follow you, until I found you?"

She looked at his hand. Then it seemed to her that her heart broke. She pressed her face to the back of his hand and tears burst from her eyes. She said with frantic but controlled passion: "O Jerome. Tell me you love me! Tell me you have not changed! Tell me that, or I shall really die!"

Forgetting everything now but this poor woman, Jerome took her face in his hands and kissed her on her shaking mouth. She put her arms about his neck and he felt their frenzied and clinging strength. He looked into her drenched eyes, so imploring, so vulnerable in their anguish.

With his lips moving against hers, he said: "My darling, my love."

Her arms fell from his neck. He wiped away her tears with infinite tenderness. He smoothed the tendrils of her hair which had escaped from her bonnet. He said: "Let me take care of

233

this, Amalie, my dearest. You must understand this is the only way, our leaving together, almost at once. Believe me, it is the kindest way. It—it will be a shock, I admit. But if we are not there to be reproached, to be reviled, matters will settle themselves more quickly."

She whispered, still gazing at him despairingly: "Your own life, Jerome. I have ruined it. The Bank—you have made a place here. Now I have destroyed everything for you."

He made himself smile indulgently. "My foolish darling. I stayed here only because of you. I shall leave it quite joyfully because of you."

But her burning thoughts still held her. "Your father—it will kill him, Jerome."

"I think not," he replied, with more confidence than he felt. "After all, he never—interfered. It may be somewhat of a shock, I admit. But he's a tough old patrician, and after a little he will be glad that we are happy. And we are going to be happy, you know."

"But how could you be happy, forever cut off from your father? He will never see you again! We'll have made that impossible for him. How will you live, Jerome? I know how hard it is to live!" The wildness was back in her voice, and the frenzied hopelessness.

"Oh, come, come," he said, glancing uneasily at the doors. "I am not helpless, or a child. And I am a portrait painter, of sorts. I could have sold dozens. Besides, I still have a little money, and we could live in France, on almost nothing. The future doesn't frighten me in the least. Not if you are with me," and he bent again and kissed her.

But this time she did not respond. Her lips were lifeless under his. She pushed him away, after a moment.

"And Alfred," she said, wringing her hands. "How could we do that to him?"

His brows drew together. "It seems," he said, with vicious lightness, "that we have already done a great deal to him."

The blood rushed to her face. She stood up, holding the back of her chair. But he had become excited at the mention of the man he hated. "Do you think I care for that pedant, that Cromwellian bigot, that stick? This will well repay him for years of stuffiness and righteousness!"

But she had become very still. "You are cruel," she said, staring at him motionlessly. "You are stupid. But they are the same thing. In spite of all your erudite conversations with your father, I have heard your cruelty and your stupidity, under all your fine words. I thought it did not matter. But I see that it does, after all."

He was incredulous. He could only stand there in silence.

But she was not seeing him now. She was remembering the night when Alfred had told her of his loneliness. She was remembering his moved, changed expression, his trust, his unconscious pathos, the touch of his hand, almost humble in its simplicity, her understanding that he had never spoken so to anyone before, his gratitude that he could speak and have her sympathy, his happiness in his belief that he had discovered a friend. She had come perilously close to loving him then, in her compassion and in her sudden knowledge of his integrity and unaffected and hidden desire for the affection of others.

Jerome was alarmed at Amalie's expression, and he momentarily lost his anger against her for what she had said. He took a step towards her, but she stepped backwards, away from him.

"You have always hated Alfred," she exclaimed. "You never understood him, or cared to understand him. You jeered at him, deliberately misinterpreted everything he ever said; you attempted, always, to make him appear a fool. And then, when you had deceived yourself into believing that the man of straw you had created was the real man, you despised him. But you have never deceived others."

"Very clever," said Jerome softly. "So I am a contemptible man, without honor or pity or sensibility. I have attacked a hero, out of sheer malice. It is very noble and edifying to hear these sentiments from you. But, of course, you have completely forgotten that you married him for brazenly mercenary reasons, exchanging yourself boldly for what he could give you.

"And now you have the audacity to call me cruel and stupid. Don't you think the same epithets apply to you also?"

Her face had become pinched and gray. But she regarded him without wavering.

"Yes," she said clearly. "We are both disgusting wretches. It will be better for Alfred never to see either of us again."

He leaned back against the desk and smiled affably. "And that, my pet, is what I have been attempting to tell you."

They looked at each other now without love or passion, only with understanding. Jerome was wryly amused. But he was also secretly and deeply alarmed at Amalie's color, at the stark agony in her eyes.

"Is it settled, then, that we must go away at once?" he asked.

She was twisting her bonnet strings in her tremulous hands. "No," she said. "We must first talk to Alfred. We must tell

235

him. We must make him see that he is not suffering any loss in my going."

Jerome pursed his lips and stared into space. "And you intend to tell him just as soon as he returns?"

The ribbons were tight and drawn, over her fingers. "If your father shows improvement—yes. The proper occasion must present itself. It will."

"I presume," he suggested sardonically, "that you will first inform me of the 'proper occasion' so I can brace myself? Or will this delightful conversation take place between you—and your husband—in the privacy of your bedroom?"

Amalie's face appeared to dwindle, to diminish. But she answered quietly: "I will tell you. It may be only a few days, it may be a few weeks."

"And in the meantime, you will maintain the most amiable relations with my family and with your husband?"

He shook his head. "My darling, isn't that too much to ask of me? I have a nervous constitution. I don't enjoy the prospect of sitting on a pile of dynamite with the fuse hissing somewhere off in obscurity."

Then he added, with virulent disagreeableness: "Or perhaps you would prefer something else? You would prefer, perhaps, to forget and to continue your life as before, in my father's house? Is that the secret alternative in your mind?"

Amalie uttered a faint exclamation. But Jerome had become excited again. He came close to her, and she retreated still a few more steps. "Well, let me tell you, my dear, everything is not in your own hands. I have a few ideas of my own. You are not going to make a fool of me."

He turned and went abruptly to his desk. He flung the half-smoked cheroot into his wastebasket, lit another. It infuriated him that his hands were uncertain.

"Perhaps you think it might be pleasant to deceive your noble husband on other—occasions, with me as your compliant accomplice. Perhaps I have underestimated your cleverness, my pet."

Amalie did not stir. She might not have heard him at all. She only gazed at him with intensely purple eyes.

"Or," he continued, with cold violence, "you would think it most obliging of me if I removed myself permanently from your vicinity, and never returned to my father's house?"

He waited. But she did not speak. He studied her intently for a long procession of moments. Then he exclaimed: "Amalie! My darling! Forgive me. I know what I have been saying is not true. But you have failed to consider me in the least."

The bonnet strings fell from her fingers. She put her hands over her face.

He did not know what to do. He rubbed his forehead miserably. He wanted to take her in his arms, but that seemed impossible just now.

"Why won't you trust my judgment?" he pleaded. "I am stronger than you, my dearest. See here," he added, with sudden animation, "I have another plan. If you are so determined to be 'honorable,' why do you not go away first and stay with a friend of mine in New York, or go to Saratoga for a few days? In the meantime, I will talk to Alfred myself and thereafter join you? In this way you will be spared all—unpleasantness— and I assure you that I am quite capable of managing the situation alone."

She dropped her hands. Her cheeks were streaked with tears. "Thank you, Jerome," she whispered. "Oh, thank you! But I cannot do that. I cannot run away like a thief. I owe this last thing to Alfred."

She looked blindly about for her reticule. It was on the chair she had left. She picked it up. Then she turned to Jerome, imploringly. "Please, please," she murmured. And flung out her hand.

He was silent, while she, in turn, speechlessly pleaded with him. Then, when she saw that he would not soften towards her, or understand, she went to the door and left the room.

CHAPTER TWENTY-EIGHT

Dr. Willis Hawley regarded Amalie with kindly and concerned worry. He leaned back in his chair. He had pushed aside a vase of early roses from his own old garden, and the warm study was permeated with the sweet and overpowering fragrance.

The physician was an elderly man, with a brown face and a thin white beard, and with curiously alive eyes the color of old amber. He was not only physician to the Lindseys, but a friend of many years. He was especially fond of Amalie, for he was a bachelor and had a considerable taste in women.

He said regretfully: "Well, now we know definitely." He added, with more cheerfulness: "But there is plenty of time, you know, Miss Amalie. You are still young. Twenty-three it is, isn't it? Of course, I have always believed that it is best for a woman to have her children between the ages of sixteen and twenty-three, when she is at her most vigorous and can take a joy in her offspring. Older women are less—flexible, not only physically, but mentally. And flexibility, I have discovered, is absolutely necessary if one is to endure the riotous company of children."

He smiled at the woman opposite him, but his eyes were still anxious.

"But should you have your first child at twenty-five, that is not too late. Your family, then, will be necessarily small, for the hazards of childbirth should not be undertaken indiscriminately after thirty. There are many who disagree with me, but unfortunately, perhaps, the facts are in favor of my opinion. Tumors, various ailments of many kinds, beset a middle-aged woman, in her early thirties, and make childbirth distressingly hazardous."

Amalie tried to smile. The doctor's keen eye detected her profound exhaustion and illness. He said, more gravely: "But there is a much more serious matter than this disappointment, which is temporary, I hope. You are not well. I have noticed, upon my visits to Miss Dorothea, that you have been failing, my poor child. It is not anemia, nor any organic trouble, I am certain. I might even say that the root of the affliction is unhappiness. But that, of course, is preposterous." He tapped his fingers tentatively on his desk, but the shrewdness of his gaze did not diminish.

Amalie forced herself to say: "I—I am not unhappy. But I am very tired."

"Of course, of course! I know how devotedly you have cared for old William, and now for Miss Dorothea. But I may tell you frankly that Miss Dorothea is in no danger. Middle-aged ladies are frequently petulant and demanding, and reek with hypochondria. I have sometimes thought that ladies between the ages of thirty-five and fifty ought to retire to some nonsectarian convent and there await the time when they have recovered their equanimity." He laughed richly. "So, you must not worry unduly about Miss Dorothea. I might even suggest a masterful neglect of her, for your own good. The air, the sun, quiet walks and drives, visits to good friends, simple meals, sleep—all these will restore your health. For," he added, with fresh gravity, "you are not well. I am afraid that, if you do not take care, you may become extremely ill."

"I do not intend to die, dear Dr. Hawley," said Amalie, with a smile which struck the doctor with fresh apprehension for her.

"Oh, certainly not, certainly not! You have a most robust constitution. But you have been much too confined." He rose as Amalie rose. "I have a tonic for you, my dear child. But it will be of no benefit unless you take better care of yourself."

He walked to the buggy with her. He noticed how feeble was her step, and how her head drooped, and how uncertain her hands were as he assisted her into the vehicle. He must talk to Alfred, he reflected. The girl was extremely ill. Her color was quite dreadful, and he, Dr. Hawley, did not like the mauve swellings beneath her eyes. He shook his head slightly. Some hideous malaise of the body or of the spirit was tormenting her, and he suspected the latter. He remembered seeing her on the village streets before her marriage to Alfred Lindsey, and he had profoundly admired her dauntless carriage, her upflung head, her shining eyes and vividly pale complexion. She possessed none of these things now. She moved as if broken, too listless, too exhausted. It was very puzzling, very disturbing. He knew Alfred well, and thought him an honorable, just man with hidden attributes of kindness and fidelity. Had something happened to that marriage?

He watched Amalie drive away, and returned to his quiet brick house, shaking his head. Yes, he must have a talk with Alfred, and immediately upon the latter's arrival home. He felt quite angry about Dorothea. Was that pestilential woman annoying the poor girl? That could hardly be true, for he was aware that Amalie had a very vital character and no vulnerabilities.

Amalie allowed the horse to draw the buggy home without any direction on her part. Indeed, she was incapable of control. Her thoughts drifted across her mind like huge tormented shapes of anguish. She found no consolation or hope anywhere, but only desolation and crushing sorrow. Her naturally resolute character had always been sustained by a kind of single-hearted and guiltless courage, by the knowledge of her own peculiar integrity. But now both courage and integrity had gone. There was nothing left but grief and a despairing remorse.

I have no one to blame, not even Jerome, she thought. I knew, the first night I saw him, that we belonged to each other. He, at least, was honest enough to accept that. He asked me to go away with him, before I married Alfred. I knew that I could make him marry me; a woman always knows that. But—he had no money, no immediate prospects. So I am more guilty than he. Had I believed, then, that his father might eventually forgive him for running off with me, I should have gone. But I was too afraid of poverty and misery and uncertainty. I was a coward. We pay more, in the end, for our cowardice than we do for our crimes.

I cannot be a coward now. If there is any honor to be saved from all this, then I must not be a coward.

But in spite of this resolution, she could look at the future only with despair. And the despair was not solely for herself but in the main for Jerome. In spite of what he had said, she knew that his interest in the Bank was not a casual or expedient thing. His love for his father, too, was not to be overlooked. When she went away with him, his life here would be ended, and he would never see his father again.

How can I make it up to him? she thought, with intense suffering. How can I make him finally believe that I was worth the abandoning of his whole life, and of Mr. Lindsey? Will he come to hate me?

At this, she felt an overwhelming torment that was unendurable. The whole warm summer landscape about her dissolved as if seen under water. She had only one alternative: to run away alone, secretly, with just a note to Alfred that she had decided that her life had become too dull for her taste, and begging him to forgive her and not to try to find her. Jerome, then, and all his family, would continue their lives in peace, and eventually, she would be forgotten, the mistake of her first coming not remembered.

They will forget me, she thought. Alfred will be dreadfully hurt. But he, too, in time, will forget me, and as soon as he can. Mr. Lindsey will not understand. But he will forgive and forget me, also. And Jerome—he will marry Sally, dismissing me as a fool. But he will forget, perhaps more quickly than the others.

But now her torment became truly unbearable. She did not have the courage to leave Jerome. At least, not yet. Give me a week or two more, she prayed. Just a few more days to see him and hear his voice. I know I am cowardly and weak. But I must have just this little more time.

The buggy was climbing the slopes now. Amalie lifted her aching eyes to Hilltop, beaming in the late afternoon sun, the shadow of the trees mottling its warm gray walls. How impregnable and kind it was, how secure and welcoming! She could not bring misery and shame to that house. She must go away. She was weeping more quietly now, and her tears stopped as her determination strengthened. It was much better for one to suffer mortally, than several. She had no illusions that Jerome would speak, after she had gone. She knew him too well. He was too selfish, too expedient, too unscrupulous. He was, moreover, a realist.

She needed only this one contemptuous thought, this one embittered reflection, to make her resolution firm. She was only human, however, and her knowledge that Jerome would forget her easily, shrugging any memory of her aside, perhaps with gratitude and relief, filled her with wild anger. She remembered his uneasy coldness when she had entered his office, his furtive glances at the doors, his careful withdrawal. She would not remember anything else. She needed this to sustain her.

She left the buggy at the stable. She discovered that a terrible weakness had come over her, and every step towards the house was made by a supreme effort. She could hardly push open the heavy oaken door, and the mild exertion made her heart beat suffocatingly in her throat. The hall was warm and dim as the door closed behind her, and silent. It seemed that the house slept. The library door was open, and she saw the sunlight striking on the dim red-and-blue morocco of the books on the shelves and lying in long bent fingers on the dark carpet. She could hear the rustling of trees near the French windows, the distant clucking of drowsy fowl. All else was wrapped in shining silence.

Amalie stood at the foot of the oaken staircase. She had not realized how much she had come to love this strong house, its peace and security, its fastness and protection for her whose life had been so beset by poverty and hopelessness. Stifled, torn again by sorrow, she unloosened her bonnet strings, and let her bonnet fall from her hand. After tomorrow, perhaps, she would never see this house again, never feel its quiet walls behind her, never sleep again in an unthreatened bed. Where shall I go? she thought numbly. What shall I do?

She looked up the stairway, waiting warmly in the dusk. She saw the sunlit corridor at the top. She began to climb, and every step was agony, for she was overcome with a final weakness. The bonnet trailed by its ribbons, which she held in her hand. Her head was bent. She felt the thickness and richness of the carpet under her feet. She was already an exile, already an intruder who had no right in this house.

The door of her room was closed. She pushed it open with a hand which had lost its strength. Dorothea sat there, near the window, her big black-clad arms folded across her grim breast. Amalie saw her mouth, its bitter hatred, and its infuriated knowledge. She saw Dorothea's eyes, burning in her gray, gaunt face under the fluted cap.

Amalie, on the threshold, did not move. She could only say to herself: She knows. She felt the floor moving and dipping under her feet, the thickening of her throat, and could hear her own loud, short breath.

"Where have you been?" said Dorothea, and even in the half-fainting condition that was overwhelming Amalie, Dorothea's voice sounded strangely quiet to her.

She made herself close the door behind her and advance towards her dresser. She put down the bottle which Dr. Hawley had given her. And now she had gone beyond any feeling at all, any pain or terror. She kept her hand on the bottle, and faced the other woman, her face deathly white and calm.

"I have been to see Dr. Hawley. He gave me this tonic." Her voice was expressionless and dull, but every word had been like a knife in her throat.

She knew that Dorothea was beside herself and could not restrain her fury and hatred very much longer. The two women regarded each other in a sudden and terrible silence.

Then Dorothea said, still very quietly: "Did you see—him?"

Amalie could not speak. Her fingers tightened about the bottle. She leaned back against the dresser, for her feet had begun to slide out from beneath her.

Dorothea moved very slightly, but that motion revealed the frenzied state of her mind even more than a violent gesture would have done.

"So you did see him. You sneaked away from this honorable house while I slept. You ran away—to see him. Shameless, abandoned woman." Her voice did not rise. It had an uninflected, even a slow and thoughtful quality, which was extraordinarily frightening, like the voice of madness.

Dorothea lifted her arm stiffly and pointed her finger at Amalie. "I have known about you two for a long time. I have tried to hide my knowledge—for Alfred's sake." Her voice broke now, cracked with savage pain. "I have kept silence—for his sake. It was my plan to keep this silence, unless you made it impossible." She paused. "You have made it impossible."

Even after she had finished, her finger still pointed inexorably at Amalie. It was as if she had no volition to drop her hand, as if it had become frozen in its attitude of denunciation and she possessed no further power over it.

Amalie said, softly: "I am going away—alone. Tomorrow. None of you need ever see me again." She closed her eyes suddenly, for she could not bear to look at the hand extended against her.

And then she heard Dorothea say, as from a great distance: "You believe you can run away, like the vile coward you are, and leave your accomplice to face the results of his crime—alone?"

Amalie did not open her eyes. She said faintly: "Alfred—need never know. You have only to keep your silence. When I am gone, you can all forget me. Jerome will never speak." She waited, then she added: "After all, he is your brother."

She heard a slight rustling movement. But it was some moments before she could lift her eyelids. She might have started back if the dresser had not prevented her, for Dorothea was standing close to her now, looking at her with an almost inhuman hatred and gloating.

"No," said Dorothea, "he is no longer my brother. So, you thought you might save him, leave him here in peace, to laugh secretly at Alfred! No, no, my dear woman. He is not going to escape the punishment of his villainy." And she shook her head with a stony and malevolent amusement. Amalie saw her eyes, and she thought, with a quick and leaping terror: She is insane! She fell back against the dresser until the back of her head almost touched the mirror, over the gilt and crystal bottles. A desperate panic seized her. Her eye darted to the door.

Dorothea reached out and grasped her arm. She shook her head violently, smiling.

"I cannot prevent your going. But—I can tell Alfred and my father. Your lover will not dare remain here, for he will know that Alfred will kill him. Go, if you wish. Run away, hide. But if he remains, you will be guilty of more than adultery. You will be guilty of murder."

Her iron fingers crushed Amalie's flesh. They stared into each other's eyes.

"Your father," whispered Amalie.

Dorothea's face tightened malignantly. "My father!" The grip on Amalie's arm had become agonizing. "Do you think I care for anybody but Alfred?" And now her look was wilder, more malefic than ever. "I have never cared for anybody, in all my life, but Alfred. When he married that young fool who died, I thought there was nothing left for me to live for. When she was laid in her grave, I was happy. I thanked God." There was something obscene, now, in her low voice, something

243

chuckling and delighted. "I knew that in time he would realize that we loved each other——"

In spite of her terror, in spite of her growing faintness, Amalie was astounded, revolted and incredulous. She listened to the sudden spilling torrent of Dorothea's passion, the cataract of her thin, shrill words. She could not look away from the jerking light in the demented eyes. She wanted to put her hands over her ears, but they were nerveless with shock.

Then Dorothea shook the aching arm she held until Amalie could hardly restrain a loud cry of pain. She felt Dorothea's breath in her face.

"And then," cried Dorothea, "you came! You indecent and disgusting creature! You seduced him into marriage with you; you plotted to ruin and destroy him! You took him from me, and now you think you can disgrace him forever, without penalty to yourself! But you fail to reckon with me!"

She shook Amalie with even more violence, and Amalie had no strength with which to resist her.

"You took away my life! You took all hope from me! You accepted the name of a good and noble man and besmirched it! It was not enough for you, all he had given you. You must betray him behind his back and laugh at him in secret. But you fail to reckon with me!"

Sheer terror now gave Amalie the force to enable her to wrench her arm from Dorothea's grasp. She sidled along the edge of the bureau. She exclaimed, watching Dorothea with enormous eyes as if their gaze might restrain her: "I am going away. I will go now. But, for God's sake, don't hurt Alfred more than he has already been hurt. What does it matter about Jerome now? If you—you ever cared for—Alfred, have pity on him now. Don't tell him. Let him forget me."

But Dorothea would not let her escape. She moved with her. She laughed aloud.

"No! I shall tell him everything, so he can do justice on that man, even if you are not here."

Amalie stopped. She clutched the edge of the bureau with slipping hands.

She murmured: "You do not love him. You never loved him. You hated him, when he married the first time, and you hated him even more when he married me. You want to revenge yourself on him because he preferred other women to you. Can't you see that? Can't you be sorry? Can't you have a little pity for him?"

Dorothea straightened as if she had become rigid. Then she

lifted her hand and struck Amalie full in the face.

Amalie did not wince, did not cry out. She stood still, in absolute silence, and the whiteness of her cheek slowly reddened into the full fingerprints of Dorothea's hand. There was no anguish, no terror, in her eyes now, which deepened to dark and glowing purple. She said clearly: "You have called me shameless and disgusting. But you are more shameless and disgusting than I. It is you who would ruin Alfred and break his heart, not I. And only out of vengeance and hatred."

Dorothea lifted her hand again with a frantic gesture, as if she would strike Amalie down. But Amalie smiled contemptuously.

"Do not touch me again, Dorothea. For, if you do, you will be sorry." Her hand closed on a candlestick on the bureau behind her. "And now you will listen to me. I have told you I will go away. But I shall remain until Alfred returns and until I have told him myself. I have a little more pity for him than you have, and I swear to you that if you denounce me before I have spoken to him first, I shall tell him of the scene in this room and what you have told me. You will never dare to speak to him again. He will know everything, and he will reproach you for having been the cause of his ultimate misery and pain, for he will know that but for you his suffering would have been less."

She caught her breath. She regarded Dorothea with proud disgust. "Keep your silence. When I am gone, and forgotten, and he has divorced me, he will turn to you for comfort."

Even in her madness, Dorothea heard. She stepped back. She stared at Amalie fixedly. Deep within her eyes the light of sanity, of shrewd calculation, of reflection, began to appear.

"And now," said Amalie, sick to very death, "please go out of my room. Leave me alone. I—I am ill, I think. I want to rest."

Still staring at her, Dorothea backed away slowly. She reached the door. She fumbled for it blindly. Then she went out, looking at Amalie to the very last until the door was closed.

Amalie stood against the bureau for a long time, unable to move for fear she would fall. Then she pushed herself to her feet. She went to her rosewood desk. She wrote calmly: "I have another plan. When Alfred returns I shall tell him, at an opportune time, that I find my life with him insupportable, and that it will mean unhappiness for us both if I remain with him. I shall tell you where you may find me, after a suitable period of waiting, when you are able to leave without suspicion. I can think of no better plan, and I am certain that upon reflection you will agree that this is best for all of us."

She folded the paper, placed it in an envelope, and sealed it. All her movements were without hurry. She held the envelope in her hand, then rose quietly and rang for a maid. She asked the maid to summon Jim. While she waited for Jerome's valet she stood in the center of the room, staring at nothing, and thinking to herself: It is quite easy, if one refuses to think about anything.

Jim tapped softly on her door, and she went to it, composed and smiling. Without speaking, she gave him the envelope. He glanced at it quickly, then at the young woman. His simian face wrinkled, but he bowed and retreated.

When Amalie was alone again, she went to her bed and fell upon it, face down, her open eyes pressed into the pillow.

After a long while she heard the dinner bell ring, but when she attempted to rise she found it impossible. All her fortitude was gone. She lay on the bed in a state of complete shock, unable to move, her breast hardly rising with her slow breath.

CHAPTER TWENTY-NINE

When Jerome returned from the Bank his acute sensibilities informed him, or he imagined they informed him, that there was something ominous in the air of the quiet house. He saw neither Amalie nor his sister. All the rooms were still and empty, filled with the warm glow of the sunset. The windows stood open, and breezes as soft as silk and as sweet as the blossoming earth blew through every corridor and door. Jerome could hear the cook's canaries singing prodigiously in the kitchen. Whistling thoughtfully, he went up the staircase to his room, looking down for a moment, on the second landing, at the deserted hall below, and listening to the ancient grandfather clock as it ticked loudly in the silence. A faint beam of light struck on its round and polished pendulum, which reflected the beam in golden intensity.

His door opened soundlessly as he approached it, and he saw that Jim was waiting for him, very sober and wrinkled. Something in the little man's sober air prevented Jerome from greeting him affably. Suddenly alert, he closed the door behind him. Without speaking, Jim gave him Amalie's letter.

Jerome held it in his hand, unopened. But he regarded Jim with penetration. Jim stared back at him somberly. Jerome frowned. He opened the letter, read it quickly. Then, as Jim watched him, Jerome deliberately tore the paper to small pieces, went to the cold hearth, dropped the tatters upon it, and carefully lighted the little pile with a struck match. He stood and watched it being reduced to safe ashes. He turned back to Jim with a bland smile, went to a chair, sat down and produced a cheroot. Jim came forward quickly and lit it for him. Jerome puffed tranquilly and studied his man amiably.

"Jim," he said, "how would you like to return to New York?"

"For a visit, sir?" said Jim, in a tone of such hopefulness that Jerome was not deceived. He shook his head a little.

"No, Jim. For good. You are delighted, of course."

Jim said nothing.

"You were quite right, in the beginning," Jerome continued, with an expression of great candor. "We ought not to have remained. I was wrong in insisting. This is a damned dull place, and I have, frankly, had enough of it. So it's back to New York for us, eh?"

Jim blinked, but he said in a voice of low firmness: "I think, sir, it's too late to go back."

Jerome scowled, and his eyes narrowed. "Now, what the devil do you mean by that, you rascal?"

Jim glanced at the small mound of ashes on the hearth, and Jerome followed his glance. He took the cheroot from his mouth, slowly. But Jim said quietly: "If you go back, sir, it'll be after the wedding?"

Jerome stood up. "I am afraid, Jim, that there will be no wedding. Not for a while, at least."

Jim did not seem surprised, but his nutlike face wrinkled despondently. He said: "I thought not, sir."

Jerome walked up and down the room, smoking abstractedly. "I see," he said, at last, after a few turns. He stood before his valet. "Jim, you aren't a fool. What would you suggest? Things are in somewhat of a pickle." He smiled wryly.

Jim shrugged. "You wouldn't take my advice, sir, beggin' your pardon. It would be improper to suggest anything." Jerome waited. The little man sighed. "If it was anybody but you, sir, I'd say to him: 'Stay here and weather it out, you bloody fool. Stay here and keep your mouth shut. Mum's the word, and the man was never hanged who held his tongue. Let the storm blow over. Batten down the hatches, and take down the sails, and let 'er rip. There's cargo aboard as should be saved.'" He

247

paused, grimacing dismally. "But I couldn't say that to you, sir."

Jerome walked up and down again. "I love your metaphors, Jim," he said. "They are so colorful. But, like all metaphors, they aren't specific. 'I couldn't say that to you, sir.' Very good, Jim. I'd glad you didn't. I am a pragmatist, Jim. I like diagrams and maps, closely annotated and marked. No, I don't like metaphors. The imagination has a tendency to fill metaphors, like a handful of peas in a pot. It rattles around too much, and forms no pattern. Be specific, Jim. Unroll the map and show the directions which, I hope, are noted in words of one syllable."

Jim straightened, looked at Jerome with hopeful courage. "Well, sir, here's the map, and it's plain to see. If—if not too many know, keep mum, ride the storm. You've got a valuable cargo, and that's the Bank, sir, and you like the Bank, and it's your life now. You've got a fine passenger aboard, too, and that's Mr. Lindsey, and you've sworn to take him through. All your treasures, if I may say so, sir, is on that ship, and if it goes down, you go down with it, and there's no saving of any part, not even yourself. That fair mithers me, Mr. Jerome. We've been through thick and thin together, and got out of blasted scrapes together, leaving only a little skin behind." He smiled mournfully.

"Go on, Jim." Jerome's voice was very affable.

Jim took more courage. "The—the country where you're headed, sir——" he shook his head, "it might be prodigious attractive, but I fancy it's full of bogs and moors and lost places, with no shelter on it, and no escape."

Jerome smiled at him with great admiration. "I do love your metaphors. By the way, where did you pick up all this seaman's lingo?"

"I was a sailor, sir, very briefly, at one time."

"You mean you were transported?"

Jim made a grimace. "It's a crude way of expressin' it, sir. But upon reflection, I believe you could call it that." He tried to smile. "I prefers, sir, to say that I took a sea voyage, for my health."

Jerome put his hand on the other's shoulder. "You came back with a lot of wit, Jim. You're helping me think. But, as I was never a—seaman—I must think in terms of a landlubber. Go on from there."

Encouraged, Jim said with more boldness: "There's your weddin' with Miss Sally, sir. A lovely young lady, with a rich pa as loves you. Go on with the weddin', and collect the cash. Money'll fill the bill for a lot of other things as has no cash value, and cash value's what's important, in the long run, in spite of what the parsons say. Why," and he became quite animated, "there was a lad as I knew, who was—takin' a voyage for his health when I was—who was quite the highwayman! Stowed away the goods neat, and they never found it. When he got back his health, after a number of quite profitable years in Australia, sir, and could return to the old country, he bought hisself a run-down County place, good acres and an old house, and became quite the squire, and married the local vicar's daughter. No one is more respectable now, sir, and more admired. Goes to church every Sunday, and is an example to his tenants. Three sons, now, strappin' young chaps as would do any father's heart good."

Jerome burst out laughing. He struck Jim several times, with heartiness, on the shoulder. But the little man had become very earnest and eager.

"So, sir, it's my advice that you keep mum, and let it blow over. What the tongue holds back never hurts anybody. Things pass, and they are forgot. It's dangerous to keep a fire burning in a wood. Just put out the fire, and the wood still stands. So marry Miss Sally, and let everythin' wag on. No one's hurt yet. You don't have to live in this house, sir, while—while Mr. Alfred's here. Unless your pa leaves you the house. But that's for the future to settle. Maybe it won't be pleasant for a while, watching a bull graze in your own pastures. But it's better than baiting the bull, and gettin' out the neighbors with pitchforks. Better," he added, with deep gravity, "than doin' a fine old gentleman in, and breakin' Miss Sally's heart, and makin' bloody enemies, and walkin' into a bog with your eyes open."

"That," said Jerome, with high admiration, "is what is known as expediency."

But Jim said urgently: "Mr. Jerome, you're not a young buck with green grass in your hair, and willin' to throw away your life just to toss in another man's bed! There ain't a woman alive, sir, as is worth a man sinkin' himself in a pit for! It's excitin' for a while, I admit, but the mornin' always comes, and there's always a reckonin', and it's usually a nasty one. Besides, you wouldn't be doin' the lady much good either. Women can be sensible, sir, more sensible than many men. Put it up to 'em, and they're always the practical ones. So, let the lady forget, too, and she'll thank you for it later."

Jerome sat down. He crossed his legs and stared at his foot. "I am afraid you're not romantic, Jim."

"Neither are you, sir," said the little man, with a hopeful smile. "You never was. I've seen that. It's a good thing, too. It's much better to be kind and sensible."

Jerome rocked his foot gently, turning his head from side to side to watch a finger of sunlight glisten on his boot. But his face darkened and tightened, and his black brows knotted together. Jim watched him with passionate hopefulness.

Then Jerome said thoughtfully: "I don't know whether your advice is honorable or dishonorable, Jim, or just intelligent. I suspect the last."

All at once, he seemed profoundly exhausted. He stood up and walked towards the windows, and Jim noticed that he limped a little, as if his leg ached and he were enormously tired and ill. He's hard hit, then, thought the valet, with a sudden and frightened sadness. It's not just a roll in the hayloft, for him, or a scramble under the hedges. I've never seen him like this. And what of the poor lady? It was a bad day when we came here!

He anxiously watched Jerome standing at the windows with his back to the room. He saw Jerome's fingers tapping on the polished panes. He heard the faint and restless tattoo. What was the master thinking? He was not one to let his ruddy emotions run away with him. He had a level head, that one, and straight on his shoulders. He had always been one as considered everything, cool-like. If such an immense struggle was taking place in Jerome, then this affair must be of colossal proportions and not a little thing of heat and casual passion or any minor folly. Did he really love that poor lady with the large purple eyes and the lovely throat? Was the thing that had them both too huge for expediency?

Jim shook his head mournfully. It was indeed an evil day that had brought them here, together. Jim did not believe much in "love." He had never encountered it before, except in its lighter and gayer episodes in Jerome's career. Now he almost believed in it, and it terrified him. It could, then, destroy lives and tear up the foundations of strong houses; it could make fools of men and fugitives of women. It was something beyond the control of any realism, of any pleading of reason, any law or creed. It was even something beyond the wild and frenetic matings of savage beasts, which lasted a moment and then were forgotten.

He's always forgotten the women before, thought Jim, despairingly. Why could he not forget this one, for his own sake, and hers?

The dinner bell pealed softly, reverberating through all the quiet rooms, in which the dim shadow of twilight was settling. Jerome turned away from the window. Jim could not see his face plainly, but he could feel the other man's intense weariness, and he knew that he had come to no conclusion.

Jim said: "The ladies won't be down to dinner, I'm told, sir. Miss Dorothea is indisposed, and Miss Amalie has a severe headache. Shall I bring up your tray, or will you go downstairs?"

"Bring up a tray, by all means," said Jerome. His voice was abstracted. He added: "Bring up one for yourself, too, Jim. We'll eat together."

He hesitated, and then Jim could feel, rather than see, that he was smiling in the dusk. "Jim, I don't know what to do. I only know we've got to wait and see how things arrange themselves."

CHAPTER THIRTY

Mr. William Lindsey had been an earnest protagonist of Descartes' theory of a *"clara et distincta perceptio rerum."* He had often told his son, Jerome, that only the man who applied this ideal in his life was truly civilized. He also quoted, in this connection, his favorite Addison, who prided himself on being a calm spectator of other men's passions and hot idiocies and stresses. Again quoting Descartes, Mr. Lindsey would say that it was necessary to withdraw from men, at least temporarily, to obtain a proper perspective not only upon one's own affairs, but upon the affairs of the world generally.

Jerome remembered this wryly, while strolling over Hilltop's grounds that evening. Detach oneself? How? Wherever one glanced, whether at the sky or at a stone, at a face or a problem, everything was colored by the individual psyche. Rather than Descartes or Addison, Jerome quoted Decimus Magnus Ausonius: "What way of life shall I now follow?"

Mr. Lindsey had always been certain, with Confucius, that good manners solved all sorts of difficulties, and made a clear path through the jungle of human emotions. With acrid amusement, Jerome speculated on the uses of good manners in his present predicament. Good manners demanded a basis

251

of good taste. Jerome could only assure himself that, in so far as good taste was concerned, he possessed none.

This startled him, for he had egotistically prided himself on the impeccable good taste which had served him so well that he had never before been involved in impossible complications. But, damn it, he thought, if one exercises good taste relentlessly, one inevitably becomes desiccated. Good taste prevented hot embroilments, but it also prevented a man from living fully. It demanded moderation and lukewarmness in all passions, all desires, all hopes. One might as well live on tepid mutton soup, he thought.

He stood on the slope below Hilltop, in the grove of pines. And it came to him forcibly, and with a sort of passionate exultation, that in his abandonment of good taste he had, for the first time, known what it was to live. Bad taste had forced the drawers of Alfred's secret files, and had brought Jerome, for the first time, into contact with the lives and the miseries and the frustrations of others. Bad taste had entangled him with the wife of his cousin, his adopted brother. But this entanglement had brought him the first deep passion of his life, his first physical and mental and emotional fulfilment. There was definitely something wrong with the exercise of good taste.

Five months ago, he reflected, he could have withdrawn himself without much difficulty. A woman unknown could be sentimentalized about, and deserted with only a touch of sweet melancholy. But a woman intimately known, understood and felt, became part of a man's flesh and blood, and he could no more abandon her than he could voluntarily abandon himself. Even if he willed it consciously, he could not really leave Amalie. He would be leaving a great part of himself behind, and would be only half a man.

Nor could he leave the Bank. With profound amazement, he understood now that for some inexplicable reason he was bound up with the Bank and its problems. He had finally looked reality in the face, and it excited him. He did not quite comprehend, as yet, why he was so concerned with the affairs of Riversend, and he had a secret conviction that part of his concern lay in his detestation of the smug and iron-willed Alfred. However, he found that power to control and order the affairs of others, especially those others who were at the mercy of Alfred Lindsey, was unexpectedly sweet.

He could not leave his father now either. Nor his home. He glanced back at Hilltop, dim against the fading evening sky.

How had he ever complacently entertained the idea that Alfred should inherit Hilltop? How had he ever been agreeable that Alfred should be Mr. Lindsey's son, his heir, his successor? He, Jerome, had come to that house as a usurper. Who had made him feel so? Alfred? Dorothea? Himself? He knew now that it was himself.

He had an inheritance here, and sharply and clearly he decided to fight for it. He had a woman here, and he would fight for her also.

He had always winced away, laughing, at the very smell of battle and unpleasantness. And so, he had been rootless and uneasy, a superficial fool engrossed in the pampering of mean little vices. He was no longer young. All at once, his self-styled rôle of smiling epicure and exquisite and trifler with the arts seemed foolish and ridiculous. It surprised him that he had learned nothing from war. And then it came to him that since the war he had been chronically uneasy and dissatisfied. The war had started him on the way home. He could see it clearly, at last. Without the experiences of war, which had unconsciously touched him deeply, he would never have been embroiled with the affairs of this house and this community.

He sat down on the warm dark grass and smoked steadily. The pattern which had been so confused was brightening into order. It surprised him, amused him somberly.

Jim had presented the problem as a choice between his new life and Amalie. Amalie, too, could see nothing as inevitable but flight, after a gesture in the face of honor. Jerome saw no distinction between Amalie and the new world of his desires. They were one and the same.

When the family returned, there would have to be an open consultation. Certain facts might have to be suppressed, for the sake of decency and future harmony. But both Alfred and Mr. Lindsey would have to be impressed with the fact of the attachment between Jerome and Amalie. Jerome did not doubt that he could present the problem with dignity and reason. Certainly, there would be a stinking uproar, but he and Amalie had only to stand their ground quietly and openly.

After all, Jerome reflected, I am my father's son. My father is not an impulsive and irrational man. He loves me and is fond of Amalie. Forced to the wall, to make his choice, he will inevitably choose me. It is just the next two months or so, in all likelihood, that will be unpleasant. It will be a new experience for me to face unpleasantness and stare it down, and I do not expect to enjoy it. But it would be cowardice to run away.

Moreover, flight would bring catastrophe.

He had only to convince Amalie now. He got to his feet and went slowly back to the house. There was no sign of his sister or of Amalie. Someone had lit a lamp or two in the library, and the soft light streamed out upon the fresh grass. He rang a bell, sent for Jim. The little man came quickly, eagerly and full of hope. But something in Jerome's face frightened him.

"Jim," said Jerome, "I want you to go to Mrs. Lindsey's room and ask her to come downstairs to me here."

Jim's fright increased. He regarded Jerome imploringly. "But the lady 'as retired, sir."

"Unretire her then," said Jerome. "Go on, be off with you, Jim."

Jim was incredulous and shaken. He could not recognize "the master" in this pale man with the grim mouth and inflexible eyes. Something "was up," and Jim did not doubt that it was alarming. This is what happened when a man got himself "mucked up" with women: it changed a chap, put a new face on him. Almost slinking, Jim went upstairs to summon Amalie.

Jerome walked up and down the library. He felt a quite pleasant and exciting strength, and exhilaration. He had discovered that it can be an agreeable and exciting thing to make hard decisions and do battle for them and to impose one's will on another.

The house was quiet, filled with the warmth of the past day, and the old familiar smell of wax, flowers, grass and leather pervaded the library. The nose, thought Jerome, is the sense closest to memory. He remembered walking like this, up and down over the thick carpet, many times in his almost forgotten youth and boyhood, waiting for his father to come down and listen to his, Jerome's, own explanation of some recent enormity of which he stood accused. There was the same reassuring and homely scent in the room then as there was tonight, the same green leaves outside illuminated by the soft lamplight, the same gleam on the opened French windows. He paused in his pacing. He could almost hear his father's hesitating footsteps on the stairway, his low dry cough, and could recall his own faint apprehension and angry defiance. How had he ever forgotten? Was it really possible he had believed that this house bored him and wearied him, and had no ties for him? He looked at the high shelves of blue and crimson books standing serenely in the light, and they were dearly familiar to him. This was his home. He would fight for it, and he would win. He would fight for the gentle sound of the wind in the trees, the feel of the carpet under his feet, the texture of the leather chairs, the glimmer of the brass andirons on the hearth. When a man went to war, and fought, it was for these things, and not for any ideal or abstract patriotism.

He heard a slight sound. He looked up to see Amalie on the threshold of the library. She was very white and still, in her gray cotton frock with the cream-colored collar and cuffs. Her black hair was rolled in a severe chignon on her neck. Her eyes were heavily shadowed, her lips without color. Jerome stood and looked at her for several moments before he said, gently: "Come in, Amalie. I must talk to you."

He did not move towards her, but only watched her as she came farther into the room, and then sat down. Her arms lay listlessly on the arms of the red-leather chair. He sat down near her, leaned towards her, and smiled.

It seemed incredible to him that only that afternoon he had glanced about him furtively when she had entered his office, and that he had been fearful of opening doors. Fear made disgusting cravens of men, he thought. One had only to determine on battle to lose fear. Why, his incredulous thought continued, it seems that I have been afraid all my life! Afraid to live, afraid to believe anything was worth fighting for, afraid to desire, afraid to be touched by real passion and real emotion! What a skulking and ignoble creature he had been, and how lifeless, how attenuated, despite all his elegant attitudes and debonair posing!

He almost forgot the white-faced woman opposite him, in the fierce and exulting contempt he felt for himself, and so he did not see how her eyes widened with a kind of exhausted and startled wonder as she watched him and recognized that some change had come over him during the past few hours. When he reached out and took her hand, she did not shrink away, but let him have it with a tired but complete surrender, as if she felt his new strength.

"My dear," he said, "I have been doing a lot of thinking. A very strange experience for me. And so, I've decided we are not to go away. This is my home. I intend to remain here, with you."

Involuntarily, she tried to pull her hand away, but he held it more firmly. Her blanched lips moved without sound, and her eyes filled with tears.

He gazed at her steadily, with a comforting smile. "You see, love, this is my home; I know it at last. This is my father's home, and I intend to stay near my father. You were

255

quite right: we cannot run away like criminals. We will face it out, together. When Alfred and my father return, we will tell them of our feeling for each other, and demand your release. Alfred cannot refuse; my father, I know, will help me. It will be very disagreeable for a while, I admit, and exhausting. But in the end, all things will resolve themselves, with dignity, if we only have the firm conviction and the courage."

She whispered: "Jerome." She tried to smile, and he found her effort almost unbearably touching. He kissed her hand.

He exclaimed, with a sudden quickening: "My darling, do you realize how much I love you? Only now do I realize how much, myself. What at first was infatuation is now something much more steadfast and permanent, for I know now how much integrity you possess, and how much honor and courage and pride. We'll make for ourselves a fine life, I promise you, serene and kind and strong—for us, and for our children. You do believe me, do you not, Amalie?"

"Yes." Her voice was only a murmur, but her whole face shone vividly. After a moment, she said: "I was afraid you did not want me any longer. That was the only thing I could not have endured."

She looked about her at the panelled walls, the books, the great fireplace, the lamplight, and her mouth shook, and she could not speak again. However, with his acuteness, he saw what she saw, and it gave him understanding contentment.

"It is only the homeless who have the capacity to love a home," he said.

"Yes. Home." She sighed deeply and smiled.

He took her face in his hands and kissed her lips gently, and she put her arms about his neck. They both thought how different this was from that night of storm and hunger, and how tenderness had replaced the first fury and passion.

They sat close together, and Jerome said: "I have had a letter from my father today. Alfred——" he hesitated, "is obliged to remain in New York for two or three weeks longer. My father has asked me to go to Saratoga and bring him and Philip home. It will not be too hard for you, to be alone for a few days, Amalie?"

"No." Her face was sad again. "Philip. I love Philip so, Jerome. How can I bear to have him estranged from me? He trusts me, and loves me, and he has been so lonely."

He was quickly jealous and frowned. "Oh, Philip. You need not fear for Philip. He has quite a mind of his own. Even his —father—could not prevent him from seeing you, if he wished. Good God, my pet, you must think only of us for a while!"

But her sadness was heavy in the droop of her head. "If it were only possible for us to be happy without bringing unhappiness to—others. Sometimes I think I do not have the courage to look Alfred and your father and Philip in the face, and tell them——" She drew a deep breath. "Perhaps we ought to have waited."

"For what?" he asked, with his quick and angry impatience. He tried to control his temper. "There is no use, now, in mutual recriminations and accusations, Amalie! That will get us nowhere. We must deal with things as they are. We must look at the facts, and proceed from there. I have no doubt that matters will be mighty unpleasant, perhaps for some time, but we must face them. Are you trying to tell me you have lost your fortitude?"

"No," she answered steadfastly. "I am only sorry that we must hurt those who trust us. If I could only be sure that they will not hate us too much!"

He smiled unpleasantly. "That is a possibility we must face also. And the sooner the better."

She stood up and walked restlessly but slowly up and down the room, twisting her hands together. Then she stood before Jerome, and she was paler than before.

"There is another thing I must tell you, Jerome. Dorothea —knows."

He regarded her with disbelief. "But how? That is impossible. There was no one in the house that night——"

She flushed and looked away. "Nevertheless, she knows. She knew I saw you today, and she accused me of everything. I did not intend to tell you. But I think, now, that you should know."

"Damn," he said, softly. "That complicates things." He stared at her. "So that is why you are so shaken." He took her hand firmly. "You must tell me all about it, at once."

She told him, in a low voice thick with shame, and he listened with increasing rage and mounting hatred for his sister. When Amalie had finished, he took several steps away from her towards the doorway, but she caught his arm.

"Wait, Jerome," she pleaded. "I think we need not fear Dorothea. She—wants Alfred. She will gain nothing by premature accusations against us. I—I have persuaded her that the less she pretends to know—about us—the more likely it is that Alfred will turn to her. If he believes she knows too much

257

about his humiliation, he will avoid her. She understands that now. She will say nothing. I beg of you not to speak to her, nor allow her to know that I have told you. I should not have spoken to you about it at all, except that I thought it might clear the air, and make any antagonism she displays less puzzling to you."

"So that is why she has been so confoundedly vicious," he said, reflectively. "The lusting old hag! Well, she deserves Alfred, and he deserves her. I could wish neither of them a better punishment."

"Jerome!" Amalie's voice was a cry of pain.

But he was excited. "Don't be so damned tender-hearted, for God's sake! Your Alfred is no saint, no man of rectitude and nobility! I have looked at his books and his ledgers. Do you know what he is doing to this community, this town? He is stifling it, throttling it! He is keeping the people half-starved and hopeless; he is driving the young men and women away to more thriving parts. He is preventing Riversend from becoming prosperous. He wishes to keep it in a kind of agricultural serfdom, for the benefit of himself and his greedy friends. The whole damn place is decaying! Oh, it is very agreeable for him, to be bowed to and scraped to as a powerful local squire, and it is agreeable for his friends! He grabs farm after farm, forecloses mortgages ruthlessly, rents out those farms to sharecroppers whom he gouges and subjugates, and is so damned smug and righteous about it that I wish nothing more but the opportunity to bury my fist in his face! That is the pious gentleman you would spare, Amalie, and of whom you know nothing."

She was silent. She was thinking of the stories she had heard in Riversend, when she had taught school there. She was remembering how Alfred had opposed adding another room, and more pupils, to that school, and another teacher or two. She was remembering the Hobsons, who would have been dispossessed but for her intercession. She was remembering despairing and bitter faces, the cowed faces of wretched farmers, the hunted faces of small shopkeepers in the town. And she was remembering that it was Alfred's name that had been spoken with hatred and misery.

But Jerome misunderstood her silence.

"I tell you," he said, with grim determination, "that I will do all I can to frustrate him! You may as well know that now. I am his enemy. I will remain here, and work, and will gain friends who hate him, and everything that he has done will be undone."

She lifted her head and regarded him fixedly.

"Yes, you may look at me, my dear, as if I had stuck a knife into your darling! But you must understand what I intend to do."

She put out her hand and laid it on his arm. "Jerome!" she cried, softly. "Do you mean that? That is why you are staying? You really wish to help Riversend, and the farmers? You are not just staying—for your inheritance? You really want to do all this?"

They looked into each other's eyes. Then Jerome smiled. He put his hand strongly over the hand on his arm.

"Yes, dear," he said.

She began to cry again, and he knew she was crying with joy and amazement. He took her in his arms and pressed her cheek against his. She clung to him quite wildly.

"You don't know how happy you have made me, Jerome. And there is so much I can tell you, from my own experience."

Still almost afraid to believe him, she drew back so she could see his face.

"It is like a dream," she said. "I did not know that you thought these things about Riversend. I thought it was just hatred for Alfred. I've misjudged you, Jerome. Forgive me."

CHAPTER THIRTY-ONE

Dorothea Lindsey was having a very strange dream.

It was half memory, that dream. She was sitting in her mother's room, a young girl again, and there was a child in her arms, and that child was Jerome, dark and restless and vigorous in a Scotch-plaid silk frock with a white lace collar. He had not yet been promoted to bifurcated garments, and apparently resented the fact, for he was screaming: "Pant'loons!" at the top of a very loud and disagreeable voice. Dorothea was struggling with him and scolding him and hearing soft and lilting laughter. She heard a rustle and saw her mother again, young and fragile and very sweet-faced.

Her mother wore white silk and lace, with a violet shawl over her shoulders. Her hair lay in heavy ringlets over that shawl and in a mass down her back. Dorothea felt a pang of adoration and sadness as she looked at her mother's face.

The room seemed to darken, and her mother's voice came as if from a far and echoing distance, full of sorrow: "Dorothea, my love, you must care for your little brother, if I am called away. I know I can trust you, my dearest one."

Dorothea heard her own voice, faint with despairing premonition: "Yes. Oh, yes, Mama."

The room steadily darkened, and now her mother was only a white and spectral shadow in the dim room, only the faintest of rustles. Terror seized Dorothea; Jerome was no longer on her knees. He had disappeared, yet she knew he was somewhere near, watching with cold and inimical eyes, full of mockery and hatred. Dorothea's mother began to speak, and her voice was chill and far-off, filled with urgent grief and pleading: "You must care for your brother, my love. You must remember me. For my sake, you must not desert nor injure him."

Dorothea cried out: "Oh, Mama, you do not know Jerome! He has hurt us all so terribly! You must not ask this of me, Mama!"

But her mother's voice, dimmer now, far off as the stars, pleaded: "You must help your brother, Dorothea."

Dorothea woke, trembling and chilled and sick. Her room was in deep darkness. Trees rustled against her windows; she saw the sharp fingers of moonlight through the draperies. She sat up in bed, struck a match and lighted her bedside lamp. It was then that she became aware that she had heard a low but insistent knocking for some time, and that this had apparently awakened her. She glanced at the clock on the mantelpiece. It was midnight.

She caught up her shawl which lay at the foot of the bed and flung it about her shoulders. She called out huskily: "Who is it?"

"Jerome."

Dorothea stared at the shut door. Her heart pained her with its sudden swift beating. She looked about the room. Her mother had gone yet she seemed to be present, her large eyes imploring. Dorothea moistened her parched lips and said: "Come in." She lifted herself up on her pillows, ran cold hands over her dark and graying hair, flung back her heavy braids. The door opened and Jerome entered, closing the door behind him.

The urgency of the dream was heavy upon Dorothea, and she could only regard her brother with confusion and wretchedness rather than with her old wary antagonism. He came towards the bed, found an old rocker and sat down. He began to rock slowly. His expression was alert, narrowed with malevolence. He studied his sister fixedly without speaking.

Dorothea heard herself saying confusedly: "I was dreaming about our mother and us." She pressed her fingers against her eyes as if to shut out the memory. She shivered. She said, her fingers still against her eyes: "You were screaming about pantaloons. You were always screaming about something, Jerry." For the first time in years, now, the old childish nickname slipped out, and it was said with weary softness.

Jerome said nothing. He casually and deliberately lit a cheroot, crossed his legs, regarded the ceiling. Dorothea dropped her hands and saw her brother clearly. Her heart was still beating with swift pain, and its tremors shook all her body. Tears moistened her eyelids. She remembered the dream and the voice of her mother. She cried out: "Jerome! Mother asked me years ago to care for you, always. She asked me again, tonight."

Jerome smiled unpleasantly, still regarding the ceiling. "Yet you intended to do a very bad job of it, didn't you? You intended to injure me as much as possible. That is why I came to see you tonight, at this ungodly hour."

Dorothea was silent. But her hands seized and clutched the bed-coverings.

"Let's not be sentimental, my dear Dorothea," said Jerome. "Let's speak outright. You've been my enemy for years. I was never yours, for I never considered you important enough. But you've become important just now. And so, I've come here now to warn you to leave Amalie alone, to keep your mouth shut, and to let me manage my affairs in my own way. If you don't—then I'll find means to make you very sorry indeed."

Dorothea drew a sharp dry breath. Her hands tightened on the bed-coverings and twisted them. But she could not rid herself of her dream. She felt faint and sick and full of terror.

She said, almost indistinctly: "Then she has told you I know?"

"Yes." Jerome stood up. "She has also told me how you assaulted her, struck her. And so, I must remind you that our affairs are our own, not yours. If necessary, I shall be forced to make that very clear to you."

Dorothea murmured: "She is a wicked woman, and you are a wicked man." But her voice was low and exhausted.

Jerome eyed her curiously. There was something here he

could not understand. He had expected his sister to shriek accusations at him, to denounce him with viciousness and fury. But she only leaned back against her pillows, her gaunt face quite haggard and ashen, and her eyes were dim.

To his surprise, she lifted her hands slowly and, with their palms up, seemed to be extending them to him. He saw tears on her lined cheeks.

"Jerome," she whispered. "Will you listen to me a moment? Perhaps I have been too rigorous towards you in the past. Perhaps I have been too stern. I thought it necessary, my duty. Perhaps I was wrong; I might have been a little softer, a little kinder." She swallowed and for a moment could not continue.

Jerome came and leaned against the carved post at the foot of the bed. His face was expressionless, but he watched his sister intently.

"I tried to do my duty," she went on, still in that husky whisper. "I may have expected too much, been too censorious. There were times when I forgot you were my brother. But you made me feel that you were my enemy. We never understood each other."

Jerome shifted a little, but his curiosity increased. Also, he felt a slight compassion and shame for his sister. This annoyed him. He had come here ready for battle and threat, and she was disarming him.

"I ought to have remembered, at all times, that we are both the children of our parents, and that our blood is the same," continued Dorothea weakly, her head drooping towards her breast. "But we were by nature antagonistic. I am the elder, and so the onus of our estrangement is upon me."

She lifted her head, and now her wet eyes flashed and deepened with strong pleading. "Jerome, let us not forget it again, that we are brother and sister. Nothing else must matter, must it?" She shifted towards him a trifle. "We are all one family, Father, you and I, Alfred and Philip, and no stranger must separate us! Tell me you understand, that you agree? Let that —woman—go. She is anxious to go, as she told me. Let us forget her, all of us, as we might forget a hateful dream. Let us all be together again, friends under one roof. And I swear to you, Jerome, that no word of all this horror shall ever come from me, to anyone."

Jerome drummed his fingers on the bedpost. His face was hard and shut.

"Thank you, Dorothea. I may as well tell you that I do not

intend to run away. I intend to remain here, as my father's son and my father's natural heir."

Dorothea's eyes glowed with joy and relief. She stretched out her hand to her brother. But he looked at it coldly for a moment, then looked away.

"Jerome! Then we can all forget, and you will be here with us, and we shall have peace and harmony again!"

He felt a wincing in himself at her loud and joyful voice. His lips tightened. He said: "I hope we can forget—after a while, Dorothea. I hope we'll have 'peace and harmony again.' That is my strongest hope." He paused. "But Amalie is not to leave. We are both going to ask Alfred to release her. Later I shall marry her."

Dorothea was stunned. Her mouth fell open with stupefaction; her eyes blinked. Then she seemed to diminish, to shrink upon her pillows, to become old and wizened. Her lips moved, but her throat closed on a spasm.

"You have only to keep quiet," said Jerome, with a new discomfort. He became absorbed in the carvings of the bedpost. "Then no one will be much hurt. When Alfred returns, Amalie and I will talk to him. My father is fond of Amalie, and I am his son. I hope, and expect, that he will help us. He is a realist, not a sentimentalist. Things may be confused, and unpleasant, for a little time, but they will resolve themselves." He hesitated. "If you care for Alfred in the least, you will understand that he can never be happy with Amalie. She does not love him, and he knows this. To continue with such a marriage can only bring him unhappiness and dissatisfaction." He returned his eyes to his silent sister. "There can be happiness for him, later. I think you understand what I mean."

Dorothea put her hands over her face. She whispered hoarsely: "You actually intend to marry that woman, to keep her under this roof, an insult to your father and to your sister? A woman like that?"

Jerome said grimly: "You must not speak of Amalie so. I intend to make her my wife. If you cannot forget your hatred for her, and your jealousy, you can at least hide them. There is no use, I know, in my attempting to refute the false opinion you have of her. I can only assure you it is wrong."

Dorothea muttered: "No! No! She cannot remain here! She cannot marry you! It is something I could not bear."

"Nevertheless," said Jerome, with hard relentlessness, "you must bear it. That is what I have come to tell you. I am glad that you have shown some reason, and that you do not intend to try to injure me. It is more than I expected. And so, I thank you, and I myself will attempt to show you some kinder consideration as my sister. I hope you may be happy in the future. If you are reasonable, and just, and have some regard for yourself, as well as for me and for Amalie, I am sure that you will finally get what you want."

Dorothea dropped her hands. She was weeping bitterly. "Jerome, that terrible woman can bring you only misery and ruin! Please believe me. I—I promised our mother to help you. I cannot refuse to do so. She wishes me to protect you from that odious creature, that appalling drab. I know it! She spoke to me only a moment or two before you came." Her voice broke, and her tears came faster.

Jerome frowned. He could not make his voice harsh, and was angry at its involuntary gentleness. "Dorothea, it might be that our mother wished you to help me, in my own way, by your silence, by your acceptance of my plans."

But Dorothea shook her head with desperate violence. "You are wrong, Jerome."

Jerome sighed with impatient exasperation. He sat down on the edge of Dorothea's bed. "Listen to me, Dotty. You must understand. Amalie and I love each other. We have loved each other from the very first. We did not know that, in the beginning. We know it now. We intend to marry each other. Nothing can change that. You must see it. Accept that fact, and everything else is clear. If you do not help us, then we must go away, and Alfred must be humiliated forever, and he will never recover from it. It will probably kill our father. It all lies with you. And you, you must remember, will gain nothing but remorse and loneliness, and the memory that, but for you, everything would have been well."

Dorothea gazed at him through her tears. She said in a low tone: "I hate that woman. I wish she might die. I cannot reconcile myself to the thought that I must see her all my life, in this house."

"But you must reconcile yourself to that very fact."

Dorothea's tears came in a fresh outburst. "There is nothing, no sense of honor, no decency, no proper regard for your father and for your sister, that can change your mind?"

"No." He rose.

She felt his implacable determination. She wrung her hands and wept aloud.

Jerome waited. His sister's tears disturbed him more than he could have thought possible.

"What of Sally?" stammered Dorothea.

Jerome glanced away. "I must talk to the General. As soon as possible."

"Have you no honor, Jerome, that would prevent you from inflicting such pain upon that young girl, and such mortification? Have you forgotten that you are betrothed to her?"

"It was a mistake, Dorothea, one of my many mistakes. I am sorry for Sally, but I should have made her a detestable husband."

Dorothea moaned: "How terrible all this is! If only none of us had ever seen that woman!"

Jerome knew now that his sister would not lift her hand against him or Amalie. He approached her, and kissed her forehead gently.

"We can't change things, my dear. We can only accept them. Be reasonable. I am going to Saratoga for my father and Philip. Alfred must remain in New York for a few weeks longer. Try to control yourself, until matters are settled. You will be doing all of us a tremendous favor, including yourself. I can trust you, Dotty?"

She put her hand on his shoulder. Her streaming dark eyes implored him. Then despair filled them, and they closed.

"Yes, Jerome, you may trust me. But, oh, Jerome, if things could have been different!"

CHAPTER THIRTY-TWO

"We have nothing to fear from Dotty," said Jerome. "While she is not exactly imbued with love and light for either of us, I have convinced her that it is to her best interests not to interfere."

He stood with Amalie in their favorite spot on the other side of the tall pines. The Sabbath peace stood in shining silence about them, and they could hear the faint fairy tinkling of the bells in the valley. The long yellow sunlight lay over the hills, flowed down the slopes, sparkled on all the trees.

Jerome held Amalie's hand tightly and smiled down at her.

"I am going for my father and Philip. Then, when Alfred returns, it will all be settled. In the meantime, don't worry or fret yourself, my love."

"It is not easy to think of disrupting so many lives and yet remain calm," she answered.

He smoothed the thick masses of her black hair fondly. "No, it is not easy. But nothing in your life has been easy, has it? There are some people who invite thunderbolts, and I think you are one of them. There, now, do not look so distressed. You must remember that the meek and the humble and the timid live vegetable lives. It is only the dauntless who attract the attention of whatever powers there be."

"I don't feel particularly dauntless any more," she said, smiling miserably. "In fact, I am vulnerable all over me. I am full of chinks. I believe I have not been without courage in the past, but then, the young are courageous either because they lack imagination or because they feel, in their exuberance, that nothing can defeat them."

"You still don't lack youth or imagination," he said, and he ran his fingers softly over her smooth cheek. "And you are quite healthy, even though you are so pale lately." He put his arm about her waist and drew her quickly to him. "Vapors would never become you, and I don't advise you to try swooning. Not with those shoulders and this chin and this height."

She tried to laugh. "I am really very delicate, Jerome. My appearance is a great fraud."

He held her face in his hands. "What beautiful pansy eyes you have, my sweet. Such gentle eyes, too. I never knew how gentle they are. They were usually flashing at me in a particularly hostile fashion."

"That is because you were particularly odious, dear Jerome. I think you, too, are a great fraud."

When he did not reply, she said, with emotion: "I always thought I was very astute in judging character. But I misjudged you."

"Oh, but you didn't. Don't make a hero of me, my pet. It is just that I have found a new interest in life; two interests, to be exact." He thought of Alfred, and the old expression of cruelty returned to his eyes. "Don't be sentimental, Amalie. If you begin by expecting excellent things of me you are going to spend a life of disappointment in this house."

When Jerome had gone to Saratoga a heavy somberness settled over the house. Dorothea went to her room immediately upon completing her household tasks. She seldom spoke to Amalie, except when necessary, and her voice, if polite, was dull and remote. This saddened Amalie, but she saw no way to assuage Dorothea's antipathy for her, and her profound if unspoken hatred. Dorothea had accepted the inevitable with her usual austerity, but her bitterness was only too evident. She had an air, too, of making her own personal plans, and this gave Amalie moments of secret anxiety.

The servants sensed the tension in the house. They knew it lay between the two women. They did not have any fondness for Amalie. She had come from their own "class," and they resented her new estate. She was an "upstart," and so they were as impertinent to her as they dared to be. If she was distant with them, she was "puttin' on airs." If she was kind, she was "trucklin' to them." In either event, they were determined that she should understand that they were familiar with her origin. The static and silent hostility between Dorothea and Amalie gave them their opportunity. They talked over the situation in their own quarters, and speculated curiously upon the cause. One and all, they sided with Dorothea against the stranger. Even Jim's influence was not enough to soften them, and he soon shrewdly desisted from his defense for fear of arousing suspicion regarding his master. However, it was he, rather than any of the others, who answered her bell, which might have been ignored save for him.

Amalie soon became aware of the atmosphere in the house, yet she held her temper. But she kept her private dossier, for she was only human. She was grateful for Jim's politeness and his readiness to carry out her wishes, and she was also uneasily embarrassed, suspecting the cause. She rang her bell as little as possible.

Slowly she realized that Dorothea, in spite of the openly impudent and fractious servants, was placing more and more responsibility for the house upon her shoulders. When one of the stableboys was outrageously impertinent to her, and she threatened to discuss the matter with Dorothea, he grinned in her face. Now, added to her grief and anxiety, was a nameless fear. She wondered what Dorothea was plotting in her room. She had been convinced by Jerome that Dorothea would make no move to ruin her or Jerome, but she knew instinctively that Dorothea's own plans would not bring her, Amalie, much comfort.

She longed for, but dreaded, the return of the family. Jerome, she knew, would not discuss the matter with Mr. Lindsey until Alfred had come home.

Almost hardest of all to endure were Alfred's loving if stiff letters. She replied to them as briefly as possible. He was enjoying himself in New York. He was being entertained by Mr. Regan, who was "very civil." He was also the guest on several occasions of Mr. Regan's friends. Shyly, and obscurely, and in very euphemistic language, he hinted of "his hopes" for himself and Amalie. She did not reply to these, except to say that Dr. Hawley believed her health was not as sturdy as it should be, but that he, Alfred, must not worry.

She knew that Jerome could not write her directly. But he gave messages to Jim, and the wrinkled little man relayed them to her. Mr. Lindsey, who had been profiting from his stay at Saratoga, had had a relapse. His arthritis was very bad. He could not return home immediately. It would be at least another two weeks or so. Philip, however, was splendidly well.

Amalie, who had been praying for a reprieve, now found the endless days almost unendurable. Her nerves became ragged. She was subject to fits of nausea. Sometimes, when awakening in the middle of the night, she discovered that her whole bed was in a slight tremor because of her involuntary trembling. Finally, she could hardly sleep at all. Her nausea increased. She fled from the table as soon as possible. She forced herself to work hard, to drive about the country in the buggy, to read for hours, to mend, sew, embroider. She visited her old friends, the poverty-stricken farmers and townsfolk. She did not accept the many invitations from the Widow Kingsley and the family of General Tayntor. Once, Sally called upon Dorothea. Seeing her from her window, approaching in her smart trap, Amalie left by the rear of the house and remained away for two hours.

Life took on the dimensions and the terror and atmosphere of a dreadful nightmare, an isolated nightmare in which she moved among malefic shadows and grinning faces. The summer advanced in golden heat and shimmering lights, but she saw none of it. Her exhaustion had become like a disease. She sickened at the sight of food, feared the coming of the night. She lost flesh and strength, and now there were deep lavender hollows under her eyes.

She felt herself completely friendless. Jerome had been gone for three weeks, and there was no immediate sign of his return with his father and Philip. Alfred wrote that his negotiations with Mr. Regan were unavoidably extended. Finally, she found that days would pass with hardly a word being exchanged between herself and Dorothea and the servants. The house assumed a strange quality, as if it had retreated from her and its walls had become insubstantial.

Her sickness became stronger. She debated whether or not she should call upon Dr. Hawley. But the thought of entering the village made her shrink. There was no comfort for her anywhere. She wandered through the house like a specter. She hated the sight of her thin white face in the mirror. She was conscious of mysterious disturbances in her body, curious stresses and aches and throbbings.

July came, in heat and thunder. Amalie could scarcely endure it. Her clothing seemed made of haircloth. She seldom saw Dorothea now. She dared not venture out of the house during the day because of the fiery sun. But sometimes, in the evenings, she crept from the house and lay in the cool pungent depths of the pines, giving herself up to complete terror, grief and sickness. Sometimes she would lie like this for hours, staring dry-eyed at the burning white moon, or watching the wide heat lightning flashing through the dark sky. Sometimes she slept here, and did not awaken until the ghostly mists of the dawn were trailing in pearly scarves over the hills.

One morning she summoned enough strength to visit the gardens and return with a basket of roses. She arranged them in the library vases. She heard a small sound and, trembling with weakness, turned to see Jim sliding into the room. He wore a furtive air. He came to her as she stood by the long table, glanced behind him quickly, then whispered: "Ma'am. Mr. Jerome will return on the thirtieth, he says."

Amalie's hands remained among the roses. She gazed at Jim in pale silence.

He studied her with anxiety and fondness. "If you'll pardon me, ma'am, but you're ailin'. It's the heat, perhaps? Sometimes I can't abide it."

She tried to smile. She thrust roses into cool water. "It is bad, isn't it, Jim?"

He was silent. He shifted about on his small polished feet. Then he cleared his throat. "The master won't like it at all, ma'am."

A thin color ran into her cheeks. "What do you mean, Jim?"

"He told me to look after you, Miss Amalie. He'll not like to see you like this. He'll blame me."

Her color deepened, and her throat closed. Then she said, in a low tone: "Why should he blame you, Jim? Please don't speak of it."

He came closer to her, staring at her earnestly. "Ma'am, I want you to know you've got a friend in this 'ouse."

She was so weak now that tears came easily to her eyes. "I know I have, Jim, and thank you."

He was touched and sighed. "If there's anythin' I can do,

ma'am, you've just got to let me know."

"Yes, Jim." She touched his arm with her chilled fingers, then moved away, her head high. He followed her with his eyes, and sighed again. A lovely young creature, this, and a lady, for all they said in the servants' quarters. He did not blame the master much. But still, it was a bloody mess.

The next day, Amalie received a jubilant letter from Alfred that he was on the way home.

The news unnerved her completely. When she tried to get up the next morning she discovered she was too ill, overcome with a sick apathy which she could not shake off. And so it was that Alfred found her, almost unable to speak, unable to lift her head from her pillows.

CHAPTER THIRTY-THREE

Alfred sat with Dorothea on the terrace in the warm twilight. Dorothea wore a light gown of gray poplin with a white muslin fichu. She had removed her frilled cap, and her thick dark hair was wound about her head in heavy braids. She seemed, to Alfred, everything that was austere and majestic, safe and secure, in his life, full of the common sense he prized and the stability which was his god.

In her presence he felt at ease and comfortable, for he knew that she was his friend and that he need not speak fully and meticulously to gain her comprehension. She appeared to understand him when he spoke only a few words, or made one of his stiff slight gestures, or exchanged a glance with him. Dorothea was well aware of this, and it added bitterness to her grief. How could a man be so blind as to overlook the true possible source of his happiness? she would reflect to herself with somber rebellion against Alfred. He has always spoken to me of his difficulties, his problems, and his uneasiness, she thought, and constantly comes to me for consolation and sympathy. We have understood each other from childhood. Yet, he has married two women and found nothing but unhappiness in them, and still he does not understand in the least! I have been an ear to him, and a kind eye, and a companion. But at the first flick of a frivolous petticoat he is off from my side. Even when he returns, full of wounds and bewilderment, he is not aware that I, and I alone, understand him and am part of him.

Dorothea reflected that men were fools, and this ancient conclusion of millions of women before her seemed to her a fresh revelation that ought to be taught women-children in their cradles. Men are obtuse, she cried to herself. A youthful cheek, a soft treacherous laugh, a slender ankle or the flirt of a curl have power to reduce them to driveling idiots and to set them gamboling like drunken goats in strange pastures. But always it is to women like me that they return temporarily, to be soothed and comforted, and always it is from women like me that they run at the first bending of a little distant finger.

Her hands, even in the dim twilight busy with her knitting, paused. She stared before her fixedly, and her face flushed hotly. She had just reached a most improper and indelicate conclusion. For men's sake, women like herself ought to be slyly determined and grim. They ought to go forth to these men boldly, and say to them: "You are a fool. I am the woman for you, and I am obstinately set on marrying you. You may flee from me, but I will follow. I shall be your shadow. I shall haunt you implacably. Until you succumb; until you surrender. And the day will come when you will thank me, and know me, and we shall be happy together."

What an indecorous thought! But one must accept it, in the name of common sense, and in the name of the welfare of these lumbering but beloved imbeciles. She thought: Even if he is released from that woman, he will stumble about miserably, until he comes upon another like her, and I shall lose him again. No! This time I shall succeed, if I have to face him down immodestly and announce that he must marry me.

Her heart was misbehaving with such intensity that her breath was short, and the dark heat increased in her face. Alfred, of course, was completely unconscious of his cousin's thoughts. He knew only that it was soothing and kind to be here with her in the twilight, and that the uncertain lines of her figure gave him comfort in his present anxiety and pain. Dear Dorothea! She was always there, his sister and his friend, utterly without sex for him, and that was so consoling!

He had been telling her of his successes in New York, and the edifying conversations he had had with Mr. Regan, who was so excessively civil and thoughtful. But even as his voice warmed, there was an abstracted note in it which Dorothea's acuteness easily discerned. She knew he was thinking of that woman, and in the growing darkness her lips pressed themselves together.

To her, as to all women of her generation, divorce was abhorrent, a shameful thing not to be spoken of even in whispers by genteel females. Yet now, in her new determination, she contemplated it with almost savage resolution. Marriages like these were crimes against society. They were crimes against the stupid men themselves, committed ignorantly and blindly. Now she regarded divorce for Alfred calmly, even exultantly. It was her opportunity; she would take it. She waited only for the proper moment, and she knew it would come very soon. She thought: Divorced men and women can rarely marry again. Fiddlesticks! What absurdity! As well refuse one who has recovered from a dangerous disease or a great wound! Of course, there will be unpleasantnesses, and scandals, and much raising of hands. But sensible people do not allow the opinions of strangers to guide them in their lives.

These revolutionary thoughts did not excite her as they might have done in the near past. They only exhilarated her, made her pose her head quite grimly and click her needles with renewed vim. And now her heart was beating with a kind of wild and unrestrained happiness. It was necessary to endure only a few short months of disagreeable events and disturbances, and these were a small price to pay for a whole lifetime of contentment and fulfilment.

The influence of the dream of her mother was still powerful upon her, and helped keep in check her chronic hostility towards her brother. She felt around her the strong walls of the house where she had been born. She and Alfred would make their lives here, with Philip. Jerome and that abominable woman would live elsewhere. She, Dorothea, did not care. Jerome would find it quite impossible to live in this community, because of public opinion, even if the divorce were consummated with great delicacy and private reticence. A divorced woman was always a pariah. Undoubtedly, they would leave Riversend, and that would hurt her father. Well, that must be expected and accepted. She, Dorothea, would do nothing to injure Jerome, or disgrace him. She sighed.

Alfred heard her sigh. He had long since ceased to speak. The twilight deepened. He cleared his throat. Dorothea thought: Now he will speak of her, and I must be ready.

She heard him shift in his chair. "I am calling Dr. Hawley in tomorrow, to see Amalie," he said.

Dorothea's needles clicked louder.

"She is in a most deplorable condition," he continued anxiously. "Much worse than when I left her. At that time, I had my hopes that——" He paused, catching himself hastily. He had been at the point of mentioning a matter it was not decorous to discuss with an unmarried female.

Dorothea inhaled determinedly. "You mean, do you not, Alfred, that you hoped Amalie was going to have a baby?"

Alfred was overcome with embarrassment. He gave his cousin an apologetic but reproving glance. She did not see it, however, because of the increasing dusk, and though she felt it she ignored it.

Alfred coughed. "You might call it that," he admitted remotely.

He added, when Dorothea remained silent: "But she tells me that—that my hopes were, unfortunately, unfounded. She has visited Dr. Hawley, and he has given her a tonic. But I may as well confess to you, Dorothea, that I find her appearance alarming. She has lost much flesh and her color is very bad." His voice was measured, but Dorothea heard his urgent anxiety. "Do you not agree with me?"

Dorothea dropped her knitting into her lap. She looked before her. Then she said, very quietly: "Amalie appears to me to be suffering from some great unhappiness."

Alfred moved quickly. Dorothea felt him turn fully to her. "Unhappiness!" he exclaimed, and there was a break, repudiating and angry, in his voice. "Why should she be unhappy? I have given her whatever she has desired. I—I love her very much. There is nothing I would not do for her."

Dorothea felt the taste of bitter salt in her mouth. She picked up her knitting again. "Sometimes that is not enough," she murmured with apparent composure.

"Not enough! What else can I do? I would give my life for her, Dorothea!"

Dorothea's heart burned, and tears moistened her eyelids.

"That is not always enough," she said. "Amalie did not love you when she married you, Alfred. You knew that and spoke of it freely. Perhaps she still does not love you."

You fool! she cried inwardly. Why do you waste your life on such a creature, when I am at your hand, loving you, asking nothing more than to serve you, to dedicate myself to you! Yet you sit beside me and talk of "love" for that abominable woman, and pain me more than I can endure!

Alfred was saying, hoarsely but with pathetic insistence: "You are wrong, Dorothea. Amalie does love me. We were very close, after Uncle William's illness. We understood each other. She begged me not to leave her, when I had to go to New York. I could not take her—because of my unfounded

273

hopes. You do not understand how it is between a man and his wife, Dorothea. My wife," he added, with such a desperate yearning in his words that Dorothea could not prevent herself from tossing aside her knitting and clasping her hands together in a kind of anguished convulsion.

She said, quickly and with involuntary force: "Alfred, I know Amalie is unhappy. You ought not to have married her. Please forgive me for speaking so freely, but you are my cousin, my adopted brother, and if there cannot be truth between us, there can be no truth between any others. She is much younger than you, Alfred. She thought she wanted what you represented. But she does not want it now. She is perishing of grief, because she feels she is—is wronging you. But she desires to be free."

Alfred did not speak, but she sensed the confused violence and misery in him, his sudden hatred for her, his bewilderment. She felt him closing his mind against what she had been saying, and denying it, in his wild sorrow. So she leaned towards him and laid her hand on his sleeve:

"I know you have believed that matters were not felicitous between Amalie and me, Alfred. You were right, in a measure. But that is because I always knew that Amalie was wrong for you, exceedingly wrong, and that you are wrong for her."

He drew away from her, but with her new prescience she was not offended. She knew his gesture was the instinctive recoil of a hurt organism.

"Has she told you of this?" he asked, his voice muffled. "She has confided in you?"

Dorothea hesitated. Then she sighed, over and over. "Not in actual words. But in a certain manner. In certain gestures. In a certain way of walking—speaking——"

She thought of what she had seen through Jerome's window, over two months ago, and the memory was like the sudden upspringing of a fire in her mind.

"Nebulous!" cried Alfred. "She is only lonely."

But not for you, thought Dorothea, mournfully.

She sat back in her chair. "Perhaps," she said. "But I am afraid it is not loneliness for you."

He laughed harshly. "For whom, then? Her old life, her old friends, her old insecurity and poverty?"

"Perhaps."

There was silence between them, then, for a long time. Now Alfred stood up and began to walk slowly back and forth over the terrace. He blotted out the pale moonlight as he passed before Dorothea, for the round argent moon was rising over the copse of pines. Dorothea was, all at once, quite ill. Strength left her hands; they fell flaccidly on the abandoned knitting. Her gray skirts fluttered about her ankles in a new soft wind. But she was aware only of this disconsolate and bewildered man pacing back and forth before her.

"Why don't you ask her whether she wishes to leave you?" she said, almost inaudibly.

He stopped in front of her, abruptly.

"What are you saying, Dorothea! Are you insane?"

She tried to see his expression, but she could discern only the pale suffusion of his large face.

"I cannot bear to see you so unhappy," she said, and her voice was low and wretchedly pleading. "I—I am fond of you, Alfred. I remember how contented we all were, in this house, before—she—came. Now there is nothing but anxiety and doubt and discord. It is not that I resent her position in my home. I do not. I have done my best for her. But I know that she has brought unhappiness here, with her, and in herself, and to you. Think, Alfred, and you cannot deny it."

But his own anguish and his secret acknowledgment of the truth in Dorothea's words excited him, made him frantic.

"You have always hated Amalie! I knew that from the beginning. I saw your hatred in your eyes, Dorothea, from the first moment I brought her here, before we were married! How can you be so base, so mean? If my darling is unhappy, it is because you have made her so!"

Dorothea was stupefied at these cruel and hasty accusations, and her pain flared up savagely. She rose to her feet. She faced him fully.

"You are unjust, Alfred, and in your heart you know it. It is true that I was never reconciled to her coming to my father's house——"

"I knew it!" he exclaimed. "It was always 'my father's house.' You resented my presence here, but endured it. But you could no longer conceal your resentment when I brought a new mistress within the walls you considered your own!"

She stretched out her hand and caught his arm. "Alfred! How can you speak so! So unkindly, so unjustly! You know your words are false; you know that I—we—have had nothing but love for you. This is your home, Alfred. You are my adopted brother, the adopted son of my father, who loves you. But you brought a stranger to this house, Alfred. Had it been anyone else I should have been reconciled, I should have been glad, for your sake. If she had made you happy. But Amalie has not made you happy. Long before you left for New York you appeared worn and uncertain and anxious. She was not one you could understand. You felt her strangeness. It is not your fault. In a way, it is not even hers. The marriage itself was a folly."

He tried to stiffen himself against her, but her voice, soft, imploring, urgent with some secret suffering, stirred him in spite of himself. He drew away from her, but gently.

"Perhaps I was unjust, and too harsh, Dorothea, and I am sorry. But you are wrong about Amalie and me. We love each other. It is true that she had a very odd and unusual life before marrying me, but it was a life she was willing to abandon. Perhaps I have been too absorbed in business, and she has been lonely."

He paused. Then, in a quickened tone, he continued: "I have neglected her. I will tell her that in September we shall visit New York. She is a female of much sensibility, and of an ardent temperament, and this quiet house on the hilltop has been too intense a contrast with her eventful former life.

"Dorothea, my dear, I have asked nothing more of you than that you be kind to Amalie. Perhaps she has not responded, or has misunderstood you, and misinterpreted your reserve——"

Dorothea, in spite of the gathering darkness, looked at him in profound despair and intense agony. She clenched her hands at her sides to prevent them from seizing him; she pressed her lips together to prevent her voice from crying out to him her whole reckless longing and love. Tears blinded her; the milky moonlight became a pearly mist. It was some time before she could speak.

Then she said: "Alfred, Alfred, I—am so sorry—for you."

But he had recovered some of his cheerful assurance. "Dear Dorothea, do not speak so tragically. You have no reason to be sorry. I am very happy, indeed. I am beginning to believe that my anxiety for Amalie is unwarranted. You tell me it has been very hot here, and as I said before, it has been lonely for her. But you did say that Jerome and Uncle William and Philip will return on Friday? How lively the house will be then! And Jerome's marriage to Sally in September—we can plan on all manner of festivities."

"I do not believe that Jerome will marry Sally," she muttered, completely weakened by her own emotion, and turning away.

"What?" He stared at her as she sat down. "What are you saying, Dorothea?"

She shivered, as if the wind had become cold. Alfred came to her chair.

"What are you saying, Dorothea? This is incredible!"

She turned her head away from him. "I believe Jerome is wiser than you, Alfred. I believe he is coming to the conclusion that he and Sally would not be happy together."

"Incredible! Did he tell you this?" Alfred's voice was stern and censorious. "Has the girl jilted him? Speak, Dorothea!"

She was frightened, and detested herself for her lack of self-control. "I do not know, Alfred. Jerome, however, seems restless. Perhaps he will go away—— He has not visited Sally very often recently."

" 'Go away'?" Alfred repeated. For a moment his pulses quickened, and he felt a sense of heat about his throat. But he severely repressed his natural reaction to the thought of Jerome's leaving. "How can he go away? He has given his word to Sally. Has she jilted him?"

But Dorothea's weakness had increased almost to prostration. She exclaimed: "Alfred, do not ask me more! It may be only my imagination. I do not know! I only know I am very tired."

She got up again, looked about her as if blinded.

"Certainly it is your imagination, Dorothea. I am really surprised at you. Jerome was always restless. But the wedding plans are all made, and I know that there has been no change whatsoever. Why, I saw General Tayntor this morning, on the way home. He was very civil, even jovial, and spoke of the wedding. My dear cousin, you must not let female instability of temperament overcome you."

Dorothea felt a swift and passionate scorn for him which momentarily swallowed up her sorrow and fear. She cried: "Oh, Alfred, do not be so obtuse! You have been away for two months, and there have been currents you have not been here to discern!"

She bit her lip then, and drew in a deep, sharp breath.

"What are you trying to say, Dorothea?" Alfred came closer to her, spoke more quietly but insistently.

"I do not know what I am saying!" she said wildly.

"I can see that." He was very stern. Then he softened. "You are tired, Dorothea. You, too, perhaps, have been lonely. It has been too much for both of you."

He took another step towards her. "I know your kind heart, Dorothea. You have been anxious about Amalie. But do not worry. I will send one of the stableboys to Dr. Hawley tonight, to ask him to come in tomorrow morning."

But she caught up her knitting, paused as if confused and stunned, then left him. He watched her go. He saw the door close behind her. He sat down and gazed unseeingly at the moonlit slope before him.

All at once he was prickling with uneasiness and depression. His head began to ache. He thought: There is really no satisfaction at all in living.

The thought, revolutionary, alien to his nature, frightened him, made him sit up rigidly in his chair. He looked about him in bewilderment, touched by a peculiar atmosphere of tumult and of sinister, unsaid things. How very odd of Dorothea! He had not thought it of her.

He rubbed his aching forehead. The wind whispered, moved, lifted, all about him. His depression increased. Then, quite suddenly, there seemed a shift in plane, and everything about him took on a sort of unfamiliarity, a tenuousness, a remoteness. He was a stranger to melancholy, but now he felt it beating heavily in his blood. The moonlit slope seemed to retreat, became as vague as mist. The walls behind him were frail as cloud. Even the scent of the earth had no memory for him. It was as if he dreamed.

He got up hastily. He threw back his shoulders. He said to himself: Dorothea's humors have been too much for me.

He entered the quiet, dark house, which held the warmth of the July day. He heard, as Jerome had heard, the loud ticking of the clock. His new weariness weighed him down as he climbed the stairs to his room. All the strong order of his life had been disrupted; strange shadows had been flung across familiar paths; unknown and whispering voices murmured in and about him.

A single lamp burned in the room he shared with Amalie. He crept across the carpet to the bed. Amalie slept. He saw the thinness and whiteness of her cheek, the hollows under her eyes. He stood there and looked down at her.

One of her hands hung listlessly over the side of the bed. Her black hair was tossed thickly on the pillows. She sighed faintly, once, then again and again.

Terror suddenly engulfed Alfred, and tearing love and passion. What if Amalie were dying? There was such a gaunt hollow under her cheekbones, such a sharpness about her chin. He knelt down beside the bed and stayed there for a long time, seeing nothing but his wife, and hearing nothing but his fear.

CHAPTER THIRTY-FOUR

Amalie awoke, lifting eyes heavy with lassitude. The sun thrust a bar of hot yellow steel through the parting in the draperies. It burned sharply on the carpet, touched one bedpost with fire, struck a spot on the mirror opposite like a small and blazing explosion.

Amalie discovered that she was still alone. Alfred had spent his first night at home on the small couch in the dressing-room in order that he might not disturb her. She raised herself on her elbow, feeling the warm moist weight of her hair on her neck and shoulders, and sickening under it. Her whole body was invaded by that sickness. She lifted the massy hair a moment with her two hands, but the air about her was hardly less oppressive. She heard the tinkle of the ormolu clock on the mantelpiece; it was only seven. The fowl were clucking drowsily at a distance. There were subdued sounds of morning activity on the stairways and in the rooms below.

The room was dusky except for that burning and hurting bar of light, and Amalie, as she looked at the mirror beyond, saw her face in it, ghostly, haggard and completely ravaged. She fell back on her hot pillows and moaned under her breath. All at once consciousness seemed too terrible to bear; she closed her eyes, pulled the warm sheet over her shoulders.

The dressing-room door opened softly, and Alfred tiptoed into the room in his crimson silk dressing gown. With the instinct of love, he knew she was awake. He came to the bed. She felt his shadow, dark against her eyelids. She opened her eyes sluggishly, and when she saw him his whole silhouette suddenly melted with the flood of her tears.

He drew a small armless rocker to the bedside and sat there, watching her with intense gravity and sadness. He did not speak; he waited. She wiped her eyes, then stared at him blindly.

He said, at last, very gently: "What is it, my darling? Are you in pain? Are you ill?"

She stirred, tried to lift herself on her pillows. He stood up and helped her, competently. The effort had exhausted her;

her color became even more gray. Alfred said, in the quick loud voice of fear and anxiety: "I have sent for Dr. Hawley. He will be here at nine. My God, Amalie! What has happened to you? I am your husband. Can't you tell me?"

The long bar of light brightened until the room was suffused with a warm incandescent dusk. Amalie saw that Alfred was extremely agitated, his broad strong face pale, his hazel eyes strained. She thought: I ought to tell him now, while we are alone. But Jerome has forbidden it. Is he wrong?

Surely it would be easier, in the quietness of this room, to confess to Alfred, to plead for his understanding, to soften his first furious anger. But her lips and her tongue were numb and stiff. She could only wring her hands on the sheet.

Alfred waited for her to answer him, then, sighing, he went to the silver pitcher and bowl on the commode, dipped a linen towel in the cool water, and returned with it to the bed. With slow and gentle hands he wiped Amalie's hot, white face. He smoothed back her hair tenderly. Then he sat down again. Now his expression was set and stern.

"Amalie," he said, "I had a talk with Dorothea last night. She told me that you are unhappy. My darling," he continued urgently, "you know I live only for you. If you are unhappy, you must tell me, so I can help you."

His heart was hammering with renewed fear and apprehension, even while his mind repudiated Dorothea's words. He leaned towards his wife and took one of her cold hands.

Amalie bent her head, and the veil of her black hair swept across her cheek. She whispered: "Yes. Yes."

Alfred's fear heightened. "Yes what?" he exclaimed, quite sharply. "What do you mean, Amalie? Am I to blame for something, for something which has changed you so terribly, and has made you so ill?"

Her head bent even lower. "Oh, no, no, Alfred. It is not you. You are everything that is kind and good. It is I who am wrong."

Alfred was silent, but his hand tightened about hers.

There was a subdued knock on the door, and Jim entered, carrying Amalie's breakfast tray. Alfred frowned on him. What the devil was Jerome's man doing here, instead of a female servant? He stood up, and coldly took the tray from Jim. "I will be down shortly for my breakfast, Jim," he said. He watched the little man retreating and he thought there was something furtive in his quick movements and sidling.

Alfred looked down at the tray with concern and distaste.

There was only a plate of hot toast there, and a silver pot of tea. "Is this all you eat in the mornings, Amalie?" he asked.

She pushed back her hair with a languid hand and closed her eyes on a wave of nausea. Alfred laid the tray on her knees. He was more alarmed than ever. "This is nonsense," he said. "No wonder you have failed so. But eat this, and then you must go downstairs with me for a real breakfast."

He was human enough to be filled with a quick, sharp bitterness. He had come back to Riversend full of triumph. He had anticipated telling Amalie what had happened in New York, the kind and civil words and invitations of Mr. Regan. He had been confident, had felt new and exultant strength. He was returning to a loving friend, who would rejoice with him. But he had returned to a desperately ill wife, a woman who looked close to death, who had no will to speak or to greet him.

Suddenly, this very fact filled him with enormous fright. But he forced himself to pour Amalie's tea. He lifted the silver cover from the toast.

"No. Please," said Amalie, in a voice of husky misery. "I am afraid I do not want it."

"Nonsense. You are pining away." Again, bitterness and anger came to him, as well as fear. "You have neglected yourself. We must stop this foolishness. Am I not your husband? If something is troubling you, you must tell me. And I want to know at once."

He waited again. But Amalie only looked emptily at the tray on her knees. Alfred moistened lips suddenly dry and salty.

"Once, you asked me to take you away from this house, to build a home for you, and me, and Philip." His voice broke; his jaw became rigid with his harsh self-control. He went on, more quietly, more firmly: "I know that things may not be well for you here, under Dorothea. She is a little—difficult. I know that she resented you, and perhaps still resents you. You are not mistress in this house. I was wrong, perhaps, in insisting that we remain, even though Uncle William gave me the impression that eventually this house will belong to me." He paused. "Amalie, my love, if it will make you happier, we will leave. I will build you a house wherever you desire it, and we can be alone, you, and I, and Philip."

Amalie's fingers touched the warm teacup. She tried to lift it, but it seemed too heavy for her. Alfred, watching her closely, sighed, raised the cup to her lips. She drank a little. He replaced the cup in its saucer.

"Is that what you would wish, my darling, to have a home of our own?"

She thought: If only I had never seen Jerome!

She forced herself to speak: "Alfred, I am allowing you to believe that something is the fault of Dorothea. It is not true. She—she has been remarkably kind. If she resents me at all, it is my fault."

"Well, then," he said, with a cheerfulness he did not feel, "that is settled. But you have still not answered my question."

Amalie's exhaustion and misery prostrated her. She murmured: "Let me wait a little, Alfred." She looked at him fully now, and it was more than she could endure to see his kindness and concern, his love for her. She said: "Alfred, you ought not to have married me. You are too good for me, and I am afraid."

This so touched Alfred that some of his fear and alarm disappeared. "Nonsense! We shall have the happiest life, my darling. I will not press you now, but I do hope that soon you will help me to decide whether we are to stay here or not. I want only the best, and the most satisfying, for you."

He left her side and began to walk up and down the room, his hazel eyes sparkling. "We can have whatever we wish. Mr. Regan complimented me on the soundness and the increasing assets of the Bank. Of course, he has the daring and cosmopolitan mind, and cannot always understand the caution and conservation necessary for a rural banking house, but I think, all in all, that he approved of my policies."

Amalie bestirred herself out of her lethargy to say: "I am sure that Mr. Regan could do no less than to approve of you, Alfred."

He stopped near her to smile down at her. "Thank you, my dear." It was coming out very well, now. She was taking an interest in his words; there was something like hope in her eyes. "Do eat some toast," he urged. To please him, she did so, though it sickened her.

"I ought not to have left you," he said tenderly. "I ought to have taken you with me. But I thought—I thought——"

"Yes," she said, with bitter simplicity, "you ought to have taken me."

Again he was pleased and touched. He stretched out his hand to lift a lock of her hair, which he fondled.

"But that was because I had hoped we were to have a child, and you must be protected, my love. However," he resumed briskly and with a shy smile, "perhaps we can have our hopes again, in the future."

Amalie pushed away the tray. She appeared faint and weak again. Alfred put the tray on the table. All his concern returned, but he said sturdily to himself: Females often have these strange vapors, I have heard. They are so delicate and susceptible. She will be better, now that I am home. I still believe that Dorothea has been oppressive, and that my darling has been lonely and depressed.

He could feel the gathering heat of the room. He saw the moistness on Amalie's white face, the pallid drooping of her mouth. He hesitated. "You are sure that you cannot join me at breakfast?"

"No. Please." She closed her eyes. "I think I prefer to remain in bed for a little longer, Alfred."

"Yes. Perhaps that is best. Dr. Hawley will be here at nine, and we must have his opinion."

He bent and kissed her forehead, and then her lips. Her hands clenched under the sheet to control her instinctive shrinking and the pang that seemed to divide her heart. Then he retired to the dressing-room, where he dressed for breakfast. Amalie lay rigid and still, listening to his soft humming, his subdued movements. When he opened the door again, she pretended to have fallen into a doze.

She heard him go down the stairs. Acid tears burned her eyelids. Then she forced herself out of bed. She stood by the window and looked out. The grounds below were inundated with radiance. Charlie, Jerome's little dog, was chasing some pigeons. Amalie could hear the distant whistling of a stableboy. The roofs of the barns were ruddy, and the weathercock upon the highest roof moved gently in the warm breeze, catching a blinding glitter as it turned towards the house. The valley below floated in a heat-haze beneath a sky like a hot opal.

Amalie stood by the window for a long time. She heard the sleepy chirp of a bird, the soft cooing of pigeons, the bright moving of the breeze. But all these sounds were faint and warm, and full of peace, hardly disturbing the shimmering cataract of light that fell on the earth and the house and the trees weighted with slumber.

Amalie turned from the window. She had pushed aside the curtains, and the large pleasant room was filled with light. How welcoming it was, how much her home, the first home she had ever known. She began to shiver in spite of the heat, and she was transfixed with pain. No matter what happened in the terrible future near at hand, this house would never be home for her again. It would remember how she had stricken it, how she had filled it with hatred and clamor and bitterness. All the portraits on the walls would repudiate her; every wall would shrink away from her.

She bathed her face and hands, combed and brushed her hair and then twisted it in long black braids that fell far below her waist. She fastened a long dressing-gown of pale-blue silk about her. Then, overcome once again by that strange weakness and fainting sensation, she sat down in a chair near the window, her hands slowly but strongly wringing themselves together on her knees.

But she had endured so much that she was conscious now of her suffering only as a huge and disembodied pain, suffused and no longer sharp. She began to rock a little, her face stiff and passive between the black braids of her hair. She watched the sunlight dancing on her blue silk thighs and glinting on her wedding ring.

All at once she had a poignant sense of approaching calamity, loud and terrible. She sat up straight in her chair, shaking violently. Some mysterious instinct warned her. She started to her feet, staggered, caught at the curtain beside the window. Her instinct sharpened. She must get away from this house at once! She looked about the room wildly, put her hands to her ears as if to shut out some roaring and impelling voice. She ran to her wardrobe and tore out a light gown of flounced dimity tied with cherry ribbons. She snatched a wide hat of yellow straw from the wardrobe shelf, a pair of black slippers from the floor. She laid out her lace petticoats, her stockings, her corset. Her hands were trembling and fumbling. She did not hear the grating of Dr. Hawley's buggy on the gravel drive below. She did not hear his voice and Alfred's rising up the staircase. When the door opened she started back so frantically, clutching a petticoat to her breast, that she had the air of a prisoner caught in the midst of despairing flight.

"Well, well," began Dr. Hawley, cheerfully, "so here we are!"

"She seems to be better," said Alfred, with pleased surprise. "You decided to dress, my love?"

But Dr. Hawley had paused on the threshold. His smile disappeared; his eyes narrowed with stern anxiety. He saw Amalie's face, frenzied and distraught. He saw her eyes, darting from him to her husband like the eyes of a cornered animal.

Alfred moved towards his wife, but Dr. Hawley, who had a strong instinct of his own, caught his arm. He tried to speak easily. "Alfred, may I talk to Amalie, alone? Would you wait outside for a few moments?"

Alfred stopped. He turned to the doctor, frowning.

"You see," said Dr. Hawley, with elaborate casualness, "a lady sometimes tells her doctor—things—which might embarrass her before her husband. I must insist upon it, Alfred."

Alfred was bewildered. He stared at Dr. Hawley, then slowly turned to Amalie. She had shrunk back against a bedpost, still clutching her petticoat, her blue robe twisted about her body. Her expression was stark, hunted, and unfamiliar to him.

"What is it, Amalie?" he cried. "What has happened?"

Her lips moved in a whisper: "Nothing. I was about to dress. You—you startled me."

Alfred relaxed a little. "Well, you must not, until you have talked to Dr. Hawley and he has decided whether you are to remain in bed." But his heart had begun to beat with a kind of curious dread and alarm. He glanced at the physician pleadingly, as if to say: You can see how she is.

Dr. Hawley nodded, and gently and firmly pushed Alfred towards the door. "It will take only a few moments," he said, reassuringly. "Then I'll call you immediately."

To the last, Amalie saw Alfred's pale and anxious face, until the closing door shut it away from her. Then she sank down upon the side of the bed, still clutching her petticoat, and her head dropped forward.

Dr. Hawley stood near the door and watched her for several long and silent moments. The sunlight washed into the room. There was no sound.

"Why are you frightened, my dear?" asked the doctor at last, in a gentle voice.

Amalie replied faintly, not lifting her head: "I am not frightened."

He advanced towards her. "Yes, you are. And you are very ill."

He took her hand, felt its coldness, felt the pounding beat of her pulse. He regarded her gravely. Then he drew a chair close to her, and sat down.

CHAPTER THIRTY-FIVE

Alfred paced uneasily up and down the dim heat of the upper hall. At intervals he wiped his damp face with his linen kerchief, which smelled freshly of lavender. He was annoyed that his knees were sometimes seized with a tremor, and that he felt slightly sick. Amalie, then, was much more ill than he had suspected. He remembered the doctor's voice, the touch of his restraining hand. Dr. Hawley was not given to dramatics. Even during crises he was usually calm and casual.

During his pacing, Alfred often stopped by the bedroom door, straining his ears. But he heard very little beyond a subdued and questioning murmur. The grandfather clock below chimed the quarter-hour. Alfred glanced at his watch. He ought to be at the Bank now, with his despatch case of papers. He was not accustomed to being home on weekdays, and this gave him a disturbing sense of unreality. He stiffened his legs to restrain the fits of light trembling that occasionally shook them.

What if Amalie were going into a decline? What if her heart were failing? He tightened his hands in his pockets. No, he had done nothing to deserve this terror. God could not be so cruel. He looked about him at the quiet walls. He leaned on the banister to stare down at the sun-dappled hall below. He heard the muffled clinking of china and silver as the servants removed the breakfast service from the dining-room, where he and Dorothea had just breakfasted.

All at once he had a strong hunger for Dorothea's calm and sturdy presence, for her reassurance. He started down a step or two. But he could not continue. At any moment Dr. Hawley might emerge from the room and find him gone. He said to himself: I must be sensible. I am alarming myself unduly. In any event, I shall not be helping Amalie if I become hysterical.

He heard the swinging of a door downstairs, and saw Dorothea's white ruffled cap below him and the firm outlines of her tall, black-clad figure. He heard the jingling of her keys, the rustle of her black bombazine apron. He called down to her softly, his heart rising a little with relief. She looked up at him, then began to mount the stairs.

"I heard Dr. Hawley come," she said, composedly, her dark eyes searching her cousin's face. "What is wrong with Amalie?"

He made himself smile. "I do not know yet. I am still waiting." He paused, then said with rare impulsiveness: "Stay with me, Dorothea. I was looking for you."

He is afraid, she thought, with bitterness and sympathy. He is afraid for that slut, who is only feeling the weight of what conscience she possesses.

"Do not distress yourself," she said, making her voice very natural and quiet. "I have been alone with Amalie all these weeks, and I assure you that she has not been very ill."

"She appeared so this morning," he said, with weariness. But his expression was both pleading and questioning.

Dorothea shrugged. "The excitement of your return, perhaps."

She hesitated, then touched Alfred's sleeve briefly. "This is not like you. You are doing no one any good by having the vapors. And again, I assure you that Amalie is not very ill. She has been suffering from the heat."

He looked down at the strong veined hand on his sleeve, and then, again with an impulsiveness unusual for him, he pressed his fingers over it. "Dear Dorothea," he said, with gratitude.

He was surprised when she snatched her hand away, when her austere face flushed crimson. And as she colored so, her cheeks became less gaunt, more full, and her eyes, oddly flashing now, appeared vivid to him, and young. Dorothea, though slightly his junior, had always seemed older; he had thought of her as his elder sister. Now, as she stood before him, straight and tall, he felt the impact of her sex, and something about her that was strangely unfamiliar.

"What is wrong?" he asked, confused.

She did not speak immediately, and then only in a strained and muffled voice: "Nothing. Nothing, at all, Alfred. But I wish you would not treat me as if I were your grandmother." She gave a short, unmirthful laugh. "After all, I am not quite thirty-nine, Alfred."

Females were certainly unpredictable, thought the bewildered Alfred. Here, in an instant, Dorothea had turned from a sexless rigid figure of salt to the living form of a woman. The "elder sister" had become strange to him, had become endowed with a kind of stern beauty he had never discerned before. Her very dark eyes sparkled in the dusk; he saw the swell of her bosom, the knot of thick braids at the nape of her neck. He felt heat in his cheeks when he saw that her pale mouth was coral with dusky color.

"I am sorry," he said, though he did not know why he

287

should be regretful. "Certainly, you are younger than I. But you have always been so reliable, my dear, and so competent——"

"Perhaps," she interrupted dryly, "it would have been better for me not to have been so reliable and so competent."

But she smiled, as if deeply gratified and oddly amused. She looked at him tenderly. "I am not going to be quite so responsible," she warned him. "I am going to develop a few vapors of my own, and call for the smelling salts. I think I shall buy a few delicate scarves, and I really think I shall discard this cap." She put her hand to her head and deliberately removed the cap. Her hair, with its few threads of white, was sleek in the dim light, and her head had for him a new nobility, in its uncluttered contours.

"It would be—unsuitable," stammered Alfred.

But she replied sturdily: "How do you know what would be unsuitable for me, Alfred? Have you ever really looked at me? Or have I just been a convenience for all of you, in this house?"

"No, certainly not," he said, with even more confusion.

Dorothea smiled again, that new secret smile. She held the cap in her hand and glanced down at it with distaste. "Perhaps if it had not been for this cap," she said thoughtfully, "I might have been married."

He was startled. "Are you serious, Dorothea? Have you ever desired to marry?"

She lifted her eyes to his face, and they flashed scornfully. "Most assuredly. I am giving it very attentive thought lately."

This novel idea so distracted him that he did not hear Dr. Hawley emerging from the room, and started when he heard his subdued and cheerful voice. He turned to the physician, and the latter's smile, his chuckle, filled him with such relief that he felt weak. Dr. Hawley smiled at him and then at Dorothea.

"Well, well," he said, "so we can have hopes, after all. The happy occasion—er—must have occurred just before you left Riversend, about two months ago." He put his hand on Alfred's shoulder, and gave him a slight push. "This time, I think we can make our plans. I do, indeed."

All at once every sound in the house appeared to fade, to die away, and there was a profound and echoless silence all through it. The dim air became spectral and very still. The doctor felt it all; it was part of the unfathomable silence of the man and woman before him, their ghostly faces, their fixed eyes.

Dorothea thought, with a numb lack of emotion: Then, it is no use, for me. The crushed cap in her hand seemed made of crumpled steel, every edge biting into her flesh. There was a sick fluttering in her chest, a thickness in her throat. She leaned back against the banister as if unable to stand upright.

But it was at Alfred that the physician was staring. He could not understand that immobile face, that rigidity. He said, in a louder and more insistent voice: "Don't you understand, Alfred?" He glanced uncomfortably at Dorothea. "Your wife will present you with an heir, in about six and one half months, I believe." After all, damn it, Dorothea was no young and delicate female who must be protected from the facts of life.

Then Alfred was saying huskily: "That is impossible. You are mistaken."

The doctor smiled irritably. "Well, I'm not. I've just completed—ah—quite an intensive examination of Miss Amalie. And I have questioned her very closely. You can be assured, this time."

Alfred said nothing, but the grayness deepened on his face, and his eyes appeared to have retreated far back into their sockets. Then, with a terrible effort, he repeated: "You are mistaken. I know you are mistaken. It is impossible."

He caught at the smooth banister behind him and leaned against it. His voice came louder now, with an undertone of dull savagery: "I know it cannot be."

The smile left the physician's face. He saw the shaking outlines of Alfred's mouth, his flared nostrils, the sharp points of his sunken eyes. Dr. Hawley glanced at Dorothea. She was raising herself slowly from the banister against which she and Alfred were leaning. She looked steadily at Alfred and then at Dr. Hawley. She opened her mouth, but no sound came from it. Then she covered it with her hand, in a quick and frantic movement.

My God, thought Dr. Hawley. There is something very wrong here. He said: "May I talk to you alone, for a moment, Alfred? Is there somewhere we can go?"

Alfred gestured stiffly at the closed door of Mr. Lindsey's room, then without waiting, he went to the door, opened it, and disappeared inside. Dr. Hawley, startled, watched him go. Then he turned to Dorothea.

Dorothea was gazing at him steadily over the hand she still held pressed to her mouth.

"I don't understand," murmured Dr. Hawley, with an aimless gesture.

289

Dorothea dropped her hand. Then she moved away towards her own room, walking unsteadily. The door closed behind her.

"Well," said Dr. Hawley, aloud, "I'll be damned."

He followed Alfred into Mr. Lindsey's room. The curtains had been drawn weeks before, and only the duskiest of light filled it. The furniture was covered with ghostly dust cloths. A faint edge of sunlight shot through the curtains, touched the floor like the tip of a bright sword. Alfred was standing with his back to the door, and when he heard it close behind Dr. Hawley, he spoke clearly but expressionlessly: "I have told you it is impossible. You must tell me you are mistaken."

Dr. Hawley saw the breadth and stiffness of his strong shoulders; he saw the clenched hands which hung at his sides. Now he discerned that there was an air of suppressed and dangerous violence about Alfred's back, and in the fixed posture of his head and neck.

"Alfred," said the doctor quietly, "I am not mistaken. I am sure of that. I am an old man." He paused. "This is very strange to me. I thought you would be delighted."

Alfred said, still without turning: "I should be delighted—if it were true. But it is not possible that it is true. I have not—not—I have had nothing to do with my wife for months. So you must understand that it is impossible."

Dr. Hawley was suddenly weak. He fumbled for a chair and sat down in its swathed depths. He pulled out his kerchief and passed it over a face that was cold and damp. The sword point of light on the floor danced before him, expanded, dwindled, became blinding. He muttered: "Perhaps I am mistaken, I—" Then he could speak no more.

Alfred turned slowly. The doctor saw him, looming larger than life-size over him, diffused, wavering, like a stony statue seen through mist. He saw Alfred approach him soundlessly, stand before him. There was a deep silence in the room.

"No," said Alfred, after a long time, and very quietly, "I see that you are not mistaken."

He waited. But the doctor only sat in his chair, an old and stricken man, twisting his handkerchief over and over in his fingers.

"You have told—my wife?" said Alfred, and his voice came as from a long distance, and was still very quiet.

"Yes, yes," replied Dr. Hawley. Sweat started out over his face.

"And what did she say?"

290

Dr. Hawley was silent. Of course, this was all a dream, a nightmare. He would awaken in a moment, gasping.

"What did she say?" the question was repeated inexorably.

Breath entered the doctor's lungs painfully. "She—seemed a little stunned. She is very ill." He wrung the handkerchief more tightly over his fingers. "My God! But it is still possible that I am mistaken. I must be mistaken!"

"But you are not?" said Alfred, gently.

Again the doctor could not speak.

"She did not say—who might be responsible?" And then Alfred's voice was brutal and maddened, though still very quiet. He had begun to beat one fist slowly into the palm of his hand.

The doctor was suddenly conscious of the grotesqueness of his nightmare. What were they saying, he and Alfred? What demented words were passing between them? He forced himself upright in his chair. "I must be wrong!" he cried. "God forgive me!" He gasped. "There have been mistakes, before——"

Alfred walked firmly to the door, opened it, held it open. "Good afternoon, Dr. Hawley," he said.

Dr. Hawley pushed himself to his feet. He was trembling. The floor tilted under his shaking legs. He reached Alfred. He looked up at him. What lay behind that fixity, that inhuman calm, that lack of expression?

He exclaimed: "Alfred, you must be reasonable! It is quite possible that I am wrong. In any event," he added, his voice sinking, "she is terribly ill, the poor creature. There are symptoms which are misleading——"

But Alfred stood by the door, waiting. The doctor passed through it. The empty hall trembled about him as if filled with fog. He turned to Alfred in one last despairing effort: "If I am right, be merciful. Remember——"

Alfred did not speak. The doctor moved away feebly. He held to the banister as he went downstairs. Alfred remained by the door of his uncle's room until he heard the outer door close. Then, walking steadily, he went back to his own apartments and entered.

Amalie was fully dressed. Moreover, she had filled her old straw valise with some hastily packed clothing. As she heard Alfred enter, she almost leaped into the air with terror, then swung about. Then, as she saw his face, she stood before him in silence.

CHAPTER THIRTY-SIX

If there had been the slightest doubt in Alfred's mind before, there was none now, as he saw Amalie's preparations for flight.

He shut the door without a sound and stood with his back to it. He contemplated his wife, saw the wild terror in her eyes, the drawn whiteness of her face under the wide brim of her hat. The pretty sprigged dress billowed about her, and was agitated as if by a slight wind. She had pressed her hands into its folds; she was retreating from him, step by step, not looking away from him. Then her retreat stopped; she appeared to grow a little taller, straighter.

Alfred looked at her throat. It was full and beating. His fingers tightened into fists.

He said, almost gently: "It is true, Amalie?"

There was no terror in her eyes now, only a frozen steadfastness.

"Yes," she said.

"Did you know it before Dr. Hawley came? Did you know it before I returned?"

"No." She lifted her head with a kind of stern resolution. "Had I known it before, I should have left days ago."

Then she said: "Forgive me, Alfred."

He regarded her almost musingly. "Who is it, Amalie?"

But she only said: "Forgive me."

He had felt only an enormous numbness before, but now it began to quicken savagely into murderous anguish. He stared at her incredulously. The light brightened in the room, so that Amalie seemed to stand in an aura of radiance.

"You did this to me, you, my wife?" His voice thickened. "Why, Amalie?"

But again she only said: "Forgive me. Forgive me."

He said softly: "Don't say that again, please. I might kill you if you do. I want only to know why you did this, why you betrayed me, why you have dishonored me. You see, I must understand, or I won't know what it is that I shall have to do with you, with everything."

He still stared at her incredulously. This was Amalie, his wife, whom he loved. This was the woman he had married, with whom he had lain, for whom he had planned, to whom he had given his name. This was the woman who had convinced him not only that she was his wife, but that she was his friend also.

"You must tell me," he said. "I must understand. What have I done to you?"

"Nothing. Nothing! It was nothing you ever did, Alfred." She put her hands to her throat. "It was only me. I was wrong, evil, contemptible. You should never have married me, Alfred."

He put his hand to his eyes and rubbed them, shaking his head dazedly. "No, I see now that I should not have married you. But I did. And you married me, of your own wish. That is what I cannot understand."

She saw that soon he would not be able to control himself, and pure animal terror seized her again. If only she could reach the door!

He had dropped his hand. He came towards her for a few steps, and she could not move.

"Don't be frightened," he said. "I don't intend to hurt you, Amalie. I only want to know the name of—the man. I want to know all about him."

She shook her head slowly, automatically. "You must let me go, Alfred. Let me go out of this house in peace, and then you can forget that I ever lived. That is what I have been hoping for, praying for——"

"You? Pray?" He spoke with loathing. "How is it possible that you have ever prayed, Amalie? How could you ever have dared to pray?"

She did not answer him. Her face was even whiter under the brim of the hat.

He looked at her steadily. And then he was overpowered by his hatred for her and the frightful pain of his love and passion and of his own dishonor. A spasm wrenched his mouth, made his eyes flicker. He aged in those moments.

"You may leave this house immediately," he said. "But first I want to know who your—who the man is. You must give me his name. You must give it to me at once, or I am afraid that I shall kill you. You must tell me everything, how long you have known him, where you first saw him, where and how you betrayed and disgraced me."

He waited. But she remained silent.

"His name, Amalie?"

"I can't tell you," she whispered. "If I tell you, nothing— nothing will be endurable for you again. It is for your sake that I cannot tell you. Let me go, Alfred."

He came closer to her, and when she saw his eyes clearly

she closed her own as if to shut out the sight of death itself.

But she spoke quickly, breathlessly: "Even if you kill me, I will not tell you. Nothing can make me tell you."

She thought, please God, whatever is to happen, let it happen now. I am tired.

Even when he caught her throat in one hand and struck her fully and heavily in the face, she felt nothing but her tiredness. She felt nothing at all. Darkness rushed against her eyes; it smothered her. She did not even feel herself fall to the floor. She lay in a swimming pool of blackness, which slowly revolved. From far off she heard a cry, heard it repeated, heard the sound of a dim struggle about her. The cries and the struggle seemed to go on endlessly, and she had no interest in them. She was intent on drowning herself in the deepening pool, and on knowing nothing.

At last, after what seemed an eternity, the pool rejected her. A burning light beat against her eyelids. She opened her eyes. And she saw that only a few moments must have passed, and that from somewhere Dorothea had appeared.

Dorothea had thrown her arms about Alfred; with unsuspected strength she was pulling him away from Amalie. She was crying out against him. Amalie heard her voice, beseeching, accusing, weeping.

"No, Alfred, you must not touch her again. You must not do this to her! If you kill her, what will happen to you? She is not the only one to blame, believe me!"

Alfred attempted to push her aside, to free himself. But she clung to him with greater strength. She pressed her head against his neck. She kept her grip on his arms.

"Listen to me, Alfred," she pleaded brokenly. "There is something I must tell you. Just listen for one moment and then you will understand why I did not tell you before."

"Go away, Dorothea," said Alfred, pushing his hand against her head.

"But you must listen to me, Alfred. I heard you ask her for his—name. If you will just wait, I will tell you myself."

Alfred was suddenly quiet. He held Dorothea away from him. She was weeping uncontrollably. Amalie raised herself on her elbow. She cried out: "No, Dorothea, no! You must not tell him!"

Her head was swimming. Something warm and sticky was oozing over her lips and chin, something salty and sickening. Somewhere a horrible pain was beginning to strike at her.

But neither seemed to have heard her. Alfred was looking

at his cousin. He held her arms in his hands. He shook her. "Tell me, Dorothea."

"No!" pleaded Amalie. She tried to get up, but fell again. On her hands and knees, then, she began to move towards them, shaking her head from side to side. Nothing mattered but that she must stop Dorothea; she must reach her at once. The few feet of space enlarged endlessly before her; she seemed to travel leagues.

"You must listen, Alfred," said Dorothea slowly and steadily. "It happened just after you went away. I—I saw them together. I thought it all over. I thought that perhaps if you never knew, it would be better for you. I hated them. I wanted them to suffer. But I decided to keep quiet—for your sake. For, you see, they told me that when you returned they would tell you, and that they would go away. They would tell you that they loved each other. I—I don't know the whole plan. But we all agreed that nothing should be said that would hurt you, like this. And Alfred, you would never have known the full truth but for Dr. Hawley's coming." She wept again, but quietly. "I did not know that—that this had happened. And I do not think that she knew, either."

Alfred said, almost inaudibly: "What are you trying to tell me, Dorothea?" And now he was as gray as stone.

"Dorothea!" cried Amalie. She had finally reached the woman. She grasped her dress in her weak hands.

But Dorothea apparently did not hear her or see her. She was looking only at Alfred, and he at her.

"Alfred, have mercy upon her. She tried to avoid him, but he pursued and tormented her, from the very day he came here. I—I do not believe that she intended to betray you. She ran from him at all times. But there was the day of the storm, and he contrived to return, when he knew I was away, and she must have been frightened. I—I do not know exactly. But I do not believe she plotted to betray you."

Alfred dropped her arms, stepped back. He regarded his cousin steadfastly. "You are not trying to tell me, Dorothea——"

"Yes, Alfred." She extended her hands to him in desperate pleading.

"Jerome," he whispered.

Dorothea put her hands over her face.

Amalie let Dorothea's dress slip from her grasp. She lay in a curled heap upon the floor, blind again, sinking into darkness.

CHAPTER THIRTY-SEVEN

Alfred Lindsey looked about the neat bare bedroom in the Hobson farmhouse where Amalie had spent the last two years before her marriage to him.

Here, in this house, he had courted Amalie, had been refused once, twice, and then suddenly accepted on his third proposal. He knew every wall of this gray, clapboarded home, the scrubby lawns about it, the long fields and spindly woods of its twenty-five acres. He knew it, not only because of Amalie, but because he had had it scrupulously surveyed when he had been about to foreclose on Josiah Hobson.

He had not foreclosed it. The farmer had Amalie to thank for this. He had advanced loans on the coming harvest, a precarious thing to do, for Hobson was not a spectacular farmer. It was also something quite against Alfred's cautious and judicious procedure in the case of other failing farms. There were some men, he knew, who, no matter how well versed in farming or how tied to the soil, were, for some mysterious reason, unable to produce good crops or were dogged by unremitting failure. However, after his help to Hobson, the farm had suddenly prospered.

Mrs. Hobson was a neat, clean woman, and the little farmhouse was immaculate, despite her brood of children.

Here, in this room with the bare wooden walls, the low sloping ceiling, the tiny windows, the polished but uncarpeted floor, Amalie had slept, and here she would sleep again, for a little while. Alfred saw the maple spool-bed with its white cotton counterpane, fringed in white by Mrs. Hobson's gnarled hands; he saw the small maple dresser, with its flawed mirror, the one rocking chair with its embroidered cushion. Little white curtains blew in the wet, strong breeze which came through the windows. The thick trees outside, heavy with rain, filled the dim little room with subaqueous and spectrally green gloom.

Alfred deposited Amalie's old straw valise on the floor. Mrs. Hobson, who had asked no questions, and knew she must not ask any, bustled in meekly behind Alfred and Amalie, carrying a plain kerosene lamp. She placed it on the table, glanced timidly at Alfred and Amalie, then left the room.

Amalie removed her bonnet and shawl, and hung them on one of the nails driven into the wall, where much less than a year ago she had hung her meager wardrobe. The little lamp had dissipated the green and shadowy half-light, but it had not conquered the chill gloom of the early evening. Amalie proceeded to open her valise; she brought out the plain coarse clothing she had placed there the November before. She put the few garments in the old drawers of the dresser. She had brought nothing of what Alfred had given her, not even her wedding ring. She had worn that shabby shawl, that blue velvet bonnet, when she had gone to his uncle's house. The dress she wore, of a rough brown cotton, had cost her two dollars only a year ago. She had thought it becoming.

Alfred watched her slow but measured movements in silence. She closed the drawer. She laid upon its top her old pathetic pincushion in the shape of a huge strawberry, her black hairbrush, her comb, her pin-tray of china dimly painted with violets. She had nothing else.

There was a door in Alfred's mind, an iron-hot door, behind which lived Jerome Lindsey. Alfred had sealed him up there, for a while. For his own sake he would not, dared not, think of him. It was a door which in a few days he would open, but could not, just now. If he did, he might lose his mind, all sense of proportion, all sanity, or so he thought, and he was not far wrong.

However, as he looked about the room, saw the shawl and bonnet on their nails, saw the sad pathos of Amalie's few possessions, the iron door opened a little, and something like murderous madness issued from it. To this, then, had Jerome brought Amalie, to this he had reduced her again. To this, Alfred was convinced, he meant to abandon her. No! cried Alfred in himself. No, not even if I have to kill him. He closed the door quickly, feeling the fire of it on his hands, for he had not yet decided that he must not kill Jerome, anyway. There was such disgust in him, such hatred, such repulsion and rage, that there were moments when he seemed to be disintegrating, when nothing but Jerome's death would satisfy him.

He and Amalie had not spoken to each other again since that terrible day in their room. Whatever brief commands Alfred had had to convey to Amalie had been given through Dorothea. Until today Amalie had remained in her bedroom; Dorothea had brought her her meals in silence. Nothing had passed between the two women except Alfred's commands. The servants saw nothing of Amalie. She lived in a shell of silence, shut off from the rest of the house. Nor had she appeared to care, thought Dorothea. She had been immured in a kind

297

of paralyzed lethargy, sitting motionless for hours in her chair near the window, and Dorothea knew, instinctively, that she sat there during the nights also. When Dorothea called for the trays, they were often untouched, and she was obliged to carry them away, the cold meats congealing in fat gravy, the bread icy, the teapot chill to her fingers. Dorothea made no comment on this; her face was unmoved and stern. But several times she had encountered Alfred in the hallway, and together they had looked at the trays, unspeaking, not exchanging a glance. Finally Dorothea came to the bitter conclusion that Alfred deliberately waited there, in order that he might inspect the tray. At any rate, after that searching look, he would turn away, and re-enter his own rooms, his broad but thinning face as set as steel, and as expressionless. When he joined Dorothea at mealtime, he hardly touched his own food, and would sit opposite her, in the candlelight, as if sunken in a lethargy and far abstraction similar to Amalie's. He had never cared for "spirits," but Dorothea, with sad disgust, saw that at the table he now drank several glasses of Mr. Lindsey's old wine, which, however, did nothing to lift the somber and dazed fixity of his eyes.

Dorothea, her own spirit laden and almost broken by the calamity which had fallen upon her father's house, her own heart wild with apprehension and fear, did everything she could to force a normal aspect on household affairs. She tried to infuse normality into her voice when talking briefly with the servants. She had told them that Mrs. Alfred was ill, and that nothing must disturb her. The servants obediently imitated her attitude, but she knew that they whispered and wondered among themselves. Surely, it had been impossible for them not to have heard Amalie's cries, and her own, and Alfred's savage and distracted voice on that hideous day. She conjectured how much they knew; then would shrug despairingly. The whole world would soon know. In the meantime, it seemed best that as little as possible should escape to the inquisitive servitors.

She noticed that Jim, Jerome's valet, was rarely in evidence. Sometimes she thought that she saw his thin and meager form drifting far off down some corridor. But he kept out of Alfred's sight, and this filled Dorothea with foreboding. The horrible little man, then, knew something. Would he find some way to warn Jerome? But no, that could not be. No letter could reach Jerome in time to prevent his returning.

There were so many terrors now in Dorothea's sleepless mind. She hated her brother; she would spare no fearful thought for him. He must be justly punished. But what of her father? How much could he be spared?

She had convinced Alfred, she wearily hoped, that the less uproar, the less catastrophe, that occurred in this house, the sooner the healing, the sooner the adjustment. At least, he had listened to her with quiet politeness, looking at her with his dead and sunken eyes, but he had made no comment. As for herself, she was making no plans, and she shrank from any personal thoughts.

She hated Amalie; she was certain of this. But when she took the trays to her sister-in-law's room, when she saw that empty bruised face and those filmed eyes, something contracted savagely in her heart, and something like virulent anger against Alfred pervaded her. He had struck and beaten a defenseless woman; he had married her face and drawn her blood. During one frightful moment, she, Dorothea, had barely been able to keep him from kicking her as she had lain at his feet. Only by sternly recalling Alfred's provocation was she able to forgive him. For Dorothea had always been quite a "blue-stocking," and had often furiously resented the oppression of her sex by men, the limitations of women's opportunities, their defenselessness before the law, their often hopeless lives. She had burned with rage more than once at the memory of women she knew, whose fortunes had been arrogantly seized by new husbands, whose children had been abused by their fathers, whose relatives had been arbitrarily forbidden the houses bought by their own inheritances. They had recourse to no law; they were chattels, mere animals at the disposal of their masters.

It had frightened and repelled Dorothea that she had been able to pity Amalie; it threw her into the wildest uncertainty when she discovered that she had had to check herself, on several occasions, from speaking to Amalie with concern and sympathy. These generous impulses, born of secret and unsuspected understanding and compassion, and of indignation against men, turned, frustrated but still powerful, against her brother, Jerome. She hoped that Alfred would punish him, short of murder. But she could not be sure that Alfred, in his malignant hatred, humiliation and dishonor, would not kill Jerome. She had never suspected this side of Alfred's nature, and it terrified her. Sometimes she looked at him wonderingly, as one looks at a baleful stranger.

Three or four dreadful days had passed, during which a kind of plague of silence seemed to have descended on the house.

But Dorothea waited, knowing that Alfred was slowly but inexorably making some plan. When he finally announced to her that he was taking Amalie back to the Hobson farm her relief was almost hysterical, though she did not quite know why. She had conveyed this information briefly but coldly to Amalie, who made no reply. However, on the designated late afternoon, in the midst of a heavy rainstorm, when she went to summon her, Dorothea discovered that Amalie was quite prepared. She was, in fact, waiting for Dorothea, sitting in her chair, clad in the poor garments in which she had come to this house, waiting quietly, submissively, silently, as if she had lost all volition of her own, all emotion, all fear and thought. It was as if she had died on that appalling day, and her body was still retaining some faint but involuntary movements, which responded automatically to the commands of others.

The servants were not visible; Dorothea had seen to that. The house, dim and silent, echoing murmurously with the rain and wind outside, seemed deserted. Alfred was waiting below, pulling on his gloves, his greatcoat buttoned against the damp chill. He had not looked directly at Amalie. But he had taken her valise from her hand, and she had weakly surrendered it to him. Dorothea watched them go, and could not understand the sick pain which weakened her.

It was wise of Alfred that he had decided to take Amalie himself, for servants gossiped. The buggy curtains were drawn; they had sat side by side for the last time. For all the notice Alfred took of her, Amalie might not have been present. He stared straight ahead, grasping the reins, guiding the horse down the flowing roadway to the valley, hearing the brush of wet branches against the top of the vehicle, smelling the cold and heavy moisture of the countryside. Whatever his thoughts, he betrayed none of them. If he was aware of the broken woman at his side, he gave no sign at all. A cool wind, penetrating through the curtains, had blown a fold of her brown dress over his thigh. He had not recoiled; he had not moved. But his muscles stiffened, held themselves tense, as if to repudiate the fabric, or, perhaps, not to disturb it.

Alfred was to remember that ride all his life, and he never remembered it without the freshness of new agony and sorrow and despair.

The Hobsons, informed briefly a few days before to expect Mrs. Lindsey, were waiting. They seethed with curiosity and speculation. But they knew Alfred too well. They would not gossip, for fear of his wrath. They would not question. It had been implied to them that to do so would mean their ruin, and because of the weather, the success of the crops was not too certain. Mrs. Lindsey, they had been told, would remain with them for a few weeks, or less, perhaps. They were to care for her but speak to her as little as possible.

And now Amalie and Alfred stood in this room, which was filled with the struggling beams of the small and odorous lamp. The curtains flapped. The air was desolate and sterile, full of grief and wretchedness. The little house was very quiet, and even the children's voices could not be heard.

Amalie, finished with her unpacking, had seated herself in the little straight rocker. She was rocking slowly, mechanically, staring straight before her, her hands, the palms upturned in a poignant attitude of utter relinquishment and abandon, lying upon her knees. Her profile was towards Alfred. She seemed completely unaware of his presence. He saw her bruised and swollen cheek in the dusky lamplight; he saw the unblinking fixity of her eyes.

Moments went by as he stood there and listened to the wind and the rain and the faint creaking of the rocker. And then, all at once, an explosion seemed to burst in his heart, an explosion of agony and sorrow and passion and love. He knew now, that whatever happened, that no matter how ruthlessly he had been dishonored and betrayed, he would never forget Amalie, never cease to love and desire her. And never would he be able to overcome his remorse; never would he forget his sudden and terrible desire, now, to take her in his arms, to kiss her bruised cheek and poor lips, to weep out his plea for forgiveness, to urge her to let him send her away until this horror was over and then to let him bring her back to his love and protection.

The force of his own emotions staggered him, made him feel faint and ill. He forced himself to retreat from her, to turn away his eyes from her. With hands that trembled violently, he laid a heap of gold and silver money on the dresser. Whether or not she heard the jingling, he could not tell. At least, from what he saw of her in the dresser mirror, moving slowly back and forth in her chair, her expression did not change.

He turned away from the dresser. There was nothing to keep him here now. But still, he could not leave. He looked steadily at his wife.

I must go, he thought. But he did not move. The wind and the rain grew stronger. The lamp flickered. And still Amalie rocked, as if under some hypnotic spell. Was she waiting for him to speak? He thought not. He believed she was not conscious of him at all, but was lying at the bottom of some awful pit, senseless, moving only feebly.

And then he said, hoarsely: "I am leaving you some money. I believe you have agreed to remain in this house until after the divorce. I believe you understand that this is the one thing you can do for me, the last thing."

Amalie's white lips moved. She said: "Yes." But she did not glance at him, nor pause in her rocking.

Again there was only the sound of the wind and the rain in that miserable little room. He was leaving her here, now, in this chill and dampness, in this poverty and abandonment. His throat tightened; he thrust his fists into his pockets.

"Is there anything else you wish?" he asked in a low tone.

She shook her head slightly.

The explosion of pain brightened in him, so that he saw splinters of it before him.

"Is there nothing I can do for you before I go?"

Again she shook her head.

He moved towards the door. At the threshold he paused, turned towards her again.

He could not help saying: "Have you anything to say to me, Amalie?" And his voice broke.

Her rocking stopped abruptly. Then, very slowly, she turned her face fully towards him, and for the first time he saw life, wild, mournful and strong, in her eyes.

"Yes!" she said. "Forgive me, Alfred. You have not told me that you forgive me."

He was silent. He was trembling again, more violently than ever. He looked at her mouth, half open, shaking.

"Oh, Amalie," he said, and then again, "oh, Amalie."

But she did not move, only stared at him, eagerly, pathetically.

"I forgive you," he said. "Yes, I forgive you, Amalie."

She smiled, gazed at him fully, as if she saw him again, and not some blurred image shifting before her.

And then he said a strange thing: "And do you forgive me, Amalie?"

"There is nothing for me to forgive," she said, clearly, gently. "You have given me a little peace, Alfred."

His own desolation and grief were unendurable to him. He took a step towards her.

"Amalie," he said, "if you need anything, at any time, anywhere, will you let me know?"

But she said, and her gaze was very steadfast: "No. You must forget me as soon as possible."

He could not restrain himself from crying: "But what will you do, Amalie?"

She shook her head a little. "I do not know yet. But I shall find out soon, I know. Go home, Alfred. Don't think of me again."

And then she turned away from him, and resumed her rocking.

He went out. He never remembered the drive home, the return to that desolate house which for him was empty forever.

CHAPTER THIRTY-EIGHT

Though Jerome had spent much time with his father in Saratoga, he had carefully refrained from discussing with Mr. Lindsey the subject of the Bank and his own plans. For the old gentleman, to Jerome's alarm, appeared much weakened and much frailer, despite the waters of Saratoga and the quiet and luxury of the great plushy hotel. Mr. Lindsey had not complained; he had assured his son that he was feeling "much stronger." But when Jerome consulted the physician, he was informed that Mr. Lindsey's already damaged heart was steadily if slowly failing, and that any unusual excitement or anxiety might cause a sudden collapse.

Jerome decided to defer any discussion with his father until they had returned home. There, after a rest from the journey, he could outline his plans and urge support. He saw that this was necessary. Mr. Lindsey must know. And Jerome's own mounting enthusiasm and excitement were now overcoming his native wiliness and cunning.

Then, on the very day that they were to leave for Riversend, Mr. Lindsey received a delayed letter from Alfred, from New York, saying that he, Alfred, was returning home at once, his business concluded. "I thought of going to Saratoga myself," he had written, "but now that Jerome is with you, and since there are certain pressing matters which must be attended to at once, I have regretfully decided that Jerome can attend to any emergencies which might arise. I hope and trust, however, that none will occur."

So, thought Jerome, the gray man is already in his stony roost, and I must talk to my father now.

He had only four hours before the train left. Mr. Lindsey sat in his great quiet room, with Jerome, waiting. The old gentleman had been giving his newspapers a thorough reading. He and Jerome were alone, for Philip had gone for a last stroll over the hotel's handsome grounds. Jerome seemed absorbed in a volume of Charles Lamb.

"How well my dear son is!" thought Mr. Lindsey, with tranquil gratitude. "He has dropped years. He is a young man again, with life and vitality. He has lost that hard look of his, that elderly cynicism, that desiccated appearance of restlessness. There is an air of enthusiasm and exuberance about him which I have not seen since he was a youth of eighteen."

Jerome was thinking: I must establish myself, now, before hell breaks loose.

He looked up, smiled at his father. He glanced down at the book he held.

"Charles Lamb," he said, unnecessarily.

"Ah, yes, Lamb," sighed Mr. Lindsey. "Unfortunate young man!"

"Truth-tellers and those who perceive the truth are usually unfortunate," remarked Jerome.

Mr. Lindsey smiled. "Are you trying to tell me that you are an unfortunate?"

Jerome laughed. "No. Not yet, at any rate. May I read you this small selection?"

Mr. Lindsey's smile became aware and amused. "Jerome, you are never casual. Read me the selection, and I will try to guess your underlying motive."

Jerome laughed again. He began to read: " 'A garden was the primitive prison, till man, with Promethean felicity and boldness, luckily sinned himself out of it. Thence followed Babylon, Nineveh, Venice, London, haberdashers, goldsmiths, taverns, playhouses, satires, epigrams, puns—these all came in on the town part, and the thither side of innocence.' "

Mr. Lindsey folded his transparent hands. His smile still lingered. "Well?" he said, when Jerome had finished and was regarding him expectantly. "So we are on this side of innocence, you are implying? The day of the 'garden' is done?"

"Yes. Yes, of course. But Alfred doesn't realize that."

Mr. Lindsey was silent and suddenly grave. His piercing light-blue eyes fixed themselves attentively on his son.

"In other words," Jerome continued, "Alfred doesn't realize that civilization has moved from the cathedral to the market place. He doesn't know that change has come. He is like the man who loves changelessness and soon discovers that he has become a grave-digger."

He waited. But his father did not speak. "So," he said, "Alfred is archaic."

Mr. Lindsey stirred. He put his thin fingers to his mouth and absently rubbed it.

Jerome arranged himself confortably in his chair, like one who is about to embark on a pleasant but inconsequential discussion with a dear acquaintance. He said musingly:

"Alfred represents the passing agrarian conception, feudalistic, aristocratic. He believes that power and wealth derive solely from the land. For that reason, it is very essential for him to prevent any invasion of our community by the new rising industrial spirit, which threatens his fastness. That is because, unconsciously, he feels vulnerable. His kind can only exist and flourish in the atmosphere of the status quo."

He paused. But Mr. Lindsey was still thoughtfully silent.

Jerome continued: "He is not only afraid of the new industrial spirit—its dirt, confusion, and so on—but he knows that it is a menace to his precarious security. So long as things remain the same, he will always be in control of life and circumstance. You see, it is necessary for him to dominate things, because of his lack of inner security and imagination. He lacks adventure. He knows that if he continues in the old way, he risks nothing, and he and the Bank (which has become a projection of himself) will remain secure. He isn't attracted to expansion and to the financing of new industries in Riversend, for to him they represent diffusion, and diffusion, he thinks, will dissipate some of his tight control, and make him less omniscient, less pettily powerful."

"Ah," murmured Mr. Lindsey. Jerome could guess nothing from that noncommittal sound.

"You do not agree?" he asked, with real anxiety.

Mr. Lindsey said: "I am interested in your very clever analysis of Alfred. Whether it is true or not, I am not yet prepared to say. But your conversation, as ever, is very lively. Pray go on."

Jerome took what comfort he could from this ambiguous remark.

"Well, then. Alfred has the British idea that value lies only in land, though even the British are now changing, and becoming industrial. It is necessary for us to get there first, if America is to become the great republican empire I believe she can become.

305

"During my years in New York, particularly since the war, I often heard discussions between Jay Regan and his other pirate friends. I wasn't much interested at the time, and thought the conversations boring, but politeness insisted that I listen. I thought I had forgotten it all, but much of the talk now returns to me insistently and with pertinent and exciting meaning.

"I know now that these men no longer dreamt of an agrarian America, a country of small towns and villages, but of the building of an industrial empire. The day of feudalism had passed, not only out of law, but out of the minds of men, and the war gave impetus to this final death of an outmoded idea. I gathered that a new democracy was coming into being, a capitalistic-industrial democracy, with such opportunities for the enterprising individual that it was impossible to be too extravagant about them. The emphasis is passing rapidly from the garden to the town. From the barn to the factory."

Mr. Lindsey coughed, as Jerome paused. "I see. But you and your friends have forgotten one thing: Man is more than factories. He is life. (I do not know whether it is true that America is passing from the garden to the town, from the barn to the factory, as you have said.) And I fear that many of your friends will forget that fact, in their enthusiastic pursuit of—what? Profits?"

"Expansion, not only of industry, but of the individual," said Jerome, quickly.

Mr. Lindsey smiled slightly. "In an agrarian society, man is comparatively free. In an industrial society he would, I fear, be the bondsman of a few. His land has been his shelter. His streets, I am apprehensive, might become his prison yard."

Jerome thought this the rankest sentimentalism.

"Father, I have lived in the larger cities. I have felt the stir and urge of expansion and growth, since the war. I know that the future is in industry and transportation and building, in expansion not in concentration. And now I know that banking must be a medium for adventure, to finance new industries, and to encourage every idea which promises a return upon the investment, and also a chance to expand into new fields, new inventions, new enterprises.

"The banks are beginning to realize this. But not our Bank. Because of Alfred. As you know, he has persistently refused to allow factories to be established in Riversend. He sees the arching of the new tide above his head, and he is terrified. He does not realize that he will be inundated by the tide, and the Bank with him, and the community, too.

306

"Of course, there are many like him. And these are the danger to America, the gray men, the little stone dwellers in the little stony towers. America will not be balked by them. But they can do much damage to the new dream, the new destiny, before they are finally eliminated. It is sad that in their elimination they will eliminate others too."

"Such as our Bank," suggested Mr. Lindsey wryly.

Jerome nodded. "Yes."

Mr. Lindsey sighed, moved in his chair.

"Alfred and I have had many discussions," he said reluctantly. "I know he believes that only land is stable. He believes that speculative business and industry are built on nothing but greed and reckless adventurousness and disregard for solid values. They are precarious. They are rootless. He prefers something which can be relied upon to yield small but stable profits. Yes, I can see his point of view."

But Jerome was suddenly elated. In spite of his father's reserve and noncommittal words, he felt a stir in him, a reluctant and secret agreement with his son.

"I know what is wrong with Alfred," said Jerome. "He was poor for so long that he is instinctively afraid that by adventurousness he might lose what he has gained. He is afraid to risk anything, even for the promise of greater prosperity for himself and for the community. He has no flair for anything, not even for living, and that is what happens to a man who has known a restricted and cheeseparing youth. I wouldn't mind what he is doing to the Bank, to Riversend, if it wasn't threatening me, also, and you, and the things you initiated, long ago."

Mr. Lindsey smiled involuntarily, but his eyes were sad as they studied his son. "You are afraid, aren't you, Jerome? You feel that men like Alfred threaten some inner integrity of yours, some fortified individuality, some freedom?"

For the first time in many years, Jerome actually blushed at this shrewd and subtle understanding.

"Ah, yes," murmured Mr. Lindsey, as if in agreement with some silent comment he had made to himself. Then he became quite alert, almost vivid.

"Jerome, what plans have you?"

Jerome had not expected this sudden, this interested and lively, capitulation. He had expected to argue long and tenaciously with his father, to plead earnestly for the latter's understanding, at the most.

So he could only stare for several moments at Mr. Lindsey,

and his dark eyes, restless and extraordinarily alive, jerked in his narrow face.

And then, briefly, swiftly, stammering through the rush of his words, running to get paper and pencil, talking loudly, eagerly, passionately, he outlined a few of his ideas. Mr. Lindsey leaned forward to watch, to hear. There was a flush on his transparent old cheek, a quick blue fire in his eyes. He seemed to shake with new life, as if his youth had suddenly returned to him with all its promise of adventure and glorious risk and hope.

Yet when Jerome had finished, and an electric silence filled the big warm room, Mr. Lindsey only sat back in his chair and was silent. But the flush remained on his cheek.

Finally, smiling deeply, he said: "Jerome, you certainly sound—convincing."

Jerome laughed, somewhat excitedly. "You mean 'plausible,' do you not? I have always admired your precision of speech. Is this new slovenliness old age or just good manners?"

Mr. Lindsey chuckled: "Well, I have always thought a well-mannered man slovenly. He is afraid to take up issues; he side-steps challenges."

But Jerome waited impatiently. Mr. Lindsey glanced at his watch. "I believe it is time for us to prepare to go to the station, my boy."

He paused. He twinkled as he saw Jerome's impatience and passion. He said: "I am afraid Alfred is a well-mannered man."

CHAPTER THIRTY-NINE

Mr. William Lindsey had long ago retired from active life, not only physically, but mentally, as he now realized with considerable ruefulness. Was it conceivable, he conjectured, that it was impossible to retire from one part of one's nature without retiring from the other? He loved his native New England philosophers; he had always profoundly admired the theory of "high thinking and plain living." He had retired, as he thought, to "high thinking," and smugly believed that in so doing he had acquired "plain living," by simply doing nothing. But plain living, he began to suspect, meant a truly arduous life, stripped to its bare essentials, as a ship is stripped for action. It meant the abandonment of enervating frivolities and futilities. But it did not mean the abandonment of participation in struggle. That had been his error.

Therefore, he concluded, somewhat dismayed, if he had not really retired to plain living, he had been doing no high thinking, despite his books and his meditations. He had substituted quotation for actual contemplation. Was it Jerome who had once suggested that the truly dangerous men were the cloistered philosophers? And was it true, as Jerome had elaborated, that cloistered men gave off a paralyzing effluvium that poisoned other men in their vicinity and inhibited their energy?

If I continue along this line of thought, meditated Mr. Lindsey, I shall surely convince myself that I am a villain, a despoiler, and I shall either become very vain or hang myself.

At any rate, he had begun to think very actively since his talk with Jerome, and from the painful twinges he experienced, and the excited weariness, the groanings of his mental machinery, grown rusty and stiff from disuse, he became thoroughly convinced that he was slowly awakening from a long period of torpor. How many years it had been since thinking had imparted such exaltation to him! If thinking leads only to dejection and deeper inertia, then it must be that such thoughts emanate from the living dead. Real thinking stimulates the mind, causes the blood to flow faster, the heart to beat more swiftly, the muscles to flex involuntarily, the head to hum with exhilaration. Mr. Lindsey was experiencing these phenomena, and it was very agreeable, though very disturbing, and tinged with a kind of not unpleasant despair. How long it has been since I have felt despair, he remarked to himself. I feel quite young again!

Though he did not agree with all that Jerome had said to him that morning, he was excitedly grateful, and, with simplicity, full of wonder. Was it possible that this only son of his, who had carefully cultivated a reputation for profligacy and recklessness, for irresponsibility and extravagance, had suddenly been transmuted into an alert and eager man of affairs, interested in finance and industry and the future of America? Mr. Lindsey instinctively distrusted sudden reforms or startling mutations in character. He reminded himself that the prodigal son had not returned to his doting father until he had lain with the cattle and eaten with the swine. Nor was William Lindsey so sentimental that he tried to persuade himself that perhaps he had not "understood" Jerome. He understood him too well. It is evident, he thought, that behind all this miraculous concern for others is a very secret fear or a driving hatred. He did not believe that Jerome was ambitious. He came back to the fear and the hatred, and the thought depressed him more and more as his conviction grew. He recalled Jerome's dark blush that morning, and became increasingly uneasy.

No matter, he consoled himself at last. I doubt very much if, upon investigation of reformers and saviors and martyrs and crusaders, there would not be discovered some private, and less estimable, impulse behind the self-sacrifices and trumpets and holy words. Then he told himself that he was an Emersonian cynic, and that while, like Emerson, he respected and defended the integrity of the individual, he had no partcular fondness for humanity in the mass and little belief in its more noble and more disinterested incentives.

Like all thinkers who are disturbed by distrustful and realistic thoughts. Mr. Lindsey hid his meditations now under fatuous words. He turned to Jerome and said simply, "I don't agree with all your arguments, my boy. But I am delighted that you have these convictions. For, you see, when you first told me you wished to go into the Bank, I had a strange sense of foreboding." He smiled his pale New England smile. "I am afraid that I am something of a romantic, after all."

Jerome gave him a sharp and furtive look. They were on the way back to Riversend. In fact, in less than an hour they would arrive. Philip sat opposite them on the dusty cushions of the train, reading. The sooty windows looked out upon a darkgreen, drenched countryside. The pale rain trembled like a dully silver curtain between heaven and earth, faintly sparkling and quivering. Low mauve clouds, in thick and swollen folds, threw a dim lavender twilight over hill and meadow and quicksilver stream. Far to the west, where the sun ought to have been shining, the heliotrope sky was hung with a shield of diffused and dusky copper.

Mr. Lindsey studied with fondness Jerome's arrogant, brooding profile. He said to himself: "How young he has become, and how vital! He has lost years. He has regained his youth. It seems that a man must have a single-hearted obsession if his soul is to be virile. I only hope that he may retain this obsession!"

Jerome was speaking abstractedly: "I ought to have returned sooner." He turned to his father, smiling. "I ought to have seen Amalie first." His words were casual, but he watched Mr. Lindsey closely.

Whatever foreboding Mr. Lindsey might have had in the past was gone now. He chuckled. "Ah, yes, Amalie is all in a woman that a man might desire. I used to think, myself, that

310

it was unfortunate I am no longer young and strong and ardent. If, for instance, I had known her twenty years ago, you and Dorothea would have had a stepmother immediately, had Amalie given her consent."

Then he looked distressed. "Have you noticed, Jerome, how pale she has become, and how listless? Dorothea, in her letters, mentioned this and ascribed it to the very hot weather. Let us hope the dear girl has recovered. Doubtless, also, she missed Alfred."

Jerome moved restlessly. He glanced at Philip, who, at the mention of Amalie's name, had lifted his head alertly from his book.

"Is Mama ill?" he asked, with faint but strong alarm.

"No, no," said Mr. Lindsey soothingly. "It is just the weather, it seems. She will be very happy to see us, I am sure."

Philip smiled, Jerome stared at him. Damn it, the boy did, indeed, resemble him, Jerome! He might have been looking into a mirror which reflected his own face of twenty years ago. Philip, feeling his eyes, looked at him quickly. Jerome, with discomfort, turned away. Yet he had a most curious thought: Philip, at least, would not blame either him or Amalie. Philip was Alfred's son of the flesh, but his mind was not his father's.

He said to Philip: "Will you get me a glass of water, please?"

Philip was only too pleased. His old admiration for Jerome, for his colorfulness and easy kindness and insouciance, had returned during the last few days at Saratoga. Jerome never treated him as an invalid, or a cripple, as did the others in the family. He had a way, too, of looking directly into Philip's eyes as one looks at an equal in mind and ability, and his interest in the boy's music and studies, his awareness of Philip's sensitivity, were genuine and open. So Philip rose hastily, put aside his shawl and book, and standing as straight as his poor deformed back would allow, went off for the water.

Jerome turned to his father and said quickly: "I am afraid it is more than the weather that troubles Amalie. I am afraid she is unhappy."

"Unhappy?" exclaimed Mr. Lindsey, in a low and troubled voice. "But why? Alfred is devoted to her. She married him for what he could give her, and he denies her nothing. I think you are wrong, Jerome. I noticed a distinct fondness between them, after my illness." He frowned. He was remembering Amalie's face, her sunken eyes, her lassitude, and he was remembering with new and acute alarm.

Jerome shrugged. "Nevertheless, she is unhappy. I know that

marriage should never have taken place. I feel it would be best for both of them if they separated."

Mr. Lindsey was both outraged and indignant. "Nonsense, Jerome. What a disgusting thing to say! Marriage is irrevocable. Amalie is a female of sense and discretion, and I am sure that no such thought has ever entered her mind. When she has children any difference or incompatibility between herself and Alfred will disappear."

He was annoyed. He stared at Jerome closely. "What are you trying to say?" he demanded. "Has either Amalie or Alfred hinted anything to you?"

"No, no. Certainly not. It is just a feeling I have." Jerome was angered. He had thought to "pave the way," to prepare his father. Now he saw that he had lost much of what he had gained, and Mr. Lindsey was distrustful of him.

"Don't meddle," warned the older man. "It is not only dangerous, it is bad taste."

"And good taste is sacrosanct," said Jerome.

Mr. Lindsey smiled. "Well, for the civilized man, it is a very adequate substitute for ethics, morality and religion."

Philip returned with the water, and there was an expression of boyish gratification on his face as he watched Jerome drink of it deeply. Jerome was attracted by that expression. "Tell me, Phil, do you believe I am guilty of bad taste?" he asked, more to divert his father's scrutiny than anything else.

"I think your taste is wonderful, Uncle Jerome," said Philip with a smile.

"And I think he is a meddler," said Mr. Lindsey. But he smiled again, with less distrust. "A frustrated meddler, Philip."

"So was Luther, and Savonarola, and John Huss, and perhaps, even Jesus," said Philip, shyly, but with stoutness.

This so amused Jerome that he burst out laughing, and Mr. Lindsey, after a confused moment, joined him.

The heavy wet twilight had settled down determinedly when they arrived at Riversend. Jerome had sent a telegram to Alfred, informing them of their hour of arrival. But the carriage which awaited them, running with mercurial drops of rain, was empty of all but the coachman. The station, too, was empty. For all the lush green of the trees, there was a look of desolation over the whole August countryside. The village seemed to have withdrawn; the street lamps flickered in the strong wind.

Mr. Lindsey asked the coachman for news of the family. The man spoke cautiously. (He had been warned by Alfred.)

Miss Dorothea had one of her bad colds again, and was in bed. Mr. Alfred would have come himself, but he had been suddenly called away to Horton Hills on a matter of importance. He would return that night. He hesitated when asked about Amalie. The young lady, said the man, with a slight embarrassed cough, was not too well. But Mr. Alfred would explain everything when he came home.

"Dear me," said Mr. Lindsey, depressed. "It seems we have returned at a bad time." He was exhausted by the short journey. He lay back in the seat, closing his eyes, hearing the painful and irregular throbbing of his heart. A somber sense of foreboding came over him.

Jerome was silent. The sense of foreboding in his father was stronger in himself. To him, the darkening countryside had an inimical look. Philip, too, was quiet.

Just before entering the rise that led to Hilltop, they passed the home of General Tayntor. The General was fond of his long daily walks, even in the rain. He was just entering his gates when he saw the Lindsey carriage and the faces of the occupants behind the streaming glass. He stopped suddenly, as if shot, and stared at them, his hand on the gate.

"Isn't that the General?" asked Mr. Lindsey, with pleasure. He indicated to the coachman that the carriage should pause, and he began to struggle with the sliding window.

But the General had come to life. He flung open the gate and closed it violently behind him. They saw his tall figure melting into the wet gloom.

"Is it possible that he did not recognize us?" asked Mr. Lindsey, ceasing his struggle with the window.

Jerome's own heart had begun to beat with thick strong strokes. Something was wrong. He had seen the General's face in the light of the last lamp. He signalled the coachman to continue. The carriage rolled on.

"It's dark and wet," he said, "and there was no definite date set for our return home."

"But surely he knows our carriage," protested Mr. Lindsey.

Jerome began to talk of something else. But he was weak with alarm. He argued with himself. His foreboding only increased. He signalled the coachman again, and pushed aside the glass which separated him from the man. "Are you sure everything is all right at home?" he asked.

The man did not turn his head. He only clucked at the horses more vigorously. "Why, surely, sir, Mr. Jerome," he answered. Jerome replaced the glass. But he was not satisfied. All his senses were alerted, like soldiers at the sound of an enemy trumpet. The General's face floated before him. Jerome had been the nearest to the old man. He had seen fury there, black rage and hatred, suppressed murder. And all of this had been directed fully, and with deliberation, into the eyes of Jerome.

Jerome was not one to shrink from alarming crises. He preferred to go out to meet them. He was certain now that something had happened at Hilltop. The carriage was climbing the long rise. He saw the house at the top. It was dark. Only one window was lighted. The rain was increasing in intensity, and the wind. Now, to Jerome at least, there was something sinister in that dim pile on the hill, something ominous in its cold and unlighted windows.

He controlled himself sternly. Something was most terribly wrong. He could not forget the General's face. Had Amalie spoken prematurely to Alfred? Yes, that must be it, and gossip had travelled down to Riversend, and to the ears of General Tayntor, father of Sally. But if Amalie had spoken (and, God in heaven, what had she said?), Alfred was too discreet, too egotistic, too vain and prideful, to have broadcast the news to all and sundry that his wife was tired of him and wished to leave him. A grotesque picture of Alfred flying wildly all over Riversend, shouting the dolorous news, and beating his breast, occurred to Jerome. He had to smile at the absurdity. If Alfred did anything at all, it would be to keep his mouth shut and lock himself up in his own secret counsel. And Amalie, with her protectiveness towards Jerome, would never have told her husband of that thunderous night in May, nor would she even have mentioned Jerome to Alfred. There was something else. Jerome's imagination, always lively, painted fantastic pictures, which his common sense immediately dismissed. Unless Dorothea had told Alfred? No, Jerome was certain she had not. At the last, she would remember that Jerome was her brother.

He began to sweat in the sticky confines of the carriage. He recalled the coachman's words about Amalie: "The young lady was not too well." Little enough, but reassuring. Amalie was still at Hilltop. She would not be there if she had told Alfred anything at all.

Nevertheless, apprehension grew stronger in Jerome. When the carriage drew up at the door, he bounded out, impatiently assisted his father. He flung open the door of the house. The hall lamp was lighted. The clock struck eight, slowly and sonorously. A low fire had been lighted against the dampness, and the air was hot, almost stifling. But there was no sound, and there was no one in sight.

"It is good to be home," said Mr. Lindsey wearily. His thin and transparent face was heavily shadowed at the cheeks by exhaustion. He allowed Jerome to help him up the stairway. There was a last vibration in the air as the clock ceased striking. The vibration, to Jerome's ears, hung in the silence like a warning voice.

They encountered no one in the upper hall. It was as if the house were completely deserted. Philip went into his own room, and the quiet shutting of the door echoed through every corridor with a dull booming. But Mr. Lindsey's room had been prepared. There were late roses in glass bowls on the tables, and another low fire on the hearth. His bed had been turned down.

"It almost seems as if we were unexpected," said Mr. Lindsey, "except for my room. Dorothea must indeed be ill. And where are all the servants?"

"Never mind. Let me help you undress," said Jerome, somewhat thickly. He was positive now that something terrible had happened, and again he literally sweated with his urgency to go out to meet it, to grapple with it openly. He seized the bell rope. "We'll soon have someone here with tea for you. And that reminds me: the train was nearly an hour ahead of time. It is possible that we are not expected for another hour."

"Yes, of course," murmured Mr. Lindsey, only too glad to slip between the cool, lavender-scented sheets. "But there is such a curious atmosphere here in the house. Deserted. I do hope that Dorothea is not too ill. But then, the coachman would have told us."

Jerome piled the pillows neatly under his father's tired head. Then he listened, alertly. Was that the front door closing? There was another vibration in the air, stronger, more ominous. But no footsteps ascended the stairway.

Mr. Lindsey smiled at Jerome. "You have hands as tender as a woman's, my dear boy," he said, with deep satisfaction.

There was a knocking at the door. Jerome sprang to open it. But before he could reach it, Jim, his valet, appeared on the threshold with a steaming silver tray.

"Jim!" exclaimed Jerome, with gratitude and relief.

The little man was almost pallid under his brown skin. He kept his eyes on the tray. He brought it carefully to Mr. Lindsey's bedside table. Mr. Lindsey smiled at him. "Good evening, Jim. It seems we returned at a bad time."

Jim started slightly. His hands shook as he removed the silver covers, which hid a delicious and delicate supper. "Yes, sir, Mr. Lindsey," he croaked. "Rather a bad time. With sickness and all. Miss Dorothea is in bed, and——" He paused.

Jerome had been regarding him with silent intensity. In some curious way, he knew.

Jim looked haggard, frightened and old. Jerome watched him pour Mr. Lindsey's tea. Then the little man glanced up at him, and there were warning and fear in his nut-brown eyes. "Not yet," he seemed to say, desperately. Jerome moved slowly towards the door, his hands clenched at his side. He listened. There was still no sound in the house. But someone had come in? Alfred? And why did he not come up to this room? He must know that the family had returned.

Jim put sugar and cream into Mr. Lindsey's tea. He asked whether there was anything else he could do. Jerome said quietly: "I will change, myself. And, Jim, will you bring me a tray, too?"

"Yes, sir, Mr. Jerome," said Jim, in a dull voice. He moved towards his master. Their eyes fixed themselves on each other. My God, thought Jerome. He went out into the dim corridor and listened. Still no sound. He leaned over the banister. The library door was closed, but there was a light under it. So, someone, Alfred (?), was down there, waiting. Waiting for what? He felt Jim pluck at his sleeve.

"Sir, please come into your room, quiet as you can," the little man whispered. "There's bad trouble here. But it doesn't do to dwell on it. I'll tell you."

They went into Jerome's room. Nothing was prepared here. No fire, no flowers. The curtains were closely drawn. Jim shut the door soundlessly behind them both. He motioned to Jerome to tiptoe to the center of the room. Now fear was on the Cockney face, fear that sharpened into lively terror and despair.

"I tried to warn you, sir. I sent a telegram. You didn't get it?"

"No." Jerome was whispering also. "Out with it. What the hell is the matter here?" He paused. "Where is Miss Amalie?"

Jim put his hand urgently on Jerome's arm. "Wait a bit, sir. Let me tell you." He cocked his ear at the door. But there was only silence. Jim came closer to his master.

"It was less than a week ago, sir. I don't know it all. They try to keep it from me. Mr. Alfred had come 'ome. The young lady was ill in her bed. Mr. Alfred was alarmed. He told one of the lads to go for the doctor. That was Monday night."

"Yes, yes. For God's sake go on, you fool!" exclaimed Jerome softly.

The little man wrung his hands. His face twisted. "I don't know it all, sir. I tried to listen. But it was no go. I only know the doctor comes the next mornin'. I saw him go. Then, later, in Miss Amalie's room, I heard her scream. It was pitiful, like. I didn't hear anythin' else, though I listened. And then, after a bit, I heard Miss Dorothea in there, talkin' to Mr. Alfred. Confused, like. They spoke low, and I couldn't put my ear to the door, for there was others listenin' now, all the lasses movin' and bobbin' around on the backstairs, and pokin' their heads up into the hall, and whisperin' to the lads who was in the kitchen."

"You heard Miss Amalie scream?" asked Jerome, almost inaudibly. "Do you know why she screamed?"

Jim shook his head. "That was all as I heard, sir. But I saw Mr. Alfred later, and he looked like death, sir, that he did. Moved like in a dream. Didn't go to the Bank at all. Still hasn't been. And Miss Dorothea took to her bed last night. But before that, somethin' else happened, and it's bad."

He shook his head distractedly. "It was given out that Miss Amalie was ill in bed, and Miss Dorothea took her trays in and out. And she locked the door behind her."

Jerome drew a deep breath. His heart was beating so fast that he had a sensation of smothering. But now a terrible rage was rising in him, and reddish wisps of mist began to float before his eyes.

Jim was whispering again: "Then, two days ago it was, Mr. Alfred took away Miss Amalie, in the buggy."

Jerome caught Jim's arm fiercely. "Where is she?"

Jim shook his head again. "That I don't know, sir. Nobody knows. There's been lots of talk. Nobody knows wot it's all abaht. Even in the village. Mr. Alfred went to see General Tayntor, one of the maids 'as told us. I've told you all I know, sir."

Jerome did not speak. He stared savagely before him. His quick imagination was filling in the gaps of Jim's communication.

"There was Mr. Alfred's lawyers here, too, sir, shut up with him, like, in the library. That was last night."

Jerome looked at the door. He pushed Jim aside. He went out of the room, he went into the hall, he ran quickly down the stairs, making no effort to hush his steps. He reached the library door, and flung it open.

317

There was a fire here also. And there was Alfred, standing before it, with bent head. He had been out, for his tall hat, his gloves and cane, were laid on a table nearby.

He heard Jerome enter. He watched him close the door behind him. His face was ashen, heavily furrowed. But when he looked at Jerome his hazel eyes burned and flashed with hatred, though he did not move nor speak.

"Where is Amalie?" asked Jerome, and he advanced towards his cousin.

Then he stopped, and the two men looked at each other in a silence which grew more frightful with every slow second.

Mr. Lindsey, lying weakly on his pillows, suddenly lifted his head. He had heard Jerome's hurrying footsteps; he had heard the closing of the library door. He let his head drop back. But something began to thrill and tremble in him, and he could hear his own heart, like a strong and heavy drum. He threw aside the covers, and, with a most enormous effort, thrust his feet into his slippers and put on his robe.

CHAPTER FORTY

Alfred's lawyers had advised him well and with realistic shrewdness, and Alfred, after the first bitter rebellion and frustrated rage, had listened. "Remember, Alfred," one of them had said quietly, "that Jerome Lindsey is the old gentleman's son, and that blood is still thicker than water. Go cautiously. Young Lindsey has succeeded in ingratiating himself with his father; it's town gossip. He is firmly affixed to the Bank now, and he has powerful friends, not only in Riversend but in New York. Didn't you tell us once yourself that Mr. Jay Regan is one? And didn't you say that Mr. Regan expressed deep interest in him, when you were in New York? Go cautiously.

"You've had the worst provocation that any man can have, and if you forgot yourself completely, you'd have considerable sympathy. But sympathy doesn't last long. If, after all your years of work, you lose your place in the Bank, your sympathetic friends will dwindle away. This woman, your wife, has betrayed you. Granted. But she hasn't 'shamed' you, as you keep repeating. She has only shamed herself. The sooner you forget her, the better. The less violence and recrimination, the less you will get the old gentleman's back up. Keep remembering Jerome Lindsey is his son. We aren't advising

318

you to stay on amiable relations with the man who cuckolded you; that's beyond human nature. But the adjustment, the new arrangement, will come later. There is always the strong possibility, too, that he will find his position in this community untenable, and if you control yourself, it is very likely that the old gentleman will send him away immediately. After all, he has wronged you, and Mr. Lindsey is a man of honor. Your forte is dignity and silence. This is your home, your community. If you exercise restraint, you will command the admiration of your friends."

Alfred's strong if hidden egotism, his natural caution, his dominating ambition, warned him that his lawyers spoke wisely. He expressed impatience for his divorce. He would give Amalie money, a small but sound sum, on the condition that she leave the community immediately after the divorce. The lawyers settled on the sum of five hundred dollars. The divorce would be expedited. There would be as little food as possible for gossip. Of course, there would be talk. But, the lawyers reiterated, he himself had only to maintain a proud silence.

They, and Alfred, left out of consideration the results of his first meeting with Jerome.

The lawyers, usually so astute, also left out of their calculations the fact that Alfred had for his wife the deep and phlegmatic passion and love which only a silent and restrained man can possess, and which he cannot overcome. They knew nothing of Alfred's compassion for Amalie, his tearing anguish at the very thought of her; they did not know that he had developed a theory, born both of his love and his egotistic self-protectiveness, that Amalie had been more guiltless than guilty, that she had been the seduced, rather than a willing accomplice in his shame.

Nevertheless, the lawyers' advice had been received by him with more reason than they had expected. If Jerome had not returned, if, indeed, he had not burst in upon his cousin with the open challenge of his demand for Amalie, Alfred might have acted to the entire approval of his lawyers.

But when he now saw Jerome, when he saw that dark and arrogant face, those infuriated eyes, that attitude of contemptuous rage and brutal disregard for the man he had wronged, all the advice of the lawyers was lost.

For in one flashing and terrible moment Alfred saw the essence of all his years with his cousin. He felt, in one vivid condensation, his old secret jealousy and envy, the tortures which the light and disdainful Jerome had endlessly inflicted upon him, the chronic fears which had dogged these last few months. A thousand sharp scenes shifted before him, and he heard Jerome's old laughter echoing from their very youth together, laughter cruel and merciless and completely genuine. He remembered all the taunts, all the stinging jests, all the glances of amused contempt, all the delicately vicious words and ridicule.

But all these things were only the backdrop to the fiery and disordered thoughts which raced through his mind now, all the male and lustful thoughts, all the male jealousy and murderous hatred. This was the hated man who had made him, Alfred, a contemptible and laughable figure; this was the man who had put his hands on Amalie's bare flesh, had kissed her, and lain with her—Amalie, his wife! This was the man who had inflicted the worst and most hideous wrong any man can inflict upon another, a wrong which struck lethally at all that makes a prideful human being: his dignity, his self-respect, his sense of property, his protected individualism, his integrity, his wholeness.

There was no reason left in Alfred now, no caution. The primordial man, rising heavily and fiercely from under all the stones of civilization and convention and self-interest which had been heaped carefully over him, stood naked and terrible in Alfred's person. And it was this atavistic creature, clearly seen, which had caused Jerome to stop suddenly, and to look at his cousin in a sharpening and ascending awareness of the presence of something which would most probably try to kill him.

Yes, a voice said clearly in Jerome's mind, he will kill you, if possible. Jerome's first emotion was incredulity. He had, absurdly enough, hardly thought of Alfred at all, except as a lumbering and faintly ridiculous figure, the unimaginative business man, immune to the passions of those with more quicksilver natures. Alfred was only a tiresome obstacle. He saw now, with increasing incredulousness, that he, Jerome, was a fool, and that his folly might cost him his life, ludicrous as the very idea might be. It really was possible, he said to himself, that this heavy-faced but wild-eyed man had loved and cherished Amalie with an abominable, but very powerful, passion, and that he was quite capable of strong male lustfulness, and the excesses which that lustfulness held in potentiality.

And so they looked at each other across the little space that divided them in this lamplit room, and Jerome thought: He is mad. The thought was cold and clear and quick. Other thoughts followed swiftly: He is stronger than I, and heavier, even though he is older. Besides, there is my leg.

He forgot Amalie in the pure instinct that awakens in a man when his very existence is threatened. He could only stare at Alfred with intense awareness and calculation. Alfred had not moved. Yet every nerve in Jerome's body was thrilling and singing in the knowledge that possible death stood only five feet from him. Alfred's face, for all its ashen look, was almost expressionless. It was his eyes that held his cousin's fascinated attention, and it was those eyes that made Jerome feel the first real terror of his life.

He still could not believe it. He could not make himself accept the fact that in this room where he had spent his childhood and his youth he might die at the hands of a man he had always despised. He recognized the leaping terror in himself, in all its vital freshness and newness, for not even in war had he known real fear, nor ever before.

Alfred, in turn, looked at Jerome. He did not know of his cousin's pure animal fear. He saw only that slightly lifted face, the stiff outthrust chin, those narrowed and penetrating eyes which did not leave his own face for an instant. He saw that the muscles about that insolent mouth had sprung out in thin cords. And then, suddenly, he knew that Jerome was afraid.

He was afraid, this blackguard, this wretch, this evil and despicable man! He was afraid, for the first time, of him, Alfred Lindsey!

Alfred said: "She is going to have a child, your child."

Jerome did not speak. He was not deceived by Alfred's voice, dull and quiet. Suddenly his eye leapt aside, looking for a weapon with which to defend himself. Alfred's words had not reached his complete consciousness. In fact, he hardly heard them.

Alfred saw the swift side glance. He followed it with his own eye. He saw his heavy cane on the table near him. His hand darted out, seized it. Before Jerome could move, or even lift an arm, Alfred had struck him savagely and heavily across the face.

Jerome staggered back, raising his arm to shield his face. He did not feel the pain, but the stunning force of the blow sent him reeling. He heard a roaring in his ears; his vision was clouded, and through fog he saw Alfred looming over him. He saw his cousin's arm lifted again and again, and yet he did not feel the blows that battered him. He had only one thought: escape. For now he knew, completely, that if he could not get away, if help did not come, he would surely die.

Far off, in the dim reaches of space, he heard a cry, a multitude of cries. He no longer saw Alfred. He was floating in semi-darkness, and he was conscious for the first time of an unbearable agony. He felt himself tossed and thrown off, sailing, swimming, and he saw before him a cloud of darkness which rushed closer and closer, spreading out and about him. Finally, it engulfed him, and he sped into it, far from the pursuing agony of his own flesh.

It was not until late the next day, when he awakened, that he learned that his father, impelled by some mysterious instinct, had left his bed and come downstairs, that he had, in fact, by his appearance, by his cries, saved his son's life.

CHAPTER FORTY-ONE

Even had Amalie been physically able to stroll about the Hobson farm, the weather would have prevented such excursions. The first days of August were unseasonably chill and wet, filled with a green and sepulchral gloom. The tenebrous sky was all gray folds, marbled with dark veins, and the earth dripped constantly.

Amalie, from her low little windows, could see the soaking meadows, the melancholy cattle huddling under drowned trees, the cloudlike outlines of distant hills. But, for her, the days were all the same. She was counting them, one by one. And as each day passed, she grew more feverish, more sleepless, more taut with extreme nervousness. She was only faintly aware of the Hobsons, though she smiled at Mrs. Hobson and the children whenever she saw them. She was given her meals in her room. Had she been less emotionally intense, straining all her thoughts and senses beyond the farm, she would have discerned that she lived in virtual isolation, and that the Hobsons avoided contact with her. They had been given their orders: Mrs. Lindsey was to be kept apart, allowed no visitors, not to leave the farm, and not to be engaged in conversation. Her presence amid this family was to be a secret from the whole community. No one must know that she was here.

If the Hobsons had feared that Amalie might do some questioning herself, or might prove restless or intractable, she gave no grounds for this. She only sat by the windows, not reading, not drowsing, her eyes fixed on the swimming countryside and the long winding road that led to the town.

She was counting. The days went by. Today, she said to herself, Jerome has returned to Riversend. What is happening there? He will know; he will be told. She shuddered away from that scene, and feverishly turned her mind beyond it. Tomorrow he will come. Or the next day, at the most.

It did not occur to her that Jerome might not be told of her whereabouts.

Friday came. It expired on the dark evening horizon in a tremendous rainstorm. Amalie did not even doze that night. She lay in her bed, trembling, her aching eyes fixed on the shadowy windows; she listened to the wind and the rain and the far wailing cry of a midnight train. When the white dawn came, she was prostrated. But she forced herself to dress, arranged her thick braids about her head, and seated herself again at the window. Today he would surely come.

But the day passed, hour by streaming hour. Her trays stood untouched on the dresser. The room was very cold, but Amalie did not feel it. Her breath steamed the window; as it formed she rubbed away the mist with her fingers. The road was a river of brown and running mud. It remained empty. When twilight came, she was still there, staring. Farmer Hobson, going to the barns, saw her white, fixed face, gazing beyond him, unaware of him, and it "gave him a start." It was like a ghost's face, he said to his wife, with sullen anxiety. He and Mrs. Hobson began to whisper together in the kitchen. They had not dared to question, even among themselves. But now the faint slow indignation of the country-folk began to awaken in them. Something was wrong. Something had happened to Miz Lindsey. They did not get to town very often, and they had been warned not to talk. Alfred was paying them twenty dollars a week for harboring his wife; that was an enormous sum, and a man did not quarrel with enormous sums even when old loyalties and old affections began to stir uneasily in him.

But the Hobsons owed Amalie a great deal; she had nursed them in illness, had prevented their farm from being foreclosed; she had given nearly half of her small salary to them when they needed medical aid and clothing. She had sat with them in their poor clean parlor, had coached their one intelligent boy, had helped Mrs. Hobson with the younger children, and had sewn for her and them. They recalled how bright her strong face had appeared in the light of the fire and the kerosene lamps. They remembered how she had gone to the barns with Mr. Hobson, singing, helping him milk when his wife was "poorly." She had ridden their horses; she had helped with the plowing, for she was as vigorous as a young and healthy man. She had hoed the potatoes, assisted in the haying, helped in the kitchen at harvest. They had loved her, and she had loved them.

And now she sat like a dumb white desperation in her room, not speaking, only looking at them with dazed and sunken eyes from which the purple tint, once so ardent and sparkling, was fading. When she spoke, it was hardly more than a whisper. They knew that she remained by the window, staring out of it for hours at a time. For whom was she waiting? Her husband? They hated Alfred, did the Hobsons, and were terrified of him. They recalled his lowering expression, his harsh voice, his peremptory commands. Yes, something was wrong with Miz Lindsey, and she was dying in that little room with the sloping roof. But they did not know what to do.

On Saturday afternoon, Mr. Hobson went to town. He returned earlier than usual, and called to his wife, horror-stricken. They crept to their own room, and whispered together for over an hour. Once or twice Mrs. Hobson exclaimed feebly and pitifully. But Amalie did not hear, and these friends did not dare tell her.

"And so, she's got to stay here till he rids hisself of her," Mr. Hobson said to his wife. "And after all this! It's a mercy that feller wasn't murdered—— And his poor father, and all."

Mrs. Hobson was aghast. She felt some natural, countrywoman's aversion for Amalie's "sin." But this was swallowed up in the more dreadful news that had followed her husband's revelations.

"I guess she's waitin' for him up there, all the time," said the good woman, shaking her head. "And he don't know, and he couldn't come—now. Not for a while, anyways. Could be we could tell her?"

"No. We can't tell her nothin'. Not in her state. Better let things take their course."

But Mr. Hobson, who was a slow, taciturn man, began to form his own plans.

Amalie sat by her window again on Sunday. The first pale sun for many days fell in thin and shallow light over the meadows and the hills. She heard the dim clanging of the town bells. She saw the road, hung over with a faint bright mist, winding down to Riversend. But no one came down the road. She remained there all night, watching and waiting, not knowing that Mrs. Hobson hovered, wringing her hands, outside her door.

A dark fog fell over Amalie's eyes. She could not rid herself of it for a long time. When she finally emerged, she was numbly astonished to see that the sun was shining, while only a few moments ago it had been twilight. Monday morning had come.

Mrs. Hobson came in with a pitcher of hot water and fresh towels. Amalie turned her head slowly towards her. Mrs. Hobson looked at that ghastly face, at the sunken cheeks where a mauve shadow had been deepening day by day, at the empty and swollen eyes. She could not restrain herself. "Miz Lindsey!" she cried. "You've not to take on so! He'll come! You'll see!" And then she put her hand over her mouth, in terror at her own words.

Amalie shook her head. "No," she murmured. "He'll not come. I know it."

She forced herself to her feet, swaying like an old sick woman. Mrs. Hobson caught her arm, compassionately. She helped Amalie to the bed. She washed her tenderly; tears ran down the sun-darkened face of the farmer's wife. "He'll come; you'll see," she said, over and over, in a hushed voice. But Amalie only smiled mournfully, pushing back her black hair with her thin hands.

She refused to stay in bed. Mrs. Hobson helped her to dress in her brown alpaca frock, and to brush and braid her hair. It was at her desperate insistence that Amalie compelled herself to eat a little bread and drink some hot coffee. Then she sat again at the window, her face pressed against the glass, her arms folded on the window-sill. Her eyes were fixed unwaveringly on the road.

She did not think. All the pressure of her bruised mind was fixed on Jerome, and on the road by which he must come. She thought of nothing else. She was like Hero watching for Leander. She was not conscious of the passage of the hours, nor of the low voices of the farmer and his wife. Nothing existed for her but the road that led to Riversend.

He will not come, now, she thought vaguely. He came home on Friday, at the latest. If he had wanted to come he would have been here three days ago. He promised me. He said he loved me. But he lied. Now he wants only to forget me.

She saw a speck far down on the winding road. She leaned

forward, the better to see. Yes, it was a buggy! She saw the newly bright sun glancing off the horse's back. She pushed herself out of her chair, a deep sob in her throat. "Jerome!" she cried, fluttering her hands at the window. And then she saw that the buggy was a strange one. But she stood there by the window, staring blindly.

A short and elderly man was alighting now, near the corner of the farmhouse. She recognized him. It was Mr. Eli Kendricks, one of Alfred's lawyers. He bustled towards the door, carrying a dispatch case with him, his brown suit pulled tightly over his stout and busy contours. Amalie heard him talking to Mrs. Hobson, then she heard his brisk firm footsteps on the stairs.

He entered, wearing a grave smile. He saw Amalie turning to him slowly. The words of formal greeting which he had prepared stuck in his throat. He thought: Good God, the poor creature's dying!

But there was a job to be done, and he was not one to waste troubled and compassionate thoughts on a defendant. He cleared his throat as he laid down his dispatch case. He wished she would not tear at him with her eyes like that—hungry, desperate, pleading eyes. Wants news of that bastard, he thought, grimly. Looks like she's been waiting for him.

He said, making his voice as detached as possible: "Mrs. Lindsey. Your husband has sent some papers for your signature." He busied himself with his case, and fussily withdrew a sheaf of papers. "Just a formality. You'll read them, please, if you wish, and then sign them."

He put a bottle of ink and a pen on Amalie's dresser and extended the papers towards her, trying to quell the quite unprofessional pity that struggled in him.

But Amalie shook her head. "It's all right," she said, feebly. "I don't need to read them. But I'll sign them, please."

"Quite out of order, Mrs. Lindsey," he said, with false briskness. "Law's a peculiar thing. You'll have to read 'em. Quick, if you want to. Just glancing over 'em."

She stretched out her trembling hand; it was almost transparent, he saw. She took the papers obediently and tried to read them. But only a phrase or two reached her consciousness. "——acknowledges and admits that the child she is to bear is not the child of her husband, Alfred Lindsey, of Hilltop, Riversend, N. Y.——refuses to divulge the name of her guilty partner——agrees not to contest the proposed divorce——"

Mr. Kendricks reflected, without the previous satisfaction he had felt, that this was a damnable thing to do to the poor young creature. He and his partner had discussed the matter with Alfred, completely. It was better for the family, for its reputation, to keep Jerome's name out of the messy proceedings. Least said, soonest mended. The family must close ranks, however bitter the pill Alfred must have to swallow. Anyway, the dirty devil had had his punishment, with the beating, and his father——. Let the matter die down. Conclude the divorce; let the woman go, and be damned to her. Close ranks. There was the Bank to consider, and Master Philip, and Miss Dorothea.

But Mr. Kendricks, to his professional horror, discovered that he no longer wished Amalie to be "damned" and forgotten. He shook his head. He had practiced law for many years and this was the first time he had wasted pity on the defendant.

Then, to his astonishment, he saw that Amalie was smiling. It was like a frail light on her ravished face, that poor smile. She was saying: "I am so glad." And he knew that she was glad that Jerome was not mentioned, that he was not named as co-respondent in Alfred's suit for divorce. Damn him, thought the lawyer savagely, with the feeling that Jerome had not been sufficiently punished. And damn *him*, thought the lawyer, with a clear vision of his client.

He said: "Then we'll just sign the papers, and I'll go, Mrs. Lindsey." He paused. "And there's just another little matter. Mr. Lindsey will give you one thousand dollars immediately after the divorce, on the condition that you will leave Riversend at once." Five hundred dollars had been the amount, but the lawyer, again quite unprofessionally, had generously increased the sum.

"Oh, yes, I'll go away," said Amalie, with piteous docility. She signed the papers. Her signature was faint and shaken. "But I don't want Alfred's money. Please tell him that."

"But what'll you do, ma'am?" protested the lawyer.

Amalie looked through the windows. Now her voice came stronger and clearer: "I'll find a way. I've had to fight all my life. I can fight again."

Her shoulders straightened, lifted. She had forgotten the lawyer. She was not seeing the road now, for she knew that Jerome would not come. It did not matter. She was alone again, as she had always been alone. She was not afraid. She put her hand to her body. No, she was not alone. Somewhere, somehow, she would find a way to provide for herself and for Jerome's child. For the first time, she thought of the child, helpless and weak, dependent on her, and a living thrill of resolution and new joy ran over her. She would protect that child and ease its way. She would fight for her child, and make certain that such terrible things should not attack it; it should not be vulnerable to life as she had been vulnerable.

Mr. Kendricks still hesitated. Perhaps he could give the poor girl a word of encouragement, a slight hint. But no, it was better this way.

Amalie was turning to him, and her smile was alive and aware. "Thank you," she said.

She twisted her fingers together, and her smile died. "May I ask just one question? Is Jerome Lindsey home? And is he well? That is all I want to know."

Mr. Kendricks was acutely uncomfortable at this awkward question. And so he answered surlily: "The—gentleman—is quite well. He returned home last week."

Amalie was silent. But her eyes implored him, held him.

Mr. Kendricks, to avoid that pathetic gaze, returned the papers to his case. He searched for his hat, mumbled, put it on his head.

Then Amalie was saying softly: "And Mr. William Lindsey? He is well? He—he is not too unforgiving? And Philip?"

The lawyer turned a bright scarlet. He did not know where to look. Then he said quickly: "Mr. Lindsey is—well. I—I am sure he forgave you———." He turned abruptly. "And now, good-day to you, ma'am."

He went as fast as possible down the stairs, out of the house. He jumped into his buggy, turned the vehicle about, and drove away. He discovered he was sweating.

He had the papers. It would not be necessary for that poor girl to appear in court. The divorce would be granted by default. He, Kendricks, was glad of that. He could not have endured it to have seen her stricken down again, before the eyes of a ravenous courtroom, guilty though she was of the worst sluttish conduct. But what was to become of her? It was all nonsense, her refusing that money. She would take it; she would have to take it. Two thousand dollars, said the lawyer savagely to himself.

Amalie did not stand by the window now. She went to her bed and lay down upon it, gazing at the ceiling, lying as rigid as a corpse. She tried to recall more of what she had read in

328

the papers. The divorce was being expedited. It would be granted on Wednesday, the day the suit was to be brought. She understood that. She had no defense. She had only to remain here, in case any unforeseen circumstances should arise. It was the last thing she could do for Alfred. To help him, to spare him, she would gladly appear in court, to confess herself before judge and jury and all her enemies. If nothing arose which demanded her presence, in the event that the judge was not touchy about law, she could go away, silently and unseen, and they would all forget her. She had understood, without having been told, that the implication to be conveyed to the court was that she had gone into deliberate and guilty hiding.

She did not know when night came. She did not know when it was morning. She knew only that an enormous sickness had come to her, shot through with pain like lightning. Through clouds of suffering she was occasionally conscious that Mrs. Hobson was ministering to her. She felt hands that lifted and moved her, cold wet cloths on her head. Between these periods of consciousness, she knew that she was so tired that she could not turn her head, and that some far-off shadow was approaching towards her over vast distances. Once the thought occurred to her: I am dying. It did not frighten her.

Once or twice she saw sunlight. Then she would sleep, and again, the sunlight was there, fixed, unmoved, unchanging. This surprised her childishly. Time was standing still. It was always day. Or, perhaps, she slept only for an instant or two, and awakened to daylight. But it was odd to see Mrs. Hobson, and then not to see her; sometimes Mrs. Hobson's face melted into Farmer Hobson's, and then into the face of a strange young countrywoman with firm and capable hands. It was very confusing.

Her eyelids were so heavy that she could hardly raise them.

After a long time she heard louder voices, protesting voices, and then a strong and vibrant silence. Someone was in the room; someone was sitting beside her, holding her cold hand. The touch of the strange hand was warm and firm and strong. She smiled. She forced herself to turn her head. She opened her eyes.

Jerome was sitting by her bed, looking down at her. When he knew that she saw him, he dropped his head to her pillow and held her to him, without speaking.

CHAPTER FORTY-TWO

Amalie sat up on her pillows, and obediently drank the broth which Jerome held to her lips. She was too weak to speak much. But when she smiled at him her whole face turned bright and radiant. She could not have enough of seeing him.

She knew that he had not left this house for two days. With deep comfort, she could be sure that when she awakened, at any hour, he would be there, either in the sunlight or in the lamplight. His features had grown clearer each time, until now she could see his dark face clearly. It was not until the third day that she saw the long red wound on his forehead, and another, just beginning to heal, on his cheek. One of his eyes was still swollen and bruised; his left arm was in a rigid contraption of wood and linen.

It was then that she came fully to life, crying out. He had lifted her with his right arm, pressing her head against his shoulder so that she might not see. But she had struggled with him, had pushed him away with new strength, had cried out her accusations against Alfred, had demanded, with desperate pleading, that he tell her all that she must know.

But there was much that Jerome could not tell her yet. He told her that Alfred had assaulted him. But he dismissed the matter lightly, for he could not bear the horror and anguish in her eyes. "After all," he said, "Alfred did have some provocation." He even smiled. "It could have been worse."

"But he might have killed you!"

Jerome shrugged. "I doubt it. He is too careful of himself. He only wanted to slash at me a little." His bruised mouth tightened grimly as he recalled that night. There was no need for Amalie to know the details.

Amalie searched his face, tears running down her cheeks. She saw that Jerome was much thinner and paler than she had ever seen him, even during those February days when his father had not been expected to live.

"He took me unawares," said Jerome, with natural male egotism. "He struck me down before I knew what he was about. Otherwise, I might have done a little mutilating, myself."

He was glad that Amalie was still too enfeebled to sense the full implications of what he must now tell her. He sighed. He looked down at the black broadcloth of his clothing.

He told her that the divorce had been granted three days ago.

He told her that he had not known where she was. But he did not tell her that for three days he had not been conscious of her with any clarity, and that for those three days he had lived in a hell of pain and sorrow and despair.

He had sent Jim to the town for news of Amalie. Jim had ascertained that Amalie had taken no train from Riversend, so they both concluded that she must be somewhere in the vicinity. No one, discreetly questioned by Jim in Riversend, knew the girl's whereabouts. For hours at a time, Jim and Jerome had discussed the matter carefully, eliminating, conjecturing. Then Jim had suddenly, and awkwardly, been accosted on a street in Riversend by Farmer Hobson, who had pulled him aside with many doubtful and sidelong looks. Jim had been allowed to see Amalie, but the poor creature had not recognized him. "Brain fever, it was." Jim had returned to Jerome with the news.

"I could not come immediately," said Jerome, and he looked away from Amalie. His eye fell again on the somberness of his clothing. "I—I wasn't capable of moving just then. Doctor's orders. My arm was broken in two places. My face had been stitched——"

There was so much that he could not tell her yet. He must hold this devastating pain still, so that she would not suspect until she was stronger.

But he did say: "The house is ours, if you wish it. Alfred and Philip have left. They have taken up temporary residence in the old Anstead house. With Dorothea. We can go home just as soon as we are married. And that will be when you are stronger. We'll have to be married in Pennsylvania. A matter of law. The judge here will not contest that marriage; no one will."

Amalie listened, weeping silently. But she understood. The guilty party to a divorce could not be married in New York State within five years, except by special permission of the court. The judge was in a bad position. Alfred was his friend. But there was the child to be considered. A marriage performed in Pennsylvania, then, would not be questioned. Amalie and Jerome could return to Riversend, and no one would molest them.

"But your father," whispered Amalie, pushing back the pain that she must face when she was strong enough to remember that she and Jerome had driven Alfred and Philip and Dorothea from their old home. "What of your father? He has not gone with—them?"

Jerome got up abruptly. He went to the window. There was a smarting in his eyes, a heavy load on his heart. "No," he said quietly. "My father did not go with them. He—stayed."

"Then he has forgiven us!" exclaimed Amalie with joy.

"Yes, my dear, he—forgave—us. I—I have just learned about his—will. His lawyers told me. Alfred and I were to have the house together, or to sell each other our share, if we did not wish to live in the house jointly." Jerome's voice was low and stifled. "I think Alfred will prefer to sell me his share. We are to share the Bank, too. That is going to be a little hard. But somehow, matters will adjust themselves. They always do. However, that is something to arrange in the future. The first thing is our marriage." He paused. "So, you see, my father understood. Somehow, I think he always knew."

There was the strangest silence in the room. Jerome still looked blindly through the window. He heard no sound behind him. At last he became aware that Amalie had not spoken for a long time.

He turned quickly. Amalie was sitting up in bed, white as her sheets, her eyes staring fixedly at him. He went back to her with an exclamation. But she held him off with her hand.

"Jerome," she murmured. "Jerome, your father is dead."

This was what he had wished to spare her, and this was what he had stupidly betrayed. He sat down on the bed beside her, cursing himself. He searched in his mind for lies, for comfort. But she looked at him, and he could say nothing.

She turned away from him then and buried her face in her pillows.

He began to plead with her; his words rushed out. But he dared not touch her. He stammered and stumbled, running his right hand distractedly through his hair. It was not unexpected, that death, he said. His father's heart had been failing steadily. It was only a matter of time. Even if these events had not occurred, he would probably have lived only a little longer. Now he, Jerome, must tell her everything. He must tell her that William Lindsey had unaccountably come down to the library, and had saved his son's life. He must let Amalie know, in full, that Mr. Lindsey had collapsed after a brief and feeble struggle with Alfred, that Alfred, forgetting the unconscious man at his feet, had carried his adopted father upstairs and had laid him on his bed, and had then summoned Dorothea and Dr. Hawley. (Jerome had learned this later, from Jim.) Jerome himself had been left to lie in the library, forgotten except by Jim, who was not capable of moving him. But Jim had ministered to him as well as possible, and when Dr. Hawley had come downstairs at midnight, Jim had called to him. With the physician's assistance, Jim had been able to get Jerome to his room and to his bed, and the exhausted Dr. Hawley had stitched his gashes and set his arm. For days Jerome himself had known nothing of what had occurred. Jim never left him. The little man nursed and fed him, changed the dressings on his face. The rest of the household was absorbed in the dying old man.

It was on the fourth day that Jerome was remembered, and a servant was sent to bring him to his father.

But Jerome could not tell Amalie of that scene by his father's bed. He never could tell anyone.

He was silent now, remembering. Amalie turned slowly towards him, speechless and still. She waited.

After a while, Jerome continued, speaking in a dull and weary voice. He and Amalie must not feel themselves too guilty of Mr. Lindsey's death. Mr. Lindsey had sent her his love before he died. He had urged Jerome to tell her that he had known for some time that he was dying, and that nothing could save him. He was glad that his son and Amalie were to be married. He only wished that he could see that wedding, and welcome them to their home. Amalie would understand, Mr. Lindsey had said, when she knew of his will.

Jerome took Amalie's hand. She did not shrink from him. But she whispered: "Alfred. How terrible it must be for him."

Jerome thought of his cousin, and his face involuntarily twisted with hatred. He averted his head. "But Alfred knew, too, that my father could not have lived much longer. Dr. Hawley assured him of that. I don't think you need worry about him too much."

Amalie was crying again, and Jerome could not comfort her. She was remembering Mr. Lindsey, and his love and kindness. She was certain that she could never enter that house again, where all those frightful things had taken place, and where Mr. Lindsey had died of the shock. She saw the old man clearly, his gentle smile; she heard his fond words, his subtle understanding silences. She and Jerome had killed him, had filled his last days with horror and misery.

"No," she said to Jerome, "we shall never be able to forget. That is our punishment."

"I tell you, my darling, he had no reproaches for us. He said his only regret was that he would not see our child, his

333

first grandchild. You must know, Amalie, how kind he was, and how happy, at the last. When I asked him to forgive us, he laughed a little, as if I were absurd."

He did not tell Amalie that his father had said almost at the last: "If you will only understand, Jerome, that no man can injure another with impunity, that cruelty done with malice and deliberation is its own punishment, that when a man strikes at another he strikes, not only at himself, but at those he loves, then all this will have been worth the suffering."

No, there was much he could never tell her, even to the day of his own death. He and his father had been alone, and Mr. Lindsey had talked tranquilly, quietly. He had thought only of his son, and not of himself and his own anguish, and that had been the hardest of all to bear.

He could not tell Amalie of the funeral, of how he and Alfred had stood opposite each other, over the open grave, listening to the words of the minister, and of how the rain had streamed down unrelentingly in that dark and lonely cemetery. That was something he could not dwell on too long as yet.

Alfred had stood there, a figure of gray stone, looking down at the grave, his arms folded on his chest. Dorothea, weeping and desolate, had stood on one side of him and Philip on the other. No one had so much as glanced at Jerome, leaning there on his cane, his arm in a sling. No one but Philip. Jerome had met the boy's sorrowful eyes, and he had seen that there was no reproach or disgust in them but only compassion and fondness. Behind the mourners stood their friends, but not behind Jerome. He had stood alone, as though he were a leper. No one had spoken to him, or appeared aware of his presence. No one but Philip. For, after the ceremony, Philip had somehow managed to reach him and touch him, and had whispered: "Please give—Amalie—my love, Uncle Jerome."

Philip had then drifted back to his father and the others, and Jerome had been abandoned. The friends had followed Alfred and Dorothea and Philip and the minister. Jerome was alone. The gravediggers, waiting to shovel the wet black earth on the coffin, had looked at him with curiosity and uneasiness. Then they, too, had wandered away to a discreet distance, whispering among themselves.

Jerome had stood there, looking down at the coffin. The rain had poured steadily into the gathering darkness. The bending willows were fountains of green water. The wet and heavy air was full of the deathly scent of the funeral flowers. The gravestones near by glimmered spectrally in the streaming

334

dusk. The intense and mournful silence of a cemetery deepened all about Jerome, and he heard the dripping water, the hiss of wet and uneasy trees.

He had turned away at last, but not for a long time. He had gone back to the gates of the graveyard. Jim was waiting for him in the buggy. There was no one else.

He had returned to his desolate home. He had gone directly to bed. The next morning, when the first light of the dawn had come, Jim came to him to whisper that Alfred and Dorothea and Philip were leaving that very day. They would not remain under that roof with the man who had brought such catastrophe to them and to this house.

No, there was much he could not tell Amalie, and never could tell her. He sat beside her, kissing her gently, smoothing her hair, and she clung to him, weeping. But he was barely conscious of her now. His pain was still too great and too new. It would take years for him to forget, even in a small measure.

He thought: How is it possible for me to take up life again here? What will happen to us? The whole township is full of hatred and vengefulness. He thought of leaving, of abandoning everything to Alfred.

And then he put Amalie aside and went to the window again. He looked out at the warm quiet twilight which had succeeded the violent rain. He thought: I will not go away. There is work here for me to do. He shall not drive me away. If there is any driving away that must be done, then I shall be the driver.

There was another thing, too, which he would never forgive: his sister, Dorothea, had appeared on the witness stand and had testified to her brother's guilt and to his adultery.

PART THREE

CHAPTER FORTY-THREE

Amalie Lindsey acknowledged that the landscape below Hilltop, while quite lively and animated and exuding an air of bustle and enterprise, had not exactly been improved, esthetically speaking. The rural silence and symmetry, the grand proportions of land and tree masses (so reminiscent of European landscapes) had been jarred and changed, and the change was not entirely for the better, still esthetically speaking. America was in the process of scarification and while doubtless this was bringing prosperity and excitement and new anticipations to millions of people, it was an offense and a sadness to those who believed that beauty (for perhaps a few superior souls) was preferable to large wages and hope and a steadily increasing rate of employment.

Where, for instance, there had been a thickly wooded section of streams and trees near the base of this hill, there was now a flourishing factory, owned and operated by the enthusiastic King Munsey, who manufactured farm implements. Its four chimneys spouted an offensive smoke, of a particularly obnoxious odor, against a once untroubled and gentle sky. The stream had lost its blue clarity and was stained with oily purple, brick-red and poisonous yellow, and the vegetation along its banks, once all bending willows and wild iris and yellow waterlilies, was dwindling away into masses of sooty weeds. Mr. Munsey, in his eager haste, had done nothing about the hundreds of tree stumps surrounding his factory, stumps which had once borne the proud trunks and the clapping leaves of noble trees. Yes, the once lovely woods were now an eyesore. Amalie acknowledged that. But she also acknowledged that, due to Jerome's inexorable insistence, the broken shacks which had once stood near the edges of the woods were gone, and that these were now replaced by miraculous little white stone and wood cottages, surrounded by neat small gardens, wherein lived the workers of Munsey's factories. Mr. Munsey had been implacably advised that he was to bring no "Homestead" scandals to Riversend, and that his workers were not to live in a kind of prison stockade such as had been the reason for the ill fame of various Pennsylvania manufactories. He and Jerome were now good friends, but there had been a severe battle in the beginning.

"These brutes don't know no better," Mr. Munsey had protested, almost in tears, and with more passion than grammar.

"I don't care if they don't," Jerome had replied. "I have myself to think of."

This had been a little too obscure for Mr. Munsey, but he had finally complied. Had he not, he would have been deprived of this perfect site. However, when newspapers, even in the City of New York, had praised this "innovation, this new and Christian respect for the rights of man, however humble, this humanitarian regard for the welfare of the worker and his family," Mr. Munsey posed for metropolitan photographs and modestly allowed himself to be eulogized as a "benefactor of man." He had had another desperate, and private, struggle with Jerome over the matter of unions, which he called "nihilistic and an infringement on the rights of capital, leading to anarchy and insolence and oppression by the ignorant masses." But Jerome had succeeded again, and when tearfully questioned by Mr. Munsey, had again made the bewildering remark that he "had himself to think of." However, when Mr. Munsey was further eulogized as representing the "new industrialist, who knew that fair play and fair dealing and a proper regard for the dignity of labor furthered the cause of amicable and prosperous relationships between the worker and the employer," Mr. Munsey did not mention Jerome.

The south end of Riversend now boasted a small but flourishing steel mill, a manufactory of harness and hardware, a big railroad shop, a wheat-flour mill, a brewery which found the spring water in that locality excellent for the "demon rum," and a carriage factory. Extending far beyond these business buildings lay the pleasant "garden" sections occupied by workers and their families, rigorously policed and kept in neat physical and moral order. Each of the new owners of the factories had had their passionate but fruitless struggles with Jerome. However, as he brought agreeable notice to them as "benefactors of mankind," they swallowed their indignation, gorge and natural hatred, beamed resplendently for photographs and graciously granted interviews to the reporters of metropolitan newspapers. Riversend, therefore, had become a "model manufacturing community."

The tradesmen had come to town, and if they were ignored by the old aristocrats, and bitterly resented, they were obtuse enough and prosperous enough not to know they were being snubbed and ostracized.

Jerome, of course, had his violent and unsleeping enemies, and among them were numbered nearly all the clergymen of the community, who declared that he was "flying in the face of Providence by encouraging rascals and the humble to rise above their God-given station in life." When Jerome managed to make the manufacturers disgorge a certain sum of money every year for the building and maintenance of several small but well-attended schools for the benefit of the workers' children, this was considered his most heinous, un-Christian act. He was a "revolutionist." Soon, with all this gratuitous schooling and "impudent" supervision of their lives, the nameless and the coarse and the vulgar and the traditionless would believe themselves as good as their betters. But his worst and most unpardonable act was when he, by undiscovered and doubtless reprehensible means, aided in the suborning of various gentlemen in the State legislature, with the result that compulsory education to the age of fourteen years because a State law. This, cried the appalled and the horrified, usurped the rights of parents, deprived said parents of the fruits of employment of their young, and encouraged idleness and irresponsibility on the part of boys and girls who had better be at work in the factories, in their parents' homes, or in the fields, rather than acquiring an education which would unfit them for their future stations as domestic workers, farm hands and patient manipulators of machines for twelve hours a day. But the workers, sending their children to school, were apparently oblivious of the doom about to fall upon their offspring, and upon themselves, which confirmed the dire apprehensions of those born to educate their children and to pass on to them fat estates and comfortable houses.

There was not a spot upon the erstwhile tender landscape which did not steam or smoke, reflected Amalie, with a smile that nicely combined both ruefulness and satisfaction. And this was all the doing of Jerome, her husband. He had accomplished it all, not without fury, threat and blackmail on his part, and with the aid of those who had, at first, declared their undying hostility to him, and their determination to punish him for his "crime" against moral society, and his effrontery. But when he had demonstrated to these enemies the sound profits which would accrue to them, their love for rusticity and their edifying morality had suddenly vanished.

There had been a very bad time, during the panic of 1873, when it seemed that the flourishing but still precarious industrialism of America must collapse. Then the enemies of industry had been triumphant. The land, they had declared, was never subject to fluctuations, was never sterile. A civilization based purely on agriculture was a civilization which never went hungry. But a raucous and rootless civilization, dependent on the churning of the "devil machines" within brick walls, was vulnerable to every sensitive wind that blew from Wall Street.

"The fault," said Jerome, "lay not in industry, but in those who manipulated it without ever dirtying their hands, or condescending to understand it."

He had almost bankrupted himself to keep the new horde of workers in food and under roofs. He had bought huge blocks of stock in the youthful industries of Riversend, in order to keep them from going under. He had emerged, somewhat shaken, at the end of the panic, with a fortune quite depleted. Within five years, however, he was an enormously rich man. He was on the board of directors of every factory in the township. This wastrel, this loiterer on the fringes of a more sober and industrious society, this drinker and carouser had become a power in the community.

But this community, though accepting him with new fondness (tenderly aware of profits), drew the line at Amalie. He was invited, fawned upon, adored, respected, treated with the fondness accorded a precocious prodigal (who had returned, not from the swine, but with pockets full of gold). But Amalie was not invited, save by her old friend, the Widow Kingsley, and the stout and bedecked wives of the vulgar "commercialists" who had invaded Riversend at the invitation of her husband. Neither Jerome nor Amalie resented this. They thought it hugely amusing. Amalie was a "divorced" woman, once openly convicted in public courts as an "adulteress." Jerome had not been divorced, and adultery was the natural prerogative of the unattached man. The Widow Kingsley, however, quoted Benjamin Franklin very stoutly: "Where there is marriage without love, there will be love without marriage." But then, said her resentful friends, the Widow had always been eccentric, and loved to attract attention by startling aberrations. If she wished to attract attention by her devotion to the "scarlet woman," and even to stand as godmother to her first ambiguous child, and to the second, then it was the duty of her friends to ignore her activities as one generously ignored the fact that there had been a hanging in a family.

Amalie, standing slightly below Hilltop this hot and sultry August morning, could turn to her right and look at the western suburbs of Riversend. There, amidst thick and well-planted trees and excellent landscaping, stood the rococo and resplendent brick and stone homes of the new and resented industrialists and their families. Amalie could see the red roofs of the pleasant big homes, and see the sunlight reflected on minute windows far below. It was a community apart, blissfully and robustly unaware that it was apart, or not caring. It was called Hilltop Gardens, in deference to the man who had made all this possible.

She turned to her left now, and far down on the hill which harbored Hilltop stood the quite new, severe but handsome residence of Alfred Lindsey. He had built this home some eight years ago, and there he lived with Dorothea as his dear sister-housekeeper and his son Philip. He had not married Dorothea. He had married no one. Dorothea was more than adequate as cousin-mother to Philip, who had lately returned from Harvard, and it had never occurred to even the more lewd-minded of the community that there might be anything even slightly questionable about Dorothea's presence in her cousin's home. Dorothea ably demonstrated that one could be as pure as ice and as chaste as snow and efficiently escape calumny.

There were some, not without sympathy, who wondered why Alfred had built this house, half-way down the slope from Hilltop, within easy view of the home from which he had practically been evicted by his cousin and the latter's paramour. Some said he did it to "remind" them perpetually of their crime against him. One or two others had their secret conviction that it was because he could not endure being too far

340

away from Amalie and the house which he had loved. In any event, he never enlightened anyone. Dorothea believed he had built here rather than move too far from the town or be encompassed by the vulgar newcomers.

But though Alfred's house was less than three-quarters of a mile from Hilltop, Amalie had seen none of that household close by, nor encountered any of them, for ten years. Sometimes, on very clear days, she could see a toy figure or two in the gardens, but could not distinguish them. Once, on one of her very rare excursions into Riversend, she had seen Philip at a distance. Then he had gone away to school, and then to Harvard. Again, she thought that she saw Alfred only a street or two away, but he had suddenly disappeared, like a ghost. She lived apart from Riversend, except for dining with the Widow Kingsley three or four times a year, in Jerome's company, or entertaining, very occasionally, the wives of Jerome's new industrial friends and associates.

When she and Jerome desired diversion, they went to New York or Boston or Philadelphia, and twice they had gone to Europe for six months at a time.

She lived immured, to the grim satisfaction of old Riversend, who believed her to be moping and drooping at Hilltop, from very loneliness, and wistfully hoping, day by day, that she might be forgiven and that one of the established, aristocratic ladies might come to call on her. It was well for the still lacerated sensibilities of these ladies that they did not know that Amalie existed very happily and comfortably at Hilltop, and desired nothing more than that she never encounter her old "friends" again, or that when she did think of them, she hoped fervently that they would continue to wall themselves up in their outrage against her. They could never understand that some natures are congenitally proud, reserved and self-contained, finding their world only among those they love.

On the few occasions when she had been seen in Riversend, she had created talk for days. There she had gone "sweeping insolently," decked out in Paris gowns and jackets and furs and feathered bonnets and lace parasols, and no one deigning to cast her a glance. There was absolutely no use, they said to themselves, in her ever attempting to ingratiate herself with them. Let her roll along in her carriage, meeting Jerome at a corner quite some distance from the Bank, and smiling out from under the shadow of her elaborate parasols. No one would speak to her or acknowledge her existence. Of course, they said, it was natural for so low-born a creature to be insensible for a long time to the contempt and scorn in which she was held. But eventually, without doubt, she would realize what a pariah she was, and that would most certainly overcome her with a complete awareness of her perpetual disgrace and throw her into the deepest melancholy. That would be her punishment.

For the sake of Jerome, who held too many of them in his power, the "old" community was severely but graciously willing to accept her children. Invitations were extended to the very young Mary Maxwell Lindsey, but always a gracious reply from the young lady's mama was returned: "We believe that Mary is not yet of an age when she should attend even children's parties." However, it was tacitly understood that when young Mary was older she would be accepted in decent society, despite the ostracism of her mother. Jerome was no fool, said his expedient friends. He knew that it would not be well for his children to be alienated from their proper companions. Besides, Mary would be quite an heiress, and she was her father's darling, though he had a younger child, a son.

For some reason, Amalie was not resentful of the fact that Alfred had built within eye-reach of Hilltop. She often sat on the terrace and looked down at the house, with a strange if tranquil expression. Once Jerome had caught her like this and had said, most disagreeably: "I shall buy you a pair of binoculars, so you can distinguish them more clearly." Amalie, her eyes twinkling, had demurely accepted the offer, and when Jerome had actually given her the binoculars, she had thanked him with more warmth than he liked. He never knew whether she used them or not, but had his suspicions that she did.

Amalie did. She would sit for a long time, the binoculars clamped to her eyes, herself concealed from her own home by the copse of pines. She could see Dorothea very clearly now in the garden, either strolling alone, or with Alfred. Their faces were only small blurs, but they moved easily and quietly, and Alfred often made one of his familiar stiff gestures. When Philip was home on his holidays, Amalie could see him, sitting alone under bending willows, a book on his knee, his eyes fixed on space. Amalie felt her only sadnesses then, and she would drop the binoculars with a sigh.

She and Jerome rarely, if ever, spoke of their alienated kinsfolk. But sometimes, when they were alone together before the library fire, Amalie would see that Jerome had dropped his book and was staring before him with quiet savagery. Then the two ugly scars, one on his forehead and the other on his

342

left cheek, would glow as raw and scarlet as if they had been newly inflicted. Amalie knew that he hated Alfred and Dorothea with a voracious hatred, and that he felt his impotence to injure them. It did not matter to him that Alfred, with proud and touching dignity, and with his old sense of justice, had abandoned Hilltop to his cousin. Alfred might have made matters cruelly awkward indeed, for the house had been left to them jointly. But he had remembered, as always, that Jerome was William Lindsey's son, and he had stepped aside. Amalie knew that Jerome had offered to buy Alfred's interest in the house, and that he had been coldly refused. She knew, with secret and inner shrinking, that this grip Alfred was retaining on Hilltop maddened her husband, and she feared, not without a sense of justice, herself, that it was for this very reason that Alfred would not relinquish his share. Amalie and Jerome might occupy this house and own a half interest in it. But Alfred would have them remember grimly that their enemy, living quietly below them, was master, in part, still, and that they lived there, unmolested, by his contemptuous and magnanimous consent.

Each year Alfred paid half the taxes on the estate. When Jerome had had some improvements made—very costly improvements in the way of extra bathrooms, gas and a new well, a new roof and some extensive landscaping—he had been visited by Alfred's lawyer who formally advised him that Mr. Alfred Lindsey insisted upon paying half of the cost. "His interest, you know, sir," the lawyer had said. "He must protect his interest." And the lawyer had smirked. However, Jerome would not accept this or the humiliation attendant upon it.

Mr. Lindsey, who had had a very strong sense of British tradition, had left the house jointly to his son and his nephew, with the proviso that should Philip die, and should Alfred have no more sons, it would, in the event that Alfred predeceased him, belong entirely to Jerome. Should Jerome have a son, however, that son would retain his father's interest in the house. After the death of both Jerome and Alfred, if their sons survived, the double interest would continue.

When Amalie had presented Jerome with his son, little William Lindsey, Jerome's satisfaction was intense. The child was beautifully formed, which led Jerome to make so savage and vicious a remark that Amalie had felt a strong, if temporary, repulsion for him. Jerome was proud of his son, and loved him, but not as he loved his daughter, Mary.

Amalie was thinking of many of these things this morning,

and they distressed her. She had filled a shallow basket with the garden's best blooms, for Mr. Lindsey's grave, for this was the anniversary of his tragic death.

This August day was not the spectral day, awash with water, that it had been on that terrible occasion ten years ago. The sky now was incandescent with light, so that the whole landscape lost hard contours and seemed made of pure bright light also. The trees were heavy with heat, motionless. A hot breath blew up occasionally from the parched earth. But the gardens glowed with color. Delphiniums were spears of brilliant blue against the red brick walls; early chrysanthemums splashed yellow, tawny pink and burning white in the perennial beds. Pears, with pink cheeks, hung from laden stems like ovals of plump freshness. Marigolds and sweet alyssum bordered every flagged path. The roses were expiring in a last violent bloom, and Jerome's new marble fountain threw sprays of light into the burning air.

Amalie's basket was heaped with fragrance. The gardeners had watered the flowers, and globes of mercurial light stood on tinted petal and green crisp leaf.

She went into the house and encountered a maid. She enquired for Mary. But Mary, as usual, had disappeared. Amalie uttered an impatient sound. Jerome encouraged the little girl in her seclusiveness and disappearances, for she resembled his father, and Jerome remembered the retiring nature of Mr. Lindsey. Amalie went into the library. The curtains had been drawn against the heat, and the room had a cool dimness pervading it. The leather chairs stood apparently empty. But Amalie, carrying her flowers, knowingly made a tour of them. As she suspected, Mary was crouched in the depths of Mr. Lindsey's old red-leather chair, and she was reading.

"Well," said Amalie, "you are a most odious young lady. I thought you were to help me gather the flowers for your grandfather's grave."

Mary put aside the heavy book and speechlessly uncoiled herself from the chair. She was less than ten years old, but she was very tall for her age, and unchildishly shy and silent. She said, in a soft but oddly penetrating sweet voice: "I'm sorry, Mama. I did not know it was so late."

"You never know. You are so very tiresome, Mary. I hoped to walk, but now we'll have to have the buggy. Look at your frock. Out of respect to your grandfather, you ought to have changed to something fresh."

The child looked down at her dress with a bemused expres-

344

sion, but did not speak. She was somewhat afraid of her mother, who was usually impatient with her. But when Amalie stretched out her hand and smoothed the mass of hair on the childish shoulders, Mary detected more love than annoyance in the touch. She smiled shyly.

Amalie sighed. "Do go and find Jim, Mary, and ask him if he will drive us to the cemetery. And tie on a broad hat. The sun is very hot."

She put the basket on the long oaken table and left the room. Mary watched her go. When she was alone, the child approached the basket and delicately fondled the flowers. Roses, delphiniums and early chrysanthemums made a splash of vivid color on the dark oak. Mary bent her head and sniffed deeply of the scent. A look of wild, frail pleasure stood in her eyes, a kind of innocent amazement and joy. She held back the thick smooth mass of her pale bright hair as she inhaled the fragrance repeatedly. She murmured incoherently, feeling a sort of exquisite pain. It hurt her, now, that these lovely things had been torn from their beds to deck a cold, uncaring grave. She glanced about her swiftly. Then she withdrew a single dark-red bud, thrust it under her ruffled pinafore, and ran out of the room. She climbed the great oak staircase with held breath. She saw no one. She peeped into the bedroom of her mother and father. As she hoped, Amalie had gone for a last fond look at little William. Mary found a water glass, filled it from the pitcher, inserted the rose, and placed it on her father's dresser. She surveyed it with profound pleasure for a moment, then pulled the bud gently towards her and kissed it passionately.

Her eyes, so like her grandfather's, sparkled deeply. But they were not frosted over, stilled, as Mr. Lindsey's had been. Their light blue was quick and intense, like running water under a summer sky. They changed, deepened, paled and darkened, with all of her silent but ardent moods. Her springtime was swelling in her, but it was a soundless springtime, deep and waiting, pregnant with future potentialities. So Mr. Lindsey had been, in his youth, and this Jerome suspected.

She saw herself in her mother's long pier glass. She had a small face, pointed and delicate, exquisitely flushed and sensitive, but with a curious look of inner strength. Yet it was not a noble face, as Amalie's was. There was a hint of rigidity in it, for all its sensibility and its childish fluidity. Later it might be hard and cold, as Mr. Lindsey's had been on occasion. Now it was sweet and pure; in spite of its patrician delicacy of feature it was not vulnerable. A light of swift intelligence touched the eyes, the curves of the small pink mouth, the nostrils of the thin straight nose. Jerome called her his "Little Beauty," with pride and egotism. Quite without personal vanity, she knew that she was indeed beautiful, but she was glad of it, for it pleased her father. Sometimes he called her his "small New England vestal," but though he smiled as he said this she was not too certain that there was admiration in his voice. It was very puzzling.

She shook back the veil of silvery-blonde hair from her hot cheeks. A few radiant tendrils of it stuck to her damp forehead. She would have to comb it, and that was a nuisance. In the curtained light of the room, her hair appeared almost white, so pale was its fair color.

Yes, as Mama had said, her frock of blue-and-red gingham was rumpled. She smoothed it with her small narrow hands. She pulled out the ruffles of her pinafore. Then, with Amalie's own impatience, she untied the pinafore and threw it carelessly upon her father's favorite chair. He was to find it later and to hide it hastily from Amalie's censorious eye. It touched and delighted him when he found these small evidences of his daughter's secret visits to his room.

Totally forgetting that she had decided to comb her hair, Mary ran down the stairs again, and hurried to find Jim, her favorite, and to inform him that he was to drive her and her mother to the cemetery.

In the meantime, Amalie had gone to the nursery. Little William, five years old, lay sleeping in his crib. She bent over him, her heart melting. If Mary was her father's darling, here lay her own Benjamin. The little boy was big and sturdy, still retaining the plumpness and roundness of babyhood. He slept lustily, and with complete abandon, his thick black curls spilling over the white pillows, one rosy fist clenched under his scarlet cheek. Black lashes fringed his lids; beneath them were sleeping eyes of dark purple, like his mother's. His mouth was large and strong, obdurate even, and the lines of his full face, even so young, betrayed that some time it would possess the strong clean planes of Amalie's own face. The child exhaled the sweetly innocent and animal scent of clean young human flesh. The sheet was wound about his limbs, for he slept vigorously. She touched the damp warm curls with a tender finger, crept out of the room, shut the door behind her.

Amalie moved swiftly away from the nursery door. She was filled with a sense of the most profound satisfaction and completion. She stepped in her room to tie on a wide straw hat. She surveyed herself dispassionately, but not without pleasure. She was thirty-two now, and childbearing had not injured her full if slender figure. Rather, it had given her a richness, a fruitfulness. Her white lawn dress, sprigged with tiny clusters of red rose-buds, enhanced her natural handsomeness, and she eyed the slenderness of her waist, the curves of her high full breasts, complacently. Her throat, rising from the low ruffles of her bodice, was still without lines or flaccidity, and showed full and white. She saw her smiling mouth, full and ripe as a fresh plum, and her clear and vibrant pallor. Her eyes shone vividly; her dark and glimmering hair was neat under her hat. It disturbed her, however, to remember that she had a few white hairs near one temple. But then, Jerome, at forty-five, was completely gray, and this only added to his distinction. As she thought of her husband, her whole face melted, became young, almost breathless. Even the occasional angry quarrels which occurred between them, and which disrupted the peace of the house, only added to their passion for each other. There might be contentment here, indeed, but there were furious up-heavals also, and no real tranquillity. Amalie laughed a little and went downstairs.

She stood in the lower hall after she had retrieved her basket of flowers from the library. Sometimes she was haunted by ghosts, the ghost of Mr. Lindsey, the remembered footsteps of Alfred, heavy and sure on the stairs, the austere voice of Dorothea, the quiet, deformed shadow of Philip. But Mr. Lindsey's ghost was always kind and understanding, and Philip's remembered presence was gentle. She shook her head and sighed, recalling that she never passed the door of the room she had shared with Alfred without a faint inner shrinking and quickened step. Mary slept there now, in the very bed where her mother and Alfred had lain. Jerome, who was no sentimentalist and saw no shadows on his bedroom walls, neither understood nor cared about Amalie's aversions in this direction. Mr. Lindsey's room had been converted into little William's nursery. Dorothea's room was empty, as were two others on the same floor. These were "reserved" for guests, visiting financiers and industrialists from New York, friends of Jerome's. Philip's room was Mary's "playroom," elaborately furnished by her doting father, her sanctuary to which none except Jerome came with her complete approval. He had given her on her fifth birthday an extraordinarily beautiful little piano, all rosewood and ivory, for she had marked musical gifts. All the rest of the furniture was of rosewood also, carefully selected by Jerome.

Amalie, in the hall below, frowned. She was always repressing a most shameful and secret jealousy. Well, some day Mary would marry, and Jerome would have to relinquish his treasure to another man. Amalie laughed in spite of herself, shook out her flounces, and went out.

The buggy was waiting. Jim, more gnarled than ever, his last fringe of hair quite white, was chattering loudly with Mary. He had brought out the two-seated open surrey, and Mary sat beside him, in front, bare-headed, her bright silvery hair flowing in a warm but strong breeze.

"You forgot your hat, you tiresome child," said Amalie, as Jim jumped out stiffly to assist her. "Go in at once and get it. You will have a sunstroke, and your father will blame me. Your cheeks are already too flushed."

CHAPTER FORTY-FOUR

A heavy hot wind had blown up and was now tossing the trees and whitening the grass and turning the few white clouds into driven caravans. The burnished sky brightened into a deeper blue under the flailing of the wind, and the rushing sun hurled shadows wildly over the hills and the valley.

Amalie and little Mary clung to their wide hats as the carriage ambled towards the cemetery. When they climbed down to the ground, the warm and roaring wind flung their frocks about them into sculptured lines. Jim and Amalie struggled with the old iron gates. Jim returned to the horse, and Amalie and her daughter, carrying their flowers, moved down colonnades of ancient trees.

Here the wind was less violent, broken by sturdy trunks and low walls. But the flat canopies of elms swung against the sky, ragged and disheveled. The gravestones glittered whitely in the sun. Rabbits and squirrels scurried across the grass. The populous loneliness of death lay all about them, the green mounds lying in light or in deep shade, the silence here as silence is nowhere else.

The Lindsey burial plot lay at the far end of the cemetery, near an ivy-covered stone wall. The Lindsey gardeners took care of this section, and it was neat and trim, the headstones polished and clear. A semicircle of tall frail willows drooped to the green earth, guarding the graves and sheltering the white-marble benches. Here stood urns full of ferns and geraniums and bright phlox. There was a small artificial pool, constructed of flat stones, where birds gathered and splashed themselves and gossiped melodiously. After the death of his beloved wife, Mr. Lindsey had had a life-size statue carved, of white stone, in the form of a cowled bent figure with folded hands. This statue stood between two willows, contemplating the graves with hidden face. The folds of its garments were green with lichen.

Amalie went to Mr. Lindsey's grave, accompanied by her little daughter. She stood there and read the script on the headstone: "William Montgomery Lindsey, 1800-1870." That was all. There were no flowery sentiments on any of the stones. Amalie laid the flowers gently on the grave. But as she bent to do so, she saw that someone else had been there before her. There was a sheaf of white summer lilies already there, at the head, only a few lilies, but exquisite in their pure whiteness and stillness.

"What pretty flowers," said Mary, with love and regret. "What a shame to let them die here, where nobody can see them."

Amalie secretly approved of this realism, but she said with hypocritical reproof: "Don't be silly, Mary. We see them, don't we? The flowers are for the living, not the dead."

"Then why put them there?" asked the girl, in her high, sweet voice. "Why can't we take them home? We haven't any lilies like these."

Amalie was about to embark on a reproving lecture about robbing graves, even of flowers, and then did not speak. Jerome was right: it was foolish to be sentimental with children. They always saw through it, and laughed at you in their hearts.

She said: "Well. If you want one or two of the lilies, take them, for heaven's sake!"

Mary eagerly selected two and held them adoringly in her small arms. She buried her nose in the petals and it acquired a golden powder of pollen. "Grandpa won't mind," she said.

"No," replied Amalie seriously, "I don't think he will. I think he'd like you to have them."

Mary gave her a quick strange look, as though surprised at these words. It was also a startled and grateful look. It was the look of one who is with strangers and then hears a familiar and understanding voice from an unexpected source. Amalie was both touched and annoyed. She did not consider herself without subtlety and sensibility; yet her child was not at ease with her, and was always faintly on the defensive. This was not flattering to one who had the gift of delicate perception, and Amalie's vanity was injured. She recalled that, at times, Mary could be heard chattering volubly with Jim, and with her father, and with her brother. But Mary was always reserved with her mother. Why was this? Amalie frowned. Jerome was always accusing her of "not talking" to Mary. That was absurd. She could not understand Jerome in these moods.

There had been another time when Jerome had said: "You are on the defensive with Mary, all the time. You never say what you mean. You think you should always be the 'mother.' Try to remember that Mary is a human being too, not just your child."

This was too subtle altogether, thought Amalie with exasperation. But she regarded her daughter intently. The wind lifted Mary's silvery mane of hair and blew it across her head and face so wildly that she had a strange and unearthly look. Her small face was dreaming as she stared down at the lilies in her arms. She had withdrawn again into the hidden place where only Jerome could seem to go.

Amalie said gently: "I wish you could have known your grandfather, Mary. He was more than a good man. He was a friend."

"Oh, yes," said the child obediently, smelling the lilies again. "I know."

"Papa told you?"

Mary shook her head. "No, I just know. I feel him here."

Amalie was silent. She knelt to rearrange the flowers she had brought. The roses were already wilting in the heat. She said: "I don't think I'll bring cut flowers any more. A plant, perhaps. Or ivy. Yes, it is a shame to leave these lovely things here to die."

"We could take them home," suggested Mary, who, despite her dreaming face and shy eager eyes, was gifted with an odd practicality.

Amalie was about to advise her again not to be silly, but she caught the words back with determination. So she merely shook her head, and after a moment said thoughtfully: "No. They'd be falling apart before we got there. Best to leave them."

Mary smiled contentedly. Then she pointed to the pool. "They'd live a little longer if we stuck them in there. In the wet mud."

350

Amalie, firmly compressing her mouth, took up the flowers and went to the pool with them, lilies and all. She thrust the long stems into the mud. The green water was faintly disturbed for a moment. Amalie felt foolish. She had brought flowers to a grave, to lie with death, and now she had given them a brief new lease on life, far from the grave. But when she saw Mary's expression, she did not regret her act. Quite light-heartedly she looked down at the flowers. "The birds will like them," said Mary, with her incomprehensible return to dreams. Amalie reflected that it was useless to try to understand Mary. But one could pretend.

Had Alfred brought the lilies, or Dorothea? Did they grow these lovely things in their garden? But Dorothea had not cared for lilies—the "flowers of death" she had called them once, in Amalie's hearing. And Alfred had never shown any partiality for flowers in any form.

"I wonder who brought the lilies?" asked Amalie of her daughter.

"I suppose he did," said Mary calmly, pointing towards a bench standing deep in the shade of the willows.

Startled, her heart leaping suddenly, Amalie turned and looked in the direction of Mary's pointing finger. A shadowy, watching figure of a man sat on the bench. When he saw that Amalie had discovered him, he rose to a short, almost squat height, and came forward slowly and quietly.

"Philip!" exclaimed Amalie, and colored deeply.

"Amalie," said Philip, with composure, and smiling. He held out his hand, and gazed up at her, searchingly but gently.

Amalie hesitated, then she took Philip's hand. His clasp was warm and kind. "I haven't seen you for years," she stammered, feeling the heat in her cheeks. "How are you, Philip? You are looking well. You have hardly changed."

But Philip had changed. He was a man of twenty-four now, and though his deformed height had just barely increased, his was the face of maturity. It was also Jerome's face, but a kinder, more gentle, more thoughtful and subtle face, without Jerome's dark arrogance and cold fierceness. It also possessed something which Jerome's features lacked: a sort of tender but powerful reflectiveness, full of humor and sadness. His hair, thick and strong and short and black, might have been Jerome's hair, in his youth, and the moulding of his narrow head suggested Jerome's pride without his impatience. There was a steadfast calm and quiet about Philip, as if he had come a long way, not without sadness, but also with immovable and compassionate courage.

"And you are just the same, Amalie," said Philip softly, still holding her hand, still looking up at her with his dark and unwavering eyes.

Amalie, still extremely embarrassed and confused, withdrew her hand. "And this is our daughter, Mary," she said.

Philip turned to the child, smiling. "Yes, I know." His smile grew more sparkling, but he considerately did not glance at Amalie. "I have a pair of binoculars too."

Amalie drew in her breath, her face crimson. Then she laughed helplessly. "Oh, Philip!" she exclaimed. "Don't tell me everyone—else—knows!"

"No," he reassured her, still not glancing in her direction, but only gazing at Mary with his kind smile.

Mary was staring at him fully, her light-blue eyes candid and pleased. "You look like my papa," she said frankly. "Do you know my papa?"

"Yes, Mary," he replied seriously, as to a respected equal. "I am your papa's second cousin. My name is Philip. Philip Lindsey."

"Why don't you come to visit us?" asked Mary. She took the hand which he had extended to her. "I think I'd like you."

Amalie waited for Philip's answer. He said thoughtfully: "I have been away at school, Mary. I have just finished, this June. But now I shall be home. And if you want me to visit you, I shall be delighted."

"Where do you live?" asked Mary, pleased and interested.

"Down on the hill, below you."

Mary's silvery brows drew together. "You mean in 'that house'?" she asked, while Amalie listened, appalled.

Philip's smile broke out irrepressibly, but again, with consideration, he did not glance at Amalie. "Is that what your papa calls it? Yes, I live in 'that house.'"

Mary, oblivious of her mother's immense embarrassment, said: "Papa says I mustn't go down there. He says gray stone men live down there, and they'll freeze me up." The child smiled at Philip, as though sharing an absurd confidence with him.

"Mary!" exclaimed Amalie. "I never heard your father say that at all. You are just making it up, and you are very impolite to Philip!"

Mary turned to her with a severe look. "Mama, I'm not making it up. You always tell me I make things up. But I don't. Papa told me that. You ask him."

Amalie was silent. Philip considered the child with tenderness.

"You look like your grandfather, my dear," he said.

Mary nodded confidingly. "Yes, I know. Papa and Mama told me. He must have been nice."

At this, Amalie and Philip burst out laughing together, while Mary studied them, bewildered. Then she said, with petulance: "Mama, Philip doesn't look like gray stone, and you are all teasing me."

"Never mind," said Philip tactfully. "That's just poetic license on your papa's part. People sometimes use words to express something entirely different."

Mary nodded, pleased. "I know," she said obscurely and gave her mother a curious swift look, which Amalie, now completely demoralized, mercifully did not see.

"Let us sit down over there, Philip," said Amalie. "There is so much I want to know about you."

The three went to the bench and sat down. Mary was plainly fascinated by this new relative. She sat beside him and stared at him with clear openness while he talked to her mother.

Philip, speaking in that quiet voice she remembered, but which was now so much more mature and assured and strong, told Amalie of his years at school. He had now returned, he said, and his father wished him to go into the Bank.

"But your music!" said Amalie, in distress. "And your writing, Philip!"

Philip looked down at his small feet. "But my father has no other son, Amalie. If he—had married—again—and there had been other children, it might have been different. I might then have done what I wished."

Amalie's eyes darkened. So here was another she had injured. She had injured him without intent, but there was a pain in her heart.

"The Bank is not as important as you, Philip," she said.

Philip did not answer this. He was thinking of his father, stricken, hopeless, somber. Philip well knew that compassion frequently destroys him who feels it. But there had been nothing else to do, nothing else he could do.

"You won't like banking," Amalie continued, her distress sharpening.

Philip looked up at the soft moving fountain of the willow branches above them. "It won't take all my whole life," he said thoughtfully. "And I don't particularly care for self-aggrandizement."

"No one has a right to bury his talents," Amalie said pleadingly.

Philip smiled at her consolingly. "I'm afraid I was just a dilettante, Amalie. Just pleasant accomplishments. I can still enjoy them. Dilettantes have their function in life, but it is not to convince others that they are geniuses." His dark eye fixed itself on her, penetratingly. "Does Jerome still paint?"

Amalie colored. "Only family portraits. He has painted me and the children."

"Well, then, if he had really been a genius, he could not have abandoned his talent," said Philip. "That is the test of genius: drive. I lacked it, as Jerome lacked it. But that does not mean that we must abandon the pleasure our slight gifts give us. We can enjoy them privately, without facing the humiliation and the heartbreak of a world's indifference, or criticism."

Amalie's hand lay beside his. He put his own on it, and pressed it firmly and affectionately. Amalie's eyes filled with tears. She said: "You had more than a slight gift, Philip."

He took out his watch and glanced at the time. A frail fairy note issued from its golden depths. Mary was immediately entranced. "Oh, how pretty. Let me see it." She took it in her thin white fingers, and studied it delightedly, while Philip watched with loving amusement. She turned the watch over, and read aloud: "To dear Philip, from his loving mother—. Oh," she said, softly. "From your mother. Is she dead?"

Philip took the watch from her and replaced it in his pocket. "Yes, love, she is dead."

Amalie gazed at him, moved. "You still keep the watch, Philip."

He looked at her strongly and deeply. "Yes, Amalie. And why not? I loved the one who gave it to me." And then he added, almost inaudibly: "And I still love her."

"Oh, Philip," she murmured.

He was silent, considering. He knew that she wanted to hear of the others. So he began to speak, quietly: "My father is well. He, too, has hardly changed, except that his hair is almost gray now. And Aunt Dorothea is ageless. She grows more energetic all the time. And more devoted. I think they are quite content."

"I am glad," whispered Amalie. "Oh, I am so glad."

He nodded gravely. "I thought you would be."

Mary had been listening to these incomprehensible remarks with profound curiosity. Her mama was so strange; her face had such a funny look. And this nice Philip seemed so kind.

She said suddenly: "Can I go down to see you, Philip, in 'that house'? Or won't they like me?"

Philip considered her with the adult thoughtfulness that so pleased her. "I am sure they would love you, Mary," he said. "But they are old people. There are no children there, you see. I don't think you would enjoy it."

"But I could see you," the child insisted.

Philip gave this due consideration also. "Well, then, how would it be if I came up to see you sometime?"

Amalie's distress returned. What would Jerome say to all this? But Jerome had never had any hostility for Philip. He had been kind, in his careless and selfish way.

Mary was delighted. "Tomorrow?" she asked eagerly.

Philip and Amalie rose together. Philip said: "Perhaps not tomorrow. But soon. Yes, I think it should be soon." He turned to Amalie. "May it be soon, Amalie?"

Amalie hesitated. Then she said clearly: "Yes. Yes."

They went slowly towards the gates together, Mary holding Philip's hand. They did not speak until they had reached the gates. Then Amalie said suddenly and quickly: "Philip. Do— they—still hate me?"

Philip dropped the bar into place. He said, without looking at Amalie: "I don't think my father ever hated you, Amalie." He wished she had not been so tactless. There were things better left unsaid. He remembered, however, that Amalie had never been notable for tact, and he smiled.

He took Mary's small flushed face in his hands and kissed her cheek. To Amalie's surprise, the child did not resent it, as she usually resented familiarities from strangers. In fact, she kissed Philip in return, with touching simplicity.

"I have another child, Philip," said Amalie. "A little boy. Named after Jerome's father."

Philip suddenly thought of his father, who had no children but himself, and he, deformed. His eyes clouded.

"It must be nice—for Jerome," he said.

And now there was something in his voice which was cold and formal. Amalie felt chilled and lonely; she knew that Philip had instinctively withdrawn from her, and despondency filled her. Did Philip blame her? Did he despise her? She wanted to know desperately.

"You haven't forgotten me, Philip?" she said, with more urgency in her tone than she knew.

He was kind again. He laid his hand, that delicate fine hand, on her arm, and smiled at her fondly. He knew that she meant "forgiven" rather than the word she had used.

"I never forgot you, Amalie. And nothing, nothing, would ever stop me from loving you," he said.

Jim, waiting in the carriage, saw them, and stared unbelievingly.

CHAPTER FORTY-FIVE

"That house," as Jerome called it, had been quite unimaginatively christened The Pines, and stood upon five acres of gradually rising and level land near the base of the hill. It had been built squarely and severely of bright red brick, and was decorated with four brilliantly white round columns of wood at the entrance, reaching to the very eaves. All the exterior woodwork, including the door with its brass hardware, was white also. But its heavy, scattered pines and its red roof mellowed what might have been a certain austere grimness, and its grounds, if uninspired, were excellent. Formal flower-beds, filled with pansies and geraniums and thick low plants, were laid, rather than scattered, upon the green lawns. Another wall of pines, at the rear of the gardens, formed a natural boundary line. There was an appearance of clean angularity about the house and its surrounding acres, and there were no dark piazzas, no turrets and cupolas or fretwork, to destroy the clarity of line. The summer trees softened a certain uncompromising air, but in winter, when the evergreens had turned a darker green, and the foliage of the deciduous trees had been shed, there was a cold starkness and bleakness there which were forbidding.

Despite adequate heating by fires and stoves, the interior, though well lighted by high narrow windows, had this cold starkness, this bleakness. Dorothea had attended to the draperies and furnishings, and here, too, the angularity of her taste, her aloofness, her natural impatience with all that was soft and blurred, were disconcertingly evident. She liked dark, hard woods, and despised anything in the way of cushioning; and the upholstery, stiff, dim and reserved in color, did not invite lounging and dozing. However, she had not succumbed to horse-hair, nor to balled, velvet draperies muffling the windows. The fireplaces were not draped; there were no corner vases filled with peacock feathers or plumes, a new fashion which she found hideous. Nor had she burdened every cold table and mantelpiece with bric-a-brac, and, while her friends thought the chill play of unshaded light and the wide empty spaces of rug very uninviting, the clean and ascetic atmosphere was, in an arctic way, refreshing. Her curtains were of lace, her draperies thin and of pale color, and summer sun and white winter shadows entered freely. Everything, in short, was uncluttered, cool, and without restfulness.

If Alfred and Philip found no quiet and comfortable corners in which to read, no sense of seclusion and warmth, they were too grateful for Dorothea's excellent ordering of the house, and for her competency, to complain.

Philip at times considered the ménage to be very depressing, and when he finally returned from the university he quietly rearranged and refurnished his own apartments. Dorothea, in cold umbrage, complained that he was destroying the symmetry of her household and "making work" for the servants. But Philip, with a gentleness she could not resist, explained that he must have soft furniture and dimmed light, and warmth, for his health's sake. This was, of course, the purest hypocrisy, but Philip preferred kind hypocrisy to open and wounding battle. In other words, he was the soul of tact.

Philip knew that Dorothea adored him, as she might have adored the son of her own body. Much of her old devotion to Alfred passed to Alfred's son. She was secretly delighted that he had returned for good, that his schooldays were over. She dreamt of his marriage to a satisfactory, obedient and well-dowered wife, who would not interfere with Dorothea's management of the home. Some pale, soft, quiet girl, who would, at least, give Alfred grandsons. What if darling Philip *were* deformed? He had a fine face, he was an elegant gentleman, he was wealthy, he would inherit his share of the Bank, he was cultivated and travelled. He was a wonderful catch, in spite of his physical disability. Dorothea grew impatient for his marriage. Sally Tayntor had married the son of Mr. Kendricks, Alfred's lawyer, rich in his own right, and she already had three bouncing little girls. One of them, surely, might marry Philip's son, though they had two or three years' handicaps.

Josephine Tayntor was still unmarried; she had dimmed to pale and silent and graceful spinsterhood. She was only three or four years older than Philip, and Dorothea saw to it that the young lady dined frequently at The Pines when Philip was at home. Dorothea was full of plans.

It had been a grief almost unendurable when Alfred had informed Dorothea that he did not intend to marry again. Dorothea, at first hopeful, had finally given up hope. With her native good sense, her ability to make the best of everything, she had taken what there was left to be taken, and had contented herself with making a home for her cousin and Philip. She was no longer unhappy. She was almost forty-eight now, and her original passion for Alfred had settled into a sisterly and severe affection, capped, aproned, bombazined, and giving off a sharp clean scent of soap and lavender.

She believed that Alfred was content. He was nearly forty-nine, and all his ways were rigid and punctual. His fair hair had whitened; there were furrows in his broad square face; his hazel eyes had chilled, become frozen over with hard reserve. Even when he spoke of Jerome, his voice remained measured and restrained and cold, without any inflection of contempt or hatred or bitter antagonism. Dorothea had sighed thankfully. Alfred, too, held no hands with the past. What was done was done. The future might be paved with stones, but there were no ambushes along its quiet paths, no hot and noxious thickets, no secret byways of regret.

But Dorothea did not know that often for hours together Alfred sat at his window in the moonlight, in the darkness of his room, looking up at Hilltop, and thinking thoughts which would have stricken Dorothea with pain and sorrow. She did not know of his sleepless nights, when he sighed and tossed and stretched out his hand to the empty place beside him. She did not know that in a steel box in his wardrobe he kept mementoes of Amalie: a tall, rhinestone comb, a length of ruby velvet ribbon, a knot of fine lace which had been fastened at her neck, the letters she had written him, one of her silk stockings, and her wedding ring. This, to Dorothea, would have seemed a dangerous sentimentality.

Worst of all, it would have seemed to her, was the retaining of a lovely miniature he had had painted of Amalie during their honeymoon in Saratoga. It was set in brilliants. It was well for Dorothea's peace of mind that she did not know that the velvet back of the miniature was worn with much handling, and that Alfred often slept with it in his hand after long and motionless gazing at the strong pale face, the full red lips, the intent purple eyes.

Life ran smoothly and silent and with expert efficiency at The Pines. No feverish currents were here, no alarums, no midnight disturbances, no turbulent uneasiness. All was peace, courtesy, pleasant amenities. Amalie was never mentioned; her memory, for Dorothea at least, never walked the long chill corridors, never smiled in mirrors. She was a loathsomeness which had died, which had been quickly buried and forgotten.

If Dorothea ever glanced up at Hilltop, hoary and gray and warm in the sun, or with chimneys smouldering and red roof burning against bitter winter skies, she had forced herself not to think of Amalie Maxwell within those thick walls, nor of Amalie's children. The house was a house of dreams, where William Lindsey lived, immured and unchanging. Dorothea had suppressed her memories. The house was only a mirage of her youth, which had become unreal and insubstantial. She had no desire to climb the hill, to look at the gardens she had supervised, to gaze through the windows at familiar furniture and old fires. This too was done and gone.

Philip, always treated with unvarying kindness and affection by his father, had become very dear to Alfred. It no longer pained Alfred that his son was deformed, that his back was bent. He saw no resemblance to Jerome in Philip's face, with its gentle and thoughtful humor, its strong and compassionate integrity. For there was much about Philip's character which recalled William Lindsey to Alfred, and Alfred had never forgotten his uncle.

Philip, after no struggle at all, had consented to enter the Bank. Alfred had been uneasy over his son's artistic gifts. Yet, when already braced for argument and protest, he had discussed the Bank with Philip, Philip had readily agreed with all that his father proposed. If he displayed no eagerness, he displayed no disappointment or regret.

Alfred had decided, after consultation with Philip, that his son should enter the Bank in September. In the meantime, he was to "rest." Alfred discovered that Philip's presence in the house now made him return home with pleasurable sensations of pride and contentment. Philip was always so attentive, so courteously interested, so respectful, and so affectionate. Alfred's face, which had become increasingly somber and grave during these past ten years, would light up at the sight of his son waiting for him near the gates of The Pines or in the bleak square hall. They would walk together in the formal and uncluttered gardens after dinner, or sit by the library fire, discussing the Bank or their friends, or the disconcerting future of Riversend. Philip would listen to Alfred's grave complaints, his expressions of reserved disgust, his hard resignation. And always, his replies were sympathetic and thoughtful. Alfred, always so lonely all his life, always so hag-ridden by his secret sense of inferiority, always so hungry for understanding and kindness, found enormous surcease in his son. He found a friend. The days were less grim now, the nights less empty.

He never guessed that Philip, in his compassion for his father, in his determination to bring some happiness and peace into that harsh and deprived life, was willingly sacrificing himself and all his hopes. Philip knew all that was to be known about Alfred, and sometimes he was seized with a veritable and silent anguish and pity. The stony and solitary contours of Alfred's existence stood in full view of Philip's discerning inner eye, and he had determined that he would soften them with fresh green foliage and a few pleasant gardens.

Thus so far, there had been no conflicts with his father. There was to be one tonight, and he knew it. Philip was not of a nature to be secretive or sly. His natural integrity sometimes overcame his tact.

The ghosts, long buried, must tonight be torn from their graves. It would be easy, Philip reflected, not to mention the fact that he had seen Amalie and her daughter at the cemetery, and not to remark, casually, that he intended to visit Hilltop. All that he had to do was to pay his visits in secret, and let his father live in peace. But Philip had stubbornly decided that buried ghosts had a terrible habit of leaping out of their graves at unexpected moments, and he suspected that much of his father's unsleeping pain might be alleviated if a certain air of naturalness could be given to Hilltop's inhabitants. He knew, if Dorothea did not, that Alfred often sat by his window and stared up the hill. Besides, Philip, with sudden human selfishness, could not believe that it was best not to see Amalie, or to acknowledge her existence and the existence of her children. In a way, the attitude of Alfred and Dorothea seemed to Philip absurd.

If his father could hear of Amalie occasionally, that look of frozen pain might disappear from his eyes, thought Philip, and, smiling ruefully, he told himself that he was rationalizing his own desire to see Amalie whenever he wished.

Philip went down to the gates of The Pines to meet his father. Alfred, for his health's sake, walked the less than two miles to the Bank, daily, except on the occasions of very severe weather. Philip, waiting for him, saw his tall, broad and erect figure striding swiftly, if stiffly, up the gentle rise towards the estate. Now that he was beyond the streets of Riversend, he felt that he could dispense with correctness, and he had re-

360

moved his hat in the hot August breeze. His big round head, cropped and white in the late sunshine, was held high and with a magisterial pomp. His pride, always strong, had during these past ten years become more assertive, as more and more blows had been inflicted upon it. He had met each event with stony courage, and thus had inspired respect even among those who disliked him and secretly derided him. If, in himself, he had the hard tenacity of despair, which kept every warm and fruitful tree naked in his heart, and every hope without a blooming time, only his son knew this. He was only forty-nine, and if his hair had not whitened during these years, he might have passed for much younger, so much vigor did he express in every movement, so decisive was his voice and so firm were his gestures.

There were moments when Philip, with pleasure, came to the conclusion that his unimaginative father, so pompous and so circumscribed in attitude and opinion, had begun to think. Despair, Philip thought, is sometimes the great energizer of the mind, though sometimes its flowering may be sterile. If Alfred was thinking, if the once calm and egotistic crust of his nature had been cracked by subterranean upheavals, then this nature was growing, under the surface, expanding painfully and with hidden groanings, but expanding indeed. There were moments when his dogmatic voice faltered uncertainly, when a look of self-questioning doubt would cloud his prominent hazel eyes, when his hand, lifted in a didactic gesture, would slowly drop and lie helpless. Alfred's was not a temperament to soften with age; rather, it had an innate tendency to crystallize into smaller and harder molecules. But Philip, with secret delight, thought that he often caught glimpses of a nature becoming more distrustful of its omniscience, and he knew that this distrust was the sign of a soul increasing in stature and pushing itself vigorously, if with pain, against the harsh boundaries of an old pattern.

If I can do nothing else, Philip often thought, I can help him push.

When Alfred saw Philip standing at the gate, his stride quickened. He waved his hat. He shouted: "Hallo!" Philip waved back, began to walk slowly towards his father. They met, half-way to the gates. Alfred looked down at his son fondly. He put his hand on Philip's shoulder, and together they walked to the house. Had Philip "rested" that day? Had he taken his tonic, and a quiet walk? Had he napped?

"I went to the cemetery and put some lilies on Uncle William's grave," said Philip.

"Ah, yes." Alfred's face darkened with sadness. "It is the anniversary of his death." The firmness of the hand on Philip's shoulder relaxed, dropped away. "But that's a depressing place for you, Philip. You ought not to have gone."

"On the contrary, it doesn't depress me at all, Father," said Philip cheerfully. "I like to think of the old gentleman. And, you may decide I am fanciful, but I sometimes imagine he comes to meet me there, and we have pleasant and amiable conversations."

Alfred looked uneasy; but the glance he gave his son was both troubled and hopeful. "Well. Perhaps," he conceded. "But I shouldn't make a practice of it."

"When I came home, I read quite a good deal in those books on banking you brought me yesterday," said Philip.

Alfred's smile had more spontaneity than it had had in the old days, and less smugness. "Did you? Did you find them interesting?"

"Indeed. There is quite a romance in banking."

Alfred's brows drew together doubtfully. "Romance? Romance in banking? In business?"

"I mean, it could be exciting," said Philip, tactfully. His father's face cleared with open pleasure. "Well," he said, "I don't know about excitement. Sometimes you are given to extravagant language. I presume you mean it is not without interest?"

"Yes." Philip smiled, and tried not to, but without success.

"And how is Aunt Dorothea today?" asked Alfred, as they reached the flagged walk leading to the house.

"Splendid, as usual, and very energetic. She dressed down three of the maids, and seemed much refreshed afterwards."

Alfred's smile was almost boyish. "Indeed. She is a great disciplinarian. But we must not reproach her, Philip. Discipline seems weakening in America these days. I view it with alarm."

If Philip was sometimes amusedly impatient with his father's tendency to quote aphorisms, and if he found them tedious, he never betrayed it. So he arranged a serious expression on his face, and nodded slowly. Alfred was satisfied. They entered the house with a warm sensation of mutual understanding and affection.

Dorothea met them in the square bleak hall, which was all black walnut and stiff uncushioned benches and chairs. She greeted Alfred with dignified amiability, inquired if he were not hot from his walk, and announced that cold lemonade was waiting for him, and a biscuit, until dinner time. As she spoke, she looked from father to son with more softness than she knew, then bustled off to get the promised dainties. Alfred went to his room to freshen up, and Philip wandered off to the brick terrace at the rear, sat down on a cushioned iron-filigree settee, and waited for his father to join him.

CHAPTER FORTY-SIX

Alfred had put on a black alpaca coat as a concession to the warm evening, and a soft blue cravat in place of the stiff dark one of his banking hours. He sat beside Philip and looked tranquilly over the formal gardens at the rear, beyond the stretch of uncompromising green lawn. An elm tree near by threw a fretted shadow over the warm earth, and the evening sky was a veined turquoise.

"Did you have a hard day at the Bank?" Philip asked, as they sipped their fresh lemonade.

"No. An unusually restful one. Routine and quiet business." Alfred was thoughtful. "You will like the air of our Bank, Philip. It is stable, fixed on firm foundations. Nothing febrile. But that is because our business is founded on land, on farms, on sound real estate. Nothing adventurous, dangerous or speculative." Now his expression became somber and dark, and he stared at the distant banks of delphiniums and late roses.

"Nothing dangerous," repeated Philip.

Alfred nodded. "I am really worried about the—the new spirit—which is invading America. Very unsound." He moved with ponderous restlessness. "In fact, I am sometimes afraid. I can conceive of nothing more menacing, more detrimental to individual dignity, than the threatening change, in America, from an economy based on land to a money-urban-industrial society, where men will be rootless and have their being, not under the sun, but within the dank walls of factories. Of course, I do not seriously believe that such a threat will broaden and deepen and become a universal and accomplished fact. But the tendency is there, in the minds of unstable and adventurous men who do not care for the welfare of the American people."

"Perhaps their idea of what is the 'welfare' of the American people merely differs from—ours." Philip added the last word with his usual tact, so that Alfred's first glance of reproof and uneasiness lightened.

"They don't care about the welfare of the people at all," he

363

said dogmatically. "They care only for huge profits. Now, I am not against profits," and he allowed himself a smile which on a less strong and angular face would have been almost coy. "But I believe in small, frequent and sound profits, which do not upset the equilibrium of a secure and ordered society. And I also believe that such profits can come only from the land and the people on it. Factories! Who will protect the workers there? Who will guard their health, their Constitutional rights, so that they do not become a burden to society? No, Philip, I see a faceless society emerging, a nation of homeless men, without dignity, pride, or self-respect."

Good, thought Philip approvingly. When a man begins to spin metaphors his brain is shuttling with alacrity. But, whoever would have thought my father capable of metaphors! He looked at Alfred, and saw that quickened thought had ruffled the stern surface of his face, so that it had become almost fluid.

Philip said thoughtfully: "I see your point very clearly. There is much in what you say, Father. But the year or so of law which you had me take at Harvard has afflicted me with that bedevilling propensity of being able to see the other side, or at least to understand what that side is getting at. Not that I agree. I merely see both sides dispassionately."

Alfred felt rather wary at this, but his pride in his son kept his eyes questioning and attentive. "Let us hear the other side," he said indulgently.

Philip leaned back against a cushion and looked reflectively at a distant tree. "There has been much discussion of this very thing, Father," he said. "I read of it in the newspapers and in the periodicals.

"There are some men, and they are not all greedy and exigent exploiters, who believe that a new industrial age will bring more leisure, enlightenment and freedom for the common man. They see commodities produced in such quantity, and so cheaply, that the luxury of today will be the pleasant necessity of tomorrow——"

"An evil, softening process!" protested Alfred.

Philip inclined his head. "Perhaps. Remember, I am only quoting the protagonists of an industrial and urban society.

"They picture great industrial centers, surrounded by small gardens enclosing individual homes, after a new awareness of social responsibility gets rid of the slums. They say it may be 'dignified' to have a society based on land, but that it might be more agreeable to wear cheap good shoes, to send one's children to school, and to have money in the bank."

"That is encouraging the common man to rise out of his station without the preliminaries of self-sacrificing hard work and struggle," said Alfred. "An easy urban life makes an indolent and selfish people, who think they have 'rights' without toil."

Philip pursed his lips. "Perhaps," he repeated, and this time without hypocrisy. "There is much in what you say. I am only theorizing, following the arguments of new and enthusiastic men."

Alfred became almost excited. "An economy based on the soil is an economy of natural rhythm. It is stable. It inspires confidence in the continuity of government, the continuity of personal and family life. It is an affirmation of the future."

Good, thought Philip again. He is really thinking. He has thought this out over long years. Do I agree? I don't know. I really don't know.

Philip said: "Remember, again, Father, I am only repeating the arguments of others. I am merely asking you for your own opinion. It is a fact, though, that America is tending to centralization and urbanization. It is inevitable, they say, that the economy based on soil must pass. We must, I believe, look elsewhere for permanence and continuity and for our terribly necessary security."

Alfred said strongly: "Where? In factories? In overgrown, rootless cities."

Philip shook his head. "I don't know. But perhaps men must create an economy of stable, spiritual values, of intellectualized virtues. At best, that will be dry bread, I admit, and could be digested by only a few. We'll have to find something else— I feel that the increasing rootlessness might lead to frightful cycles of panics, depressions, even to world wars. Yes, we shall have to find something—I don't know what."

He looked at his father compassionately. Alfred was thinking again. His face, if resistant, was despondent. He knows his era is passing, thought Philip, and he is afraid.

Alfred said: "I will do my best to maintain the old economy based on the soil. I am afraid that my kind is going under. But we'll go down fighting."

He stood up. Now his massive figure seemed somewhat blurred. He put his hand to his cheek, and slowly rubbed it with his palm. The disquiet in his eyes deepened, so that he had a melancholy if determined expression. He said quietly:

"You see it here now in Riversend, since—since—Jerome. The well-paid workers in those abominable industrial works don't know what to do with themselves. They have nothing but their pay!"

Philip's own eyes quickened, brightened, as he looked intently at his father. " 'Nothing but their pay!' " Yes, he thought, my father has begun to think, thank God. And this time, he is right. But I wonder if he knows how right, and how profound, is that statement of his, and how full of sinister potentialities?

Sometimes, he reflected, simple men utter prophetic words which are quite beyond their own comprehension. The whole world of ominous possibilities which had opened before Philip at his father's last words sobered him. But he doubted, with wonder, whether Alfred saw that complete and brawling and hungry world, that roaming and homeless world, that dangerous and seeking world, without stability or faith or individual responsibility.

Philip thought: Both my father and Jerome are right. And both of them are wrong also.

The dinner gong sounded. Alfred had been so sunk in thought that he started. He turned to Philip bemusedly. "Dinner," he said, as if only he had heard the gong.

They went in together. The cold and austere dining-room was filled with wan evening light, for it faced the east. The atmosphere was whitish and dusky, and its somberness was enhanced by the narrow china closets of black walnut, which stretched from floor to high, dim ceiling. The round table, with its stiff linen cloth, glimmered, as did the silver. The tall, thin windows looked out on gardens already mauve with twilight, already faint with dying color. In an unseen tree, a robin dropped his far and melancholy notes into the breathless silence.

The dinner was excellent, hearty, and quite unimaginative. If Philip sometimes longed for delicate broiled lobster, for clams baked with herbs and bacon, for meats with wine sauces, all of which he had enjoyed at Delmonico's on his frequent visits to New York, he was courteous enough not to mention it. He did not like the heavy port which was served with Alfred's dinners, but Alfred insisted that he drink it, for "blood." Philip invariably winced at the word. He saw the thin elegance of his vital fluid thickened by this abominable wine, so that it flowed more sluggishly, and his brain became smug and self-satisfied under its fumes. He drank the port sparingly. No wonder the British loved the status quo so inexorably! Red-running beef and soporific port were enough to make the most volatile man both brutal and dull. Philip thought longingly of the light, gay

Latin wines he had drunk. Ah, that was the wine for sparkling literature, for leaping statues, for grace in living and versatility in government! He recalled that he had heard it said that the Portuguese did not drink their ponderous port themselves, but exported it. He commended their perspicacity.

He waited until both Dorothea and Alfred had been surfeited, and their sensibilities lowered by the very specific gravity of their weighty meal, before he threw a lighted taper on the port-dampened wood of their reactions.

He said: "It was pleasant and quite lovely in the cemetery today. Your lilies were exquisite, Aunt Dorothea."

Dorothea said uncompromisingly: "I only grow them because you like them, Philip."

He inclined his head towards her, with a smile. "I know. And that is very thoughtful of you."

Dorothea, sternly pleased, said: "I know I should have gone myself. But I had too much to do, and besides, I cannot convince myself that my father is there, anyway."

Her gaunt face, dry and faintly lined, saddened.

Philip nodded. "I wish you had gone, Aunt Dorothea. I had the pleaure of seeing Jerome's little girl there. A beautiful child. She looks like her grandfather."

The port-dampened wood, he found, was very capable of being ignited. For both Dorothea and Alfred turned to him with an almost violent quickness, both their faces tightening, becoming overcast with a cloud of emotions. Philip calmly sipped his coffee, affecting to be unaware of the profound disturbance he had created.

"I trust," said Dorothea, in a stifled voice, her hand trembling on her spoon, "that you did not speak, Philip."

Philip raised his eyebrows in artless bewilderment. "Not speak? Why not? Such a pretty, fairy-like child. It would have been impossible not to talk to her. I was sitting in the shade of one of the willows, and she found me there."

Dorothea threw herself stiffly against the back of her chair. She glanced at Alfred. She expected to see anger in his eyes, cold fury on his mouth. But he was regarding Philip with a strange and waiting expression, his big head thrust forward slightly as if to see his son the better.

"Was—was anyone else there, Philip?" he asked, and his voice was oddly muted, as if without body.

Philip put down his cup. He said, with great naturalness: "Yes. Her mother."

Dorothea sucked in her breath. She still stared fixedly at Alfred.

Alfred turned away from his son. He ran his finger abstractedly over the edge of his saucer, and said nothing. His head was bent, his face lost in the growing obscurity of the room.

Dorothea, seeing that Alfred would not speak, cried loudly and angrily: "Philip! Do not tell me that you talked to that horrid creature, that you had any traffic with—her!"

Philip gazed at her as if intensely surprised. "Yes, I did, Aunt Dorothea. And why not? She was very kind to me when I was a boy. I have no quarrel with her."

Dorothea gaped at him with stunned incredulity. She could hardly speak, so overwhelming was her sense of outrage. Then she exclaimed rapidly: " 'No quarrel with her'! Philip, are you mad?" She turned toward Alfred, but Alfred's head still was bent. His finger still traced the edge of the saucer. Dorothea could not believe it! She turned again to Philip. She was vibrating with passion, her dark eyes furiously dilated.

"Are you mad?" she repeated harshly. "Have you forgotten what she did—to all of us? Do I need to recount it all, injury after injury? Philip, this is not like you! How can you be so insensible, so obdurate, so blind, so without decency and self-respect?"

Philip was calm. "I don't see where 'decency' enters into the matter. The lady spoke to me first, after the child found me. Should I have left them, discourteously, awkwardly? I trust I am somewhat civilized."

Out of the corner of his bland eye he watched his father closely.

Dorothea thrust her chair back from the table. "If you are so lacking in sensibility, in personal honor, in pride, then I have nothing further to say to you! I can only say that you have disappointed me profoundly." She was breathing irregularly, her pale face ablaze with wrath and suppressed violence.

She glanced at Alfred again. Why did he not speak? She continued, in a voice increasingly breathless with wild emotion: "Have you no consideration for your father? Have you no respect for him? Have you forgotten what that Jezebel did to him, the disgrace she brought to all of us? Have you forgotten that she was the cause of my father's death—the direct cause?"

Philip was very calm. "I only know that there was a series of unhappy but quite inevitable events. Events flow out of character, and character is fixed. What happened was bound to happen. I don't see where I have been guilty of any lack of consideration for my father, or lack of respect for him. He knows me too well to believe that I would deliberately humiliate him."

He paused. Alfred did not move or speak. He sat in his chair as if he were asleep.

"I do not think that Amalie was the cause of Uncle William's death. It was inevitable that he would die soon. And I don't think he held any bitterness against either Jerome or Amalie. I distinctly remember that he did not.

"In any event, Amalie was kind to me, and I loved her. Common decency demanded that I speak to her when she saw me there." He shrugged. "After all, it was a long time ago, and I believe it was for the best."

"You don't know—!" Dorothea almost screamed. She had been about to cry out the hideous fact of adultery, but caught it back. Philip was twenty-four, but she was positive that he was absolutely innocent of the darker aspects of human villainy. To her, he was still a young boy, chaste, pure and unaware of these disgusting physical aberrations.

Philip read her thoughts, and he could hardly repress a smile. He thought Dorothea naïve and pathetically absurd. It was she who knew nothing of passion and the heavy tides of irresistible lust and desire. Moreover, he was annoyed that she repudiated his manhood.

He kept his voice quiet and reasonable: "I have always been sorry that things happened as they did. But, I repeat, they were inevitable. And again, it was a long time ago. I am not suggesting that we all indulge in an orgy of forgiveness and kisses and tears. But I do believe that civilized decency demands courtesy, and that it is ludicrous to maintain an attitude of eternal hostility."

" 'Eternal hostility!' " Dorothea's voice was practically a shriek. "And who, pray, is keeping up that hostility? Your father? No! One has only to look at that huge monstrosity of a bank which that—that man—has built, hardly three streets away from our own Bank! Riversend Bank of Commerce, indeed! A grinning horror, a direct affront and challenge to all of us! Year after year, he has injured your father, reduced our Bank to second place in the community, inflicted insignificance upon us, mortified us, brought dreadful creatures into our town, dirtied up whole sections! With malice aforethought!"

Philip smiled indulgently. "Now, Aunt Dorothea, that is

silly. Jerome was after money and what he thought was progress. He considered our Bank stuffy and unprogressive. He built his own. He does not interfere with us——"

" 'Not interfere with us'!" Dorothea was almost stupefied at this enormity. "He has only taken away your father's wealthiest depositors, and the richest retired farmers, and left us with the small farmers and little business men!"

Alfred's face, in the dimness of the room, flushed, swelled.

"With malice aforethought!" repeated Dorothea, with vehemence. "It was done, all of it, to humiliate your father, to ruin him, if possible."

"Men don't build up great commercial banking houses out of sheer pique," said Philip coldly. "That is purely feminine reasoning, utterly illogical. And stupid."

Dorothea gasped. Her voice choked in her throat.

Alfred slowly lifted his head. He spoke huskily: "Philip is right about that. He—Jerome—" he uttered the name in a stifled tone, "had had his ideas all along. They had nothing to do with personalities."

"I don't understand you, Alfred," said Dorothea, close to bitter tears.

He regarded her with somber gentleness. "Let us be fair, Dorothea. I had many arguments with Jerome before—before — He was always convinced that I was wrong. I knew for months that something was brewing in his mind. I knew that he had had long talks with his father. I suspected, after a little while, that he was convincing Uncle William. I did not interfere. That would have been unjust, wrong.

"When Uncle William's will was read, I was not disturbed, nor angered. It was only just. After all, Jerome was his son, and I had my suspicions that the will had been changed, several months before—before—— I said nothing. It was Uncle William's money, and Jerome was his son. Uncle William was always just, and I realized it. You had your separate fund, established by your father, to take care of you as long as you lived. Twenty thousand dollars to Philip, and the fortune his grandmother left, to be his on his majority. Jerome and I to divide all the assets of the Bank, the—the house, the other liquid and real assets."

Dorothea interrupted passionately and illogically: "He would not sell you his share of the house, nor his share in the Bank! He even had the effrontery, after all your work, to demand that you step aside and let him become president!"

Alfred smiled somberly. "But I did not step aside, and I

370

did not sell him my share of the house. Perhaps I was malicious. I don't know.

"Through our mutual attorneys we came to a very satisfactory agreement, and I must admit that Jerome was considerate. He might have been much more vicious, had he so desired. Let us be fair. He agreed to take half of all the liquid assets of the Bank, as soon as convenient for me, through notes, maturing at very reasonable and considerate intervals, covering his share of the investments, real estate and other assets. He might have demanded it all immediately, and then I should indeed have been ruined, and completely. During the panic, he did not press for payment, and only took what I could spare. He has no hold on the Bank now. He could have retained it, and could have driven me out eventually. He did not."

Dorothea stared at him, speechless. She had known nothing of this. But her mortification, and her hatred of her brother, only increased at these revelations. That such a man as Alfred had been at the mercy of such a scoundrel, such a blackguard, such a villain! The very fact that Jerome had been "fair" only intensified her humiliation. That monster might have ruined Alfred, and his magnanimity was loathsome.

Her mouth twisted, as if it had tasted something intolerably vile and disgusting. She felt stifled with repulsion.

She stammered, waving her hand and arm stiffly as if to brush away what she could not bear to see: "And he built that horrible monstrosity to insult your eyes every day!"

Alfred smiled again wearily. "Jerome has his own taste in architecture, and even if I don't admire it, I understand he has a right to his own choice."

"Riversend Bank of Commerce!" exclaimed Dorothea, with profound loathing.

"Well, it is a commercial bank," said Alfred. He sighed. He seemed exhausted. He stood up. He looked at both of them, Dorothea and Philip, with depleted and overcast eyes. Philip stood up also.

"Philip," said Alfred, almost inaudibly, "I should like to talk to you for a few minutes. In your room."

CHAPTER FORTY-SEVEN

They went together into Philip's handsome and comfortable room, where Philip had done his best to soften the starkness and astringency of Dorothea's original taste. As Philip had a deep love for flowers, every bowl and vase in the room was filled with bright blooms and thick green leaves. The windows looked out upon the gardens, and were framed in colorful prints.

Philip courteously drew forward a comfortable chair for his father, then sat down near him. He opened a silver box and helped himself to a long neat cigarette. Alfred said: "Machine-made?" Philip smiled and nodded. Alfred said: "But one never knows what they put into those things—made in factories. When a man fashioned his own, he could be certain that they contained nothing deleterious." To which Philip replied: "Their taste is excellent. If they have included old shoes and rags, or, as some detractors say, an occasional finger or two from the hand of an operator, these have only added to the flavor!"

Some years ago, thought Philip, seeing Alfred's sudden slight smile, his father would have frowned reprovingly at such a statement. He saw Alfred's smile, but he saw its tired somberness also.

"Try one, Father," he suggested.

Alfred, with slow reluctance, but with some curiosity also, accepted a cigarette and allowed Philip to light it. During the past two or three years he had begun to smoke an occasional cigar, though he never seemed to derive much pleasure from it. He puffed cautiously on Philip's cigarette, raised his whitened eyebrows. "Mild, not bad at all," he said, as if somewhat surprised. "These are flavored with rum," said Philip. "Rum?" Alfred was astonished. "What is wrong with the flavor of the pure leaf? Have Americans become so effeminate that they cannot endure tobacco as it is grown?" Philip shrugged. "Perhaps as man becomes more prosperous his taste becomes more esthetic."

He waited. But Alfred smoked with heavy thoughtfulness, looking unseeingly through the windows. Then, after several long moments, he said: "Philip, your Aunt sometimes speaks hastily, from her heart. Her words, then, are sometimes more violent than is—necessary. You understand that?"

Philip nodded gravely.

"She means no harm, Philip. But her sensibilities and loyalties are very acute. And we owe her so very much."

"I know, Father. I have never deprecated Aunt Dorothea's contributions to our comfort and her devotion to us."

Alfred sighed. "She did not mean to offend you."

"I know."

Alfred put aside his cigarette. "I know that there is no ques-

372

tion of your loyalty, Philip. I have faith in your judgment. Whatever you do could not be questioned from a moral point of view. It is just a matter of good taste."

"I think it would be a matter of very bad taste had I insulted a child," suggested Philip gently, "or been discourteous to a woman who had been kind to me, and who had given me a mother's love, even if it had been only for a short time."

Alfred looked at the cigarette smouldering in its silver tray. "You are right, of course," he said, almost inaudibly. "It is very difficult." He hesitated. "But one can be careful not to encounter difficult situations, to avoid any opportunity for them. Heaven knows, there are situations which it is impossible to avoid. But to seek them out, to lay one's self open to them—that is a different matter."

"I did not seek out this encounter," Philip reminded his father. "If the child had not found me, I should have said nothing, I think. They were there some time before I was discovered."

Alfred inclined his head. "Yes. Yes, of course. You did what was expected of a gentleman. But—you will avoid similar occasions, I am sure."

Philip was silent. But he gazed at his father penetratingly.

"We have lived here for quite a number of years now, Philip, and this is the first—encounter. I am sure we'll spend many more years here, and not have a repetition."

Philip said quietly: "I have been invited to Hilltop. I accepted the invitation tentatively. I may go up."

Alfred turned to him quickly, as if incredulous. "Philip, did I hear you correctly?"

"Yes." Philip's voice was determined, but still gentle. "I am remembering that you own a half interest in that house, and that—later—that interest will come to me. I was born there; it is my home. My mother died in one of its rooms. My happiest memories live within its walls. Sometimes I feel exiled." He paused. "I want to see my old home again. I want to see the hawthorn tree I planted in the garden. Uncle William gave me a corner where I planted white roses. I feel they are mine. It is our home, too, as much as it is Jerome's. More so, in fact."

Alfred stared at him in confusion. He was overcome with a flood of conflicting emotions. He saw Hilltop clearly in his mind, its brick garden walks, its red wall in the rear, its old dark trees, the light of the sun on its old windows. And he was filled with an intense nostalgia and sadness.

He said: "Yes, I can understand your feelings, Philip. This

373

house is too new. In a hundred years or so, it might acquire the mellowness of a true home. But not yet, I am afraid, and not in our lifetime. That is something we must leave for our heirs. Yes, I understand."

Philip said, with deliberate hypocrisy: "I want to see Hilltop again. I want to walk in its rooms. I want to look at the things which belonged to us, which still belong to us. Perhaps I am sentimental. And I know that there are many who would despise such sentimentality, and probably they are right."

"No, no," said Alfred confusedly. He rubbed his lined forehead. "It is not sentimentality. A man's deepest instincts are rooted in his home. It is natural. I am only trying to recall to your memory who are now living in that house."

"They have no right to drive us out, to keep us out," said Philip artfully. "The house is ours, too. We have a lawful right to enter whenever we wish, thanks to your wisdom in not selling Jerome your share, Father."

Alfred was distressed, but he was also strangely pleased and touched. His tired hazel eyes brightened with satisfaction as he looked at his son. "I had to preserve your birthright, Philip. I shall never let anyone take it away from you."

Philip nodded with a strong affectation of grimness. "Thank you, Father."

Alfred really did not know whether he should be annoyed or pleased. "I did not think that you were so—implacable, my boy."

"Oh," said Philip easily, "I am just a seething pot of implacability. I want what is mine, and I intend to have it, to enjoy it."

Alfred leaned back in his chair and considered the whole distressing situation with confusion and pain and uncertainty. "You could," he suggested doubtfully, "arrange with—them— to let you go through the house and gardens, say, every few weeks. And doubtless they will be considerate and tactful enough to remove themselves during those hours, or to keep out of your way."

Philip repressed a smile. But, as usual, his father's naïvete filled him with tenderness. "That would be awkward," he said consideringly. "That might give certain people an occasion for amusement, at our expense. I think, perhaps, it would be best if I simply went up there easily and naturally and looked about, without previous notification of my coming."

Alfred frowned suddenly. "That would be the least awkward, I admit. But there is another thing: he—he might be there. He might insult you, attempt to drive you away. That is something

374

I could not endure." And his folded hands suddenly parted, became large and threatening fists, and his eyes, staring before him, burned darkly.

He will always hate Jerome, thought Philip. And it is something more than Amalie; it is of many years' growth, years crowded with hatreds and jealousies and insults and hostilities. It is instinctive, inherent, between them.

He said calmly: "How will this be? I will never go up there when I suspect Jerome might be on the premises."

Alfred relaxed his savagely knotted hands, but he said nothing and only looked before him fixedly.

Philip spoke with wiliness. "I have always admired one thing about you, Father, more than any other. You have always been just." He reflected, with cynical sadness, that a man must have one prideful and conscious virtue, and "justice" was his father's. It was a fetish with him.

At the beloved word, Alfred's last dull rage smouldered out. He regarded Philip consideringly.

"You could have made it so disagreeable for Jerome that he would have been compelled to leave the house. You could have hounded him there, subjected him to mortifications and endless harassments. But you did not. For that, he ought to be grateful. And in return, he ought not to object to my visiting my old home whenever I wish."

"He dare not object!" said Alfred strongly.

Philip nodded with satisfaction. "No, he dare not. And, besides, there is another matter. Once a year you have the place inspected by your attorneys and agents. I think I could do a better job for you. I can look for things which might escape the casual eyes of those who are not much interested. After all, I must help preserve the property."

Alfred said, softly: "I have been informed that Hilltop is in excellent condition. He—he has added many improvements, and beautified the grounds, too. One must be just."

Again, Philip reflected on the one supreme virtue which every man possesses. And he began to wonder, from these visible evidences of deep-seated pain, whether that chosen virtue did not cause its writhing possessor more anguish than it was worth, and whether or not it was completely alien to that possessor's real nature. A kind of self-flagellation, thought Philip, the gentle cynic. Each man to his individual hairshirt. What was his own? Deliberate self-sacrifice. The ugliest of the "virtues." Sometimes it made a dangerous creature of the man who harbored it.

Alfred got up and went to a window. He kept his back to his son. "Of course, you need waste no words on—anyone—on your tours of inspection, Philip." He was silent then, but Philip felt his pathetic waiting.

"Only as many as courtesy demands," Philip conceded. He lit another cigarette. He said casually: "The little girl is very pretty indeed. There is a quality about her which strongly reminds me of Uncle William. She has his eyes and his coloring, and the expression of her mouth is his also. She is all New England. Not in the least like her mother, or her father either."

Alfred did not turn or speak. But Philip felt his tenseness.

"A very cool and somewhat silent child," said Philip, meditatively. "A puzzle to her mother. I had the slight impression that all is not happiness for Amalie."

"I am really not interested in——" said Alfred, in a muffled tone. But he did not move.

Philip went on, as if he had not heard his father: "Amalie has not changed much. She has some white threads in her hair. But who is completely happy, anyway? She told me of her little boy, who is named for Uncle William." He paused. He said, with a soft and affected hesitation: "She begged me to tell her that you did not hate her."

Alfred made an abrupt movement at the window, an involuntary movement of pain. Then he was still again. Philip saw the massive lines of his broad shoulders, and they had a touchingly softened look about them, an eager and waiting look.

"I said," Philip continued gently, "that I didn't believe you had ever hated her. She seemed happy, then, and relieved." Philip did not mind lies that gave pleasure or peace to anyone, so he uttered a very large one without scruple: "She asked about you in detail, Father. I did not enlighten her much, except to tell her that you were well and content. That, too, gave her obvious happiness. She said that she always remembered how kind you were, and how good. Did you know that she has a pair of binoculars?" Philip added.

"Binoculars!" said Alfred faintly.

Philip laughed. "Yes. She admitted she spends considerable time looking down here. And not at me, I suspect."

Alfred was silent again, then he swung sharply about. His face had changed, become revivified with a kind of youthful intensity. "You are not joking, Philip?" he said, and the tone of his voice moved Philip to an aching pang of compassion.

"No, Father, I am not joking," he said. "It is true: she has

376

binoculars." He stood up and regarded his father with grave earnestness.

They stood and looked at each other in a long and searching silence.

Then Alfred said, as if speaking from some inner compulsion: "I shall never forget Amalie. I have held her—almost—guiltless."

Good God, thought Philip, with pity, does he believe Jerome raped her? Well, let him believe it if his vanity, his love, his loneliness, can so be assuaged.

Much of Alfred's somberness and weariness had lightened. He lifted his head. He put his hand on Philip's shoulder. He smiled, almost excitedly. He said: "Philip, I know I can trust your good taste, your discretion. You have always been so good. I am grateful. And we have grown so close together in these years——"

He pressed Philip's shoulder strongly. Then, still smiling, he went away. His step on the stairs was quick and light.

I hope, thought Philip, uneasily, that I haven't said too much.

CHAPTER FORTY-EIGHT

The Riversend Bank of Commerce, scornfully stigmatized by Dorothea as "that grinning monstrosity," was not in the least monstrous, nor, in its deliberately lofty dignity, did it "grin."

It was, however, designed to overshadow the Lindsey bank. There was much of the stage manager in Jerome; he knew the value of overpowering "properties." As he was also an artist, he understood the psychic impact of mass and proportion, the effect of angles, the helpless inability of the human eye to refrain from travelling up a soaring column. He knew that the English mind preferred smallness, solidity and unpretentiousness, and that the Englishman had a tendency to respect grimness and compactness. But the American mind, already affected by the vast skies and great plains and immense vistas of the new country, loved monoliths. America, he realized, was ripe for an architecture peculiarly its own: great gleaming walls, dazzling smoothness, clean strong angularity. The South had first demonstrated this new trend, in an individual architecture. Jerome intended to use these proportions of line and alabaster-like massiveness, and adapt them to the more pale and clarified light of the North.

So, the Riversend Bank of Commerce was easily the largest commercial establishment in Riversend. It had taken long over a year to build. Jerome had selected two acres of land less than an eighth of a mile from the old Lindsey bank, and had torn down the small shops and stables on that site. He ruthlessly cleared away all clutter, all brush, all spindly second-growth timber, all walls and fences. Everything was levelled, laid open to the sky. Then, in this square center of windy space, the bank was built. Pure white granite was brought in from Vermont, huge blocks carefully fitted together to form wide square walls of brilliant austerity. Hating the narrow, slit-like windows of his era, Jerome specified windows that were both wide and tall. Four enormous white columns of the granite graced the stern façade, stretching the complete height of three stories. The doors, quite gigantic, were of dully polished bronze, with grills.

The grounds were heavily seeded with grass, so that in the second summer the shining bank stood on a great square of bright, smooth green. No flower beds marred this greenness. There were no trees except two beautiful cypresses at the foot of the three low, wide, white steps that led to the doors of the bank.

General Tayntor had called the bank a "fine example of bastard Greek." But, as Jerome pointed out, there was no valid objection to adapting the noblest form of architecture to American taste. Indeed, if an impartial eye studied the bank for a few moments, it was evident that the Greek influence was only in the effect of the mass and the columns.

Riversend had been stupefied by this new addition to its somewhat insular and English architecture, all red brick, dull gray granite, or wood. It seemed to shrink back from it, to huddle away, both in suspicion and awe. It stood high and white and wide, and there was hardly a section of mid-Riversend that did not have a view of it. It took Riversend nearly five years to accept it, to come to admire it. And by that time Jerome had become so established, so much the power of the community, that had the bank indeed been a "grinning monstrosity" it would still have seemed beautiful in the eyes of the townsmen.

Promptly after the reading of his father's will, and his marriage to Amalie, Jerome had gone to New York with his bride. There he went into long conferences with his old friend, Jay Regan, and the latter's friend, Gordon Livingston, of Livingston, Hatfield and Company, bankers and investors. Mr. Livingston was a gentleman who listened with attention and sympathy to Jerome, for he was much interested in industrial banking. Jerome informed his friends of his plan, the establishing of a bank to be known as the Riversend Bank of Commerce, and that he intended to attract to Riversend as many new industries as possible. He himself intended to enter the field of financing and underwriting such industries. There was much uninvested money in the old Lindsey bank, but before he could persuade the owners to invest with him, he must prove that industrial financing and the investment of money in such enterprises as railroads, mining, and other industries of national scope, could bring a greater return than local farming and the financing of small shops. Frankly, then, Jerome asked his friends to recommend to him those securities which he, in turn, could recommend to the investors of Riversend and which he could buy himself.

He invested heavily, following the advice of these friends. Upon his return to Riversend he began to build his bank.

While the bank was being built, he cleverly disseminated rumors to the effect that "Jerome Lindsey has got onto some good things in New York." He allowed it to be circulated that he was a clever investor, that he was well on the way to doubling, if not tripling, his fortune. The big industrial and financial boom that followed the war lent verity to these rumors.

For a while, the offended gentry of Riversend kept their distance from the man who had so flouted all their pet conventions and their Victorian sense of respectability. They would have none of him. They watched his bank rising, and jeered. They saw his carriage in the streets, and turned aside. He was a pariah. But Jerome smiled to himself. The strong pungency of money covered, he knew, all other smells.

When he heard the rumor which General Tayntor was now spreading about him he laughed aloud—but secretly, in exultation. For it seemed the rumor related that Jerome had never had any intention of marrying Amalie, wife of Alfred, but that Alfred had himself forced a "shot-gun" marriage on him. Jerome, said the General, had been much in love with Sally Tayntor, but the girl, once the scandal became public property, jilted him, much to his despair.

So, thought Jerome, with satisfaction, the old devil is saving his pride and preparing the way for his forgiveness of me and his approach to me. It will be all magnanimity. He himself made no overtures to his old friends. He merely waited.

The bank was not yet finished before the General found a way to accost him "accidentally" in front of the General's own home. It was a frigid meeting, a reserved one. They mentioned no personalities. The General only remarked that he had recently returned from New York where he had heard rumors that Jerome was one of the cleverest speculators on the Street. "Of course," said the General, "that is very foolish and precarious, and I hope the rumors are untrue, for the sake of your father's memory." This remark had the ring of a covertly eager question.

Knowing that the General was the most valuable gossip in Riversend, very avaricious, and only too anxious to have the "rumors" substantiated, Jerome immediately invited his old friend to dine with him at the Riversend Hotel, that very noon. The General demurred stiffly, finally allowed himself to be persuaded. They created a minor sensation when they met together in the hotel dining-room less than three hours later.

The two carefully ignored the subdued amazement about them, and drank several glasses of whiskey before dining. By that time the General had mellowed. His fondness for Jerome had always been sincere; it came to the surface now with much laughter and many exclamations of "my dear boy!" A drink or two later, the General's arm was about Jerome's shoulder, and their heads were together, exchanging sentimental reminiscences of William Lindsey.

Two hours later they were still in the dining-room, where Jerome had ordered a very good dinner. The General had always believed that Jerome was "cagy." He now listened to Jerome's "confidences," feeling very cunning himself, and very astute. He was certain that all the sentimentalizing, and the whiskey, had loosened Jerome's cautious tongue, and did not question the things which Jerome confided to him. Moreover, they had the ring of truth.

Jerome informed his old friend that both Mr. Regan and Mr. Livingston were backing him. Of course, he said, all this was very confidential, and he trusted the General to keep the matter so. Jerome enlarged on his really enthusiastic belief in the industrial future and the rising power of American business in world affairs.

It was not his intention, he said, to extend any offers to Riversend investors to come in with him. None whatever, except, perhaps, to a friend or two, such as the General, if he could rely upon the General's discretion. The General then had an opportunity to "grow" with Jerome—the possibilities, the

380

profits, were unlimited. He, Jerome, might, upon consideration, offer the General shares in the new bank, which would entitle him to dividends instead of to mere interest.

"I intend always to have a large reserve of liquid assets," he said. "I want flexibility in investments."

Before parting with the General, he again swore him to secrecy. The General, seething with impatience to spread what he had heard, could hardly leave his young friend soon enough. Again, Jerome sat back, laughing inwardly, and waited.

The bank was hardly in operation before the large money-holders of Riversend were clamoring to open accounts. By that time, new industries, encouraged, financed and stimulated by Jerome, were already moving into the community.

"What price loyalty," said Jerome, watching Alfred's old supporters and depositors streaming into his bank. He, Jerome, received them gravely. He was both president and financial adviser of the new bank, and his manner was formal and gracious, but cool.

The shares in the bank were swallowed voraciously. The General was now a director. Riversend was stunned. Never had there been such prosperity, such excitement, so many new-comers, so loud a sound of building, so much hurry and commerce and so many rumors. The people could not grasp it all in one clutch, could not digest it immediately. It was incredible. To Riversend, for three years, it was like a dream. The farmers had new equipment, new wagons, new stock. Their wives bought a "good" silk dress, each and every one. Their children went to the new schools. Streets were laid almost overnight. Thousands of men and their families from surrounding towns, countrysides and villages, streamed into Riversend to work in the factories.

Then came the panic of 1873, and suddenly, almost overnight it seemed, the hammers and the pistons and the lathes and the machines were silent all over America.

"This," said the old intransigent enemies of Jerome, who had never become reconciled to him, who had remained loyal to the solid Alfred, "is the end of the adventurer."

But it was not the end. Jerome, as he had told the General, had retained a backlog of liquid assets. When his stocks and bonds had made him a nice profit, he had sold them, and when the panic arrived, he had good reserves, including his notes on Alfred's sound bank. He was very reasonable in this matter, not pressing Alfred when pressing might have resulted in a catastrophe. He had sound business reasons for his magna-

381

nimity. But he knew also that his forebearance made him new friends, those who were loyal to Alfred and those who would have gone down with Alfred had Jerome seen fit to exert pressure.

The panic passed. It had been only a hiatus as America lingered in the last phases of the old agrarian economy before entering the new economy of industry.

Within ten years, the Riversend Bank of Commerce had become the greatest influence in mid-New York State, the growing center of industry.

It was a feat possible only in America during the 'seventies and 'eighties.

Alfred's bank remained the small farmer's bank, the small shopkeeper's bank. It had a sound place in the community, and Jerome did nothing to destroy it. He instinctively knew that such banks are necessary to the health of a community.

He was once again the idolized and pampered pet of his old friends. That they still did not accept Amalie was of no concern, but only of amusement, to him. He had no proper reverence for "gentry." He was content that his children had for their companions the children of the new industrialists. At least, he would say, these children were of strong blood, and had vitality in their bodies. Little Mary's governess, however, was a cultivated and learned Frenchwoman whom he and Amalie had imported from France. He had plans for his daughter beyond the boundaries of Riversend. His son would follow him into the bank.

So it was, that on this August day, which had been the meeting day of Amalie and Philip Lindsey, Jerome was very content, very satisfied with himself.

He was the last to leave the bank, at six o'clock. He entered his carriage and was driven home. As usual, he anticipated greeting his family, his wife, his daughter and his son. He had everything. The carriage rolled past the old Lindsey bank, and Jerome did not give it the slightest glance. It was his past, and it was behind him.

CHAPTER FORTY-NINE

It is very pleasant and comforting to the ego to know that one has had a tremendous influence on his community. Man's sense of personal significance, always insecure at best, is given the illusion of enduring value when he perceives external evidence of his individual potency. Jerome, thinking this, knew he was no exception to this pathetic human craving to write one's name in water and see it solidify into marble.

Riversend now had two lines of horsecars. The old oil street lamps had given way to gas lamps; they flickered down many new neat streets of an evening, streets paved in parquetries of red brick. New shops had appeared and an "opera house." There were two hotels now, filled with a constant flow of "commercial" travellers. He, Jerome, was the author of all this, and he looked on it with satisfaction.

Eight years ago he had formally opened his bank. Mr. Regan, Mr. Livingston, and several other distinguished bankers and financiers from New York, had come to the opening. Jerome had invited over a dozen small bankers from the surrounding villages and towns and small cities to be present, and they had come eagerly. The industrialists with whom Jerome had been in contact came also, hopefully. General Tayntor, the Widow Kingsley, and several other reconciled friends, arrived in state. Jerome had allowed no one to enter the bank until it was complete. And he had the pleasure now of seeing their amazement, their awe, and of hearing the sincere congratulations of his New York friends.

The interior was truly impressive. The floor seemed composed of one gigantic slab of glimmering black marble. The lofty ceiling was upheld by gleaming columns of white marble polished like satin. The walls, half-way up, were of black marble. The plaster above them had been decorated with exquisite murals by Jerome himself. Here, too, he had shown an imagination beyond his immediate era, for the murals depicted men at work in logging camps, in factories, on farms, in banking houses. The colors were subdued but powerful. The cashiers' cages were of dully gleaming brass. Along the wall were arranged marble benches, separated by potted palms and rubber plants. Riversend was stupefied.

Later Jerome had held a reception at Hilltop for his friends and supporters. Never had there been such a reception and such food! After eight years, it was still an inexhaustible topic of conversation.

Jerome never tired of it, either. As his carriage glided through the streets, and he was hailed by friends and acquaintances, he acknowledged their existence with graciousness. He sat in his carriage, his gray-gloved hands folded on his cane, his tall gray hat fashionably atilt on his head, and bowed from side to side. Sometimes Amalie suspected that Jerome was losing his sense of humor, and with her characteristic candor she so informed him. When he became irritated at her words, she was confirmed in her suspicion.

"A sense of humor is the fortress of the insecure," he told her.

"It is also a safeguard against complacency," she replied.

It would have enraged Jerome had he the slightest awareness that Amalie was beginning to think that he and Alfred had much in common, unsuspected in the old days. Amalie reflected, not without ruefulness, that a man had only to be successful to lose a certain sprightliness of imagination. Was it because success brought with it an almost inevitable increase of secret personal insecurity? That was paradoxical, but it had been Amalie's observation that life was a study in astounding paradoxes.

It was also possible, thought Amalie, that when a man's environment was insecure and uncertain he must needs fall back upon himself, and the falling back strengthened him, gave him a vivacious fortitude, a sense of proportion, a feeling of impregnability. It was when a man expended himself upon his environment that he became vulnerable, however he denied it. Objectivity created cities, expanded civilization, but, carried too far, it reduced man's subjectivity, which was really his profound individuality, his intuitive knowledge that his own soul was his real fortress. The "high thinking and plain living" of the New Englanders was more than an interesting philosophy, Amalie would think. It was the secret of man's power over externals, the secret of his enduring integrity.

When she talked of this to Jerome, he listened to her intently. Then his impatience, his walking away, convinced her that, in spite of all that he had done, he was deeply and namelessly uneasy. She loved him most in this impatience. She knew he knew that something was wrong.

"You think I am constantly pursuing money," he accused her, angrily. "But no one desires a lot of money less than I." And she knew this to be true also.

When the carriage began to climb up the slope to Hilltop, this warm, red-and-gold August evening, Jerome felt suddenly deflated. This deflation was becoming more and more frequent with him. He did not know its cause. He had brought prosperity, good wages, opportunity and progress to Riversend. But there was something in all this which was ominous also. What was it?

384

He had a habit now—a dangerous one, though he did not know this—of attempting to throw the darkness of his inner malaise upon external objects, and of blaming those objects for his depressions. So now, as he glimpsed through the trees the austere red brick of his cousin's house, he convinced himself that that house was a constant festering in his flesh, a source of infection which perpetually oppressed him. A few years ago, the house had only amused him. Now it angered him.

He was in a bad mood when he arrived home. Amalie and the two children were waiting for him on the lawn. With the prescience of a woman who loves much, Amalie guessed, as he alighted from the carriage, that Jerome was perturbed. There was something in the set of his shoulders, the line of his hard and arrogant jaw. She bent towards little Mary and whispered quickly: "Darling, do not tell Papa just now about our meeting with Philip. I will tell him later."

The child lifted her large light-blue eyes to her mother's face. "But why, Mama?"

Amalie set her mouth. "Because I tell you not to," she said crossly.

Mary was silent a moment. Then, flinging her silver-gilt mane back over her shoulders, she ran across the lawn to her father, her delicate little face lifted up with an eager, faun-like expression upon it. Her gingham frock blew back in the soft wind, showing three or four frilled and belaced cambric petticoats swirling about her legs. She moved like a shadow, but Jerome saw her coming. His lowering look cleared slightly. He held out his arms to her, and she jumped into them. He swung her high and clear, lifted her up, and kissed her soundly. She wound her arms about his neck, pressed her cheek to his, almost hungrily. Her face glowed.

Moving quite sedately, Amalie approached Jerome, holding little William's fat warm hand. Jerome's hat had been knocked off in the enthusiasm of his daughter's greeting. His curling gray hair gave his dark and narrow face a distinguished look. When he was pleased, or unconcerned, the old scars on his forehead and cheek were almost invisible.

Amalie, with that trick common to loving wives, saw everything while she appeared to see nothing. She placidly accepted Jerome's kiss on her mouth. She pushed little William forward for Jerome to kiss. He put down his daughter, quite reluctantly, and lifted the small boy in his arms. The child received Jerome's caress with shyness. His dark eyes fluttered. He was relieved when Jerome set him down on his feet and he could return to his mother and the sanctuary of her skirts.

"It has been such a warm day," said Amalie casually, as they walked together up the flagged path to the house.

Jerome glanced at her quickly and suppressed a smile. He knew that Amalie had seen his irritation and was giving him an opening to unburden himself. He tweaked her ear. "Nothing's wrong with me," he said. "It's just that it annoys me more and more to see that damned house down there."

"After nine years?" Amalie's smooth black brows lifted quizzically.

"Ulcers don't get easier to bear with time," he replied. Then he felt foolish and laughed a little. "I'd like to drop a stick of dynamite on it," he added, but his tone was indulgent.

The cool and fragrant duskiness of the house soothed him, as it always did. Arm in arm, he and Amalie went up the stairs to their rooms. He saw the rosebud on his dresser, and his eyes lighted. But he did not mention it to Amalie. They chatted amiably while he changed and washed. Amalie made herself very agreeable. She tied his cravat for him and kissed him on the chin afterwards. Then, quite casually, she lifted the rosebud from its glass and put it in his lapel. "How the child loves you," she murmured. Jerome's disposition was further sweetened by this. He glanced in the mirror. "She's a minx," he said, with fondness. "She knows all the feminine tricks. I wonder what she wants this time?"

"Nothing. Do women always want something?" Amalie laughed.

"Always," he said, pinching her cheek. They looked at each other breathlessly for a moment, their old passion as ardent as ever.

Feeling that Jerome could now bear the unpleasant news, Amalie drifted away to her own dressing table and smoothed her hair. She bent forward as if to examine an incipient wrinkle.

She watched Jerome in her mirror. He was preparing a whiskey-and-soda at a special commode set aside for that purpose.

"A very small glass of wine for me, my love," she said.

She took the glass from him, and they sat down together to enjoy the drinks. There was always wine downstairs, and the children did not dine with their parents, but Jerome had decided that he preferred not to drink whiskey in any spot where Mary might unexpectedly enter. Amalie thought this ridiculous.

386

When Jerome had been fortified, Amalie said, very casually: "Mary and I went to your father's grave today."

Jerome swirled the amber liquid in his glass. He said, looking at it: "Are the graves well kept?"

"Yes." Amalie paused. Then, in a light voice, she continued: "Do you know whom we discovered there? Philip! He had been decorating your father's grave, too."

Jerome looked up sharply. "Philip? I hope he didn't have the impudence to speak to you."

Amalie raised her brows, which Jerome suddenly found an irritating habit.

"Impudence, Jerome? Why 'impudence'? Of course he spoke. In fact, Mary discovered him. I had a feeling he wouldn't have made himself known if the sharp-eyed little minx hadn't found him." She paused. " 'Impudence' was never exactly the word for Philip."

She was apprehensive when she saw that the scars on her husband's face had turned a faint scarlet. He said, in a repressed voice: "Well, I suppose you couldn't help exchanging amenities with him. I hope it stopped there."

Amalie, with a serenity she did not feel, sipped at her glass. "I have always been fond of Philip. And he was always fond of you, and you of him. Perhaps that is because you resemble each other so."

Jerome set down his glass with a thump. "Let's not be sentimental, please. I never had anything against Philip. He was only a young boy when— But I am sure you were discreet enough not to carry on any unnecessary conversation."

"It depends," said Amalie, judicially, "what you mean by 'unnecessary conversation.' We had a few things to say to each other. Philip is going into his—father's—bank."

"What? No music, no writing?" Jerome's tone was sneering, but Amalie saw his interest.

"No. I gathered he felt it was his 'duty.' "

"Another one!" Jerome laughed shortly. "How 'duty' haunts this damn family! Well, I never did have much faith in his talents, as you seem to have had."

Amalie suddenly saw Philip's grave and thoughtful face, and she was angered. Jerome was watching her curiously. "I suppose he's quite grown-up now. Has he changed?"

"He's not much taller, but he is a man. In character and in manner and in a certain way of talking, he resembles your father very much." Amalie spoke coldly. She was surprised when Jerome said, almost with kindness: "Yes. I always

387

thought that, too. Poor devil," he added, reflectively. "The New England heritage has a way of cropping out in a family's character, like granite through fertile earth. So he's going into the bank, eh? I can't reconcile that with what I remember of Philip. But I suppose he's become a stick, too."

"No. You are wrong, Jerome. He is as he was, only more so. I—I am very fond of Philip. He asked about you in detail. He seemed—interested—and sympathetic. He said to tell you that you had accomplished marvels and that he hoped to study the whole subject."

"Very condescending of him." Jerome got up and mixed another drink for himself. "I suppose he was full of lofty magnanimity, too."

"How little you understand of anyone, Jerome!" Amalie's quick temper was flaring. "What a distorted idea you must have of Philip! You yourself used to say how like your father he was. If Philip is 'sacrificing' himself by going into the bank, it is not because he feels righteous about it, but because he is compassionate."

Jerome turned from the commode and stared at her. His expression was dark, almost inimical.

"How you two must have wallowed in sentimentality!" he said. "What heart-throbbings there must have been! Such tremolos, such bathos, such sighing."

He sat down again, while Amalie looked at him, fuming and crimson.

"One such episode is enough," Jerome went on. "Let that end it."

Amalie's temper was fast surging over its boundaries of caution.

"That is not so easy, Jerome. He wishes to visit Hilltop occasionally."

Now Jerome's eyes turned vicious. "He does, eh? And I say no."

"You forget that he too has an interest in this house."

Jerome was silent. He regarded his wife blackly, and the scars were now a vivid scarlet. Then he said: "So. He wishes to come up here and spy."

"Philip? Spy?" Amalie was outraged. "If you have the slightest knowledge of him how can you say that of Philip? You seem to forget that this was Philip's home, also that he might have some affectionate memories of it." She paused; her breath was coming fast. "You can't keep Philip away, Jerome. Unless you ask him not to come. He will not come, if you ask him not to. You know that. Are you going to do that?"

Jerome put down his glass, reached for a cigar on the table beside him, and lit it. He did all these things with deliberation.

"He will respect your wishes, I know," Amalie went on, her voice faltering. "He was always so fond of you. You have only to tell him not to come, to say you prefer that he keep away. Will you be that small, that cruel?"

Jerome said: "When I cut away a certain part of my life, I make a clean job of it. I don't want messy details and frayed rags blowing about."

Amalie's distress suddenly lightened at his words. She scrutinized him closely. "We have no quarrel with Philip," she said, with gentleness. "You two have always liked each other. But he is very sensitive, and I know he won't come when you are here, if you wish it that way."

She waited for him to speak, but he did not. Amalie's temper threatened to rise again. "I did not think that you lacked perception, Jerome. I am disappointed in you."

She did not know why he laughed without any preliminary indications of amusement. "At least twice a week you tell me you are disappointed in me," he said. "You women always want to mould men to your heart's desire. I made an honest woman of you, and you made a paterfamilias of me. But that doesn't satisfy you, does it?"

She was about to make a furious reply, then was silent. For she saw that Jerome was thinking, and that his thoughts amused him, and that he smiled to himself unpleasantly.

He said, with deceptive lightness: "Well, if he wishes to come, he is within his legal rights, I suppose. Let him come, poor devil. I imagine he finds life in that dank mausoleum pretty trying. Who am I to deny him a little pleasure?" He smiled again, still unpleasantly.

"Have you arranged another meeting, my pet?" he added.

"Oh, don't be abominable, Jerome. You can be so petty. Philip may not come at all, though he isn't a prig, and he wouldn't remain away just because he thought it might offend his father. He is too sensible."

The dinner gong boomed softly through the house. Jerome rose. He held out his hand to Amalie and pulled her playfully to her feet, dragged her to him, and kissed her soundly. "I love you, even if you are a fool," he said, rubbing his chin in her hair.

Again hand in hand, they went downstairs to dinner.

But Amalie was depressed. She had wanted, sought, prayed

389

for security all her life. In her seeking for it she had made a tragic mistake. She was now mistress of this solid old house, the wife of its owner, the mother of children. She had her own carriage, her rich gowns, her jewels. Her portrait and the portraits of her children hung on the old panelled walls. She walked, mistress of everything, through the gardens, and sat under the ancient trees. But still she was not secure. She would never feel secure. Perhaps it was because she lacked, in herself, the capacity to attract security, or even to acquire it. It was like a desperate hunger in her, but when she eagerly lifted the cup of security to her lips she discovered it was empty.

Always she was aware of the winds of instability about her, a certain transience of atmosphere. Contentment, apparently, would never be hers. Was it because she, like Jerome, was too restless, too seeking, too unsatisfied? But why, when she so ardently craved permanence and roots?

They reached the lower hall together. Jerome glanced in at the library. They stood and listened to the grandfather clock, ticking away as it had ticked for over one hundred years. "There's a definite advantage in having tradition," he said.

And then Amalie knew that Jerome also felt insecure, that he, too, felt that the slightest wind might blow his rootless self out of these very walls and into bodiless space.

They went into the dining-room, where for a century nothing had been changed. They sat down and looked at the old silver, the old Limoges plates, the flowers. And then it came to Amalie that the fault was not only in herself and Jerome but in the very air of America. Tradition was going, slowly but surely. Permanence and security were dissolving. Religion was giving way to materialism, to objectivity. The roots of America were stirring in friable soil.

Jerome said: "I went through the factories today, with Munsey and the others. Things are moving fast. Sometimes I think they move too fast. I have a feeling that something is growing enormously in this country, and that it may get away from us. And that 'something' may be good or it may be bad. I don't know."

Amalie gazed at him with deep gratitude, but without surprise. She and Jerome frequently had these telepathic interludes together, when each simultaneously spoke aloud what the other was thinking. She was very moved. She put out her hand to her husband, and he took it, and they looked at each other with bright eyes.

"It is all nonsense, of course," said Jerome, "but I think

these rascals of ours ought to go to some church, and get some religious instruction. All mumbo-jumbo, and quite unscientific, but still—— Oh, hell! I don't know."

CHAPTER FIFTY

Jerome's depressed mood did not lighten, either that night or the next day.

His depressive states were invariably accompanied by a kind of disgust for himself, a kind of furious impatience. It always seemed effeminate to him to be the victim of moods, and especially alarming that these moods were increasing in intensity and frequency. His attempts to apply logic to them appeared, even to himself, as puerile. It was the naïve young, the inexperienced, who adored logic, who were ponderous, who sought common-sense reasons for the sickening malaise which seized on the human spirit and turned it into a mass of collapsing and painful inertia.

Sometimes it needed only a certain light in the sky, a certain whitening of a tree, a certain intonation in the voice of a friend, to throw him into a misery which was apparently causeless. Then it was that he could not think at all. He could only endure, with what little natural patience he had, or drink rapidly, or find some petty reason to become enraged.

There were, he knew, peaceful men who had an air of timelessness and tranquillity. He began in this connection to have a notion of the relativity of time. Time, for him, was rushing, pouring, cataracting, a roaring stream of rapids. But to the peaceful men time was without peril, a natural element like air, which flowed about them without eroding their personalities or splintering their lives. What secret did these peaceful men possess which made them go about their duties calmly, accomplishing, too, a great deal, and that with solidity and permanence? Calamity ran by them on another road to the sea. Their lives were without alarums; their families smiled serenely. They sat by their fires and sipped their whiskeys and their eyes were without heat. Much of the time, Jerome envied them. He might have felt much better had he discovered that their existence was without significance. But he was too intelligent to believe that.

There was something in him which was wrong. He did not know what it was. It was some pattern of personality. He had in his life been elated, disturbed, infuriated, downcast, exultant, despairing. But he had never been happy. Why? He had a wife and a family whom he loved. But sometimes the very sight of them increased his wild wretchedness. Sometimes he was sorry for them, that they had to be afflicted with him. Sometimes he thought of leaving everything, and running away, and losing himself forever. But he would always, he knew, carry himself with him.

He was always seeking evidence that he was "accomplishing something." This, he began to realize, was part of the nameless disease from which he suffered. He would think: A man must accept himself, and all he is, before he can have a single moment's peace. At one moment this would seem a very clever epigram. But the next moment, the epigram was only a collection of words, without meaning and clothed with preciousness.

He remembered his earlier life, when he had been rootless and languid and irresponsible. He understood now that he had only been afraid. He would always be afraid. Of what? He would always hate. Whom? And why? He did not know.

Tonight, as he rolled home in his carriage, his thoughts were dark and confused, and he recognized the signs of a particularly bad mood. He reached the slope that rose to Hilltop, and he saw nothing of the countryside; he did not even see Alfred's house. The road rose up gently, rounded a sharp curve. Philip was strolling along the side, frolicking with a small white dog.

Jerome's first impulse was to drive on, looking straight ahead. Then a second impulse came, and he ordered the coachman to stop. Hearing his voice, Philip turned; then, seeing the occupant of the carriage, he smiled with natural and genuine pleasure, whistled to the dog, and turned back.

"Jerome!" he exclaimed, reaching the carriage.

"Well, Philip," said Jerome, slightly embarrassed. He stepped out of the carriage and extended his hand to the younger man. Philip took his hand warmly and smiled up at him.

"It's been a long time, Jerome," he said.

"Yes, hasn't it?"

"I'm so glad to see you," said Philip, after a moment, and with deep and sincere simplicity.

Jerome was suddenly surprised and taken aback. He was glad to see Philip! He looked at his cousin with a sort of astonishment. Philip had become a man. He stood on equal ground with Jerome. He was no longer a pathetic boy. He regarded Jerome steadfastly, and with a gentle smile, and there was something in that smile which mysteriously lightened the blackness of Jerome's mood and alleviated his pain. He pressed Philip's hand hard before releasing it.

"You've grown up, Philip," he said. Then, quite irrelevantly, he added: "I'm glad to see you!" To be with Philip like this was like coming in out of a storm into a safe quiet place. Of course, the sensation was absurd, but Jerome held to it.

"You are back home for good?"

"Yes. Yes, I am sure of that."

"I am glad."

Again they looked at each other intently. Something is wrong with Jerome, thought Philip. The old restlessness and impatience are stronger in him than ever. Physically, he hasn't aged much. It is something else. It is something which is incurable, I suspect. He is afraid of something. I have a feeling he is bedevilled by fear, and doesn't know what he fears. What does he want? What is he running away from?

The silence was becoming a little awkward. But still, Jerome did not want to leave Philip. He said: "Amalie has told me that you intend to visit Hilltop. Could you have dinner with us tomorrow evening?"

Philip hesitated. Then he said, quietly: "Yes. Yes, I think I can. Thank you."

There was no embarrassment in his look, or in his words, and Jerome thought: But he never was a fool. You could always rely upon Philip to do the natural and reasonable thing.

A most peculiar warmth and friendliness brightened in him.

"I'd like you to see my bank," he said, "and the factories. We've made progress in these years, Philip."

Philip smiled again. He eyed Jerome with searching but compassionate curiosity.

"Thank you. I accept your invitation at once. In fact, I intended to write to you for permission."

"You've been away so much you could hardly know what has been going on," said Jerome. Philip detected a kind of pathetic boastfulness in his voice.

"Yes, I see there have been many changes. I want to know about them."

Philip's face was polite and interested, but there was a quizzical gleam in his dark eyes which suddenly brought William Lindsey to Jerome's mind. Yes, it was true: Philip, for all his darker coloring, startlingly resembled his great-uncle in character. There was a quietness about him, a balance, a humor, a profound thoughtfulness, which made Jerome conscious of an aching sadness in himself, and a deeper attraction warmed in him towards the younger man.

Jerome laughed a little. "Tell me, Philip, do you quote a great deal?"

Philip was not puzzled or confused by this extraordinary remark. He understood at once. His smile made his eyes sparkle. He turned a little and glanced down at the valley, where the chimneys of the factories still smoked restlessly against the sky.

"Yes. Sometimes. In fact, I could quote something now. I was just thinking of something which Benjamin Franklin once said about natural wealth: 'There seem to be but three ways for a nation to acquire wealth. The first is by war, as the Romans did, in plundering their conquered neighbors. This is robbery. The second by commerce, which is generally cheating. The third by agriculture, the only honest way, wherein man receives a real increase of the seed thrown into the ground, in a kind of continual miracle wrought by the hand of God in his favor, as a reward for his innocent life and his virtuous industry.' "

His voice was casual, easy, and pleasant. But Jerome slowly flushed. He said: "I often wondered how it was possible for my father to memorize so many quotations. You seem to have acquired the gift. Is it a prodigious memory, or an inability to form original thoughts? After all, something must fill a void."

Philip burst out laughing. And Jerome, who had begun to boil with anger, suddenly found himself laughing too.

"Old Ben was still caught in the last retreating wave of feudalism," said Jerome.

"I never liked feudalism. But it had its points," said Philip. "However, if you don't care for Franklin, I could regale you with a little Thoreau and Emerson."

Jerome lifted his hand in mock alarm. "My God, no. I can quote them myself. *Ad nauseam*." He paused. "I hear you're going into the old bank, Philip."

"Yes. In September." Philip's tone was tranquil.

Jerome was embarrassed again. "You look well," he remarked.

"Oh, I am. My constitution is really very sturdy, in spite of the loving convictions of my friends."

Philip was all poise. It was Jerome whose embarrassment was becoming acute. And yet, he did not want to leave Philip.

He glanced at his carriage. "We can expect you, then, tomorrow night?"

Philip nodded. "And, if you don't mind too much, I'd like to make a tour of your fine bank, and of the factories, too, tomorrow. Unless you are busy."

"I want you to see them." Jerome climbed into the carriage. "Until tomorrow." He touched the brim of his hat and was driven on. It was only by a strong effort that he prevented himself from looking back. It seemed to him that he was leaving behind him a warm quiet spot, where he had momentarily been safe and at rest.

Philip watched him go, thoughtfully, all the pleasantness ebbing from his face. He sighed, rubbed his chin with William Lindsey's old gesture, whistled to his dog, and continued his walk.

CHAPTER FIFTY-ONE

Philip created a minor furore when he entered the marble precincts of Jerome's bank the next morning. But his manner was dignified and natural, and his voice was calm when he requested a clerk to inform Mr. Lindsey that Mr. Philip Lindsey wished to see him.

Speculation buzzed among the few customers at the bank when Philip disappeared within the doors of Jerome's offices. It rose to excitement when Jerome and Philip appeared together with every evidence of simple amity and friendliness. Every eye followed the two men as they toured the bank. Philip was very interested, and apparently unaware of the excitement he and his cousin were creating or the winds of gossip which they were stirring up with such a vengeance.

The final stupefaction came when Jerome was heard to call for his carriage and the two finally went away together.

At two o'clock they were seen together at the hotel, where they settled down at Jerome's established table and ordered luncheon. The other diners stared at them furtively, tried to overhear their conversation. But Jerome and Philip drank a preliminary glass of whiskey-and-soda before dining, and their air was excessively interested, their absorption in each other complete. It was as if they were entirely alone. By half-past two, Alfred had heard the whole incredible story. He received the news impassively and apparently without interest. Philip had informed him that morning of his intention to visit the factories and the glaring new bank, and of the dinner invitation that evening. And Alfred, as usual, had made no comment, had only regarded his son somberly. However, his faith in Philip was very great; he knew his son too well to suspect any ulterior motives in all this.

"Well, now," said Jerome buoyantly, "what do you think of it all?"

Philip smiled. "I think Napoleon was a very clever man, when he spoke about the ease with which he could build up a new army. He said, if you remember, that all he had to do was to offer escape from button factories."

Jerome frowned. "Button factories?" His frown deepened. He shook his head, pretended not to understand. "I thought you'd be impressed by what you have seen, Philip. Can't you get a glimpse of it? The future of America is illimitable. The expansion of our industrial empire will eventually liberate man from stultifying labor, give him leisure in which to enjoy himself, educate himself and consider his position under government, free him from insecurity, and fill his home with comforts and pleasures."

He waited. Philip did not speak. He sipped his drink thoughtfully. Jerome's impatience heightened. Then Philip said: "I have often walked of late, through the prettified sections where the workers in those factories live. I see the workers sitting vacantly on their stoops, gazing into space. You could say that even if they, themselves, are incapable of mental evolution, having hardened into a stagnant mold under the pressure of their former life, their children will advance, become more aware."

He shook his head. "I don't think so, Jerome. Sorry. Something is lacking in all this. I'm not sure what it is. But increased leisure, better education, more money for—things— is not the answer. I think men like you are making a grave error, but I don't know what the error is. It is huge and frightening, but it eludes me just now."

He expected a contemptuous remark from Jerome, but to his surprise Jerome was regarding him searchingly, almost eagerly. Then Jerome said, with an attempt at flippancy: "You are going to be exactly like my father. Come on, now, you have reached some conclusion. What is it?"

"You've felt it yourself, haven't you, Jerome?" asked Philip shrewdly.

"I don't know what you are talking about." Jerome looked

at the steaks which had been placed before them. He ordered a bottle of wine. He informed Philip that he kept a stock of his own wine at the hotel, for his personal use.

Philip said: "Let us get back to the button factories. Frankly, Jerome, do you think they contain in them all that a man needs for excitement, for his instinctive demand for elation and joyous unpredictability, for his primitive desire for adventure? They produce things in volume, yes. But I do not feel that producing 'things' will give man all that his nature basically craves. Somewhere, in that theory, I think, the whole error lies.

"I only know that increasing invention, the mounting thunder of machines that one hears now all over America, robs man of something which is one of his most urgent needs, and I think you ignore that need at your peril, all of you who think that mere possessions and mere money can satisfy man's subjective cravings."

"You are getting metaphysical," said Jerome. But he listened acutely. "Go on. I will try to remember that you are a scholar, and not a practical banker yet." He smiled.

Philip had become more thoughtful than ever. "When we went on the tour of the factories this morning, you said, and with a great deal of truth, that the day of endless hand labor, of laborious individual work, has passed. I feel some misgivings when I think of that. For, say what you will, and with truth if you insist, I do believe that the worker in the old days had a personal pride in what he made with his hands, what he fashioned from his own peculiar imagination. Whatever he did, he stamped with his individuality; his work was the expression of his own spirit, and no matter what it was, it was his, whosoever the purchaser.

"I have an uneasy fear that factories rob, and will continue increasingly to rob, man of his pride, his need, his needful sense of importance, his belief in his own value. I believe that it was this natural pride which made him, in the old days, endure unbroken hours of work, either on the land or in his workshop, and endure them without rebellion, sullenness, or bitter restlessness. Jerome, I noticed today that the workers seemed profoundly unhappy——"

Jerome devoted himself to his dinner. "I ordered these steaks, especially," he said.

"Thank you," said Philip gravely, his eyes twinkling. He looked at his cousin with affection. He knows, he thought. That is what is bothering him.

Jerome glanced up. "Well, go on. The workers are profoundly unhappy——"

"Yes. Jerome, I've travelled all over Continental Europe. Especially in the Latin countries. The people are dreadfully poor, yes. They are ignorant, yes. But, strange to say, they seemed happy. Materialism and factories haven't touched these Catholic countries much, as yet. I think we have a clue there.

"The Roman Catholic Church has a regard for the individual and acknowledges that he is more than his environment, that he is a distinct and prideful soul, as well as a pair of hands. The Guilds of the Middle Ages understood this, as the Church understood it. Whatever the quarrel we have with feudalism, and it is a valid quarrel, at least the worker was never bored. He made living things; his life was not occupied with dead matter. Our new industry, then, must borrow the premise of the Roman Church, that it is the individual that counts, and that his soul must never be put in jeopardy by machines, no matter how competently they work, nor how smoothly, whatever the mass of the things they grind out, hour by stifling hour."

"I still think you are metaphysical," said Jerome. "Are you advocating dirt and ignorance and disease as against clean industrialization and enlightenment?"

Philip laughed gently. "No. And you don't misunderstand me, either. I like the sound of industry; I think you are quite right in your prophecies of the future, and I am glad of it. But I don't think we need make a choice between individual happiness and pride, and mass production and objective materialism. I think the answer lies in combining both of them, and that is a tremendous task for the future."

Jerome accepted one of Philip's cigarettes. He examined it with a smile. "Machine-made. You aren't consistent, Philip."

"Oh, nonsense. Don't try to deceive me, Jerome. You know what I'm getting at, for I feel it is in your own mind too. You know very well that the rising machine age is destroying the diversity of human life. And versatility is man's most prominent characteristic. Materialism and its new apostle, the machine, will eventually destroy it, unless——"

"Unless what?"

Philip shrugged. "I don't know yet. Now, I know there is no use in crying out against machines, in denouncing their contribution to the civilizing of the world. What I do fear is that we may never be able to inject into such mass production a sense of personal pride and worth, and the individualism which man must have, unless he is to become a mere servant to his own mechanisms. With that very dreadful potentiality, man might well embark on some madness, such as universal wars, to escape the mechanical life he has created.

"Sometimes I don't think we can inject individuality and pride into factories. It is incompatible. But somewhere, somehow, we must discover something outside the monotony of factories which will give man his necessary feeling of value, his necessity to believe that he is contributing to the world something peculiarly his own. Year by year, I feel, the immensity of the need will grow, in direct ratio to the expansion of the machine. The bigger the place the machine takes in life, the smaller will man be squeezed. But man is a spiritual explosive. It is most frightfully dangerous to compress explosives. They have a bursting point."

Jerome leaned his elbows on the table and stared with narrowed eyes at Philip through a haze of smoke. He said softly: "So, Philip, you too are joining the fight against the gray men? Good! The gray men have left the land; they are invading industry now, and I hate them wherever they are. I've felt this for a long time. I could not speak of it before to anyone. I'm damned grateful to you."

His voice, for all its softness, became more intense: "Contrary to what you may have heard, Philip, I am not 'money-mad.' I've gotten a lot of it, yes, but for money as a thing in itself I have never really cared. I got along very comfortably on quite a small sum in New York and in Europe. Don't ever believe that my New England papa was lavish with the cash!"

He paused. "Yes, I discovered that a great deal of money was not necessary to a man's happiness, especially money that came to him easily. Money earned by individual effort is the only money that contains any element of personal satisfaction. That may be a pious aphorism, but it is still true."

Philip listened gravely, nodding his head. The rapport between the two men strengthened. Jerome was very excited. He looked at Philip with an expression that kindled his dark features.

He said: "I, too, have been having my fears, Philip. I have felt, with you, that the expansion of the machine is lessening man's sense of his innate integrity. I know that emotion is the basis of all men's lives. And all their happiness and emotion and drama are being sucked out of them by mechanisms. My friends would think me a heretic. But they are gray men, without imagination. Well, what is the answer? Have you come to any conclusion?"

Philip sighed. "I don't know, either. Is it heightened activity of religion? Must religion be revitalized in America? Is it a deliberately quickened interest in politics, for every man? Is it an expansion of his mind, so that he may realize that the welfare of all other men is his personal responsibility? Is it increased education, an artificially stimulated pleasure in the arts? I still don't know. I only know that man will now have to find an active life apart from his work, for his work has, in mass production, been necessarily robbed of all personal significance. Man's emotions can't be indefinitely suppressed. I think the first step must be greatly decreased hours of work in factories, so that the monotony won't drive him mad."

"Yes. I know that. The men work in the Riversend factories nine hours a day. I put that through, myself. But you've seen their faces during their hours of leisure. It's damnably confusing."

They finished their coffee in silence. Then Philip said: "I'm only a tyro. Perhaps I'm not a practical man. I really know very little about all this. I only feel something threatening in the air. I hope I haven't disturbed you too much, Jerome."

"No," said Jerome somberly. "You've only put into words what I've been suspecting subconsciously."

"I only know," said Philip, "that man can't live objectively all of the time, without danger to himself and to the whole world. There must be some outlet for his more powerful self, his subjective self. He must have some escape from the button factories. If he doesn't find it, we'll face catastrophe."

CHAPTER FIFTY-TWO

Philip looked about him slowly and penetratingly as he sat beside Jerome in the latter's carriage, which was carrying them up to Hilltop.

He had not come this way for ten years. He remembered this particular old Norwegian elm which stood by the road, its bearded trunk green with moss, its heavy limbs flung out like sinewy arms, massive with leaves. He saw how it had grown and thickened; it was a beloved friend. He remembered this small sunken depression ringed about with twisted oaks; he had lain in the thick grass there and watched the birds busy about their nests. Here was the spring from which he had drunk, holding the bright cold water in his hands and watching it run, like quicksilver, through his fingers. The carriage climbed higher and higher. There was the copse of pines, almost black against the red sunset, their forms solemn and still. And now there was Hilltop, gray and square, all the windows glittering with scarlet fire, the lawns vividly green about it. The ruddy roofs of the barn were as he remembered them, and the weathercock, and the old walls of the garden, shadowed by the drifting frail green of the willows. That might be Charlie barking in the rear. But Charlie, he knew, had been dead for several years.

Home, he thought. He was suddenly profoundly grateful to his father that he had not sold Jerome his interest in this dear house. Jerome might think it sheer malice. But Philip knew it was not. The roots of all the Lindseys had driven deep into this earth; their thoughts had grown over it like the very ivy which covered the walls. Philip, in whom a sense of permanence lived as it did not live in either Amalie or Jerome, looked at the house with a passionate contentment. Some day, he felt with an instinctive intensity, he would live here again.

Jerome, always so clairvoyant with regard to the thoughts of others, knew something of the emotion of the younger man beside him. He smiled, and now with sympathy. He let Philip look without disturbing him with so much as a word or the slightest gesture.

Amalie, in soft gray silk taffeta, looped and braided and draped, was waiting for them with the children. She was slightly nervous. When Jerome had informed her last night that he had invited Philip for dinner, she had regarded him searchingly. Jerome was not given to doing things on impulse, and she suspected most of his motives.

But she saw, though with faint apprehension, that as they descended from the carriage Jerome was all affability to Philip. She had warned Mary to behave sedately tonight, and she came forward slowly with the children, smiling, holding the two by their hands. Little Mary was dressed in her best frock of white muslin and lace, and was wearing white stockings, while a white ribbon tied back her silvery hair. Young William, fresh from his tub, was warm and sleepy and flushed, his dark curls a tangle on his round head.

Philip thought: What a pretty picture they make! Mary, with her large blue eyes which seemed to fill her face, and the mass of smooth hair which fell to her waist, made him think of

Alice in Wonderland. As for the boy, he reminded Philip of the miniature of Jerome at the age of six which had been one of Mr. Lindsey's treasures.

The children were presented to him, and he acknowledged their presence with grave courtesy. Little William, usually shy with strangers, peeped at him with interest, while Mary shook hands with him primly. Yes, it is a very prim miss, thought Philip, smiling to himself, but one capable of secret storms. New England storms, added Philip mentally, bleak and cold and glittering ice.

He watched as Jerome kissed his daughter with great tenderness, his son with casual affection.

"Philip, I'm so glad," said Amalie simply, as she touched his hand. He knew she was sincere. Her purple eyes were quite brilliant in her strongly molded face. She sent the children away then, and she and Jerome and Philip entered the house through the heavy oaken door so clear in his memory. She engaged Jerome in light conversation in order that Philip might look his fill in the cool dimness of the hall.

"Nothing has changed," he said at last.

Amalie glanced about vaguely. "Hasn't it?" she murmured.

The grandfather clock struck seven. Philip stood in silence and listened to every melodious note until it died away. How often he had heard those notes, and how many scenes they recreated in his memory! Here was the library, now. It would not have surprised him had he seen Mr. Lindsey's tall and emaciated figure in that old red-leather chair and he heard his quiet cool voice.

Everything was poignant to him: the tall French windows, which were only frames for outdoor scenes of gardens, trees and grass, the high shelves of books bound in blue and red morocco, the long oaken table with its old lamp, the immense fireplace, cold now, and surmounted by the portrait of Jerome's mother. How strange it was that a mere set of andirons, the mere drape of a remembered curtain, the mere smell of flowers and earth and trees, the mere dull patina of panelled walls, could strike so passionately on a heart!

He sat down on a chair where he had sat a thousand times, and all its contours were familiar to him. He drank sherry from a glass whose intricately cut surface made him raise it, as he had done so often before, to catch the light on its prismatic facets. One of Mr. Lindsey's books, a thin volume of Keats, lay open on the round oak table beside him. It might have been laid there by the old man only an hour ago. His rack of pipes was here still, burnished, dimly fragrant with his special brand of tobacco. Something perilously close to grief clouded Philip's eyes for a moment. And so he missed the glance of understanding which passed between Amalie and Jerome.

They talked together amicably and with laughter, and to Philip the past ten years seemed like a dream. At any moment now his father or Dorothea might enter. When he heard the dinner-gong he did not start. It was natural and right that he should hear it. He had never been away.

It was Jim who opened the dining-room doors, and Philip stopped to speak to him, to shake hands with him. Jim, like oak, had merely darkened, become more weathered. "It's good, that, to see you again, Mr. Philip," said Jim. And Philip answered, with a strange smile: "Nothing has changed, Jim, not even you."

It seemed odd to him that only three places were set at the table, and a kind of psychic restlessness filled him. Jerome sat in old Mr. Lindsey's place now, and Amalie in Dorothea's. As for Philip, he sat where his father had sat; he wished they had set his place where once it had been. Then he could have seen the heavy mahogany sideboard with its remembered silver. Now he was depressed, for this was the first strangeness he had encountered, and it was wrong. But he fixed his attention on the old silver bowl in the center of the table, filled with roses. The same roses he had known; they had not withered nor dropped a leaf. He smiled.

Amalie, who had expected some constraint, was happy to discover that there was none between Jerome and Philip. But then, Philip had always been tactful and diplomatic; his manners had always been so gracious, so in command of the immediate moment. He is a gentleman, thought Amalie, with fond gratitude. She had never found Philip's deformity repugnant; in truth, like all others who came to know him, she never saw it. She saw only the large, well-formed head with its thick dark hair, crisp with waves, as was her own son's hair. She saw only the high broad forehead below it, a truly noble forehead, the black thoughtful eyes set deeply and strongly in their large sockets, the dark slender face and aquiline nose, the good firm mouth with its lines of humor and tolerance. If that head was settled too low in broad and crooked shoulders, it did not matter in the least. One saw only that fine face, which resembled Jerome's so startlingly and yet was so much more mature, so much quieter and more reflective.

Philip's thoughtful nature, so gentle and yet so profound,

his mind, so tolerant and so just and so subtle, filled Amalie with peace and contentment. She knew that he had depths of sternness in him, but no malice, no implacability. He would always understand rather than blame. He was a good man. It came to Amalie, with astonishment, that it was a strange and excellent thing to know a good man. Such a man was "the shadow of a great rock in a weary land."

Jerome, she saw, was not insensible to Philip's qualities. He talked to Philip with a simplicity and sincerity she had not heard from him for a long time, if ever. He seemed to take pleasure in Philip's company; some of the restlessness had left his eyes, the darting expression of seeking and dissatisfaction. She listened to their voices with contentment, and wished sadly that Philip might always sit at this table. It would be a boon to Jerome.

They sat on the terrace in the twilight after dinner, sipping brandy. Philip watched the lavender shadows stealing over the earth; he watched the silver curve of the moon rising over the copse of pines. The murmur of the trees was music in his ears. It did not seem possible that he must leave this dear place and go—home? This was home.

He must leave soon for his exile. He listened courteously while Jerome spoke of his children, and particularly of Mary. "The minx has quite a musical gift," he said, with an elaborate affectation of amused indulgence.

Philip was immediately interested. "I should like to hear the child play," he said. "But, of course, it is too late."

Jerome rose with alacrity. "No. I don't think so. Has she gone to bed, Amalie?"

Mary had indeed gone to bed, but Amalie went to fetch her. The girl came down swathed in the white silk ruffles of a pretty dressing gown, her blue eyes wide and bright. Philip took her hand, and speaking to her in the tone of pleading apology he might have used to a woman, said: "Mary, I am so sorry to disturb you, but I have heard that you play splendidly. Would it be too much if you played just one selection for me, before I go?"

The faintest of blushes ran over the child's face; she dropped a small curtsey. "Thank you. It will give me pleasure," she replied, with the artificial poise of a well-bred young girl. She smiled at Philip primly, and without embarrassment sat at the piano. A servant had lit the great gas chandelier in the music room. Philip regretted this; he much preferred the old soft candles sparkling among crystal. This bare bald light, faintly flickering, did not please him.

Mary flung back her hair with that stiff precision of hers which Philip found so enchanting. Then a look of absorption came into her eyes, a dreaming look. Her small white hands moved softly over the keys, seeking and murmuring. Philip began to recognize a theme of Chopin's. But the child was improvising; it was as if her mind wandered among the beautiful remembered thoughts of others and was constructing from them a new pattern of her own.

Philip listened and was astonished. The technique was both childish and mature; a little run of notes here, infinitely sweet but simple and uncertain, and then a few bars, strong, sure, original, rushing from the keys with a fervent and triumphant sound as though they came from the passionate meditations of a woman. Mary's head was thrown back; it was evident that she was not aware of her parents or of Philip. She was entranced in some dream of her own. Her delicate profile was stern and pale, almost as if hypnotized in its rigidity. It seemed hardly possible that that melodious thunder of notes came from those small frail hands. Philip drew closer to her, his head bent and listening, watching the child intently. She did not see him; she was aware of nothing but her music. Beyond the windows the night was still and warm and dark; the music invaded it like a loud and harmonious voice.

Then abruptly the piano was silent. It was as if some beautiful and violent meditation had ceased before it had come to any conclusion. Mary turned from the instrument, and her silvery curtain of hair fell shyly over her cheeks. She looked at her father.

Jerome smiled at her proudly, then turned to Philip. "Completely undisciplined, of course, but her teacher says she has talent. What do you think?"

"Extraordinary," said Philip. He regarded the girl with gravity, then was still. She stood up, hesitated. Then she said in her soft, light voice: "My mama says you play, too. Would you play for me?"

Philip bowed. "It will give me the greatest pleasure, my dear."

He sat down before the piano. Here was the nick he remembered, below middle C, a deep dark indentation of obscure origin in the old mahogany. The four yellowed keys in the next octave had deepened in tint. He remembered a servant attempting to bleach them with a solution of lime. He remembered, too, the rich sheen of the wood, the way the stool wabbled a little to the left, so that he had had to brace his foot to remain steady. He touched the keys, and they came to life under his fingers as if in eager response to an old friend.

He began to play the second part of the first movement of Schubert's Symphony No. 8 in B minor, the allegro moderato. Now the keys responded with a great ardent cry, a wild and discordant imploring that tore at something primitive and terrible in the human heart. It was an invocation, threatening and savage, to primordial gods, a protest of terror and defiance both heroic and despairing. Then, mingling with these cries moved a gentler and more majestic theme, soft and compassionate, as if strange and nobler gods answered, and one saw an agonized and barbaric head turning in chaos to listen, to be silenced, to drop clenched and uplifted hands. Louder, deeper, sweeter, spoke the gods of pity and beauty and tenderness, so that the fury sank into nothingness, and the voice of barbarism, uncertain at first, entered the prayer of peace in faltering murmurs.

Mary had moved so close to Philip that now she almost touched him. She fixed her eyes on his face; her mouth had opened slightly, as if she found it difficult to breathe. Jerome had taken Amalie's hand; she felt its involuntary hard pressures, its heat and tremulousness. But he, too, looked only at Philip.

The sweetness and majesty were now almost unbearable, stately and exultant. Mary's face was wet with tears. She bent her head, and a long pale lock of her hair touched Philip's shoulder. When he had played the last note and had turned to her, smiling, she looked into his eyes. His smile abruptly disappeared. He lifted his hand as if to touch her, but she fell back, made a faint whimpering sound, turned suddenly and ran from the room.

"I have frightened the poor little creature," he said, rising from the stool, and looking at Amalie and Jerome with concern.

"Oh, no," said Amalie. "She is so sensitive, and music often disturbs her. But I've never seen her so moved; she is such a repressed little thing."

"All New England," said Jerome. He seemed abstracted. "You certainly haven't lost your gift, Philip. And now you are going into that bank!"

Philip's expression became withdrawn and polite. "A man has to be practical," he said, with formality.

His host and hostess regarded him in perturbed uncertainty.

He drew out his watch and glanced at it. "I must really go now," he said. "And thank you for a delightful evening." He paused. "Are you sure I haven't frightened the child?"

They reassured him with affection. Jerome called his carriage for Philip. They shook hands. Jerome said: "I have enjoyed your coming, Philip. Please come often. There are so many things we need to discuss. And, in the meantime, will you think of some solution to our problem?"

CHAPTER FIFTY-THREE

When Philip arrived home, he found his father reading in the chill library where summer heat never seemed to penetrate.

Alfred put aside his book, the *Meditations* of Marcus Aurelius, and greeted his son affectionately. Philip sat down on one of the stiff chairs, always so unfamiliar to him. Alfred suggested a glass of wine, an unusual procedure, and Philip assented. His father appeared very tired and gray, but gentle.

"I missed you tonight, Philip," he said. He looked about at the forbidding walnut walls, at the narrow and gloomy windows, at the crimson Brussels carpet. He added, in a lower voice: "Was it so hard to come back here?"

Philip glanced at him swiftly, with hidden compassion. As his father's character mellowed, became softer, more perceptive, less dogmatic and didactic, rounded by grief and by long secret meditations and uncertainty, Philip's love for him increased.

He replied, with his customary simplicity: "Not too hard. You were here, waiting for me."

Alfred turned the wineglass about in fingers that trembled slightly. Then he said, almost inaudibly: "Thank you, Philip."

"Wherever you are, Father," Philip continued, "will be home for me."

Alfred said nothing. He could not speak.

After a while he put aside his glass of wine, almost untouched. He stared at it somberly. "I don't like this house, Philip. I don't know what's wrong with me. When we built it, it seemed to me that it was everything I wanted. It is my fault if it is what it is—cheerless, cold, uninviting. I don't know how I came to arrange it so. There is not one room which I did not expressly order——"

He sighed, slowly turned his eyes from wall to ceiling to

floor. He looked at every formal table, every lamp, every chair. Then he shook his head numbly.

"There are not enough people here," said Philip, with pity. "But I am home now, for good. We must have some parties, young people and such. A house needs the sound of life."

Alfred sighed again. "It needs life in its inhabitants. I am afraid I have never been very alive, Philip."

Ah, but you are now, thought Philip, with sad tenderness. It seemed to him that his father had shed some horny external skin, and had emerged vulnerable and susceptible to new winds and stronger airs.

"Is Hilltop the same as ever?" asked Alfred, in a low voice, gazing at his polished boots.

"Yes. Just the same. I expected you to come into the library or the dining-room at any moment. It seemed wrong that you were not there. I sat in your place."

To his first surprise, then not at all to his surprise, Alfred looked up swiftly, and he smiled. "Good. I am glad of that, Philip. Yes, I am very glad of that. It seems proper."

His square, strong face had brightened. His tired hazel eyes beamed. "It was probably an accident, of course. I can hardly think—they—did it by design."

Philip told another of his compassionate lies: "On the contrary, they pointed the fact out to me, called my attention to it."

The light in Alfred's eyes increased. "Ah, she would do that! It is just like her. She always understood. I didn't, then. But—Amalie—could always be relied upon for the delicate and sympathetic touch. Yes, she always understood."

Philip had not thought so in the least, but now he began to wonder.

"Uncle William always remarked on Amalie's subtlety," continued Alfred, with rising animation. "I didn't understand at all. I am afraid I was a heavy, dull fool, Philip. If I had had any perception at all, any delicacy, things might have—" Now his face clouded with its old somber grief.

Alfred stood up. He walked up and down several times, slowly and ponderously, his hands in his pockets. "In those days, I thought only of success, of making money, of—of—" He stared at his son with acute astonishment. "Of 'justifying' myself, of 'proving' myself. What was I trying to prove? It seems very vague to me now, very puerile. You see, I always felt so insecure, so inferior. I think I wanted to prove to Uncle William that he was not making a mistake in me."

He paused by the table near his chair, lifted the wineglass, drank quickly. Philip sensed an excitement in him, an involuntary compulsion.

"Only a very strong, a very wise man, Philip, can rise above his early beginnings, rid himself of the wisps of self-doubt, the heart-burnings and struggling ambition. Only such a man can go on, forgetting; only he can grow and expand in character. I was not such a man. I could only remember how poor my father was, how vague and chronically unsuccessful, and how he was Uncle William's beneficiary. I remember my shame, in my boyhood, that I had a father who received what was virtual charity from his brother. And I think I felt that I—must have some of his character in me. When Uncle William gave me my opportunity, I wanted to show him that I wasn't such another as my father but had something of Uncle William himself in me. I—I tried too hard, Philip. I could never forget. I had only one drive in me. I drove myself too much, too fast, too mercilessly."

He lifted the decanter of wine and poured his empty glass full again. He held the glass in his hand. He regarded his son with oddly fervid eyes.

"Every other potentiality I had was suppressed in the one vehement desire to please Uncle William, to make up to him for his disappointment in Jerome. That is what I thought then. But now I know it was to hide my secret fear of my own lack of confidence, my own insecurity, my own belief that I wasn't much of a man, after all. Not endowed above the average with brains. Not imaginative. Only a dull, dull fool, obdurate and greedy."

Philip leaned back in his chair and listened quietly and with profound attention. Alfred saw the love and comprehension in his dark eyes, and something rose up in his throat. His voice was thick when he went on:

"That was behind my hatred for Jerome. It seems so odd to me now, knowing this, after all these years. Jerome had self-confidence; he always knew what he wanted. He—he was strong, Philip. Nothing external mattered to him, neither money, nor 'self-proof' nor 'making his mark.' He was secure in himself."

Philip stirred. "No. I know now that that is a fallacious idea."

Alfred stared at him. He seemed about to protest, then was silent. He looked at the ruby fluid in the glass he held. "I see," he said softly. "Yes, I think I see."

He glanced about the room, slowly, thoughtfully. "It is very strange. I don't seem to want anything very much any longer, Philip."

He added, trying to smile: "Is it because I am getting old, my dear boy, or just very tired?"

Philip shook his head. "You aren't fifty yet. You are neither old nor tired. I just think that you have become strong and wise. Uncle William had that strength and wisdom."

Alfred did not speak for a moment, then he said: "Thank you, Philip. Thank you. I have never heard anything so kind before."

There was a stern rustle at the door, and Dorothea entered the library. Philip rose. But Dorothea ignored him, outraged as she was.

"It is getting late, Alfred," she said. "You know you will have one of your headaches if you don't go to bed at once. You mustn't let those who are so inconsiderate of your feelings and desires impose upon you."

She stood there, tall, gaunt, stately, her accusing gaze fastened implacably upon Alfred, and waited. She was accustomed to having Alfred say, almost with meekness: "You are right, Dorothea."

But Alfred only smiled at her fondly. "I am not in the least tired, Dorothea, and I don't think I shall have a headache. It is not eleven o'clock yet. I am quite wide awake."

Dorothea's eyelids flickered. Philip was watching her with amusement.

"And Philip is not imposing upon me, my dear. He and I were having a most interesting discussion."

"Doubtless," said Dorothea, with acid irony. "But I am not interested in the 'interesting discussions' of those who have so little proper regard for their fathers, so little understanding of propriety and decency. I refuse to acknowledge their existence. They are outside the pale of my understanding."

Philip, the tactful, did not attempt to protest. He knew that Dorothea was impatiently awaiting an opportunity to turn upon him, to upbraid and denounce him. When he did not give her this opportunity, she was nonplussed and angered. She tossed her graying head.

"Are you going upstairs now, Alfred? I should like to turn off the gas. One cannot leave such things to ignorant servants."

Philip waited with quite an absurd anxiety. Would his father, as usual, see the "justice" of Dorothea's remarks, and give in?

Then Alfred spoke, and Philip felt an almost equally absurd relief. "Now, Dorothea, I think I am quite capable of turning off the gas. I won't blow it out, I promise you. Philip and I haven't finished our discussion. But, please don't trouble yourself to wait until we go up. You get up early, and I think you ought to retire now."

Dorothea drew in her breath. Then she turned rigidly, lifted her head high, and went out of the room.

Alfred watched her go. He was smiling. He said: "Dorothea is a good woman, bless her, but somewhat inflexible. Sit down, Philip, and tell me more about Hilltop. Have they changed the gardens, or cut down that old elm that used to scrape the roof on windy nights?"

CHAPTER FIFTY-FOUR

The winter day was all fiery blue and white. The holidays, long since over, had been forgotten, and the townsmen looked forward to the spring. Jerome, from his office windows, could see the thick white plush of the snow on the great lawns which surrounded the bank. The two cypresses stood, dark green pillars, against all that purity and blueness, like guardians at a temple.

The office was warm and pleasant, spluttering logs of applewood roaring in the fireplace. Jerome and Philip and General Tayntor sat at a small table and sipped brandy. Papers were spread upon the table, papers which the General was regarding skeptically, his white brows raised high towards the thin white hairline above his wrinkled forehead.

The General had weathered, rather than aged. His long and emaciated body had lost little of its soldierly erectness, its hard and bony contours. His wicked and ruddy face had thinned, but it still wore its air of twinkling cunning and knowingness, and his tiny blue eyes were still vivid and sparkling.

He tapped the papers with a lean finger. "This will cost a lot of money, this infernal 'Riversend Community' of yours," he said. "Who's to foot the bill, eh? Ho! 'Riversend Community,' by God! What for? Nonsense. Who cares?"

He said, leaning forward to accept a light for his cigar from Philip: "A lot of money. There'll be rumors about the bank.

411

Can't afford it. No bank can afford it."

Philip glanced humorously at Jerome, who said: "You've got a lot of money, General. You're almost a millionaire, and you have me to thank for it, to a great extent. What the hell do you want with all that money, anyway?"

The General grinned. "You mean, I'm an old man, and I've got enough? Nobody ever has enough. Money's a fine substitute for what sentimentalists think children are. Children! Waste of time. Wish I'd known it before. What use are children to a man?"

He turned to Philip. "What's all this? What does your dad think of this, your being here as cosy as a bug in a rug?"

Philip said, smiling: "My father now reads Marcus Aurelius."

This tickled the General immensely. He shouted: "The accountants ought to examine his ledgers then, by God! Marcus Aurelius! Haven't come to that yet myself." But he eyed Philip curiously. "He's got no objection to all this friendliness, eh?"

Jerome frowned, but Philip seemed amused. "My father respects my judgment."

"First time I ever heard of Alfred Lindsey respecting anybody's judgment but his own. Think I'll mention this to the State examiners."

Philip indicated the papers. "I'm willing to put up twenty thousand dollars of my own—not from my father's bank, either. Jerome will do the same, or more. We thought you might wish to contribute, for the good of the community. The Widow Kingsley is willing to advance ten thousand, and there are others. When you consider it over a long range, the scheme will pay its own dividends. The workers, as Jerome has shown you, are really invested capital. I'm surprised that employers haven't realized that before. When a man is clean, interested and happy, and has something to look forward to besides his daily monotonous work, he produces more. It is boredom and hopelessness that make a worker restless and discontented, and that lead directly to large labor turnovers, indifference, wastefulness and resentment."

"Visionary! Anarchistic! What's a damned worker for? He's expected to work, and that's all, and the hell with him."

Philip said coolly: "We are making an experiment, an experiment in humanity. An experiment in human coöperation."

"Ho! Damn humanity! I've said it all my life, and I say it again. It's come to a pretty pass when you pay a man more than he's worth, then must worry about his soul! His soul, by

412

God! This cattle hasn't any soul. Isn't it enough that Jerome's been kicking the employers of labor in the backsides so hard that he's got hours reduced to nine a day, instead of the usual ten or twelve? What more do they want?"

"They want to live, too, General. Yes, I know there will always be drawers of water and hewers of wood who won't ever want anything besides their pay and their sleep and their women. But there is also an element among them who want more, and must have it, not only for their sakes, but for ours, too."

The General looked from Philip to Jerome suspiciously, his eyes narrowed so tightly that they almost disappeared. He seemed highly edified. "It's a cute thing, this, Jerome going in for philanthropy. Can't reconcile it with what I know of him."

Jerome said, with a smile: "I'm thinking of myself. I don't like the gray men who are now beginning to control American industry. I never liked the gray men who think only of profits and of money. I've studied them down through the centuries, from the time when they were great landowners, and now when they are industrialists and financiers. I hate them. Having no life or joy of their own, they try to destroy these things in everyone unfortunate enough to be in their power. But I see you don't understand, General."

The General was silent, his eyes still screwed up, a long, slit-like grin on his mouth. He puffed at his cigar. Finally he said: "I remember a talk we had long ago, Jerome. When my girls and I came for tea at Hilltop. It was about a dream that the young men had, in America. Do you recall my saying that I had had that dream, too, but couldn't remember what it was? It was a nice dream, and it was like living in a perpetual state of drunkenness. But I don't remember what it was."

He scratched his ear. "Funny, I remember how I felt about it, but I still don't remember what it was!" He paused. "You seem to have it still, and that's a very funny thing! Very, very funny. Come on, now. What is it? I'd like to remember it."

It was Philip, rather than Jerome, who answered: "I think, if you will pardon my sentimentality, that the dream is the universal welfare of men. It's very sad that men as they grow older lose that personal sense of responsibility towards the world. No one need forget that dream. It has been written down for many centuries, in the two Testaments. How long has it been since you've read the Bible, General?"

The General slapped his hand loudly on the table and burst out laughing. "A pair of parsons, by Jesus! I never thought to

413

see the day!" He turned to Jerome, and jeered: "You wouldn't have a Bible handy, would you?"

But Jerome only smiled. The General studied him sharply and with concentration. "Come on," he said. "What's behind this? It isn't love for humanity. I know you too well."

Jerome said: "You are right. It isn't. Rather, you could call it hatred for the kind of men I've always hated. The killers of joy and gaiety. The gospel-shouters of 'Work.'"

He stood up and began to walk up and down the room. "I meet these men regularly. I wonder, when I meet them, at their barrenness of heart, their drabness of imagination, their emptiness of soul. If they can find nothing better to do with their lives than work, then they had best be dead. One wouldn't mind, but they impose their dusty laws on others, too. These dreadful creatures, out of their sterility of mind, see only ashes and blank walls, and must work to shut their awareness of their own futility out of their consciousness. Worse, they try to imprison all other men in their jails."

He stood by the window, and continued, more softly: "We all have to work, but no one should work more than a few hours a day for his living. Soon we'll need no more than that. When the American frontier is entirely conquered, when all the cities are built and great highways have been riven through rock and mountain, America will have come of age, so far as material wealth is concerned. But if something revolutionary doesn't happen, the myth of work for its own sake will persist, to the ruin of the American mind and spirit.

"What will happen? As the machine age advances and becomes more powerful, such masses of things will be produced that the market will be glutted, and panics will follow. There will have to be some limit imposed on the amount of things which can be produced. Or the working week will have to be cut very short. Otherwise, America will be smothered under mountains of things—daily growing more trivial and worthless. Men will waste their lives making foolish trinkets and unnecessary and silly luxuries. And that will be a crime committed bloodily against the human spirit and its dignity."

The General scratched his ear more vigorously, but his eyes, fixed upon Jerome, were intent and curious.

Then Philip spoke: "I think what Jerome means is that a mechanical civilization does mortal violence to the subjective nature of man. Man cannot live by machines alone, nor by the things which they produce. He must have something else. Jerome, in our proposed Riversend Community, hopes to give the local workers that 'something else.' We can't do away with machines, and we don't want to. But we can do something for men, so that the machine doesn't make them serfs of mechanisms. Work is good only when it produces just sufficient bread for survival. When it produces more than that it is evil, and those who demand devotion to work are the enemies of man."

The General chuckled. "You'll get the parsons, as well as Wall Street, down on you for that! Doesn't the Good Book say that mankind was banished from the Garden and sent out to earn its bread by the sweat of its brow in the fields?"

"That's exactly what we mean," said Philip, with his usual charm. "Thank you, General. You've expressed it perfectly. We propose to give the workers in this community a chance to 'earn their bread by the sweat of their brows in the fields.' As an escape from the factories. That is just one of our plans. Jerome will buy two hundred acres of land to the west of Riversend, and allow every worker to buy an acre, on easy payments financed by this bank. The worker and his family will then raise whatever they wish on that land, flowers, vegetables, chickens. They will not be divorced from the land. We think it a very dangerous thing for men to be divorced from the land. If men must work in factories, they must have earth to stand on afterwards, their own earth. A constantly expanding urban society is cannibalistic. It's a threat to the peace of the world."

Jerome turned from the window. He and Philip looked at each other with strong affection and understanding. The General saw that look, and he chuckled again, inwardly, but with more kindness. He tapped the papers again.

"Well, I agree with you about the land, damn it. But what about this 'education' for the factory fellaheen? Teaching them to 'enjoy' books, by Christ! Teaching them what American citizenship means! Getting the parsons and the priests to help! They won't!"

"They will," said Philip positively. "There are one or two rock-bottom preachers who are horrified. But we've talked to several ministers, and to the two Catholic priests of this community. We had less trouble with the priests: the Roman Catholic Church understands that man cannot live by bread alone but must have something nourishing for his stronger subjective nature. So these good men are going to help us. They will conduct classes in one of our buildings, not religious classes exactly, but moral ones, full of interest. They will explain man's place in nature, his duty to others, his responsibility towards the rest of the world."

The General was silent. But he shook his head slightly, over and over.

Philip was becoming somewhat excited, though his voice remained quiet and firm:

"We've talked to local teachers and to others outside. We'll have classes in the skilled trades. We'll have music recitals, made up of workers who can learn to play various instruments. Silver-work will be taught. We'll have tinsmith shops, carpenter shops. Handicraft. Woodwork. Carving. We'll have a store where these things can be sold, at a profit to the workers. Or they will make the things for their own homes. We'll offer prizes every year for the best work, the best gardens.

"We'll have discussion groups, on politics. We'll make the workers see how necessary it is to have an intelligent electorate.

"All these things will be done after working-hours, on holidays, week-ends."

"My God!" muttered the General, as if dazed. "What rot! What nihilism!"

"Playgrounds for children, laid out and made by their fathers. And for the women, instruction in household matters, prenatal care, child care, cooking, sewing, participation in the County Fairs," said Philip.

"Visionary!" cried the General. "You'll have the whole country down on your necks! I never heard such nonsense! Who cares about these cattle? You'll be laughed out of existence."

Philip winked surreptitiously at Jerome. "What do you say, General? Will you donate a few thousand dollars for this? Think of your name in the newspapers as a benefactor of man! We're going to give the matter a lot of publicity."

The General said, waving his hand as if to brush away all this: "Who is going to build all these infernal buildings for your classes and your shops?"

"The workers themselves. There are good bricklayers and masons and carpenters among them. We've talked to them about it. You never saw such excitement."

"And the money? You'll need scads of money."

"I've told you: Jerome and I will put up twenty thousand apiece, or more, if necessary. And we hope that others like yourself will help."

The General stood up to shake out his coat-tails. "You're mad," he said. He scowled. "How much? I won't put up a cent more than five thousand dollars."

Philip and Jerome stumbled over each other in their haste to shake the General's hand. The General glared at them, shook his head, pulled away his hand abruptly. "I'm going demented in my old age," he said. "You can pray that I won't change my mind."

Then he laughed. "What do the boys who own the factories think of all this, eh?"

Jerome laughed in answer. "They went into a panic, until it was explained to them that this is a private project and will cost them nothing. Worse, however, was their fear that the workers would get 'uppity.' Forget that they were born to work for their masters. Yes, the boys are in a state. We'll prove to them that they are wrong."

"But what about industrialists in other cities and sections? They'll cut your hearts out, Jerome."

"That's something we'll fight when the time comes. Some rumor of all this has gotten about. That is why I went down to see Jay Regan last week, and Mr. Livingston, and others of my backers. They didn't approve. They said, as you have said, that this is 'revolutionary,' a 'dangerous experiment.' You see, they, too, think only of their profits. They have an idea that I am insane. I persuaded them to wait a year or two, and see for themselves. We've got to make it a success." He spread out his hands, with a rueful smile. "We'll need the help of all this community. For, if we go down, you'll all go down with us, General."

The General was immediately alarmed. "I thought so! Who the hell thought of this foul scheme, anyway?"

"I did," said Philip quietly. "Jerome knew something was wrong. I thought it all up myself. We finally worked out this plan together."

The General looked at him with an irate eye. "What could you expect of a damned scholar! A bookman!"

Philip smiled. "I went to Harvard, too, General."

"You never learned such things at Harvard!" cried the General. "I went there, myself, and never heard of it!"

"You'd be surprised what you can hear there now." Philip still smiled. "You'd be more surprised to hear that many thousands of men in America are seriously concerned with the growth of the machine in America, and what it will mean to the people. They know what unrelieved materialism can do to a nation. They have the evidence of history."

He looked at Jerome consideringly, as if to seek permission for what he would next say. Jerome nodded.

"As Jerome has explained, we'll have to make this a success. We're going ahead with it. No one can stop us. And we'll need the help of all of you who have money. You can't withdraw, General. You're too heavily invested with Jerome.

"But then, we called you here today because you are a perspicacious man, of understanding. We are relying on you to influence others, also."

"Blackmail, for a lot of visionary nonsense!" shouted the General.

"Have another brandy," suggested Philip, filling the General's glass again. "Very good brandy. And another cigar." He opened Jerome's silver box and pushed it invitingly towards the old soldier.

He said: "We are going to summon newspaper reporters from all over the country. With their artists. I think you can do the honors, General. You will be our spokesman. I understand a quite famous author is going to write a book about this, too. You'll be mentioned prominently."

"'Riversend Community'!" snorted the General. His face was very red and congested.

"With you as one of the directors," said Philip.

The General drank his brandy furiously, let Philip light his cigar. Then he paused, scrutinized Philip. The poor devil was deformed, but he had good blood in him, and the deformity was not hereditary. He would also have a fortune some day— Alfred's bank. The Lindseys were the best.

He said, with his usual disarming frankness: "Time you got married, you scheming devil. What about my Josephine? She wraps me in cotton. Hate it. I'm not dying yet. Ho! How old are you? Twenty-five, eh? She's not much older. Is it a match?"

CHAPTER FIFTY-FIVE

Amalie had been enjoying a novel highly recommended for its "sensibility, perception and deep insight into human nature." The critics had loved it. It was very popular. Amalie herself found it interesting and amusing until she read the artless phrase: "Lucille asked so little of life. She wanted only to be happy. A small, small thing."

At this monstrous absurdity, at this quintessence of all that was ludicrous and naïve, Amalie uttered a profane exclamation and flung the book far from her across the brick terrace, so that it landed with a satisfying smash against the trunk of a tree. "A small, small thing," the lady novelist had wistfully called "happiness." A free peach on a tree in a boundless orchard; a little shell on a beach; a buttercup beside a garden path! How could any human being be so precious, so ridiculous, so appallingly unaware of one single day in the agony of a world?

Happiness. Not even the founders of America had declared that happiness was an inalienable right of man. Only the "pursuit of it." *There* was wisdom, *there* was understanding, *there* was sad cynicism. One only pursued it. It was rarely, if ever, attained, and then only briefly, like the sun shining for a moment through a rack of dark clouds.

The fool, in his misery, believed that some malign fate kept him from dancing in a perpetual ecstasy. The malcontent believed some alignment of baleful men plotted to shut him out of the garden. The suffering, in their blind selfishness, believed all other men possessed of contentment, of money, of health, of joy. Only a few knew that there was no happiness, no peace, no real and enduring rapture, anywhere in the world. There was no happiness even in love. Men clutched at each other in a despairing darkness, and begged for reassurance. It was the pursuit of the impossible—the shadow of it—that constituted the hope. "A small, small thing," indeed! Oh, damn fools!

She herself was a "damn fool." But a wiser one now. And a much sadder one.

She stared at the mangled book she had thrown from her. A warm summer breeze fluttered its crushed pages pathetically. She felt a kind of compassion for the book and its ingenuous writer, and for all the others who believed in the easy attainment of the unattainable.

She knew now that the one most active and terrible force in the world was fear. It was fear that compelled men to seek happiness, as an agonized body seeks a narcotic. It was fear that developed civilizations, built monuments and started wars. It was behind all the irrationality and chaotic emotions that dogged mankind. It was the fountainhead of religion. It had conceived God, or become aware of Him. It was the mother of hatred.

The old prophets had known the power of fear. All the holy books recognized it for the power it was. Against it Moses had thrown up the fortress of the Ten Commandments, instinctively recognizing that law can be a great wall against wild uncertainty, that obedience to the demands of order, and stern regulation, can give men a sense of security. Law helped a man not to think. It substituted conduct for meditation, and so saved men from madness. The repetition of prayers, an established code from which it is dangerous to deviate, hypnotize men and dull the terror of their instinctive perceptions.

Was it Jesus, or someone else, who had said: "Perfect love casteth out fear"? But there was no perfect love. There were short periods of utter self-abnegation and self-sacrifice, and during those periods man forgot himself and his terror. But it was impossible for any but a saint to live in a perpetual state of "perfect love." For men had to live with themselves.

Amalie knew that, even more than most men, Jerome was tortured with fear. Fear of what? She did not quite know. But she knew it explained his life, his periods of brutal irritability, his equally irrational elations, his cruelties, his feverish plans and industry, his concern with Riversend. Doubtless, too, it had been behind his earlier almost paralyzed mode of living.

There were some men who, hounded by the universal fear, fortified their houses. There were others, more profoundly afflicted, who fortified the whole city about their house. Jerome was fortifying Riversend; it was the wall around his fortified home.

Amalie stared at the warm trees in the distance, shimmering in wind and sun. She, too, was always afraid. Her strong old courage was, she knew, the product of her fear. But she was not as afraid as Jerome. There was in her a kind of fatalism. She no longer expected happiness, and so, at times, could be almost tranquil.

Perhaps it is because I am not so intelligent as Jerome, she thought, with bitter amusement. The more conscious a man was, the more vulnerable he was, the higher were the walls he built to protect himself. But at the end his walls were nothing, his fortifications were nothing. "He that hath no rule over his own spirit is like a city that is broken down, and without walls."

Amalie thought of the years of her marriage to Jerome. In them she had known joy and laughter and delirium and excitement. But no happiness. She had been a fool to expect it. The nearest she had come to happiness was when she had been married to Alfred, she thought, and this thought made her sit upright as if suddenly and invisibly struck. Those few days following the almost fatal illness of Mr. Lindsey, so many years ago! When Alfred had sat beside her on the bed where she lay in her exhaustion, and had talked to her gently, telling her things he would never tell anyone else, and holding her hand, while she listened more with her heart than with her mind and her ears, she had come perilously close to peace and happiness. But she had never known them again. For there was no approaching Jerome. She saw him only as he wished to be seen at a particular moment. Or if in a moment of his abstracted defenselessness she came upon him, he would direct a reasonless anger and brutality upon her, as if she had caught him in a humiliating posture or an indecent act.

But Alfred had frequently, and humbly, indicated to her his wish that she look at his spiritual nakedness, and understand and pity his deformities.

He, too, had been afraid. But his fears had been superficial, almost childish. In some way, she now knew that he was no longer afraid of anything. She could not tell how she knew. Perhaps it was because Philip had told her some things obliquely.

But she had not, she thought, loved Alfred. Perhaps that had been because of her own fears, her own restlessness, which was the symptom of her fear. In Jerome she had instinctively recognized her own distrusts and alarms. Had they pooled their—cowardice? She did not know. Even now, their lives were full of tempestuous periods of almost desperate gaiety. This did not make for harmony and contentment. Perhaps she was growing old. But she longed now for such harmony and contentment. She longed for the security they would bring, but which, with Jerome, she would never know.

We should, she thought, teach our children not to fear anything, neither sorrow nor illness, death nor disappointment, grief nor pain. But first it was necessary for the parents not to fear. How was that possible? Of course, there was God.

She stood up restlessly and began to walk up and down the shaded terrace, her hands wrung together in an unconscious gesture of misery. How teach Mary and young William that events are only water flowing about the strong keel of the human spirit? How so fortify their souls that their sails might fly gallantly before any wind? Of course, there was God.

But God, Jerome had said, was a superstition, born of fear. Amalie shook her head despairingly. Yet he had also suggested that the children attend church. She sent them to the village Congregational church every Sunday. As yet, there was no way of telling whether they were becoming strengthened against fear. There was a world of churches, but the world remained terror-stricken and full of hatred. Was it because it had never really tried religion? The mouth might be full of the Name of the Lord, but the spirit could remain starved and unfed. Something was wrong. Pews were crowded, and men emerged, later, into the Sunday sun, and looked at their fellowmen with distrust and fear and hate. Were the shepherds false, the words they said meaningless? Never, as yet, had men tried God. Until they did, they would know fear, and destroy in their fear, and they would kill, and there would be no imagining their ultimate enormities.

She heard a child's steps running through the house; a door opened and slammed, and young William, almost nine now, came towards her, shouting and laughing. She looked at him with passionate fondness, and smoothed his thick dark hair. Then she caught him to her, and cried: "My darling, don't ever be afraid! Never, never be afraid! If you are afraid, you will be a bad man, and a cruel one, and there'll never be any peace in your house!"

CHAPTER FIFTY-SIX

Here, at least, thought Dorothea, it does not change.

She was rigorously pruning the lilac bushes of their withered blooms. They hung, brown and dry, on the green branches. One could depend upon a garden, which knew no changes but the seasons and in the repetition of the seasons only reaffirmed their changelessness.

Her garden was only thirteen years old, and Alfred had said that it took much more than thirteen years to make a garden. It was unlike Alfred, she reflected, to say things like that. It was not so much his words; there seemed always to be a deeper undertone to what he said these days. These days? Dorothea paused, the sharp knife in her hand. It had been many days. Strange, how insensible she had been!

She threw the dead blooms into the basket beside her. She looked at the walls of the garden, and then at the blank red face of the house. A sudden heavy depression overcame her. She shook her head. It had been only last night that Philip had read Alfred a most melancholy poem. Dorothea knew, and cared, little about poetry, but she had listened to this. She knew of its author, for he was very notorious and very shocking, and gentlefolk quite properly spurned him. His name was Algernon Swinburne.

The poem had filled her with a formless despair, and she had listened to it unwillingly. Worst of all, Alfred, too, had listened, leaning his elbow on the arm of his chair, and supporting his chin in his hand. Dorothea remembered clearly only one verse:

> "I am tired of tears and laughter,
>   And men that laugh and weep;
> Of what may come hereafter
>   For men that sow to reap;
> I am weary of days and hours,
> Blown buds of barren flowers,
> Desires and dreams and powers
>   And everything but sleep."

Incomprehensible gibberish! She could not understand why it haunted her with an eerie apprehension, why it threw a spectral and insubstantial light over her garden. She moved her shoulders stiffly and uneasily; her crinolined skirt creaked a little.

Had Alfred found it gibberish? Why had he sat there, so still, listening to Philip read? His face had been very quiet, but very strange. The years had thinned it, brought out unsuspected sharp modeling from under once-heavy flesh. He had sat there and looked at Philip, and his eyes had been too motionless, too fixed.

She glanced down at the basket which contained the dead cones of the lilac blooms. "Blown buds of barren flowers." She shivered. "Nonsense," she said aloud. That terrible poetry, with its note of wanton deathliness! Why did the very memory of it impart a forsaken aspect to her pretty and flourishing garden? Why did it hint of decay, of mortality, of "doubtful dreams of dreams"?

The warm sun moved behind a cloud, and now the garden was robbed of color. The roses bobbed ghostly heads in a low wind; the very trees were wan. Dorothea had the strangest sensation that she had stood here for a long time and had seen death come to the earth.

Change, she thought, wretchedly. Alfred had changed. He had never been exuberant. But he had been forceful, his voice strong, almost dictatorial. He had known himself. When had he changed? She could not remember. But she saw now that he was a different man, somber, abstracted, sometimes too gentle, almost uncertain, given to weighing matters doubtfully, whereas at one time he had had an instant and dogmatic opinion. He was tired. He was very tired. She knew this now.

She felt sick with pain and grief and love.

Philip's little white dog, which had been sniffing busily among the shrubs, suddenly emerged, barking shrilly. He ran towards the garden gates, very excited. He stood there, making the most annoying uproar. Dorothea called to him sharply. He glanced back at her, still barking. A young girl was leaning on the other side of the gate, calmly gazing over it.

Dorothea was unnerved. She smoothed back a lock of her heavily streaked hair. She said coldly: "What is it? What do you want? Are you looking for someone?"

She approached the gate slowly but determinedly. Doubtless this was one of those insufferable new young people from the valley. A most impossible intruder. Dorothea decided to send her packing immediately. She repeated: "What do you want?" and bent down to take the little dog in her arms.

The girl was very tall and slender in her printed muslin dress. Her very light hair was tied back with a blue ribbon the color of her eyes. She had a delicate cool face, firm and finely cut. She said: "Philip lives here, doesn't he?"

"Philip?" Dorothea frowned. She stared at the girl forbiddingly. But her heart had begun to beat in the most curious way, as if it had responded to some instinct as yet unsensed by Dorothea's conscious mind. "Who are you, my girl?"

The girl smiled. Dorothea was suddenly dazed and upset. She had seen that slow and thoughtful smile before, she could not remember where. But it was very familiar.

"I am Mary Lindsey," said the girl. "And you must be my Aunt Dorothea. My real aunt. Not Philip's."

She put her hand on the gate and opened it, and stepped inside, moving with surety and poise. Dorothea watched her, numbed. The dog barked wildly. Dorothea put her hand on his head and pressed it so harshly that he yowled briefly.

Mary tossed back her hair; the sun, coming out from behind its cloud, shone suddenly and brilliantly on that pale bright mass, which hung far below her waist. "How do you do, Aunt Dorothea?" said Mary formally.

She has my father's face, thought Dorothea. She has his eyes, and his movements. She is my own flesh and blood, my niece.

Dorothea was almost gray with shock; her gaunt cheeks drew in.

424

Mary was glancing about her at the garden; she looked at the house seriously. "I wonder why I was told I mustn't come here?" she asked, in a musing voice which was almost neutral in its timbre.

Dorothea found her own voice. She said, faintly but bitterly: "Have you asked your father?"

Mary smiled a little. "Yes. He was very indefinite. It seems he doesn't like anyone here but Philip." She studied Dorothea coolly. "You don't seem very formidable, Aunt Dorothea."

Dorothea put down the dog, who frolicked to Mary and sniffed her eagerly. Mary touched him lightly with her slender foot.

"I have just come home from Miss Finch's School on the Hudson," she said. "I thought I'd come to see if Philip were home."

"He is not." Dorothea spoke as if half stifled. "He is at his father's Bank." She hesitated. Her eyes had dimmed quite unaccountably. "So, you are Mary."

"Yes." The girl's smile, even if it was cold, could be charming.

"And, let me see: you are about fourteen, aren't you, child?"

"Almost. Next February."

"A young lady," murmured Dorothea.

Mary inclined her head with stately graciousness. "Yes. I am going to marry Philip when I am seventeen or eighteen."

Dorothea was stunned. Blinking her eyes, she stared at the girl.

"I haven't told him yet, of course," Mary continued. "But I shall soon. That is why I came down here. I think it is so silly that I shouldn't know my own aunt and Philip's father."

Dorothea glanced involuntarily at the house. It so happened that Alfred was home today, with one of his severe headaches. Dorothea was alarmed. Alfred must not see this strange girl. She turned to Mary abruptly. But when she saw that fair and composed young face, she could not say what she had been about to say.

"I think," she said, her voice breaking involuntarily, "that you ought to ask your father's permission to come here, child."

"He would not give it to me," said Mary, smiling again. "I know that. It's so foolish. Aren't you going to kiss me, Aunt Dorothea?"

She came up to Dorothea, and she was almost as tall as her aunt. Dorothea regarded her with stupefaction. She saw that Mary was presenting her cheek; she could see the frail color under the fine and vibrant white skin. To her further stupefaction, she found herself bending towards the girl. Her lips touched flesh as soft and sweet as a rose.

Something happened to Dorothea then. Something melted and flowed in her like tears, full and uncontrollable. She put her hand on Mary's shoulder and looked into those aloof blue eyes. She said: "Mary. Mary."

Mary's smile became gentle. "Aunt Dorothea," she answered softly.

Then Dorothea, her eyes moist and aching, said hurriedly: "My dear, you must not come here again without your father's express permission. It would be wrong and undutiful."

"I have every intention of telling Papa that I came here," said Mary primly. "But he was not at home this morning, and I could not ask him then."

That, Dorothea thought with mournful irony, is what Papa would have called sophistry. Mary had a pure and untouched look, a delicate transparency. But Dorothea was suddenly enlightened, and not without amusement. This was a resolute child, with quiet and determined strength, with a will and a mind of her own. She was no milk-and-water miss. There was Lindsey steel in her. She is as I was at her age, Dorothea commented to herself.

She searched the girl's face for some resemblance to Jerome and Amalie. But there was none. She is more my father's daughter than theirs, thought Dorothea, with pathetic gratitude.

"You have a little brother, too, haven't you, my love?" she asked.

Mary inclined her head with a gesture so familiar that Dorothea's heart opened on a quick pang.

"Yes. William. He is eight years old, and a bother," said Mary. "Little boys can be very annoying, and he is Mama's pet, which makes him worse."

Mary had an air of disarming frankness, but Dorothea was not deceived. The girl had potentialities for secrecy and deep reserve. She did not speak impulsively, though her words could be startling.

"I am sure that mothers do not distinguish between their children," said Dorothea, with Mary's own priggishness.

Mary laughed. Her porcelain-like features sparkled. "So long as Papa does, I do not care," she said.

Dorothea studied her with new affection and scrutiny. There was such a cleanness and freshness about the girl. One could

426

not imagine her hurried or mussed or confused. For all her appearance of fragility, she would be competent on all occasions.

"I am about to have my luncheon," said Dorothea, suddenly reckless. "Will you join me?" What did it matter if Alfred saw this beautiful young girl? Dorothea had the oddest thought that Alfred would not mind, would not be disturbed. That was part of the change which had come over him.

Mary politely, and with the most matter-of-fact manner, accepted the invitation at once. She looked about her with courteous interest as she accompanied Dorothea into the house. Dorothea saw this, and again her voice was embittered when she said: "This is not like Hilltop, is it, Mary?"

"I think Hilltop the nicest place in the world," replied the girl. "But this could be very nice, too, if there were just a little more sun in the rooms."

Dorothea said: "They do not make fabrics and rugs as they did once. These might fade if I allowed too much sunlight to come in."

"Oh, everything at Hilltop is faded. And I think it charming," said the insouciant Mary.

Dorothea was annoyed, then she hesitated. She drew back the draperies at the windows of the living-room, and let the sun pour in. She winced when she saw it splashing in golden pools upon her best Brussels carpeting. Mary nodded, approvingly.

Dorothea said: "Please sit down, my dear. I will consult the servants about setting an extra place."

Again, Mary inclined her head with that painfully familiar gesture. But though she put her hand on the back of a chair, she did not sit down until Dorothea had begun to move out of the room. A flush of pleasure touched Dorothea's lined and weary face. She went upstairs at once with a quicker step than usual. She felt both excited and pleased. She knocked on Alfred's sitting-room door. Alfred, pale and drawn, was at his desk writing in his personal expenses book. He smiled at his cousin when she opened the door and stood on the threshold. She actually came in and closed the door behind her, something which she had never done before.

"Alfred!" Dorothea spoke quietly, but with obvious excitement. "We have a visitor! She wandered down here without invitation, without any by-your-leave. I do hope you do not mind." She regarded him eagerly. "It is Mary. Jerome's young daughter."

Alfred put down his pen so suddenly that it made a sharp click on the mahogany of his desk. His eyes seemed to retreat under the eaves of his brows. He gazed at Dorothea intently.

"I have invited her to have luncheon with me," Dorothea went on. "She is such a sweet child. But it is not necessary for you to come down. If you wish, you may have a tray in your room."

Alfred saw that Dorothea was quite unusually flushed and tremulous. He could not remember having seen her like this before. He smiled painfully.

"That is not necessary," he said. "I shall be glad to join you both."

"How kind of you, Alfred! She has asked about you, and expressed her intention—her intention, if you please!—to know you. That is the sort of forward young person she is!" She sighed, still excited, and smoothed her apron. "I do not know what young people are coming to, these days! They have no reticence, no delicacy."

"Children do not need it," said Alfred, rising. Dorothea was startled at this peculiar remark from one who had been so rigid, so correct. Alfred continued: "I will go down at once. We must not leave our guest alone too long."

"I must speak to Elsie about another place," said Dorothea breathlessly, and hurried away.

Alfred went slowly and heavily down the stairs. He went into the living-room. He saw the outline of a smooth bright head, then the head turned and he saw Mary's cool and exquisite face. The girl stood up most politely, and curtseyed.

Alfred could not move for a moment. Amalie's daughter! She might have been his own, this fair sweet child with the strangely familiar blue eyes! He felt cheated, robbed, and something burned hotly in his chest, made his vision uncertain.

"I am Mary Lindsey, sir," said the girl politely. "And I presume you are Philip's father."

"Yes, my dear." Alfred's voice was low and shaken. He held out his hand to her, and she took it calmly and without shyness. She surveyed him frankly and openly. What she saw apparently pleased her, for she gave him her sweetest smile. "I think you are my second cousin, sir?"

Alfred hesitated. "Yes, that is correct, Mary. But I was adopted by your grandfather, too. So I am your adopted uncle. You may call me Uncle Alfred."

Mary's hand, soft and slender, was still in his. It was her mother's hand, firm under its yielding flesh; smooth, for all the delicate strong bones. Alfred held that hand more tightly than he knew. And Mary, always so subtle, waited patiently for release. She understood that the sight and touch of her was disturbing this quiet gentleman very much. But she did not know why.

"I am very glad to know you, Mary," said Alfred. "I hope you will come often. It is unfortunate that Philip will not be home for luncheon, but I hope you will not be too bored by us."

"Oh, I am sure I shan't," she assured him seriously. "Philip has spoken of you and Aunt Dorothea so often that I feel I already know you." She remembered her manners, sedulously taught in Miss Finch's School. "I hope you will not be bored by me, nor think it presumptuous of me to come here without express invitation."

"I do not think it necessary for you to wait for invitations," said Alfred, with equal politeness. "Please come often. We'll be delighted to see you."

She waited for him to seat himself, then sat near him, her feet primly held together, her hands folded in her muslin lap. Alfred was deeply touched by her daintiness, the outline of her firm and pretty chin, the brightness of her calm blue eyes. Yes, this should have been his dearest daughter, his dearest child, his pet and his consolation. Something in him yearned towards her; he felt that she was his own flesh. Well, he thought, in a way she is. After all, she is my uncle's granddaughter. She is a Lindsey. Looking at Mary now, he could not think of her as Jerome's child. It had been quite some time since he had felt any rage or hatred for Jerome. This was Amalie's daughter, the granddaughter of William Lindsey. For Alfred, that was enough.

He asked Mary about her school. She informed him that this was her first year away from home. Her papa had not wanted her to go, but Mama had insisted. Now Papa was quite reconciled. He thought she, Mary, had improved very much. Mary smiled indulgently at this. No, she was not unhappy at her school. She had a most excellent music teacher. The girls were often escorted to New York to the Opera, and sometimes to a play. There were so many things to see in New York.

Mary's voice, high and somewhat neutral, but very sweet, soothed Alfred's ear. He listened as if absorbed. He watched a streak of sunlight running through her hair. His Uncle William's hair, in his earlier days, had been this color, this texture. Mary turned her profile to Alfred for a moment, and its outlines, cool and clear, caught at his heart. It was William Lindsey's profile. But there was something else, too. There was a certain tilt to her head, a certain shadowy modelling about her cheekbones which hinted of Amalie.

Mary, in turn, had decided that she liked her Uncle Alfred. There was a stillness, a strength, about him of which she approved. He was not in the least a "gray man." Papa was wrong. But then Papa was frequently sharp about many people. Mary often thought him slightly cruel and malicious, but so very, very amusing. One could overlook the cruelty and malice, if one was made to laugh. Dear, dear Papa. She smiled and Alfred saw that smile, and with the old tearing at his heart he thought again of Amalie.

He said: "I once lived at Hilltop, too, Mary. Before you were born. I still remember and love it."

Mary looked at him quickly. "I did not know." She studied him seriously. "Why did you leave? There are so many rooms. I should have loved it to have Philip there."

Alfred was silent. Then, when he saw that Mary was waiting for his answer, he said: "After all, it is best for a family to be alone. Two families can often become very tiring to each other. I—I thought it the proper thing to take my own family away, and build a home of our own."

"But Aunt Dorothea is my father's sister," said Mary, puzzled. "She ought to have stayed with us."

Alfred's smile was somber. "But your—father—had your mother, my dear. He had your mother. But I had no one. So Dorothea came with us."

Mary fixed her eyes upon him penetratingly. She knew that he had not told her everything, and she had a child's natural curiosity, which had grown over the years.

"But you never visit Hilltop. Don't you like my papa, and my mama?"

Alfred stood up, stung by pain. He glanced at the door, wishing desperately for Dorothea's return. He said, in a stifled tone: "Your father and I did not have very much in common, my dear." He could not go on for a moment or two, then Mary could hardly hear his words: "Yes, I liked your mother very much. Very much. But sometimes families are incompatible. Was that the gong I just heard?"

Then, to Alfred's deep thankfulness, Dorothea rustled into the room. She looked from Alfred to Mary. She saw that Alfred was extremely disturbed and wretched. What had this strange child said to him? But Mary was all aplomb and pleasantness, and rose properly when her aunt entered.

Mary thought the luncheon very plain and tasteless, quite

unlike the spirited meals at home. The house, too, was abnormally quiet. There was no striking of a clock, no friendly voices of servants at a distance. There must be horses, and there had been Philip's little dog, but there was no neighing or barking. She heard the lonely rustling of trees. The windows in this stark dining-room faced north. Mary could see dim shadowed lawns, made duskier by evergreens. She sensed a dampness of the atmosphere and shivered. No wonder darling Philip came so often to Hilltop. The silence and the chill here must be very disagreeable to him too.

Dorothea suddenly became anxious. "But your mother, my dear: will she not wonder where you are, and why you have not appeared for luncheon?"

Mary shook her head, and her web of pale hair was slightly agitated. "I had an earlier luncheon with my brother, in his nursery. Mama is entertaining Mrs. Kingsley today, and she told me to keep William away from them. Mrs. Kingsley doesn't like children. She likes animals best." Mary considered this thoughtfully. "I don't blame her, really. Little boys, especially, can be very tiresome."

Dorothea had a sudden swift memory of her own guardianship over the obstreperous Jerome so many years ago. She, too, had often been warned to assist the nursemaid in keeping Jerome away from the guests. Her eyes became moist. She said: "Is your brother rather noisy, my love, and uncontrollable?"

"Only with Mama," said Mary. "He is very well-behaved when Papa is at home. Papa is sometimes stern with him. But when Mama is alone, William can't always be controlled. He takes advantage. He has tantrums."

Ah, yes, Jerome "took advantage," and he often had "tantrums"! How well Dorothea remembered. She smiled at Mary with sympathy and understanding. How odd that history could so repeat itself in a family! She felt a quick deep bond between herself and this calm young girl. She knew instinctively that without too much effort Mary could control William, as she had controlled Jerome.

Dorothea turned to Alfred. He was smiling at her. He too was thinking of the things that were filling her own mind. It had been a long time since Dorothea had experienced this sense of warmth and understanding, this closeness.

Then Dorothea remembered that Mary had been remiss in her duty. "But you left your brother alone, after all," she reminded her niece, with an attempt at severity. "That was quite wrong."

Mary was not abashed. "I had had enough of him, for two hours," she said. "I gave Margie, his nurse, an old locket of mine on her promise to keep him away from Mama and Mrs. Kingsley. She said she would tie him down if she had to. Of course, he roars," she added, reflectively. "But Margie can keep the doors shut."

Once Dorothea had locked Jerome in a closet. That was when Mama was so ill. He had not been frightened. He had kicked the inside of the door to splinters. Dorothea's hand held her tea-cup but did not lift it to her lips. She stared at the table-cloth, remembering.

It did not occur to her until later that she had recalled these memories of Jerome without bitterness or hatred.

Mary made a spot of radiance in the dim dining-room. It was so natural for her to be here. It was like having Alfred's daughter in the house. Alfred's daughter! He had been deprived of this treasure, this sweetness, through no fault of his own. But still Dorothea could feel nothing but sadness and regret.

Mary refused a drive home. She liked the walk. She left messages for Philip. He was not to forget that he was dining at Hilltop tomorrow night. She hoped that he would bring the copy of Shelley he had promised her, bound in limp red morocco. He had written her that he had bought it especially for her.

Mary composedly kissed her Aunt Dorothea and then Alfred, thanked them for the luncheon, and sedately went away. They accompanied her to the gates. They watched her tall slender figure climbing steadily up the hill. When she was some distance away she turned to wave to them. They both felt a poignant sense of loss, of irreparable grief. It was wrong that she should leave them. They watched the sun glinting on her hair until a bend in the road hid it from their sight.

Her name should have been Elizabeth, thought Alfred. My mother's name.

CHAPTER FIFTY-SEVEN

"Really, Mary!" exclaimed Amalie, very perturbed and exasperated. "You have no sense of proportion at all. I can't think what your father will say when we have to tell him. Unless you do not tell him."

"Oh, I intend to," said Mary placidly. "There is no use having secrets."

She regarded her mother reflectively. "He never said expressly that I should not visit Uncle Alfred and Aunt Dorothea."

Amalie sighed resignedly. "Don't use that sophistry on me, my girl. You've known, surely, that you should not go down there. You have not been in ignorance of your father's—feelings—about that family."

Mary smoothed her hair with both hands, then shook it back again.

"Mama," she said, very quietly, "I am almost fourteen years old. I am not really a child any longer. Don't you think I ought to know why there is such a feeling about Philip's family? It is all so mysterious."

Amalie was silent. The girl was right. Some day, perhaps very soon, she would hear the story. It might be garbled. People could be so merciless. Amalie knew that Mary, in spite of her surface tranquillity, had a deep capacity for feeling, for emotion. Amalie did not know what to do! Whatever she did, it would infuriate Jerome. But Jerome would be infuriated anyway, and he would blame his wife without reticence and with no mincing of words.

But, my God! thought Amalie, with despair, the actual story was bad enough without fearing it would be "garbled." The bare facts might be shocking enough. However, there was nothing that could be done about it. It would be best if Mary's mother gave her a brief and tactful outline. She thought of Jerome's anger. It could not be helped.

She said: "Mary, you are a sensible girl. And I agree with you that you ought to know about this. Otherwise, other people may tell you, and they can be unkind." She paused. After all, Mary was not yet fourteen. What could she know of human passions? Would she blame her parents? Would she build up in her mind some fantastic opinion?

Amalie, despairing again, said: "At one time, Mary, I was married to Alfred Lindsey."

Mary moved quickly. She turned on her chair and gazed steadily at her mother. But she made no remark.

Amalie twisted her fingers together. She bit her lip. Mary waited.

"We—all lived together at Hilltop then. Your father came home for the wedding." Oh, God, this was going to be worse than she had thought! "It was very unfortunate, perhaps, but

433

your papa and I—your papa and I—decided we loved each other. So, a few months later, Alfred Lindsey and I were divorced, and your papa and I were married."

"Divorced!" said Mary, too softly.

Amalie frowned. "Surely you know what divorce means, Mary. Of course, divorce is rather—unusual. But sometimes it is necessary. I found I did not really love Alfred Lindsey. It was best for all of us that it happened that way."

She could not read Mary's large blue eyes. They had not moved from her mother's face. Then, all at once, it came to her with a shock that Mary was admiring her!

"Why, Mama," said Mary, almost with wonder. "You must have been very courageous!"

Amalie actually gaped in her stupefaction.

Mary was scrutinizing her mother with profound interest. Mama was not dull then, or so strait-laced! Mama had been daring and young and strong; she had had the courage to do a most outrageous and adventurous thing. She had faced down a whole world of censure. Mary was excited, her budding sense of romance stirred. And Papa! How gallant, how irresistible, he must have been! He was not merely his children's father; he had been a romantic and dashing figure in his own right, a figure of gaiety and abandon. Mary decided that she had never loved her parents so much. Why, she had never loved Mama like this, Mama who had always appeared so correct and rigid with her daughter!

"So," said Mary dreamily, "that is why our familes don't visit. Uncle Alfred must have been hurt, wasn't he?"

Amalie moved her head restlessly. "I believe he was," she said, still dumfounded at what she had seen in her daughter's face. "But he is a very sensible man. I am sure he holds no grudge. But things are somewhat awkward, you see. So we think it best to have nothing to do with the family down there."

"Yes," said Mary, staring at the window. "I think I see. Uncle Alfred is very kind. He doesn't hold any grudges. He asked me about you, Mama. A lot of things." She was silent a moment. "Why didn't he marry again, too?"

"I'm sure I don't know!" exclaimed Amalie. "After all, he had been married twice. Perhaps he thought that enough." She stopped. "What did he ask you about me, Mary?"

"He wanted to know whether you were still pretty." Mary concentrated on her mother, with new eyes. She had never thought of her mother as handsome or otherwise. Mama was just Mama. But now for the first time Mary saw her mother's beauty, and a strangeness, a shyness, overcame the girl. She also saw her mother as a woman, not merely as a mother. "He wanted to know whether you still liked the garden. He asked me whether your favorite color still was green."

Amalie's eyes darkened. She dropped her head a trifle.

"I didn't know it then," continued the terrible Mary, "but I know it now. He still likes you, Mama."

Amalie rose. She said in an odd voice: "Mary, I don't know what we can do. Your papa is going to be very angry. I—I think you yourself ought to tell him. I think you ought to tell him what I have told you. I don't want to be there when you do."

Mary nodded. Her smile was secret and mature.

"I think he will tell you not to go down there again, Mary. And you must obey him."

"I don't think children should obey stupid commands," said Mary, with composure. "And I like to visit my relatives."

Amalie gasped. She turned quickly on her daughter.

"Why, Mary! How can you say such things? Can't you realize that parents sometimes give children commands which are beyond the understanding of foolish girls?"

"No," said Mary. "After all, I am not a child. I am old enough to form my own opinions and decide what I want to do. I think Papa will see that, too. He always listens to me."

Jerome was white with rage. He and Mary were sitting together in Mary's room. Mary had invited him there after dinner. She often had these confidences with her father. They had walked out of the library as they had often done, together, Jerome giving his wife his old indulgent and somewhat sheepish smile, as if laughing with her before going away with Mary for one of their affectionate "talks."

If Jerome was almost speechless with his anger, Mary was all calm.

"You must not blame Mama," she was saying. "She did not know I was going. In fact, I left the house without her knowledge. I fully intended to go down to Philip's home when I left. When I returned, Mama was very angry with me. I insisted that she tell me about everything. So she told me. I am not in the least shocked. I think it very exciting. And now I understand everything, and I wonder why I wasn't told before."

Mary was thoughtful. If she was at all disturbed by her father's savage pallor, and by the way the scars showed bright red on his cheek and forehead, she betrayed no signs of it. She had never seen him this way; he had never looked at her like this. But she was still calm.

"Of course," she said reflectively, "I need not have told you of Mama at all. But I think that would have been wrong. There is no sense in being dishonest and sneaky."

Jerome had never struck his daughter in all her life. Now he had the most brutal desire to do so. But he still did not move.

He only said thickly: "You little slut. You knew I did not want you to go down there, ever. It was made very plain to you. But you deliberately disobeyed."

Mary winced. For the first time in her life she was frightened of her father. She lifted her chin high, but her color was gone.

Jerome felt a tautness, a burning, in his scars. This incensed him even more against Mary. He stood up now, went to the girl, and struck her violently across the face.

Mary did not cry out, nor cringe, nor throw up her arm. She merely lifted her head higher. The imprints of Jerome's hand sprang out in crimson on her white cheek. She regarded Jerome steadily, and her blue eyes were huge unafraid wells of light now, quite inscrutable.

That look gave Jerome pause. It was his father's own expression. Suddenly he hated himself for that blow. But his voice, though unsteady, was still thick when he spoke:

"I want you to understand this, my girl. You must never go down there again. If you do, it will be at your own peril."

Mary said in a still tone: "There is something here I don't understand, Papa. If anyone should be angry, it is Uncle Alfred, not you. You took Mama away from him."

Was that contempt that shone so brilliantly from those young eyes? Jerome's rage made his head hum.

"Your mother is a fool for telling you," he said, with hoarseness. "She ought to have known that you would not understand, that you should not be told anything." He was almost beside himself. He touched the scars on his face. "Look at these, you little imbecile. Your kind 'Uncle Alfred' did this to me."

Mary was rising from her chair, unable to look away from him. She was whiter than ever. She whispered: "When he— knew—about you and Mama?"

"Yes!" Jerome was almost shouting.

"How silly," said Mary, still in that whispering tone. "He ought to have known that you and Mama couldn't help it." She put her hand to the flaming imprint on her cheek, and again her eyes shone brilliantly. "Just as you, Papa, ought to have known better."

Her dignity silenced him, overcame him with shame. He bit his lip. Then he put out his hand to his daughter. She took it without hesitation.

"Mary," he said, "you are too young to understand everything. Some day perhaps you will. Then you will know why I must ask you never to go down to that house again." He added: "I'm sorry, my darling."

He had always had complete control over Mary. The sympathy between them had been absolute. Now, in some instinctive way, he knew that something that had run between them like a strong nerve had been cut. It was almost like an umbilical cord, he thought confusedly and he was filled with pain.

"If that is your express command, Papa, then I shall obey," said Mary. She had the dignity and pride of a woman now. Yes, that was contempt in her eyes. But it was contempt for him that he could forget himself and behave childishly and unpardonably.

"Thank you, my dear," said Jerome. He went away and left her now. He had intended to call Amalie to him and to upbraid her viciously. But now he felt only misery and an increasing sense of loss.

CHAPTER FIFTY-EIGHT

When Philip went to Hilltop for dinner the following evening, he looked swiftly for signs of constraint. To his regret, and with some apprehension, he saw that Amalie, though she was gracious as always, appeared too controlled, and that there was an inimical spark in Jerome's eye whenever he glanced at his wife. But his manner towards Philip was as easy and as welcoming as ever.

Philip showed them a package which he had brought with him. "A book of Shelley, and a volume of some airs from Brahms," he said. "For Mary. I promised the child the Shelley, and forgot it for a few days." He laughed gently. "But Mary didn't forget. She came after it yesterday."

Amalie smiled uncomfortably. Jerome said, with a smile: "Mary is impatient. She is also very rigorous about promises. We've discovered that. A whiskey before dinner, Philip?"

Philip was grateful for this diplomacy. By nature adroit in human relationships, and possessed of considerable finesse in managing those inevitable awkwardnesses that occur in the smoothest society, he hated all roughnesses and gauche encounters. This was partly because he was the soul of discretion, and partly because he was so innately kind. He used graceful lies and gentle hypocrisies when necessary to salve the sensibilities of others and to create good will where only animosity had lived before. To him, a ruthless man who spoke bluntly and "truthfully" upon the slightest provocation was like an uncouth bull who charged with pointed horns and slashing hoofs, and there was no excuse for him in the delicate relationships between human beings. Philip maintained the grace of a polite minuet in his own encounters with others; he glided about stumbling dancers on the universal ballroom floor with the serene unconcern that assumes everyone is equally adept. His very presence prevented acute embarrassment from reaching the heights of distressing hostility, and the elegance and consideration of his manners had a very salutary and inhibiting effect on chronic "truth-tellers" and those who loved argument and discord for their own sakes.

Philip had always admired Jerome because the latter possessed, in a large measure, the ability to overlay the rough sand of threatening irritants with the pearly substance of good manners and civilized deportment.

He and Jerome drank their whiskey, while Amalie sipped at her sherry. The warm summer evening, still and bland, soothed spirits that had suffered from the daytime heat. Philip, dismissing the subject of Mary, complimented Amalie on the arrangement of flowers in bowls and low painted trays.

"You are the perfect hostess, Amalie," he said. "There is never a false note about you anywhere."

Jerome's eye, as it rested on his wife now, was slightly less inimical.

Philip enlarged: "At the risk of appearing disloyal to dear Aunt Dorothea, I must admit that Hilltop, under your hand, Amalie, has taken on a new and brighter air. But it is not a false air. It is as if all the old dull surfaces of the house had been burnished. You seem to accomplish the mechanics of household management with aplomb and smoothness. Do you have the trouble with servants that Aunt Dorothea has?"

"Amalie has a way with servants," said Jerome. He was not in the least deceived by all these lavish compliments, and not in the dark as to their intention. Nevertheless, because they

438

contained truth, and because he was proud of his wife, he did not mind. "She knows how to treat them. She never argues with them, but she never allows them to take liberties. Also, we pay them very well."

Philip saw Amalie's lip tremble. So, he thought, the poor darling has had a bad time with this devil since yesterday.

"You are so kind, Philip," Amalie said. Her smile was less unnatural now.

"Aunt Dorothea believes in sternness and the rod," Philip continued. "I try to tell her that that day has passed, for servants. It is no use, of course. We haven't a servant who has been with us for over five months. Well, after fifty it is impossible to change an attitude. One becomes encased in one's habits as a snail in its shell."

He inclined his head at Jerome. "I believe you, however, are the exception, my friend. Your nature becomes more flexible and understanding as you approach that nasty half-century line."

Jerome laughed with delight. "Is this your night for passing out verbal Christmas presents, Philip?" he asked. He refilled his and Philip's glass. His eyes danced.

But Philip was very serious. "No. I am merely expressing my gratitude for the fact that I am permitted to come to this house and to know you and Amalie."

Amalie said impulsively: "And we are grateful that we have you, Philip." She hesitated and looked at Jerome. "That is true, isn't it, love?"

"Oh, yes, indeed, my pet." Jerome was standing near his wife. He touched her cheek carelessly. Amalie's full red mouth became tremulous. "We couldn't get along without Philip," Jerome added, more and more delighted. "He is the only man I can talk to in all Riversend. A diplomatic scoundrel, but he has his worth."

They went in to dinner. Philip saw at once that Amalie had been at her old task of trying to placate Jerome. His favorite dishes were served. Philip complimented his hostess on their excellence. "Where do you get such beef?" he asked.

Jerome was immediately interested. "I buy it from one of the machinists in Munsey's factory," he said. "He bought four more acres from me, and he has a cow or two, there."

He enlarged on a new experiment of his, which had, in fact, been discreetly advanced by Philip. Prize bulls had been bought by this particular worker and others. Their female offspring had won State Fair prizes for milk. The farmers, dour and skeptical, had finally succumbed to the idea of scientific breeding.

The men then centered their attention on the always absorbing subject of the Riversend Community. The Community had been in full swing now for over a year. Industrialists, bankers, large landowners and those philanthropists who were concerned with human welfare had come in troops to Riversend, at first doubtful and suspicious, and then amazed. Philip, though now assistant manager at his father's Bank, had found time after his hours there to plan the whole project and to help direct it. In the past three years as many as six substantial buildings had risen on the large plot of land which Jerome had bought near the railroad. Philip had a corps of able assistants.

The land immediately about Riversend had, to quote an ebullient reporter, "bloomed like the rose." Neat acres devoted to farming, chicken raising or floriculture, had replaced the wild grazing land which for years had been lying fallow. On holidays and on Sundays, after the day's work, the hundreds of workers and their families could be seen on their way to their acres, standing, sitting, singing, in great farm wagons, sunbonneted women, sunburned children, brawny men, all with that look of deep serenity and satisfaction which comes to those who have something to live for besides their daily toil.

The quiet countryside on these occasions became alive and vivacious with voices, with the strong figures of those who dug, watered and cultivated. Owners of neighboring plots discussed fertilizers and produce, argued good-naturedly. After sundown, there was a community feast, spread out on immense wooden tables surrounded by benches. Campfires were lit. Some men had caught fish in the nearby stream; the women had brought huge pots of baked beans, boiled and roasted hams, pies, cakes, warm home-made bread. Coffeepots spluttered on the fires, and barbecued spareribs and beef. Children ran about, tired but hungry and full of health. A guitar or two struck sweet chords on the sweeter air of night, and voices sang, and dark shapes moved vigorously about the fires. Afterwards, some of the younger people danced, while their elders sat about and kept time with clapping hands. Babies, replete, slept in the plump arms of their mothers. Later, the wagons went homeward, their occupants weary but still laughing and singing, while a great golden moon swung over the trees.

In the winter, the Community houses were filled. The products of these houses had already acquired a widespread fame. Buyers from New York and Chicago and Philadelphia and Boston came for the excellent lace bedspreads, the quilts, the pottery, the painted glass, the fine woodwork and small articles of furniture, and other products. Good teachers had offered their services, but Jerome and Philip had insisted upon paying them. Now there was a permanent winter staff. In the summer, the teachers assisted on the land. There was a greenhouse, too, and in the winter the churches were as fragrant and sweet with flowers as they were in the summer.

Best of all, the factory owners discovered that they rarely lost a good worker. They discovered also that the men took more interest, even in their monotonous tasks, and that they did them better. More and more workers were buying the small neat houses in which they lived. Many of them actually built the houses themselves, as they had built the Community buildings.

All this had not been accomplished by the planners without struggle, without anxiety, without apprehension. The workers, at first amazed and suspicious, had been won over only by prolonged argument. It had been hard to convince them that anyone was really interested in their welfare, really concerned with their happiness as well as with the work of their hands.

The Riversend Community became famous all over the industrial East.

Hard as the winning over of the workers themselves had been, even harder was the winning over of the local industrialists. They had been joined in their angry protests by their brother industrialists over nearly all the country. The experiment had been decried as "dangerous, pampering, anarchistic, revolutionary, full of impractical visions." Some clergymen had denounced the Community. The newspapers had laughed at it and had filled their pages with derisive cartoons.

Then, with pomp and with dark suspicion, the Governor of the State had come.

He stayed three days, as Jerome's guest. He left full of the most extravagant enthusiasm. "Mr. Jerome Lindsey, founder of the Community, has demonstrated to the leaders of America not only the Christian character of such a project, but the healthy material advantages of it," he had said, addressing the State Senate.

No less than four books had been written about the Community. Social leaders, both men and women, came from Chicago and New York to study this revolutionary idea and, returning, attempted to persuade the people of their own cities to imitate it. The newspapers, abandoning their derision, carried large editorials about the Community.

But the fight was not yet won, and Jerome and Philip knew it. They knew that the struggle for human justice and decency and dignity will never be ended.

They talked of this struggle, tonight, over their port.

"Sometimes I think that you yourself, Philip, have taken on too much," said Jerome. "You never have a moment to call your own."

"It is my life," protested Philip. And then was silent. It was not his "life," there in his father's conservative Bank with its dull ledgers. He did his work there well, and Alfred was grateful and proud. But Philip escaped from the Bank as early as possible. He and Alfred never indulged in arguments about the Community. Philip was beginning to believe hopefully that his father was at least slightly interested.

Alfred's Bank was benefiting, too, from the Community. In the last few years Riversend had trebled its population. It could not be called a city; it was no longer a town. There were four extra cashiers on duty now in Alfred's Bank. Once, on a weekend, when Alfred could be certain that Jerome was not about, he had accompanied his son through the Community buildings, and had allowed himself a glimpse of the workers cultivating their land.

"You see, Father," Philip had said on this happy occasion, "we are preventing the concentration of industry and the complete urbanization of workers, before they can even begin to threaten this area."

"I have always denounced the divorcing of men from the land," Alfred had informed him, with dignity. "I am glad to find that others agree with me."

Philip had smiled to himself, but with affection.

A week later, Alfred had given Philip his personal check for three thousand dollars to help towards the building of a small medical clinic of which Philip had told him. "However," said Alfred, stiffly, "I wish the gift to remain anonymous."

Philip had been poignantly touched by this. He accepted the gift with a few casual words in a matter-of-fact tone. Alfred was grateful for this tact.

After dinner, Jerome requested that Philip play for himself and Amalie, and Philip consented with pleasure. They sat in the music room while Philip played a few selections from Chopin, a nocturne or two. Outside, the dark, moonless night was silent and warm. Crickets and tree-toads chirped and sang a melancholy accompaniment to the music. Once, a breeze sprang up momentarily, and the trees murmured sonorously. Now Philip could feel that a temporary measure of peace had come to Jerome and Amalie. They sat side by side, listening; Jerome stretched out his hand and took his wife's. Her eyes filled with tears, but she looked only at Philip.

A little later, Philip announced that he wished to give Mary the books. Amalie was about to call the girl, but Philip said: "Please don't, Amalie. I'll go up to her sitting-room, as usual. We like to have our little talk together alone, as you know. I haven't seen the child for days."

CHAPTER FIFTY-NINE

Philip opened the door of Mary's small sitting-room and said brightly: "May I come in, please?"

Mary was at her rosewood desk, writing precisely in her diary. She rose at once, smiling faintly. "Oh, Philip." Her young voice was restrained, but calm as always. The lamp on the desk threw a soft shadow over her face. She indicated a chair for Philip, who sat down. He held his package on his knee. Mary sat down again, more slowly than she had risen.

"I've brought the Shelley for you, my dear," he said. "And also some airs of Brahms. A copy, signed, it is alleged, by the composer himself. It is in vellum. I bought it in New York a month ago, and it did not arrive until today, with some other things. When I played the airs over this morning, I decided that you must have the book."

He held out the package to her, scrutinizing her earnestly but without apparently looking at her too closely. It was then that he saw the several small bruises on her cheek. Though he still smiled, he went cold with shock. He hardly felt her eager hands taking the package from him. The coldness on his flesh increased, but there was a stern burning in him stronger than mere anger.

The girl sat down with all her old and unhurried grace, which was so regal, so quietly elegant. She unwrapped the package, examined the contents. She lifted radiant eyes to his. "Oh, Philip! How kind of you!"

His voice was trembling treacherously, though he tried to steady it. "Not half so kind as you, Mary. It was the kindest thing to visit my aunt and my father yesterday. They wanted me to tell you how much they enjoyed your coming. I believe they quite love you."

A bright color ran over her face, and the small bruises quickened. But she did not look away from him. She said simply: "I love them too. I wanted to know them, because of you, Philip."

Philip remembered Dorothea's telling him affectionately of "that dear child's determination to marry him in three or four years." They had laughed together; Philip had never heard such a gentle laugh from Dorothea before.

He said: "They want you to come again soon, Mary."

Mary bent her head over the books. A long length of her fair hair fell over her cheek. "I want to, Philip," she said, in a low tone. "But I think it best not to."

There was a little silence. Then Philip murmured: "Your father forbade it?"

Mary nodded, her head still bent.

Philip sighed. The burning in his heart was wilder. Jerome! Philip spoke in what he hoped was a reasonable voice: "Well, then. I am sorry. He probably knows best."

Mary lifted her head; her eyes were fearless and direct, but they seemed older to him than he had ever remembered them.

"I ought to have asked him first. You see, Philip, there were things I didn't know."

Good God! thought Philip. He had a great aversion for situations which involved embarrassment and the invasion of another's privacy.

"I didn't know my mother had been married to your father," Mary went on, without hesitation. "I didn't know that she had divorced him, and then had married Papa. If I had given it even just one thought—Papa's not wanting me to go down there—I might have realized that he must have good reason to forbid me. I seem to have grown up since yesterday."

To Philip, that young and steady voice became unbearably pathetic. He said, as if defending her against the cruelty of disillusion: "My dear child!"

"Mama told me," she went on, as if she had not heard him. "She was very upset. It was very thoughtless of me."

Philip drummed his fingers silently on the arm of his chair.

He heard Mary sigh. "How hard it must have been for all of you to leave Hilltop," she said.

"Yes," he answered, speaking fully from his knowledge that Mary was now no longer a child. "It was very hard. There were so many memories. Mary, my dear, I loved your mother, too. She was the first mother I had ever had. She gave me my

444

watch." He drew it from his pocket and showed it to her. She nodded.

She said, with a faint wonder on her face: "It's very strange how you don't think of your parents ever having had a life of their own before you were born. And very stupid too. Did Mama seem beautiful to you, Philip, and kind?"

"Yes. Oh, yes, Mary." He found it a little hard to see her clearly.

She stared at a wall with dreaming eyes. "You know, Philip, I sometimes thought that Mama was a little tiresome, at times. She was just 'Mother' to me, and I was always vexing her. But now I seem to know her better. She looked sad when she talked of your father. Philip, do you suppose she ever liked him, really?"

Philip's conflict of emotions confused him. "Mary, I don't know. I really don't know. Perhaps she did. She must have, or she wouldn't have married him in the first place. Well. It can't be helped. It happened a long time ago, long before you were born. Some things are best forgotten. It does no good to dig them up after they're buried."

Mary's hands were clasped on the books. For the first time Philip saw them consciously, and he was moved by their delicate whiteness, their transparency. The lamplight shone on the girl's clear profile; her thick pale lashes threw a sharp shadow on her cheek. He thought: It is such a lovely, valorous face, so exquisite, so fine. And so proud, so nobly pure. That small firm chin had dignity, too; the shape of the brow was aristocratic, imperial, in its white and sloping contours. Something too poignant moved in Philip.

"But," she said thoughtfully, "you come here, Philip. Papa likes you. He wants you to come."

"We always liked each other, your father and I," he said. "There was no quarrel between us." He halted. He knew what the girl was thinking: There is no quarrel, either, between me and *your* father. He saw Mary smile; that smile saddened him, it was so ironical, robbed of youth. Then she turned to him, with her lucid and open look.

"There are some things I don't know yet, aren't there, Philip?"

He was extremely embarrassed and alarmed. "I am sure your mother told you all there was to know, Mary. I—I would say it is a matter of incompatible temperaments, between your father and mine. I understand they were enemies all their lives. They never understood each other. It was not just

445

your mother——" He stopped. He was always averse to discussing others in their absence. It smacked of disloyalty.

Mary was regarding him seriously. "I think I understand. But your father was not bitter about mine. Papa told me those scars had come from Uncle Alfred. Perhaps if there had been no scars, Papa might have forgotten too. They always remind him. He must have been terribly humiliated. Poor Papa."

Philip stood up hastily. "Your father is a very proud man, Mary." Then he paused. How penetrating of the child! He studied her earnestly, and again that odd poignancy moved him.

"Yes, very proud, Philip. I know that now. You see how wrong I was. I know there is something more that I haven't been told. Can you tell me?"

Philip was full of consternation. With more severity than he actually felt, he said: "Mary, my dear. Don't you think it is a little impertinent of us to discuss your father like this? Do you think he would like it?"

"Of course he would not. You are right, Philip." She put aside the books. Her expression was so tranquil that it appeared impassive.

"You will try to forget all this, Mary? It does not make any difference between you and me?"

She stood up. Her head was considerably higher than his. Her eyes were candid again, and very blue.

"How could it, Philip?" She gave him her hand. It was cool in his, and yielding.

"You will tell Aunt Dorothea and Uncle Alfred that I send them my love, and that I'll come to see them again some day, but not just yet?" she said.

"Yes, darling, I will." The poor, poor child. But she was no longer a child.

He went down the stairs slowly. He arranged his dark features into a smile before going into the library. He saw Jerome, and again that harsh burning pierced him. But he saw Amalie also, and her anxious pallor.

He said cheerfully: "The child is very pleased with the books. She wants to play the Brahms for you the first thing tomorrow, Jerome."

CHAPTER SIXTY

"Work, or business, or even the professions," Jerome said, "have become not merely the source of the wherewithal with which to enjoy life but reasons for existence in themselves."

This seemed to him to be a most terrible spiritual error. He blamed the Puritans for it, the Puritans who were masochists and hated joy and life. He had listened to Philip's account of his last years at Harvard. Scholasticism, classicism, no longer had for their aim the broadening of the human concept of the universe, the increase of delight as consciousness is increased, but were a preparation for making money. Philip had friends in Boston and Philadelphia. It disgusted Jerome when Philip cynically informed him that conversations about the arts and philosophy, and conjecture as to man's place in nature and in government, were ridiculed as the occupations of silly professors and schoolteachers, and those unacquainted with reality. Now it was "business." In defense, many Bostonians and Philadelphians had hinted that whatever had nothing to do with the capacity to make money was not "democratic," not "American." A wave of anti-Europeanism had arisen. Many had become alarmed at this. But Philip explained that it was not anti-Europeanism *per se,* but a guilty revolt against tradition, aristocracy, the arts and philosophy, which "Europeanism" represented to the lusty boars that ranged through American banking houses and industry. It was "hatred of class," explained the boars, who were rapidly establishing an "aristocracy" of their own which had its basis in cash balances only. "Classes," in Europe, had been based on family, tradition, learning, intellectual accomplishment. But American "classes" were even more rigid: how many thousand pairs of shoes or tons of pig iron or ready-made suits or locomotives or rails or silver or coal had a certain man sold during the past year?

To Philip and Jerome, this seemed a far uglier thing than the old class distinctions of Europe, and even of the earlier America. "It is comparatively easy to make money," Philip said. "The veriest peasant or pleb or rascal can do it. So, if we are not careful, the new leaders of America, the new statesmen and politicians, will inevitably come from those who have no tradition of pride and dignity and honor. We shall have mountebanks representing millions of lightless and cunning fools, without learning, without a sense of universal responsibility, and without exaltation. I foresee a time when America will have profound weight in the world. If that weight is not accompanied by thoughtfulness, intellectual perception and decent altruism, then the world will be in a sorry state indeed."

He recalled to Jerome Plato's hint for a perfect society: that a certain class of noble and learned men, of tradition and intellect, be maintained from which to draw all statesmen, all lawmakers. "They need not come from the 'old' families," said Philip, "for the 'old' families in America are almost always the descendants of mere robbers and pirates and thieves in the slaughterhouse or mining or railroad businesses. We should have monitors in all our public schools, constantly on the alert for those children, those boys, those young men, no matter what their background or their family, who display intuitive delicacy, integrity and intellect. These should be winnowed out from the mass, who will always be concerned, in our terribly out-of-joint society, with the making of money and with work for its own sake. Free scholarship to the best universities should be given these young men. Later, we should have for them governmental schools of political science, with the emphasis on history and human relationships.

"From these graduates, and from them only, should come the Senators and Congressmen, the civil servants, the Mayors and the Judges, the officers of the armed forces, and even the Presidents of the United States. This is true democracy: the free choosing of the best. Only in a true democracy can the best, regardless of background or birth, be elevated to positions of authority.

"In these governmental schools there would be no emphasis on money. Service to the nation, to humanity, would be stressed. That would be their vocation, the ideal to which they would be dedicated."

"A Brahmin class!" said Jerome, with a laugh. "Think of its dangerous potentialities!"

"There is no danger," said Philip seriously. "An inherited aristocracy is your real 'Brahmin' class. The class I suggest would be drawn from all ranks of society, from the children of laborers and masons to the children of Boston and Philadelphia society, from the children of the plantation owners of the South to the children in the tenant cottages. They would be elected to governmental positions; they would not inherit them. There would be no 'House of Lords' idea in America."

"Your idea smacks of the monastery," said Jerome, but his ridicule, as usual when with Philip, was really only a mask for

448

his real interest and approval.

"The monastery idea is not a bad one," replied Philip. "A body of dedicated men, freed of the stultifying necessity of making money, free to work for the general good and the advancement of knowledge. I have always agreed with the premise of the Roman Church: that to do his best work, a man must be liberated from personal anxieties, not weighed down by the compulsion to provide for a family.

"The graduates of my hypothetical schools would be sufficiently remunerated, so that their families would not suffer. It is not the desire for money which is the root of all evil, personal and national, but the desperate necessity for it."

He smiled. "Under this plan of mine, the venal lawyer, the greedy businessman, the intellectual failure and the incompetent could not resort to politics, nor be elected to positions of profound trust and gravity. As my graduates would be imbued with their mission, they could not easily be bought by subversive lobbies. As they would, in the first place, be good men, they could not be tempted by scoundrels."

"I have a feeling this is going to cost me money," said Jerome reflectively.

"It is." Philip laughed. "We can begin right here in the schools of Riversend. We must have talks with the teachers. Find out the best boys, not those of keen and avaricious and merely acquisitive minds. But those who are thoughtful and intrinsically decent, as well as good scholars. Provide scholarships for these boys. Tell them, from the very beginning, in their grades and forms, to what they must dedicate themselves."

He stood up and walked slowly but eagerly up and down Jerome's office. "America! I feel prophetic. This nation shall be great and heroic. It shall stand like a Colossus over the ruck of dark and malignant history. It shall, it must, know that the destiny and the dreams of all men repose in it, as a child in the mother's womb. Who can withstand America, if she lives in the sun of nobility and generosity, if all men within her borders can truly say: 'I am free'?"

He continued to walk up and down. He said musingly: "I feel mystical. America is not merely an experiment, conducted by men, in liberty and vision and hope. It is an experiment, conducted by God, to discover whether man has come of age, whether he is mature enough to order his own destiny, whether he has acquired sufficient greatness of heart to succor other men. Here is the hope of the ages. Here is the dream of the prophets. Here is the thought of Plato and Socrates, of Jesus and Buddha. It was to all men, and not to Moses alone, that God said: 'Lift up thine eyes westward, and northward, and southward, and eastward, and behold it with thine eyes.' And surely, surely, He said this of America. Surely, this is the Promised Land."

Jerome had seldom seen him so moved. Philip turned to him suddenly, eyes flashing, hands clenched. "We must keep America safe from the mountebanks, the liars, the exploiters, the haters, the fools. Here is the dream. We dare not let it turn into a nightmare, where only money and property are sacred, and man's soul is buried under the stones of materialism and lust. Something else must be taught in the schools besides preparation for making money. Something spiritual, something subjective and noble must be injected into the minds of children. Something not chauvinistic and narrow.

"We have mouthed for over a hundred years that all men are equal in the sight of God and before the law. But we have never made the children believe it. Unless we do, we are lost. That is the evidence of history. So long as one man in America is without hope, so long is the whole nation without hope. If one man lack a vision, we shall all lack it. That is the task for the future: to give all men hope, to assure them that they do not live by bread alone."

"It all comes down to the never-ending fight against the 'gray men,' " said Jerome.

"Yes. The fight against those who love only their own bellies and their own bank accounts. The fight against those who see in possessions the only reason for living. Religion, thus far, has failed to conquer the 'gray men,' or even to fight them. It must begin, this fight. It cannot begin soon enough."

Philip paused. He looked at Jerome queerly. "You are quite wrong, you know," he said. "My father isn't a 'gray man.' He only needed money. Someone should have told him, in his early days, that a man does not need to demonstrate his competence and justify his existence by the making of money. He knows that now. Yes, you are wrong."

Jerome stood up abruptly. "Let us have luncheon together," he said.

Philip sighed. They went out.

Jerome did not speak again of what they had been discussing, but Philip knew that he was thinking, and he was satisfied.

Jerome began to speak of Mary. Amalie and the girl were returning to America after a few months in Europe. They had attended the Jubilee of Queen Victoria; friends of Jerome's in England had been instrumental in presenting both Amalie and Mary at Court. "I want the girl to get a feeling of stability, of the firm integration of history," said Jerome. "She is seventeen now and she has a mind. When she returns, she wishes to go to Cornell University. I hardly thought I'd live to see the day of coeducation in America!"

"Mary has a great soul," said Philip. His face was moved. He looked away from Jerome. "I only hope she will marry as great and as good a man as she is a woman."

"Oh, I have plans for her," said Jerome, with smug satisfaction. His expression was bright with pride and love. "But there's my boy, too. He's to go to Groton very soon. My God, how time flies. Banal, that remark, isn't it? Will's twelve now, and has the makings of a rousing businessman. But Amalie's been careful of him. He goes to Sunday school, and his mother teaches him constantly that he has a duty to others above his duty to himself. Whether he is taking the lesson to heart or not, only time will tell. He has a good bank account of his own," added Jerome wryly.

After the meal Philip went back to his father's Bank. Alfred, as usual, appeared happy to see his son. Philip sat down. "I've talked with Jerome about what we discussed last night, Father," he said. "I think he will endow a few scholarships. With yours, and mine, the thing ought to be impressive."

"You didn't mention my name, I hope?" Alfred asked quickly.

"No," lied Philip.

Alfred said: "I haven't hated Jerome for years. Of course, we could never be friends, I suppose. We couldn't even be speaking acquaintances. I have never forgotten Amalie. I haven't forgotten Jerome's blackguardly way of managing the situation. But I don't blame either one of them now. Perhaps I am just tired."

He added: "I have a feeling that one of these days Jerome and I shall meet, and—things—will be cleared up."

"Yes," said Philip, with an odd glance. "I think they will."

Alfred went on almost mournfully: "You know, Philip, it seems very vindictive of Jerome that he never allowed Mary to visit us again. I quite loved the child, and Dorothea did, too. What harm could we have done her?"

"But you met her often on the road, quite accidentally," Philip reminded his father, with a smile. "And at the homes of discreet and mutual friends. Mary can be quite subtle."

"I never thought that quite honorable," said Alfred uneasily. "If her father forbade it, perhaps she should have obeyed not only the letter of the law but its spirit."

"Mary has a lot of sense, and she is a creature of reason," replied Philip. He told his father of Mary's impending return. "And I had a letter from her this morning," he went on. "And a photograph."

He took an envelop from his pocket, and Alfred seized the photograph eagerly. He saw that fine and delicately carved face, haughty in its youth and beauty, the wide fringed eyes full of spiritual light and resolution. The pale hair was not frizzed on the forehead; it lay over the fragile but strong contours of her head in long smooth waves, and was coiled in a thick and glistening chignon on the nape of her neck.

"What a lovely chin, so high and valorous," said Alfred, with love. "Her nose is exactly like Uncle William's. She has his look, too. What a sweet child."

"She is seventeen," said Philip. "Not a child. Not even in years, and certainly not in character."

Alfred put on his spectacles to read the inscription on the photograph, which was written in the sharpest, smallest script: "To my darling Philip, with all my love. Mary."

"How touching," said Alfred. "One understands that under all that pretty coldness is a really warm heart. She is much attached to you, Philip."

Philip took back the photograph. His expression was more odd than ever.

"And I love Mary, too," he said very quietly.

"Who could not?" Alfred's tone was absent. Then he said: "Philip, you are now over thirty. You never speak of marriage. You really ought to, you know. All that I have will be yours. You must have children."

Philip smiled. "I promise you I'll be married within two years," he said.

Alfred was delighted and pleased. "Josephine Tayntor—I hope?" he suggested. "Of course, she is three or four years older than you, but she seems quite immature. Or Goodwin's girl? She is only twenty-two, and you see a lot of her. She won't have the fortune of Miss Josephine, but somehow that doesn't seem to matter."

"I've already made my choice," said Philip. "Now, please don't ask me, Father, but I feel you aren't going to be disappointed."

452

The endowing of twelve scholarships by Jerome Lindsey created great excitement in Riversend. All were more than pleased, until it was discovered that these scholarships were not for the exclusive benefit of the sons of the "old" families of Riversend. Indignation ran very high in several quarters when it was further discovered that seven of the scholarships went to the young sons of a machinist, two farmers, a bricklayer, a shopkeeper, a widowed seamstress, and, finally, the fourteen-year-old boy of the town drunkard. (The other five were divided among three sons of the respectable middle class and two sons of an "old" family.)

Again the cry of "nihilism, anarchism, socialism and revolutionary," rose throughout the township.

Jerome was waited upon by several of his outraged friends. Only General Tayntor understood. The other four went away fully convinced that Jerome had some nefarious scheme to undermine orderly government.

As Jerome loved a fight, he much enjoyed these encounters.

His peace of mind would not have been much enhanced had Philip informed him that Alfred was endowing two of these scholarships, a fact which the tactful Philip discreetly kept quiet.

Jerome had selected the fine private preparatory schools for his scholars. On this occasion he had another struggle on his hands. The fine schools were at first adamant in their refusal to take the sons of nameless workers and drunkards. Jerome enlisted the aid of his powerful friends in Boston and New York. He succeeded, but the newspapers were again acrid in their comments.

"The schools I selected are the most excellent ones for the preparation of young men for their duty to their country," said Jerome to Philip. "But they have somewhere gotten the erroneous idea that such men should come from well-founded and prosperous families. It was hard to convince them that perhaps the working classes might be able to produce their quota of leaders. I quoted Abraham Lincoln to them by the yard, and they quoted George Washington back at me with equal dexterity. They also quoted Alexander Hamilton, and his remark that the people were 'a great beast.' I told them that Hamilton didn't mean just the people who worked with their hands. They told me there was no evidence he didn't mean just that. But the prexies, in the main, were sensible men. They don't like novelty; it upsets them, and there's nothing so obstinate as a pedant when something out of the ordinary happens."

Mary and Amalie had returned to Riversend. Jerome invited Philip to dinner, to celebrate the homecoming. He himself was in a buoyant mood, and it annoyed him to discover that Amalie was curiously quiet and heavy of eye. "I thought you liked Philip," he said impatiently when she displayed no animation at his news. "If you wish, we can be rude and send him a message not to come."

"Don't be silly," said Amalie. There was a grayish shadow about her mouth. "Of course, I'm very fond of Philip, and am very glad that he is coming. But it just happens that I feel slightly depressed. Are you the only one in the household entitled to moods?"

Jerome smiled broadly. "There isn't enough room in this house for two moods. And I like the moods of others to coincide with mine."

"Egotistic, as usual," commented Amalie. She aroused herself a little. "Don't mind me. But did I ever tell you I don't like the town down there? I oughtn't ever to visit it. However, it was necessary. There was a length of lace that I needed, and it so happened that Rogers' had the only match."

Jerome looked at her penetratingly. So the poor darling had been snubbed again, had she? It was oddly puerile of him to believe that such "snubbing" could depress one as strong as Amalie, but believe it he did. He kissed her fondly and consolingly and could not understand why she so suddenly clung to him and cried a little. It would have amazed him had he known that there was now no comfort in his caresses.

For, that afternoon, in Riversend, Amalie had come face to face with Alfred.

She had indeed gone to Rogers'. She left the shop, holding high her parasol of black lace, and lifting her mauve silk skirts from the dust. Her bonnet of yellow silk was tied with mauve ribbons, and she looked unusually handsome and young. She strode across the narrow sidewalk towards her carriage, and collided with someone quite violently.

"I beg your pardon," said the gentleman, with distressed courtesy. "My fault, ma'am."

"So heedless of me," murmured Amalie graciously. She

454

glanced up with a smile and encountered Alfred's shocked hazel eyes.

They were alone on the sidewalk, as it was three o'clock in the afternoon, and extremely hot, and the usual crowd of shoppers had not yet appeared. Those who passed were comparative strangers to Riversend and recognized neither Amalie nor Alfred. So they stood and looked at each other in a sort of paralysis, unaware of the few men and women who brushed by them.

It was only necessary for Alfred to lift his hat politely and pass on. It was only necessary for Amalie to murmur a single word and go to her carriage. But neither could move. They could only look speechlessly into each other's eyes. Amalie's face whitened under the shade of the parasol; even her lips lost color. Alfred turned quite pale.

They stood so close that Alfred could see the trembling in Amalie's throat, the pulsing in her temples. But eighteen years, like a swift rush of impassable water, had run between them, eighteen years of suffering and loneliness for Alfred, eighteen years of anxiety and feverish restlessness and perplexity for Amalie.

Their mutual shock held them in their paralysis. Amalie might have broken the enchantment, and, in fact, made a slight attempt to do so. But Alfred's eyes paralyzed her. They had become vivid with hunger and grief and mournful passion, and something that could only be urgent and pathetic tenderness. She felt something turn and twist in her at what she saw so simply and tragically revealed. She put out her hand to him, not so much in greeting and politeness as in an imploring gesture, utterly impulsive and involuntary.

He looked down at her hand as if he could not believe it. And then he took it and held it. He said faintly: "You haven't changed, Amalie."

"Oh, yes," she heard herself saying on a slight rush of breath. "I've changed. Oh, yes." And then her face was scarlet and shaken.

He listened to her gravely, as if what she had said was of profound importance to him. "I have changed, too," he said, after a moment.

His hand was warm and strong and very gentle. It let go her own. She was still conscious of the warmth and strength and gentleness.

She saw how tired and quiet he was, and how still. He had always been stolid; but he had never been still like this. It was

455

the sort of stillness that hung over and about Hilltop, steadfast and comforting and safe. He had aged, she saw, but he had the dignity of wisdom now, and not the old self-conscious dignity of a man unsure of himself.

He could see that the strength that had always been in Amalie's face had become a taut rigidity, as if the bones and muscles had tightened in a permanently tense pattern. Between her eyes, which were tired and anxious, there was a single deep cleft. But she was beautiful. She would always be beautiful. He would never forget her, nor the way she smiled, the way her lips broadened at the corners rather than thinned.

"You have a dear girl—Mary," he said. "A very dear girl. She must make you very happy, Amalie."

"Yes," she murmured. Then she said, in a louder voice: "And you have Philip."

What were they saying to each other? They were speaking as if in condolences! Her heart was beating too fast. The warmth of Alfred's touch was still in her hand. She could feel a burning along her eyelids.

Now he was taking her elbow very lightly. "Your carriage?" he was saying.

He helped her in. She stumbled over the mauve ruffles of her skirt. He waited until she was seated. His bare head was white in the hot sun, and he was still looking at her searchingly.

"Good-bye," she said, trying to smile again.

"Good afternoon," he replied.

He watched her as she was driven away. The street seemed to grow darker all about him. At the corner, she turned her head and glanced back. He waved his hat at her, and she tilted her parasol in answer.

The shock remained with her all the way back to Hilltop. She could not understand it. It was like a numbness all along her nerves, a darkness in her mind.

CHAPTER SIXTY-TWO

Jerome's mood that night was one of exhilaration. It was as if he had had a secret triumph over a detested enemy. Philip listened with sympathy and with an air of kind reflection. Amalie, who usually entered into any conversation with spirit, was somewhat quiet, as if very tired. But Mary, turning her sparkling blue eyes first upon her father and then upon Philip, was absorbed. Her glance, however, was a little longer upon the younger man and sometimes the radiant paleness of her face appeared to reflect a faint color. Sometimes, too, her mouth had a passing expression of sternness and resolution, which immediately melted into a warm smile when Philip turned to her.

She would look at his hand, as it touched silver or glass, with a still intensity. She would look at his profile, and draw in her breath. Then that expression of sternness and resolution would harden her face, and her fair head would lift.

It was some time before Amalie finally became aware of all this. When she did so, she was incredulous and stunned. She would shake her head slightly, in dazed denial. It was not possible! Mary was only a child. She saw Philip's gentle and tender glance at Mary, and there was nothing in his eyes that confirmed the preposterous suspicion in Amalie's mind. However, Amalie was only slightly reassured. Philip might be as detached and abstracted as he pleased. Amalie could read her daughter's expression, could feel her tenseness.

Amalie was frightened and filled with sudden maternal protectiveness for her daughter. She knew Mary very well now. She knew that the girl was not given to sudden whims, and that her mind, once made up, was as inflexible as stone. If Mary loved Philip, she would never forget him. Nor would she keep the matter a secret. For a moment, Amalie smiled involuntarily. However he tried, or even if he did not love her in return, Philip would not escape Mary. Or, if he did escape, Mary would be mutilated for life, some virtue in her forever amputated.

But she is very young, thought Amalie, trying to reassure herself. She might forget him. After all, she has seen few young men. She has no judgment.

In order to distract her disturbing thoughts she tried to interest herself in the conversation between Jerome and Philip. Jerome was in one of his scoffing moods when he derided the world and all in it. It was his usual reaction to a personal victory. His was the derision of one who had triumphed. It did not matter how small or great the triumph, and Amalie in the beginning never knew whether he had merely won a point over one of the directors of the bank or had succeeded in accomplishing something of profound importance.

He had been relating to Philip his conquest of the pedants in the matter of the scholarships. Amalie began to feel embarrassed. Such a small conquest! She could see those timid and desiccated old men, finally overcome by the determined and brilliant arguments of the excited Jerome. Amalie felt pity for the old men. Her embarrassment grew, and she could not look at Philip for fear she might see amusement in his attentive smile. But Philip was not amused; he was only compassionate. Was it possible that Jerome had lost that delicate sense of proportion which had seemed one of his most conspicuous virtues? Or was there a bedevilling something in him which distorted that virtue at times, and then almost always on some insignificant occasion?

"It is amazing how much importance these pedagogues arrogate to themselves," said Jerome contemptuously. "They appear to believe that their musty little studies are the colonnades in which Socrates sat, and that their pronouncements on petty matters are the ultimates of wisdom. I could not refrain from quoting to one of them a certain phrase from Goldsmith's 'The Citizen of the World': '—minims, the tenants of an atom, thus arrogating a partnership in the creation of universal Nature!' "

"That floored him, I suppose," said Philip, smiling. "Or did he quote right back at you Pascal's little paragraph: 'Man— is a thinking reed. The entire universe need not arm itself to crush him. A vapor, a drop of water, suffices to kill him. All our dignity, then, consists in thought. By it we must elevate ourselves, and not by space and time, which we cannot fill. By space the universe encompasses and swallows me up like an atom; by thought I comprehend the world.' "

"They comprehend nothing," said Jerome derisively. "They are unable to think. When I explained to them that I wish my boys to have a foundation in the practical sciences, they were aghast. Learning is nothing, I told them, if it is not utilitarian. Classical education has no part in a very realistic world, or, at the most, a minor part."

You did not always think so, thought Philip. And do you, in fact, really think so now? He said: "I still believe in solid learning of the academic sort. Only by understanding the long old thoughts of men can men of today understand themselves and their place in nature. Socrates is as fresh and vivid today as he was a couple of thousand years ago. The mind of man is the only constant, the only verity. Do you remember what Bacon said? 'Let men only consider: if they would apply only a small portion of the infinite expenditure of talent, time, and fortune now given to matters and studies of far inferior impor-

458

tance and value, to sound and solid learning, it would be sufficient to overcome every difficulty.' In other words, man can really add cubits to his stature by the exercise of his mind. Jesus was only cynical when he pretended to doubt the efficacy of thought."

Jerome was restless. Puffs of quick smoke issued from his cigar. He said: "Our conversation tonight is strangely familiar. My father and I used to spend hours hurling contradictory quotations at each other." He paused. "Sometimes I almost believe that there will be no place in the future for any man except the man who has excluded from his personal world everything but science and scientific evidence."

You don't believe that either, thought Philip.

They went into the library for brandy and coffee. The heat of the day had softened into a light silvery rain which whispered at the windows. Philip could hear the gentle scraping of the elm bough at the eaves. Lavender shadows filled the quiet room. Jerome had suddenly lost his usual airy volubility. He sat smoking in somber silence, frowning to himself, moving restlessly in his chair. Amalie embroidered. Mary sat and looked at Philip. Philip, as he sipped his coffee, was conscious of a growing uneasiness. There was in this murmuring atmosphere a tenseness which he could not understand.

A servant entered to light a lamp, which glowed like a small amber moon in the closing dusk. The rain had stopped. But all the world was musically adrip with sweet fresh sounds. The gentle evening sky had turned lilac and silver.

It was then that Mary proposed that she and Philip take a walk before he leave for his own home. Philip amiably agreed, glanced at Amalie for permission. She nodded with a faint smile. But she watched Philip and Mary leave the room with trouble in her heart. There had been something in Mary's clear and delicate face that renewed Amalie's apprehension.

Jerome said, after a little: "Sometimes Philip annoys me. I am afraid he is something of a pedant himself."

He is your conscience, thought Amalie, with sudden and piercing intuition. He is what is really in your mind. She said: "Oh, no, Philip is not a pedant. You know he is not, really, Jerome."

Jerome did not reply. He refilled his brandy glass. Amalie returned to her embroidery. She was vaguely disturbed because her fingers were trembling.

In the meantime, Mary and Philip were walking slowly down the road from Hilltop. They reached a stretch of fragrant pines and spruces. Overhead, the sky had deepened to a soft heliotrope, wide and calm. The moon was a white face in the sky, as she slowly climbed through tinted mists. The silent west was a lake of pale green, as deep and flat as jade, in which sailed small rosy clouds. The grass gleamed with drops of crystal; crystal hung on the pines, which exuded a strong fragrance. It was that hour of twilight which casts no shadows, so that everything seemed without substance. Even the violet hills appeared to be only banks of cloud against the cool sunset.

The pine woods were very quiet. Philip and Mary walked hand in hand. Her head was higher than his, and lifted with that prideful grace he loved so much. There was such a tranquillity about the girl, such an integrity. Philip's hand tightened on hers. He thought, with deep and simple passion: Let nothing ever hurt her! She is not a nature to endure hurt, without maiming. My darling, my dear darling.

They reached a small clearing in the little woods. There stood their favorite flat stone. They sat down on it, and did not speak for a long time.

Then Mary said, very softly: "In February, I'll be eighteen." She tossed her head, as if her silvery mane still lay upon her shoulders instead of being coiled in its shimmering smoothness on her neck.

"Yes. I know, my dear."

"I have decided not to go to Cornell, Philip. I thought I would, at first, and Papa was pleased. But I want something else now."

Philip lifted Mary's hand, and smoothed each of the white fingers separately. She watched his bent head. Now her slender pale face quickened, glowed, melted.

"What do you want, Mary?" he asked gently.

"You, Philip," she answered, and her voice was very clear.

He dropped her hand. He looked at her, white with shock and disbelief. He moved as if to get up. But she put her hand on his arm.

"You'll never ask me, dear," she said. "I don't know why. I'll have to ask you, it seems. Will you marry me, Philip?"

He saw her shining eyes, her smile, the pale brightness of her hair. He thought: I never knew a man could experience such a pain as this, and not die of it. Then he said: "Mary, look at me."

She obeyed him slowly and intently. She did not answer after she had finished her deliberate and tender scrutiny, but only smiled, as if he had said something foolishly endearing, like a child.

"I see you," she said.

Philip sighed and turned away.

"I think," she added, and now her natural voice was shaken, "that you are being very stupid, Philip. You wanted me to see your back, didn't you? You wanted me to see the way your neck is set deep in your shoulders, didn't you? Yes, I saw all this. But I see your face, too. I see all of you." She took his arm and forced him to turn to her again.

His eyes were stark and somber with pain. "I am fifteen years older than you, Mary."

"Fifteen years." She spoke meditatively. "What are fifteen years? I'm not a child, dear. I don't think I ever was."

He saw her mouth. It was very near to his. He thought: It would do her no harm, would it, to kiss her? Just once? Only once?

He moved away from her. He said: "Mary, I have always loved you. I don't think it matters so much now whether I tell you that. At least, I hope not. You are so young, Mary, my darling. I must try to make you understand. You really don't know what you are saying!" He had to stop, to catch his breath, for there was a constriction in his throat. "I thought about—this—once. But now I see how ludicrous, how shameful, the very thought was." Despair was confusing him. "You must think of your parents," he added faintly.

But Mary, looking off into the distance, only smiled with dreaming reflection. "Philip, I know a lot of things now. I know Mama married your father because he had what she wanted. I know all about her life. While we were in Europe together alone she told me everything. I know that I was born scarcely six months after she married Papa. Mama and I have grown very close. We never were, you know, until I was almost fourteen.

"Then we understood each other. Mama loves you. Papa admires you, and is very fond of you. They will be glad."

Philip uttered a sharp exclamation of denial and pain. Mary took both his arms in her hands and looked at him fully.

"All my life," she said, "since I have known you, I have loved you, Philip. Papa and I understood each other; Mama and I do now. But neither of them has my whole confidence, as you have. You are part of me, Philip. I have never been able to see, or want, anybody else. Mama understood, and that is why she took me to Europe—I think. But it was as if

I had—armor—over my heart. I thought of nothing but you. So you mustn't be afraid. You are all I have, and all I ever want."

She waited. He did not answer. But she saw his suffering, his stern repression, his denial and misery. She said: "You'll have to trust me, Philip."

She held out her hands to him, palms up, in a simple and touching gesture of pleading surrender. He took them, held them with desperate strength.

"How can I take you, Mary? You are so young, so—unknowing. It would be a crime."

"Oh, why!" she cried, loudly and impatiently. "You are insulting, Philip. Philip, my darling! Look at me, really look at me, Philip!"

"I have never done anything else but look at you, Mary. I—I had my hopes, my silly dreams. But now I've had time to think."

She laughed with sweet triumph. "You think too much. Are you going to marry me, Philip? Or must I haunt you up and down Riversend until public opinion compels you to make an honest woman of me?"

Again she waited. But he did not move. His eyes, however, stared at her with passionate wretchedness and hunger. Then, sighing with indulgent impatience, she put her soft young arms about his neck, bent her head, and kissed him full upon the lips.

Still, for several long moments, he did not move. Then he caught her to him with a kind of wildness and abandon, and pressed his cheek against her hair.

CHAPTER SIXTY-THREE

"You did—what?" said Amalie incredulously, pushing back a lock of hair, her familiar gesture when baffled.

"I asked Philip to marry me," replied Mary, with her usual crystal composure.

Philip said: "Please, Amalie. It wasn't quite like that. Mary makes it sound so bald. That is because she is so direct."

Amalie had begun to smile. "You misunderstand me, Philip. I was surprised that you hadn't asked her, and that you made it necessary for her to ask you."

Her smile remained steady, but her eyes were anxious and abstracted.

They were together, these three, in Amalie's small sitting-room. The late August twilight deepened outside the opened windows in purple and lush green shadows.

"I knew Philip would never ask me," said Mary calmly. "I knew it was no use to wait."

"But how—improper," murmured Amalie. She seemed tired. She rested her head against the black-and-red tapestry of her low rocker. She was forty now, and her natural stateliness had increased with her years. A startling white lock ran through the thick masses of her black hair, from the peak on her forehead to the nape of her neck. Her strong face was hardly lined; her violet eyes were steady and full of vigor. Only her mouth, though still ripe and rich, betrayed a chronic sadness and restless despondency. These disappeared when she smiled; then her features sparkled with merriment and humor.

Philip thought that not even Mary had this splendor of Amalie's. Her green silk gown, tight of bodice, tight and prim to her ankles, was caught towards the back in falling tiers of drape and ruffle. The smooth and shining cloth outlined her long thighs; her ankles were the ankles of a girl.

Mary, tall and straight, even stiff, on the edge of her chair, was very slender in her youthful immaturity, her blue voile dress classic in its gentle folds. If Amalie had splendor, this girl had a patrician grace, valiant and pellucid.

There is something to be said for having a mind without doubt, thought Philip. Mary might frequently give battle, but she would always have an inner peace. That peace had been denied Amalie. She had too much imagination.

"I can't see that I was improper," said Mary simply. "Someone had to speak. It had to be me."

Philip laughed, somewhat embarrassed. Then he said: "Amalie, I am so glad that you don't mind."

"Mind?" Amalie lifted her brows. "I am grateful. I've always loved you, Philip. I am proud that you want Mary."

She moved restlessly. She looked at her slippers. "I want to ask one thing of you both, however. I want you not to speak of this to your father, to Jerome, until Mary is eighteen. That will be next February."

Mary's fair brows drew together. "But why, Mama?"

Amalie glanced at Philip. She said, and her voice was not quite candid: "Mary, you are still only seventeen. Until a girl is eighteen, she seems a child to her father. He would be outraged at the thought that you are thinking of marriage."

"I quite agree," said Philip.

Amalie's eyes, unwillingly lifting, met Mary's. You will then, said those eyes, be your own mistress, when you are eighteen. And Mary's eyes replied: I see. I know.

"If you think it best," Philip went on, "then it is best, Amalie." He hesitated. "Do you think Jerome might have any objection? After all, I am nearly fifteen years older than Mary. Jerome might think that too elderly." He smiled with an eager anxiety. "And, of course," he added, with painful hesitation, "there are other things too."

"None are important. None exist, except in your own mind," said Amalie. Her face had clouded. Then she stood up suddenly, and Philip rose also. Amalie took his hand, bent her head and kissed him. "Dear Philip," she said, and her voice faltered.

She kissed Mary then, touching the fair smooth head with a tender hand. "It was only yesterday that you were a most provoking little girl, darling," she said. There were tears in her eyes. And the trouble and fear in her heart became sharper, more alive.

Philip walked home slowly that evening, under a moon that threw a brilliant wash of silver over the quiet world.

Far below in the valley he could see the chaotic tiers of light which were the windows of the Riversend Community buildings. They were set in a small park-like tract of land, lovingly kept by hundreds of appreciative hands. Now that the days were drawing in, the workers were flocking to the buildings again, there to work, to read, to listen, to sing, to laugh, to play, to boast of harvests and to plan work for the winter.

The night was sweet, warm and quiet. But Philip was filled with a curious uneasiness, a sense of foreboding. He could not shake it off. He had just become betrothed to a girl he had always loved. For the first time in his life, the future had potentialities for beauty and fullness and excitement. He had become a whole man, was no longer merely a scholarly spectator.

Yet he was troubled. He knew that part of this came from a growing apprehension as to Jerome's reaction to this betrothal. Much as Jerome relied upon him, and liked him, and confided in him, Mary was his ewe lamb, his darling. Philip thought of himself with dispassionate coldness. What had he to offer Mary? Not strength of body, nor youth, nor ardor. He saw himself as Jerome would see him.

He had at first decided not to tell his father of this betrothal until February. But now he felt that he must tell him. He wanted some reassurance from another.

He found Alfred alone in the chill and lonely house, reading in the narrow library. Alfred looked up with his usual pleasure when his son entered the room. He is so lonely, thought Philip. I leave him too much. I am always at Hilltop.

He sat down near Alfred, who immediately asked about Amalie and Mary. Philip answered with constraint. Then he leaned towards his father and said:

"I must tell you something, though it must remain a secret between us. When Mary is eighteen, she and I are going to be married."

Alfred's book slipped from his hand. It dropped to the floor. His pale seamed face became blank, disbelieving.

"Yes," said Philip, nodding his head, his heart sinking at his father's expression. "I hope you don't mind too much, sir."

"You say you are going to marry Mary?" said Alfred slowly.

"Yes," said Philip again. He stood up, as if forced to his feet. "We have spoken to Amalie. She seemed—glad. She even seemed to have expected it."

Alfred was silent.

"You disapprove, Father?" Philip's question was almost an exclamation.

Alfred regarded him fixedly. "No. No, I am very happy, Philip." But his light hazel eyes were full of deep trouble. "But what of Jerome?"

"We'll tell Jerome in February."

Philip waited. Alfred was silent again. His eyes did not leave his son. Then Philip could endure it no longer. He cried: "You think it disgusting of me? You think it contemptible? You look at me, and think: This poor creature dares to think of marrying that lovely girl, that child?"

Alfred started as if something sharp and fiery had touched him. He got to his feet. He said: "No, Philip. I'm not thinking that. How could you believe such a thing? You are my son, and to me you are perfect, not only because you are my son, but because of what you are."

Philip sighed.

"I am thinking of Jerome," said Alfred, with pity.

Philip walked to a table and began to lift and lay down various small objects upon it. "I've been thinking of Jerome, too," he murmured.

He heard his father's voice then, strong and firm as it had not sounded for years: "It doesn't matter, Philip. We'll find a way."

He paused, then exclaimed: "Why, how wonderful this is! I can't believe it! That dear girl, my daughter! Philip, look at me!"

CHAPTER SIXTY-FOUR

It was on the fourth of January, 1889, that Dorothea Lindsey died.

There had been no preliminary warning, except that Dorothea, who rarely if ever complained, had remarked to Alfred, the day before, that she was extraordinarily tired. It had been the holidays, she had said, as if in apology. Besides, she added quizzically, she was not as young as she had been, and that when a woman had lived fifty-four years she might be pardoned for feeling her age.

Alfred had repeated after her: "Fifty-four years!" He was very slightly older than Dorothea, and had not thought of time in relation to himself. He had been somewhat shocked and sobered. Why, it was only yesterday that he and Dorothea had talked seriously together as they strolled about the grounds at Hilltop. How old had they been? Dorothea had been eighteen, he nineteen. He had been full of plans, and Dorothea had been all sympathy and gentleness. The intervening years were like wisps of foggy mist. Through them, he could see himself and Dorothea, young and fresh and strong.

Alfred slept only fitfully that night. When he awoke in the morning he was very tired. Feeling his age! But he had not felt his age yesterday. He and Philip went down to breakfast. They were informed by a maid that Miss Dorothea was not feeling well, and that she had requested a tray in her room.

Alfred expressed his regrets. He and Philip prepared to leave for the Bank. The sleigh was waiting for them, heaped with its furry robes. The bright blue morning was just beginning to illuminate the world of snow; every fir tree was weighted with white. So pure and clear was the air that they could hear the busy sleigh-bells in the village, as others glided to their business establishments.

Alfred suddenly discovered that he had left his dispatch-case on the hall table. Philip was already in the sleigh. Alfred's first impulse was to send the coachman for his case. Then, not exactly knowing why, he turned and went back himself.

The narrow bleak hall was only duskily lighted by the radiance outside. Alfred's case was on the stiff oaken chair near the door. He lifted it. Then a strange thing happened. He felt that someone was with him in the hall.

He stood and listened. He heard nothing but the mysterious accelerated beat of his heart. It sounded like a quickening drum. He could see the dimmed light trying to struggle through the slit-like stained-glass windows on each side of the oaken hall door. Through the door to his left he saw the somber library; one of its windows looked out upon a blindingly shining world of blue and white. There was not a whisper or a movement that he could hear in all that tall and gloomy house.

Yet someone was here with him in the hall. An odd tremor passed over Alfred's flesh. His heart beat louder. He looked about him searchingly. He felt the closeness of some unseen personality; that personality came nearer to him, gliding without the slightest sound. Alfred stepped back involuntarily towards the door, his hand clutching his case. Then he could not move. Some other sense held him still, waiting, listening, feeling, with an intensity he had never before experienced.

Then he knew. He said aloud: "Uncle William!"

The unseen personality seemed to glow gently all about him, as if pleased at recognition, and radiating affection. Alfred said again, even louder: "Uncle William? It *is* Uncle William?"

He was no longer afraid. He was almost happy, almost excited. He exclaimed: "Uncle William! What is it, sir? Is there something you want?"

He looked about him, quickly, eagerly. So concentrated, so strong, was the influence of what was still unseen, that Alfred's eyes darted urgently into every corner. Had Mr. William Lindsey suddenly appeared before him, Alfred would have felt no shock, no terror, but only joyful recognition.

He felt kind laughter near him, though he could not hear it with his ears. He felt an increase in tenderness. A warming glow came over him, as if he had heard affectionate words promising happiness and comfort. "Yes, yes," said Alfred softly. "How good of you, Uncle William. I am so glad you have come here."

Was that a sigh, a murmur, he had heard? He strained his ears. The personality was retreating from him. He followed its

467

going. It had reached the stairs. Alfred moved too, involuntarily, as if hypnotized. Suddenly, the personality had gone. Alfred reached the stairway, tried to peer up into its dim height. Then something impelled him to race up the stairs with the speed of urgent youth.

A maid, her arms filled with sheets, was just going into Alfred's room. She turned and stared at Alfred with astonishment, frightened by his grim white face. Here was her master, coated and hatted, his case in his gloved hand, as she had seen him, only a few minutes ago, leaving the house. Now he was staring at her wildly.

"Miss Dorothea!" he exclaimed. "How is Miss Dorothea?"

The girl, taken aback, stammered: "Miss Dorothea? I took away her tray just a while ago, sir. She was sleeping. She hadn't touched her breakfast."

Alfred swung about abruptly. He opened Dorothea's door with urgent swiftness. Dorothea lay upon her pillows, very still, her eyes closed. There was no sound of her breathing. Her face was the color of wax, with greenish shadows.

Alfred stood beside the bed and looked down upon her. He stood like that for a long time. Dorothea was smiling faintly; her gray braids were spread over the pillows, like the braids of a girl. A long time passed. Alfred could feel nothing but numbness and quietness.

At last he became aware that Philip was beside him, his hand on his arm, speaking softly. Alfred turned to him dazed.

"Uncle William was here," he said. "He came for Dorothea."

CHAPTER SIXTY-FIVE

"You are surely going to the funeral, Jerome?" said Amalie.

"No, I am not," he said. "Why should I?"

Amalie was stunned. She glanced at Mary, who sat at her mother's right at the breakfast table. The girl was looking steadily at her father. She was quite pale, and her crimson wool frock enhanced that paleness.

"Aunt Dorothea is your sister, Papa," she murmured.

Jerome, unperturbed, drank his coffee. But Amalie knew he was angry. He put down his cup. His dark eyes were narrowed and full of hard malice.

"Look here, my girl," he said roughly, "let's not be sentimental. I haven't seen 'Aunt Dorothea' for over eighteen years.

I don't care to see her now that she is dead. I'm no sanctimonious fool who goes blubbering to the funerals of enemies."

Amalie and Mary were silent. But they continued to regard him fixedly.

"Moreover," said Jerome, "I want no member of my family going down there either."

Mary said quietly: "She is Philip's aunt, by adoption. We owe something to Philip. He was very fond of her."

Jerome struck his thin brown hand on the table. "Philip's fondness has nothing to do with us. He isn't a fool. He understands. Let that end it."

Amalie found her voice, but it came from her white lips trembling and muffled: "Your sister! She never harmed you, Jerome. She took the place of your mother. She tried to be fond of you, but you always hated her. Oh, what can I say? Is there no natural feeling in you, no kindness?"

Jerome stood up. He stared at his wife almost malignantly. "Sentimental twaddle! Whimpering idiocy! 'Natural feeling,' by God! Because I refuse to be mawkish you come whining to me like an imbecile. I want to hear no more of this, do you understand? Both of you?"

Mary rose silently and went out of the room. Jerome watched her go. Then he swung upon Amalie savagely.

"So, you've finally succeeded in turning my daughter against me, haven't you? That makes you feel very contented, I suppose. You've misrepresented me to her for years now, done all you could to separate us. I presume you are happy at last."

Amalie stood up also, and leaned against the table. "How can you say that, Jerome?" she whispered. "How can you be so cruel?"

She stopped. Her purple eyes became very large and intense. "Cruel," she repeated, still in a whisper.

But Jerome was enraged. "You deny it, ma'am? You deny that you have poisoned my daughter's mind against me, ever since she was fourteen years old? I've seen it, and watched it for years. I haven't been so blind that I couldn't see. And now you take this maudlin occasion to emphasize to her that I am a 'cruel' man, an insensible father, a bad brother. My God!" he added, with disgust and increasing rage.

Amalie was paler than before. But she said steadily: "Your father would want you to go to your sister's funeral."

"Don't talk like a fool!"

Amalie drew in a deep breath. She appeared weak. She said: "There is another thing. You can offend a community's

469

morals, if you wish, and can be forgiven. But you can't offend its etiquette, its good manners. So——"

" 'Morals'!" ejaculated Jerome viciously. "What do you know of 'morals'?"

Amalie shrank back.

"You are an excellent one to talk of morals," Jerome continued. "You haven't any. If you had had the slightest moral sense you would not have gone treacherously behind my back and turned my daughter against me."

"You are wrong," said Amalie. She was trembling. "I did not turn Mary against you. If she is not what she was to you, that is your own fault, not mine."

She was stupefied, incredulous. Was this Jerome, her husband, the man she loved, this evil-eyed stranger with the gray hair and tight dark face? Was this actually hatred for her which she saw in his eyes, a leaping and merciless hatred?

How had she not known that he was cruel? Surely, she had known! But she had crushed down the knowledge. She could keep it down no longer.

Her voice was steadier now, and she looked at him unmovingly: "You are a cruel man, Jerome. I don't think I ever acknowledged it before, even to myself. I can forgive anything, Jerome, but cruelty. Anything."

Yes, that was true, she thought. She could not forgive cruelty, could find no justification for it. It was the most evil, the most wicked, the most unpardonable thing. A cruel man had no virtues at all. Cruelty prohibited them. A cruel man was dangerous, treacherous. He might have passions, but he could not truly know love.

Amalie's tortured mind, swift and sharp now, ran over the years. She thought of all that Jerome had accomplished for the good of thousands of desperate men and women. If he was really cruel, why had he done this? Then she knew. It had been because he had hated Alfred. Good had been the excellent fruit on a poisonous tree. Was that possible? It seemed that it was possible. What Jerome had done had not touched his heart. Because it had not come from his heart. It had come from his restless and unrelenting soul.

She knew he was not happy, because he did not possess the capacity for happiness. He was restless because it was not possible for him ever to feel peace. There was something unresolved in Jerome. And that was because he was cruel.

Amalie was terrified. How was it possible to live with Jerome in any sort of affection or amity, now that she knew he

470

was cruel, now that she had acknowledged it?

"So I am cruel, am I?" said Jerome, in a pent voice. "So that is what you have been telling Mary all these years, eh?"

Amalie could not speak. There was a pain in her breast that was almost past enduring. There was a sickness in her throat.

She thought: How naïve I am. How little I have known about the deviousness of the human soul! I don't know anything—nothing at all.

"No doubt," Jerome went on, "you are thinking regretfully of the tender first husband you so easily betrayed and abandoned. Why not tell him? It would give him a great deal of satisfaction, I am sure."

His manner, his face, his glinting eyes, were filled with ugliness. And with mysterious fear.

During all these years Amalie had believed that Alfred was the one beset by a secret knowledge of inner inferiority and insecurity. Yet now she understood with sudden illumination that, to a great extent, she had been wrong. Alfred's insecurity had arisen from his sense of gratitude to his uncle, from his devotion to William Lindsey. Otherwise, he had been strong. He had acquired wisdom. This she had learned from Philip.

But Jerome would never be wise. He would always be at odds with the world. He hated because he feared. He hated because he could never trust.

Compassion rolled over Amalie like a smothering wave. She held out her hands to Jerome. "Oh, please don't, darling!" she cried softly. "I am so sorry."

But Jerome could not be moved. He gave her another malevolent look. Then he turned and went out of the room.

Amalie remained alone for a long time.

It seemed to her that she had been alone for so long. She had been alone all her life. She was filled with desolation, the awful desolation that comes to one who understands with remorseless finality.

I am tired, she thought. I am so tired of trying to understand, of trying to be happy. There is something unresolved in me too.

CHAPTER SIXTY-SIX

Dorothea was buried on January seventh, in the family plot.

The day was all crystal and white and glittering blue. The black pines of the cemetery blazed with icicles. The grave was a raw black gash in the pure earth. Scores of Dorothea's friends had come here. She had never inspired much love, but she had inspired respect. Her life had been above reproach. These were cold virtues, but at the last they were appreciated.

Some whispered that Alfred seemed very calm and resigned. He looked at the grave, at the heaps of ferns and hothouse flowers waiting on the brink. Some said he was stunned, numb, inconsolable. How else could he keep from betraying some grief at the sight of the coffin of the cousin, the sister, who had served him so faithfully, and with such affection?

Philip, his son, stood beside him. Poor misshapen creature! thought the friends. Poor Alfred Lindsey. He had nothing at all in the world to comfort him, thought the sentimental. His first wife had died, his second wife had betrayed him. He had no strong sons, no pretty daughters, to give him consolation and hope.

Philip could sense their commiserating thoughts quite clearly. "No consolation and hope." But what consolation or hope was there in living? The only inevitable thing at all was man's suffering and man's death. Yet, when these came to him, the average man was stunned and incredulous and despairing. He had made no preparation for them in his life, as did the Chinese. He had no philosophy for the inevitables. They were catastrophes and calamities, the inexplicable, the events that ought not to have occurred. Yet man should know that he would suffer, that he would face death and lose to death all that was significant and dear to him. To prepare for agony, for parting, ought to be part of the education of every human being. Without this education, man lost his dignity, for in pain and loss he was revealed to others and to himself as a creature who was ill-prepared.

Nor did religion so prepare a man, though the holy books spoke extensively of suffering and death. But the emphasis was always on life. Religion took no real stand on the negatives. Man cannot live by the positives alone, for they are only a portion of life. The moon, thought Philip, has a dark face and a bright one, but they are one and the same thing. No one emphasizes that. Thus man laments in bewildered agony at sight of the dark face, and can find no consolation and no hope.

Alfred, dressed in black broadcloth, his head bared to the winter sun, leaned on his ebony cane and looked at the grave. Good-bye, dear Dorothea, he said in his heart. I know you are happy. I wish, my dear, that I might have been able to give you some happiness here. That wish is all I can send to you.

How obtuse I was! There were so many times when I might have smiled at you, and laughed with you. But I did not. Why? I don't know. I think it is because we never accept the fact that inevitably death must come, and that all the things unsaid and undone will stand beside and around us like closed graves.

He remembered that Dorothea had wanted to plant yellow daffodils along the left side of the house, but that he had had one of his rare moods of obstinacy on the subject. Why, daffodils had only one blooming, bright and golden to be sure, but for such a little time, and then their seared foliage remained an eyesore for the rest of the summer. A blankness was left behind. But now, with deep poignancy, he wished that he had let Dorothea have those daffodils along the house. Poor Dorothea. He thought of the daffodils, and all at once he seemed to see Dorothea's secret nature completely revealed. She had loved the flowers for their cool springtime blooming, for their vehement and passionate golden life, for their joyous affirmation in the renewal of summer hope. His bitterest grief came to him then. He ought to have let her have the daffodils. Well, he would have them planted where she had wished them. He would have them planted on her grave. The yellow cloud of them would dance in her memory.

The minister had concluded his prayers. He threw a handful of mingled mud and snow onto the coffin that lay in the grave. The mourners moved restlessly. They instinctively did not like that gesture. They huddled closer together, and turned their eyes away. They will not look at the inevitable, thought Philip. They will pile up the fires higher when they go home, and many of them will order stiffer whiskeys-and-soda, and quite a few more will invite friends in for the evening, and they will talk and laugh a little louder than usual.

Suddenly there was a murmur of surprise among the mourners, and a stir. A tall young girl in sealskin jacket and wearing a round sealskin hat was moving towards the grave. Her arms were filled with hothouse lilies and roses. Mary Lindsey! They stared at her in disbelief and active curiosity, and also with peculiar relief, as if she had saved them from the necessity of looking at the grave. But Mary did not return their stares. She looked steadily before her, her wide blue eyes lucid and quiet. She went directly to Alfred and Philip. She smiled at them tenderly.

"Mary," murmured Alfred.

"My dear," whispered Philip.

She stood on tiptoe to kiss Alfred's cheek, and then kissed

Philip. She turned to the grave then, and dropped the flowers upon the coffin. "Good-bye, Aunt Dorothea," she said softly. She stood between Alfred and Philip, her arms linked in theirs, and she smiled again.

She went home with them, to the dark, quiet house. She stopped when Alfred stopped. He pointed to the left side of the house. "I'm going to plant daffodils there," he said. "Dorothea wanted them."

Mary glanced at Philip. There were tears on her lashes. She took Alfred's arm again, and the three of them went into the house.

The servants had allowed the fires to burn low. Mary briskly tossed coal upon them. She lighted lamps. She moved about quickly and lightly. To Philip, at least, it appeared that she left a trail of frail brightness behind her. A maid hurriedly brought in tea and fresh hot biscuits and jam, and Mary served them. Philip and Alfred had sat down, overcome with heaviness and despondency, watching the girl, but now, as she poured their tea and laughed a little and spoke with casual cheerfulness, they forced themselves to respond, for very politeness' sake.

"It seems I'll have to take care of you two," she said, sitting on the edge of a chair and sipping her tea. "Aunt Dorothea would be much annoyed if she knew that you were sitting here in what she called 'the dumps.'" She paused. "After all, one must go on living." She glanced at them artlessly, then smiled. "The only question is: Why?"

"Why?" repeated Alfred heavily.

But Philip found himself smiling, in spite of himself.

"I think Mary is laughing up her sleeve at us," he said.

Alfred tried to be shocked. But he failed. A renewed warmth was penetrating him. He began to feel some consolation and peace.

"One must have some reverence for the dead," he said uncertainly.

"Reverence?" Mary's eyebrows went up. "Why more so than when they were here? They're probably just as nasty or nice or kind or foolish as before. They are just the same. Except that they are beginning to learn a few more things. It would be interesting to know what Aunt Dorothea is learning right at this moment." She laughed a little. "Probably she is resisting some idea which doesn't coincide with her preconceived beliefs, poor darling."

She added, a little more seriously: "Of course, we all miss her. She knows that. She knows we can't help it. But she would think it very silly to weep and wail over her going. Aunt Dorothea had such character."

When a few friends came to sit and condole with the bereaved father and son, they were aghast to hear laughter in the drawing-room. They found Mary happily refilling teacups and plates. They found Alfred and Philip smoking, their expressions comforted and amused.

"She is like her mother," they said later, when, both shocked and discomfited, they had left the house. "She has no reverence or decency. I am surprised that Alfred encouraged her. As for Philip, he always seemed so proper and conventional. Yet, there he was, laughing at some foolish remark she made, and rising to greet us as if we were most unwelcome."

CHAPTER SIXTY-SEVEN

Quarrels between Jerome and Amalie were usually hot and brief, ending in reconciliation and laughter.

But this quarrel, though apparently passing, did not end in laughter. It ended in a kind of queer silence, like a truce.

Amalie, with her profound understanding, knew that she had struck deeply at Jerome with her accusation of cruelty. He could not forgive her because he knew that she had spoken the truth. She had made a breach between them which could never be healed.

The dark days of January and February were wretched ones. Jerome went to New York alone, on business. He did not invite Amalie this time. On this journey, he also took his young son away to school.

"At least," said he to Amalie, "you won't have much opportunity to turn William against me."

Amalie did not reply to this. She was very weary these days, sunken far into despondency and silence. She missed her boy. But she missed something else more urgent and passionate. She missed what she had believed was Jerome. It did not matter that the man of her imagination had never existed. She felt the loss as intensely as if he had died and a stranger had taken his place.

Though she knew that Jerome was as miserable as herself, she was powerless to do anything at all about it. She was too tired.

Mary was her comfort now, sweet, cool young Mary with her neutral voice, her eyes that never clouded for very long. Mary did not speak of that day in the dining-room when Jerome had lashed at his wife and daughter with such ugliness and fury. She did not speak of Dorothea. When Philip came, she greeted him with a brightening of her whole face, but her words were always calm and matter-of-fact. It seemed to Amalie that something strong and sure was ordering the household now. Something clean and practical was sweeping away cobwebs of wretchedness and darkness. Amalie would watch Mary and Philip together with a content she had not known for years.

Within a few days Jerome would return. Mary and Philip had decided that they must tell him now of their plans for themselves. Mary showed no perturbation. She knew what she wanted. She had decided what to do. In a character of such clarity there could be no fear or apprehension. Sometimes Philip and Amalie caught themselves exchanging glances of rueful amusement and anxiety. But in spite of themselves they could not help but contract some of Mary's decisiveness and tranquillity. She almost deceived them into believing that Jerome would receive the news placidly.

After all, Amalie would think, as she lay alone in the night, Philip has been Jerome's best friend, his only real confidant. They understand each other; there is a real affection between them. What objection could Jerome have to Philip? Years? Deformity? They were nothing. Jerome was subtle; he never saw these things in Philip. Money? Philip had plenty of that, and would have more.

But there was Alfred. It was Alfred that Jerome could never overlook. Amalie knew that Jerome thought of his cousin each time he saw his scars in the mirror. At these times Amalie found that she could not blame Jerome too much. Had Alfred faced him, man to man, that frightful day in the library at Hilltop, had they struck equal blows, then Jerome might have forgotten. But Alfred had not given Jerome a chance; he had lifted his cane against him as a man lifts a cane against a loathsome dog. He had beaten Jerome down, as a man would beat down that dog.

It was very strange. Alfred had had the most intolerable provocation. Jerome had been victorious in his betrayal. Yet Amalie, with wondering perverseness, understood that in some way Jerome had been wronged. It was very confusing.

On the day of the night when Jerome was to return, Amalie said to Mary: "Let us get it over with, child. I confess that I can't stand this much longer."

Mary smiled. "Dear Mama," she said. "There is nothing to be afraid of. I am just going to tell Papa that I am to marry Philip, and soon. That is all."

That is all. It was not so simple. Nearly half a century of hatred and animosity stood behind the girl's unworried words. What could she understand of that?

With some irritable impatience, Amalie exclaimed: "Mary, sometimes you do speak like a child! Because you have had so little experience in living, you presume that there is no such experience. You have had only a small contact with human beings, and because your range is so limited, you naïvely believe, like a child, that the world is two-dimensional. You see only what you want; you cannot understand that there are imponderables which are powerful enough to deny you your desires."

Mary regarded her straightly and quietly. "Mama," she said, after a moment's reflection, "I refuse to allow the 'imponderables' of others to hurt my life. Yes, it is simple, to me. I love Philip, and he loves me. Neither of us is responsible for anything that happened to you, or to Uncle Alfred, or to Papa. I —we—aren't going to let what happened destroy our own happiness. The very idea is not sensible! If anyone is hurt, it is not our fault." Her eyes became more penetrating, a little hard. "You do not object to Philip marrying me, Mama. Nor, I know, does Uncle Alfred. Who, then? Papa? I don't know whether he will. But if he does object, it really does not matter to us. He won't be permitted to interfere with our lives." She added: "He did not let anyone interfere with his."

Amalie had long ago begun to believe that she was invariably seduced by logic. So she listened intently to what Mary was saying.

The girl continued: "It seems to me that too many people allow 'imponderables' to thwart them. And they are always the 'imponderables' of others! The thing to do is to look at the problem simply."

Amalie said: "No matter who is hurt? That is a ruthless point of view, Mary."

But Mary replied calmly: "It may be ruthless, but I think it is sensible. I don't believe anyone should take happiness at the expense of another human being. No. But my marrying Philip will not destroy Papa's happiness, nor injure him, nor

477

wound him. Nor has he the right to demand that I let my own happiness go in order that he may enjoy to the end of his life a feud of his own making. No one has the right to interfere with the peace and happiness of anyone else, just for his own selfish reasons and prejudices. That is a crime."

"Suppose that your father disowns you for marrying Philip?" asked Amalie thoughtfully.

Mary gestured slightly with her narrow hands and smiled. "I doubt that he will. But if he does, he will lose more than I. I'll feel very sorry for him."

She left the room to put on her coat and hat for a walk in the shining cold. Amalie was left alone by the library fire. The worst thing about being logical, she thought wryly, was that one ended up in confusion. One saw too many sides. She respected Mary's clean ruthlessness, but it was ruthlessness just the same. She also admitted that Mary had a right to her own life and her own happiness. But did she not owe something to her parents?

There is something to be said for simplicity of purpose, Amalie continued to herself. Perhaps that is what has been wrong with me: I never had simplicity of purpose because I never really knew what I wanted. I began in a muddle, and I am ending up in a muddle. Jerome and I were ruthless. But it was a murky ruthlessness. At least Mary is clean and sharp like a knife blade. And I am quite certain that she would never be cruel, or helplessly brutal, or devious. As we were. Perhaps there is something to be said in favor of single-mindedness.

When Mary returned to the library, clad in a red merino frock that was short to the ankles, for walking, and in her black seal coat and round hat, Amalie held out her hand to her with tender impulsiveness. Mary kissed her calmly. She disliked all impetuousnesses, especially those based on sentimentality. She pulled up her gloves and smiled composedly. "It is such a nice afternoon for a walk. I am taking one of the dogs."

"Mary," said Amalie, "you are quite right, my darling. Take what happiness you can. Don't grow murky or confused. If you do, you might become a cruel woman, helplessly cruel."

Of course, thought Amalie, the girl was too young and inexperienced to understand. But Mary was regarding her mother with serious thoughtfulness. Then she nodded her head slowly. "Sometimes one can't help being cruel," she said. "Sometimes life can be so crushing that, to rescue one's self, one must be cruel."

Amalie went to the window to watch her daughter go romping down the hill with a cavorting dog. Her eyes were filled with tears, and her heart with aching gratitude.

CHAPTER SIXTY-EIGHT

Jerome returned home in much improved spirits. He had brought Amalie a beautiful cameo brooch from New York, and Mary an ermine jacket, a muff and a small bonnet to match.

He greeted his wife with that lightness and geniality which she had come to know as his reactions to an uneasy conscience. And acting subconsciously on the principle of feeding a condemned man his favorite dishes, she had ordered an elaborate dinner for him. Jerome looked at them quizzically. "Is this just a welcome home, or am I expected to give something, or to overlook something?" he asked, as he began to carve the stuffed goose.

Amalie colored, but Mary smiled affectionately. "All of them, Papa," she replied, with placid composure.

Jerome paused with the knife in his hand, then he began to laugh. He put down the knife, and reached over to Mary to pinch her cheek. "At any rate, I can be sure that anything you want would be harmless, my pet," he said. "What do you wish to exploit me for this time?"

Amalie glanced at Mary, but the girl was still placid. "I suggest we enjoy our dinner first," she said. For a moment her eyes softened almost regretfully as she looked at her father. She patted Jerome's hand. At that maternal gesture, he was flattered and much amused, and tried to catch Amalie's eye for a smile. But Amalie was playing with the stem of her wineglass.

Jerome, in high good humor, relayed messages for Amalie and Mary from William. "The boy settled down in his school like a caterpillar in its cocoon. When I finally left he was already bullying a few other boys. And I was always afraid he had a streak of timidity in him! He isn't like my father. He isn't like me, or like you, Amalie. Who, then?"

"Aunt Dorothea," suggested Mary, tranquilly.

How tactless! thought Amalie. But to her surprise, Jerome was smiling. "How could you know?" he asked Mary, indulgently. Then he added: "By God, my pet, I think you are right!

I was always puzzled by a certain familiarity— There must have been a brigand or something like that in the family tree."

Amalie was greatly surprised. This time Jerome had not been angered by the reference to his sister, but only amused as he admitted the resemblance between Dorothea and young William. Then, he had always secretly admired Dorothea! In spite of the incompatibility and the resentment and suspicion and hatred! Why had he admired her for her indomitable arrogance and inflexible character? Because there was a lack of these traits in himself? Again Amalie felt a sad pity and tenderness for him.

Jerome was speaking of his visit to Jay Regan and his other friends. He had dined with the Governor. His women listened with unusual and attentive politeness.

"There is something which Philip wished me to do in New York," said Jerome. "I thought he might be here tonight. I wrote him when I should be home."

Mary said smoothly: "He couldn't come tonight, Papa. He was very sorry."

"I am, too," said Jerome. "And disappointed."

Mary glanced at her mother. She said: "You are very fond of Philip, aren't you, Papa?"

"He and my father are the only men I ever trusted," he replied, and his voice was gentle. "The same integrity, the same calm logic and subtlety. One can rely upon Philip, trust him implicitly. I miss him tonight, I have a lot to tell him."

"You never find him distasteful—in any way?" asked Mary.

Jerome lifted his head and frowned at his daughter. "You mean his deformity? I did not think you so trivial, Mary! I am surprised at you. Philip is a man in every fine sense of the word. But then, you are young, and given to putting too much stress on externals. I never notice anything about Philip but his character."

Amalie put down her fork and listened with painful attention. Something like a sigh came from her. Again her eyes met Mary's.

Mary said meekly: "You are quite right. Papa. Perhaps I am trivial. I almost forgot: I have a message for you from Philip. And I'd like to give it to you alone. If Mama does not mind?"

Amalie said, almost hysterically: "Oh, I do not mind in the least, Mary! I am sure it is private."

"I can't imagine any message from Philip which would exclude your mother," Jerome rebuked his daughter.

"I am sure Philip meant no harm. It was just that he said it was somewhat—private. He said nothing about Mama."

"How single-minded you are, pet," said Jerome. "Because he did not specifically mention your Mama being present, you concluded he did not wish her to be present. You have a rigorous mentality, Mary."

"My New England conscience," suggested Mary. "So after dinner could you come into my room, Papa, and listen to the message Philip sent you?"

Jerome was pleased. Mary had not invited him to her "private consultations" for a long time. He stared at his daughter with deep love. He gave Amalie a look which was compounded of smugness, satisfaction, and almost childish triumph. Amalie sighed, smiled faintly. She touched her forehead with her crushed handkerchief.

Jerome did not notice that his wife ate hardly a morsel of the good dinner she had ordered for him. But Mary, Amalie observed, ate with her customary good appetite. Could anything shake the child very much? Perhaps. But probably it would not destroy her appreciation of food. Was this because of a lack of sensibility, or because nothing could divert Mary from any purpose she had decided upon? Almost enviously, Amalie decided it was the latter.

When the meal was over, Jerome followed Mary into her warm and pretty room. She drew a comfortable chair forward to the fire for him. She lighted his cigar daintily. He watched her with fondness. Her quiet dark-brown frock had a collar of Irish lace, and there was a touch of the same lace at slender wrists. Her pale smooth hair gleamed in the lamplight. Her long and delicate face was serene, her blue eyes were smiling and steady. Again, Jerome was struck by the singular resemblance between this young girl and his father. She bent her head in the old familiar way. Her broad, thin shoulders were set like her grandfather's, in a straight, proud elegance. She is, thought Jerome, pure white granite, like him. His hand was a little unsteady as it held his cigar.

Mary seated herself near to him. She crossed her ankles, leaned back in the chair. The firelight struck her profile. Jerome experienced a slight dizziness. It was the profile of his father, somewhat more gently carved, somewhat smaller. His father, in his youth, might have been the image of Mary.

"You are so like your grandfather, my darling," said Jerome.

"You tell me that so often, Papa," replied Mary, unruffled.

"But you don't quote," he said. "My father always quoted."

"Perhaps that is easier than finding words of one's own," Mary remarked. "Or perhaps when one is older, the thoughts of others are more easily remembered than one's own thoughts. Or Grandfather may have been too reticent, or too cautious. When he quoted others, he put the blame, or the credit, squarely on dead men's shoulders, and left himself free from censure, or from admiration. Grandfather must have been a very modest gentleman, or perhaps a somewhat timid one."

Jerome was not sure he liked these remarks. But he was surprised at Mary's shrewd insight. He considered what she had said. Then he observed, with reluctant surprise: "I almost believe my father was somewhat cowardly! But there, that is an uncharitable thought. Let us say, perhaps, that my father hid himself behind quotations."

"That does not explain why," said Mary.

"Explanations are not always kind, my love. But what is it that you have to tell me about Philip?"

Mary put up her hands, palms down, and smoothed her hair. Then she arranged her frock. She turned her eyes directly upon her father, and without any change in her neutral voice, she said: "Philip and I wish to marry, Papa. We thought you ought to know at once."

Jerome's cigar was in his mouth. He put up his hand to remove it. It fell from his fingers onto the hearth. Mary pushed it towards the fire with the tip of her boot. Jerome was slowly straightening himself in his chair. His features were wizening, darkening, his eyes narrowing to bright slits. He said softly: "What?"

Mary inclined her head with a serious smile. "Yes, Papa. We are going to be married, Philip and I." She showed no agitation or fear, though her jaw set somewhat rigidly and she thrust out her chin.

"Are you insane?" Jerome's voice had dwindled to a stifled whisper. "Do you know what you are saying?"

"Yes, Papa. I know very well what I am saying." Mary put on an expression of puzzled surprise. "Have you any objections, Papa?"

He stood up abruptly. He had to put his hand on his chair to keep himself from staggering.

"You are insane," he repeated. He had some difficulty with

482

his breathing. There was a sick and pounding constriction in his chest, a spiral whirling before his eyes.

Mary stood up now and faced him across the hearth.

She said very quietly: "Papa, you spoke about Philip tonight. You thought I was speaking of his—deformity—in a thoughtless fashion. I was really trying to find out what you thought. So it can't be Philip's—deformity—that you object to. Nor can you be objecting to Philip. What is it? Because I am young? But I'm not really. So what is it?"

Jerome's fists clenched. He half raised his right one. It fell back to his side, paralyzed. But his expression became more malign. He was panting a little.

"Who is behind this?" he asked, getting out the words as if by tremendous effort.

"No one. Only Philip and I."

"That vile cripple." The phrase seemed more terrible to Mary because of Jerome's half-inaudible muted voice. Standing stiffly on the hearth, she flung up her head, and a light passed over her face. Her eyes flashed in the dusk.

"What a sickening thing to say, Papa." Her young voice was full of hard contempt. "But you don't mean it. You can't mean it."

Even through his rage and disbelief he heard that tone, saw the white rigidity of her face. He put his hand to his neck, swallowed thickly.

He said: "Does your mother know?"

Mary inclined her head. "Yes. We told her. She is happy about it."

Jerome murmured: "The slut."

Mary's expression changed. She moved back a step, not in fear but in repulsion. She closed her eyes to shut out her father's face, but her own remained hard and invulnerable.

Jerome, his breath catching, was speaking again, almost incoherently: "One could never trust her. I never trusted her. She has no dignity, no honor, no sense of proportion. And she did this to me, to my daughter."

Mary said loudly and sharply: "My mother had nothing to do with it. She has been wretched, wondering what you would say. We had a talk, just recently. She said I had no right to take happiness, if it would hurt you. I told her you had no right to be hurt." Now, for the first time, she felt a passionate emotion of disgust and anger. Her eyes widened, filled with strong blue light. "You can't stop us, Papa. No matter what you try. I didn't think I'd have to say this to you. I thought

483

your fondness for Philip, or some natural decency, would make you consider our marriage temperately and justly, whatever your private objections which have nothing to do with us. You make me quite ill, Papa."

But Jerome was now beside himself. "I see now, why he came here, wandering obscenely around, talking smoothly. He was after you, the filthy creature. He dared to think of my daughter! He dared to think he could bring his obscenity and loathsomeness into this house!"

Mary smiled strangely, but she said nothing.

Jerome continued rapidly: "If he ever presumes to set foot in this house again, I'll kill him. You can write him to that effect, that repulsive son of a contemptible father. As for you, I'll send you away at once, until you remember who you are and what you are. Until you get over this—this sickness. You dirty little animal!"

Mary saw that there was no reasoning with him, that anything she said would only increase his demented fury. He was beyond understanding. So she only stood in silence, looking at him steadily.

He raised his fist again. "You'll stay in this house, in this room, until I can plan what to do with you. You are not to step outside for an instant, not even on the doorstep. You are not to speak to anyone."

A flicker passed over Mary's eyes, but she pressed her lips soundlessly together.

"As for your mother, and—him—I'll deal with them myself."

Slowly, as if blind, fumbling along the side of his chair, he turned away. He put out his hands, as if to guide himself around tables and lamps. Mary watched him go. Her cool young heart seemed to open on a deathly pang. She took a step towards him, then stopped. He closed the door behind him softly.

Mary put her hands over her eyes and drew in a deep, strong breath.

CHAPTER SIXTY-NINE

Amalie sat in her room waiting. A fire burned warmly on the hearth, but she felt terribly cold. She shivered. Then she would wipe dampness from her forehead and upper lip.

The house was very quiet. She could hear the notes of the grandfather clock as it struck the quarter hour, the half hour. She could hear the snapping of the trees outside in the intense cold. The curve of a brilliant crescent moon shone in through the window.

How can I bear this waiting? thought Amalie. Perhaps I ought to have gone with them.

The stillness increased. It seemed to Amalie that she was sitting alone in empty space, helpless and abandoned. The walls of the house, the very fire, the furniture, all appeared to have retreated from her. She remembered this sense of withdrawal. And then she realized that the house had never accepted her and that this was why she had never felt peace within it.

O God, she thought, and remembered how often she had thought this, I am so tired! I am tired of all the years of anxiety and pain and confusion and uncertainty. I am tired of all this insecurity and uneasiness. What is wrong with me?

She listened. There was still no sound, no movement. A wind rose briefly, shook the windows, made the fire roar up, then passed.

Jerome and Mary had been together for a long time. What was taking place there? Amalie had not heard a voice raised, nor an exclamation. The clock chimed again.

The door opened. Jerome stood on the threshold looking at her. And when she saw his face she rose up involuntarily, as if pushed.

He spoke, very softly: "You slut."

She put out her hands before her, as if to defend herself. No, not to defend herself. It was to hide Jerome's face, Jerome's most terrible face.

"You did this to me," he said, still softly. "I ought to have known that a woman like you, without tradition or honor or decency, would do a thing like this, behind my back. Well, you can't do it."

Amalie straightened until she was very tall. She was no longer terrified or stricken. She looked at Jerome unwaveringly. Then, without hurry, she went past him and out of the room.

She went to Mary. She found the girl sitting before her small fire, motionless, very white, and very still. Mary stood up when her mother entered.

"Don't worry, Mama," said Mary gently. "I am going to

485

marry Philip. Nothing can stop me." Her eyes were shining, undaunted.

She came to Amalie and put her arms about her. Amalie did not move. She had no tears. She had only this appalling suffering in her heart.

"Stay with me tonight, Mama," said Mary, understanding. "Sleep here with me."

"Yes," said Amalie. She leaned heavily against her daughter.

Mary led her to a chair. She knelt beside her mother and rubbed Amalie's icy hands. She kissed her cheek and her numb lips. Amalie appeared unaware of it all. She stared before her emptily. Then, after a little, she began to speak:

"I don't know what to do. It was his face— He hates me. I can bear anything but that."

Mary lifted her mother's hands and pressed them against her cheek.

"Oh, no, Mama, he doesn't hate you. He doesn't hate anyone except, perhaps, himself. He is so confused."

But Amalie's broken voice went on: "All these years. It was like living, always, on the cracking crust of disaster. We both felt it. I don't know why. There was something wrong with us, both of us. I thought we could be happy." She pressed the palms of her hands together, shrank in her chair, and shivered. "We were happy. Yes, I am sure of it. But always something was there, threatening. It was in ourselves. There was something wrong. It has always been wrong."

Mary sat on her heels and regarded her mother compassionately. Amalie's eyes were wild and distraught.

"We wanted security and peace, and we couldn't have them. I don't know why. Mary, you must remember that about your father. He has been cruel because he was always frightened. Do you know what it is, to be frightened like that?"

"No, Mama. I was never frightened. Because I had no need to be frightened, as you had." Mary spoke in a deep and newly enriched voice of pity and understanding. "Poor Mama. Poor Papa."

"You can't really know, Mary. You can't really know!"

"I don't know. But I can feel."

With sudden feverishness, Amalie grasped Mary's shoulder with her hand. "You mustn't marry Philip, Mary. Not for a long time. You must think of your father. Promise me this, Mary."

486

Mary stood up. She said, softly: "Mama, Papa must not be permitted to have his senseless way. In your heart, you know that. So you mustn't ask it of me."

CHAPTER SEVENTY

The cold broke during the night. It was followed by a wild storm, a blizzard that roared in on white wings from the north.

By daylight, the world was one vast movement of wind and snow. Roads in some spots were swept bare to the earth, heaped high in others. The hills were blotted out behind an immense and agitated veil of gray. Riversend huddled under the fury; at midday, it was dark enough to light lamps. The gas lamps on the streets flared with a wan and yellow light. But the streets were empty.

Philip and Alfred were sitting together in the latter's warm office. They had been talking for an hour, and their conversation was not about the Bank.

"Yes," said Alfred, "go to his bank at about three o'clock. Of course, there is the possibility that he may not have left Hilltop this morning. This is the worst storm I have seen for nearly twenty years."

He remembered the storm on the night when Jerome had returned home, to bring such devastation and misery to Hilltop. This was another such storm, savage and screaming and turbulent. Alfred was uneasy. He kept glancing through the windows. Thick flakes of snow clung to them, to be swept off, to be replaced. The fire spluttered and crackled.

"I should have gone there last night," said Philip. "But Amalie and Mary especially requested me not to. Now, it seems cowardly of me to let them face it alone."

Alfred turned his face to his son. His pale eyes were suddenly stern.

"Philip, it appears to me that I should be the one to object, not Jerome."

Philip said nothing.

Alfred sighed. "Jerome, however, was always a vindictive and passionate man. From what I hear, he has not changed in the least. And why should he not change? He is past fifty. If a man doesn't learn wisdom and maturity by that time, then there is no hope for him. How can Jerome be so childish?"

Philip said: "We have no proof, as yet, that he *is* 'childish' about this, Father."

"No," admitted Alfred, "that is quite true. We must reserve judgment."

"It is hard enough for a man to give up a daughter he adores, even if—if everything else is satisfactory," said Philip, with sadness. "We mustn't blame Jerome too much, should he prove a little difficult. I am relying, however, on our years of friendship and understanding and work and mutual sympathy. He can't forget all that, surely."

"You would be surprised at what a man can forget under the stress of emotion," said Alfred grimly. "He can forget love and decency and honor and reason. He can do and say things which can never be forgiven. Never. Never."

He waited a little, then he said: "To many, Dorothea may have appeared hard and unrelenting. But she wasn't really. She lacked understanding of many things, but they were the small things. She had a large awareness of big issues. During her last years, especially, she became kinder, gentler. I only wish she had lived long enough to see you and Mary married. That would have made her so happy."

"You ought to have married Aunt Dorothea, sir."

Alfred moved restlessly. He flushed. "Well, I thought of it a few times, I confess. There was a deep affection between us. I —I had an idea she hoped it. But it would not have been fair to her. You see, my dear boy, I couldn't forget Amalie." He looked again at the storm. "I still love Amalie, Philip. I think I always shall."

He said, as if speaking aloud to himself: "I have seen Amalie a few times, at a distance. I thought she seemed unhappy and abstracted. I—I've never spoken to you of this before, Philip. But now I must ask you outright: Is she really happy with Jerome? Is he good to her? Kind, charitable, tender? It would give me some peace if I could know that with surety."

Philip hesitated. Then he said reflectively: "I don't know whether Amalie has the capacity to be truly happy. Perhaps it isn't Jerome's fault."

Alfred quickened. "You say she is unhappy, Philip?"

"If she is, I don't think it is Jerome's fault."

"He doesn't understand her, then," said Alfred, urgently and greatly moved. "I didn't—long ago. But the years have made me understand. Amalie needs a sense of permanence, of security. She never had it. Neither of us—Jerome or I—could give it to her. I don't know why. I think I might have, if things had been different."

He said huskily: "Yes, I am sure I could have given it to her. Eventually. When I finally realized that I didn't have to justify myself. But I didn't have time then."

Philip felt an emotion of sad indulgence. He began to speak, then paused. He stared at his father incredulously and knew the truth with a sort of blinding clairvoyance. Yes, Alfred could have made Amalie happy, happy as she had never been before. A few years, only a few years, had been needed. Alfred would have gained in wisdom, in quietness, in peace, under the happiness of being married to Amalie. There were some who were slow in maturing, and some who would never mature. Alfred was among the first, Jerome among the second. If Jerome had never returned to Hilltop, then, in a few years, there would have been peace there, and contentment.

Philip's heart ached. Then he said to himself: But if that had happened, Mary would have been my sister!

Could he, Philip, be sorry? If he had the choice, would he wish things might have been different? Perhaps, he thought. Perhaps not.

The door opened, and an excited clerk appeared. "Mr. Jerome Lindsey is here, sir, and wishes to see you and Mr. Philip!"

"Jerome!" exclaimed Alfred, starting up. Then he paused, turned to Philip mutely.

Philip had paled. "Send him in," he said.

The clerk went out. Philip put his hand on his father's arm. "Please," he said, "let us be as calm as possible. It is evident that Jerome isn't in the least calm. Otherwise, he would never have come here. I can rely on you to keep your temper, Father, under any provocation?"

Alfred bent his head. He sat down again. His hands were shaking. He clasped them together, very hard, on his desk. Philip, standing, waited.

The door opened again. Jerome appeared on the threshold, his hat brim, his shoulders, white with snow.

He did not look at Philip. He looked at Alfred. He closed the door behind him.

Over the space of dark warm carpet, over the space of years of hatred and madness and bitterness, the two men regarded each other in silence.

Neither saw any change in the other. They were young again; their childhood, their early youth, their later manhood, rolled all about them like a scene dissolving into scene and sound into sound. In the flash of a moment, they remembered a hundred things, all the years of enmity, misunderstanding, hatred, envy, small triumphs and devastating victories, defeats and humiliations and shames. Their incompatible natures stood opposed, while the years tumbled and flowed past them, and only they remained the same.

Philip, always so adequate in emergencies, could not speak. Very dimly, he was aware that the fire flared up, that the lamps flickered, that the wind screamed at the windows. The silence in the room became like breath held to suffocation. But, more than anything else, he was aware of Jerome looking at Alfred with eyes from which all sanity and reason had been burned away.

But Alfred was returning that implacable malignant look very quietly. His own face was gray and rigid, as if with shock at what he was seeing with his inner eye. But he was not afraid, not even alarmed. His expression was, it is true, stern and still, but it was the expression worn by one who confronts dementia and knows that, for the sake of the madman, himself, he must not be taken aback by it.

Then Alfred's expression changed. Philip saw that he was staring at the bright red scars on Jerome's face. His shock seemed to increase. His lips jerked. One of his hands half rose as if to shut out the sight of those scars. Then it fell heavily to the table again. In the silence, the sound was loud.

Jerome remained where he was, leaning against the door through which he had entered. His breath came sharply. He said, and his voice was low:

"Look here, you. I have only one thing to say: No."

Philip moved involuntarily. Jerome caught that movement. He turned on the younger man. Philip saw the flash of his teeth.

"You disgusting, contemptible, miserable cripple," said Jerome, with soft loathing. "You foul and wretched creature. Don't cross my path again. Don't ever let me see you. If you do, I will kill you."

Now he was full of uncontrollable and wondering outrage. "How dare you look at my daughter, you! How dare you think of her? You!"

Alfred had never before seen Philip shrink or fall back before anything. For the first time in Philip's life, the light went completely out of his eyes. Alfred forgot everything then, except the agony he saw in his son, the overwhelming despair and humiliation. He forgot everything but that this was his son, who was being so hideously attacked, and who had no defense. Alfred stood up, walked around his desk and faced Jerome, so that there was only a yard or so between them. His strong legs felt weak and numb, but there was a fiery burning in his chest.

"Listen to me, Jerome Lindsey," he said, without hurry. "I, too, have a few words to say. And I want to tell you now that I forbid my son to marry your daughter. I ought to have done that before. I was a fool to think you might have changed, that you might have become a man, a decent and understanding man. I see now that you'll never change. I might have known that a bad man is incapable of change, or of acquiring any kindness. Yes, I was a fool to believe that we could have anything but hatred for each other."

They stared into each other's eyes. Alfred's were inflexible and calm. Jerome's leapt about in their sockets.

Philip, devastatingly weak, leaned against his father's desk. Something bulked in his throat, salty and choking.

Alfred was speaking again: "I want nothing of your ugliness of spirit in my family. I'd be afraid. I don't want anything to remind me of your evil tongue and your bad nature. You took from me everything that was worth having. I have forgiven you, and I had hoped to forget, but you've made that impossible now."

He turned to Philip, and it was unbearable to him to see his son like this. But he said, forcing his voice to strength and sternness: "Philip, do you understand me? I forbid you to marry this man's daughter. If you do so, against my command and wish, you'll no longer be a son of mine."

He was all resolution and pride and dignity, but it was becoming increasingly impossible to endure the sight of Philip's suffering.

"Answer me, Philip. Are you going to obey me?"

Philip pressed his hand harder against his father's desk. He said: "Yes. I will obey you, Father."

My son, thought Alfred, with heavy pain. My son, my son. He took a step towards Philip, and Philip tried to push himself away from the desk. He said to his father, silently, from out of his own inner torture: It is all right. Don't be so unhappy for me. It is all right. We'll manage, somehow, together. And Alfred stood there, his hand half lifted towards Philip, and he seemed to be listening, too moved to speak.

Jerome looked from one to the other. Then he burst out laughing. There was no other sound in the room but the sound

491

of that brutal and vehement laughter. But Alfred and Philip did not seem to hear him. Philip was even trying to smile at Alfred, with gentle encouragement.

Jerome stopped his laughter abruptly. Something that greatly disturbed him and strangely tormented him was happening here. But he said, almost genially: "It is all settled then, without trouble and without fireworks. I always like to see people being reasonable. It is so much pleasanter."

Don't mind, Father, Philip was saying with his eyes to Alfred. Don't mind for me. I shan't die of it. Men don't die of such things. We'll both forget, some day.

Jerome was saying: "Yes, this gives me much pleasure. I've waited for it a long time." He concentrated his attention upon Alfred, who still looked only at his son: "You thought to work your way into Hilltop through your deformed son, didn't you? You thought you'd intrude into my life, and go snooping and spying about. It was a nice plot, but it didn't turn out the way you thought it would. It was a very stupid and infantile plot."

Alfred turned to him slowly, as if he had forgotten that Jerome was there and was surprised to discover that he was. He could not speak immediately, and then he said in a low and inflexible voice: "There was no plot. That is just in your mind. I never want to see Hilltop again. You've made it an ugly place for me. I never wanted to see you again, either, or anyone who belongs to you."

He paused, then he said, as if in rising incredulity: "I don't understand it! How can you have lived so long and acquired no charity, no kindness, no gentleness? How is it possible for a man to be so cruel?"

Jerome did not move. But he appeared to have retreated a step or two. Now all the malignity had gone from his dark narrow face. He seemed profoundly startled, as if he were listening to something else besides Alfred. His brows drew together in concentration.

Alfred sighed heavily. "I've watched you all these years. I've seen what you have done. And I've thought that you had become a different man, a better one. I don't understand it, no." He shook his head. "I'm afraid that I'm not very clever."

Again he was all dignity. Now, as he looked at Jerome, he became aware of an oddness in the other's expression. He leaned forward a little, in the dusk, to try to find out what it was. Jerome stared back at him, and his eyes had in them a peculiar intent brilliance, as if he were listening with all his faculties.

492

Alfred heard his own voice trembling uncertainly: "I don't think we have anything more to say to each other. Except one thing: I beg of you not to be too harsh to that lovely child. She is young. This was a—mistake. Let her forget."

Jerome said nothing. Alfred, suddenly uneasy and bewildered, again peered at him. He became aware that he was seeing something he had never before seen in Jerome. A kind of sober and shaken thoughtfulness, lonely and wretched, and completely vulnerable. Alfred shook his head slightly. It was his imagination, of course. The firelight and the stormy dusk were confusing him.

Then Jerome turned away, opened the door, shut it softly behind him.

Philip had sat down. He was leaning his elbows on his father's desk, and he had covered his face with his hands. Alfred studied him, and he thought to himself that this was the greatest pain that he had ever had to bear, and that it was easier for a man to suffer his own personal agonies than to see the suffering of one he loves.

He said: "Philip. My son."

Philip dropped his hands. He looked before him steadily. "Yes, Father," he answered.

Alfred put his hand on Philip's shoulder, and was miserably silent. He looked a long time at the snow-shrouded window. Then he said, almost softly: "Don't be too unhappy. I don't understand some things. I know everything will be all right. Philip, when I looked at Jerome just now, I saw something strange. It was like seeing someone come out for the first time from behind distorted shadows. He didn't hate me any more. Yes, I am sure of that: he no longer hates me. I don't know. But I do know that things will be well for you, my dear boy. Just a little longer, just a little more patience."

CHAPTER SEVENTY-ONE

Jim, huddled in the fur robes, was waiting in the sleigh for Jerome. The little old man was very wretched and perturbed. There was no standing this beastly weather, he thought. It was like the night that Mr. Jerome had come 'ome. It was still day, but the storm had so darkened the sky that it might have been late evening.

Jim was frightened too. Why had Mr. Jerome gone to that

Bank? He had not spoken from the time that they had left Hilltop. He had just sat there, like a graven image. Sat there, he had, in the sleigh, looking straight ahead with eyes like gleaming marbles. Something was wrong. Something had always been wrong since they had left New York nineteen years ago. God, was it nineteen years? The way time passed was a caution.

The gray veils of snow and wind thickened, so that the street was lost in wavering gloom. Then Jim heard Jerome climbing into the sleigh again. "We'll go home," he was saying. He pulled the robes up to his chin.

"Yes, sir," said Jim thankfully. "It's a bad day, and it'll be a worse night. No use stayin' in town today."

"No," said Jerome. His voice was muffled.

Jim turned the horses about. The sleigh floundered through piling drifts. The gas lamps flickered. The wind tore at the men's faces, at their hats, at the tight warm robes. Jim's nose was numb with cold; he sniffled, blinking reddened eyes.

It was almost impossible to see. Jim gave the horses their heads. The devils could find their own way home. The runners of the sleigh crunched and whined through the snow; the vehicle rocked and swayed. Now, as the wind struck his face repeatedly, Jim began to gasp for breath. Jerome, sunk far down in the sleigh, sat without moving or speaking.

The yellow street lamps wavered by them like faint moons seen through fog. Riversend had an abandoned, lost air. No one fought on foot against the storm, or even in sleighs. The snow hissed in the burning gale. Once a horse stumbled, and the sleigh jerked aside violently.

Amalie. Mary. Jerome wiped the snow from his face. He roused himself a little. "Can't you make them go a little faster?" he asked.

"No, sir. It's beyond me, this storm," said Jim fearfully. "They're doing the best they can."

"I must get home soon," said Jerome loudly.

Jim slapped the reins. Bells jingled. The horses, apprehensive, struggled up the slope from the valley.

I must get home, thought Jerome. Amalie. Mary. My dears, my darlings. "Faster!" he shouted.

"Can't sir, beggin' your pardon!" shouted Jim, in return. "There's treacherous goin', right about here. That ditch somewheres. Can't see where it is."

Now it was almost as dark as night. The grayness grew more impenetrable. The wind roared in the unseen pines which ran along the heaving road. The sleigh lumbered from side to side. The horses panted, groaned. To Jerome nothing at all was visible, not even Jim, who was sitting in front and desperately slapping the reins.

Amalie. I must go to Amalie. I must tell her—what? What can I say to her? I can only ask her to forgive me. How much she has known about me which I didn't know at all! She sensed it all, but I didn't understand until now.

He saw himself and understood himself with new and brilliant clarity, and he felt wonder and shame. He knew now that always he had been bedevilled by the unadmitted fear of his adequacy to meet his dreams and aspirations. He had been a dabbler in everything. Once, he had dreamed of being a great artist. Then, at some time, he had discovered that he would never be great, but only pleasantly mediocre, and the disillusionment had paralyzed him, made him inert. He had become convinced, if only subconsciously, that he would never be completely adequate and in command of circumstance. He had never reasoned out his fear, nor subjugated his egotism, which had refused to be satisfied with anything but the ultimate, the greatest. His imagination, which alone made him a superior man, had defeated him. It would not let him be content with what was within his capacities.

His vanity had made him apathetic, but he had interpreted this apathy to mean an easy and mature detachment from all the feverish strugglings of other men. And now he understood that he had been puerile: he had had the silly, unconfessed notion that men like Alfred, the "gray men," were adequate and invincible, and so he had hated them. He had rationalized his unconfessed defeat, and so had considered himself superior to the strivers, no matter for what they strove. He had despised men like Alfred, too, because of their dedication to the barren things of life, but now he knew that he had really despised them for the lack of imagination which had prevented them from guessing that they might be defeated at all. They had been content with small victories; he could never be content with anything but the most resplendent. They had not been afraid to fight. He in his youth had been afraid to fight, for fear of being ignominiously vanquished. What little joy he had known had been in these last nineteen years or so, when he had finally accomplished something and proved his adequacy. But it would have been much better for him if he had known himself then as he knew himself now.

He had remained at Hilltop, he knew, not only because of

495

Amalie, as he had thought, but because he had felt in that old house a serenity, a peace, a refuge, a sense of effectiveness. It had rested something in him that was feverish and exhausted.

If only he could have delivered himself to that old house completely, and with understanding! He might then have accomplished more, without the sense of being driven which had made him hate and struggle and destroy himself. He would have had a happier life; he would have made others happier.

He saw so clearly now how miserable he had made Amalie, out of his own unresolved misery. He saw all the ugly mistakes he had made, because he had been so blind. Mary, he thought, your father is a fool.

"What is the matter now?" he cried, as the sleigh stopped abruptly.

Jim's voice, muffled by wind, blew back to him: "Feels like a bad drift, sir. Mounting-high. Horses havin' trouble, like. There. They're clear now."

The house would be warm and bright and snug. The grandfather clock would be chiming. There would be a fire in his room. He would be returning home, complete and healed. He would call Amalie in, and he would say: "Forgive me, if you can. Forgive me for all these years, for all my folly and stupidity and all the things I did, not only against you but against myself." Then Amalie would kiss him, and she would say—What would she say? But he knew Amalie. Her face had been tired so long, and it was his fault. Would it brighten a little, when he spoke to her?

They would talk together very soon, in the firelight, he and Amalie and Mary. And he would say: "Mary, I was all wrong. Forgive me. Send for Philip."

Philip. He saw Philip cringing away from him, turning away. Philip, who had been his friend. Philip had understood. He had known all the time what was bedevilling Jerome. Out of his kindness and his own deep convictions and integrity, he had tried to help Jerome find himself. He had made confused things clear. He had directed Jerome's concentrated energy out from himself to others. Now Jerome remembered Philip's quiet and compassionate eyes. Yes, he had understood. He had given Jerome some measure of victory. If he, Jerome, had accomplished anything truly permanent for Riversend it was because of Philip.

How could I have spoken so to him? thought Jerome. What possessed me? I must have been mad. It seems I've been mad all my life.

Tomorrow I will write to Alfred. There can be nothing between us, of course. There never can be, as long as we live. But I can write him: Try to forget what I have done and what I have said. It happened a long time ago.

His cheeks were numb, and his hands and feet. The sleigh was rocking violently. He heard Jim cursing. From the tilting of the sleigh, he knew they were on a steep slope. He looked up. Was that a light in the far window at Hilltop? It was just a faint yellow glow, lost again in the snow and the wind.

Wait for me, he said to the light.

Then he had the most curious thought. His father was waiting for him, up there at Hilltop. He would find his father in the library. He would be sitting there, smoking and reading. He would look up, with a smile, laying aside his book. What would he quote now? Jerome smiled in answer. Addison? Thoreau? Whitman? Emerson? It would probably be Emerson, the young Emerson. Jerome heard his father's voice, clear and high above the wind: "Jerome, Jerome! My dear boy!"

Amalie heard the door open below. She heard a great hoarse cry. She ran out of her room, and met servants running also. And then there was Mary.

She ran downstairs. Jim, bleeding from a dreadful gash on his cheek, stood below, shaking violently, wild with terror, his clothes covered with snow.

He saw Amalie vividly in the lamplight as she came down. He saw her pause on the stairs, lifting her hand suddenly to her mouth, her eyes widening desperately above it. He saw her catch at the banister. Mary was behind her, very pale and still.

Jim staggered towards the two women, flinging out his arms. He screamed: "Help! Help! The ditch! The master's down there, in the ditch!"

CHAPTER SEVENTY-TWO

Philip came downstairs somewhat late this autumn morning. The lassitude which had been weakening him steadily during the summer months seemed especially heavy today. Alfred complained that his son was working much too hard. But he was proud of Philip, proud of all he had accomplished and was accomplishing.

Breakfast was waiting for Philip in the small narrow room

overlooking the gardens. He thought: How strange it is that all that brilliance is shining out there and in this house there is only coldness and dimness!

Alfred had gone to the Bank. Philip ate his breakfast alone, and without appetite. There were letters for him. He ran through them quickly, then caught up one with an eagerness he could not control. It was from Mary, written from New York.

"Darling Philip," she wrote, "you will doubtless be surprised that Mama and I are now in New York. We had to leave New Orleans to bring William back to his school. But that was not the only reason. Mama suddenly decided that she was very tired, and that she wished to return to Hilltop. She is not looking well at all, and I am very anxious about her. She is wearing a very sad and determined air lately. But she does not appear so numb and listless as she did during the first months after Papa's death."

Philip's eye ran swiftly over that sharp small script with its clear legibility.

He continued to read: "Perhaps I imagine it, but your letters are so short and distant. So cold. Is it because you are working too hard? If that is so, then Mama and I shall feel conscience-stricken. But we are also proud. How kind, and how wise it was of Papa, to appoint you executor of his will and his estate, and to name you as president of his bank! He knew that you and General Tayntor were good friends, and that the General, as vice-president, would have no quarrel with you."

Philip paused and looked before him. I can't go on with it, he thought. But he knew he must. He could not abandon Amalie and Mary. Love for them and duty, as his father had pointed out, must keep him in Jerome's bank, as president, until young William had attained his majority. But even then, according to the terms of the will, Philip was to be chairman. The years stretched before Philip as a great weary desert is spread before exhausted eyes.

It was not only the bank, Jerome's massive Grecian temple dedicated to finance. Philip was also director of the Riversend Community. Too much depended upon him. I haven't the strength, he thought. But he knew it was because he no longer had the heart. He wanted nothing for himself, because the thing that he truly wanted he could not take.

Mary's letter continued: "It has been so long since we have seen you. Since last February! Eight months! But, as you know, I had to take Mama away. I was afraid that she would die—

first, during those weeks of illness after Papa's death, and then during the following months. She has become so thin you would hardly know her, and it breaks my heart. But she sometimes smiles now. She smiled for the first time, about a month ago, when William said something very ridiculous. Now she even reads occasionally. But her real interest is aroused when I talk of the time when you and I will be married. In fact, it is only when I talk of this that she becomes truly alive and almost like her old self. She still doesn't speak much of Papa. At first, she could not mention him at all. But now she often says: 'Your father would like that frock, Mary. Your father would be so amused to see how much you resemble your grandfather.'

"I was beginning to be very depressed about all this travelling. But, of course, I was willing to undergo it for Mama's sake. She was so restless, even though she always appeared about to faint from weariness. But she has become quieter. When she spoke of going home I tried to conceal my joy."

The script became softer now, less certain: "Dear Philip, I am counting the days until I see you again. How wonderful it will be! And then we can make our plans. I know that you did not mention them before because it was so soon after Papa's death. But Mama says it is proper to do so now.

"I do not know the exact day when we shall return. But it will be soon. I know it will!"

Philip slowly laid aside the letter. Again he looked through the narrow window at the garden. Mary. But he could not marry her. That was impossible. Jerome had made him see what he, Philip, was, in contrast to that lovely girl. She was young. She would soon forget. In his self-abasement, he could not make himself believe that she would remember him for very long. Some day she would be grateful that she had not married him; she would be grateful to Philip himself.

The dull stone that now lived always in his chest became heavier. He rubbed his tired eyes. It had not been too hard while Mary was away, while Hilltop stood untenanted, except for servants, on its high green hill. But now Amalie and Mary were returning. Hilltop would come alive; its heart would beat again, strongly, urgently. How would he be able to endure it, never going there again, never seeing Mary except casually, never talking to Amalie?

Mary. Mary. But when he thought of Mary he thought of Jerome.

What had Alfred said, pleadingly? "Philip, you are too imaginative, too sensitive. If Jerome had truly meant those wicked things he said to you, he would not have written his will like this. He reveals in every line all the trust and affection he always had for you. Poor Jerome. He thought himself the essence of self-control, but he really was the most uncontrolled of men. I prefer to think, and I believe, that this will is more the true Jerome than the one we saw in my office. You see, yourself, how implicitly he trusted you, with full acknowledgement of your wisdom and ability.

"I have the strangest conviction that during the last minutes he spent with us something happened to Jerome. I saw something in his eyes. They had changed quite suddenly. He seemed to be listening, to be understanding. All his hatred went out of his face. When he left us, I had the certain knowledge that he was returning to Amalie and Mary, without rage, but with love and a new perception."

Philip had smiled at this with mournful cynicism.

"So," Alfred had pleaded, "go to Mary when she returns, and take up your life with her again. Don't visit your own doubts upon that poor young creature. You can make her happy. You can make Amalie happy. Your duty to them does not end with your expert performance at Jerome's bank, nor with your management of their estate."

But he never dreamt of my marrying his daughter, thought Philip. I was his friend, his confidant, his adviser. But he never saw me as the husband of his daughter. One can't forget that.

Nor can one forget, his dreary thoughts continued, that Mary deserves better than a deformed man so much older than herself. She deserves the glory and the youth of life, the happiness and the gaiety. I can give her none of them. What a fool I was, from the very beginning! If I had taken only a little thought, I'd have known. But I wanted her, and to me that seemed enough.

He went out of the house. The weight in his heart extended to his body. He walked like an old man. He stood in the road and looked far up the hill at Mary's home. He could see the tiny glimmer of the top windows, the red roof, through the trees. All at once every instinct urged him to go up there, for the last time. It would do no harm. After today he would never go there again, never.

His weariness lifted. It became a passionate thirst. Just once more, just once more to see the library where Uncle William had sat, to see the garden, and the stables! It was little enough. There was no one there but the servants.

His feet carried him up the hill. The warm October morning

lay in shining wideness about him. Leaves scurried ahead of him, like small gay creatures. Golden dust followed him. Once he turned and looked at the valley below floating in a silvery morning mist. He could see in that mist the deeper nuances of smoke, and though he could not actually hear anything but the sounds of the woods about him, he thought he could discern the rumble and noisy activity of the factories and the railroad.

He paused again, this time to look at the valley with more intentness. He thought of all that was being said about America as a "growing and maturing nation." But all at once he felt an uneasy fear. Something was passing from America. While she grew industrially, she was losing her maturity. It was as if a giant, abnormally doubling his stature, began to suffer the dwindling of his brain. What if we become the dinosaur among nations? thought Philip. Well-armored, powerful, shaking the earth with our tread, and having the perceptions of a minute if lustful intelligence? Is it possible that we reached our maturity with Emerson and Thoreau? Is it possible that we have already lost maturity, lost ripened manhood?

Are we "laying waste our powers in getting and spending"? Can it be that the world of the mind, so loved by Uncle William and his contemporaries, has lost prestige because of its intangibility? The plain living and high thinking of the New Englanders has degenerated, I fear, into the showy existence, and absence of any thinking at all, which betray the born plebeian, the born vulgarian.

The human soul has fallen into disrepute in America! Philip's melancholy thoughts continued. For lack of sustenance, it is withering. For lack of light, it is becoming blind. For lack of a vision, it is perishing. Yet that human soul wants so little, really. It wants reverence and contemplative peace. It wants books and open spaces. It wants the free sky and the wild sun. It wants a little privacy and a little music. It wants to think of God.

But that little was rapidly being taken away from the heart and the soul of America. Goods, properties, possessions: these had usurped the place of contentment. No one could possibly belittle that self-respect which manifests itself in the making of an adequate living. But an adequate living does not demand that all a man's heart and mind and soul be dedicated to the acquiring of mountainous possessions, more malignant trivia than ever were owned by a medieval prince. For his happiness a man's house need not be large, and requires only a small garden behind it, and a few trees. His children will not die for the lack of expensive carpets and gilded gew-gaws. But they will surely die, and America with them, if they lack a vision.

We have done what we could in Riversend, thought Philip, Jerome and I. Now he could think of Jerome with a faint warmth and affection which were revivifying. Yes, we have done what we could. But what of the rest of America? Who will set out to do what we have done? Who will renew the vision in our country? My country, my dear, dear country! What is to become of you, when even the poor man, the poor farmer in his field, thinks no thoughts of God and destiny and virtue and contentment, but only of acquiring money and buying malevolent nonsense with it?

Even while Philip's despondency grew stronger, he felt an old familiar stirring in him, as if he had tensed some strength and sternness in himself in order to give battle. Surely, he thought, I do not think these thoughts alone. Surely there are other men who believe as I do, and hope and fear as I do. I must find them!

His mind was clear and free. He thought of Jerome with the first poignant grief and sadness he had experienced since his cousin's death. Jerome's vehement and confused soul had had these thoughts; he had tried to embody them in the Riversend Community. Poor Jerome! Philip said aloud: "I won't forget, Jerome. I will try to do what you wanted to do, even though you were not certain what that thing was."

His step became lighter. He was not so weary. He felt wonder. Now he could lift his head and go forward with more strength. Why was this?

He was approaching Hilltop now. The house, strong and gray against the cobalt sky, stood fully above him. It had the face of a friend. Now he saw that the windows were wide open, that smoke was blowing from a chimney or two. They were preparing for the family's return.

I can be strong, thought Philip, looking at that dear house, even if Mary is not with me. I can be happy, a little later, knowing she has found youth and gaiety and love, and that she is filling this house with her children.

He moved silently along the side of the house, to look at the gardens for the last time. No one was about, but he heard the neighing of horses.

The azure October day was all bright, still air and the last expiring glory of color and peace and sweetness. How silent was the warm and golden sun! The wall of burning trees was a tapestry of dark and pale green mixed with the blaze of maples, the yellow of elms, the crimson of oaks. Philip could not remember when the flowers had been so brilliant, so numerous, so delicate yet strong of fragrance, in their refutation of their coming death. A great bee bumbled over the calendulas and the enormous red buds of the last roses, and a white butterfly perched for an airy moment over pale daisies no more snowy than he, and was one with their petals. The red brick wall was covered with rose-canes, and over it hung the burnished fruit and the dark green leaves of apple trees. The grass was high and thick, deeper and fresher than it had been in the very heart of hot August, and the lilac trees, in the midst of their fading foliage, showed the rich green buds which would flower in the spring. A pointed hawthorn tree was dropping its leaves; in the grass lay its round fruit like scarlet pearls. A few birds whistled and sang contemplatively in the mighty poplars in the near distance. Never had there been such a blue soft sky, so wide, so radiant, so nobly tender. The faint wind had a hint of chill, but it was fresh, under the warmth of the sun, and the silence was deep and all-pervading.

They call this the season of death, thought Philip. But I know now that it is the season of the beginning of life. The pods, he saw, were full of seeds; golden-brown they lay in their fragile cases, row after row. They will soon fall to the ground, and nestle there, waiting. It is the season of life. Under all this last silence the earth is busy, seeding, planting, garnering. The squirrels, too, are busy, burying nuts which in the spring will rise into young trees. Spring is not an awakening. It is only a flowering of what has been seeded in autumn, the season of life.

A deep and tender comfort filled Philip, a comfort as rich and full as the October day. Whatever came to him now he could bear with strength and peace. Somewhere in America, the seeds of good men's thoughts had fallen on fertile ground. Somewhere, some day, those seeds would be trees, sure and high and invulnerable, to keep the desert of materialism from parching America, to hold the desert at bay, to protect the soil from erosion, and to offer shelter to the tired souls of men, and fruit to their thirsty lips.

He bent and picked a last yellow rosebud, and held the sweet flower to his nose and mouth. He looked about him with contentment. Though he would never see it again, he would always remember this garden. To him, it was a holy place.

He felt the lightest touch on his arm. He had heard no one approaching him. He turned quickly, to see Mary.

She stood there, her silvery blond head bare to the sun, her fine clear face smiling, her blue eyes full of tears. She waited for him to speak; there was a breathlessness about her, a gentle and valiant glory.

"Mary," he murmured. "Mary, my dear."

She laughed a little then. "Philip. Oh, Philip. We came home last night! How did you know?"

I did not know, he thought. Or did I know instinctively?

She saw that he was looking at her gravely, almost somberly, his dark eyes steady and withdrawn. And then she knew he was in trouble. Yes, she knew he was in trouble, and understood, fully, what it was.

She took his hand. She looked straight at him. "Philip," she said, "when we found Papa that night, in that terrible ditch, he wasn't dead. We brought him home. He—died late, at midnight. But before he died, he whispered to me: 'Send for Philip. I want to see Philip. I want to see you two together, you and Philip.'"

Her eyes widened. "You didn't know, did you! But I thought you did!"

She held his hand in both of hers, and he felt the sweetness of her flesh, the strength, the sadness. She cried: "Is that why your letters were so strange?"

"I didn't know," he said. And then again: "I didn't know!"

The brilliant air brightened so strongly that it blinded him. He kissed her hands and her wrists. This was wrong, wrong! and then, all at once, he knew it was right.

"Mary!"

She bent her head and put her lips simply and gently upon his own.

"Come in, dear. Mama wants to see you. She wants to talk to you, Philip."

CHAPTER SEVENTY-THREE

Alfred exclaimed, out of his pain: "No, Amalie must not do that! She cannot do that! Leave Hilltop? That's impossible. It is her home. There is plenty of room there for you and Mary and Amalie."

"That is what I told her," said Philip sadly. "But it was no use. She said that the house had never 'accepted' her, that there was no peace for her inside its walls. So she insists upon giving me her share of it as a wedding present. She will live in a little house somewhere in Riversend, she says."

He and his father were sitting in the garden in the mauve twilight.

"You would hardly know Amalie," continued Philip, with increasing sadness. "She is so thin and white, and so feverish. But she is calm. It is almost the calmness of despair. It is, I feel, more than grief for Jerome. Sometimes she subsides into a kind of numbness and abstraction. Poor Amalie. I cannot remember when I have seen her happy. Was she ever happy? I don't know."

"But she cannot leave Hilltop!" said Alfred. Then he added, with pathetic simplicity: "I couldn't bear to think of Hilltop, and Amalie not there."

He waited, and his voice trembled when he next spoke: "Philip, tell me: Is she grieving very much for Jerome?"

Philip sighed, over and over. "I don't know. She is grieved, of course. But I think it is something else too. I think it is the culmination of a whole life of insecurity and bewilderment and confusion. I don't know what it is."

Alfred was silent. In the dusk, he could feel, rather than see, his son. He felt Philip's happiness, which was like a glow, and his renewed strength and life. God be thanked for that! God bless that sweet girl! She and Philip would live at Hilltop together. He, Alfred, might see them there occasionally. At this thought, something lifted and brightened in Alfred.

He stood up. By straining his eyes, he could catch a glimmer of light far upon the hill. Hilltop! Now, in a way, it was home for him again.

Then he stood very still, his hands at his sides, his heart hammering. He said, abruptly, in a smothered voice: "I must go out for a while, Philip. Just for an hour. Wait here for me."

There was no moon, but the stars were so bright that a long spectral shadow of frail silver lay over the earth and the hill. Alfred climbed slowly. He had to pause to rest a heart that persisted in pounding and palpitating. The way was so familiar. He knew every great tree that fluttered its dim outline over the road. He passed the deep ditch where Jerome had been mortally hurt. He stood and looked at it. Now he was flooded with pain and regret.

He went on. The windows of Hilltop glimmered more clearly. How often he had seen them like this, full of golden light! He never could forget them. He felt as if his uncle were waiting there, in the library. Philip had told him that things had changed very little in the house. It was like—coming home.

The night was cool, but Alfred's face was damp, and in him there was a prolonged trembling. When he reached the gates, he did not go in immediately. He stood and looked at the house. He saw the old familiar brass lamp shining softly in one of the library windows. Surely Uncle William was sitting under that lamp, reading.

When he lifted the brass knocker on the oak door, the sound came back to him across the years. He touched the gray stones on either side of the door as he waited. They were warm and old and strong against his hand.

The door opened and a maid admitted him to the big hall. A fire was burning on the hearth. The grandfather clock struck nine, with its old resonant notes. Firelight and lamplight gleamed on the panelled walls. Why, he had been here only yesterday, only this morning! The clock was his friend, the fire welcomed him. He was conducted to the library, and he looked at the tiers of books, at the low fire, at the dark leather chairs. He saw his uncle's chair, waiting; he saw his pipes. Something pent and tight in Alfred relaxed and warmed.

He stood before the hearth and saw the brass andirons. Nothing had changed. But why should it? He had never left this house. It was home.

He heard a faint rustling sound, and again his heart began that strong sure beating. He turned slowly. Amalie was near him. But it was an Amalie grown thin and white and withdrawn, with a numb and exhausted face and purple eyes that had wept too many tears. It was an Amalie with a snowy lock of hair running from her forehead to her nape.

In silence they stood and looked at each other. Amalie's black gown shimmered in the lamplight, revealing her still splendid figure, her dignity, her grace. She was holding out her hand to him, and there was no emotion in her eyes except endless weariness and dullness.

"Alfred," she said.

He took her hand. He felt dazed, stricken, overcome with love and compassion.

"Amalie," he murmured.

She withdrew her hand. "Please sit down, Alfred," she said. Her voice sounded faint and without its old rich timbre. She sat down across from him, where so often she had sat before, and they looked at each other without speaking.

At first her eyes remained dull and empty. Then they began to see him. She saw his strength, she saw his maturity, she saw the peace that had finally come to him across years of pain and suffering comprehension. Wonder touched her face, the wonder of a weary child. Something flowed from him to her, something reassuring and steadfast and full of compassionate understanding.

She said dimly: "You have changed, Alfred."

"Yes," he said, with softness, "I think I have, Amalie." It was intolerable to him, to see her like this. He wanted to go to her, to press that stark face into his shoulder, to hold her to him, and comfort her. "You see, Amalie, I know so many things I never knew—before."

She twisted her hands together on her knee, and he remembered that old gesture of restlessness. He saw her breast swell, as if drawing in a heavy breath: "Alfred. I think I know why you came here. It was to say that you do not approve of Philip marrying Mary?"

He was so astounded that he could not speak. Now she was leaning towards him, her eyes full of desperate pleading: "Don't say it, Alfred! Let them be happy! They love each other."

His voice trembled when he replied: "My dear, I didn't come to say that. I am glad about Philip and Mary. I hope you are glad, too."

She was amazed. She sank back in her chair. Then he saw tears in her eyes. She was trying to smile. "I am, I am, Alfred," she said softly. She turned aside her head. "And I know that Jerome, too, is glad."

"Yes, I know he is," said Alfred.

Again, there was silence between them. The low fire crackled. The old elm branch scraped along the eaves. Alfred started. It was like the knock of a friend on an old, forgotten door.

Alfred spoke: "Amalie, I came here tonight to persuade you not to leave Hilltop."

She turned her face to him, dimly startled. She shook her head. "I must, Alfred. I really must. You see, it was never really my home. It is Philip's home. And Mary's." She paused, then she cried faintly: "It is yours, too, Alfred! I have no right here!"

He went to her then, and took her hand. It was cold and damp. He held it strongly. "It is your home, Amalie. I can't bear to think of you not being here. Will you stay here, for my sake? Will you let me continue to think of you in this room, and in these gardens, and looking through these windows?" His voice began to fail him, so that it was almost a whisper: "You don't know how it has comforted me, all these years, to

507

imagine you here, Amalie."

His hand was warm and firm as it held hers, and its strength was good to her. She clung to that hand; tears were spilling over her face. She was trying to smile again. But she shook her head a little.

"Alfred, you are only trying to be kind——"

"Oh, no," he said. "No. I am trying to keep my memory of you, Amalie. That is all."

Full of wonder, incredulous, she looked up at him. Their eyes held together. Now there was only the sound of the fire and the scraping of the elm branch in the quiet.

He bent his head. "Yes, Amalie," he murmured.

Still clinging to his hand, she got slowly to her feet. She could not look away from him. She tried to speak. She made several attempts, but her lips trembled. Then she could only whisper:

"Alfred, you——"

He said: "Amalie, will you let me come again? Some day, soon? You will let me see you? Amalie?"

Had she really moved? Had she come a little closer to him? He could see the wet purple of her eyes, and the brilliant iris.

She was saying: "Yes. You may come again. And soon. You must come again, Alfred. You must always come."

Yes, I will come, thought Alfred, with deep surety. And some day I shan't go away again.

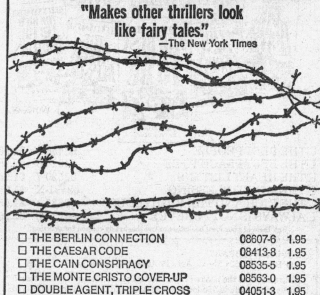

HISTORY · BIOGRAPHY
· POPULAR CULTURE

Outstanding Non-Fiction Titles

THE THIRTEENTH TRIBE 0-445-04242-7 $2.25
by Arthur Koestler

This book by a world-famous author proves that the true ancestors of Western Jewry were not Semites but Khazar warriors. "Clear and convincing."—*Newsweek*

KISS 0-445-04112-9 $1.75
by Robert Duncan

They wear seven-inch platform heels and lurid, Halloween makeup. They are the rock group that America loves to hate. They are KISS. And this is their incredible story. Illustrated with photographs.

WHERE ARE THEY NOW? 0-445-04264-8 $1.75
Yesterday's Sports Heroes Today
by Phil Berger

They were the champs, and the sluggers. They made and broke the records, drew and held the crowds, earned and lost the money. Here are 50 sports greats and what happened to them after the applause died down. Illustrated with photographs.

ROBERT ALTMAN 0-445-04262-1 $2.25
American Innovator
by Judith M. Kass

Some love him, some hate him. But no one ignores the contribution of director Robert Altman to the art of American film. From *Mash* to *Nashville* and *Three Women*, Altman's films are technically outrageous, artistically stunning. Here is the first book to take an in-depth look at this provocative and ambitious filmmaker. Illustrated with photographs.

ALL TIME BESTSELLERS FROM POPULAR LIBRARY

B-17